FEATURING MATTHEW SMITH, AL EWING & REBECCA LEVENE

THE BEST OF

TOMES
OF THE
DEAD

WWW.ABADDONBOOKS.COM

An Abaddon Books™ Publication
www.abaddonbooks.com
abaddon@rebellion.co.uk

This omnibus published in 2010 by Abaddon Books™,
Rebellion Intellectual Property Limited,
Riverside House, Osney Mead, Oxford, OX2 0ES, UK.

10 9 8 7 6 5 4 3 2 1

Editor-in Chief: Jonathan Oliver
Desk Editor: David Moore
Junior Editor: Jenni Hill
Omnibus Cover: Luke Preece
Original Covers: Mark Harrison
Design: Simon Parr & Luke Preece
Marketing and PR: Keith Richardson
Creative Director and CEO: Jason Kingsley
Chief Technical Officer: Chris Kingsley

ISBN (UK): 978-1-907519-34-5
ISBN (US): 978-1-907519-35-2

Printed in the US

THE WORDS OF THEIR ROARING

BY MATTHEW SMITH

For my mum and dad,
Who always knew... one day...

And for Emma,
Princess among Squaxx

INTRODUCTION

REWIND TO THE beginning of the 1990s, and zombie fiction, I felt, was getting short shrift. Vampires were alive and well, so to speak, thanks to Anne Rice and her ilk, but there seemed a dearth of literature featuring my favourite celluloid monsters. There were occasional dips into the undead sea: splatterpunk authors John Skipp and Craig Spector edited a couple of excellent anthologies called *Book of the Dead* and *Book of the Dead 2: Still Dead*, while Philip Nutman expanded one of his stories published in the first volume into the novel *Wet Work* in 1993. But for this twenty-year-old horror fan, I was still waiting for the apocalyptic zombie novel that thrilled as much as the best of George Romero's movies.

I'd been an aficionado of the sub-genre ever since I first saw the original *Night of the Living Dead,* but I wasn't a zombie apologist – Fulci's *Zombie Flesh-Eaters* has its moments, but nothing holds a candle to Romero on top form. I've sat through enough cheapo dreck like *Burial Ground* to know that zombies are so much more than rubbing oatmeal on an actor's face and letting them stagger around eating offal. Whether it's the excitement in seeing civilisation under collapse, the terror of infection and being consumed alive, the fascination with how people cope once the societal codes of conduct have been removed, or the exhilaration that comes from the Wild West spirit of fighting a common enemy, it's potentially one of the most interesting of all horror scenarios. There's always plenty of meat to chew on.

As the decade progressed, the zombie slowly crawled into the pop-culture spotlight, thanks in part to successes like the *Resident Evil* videogames and *The Walking Dead* comic series, and partly through a general post-millennial anxiety: climate change, bird flu, and dirty bombs all made humanity wake up to the possibility of mass species extinction, and nothing reflects the fears of the era like the horror genre. In the space of a few years, Max Brooks published *World War Z*, Edgar Wright directed *Shaun of the Dead*, *Dawn of the Dead* got the remake treatment, and Romero himself climbed back into the saddle with *Land of the Dead*. We were living in end times, and the zombie was back, back, *back*.

In 2006, I got the chance to write the zombie novel I'd been mulling over. I'd always had firm ideas of what elements I'd incorporate, such as mankind being the instigator of his own demise (no supernatural cause or passing comet sprinkling radioactive cosmic dust), and I wanted to explore the zombie's evolution, something Romero develops in his trilogy but doesn't, to my mind, take quite far enough. Borrowing themes from the films of David Cronenberg, I wanted to see how the virus that brought the dead back to life would continue to work upon the ghouls years down the line, transforming matter from one state to another. In fact, the virus is kind of like Harry Flowers, seeing the undead outbreak more as an opportunity than Armageddon, one advantageous kink in the human race's journey.

The title, incidentally, comes from an editorial aside I once read in a copy of Marlowe's *Doctor Faustus*, which argued that the doctor's cries to God as the devil comes to claim him were an echo of Christ's pleas upon the cross: *'Why am I so far from the words of your roaring?'* The phrase stuck with me, and seemed to fit with the mournful moans of these sad, shambling creatures, trapped – to quote one of my favourite lines from the book – in their own private resurrection.

Matthew Smith
June 2010

Latimer spake to Ridley as fire was kindled: "Be of good cheer, Mr Ridley, and play the man. We shall this day light such a candle by God's grace in England, as I trust shall never be put out." With a bag of gunpowder around their necks, they were burned and Latimer apparently died quickly and with little pain, but Ridley burned slowly, and desired them for Christ's sake to let the fire come unto him. They heaped the faggots upon him, but it burned all his nether parts before it touched the upper, that made him leap up and down under the faggots, and often desire them to let the fire come unto him saying, "I cannot burn," and after his legs were consumed, he showed that side towards us clean, shirt and all untouched by flame.

In which pangs he laboured till one of the standers-by with his billhook pulled off the faggots above, and where he saw the fire flame up, he wrestled himself unto that side. When the flame touched the gunpowder he was seen to stir no more.

Foxe's Book of Martyrs,
16 October 1555

PROLOGUE

Background Noise

"Did you say the stars were worlds, Tess?"
"Yes."
"All like ours?"
"I don't know; but I think so. They sometimes seem to be like the apples on our stubbard-tree. Most of them splendid and sound – a few blighted."
"Which do we live on – a splendid one or a blighted one?"
"A blighted one."

Thomas Hardy,
Tess of the D'Urbervilles

AS THE SOLDIER ran, he barely raised his eyes from the battle-scarred earth, intent on watching one foot replace the other, propelling him from danger. The rattle of gunfire had slowly faded the greater the distance he put between himself and the trenches, and the occasional mortar explosion was merely a dull thud behind him. Even so, he dared not slow his pace, despite the growing ache in his limbs. The ground was not easy to traverse; sludge becoming quagmire, plain disappearing into crater, every movement was an effort to stay upright, and to keep his boots on his feet. He had to pick his way carefully through barbed wire, sprawl in the mud if he thought he heard whisper of the enemy (and just who was that, now that he had chosen not to belong to one side or the other?). Exhaustion threatened to overwhelm him; but one notion kept him going, reassuring him as he watched his legs driving him towards that goal: escape.

Private William Steadman did not want to die.

He supposed there was a little of the childish logic in the way he kept his head down as he ran, reasoning that what he could not see would not hurt him; and rather than stop to get his bearings, he put all his effort into the act of flight itself, pointing himself in one direction and seeing where it would take him, as if he were a schoolboy released for the summer holidays. It was difficult to deny that he felt as lost and scared as if he was twelve years old, shrunken and vulnerable in an adult's uniform. But that was hardly a unique phenomenon; he'd seen his fellow soldiers – men perhaps in a civilian context he would've considered unscrupulous scoundrels and brawlers – reduced to bawling infants. Their faces had been masks of incomprehension and fear; they knew how close they were to death, how their dreams for the future, their desire to see their families again, hinged on an order. To leave the comparative safety of the trench, cross no-man's-land and embrace the German guns was to strip a man of everything he had and was ever likely to have. And so Steadman, with his own tears icy on his cheeks, had had to listen to one of the most terrifying sounds he'd ever heard, far worse than the shriek of shrapnel cutting through the air: that of grown men crying with regret and loss. It was utterly alien and impossible to forget.

He slid his way down a bank and felt the dirt beneath him crumble. Trying to regain his balance, he increased his pace, but only succeeded in pushing himself forward and tumbling headfirst into the mud. He rolled onto his back, a part of his mind yelling at him to be back on his feet instantly, but a curious lethargy came over him, as if the earth were sapping him of strength; as if, once this close to it, it would suck him to its bosom – revenge for the damage that had been wrought on its surface. He imagined lying there, relaxing his grip on life and watching the sun and moon chase each other across the sky, his body slowly sinking into the ground, becoming part of the landscape like so many other corpses had. Every morning for the past sixteen months, he'd woken and looked out on carcasses littering the battlefield, human and animal seeding the soil. What would it be like, he wondered, to join that silent sea of the dead? To succumb to the exhaustion and close his eyes one final time? The idea stayed in his head longer than he anticipated, perversely attractive. In the last letter he'd written home, he'd said how he'd forgotten what it was like to be warm and clean, to eat and sleep in comfort, not to have the tight ball of dread lodged in his gut; those concerns would just fade away if he was to give up now, if he was to relinquish the struggle to survive...

Steadman clutched a handful of mud and brought it to his nose; it smelt rotten, diseased. It served to fuel his anger and clear his mind of any thoughts of surrender. He would not sacrifice himself for this war; it meant nothing to him. As was common with most of his comrades, he knew little of the history behind the conflict, the objectives of taking part in it, or indeed how the world will have changed once everything returned to normal. They had just been shipped over to this godforsaken hole, instructed to stand in a freezing field, point their guns in the direction of the Hun, and wait until they could be told they could go home. It was difficult to picture a more futile image than two sets of opposing forces facing each other down from opposite ends of a muddy stretch of earth, while somewhere – invisible, in another world – generals bluffed and blustered. It would be laughable, were it not for the thousands of men being thrown across the lines. Then the stalemate became a massacre.

He held his commanders in absolute contempt. Their strategies were idiotic, their disregard for the troops who fought for them breathtaking. Many was the time he had seen Allied shells landing on their own attacking battalions because the advance had been planned with so little forethought, or frightened, sobbing young lads barely out of puberty executed for refusing to go over the top, obviously incapable of holding a rifle without shaking, let alone firing it. The injustice made him want to scream. He wanted to shout at the sky and pummel this sick, stinking earth. He was not some expendable, unthinking automaton they could put in front of the German bullets; as far as he was concerned, it *did* matter whether he lived or died. He thought of his parents raising him as a child, fretting when he was ill, glowing with pride when he returned from his first day at school, taking the time to show him the difference between right and wrong and the good teachings of the Lord, to be the best person he could be, and all that pain, all that effort, all that heartfelt love, blown away in an instant as he charged at the enemy and his brains splattered on the ground.

He clambered to his feet, taking deep breaths, steeling himself for the next stage of his journey. A mist was rolling in, the air chill and damp, and he assumed darkness would begin to fall within the next couple of hours. He had to find shelter if he was to last the night. He wished he'd remembered to get his watch repaired; the sky was sheathed in a thick blanket of cloud and gave nothing away, so he had little idea of the time. He didn't even know for how long he had been running. It seemed like most of the day, but he had a niggling suspicion that he hadn't covered as much ground as he hoped. The area was notoriously easy to get lost in, or to find oneself travelling in circles. He set off at a trot, intent on bedding down in the first shattered town building or abandoned farmhouse he came across.

But what exactly were his plans beyond that? He had no money, no contacts he could enlist to help him out of the country. His chance of escape seemed as slim as if he were back in the trench and awaiting that final whistle. The problem was that his desertion had been spur of the moment, a frantic bubbling of panic that eventually burst into full-blown terror. Although he had fixed bayonets in blank obedience and prepared to engage the enemy in combat, his gaze never straying to anyone on either side of him, the moment the signal came and the first soldiers went over and the shooting started, he had lost his nerve, dropped his rifle and faked injury. In the rush and confusion of men surging forward and then falling back as they were struck, he'd buried his head in his hands and played dead. As he'd willed himself to remain stationary, he could do nothing but listen to the thunderous, ear-splitting roar of the mortars, the high-pitched wail of injured men pleading for help and then cursing venomously when none arrived, and the rapid *thunk-thunk-thunk* of bullets meeting muscle and bone. When he'd opened his eyes, what was left of his regiment was several hundred yards away and he lay beneath a pile of bodies, butchered by machine-gun fire. Extricating himself slowly from the wretched heap, he'd crawled inch by inch in the opposite direction to the battle, praying silently that no one should see him and at the same time asking his Saviour to forgive his cowardice. Occasionally he would glance up, pulling corpses around him if he thought he heard anyone approaching, hating himself for his weakness. It was time consuming, arduous work, and he calmed himself through concentration, fixing his sight on some distant object, be it blasted tree or wire fence, and driving himself towards it. He was dimly aware that he was humming a hymn under his breath, a thin keening sound suggesting he was teetering on the brink of outright hysteria.

Indeed, this was insanity; he knew he had nowhere to go, knew he would be crossing dangerous terrain, knew he could give no excuse if he was discovered and was almost certainly facing court martial and the firing squad. But, he had reasoned, he had made his decision, however sudden, and should stick to the matter in hand, putting all his effort into finding a way out of this mess rather than questioning its wisdom. When he came to a secluded spot he vomited copiously, and some of the anxiety seemed to drain away with it. His mind was set, and every minute he stayed alive was a tiny triumph.

With that, he had wiped his mouth and started to run. *Onward, Christian soldier,* he had thought bitterly.

He had been fortunate, of that there was no doubt, that he had not been picked off by some lone sniper, and he was aware that his luck could not last for much longer. It occurred to him that maybe he had been seen by the enemy, but they had discerned in him no threat; they recognised a scared fellow human being fleeing for his life, someone who had opted out of the war, and who was not worth the trouble or the waste of ammunition. The thought gave him hope. He imagined others like him, from all sides of the conflict, congregating to wait out the hostilities. But such a haven amidst this hell, he realised, sounded fantastical.

Darkness was closing in far more quickly than he had guessed. Soon it would be pitch black, and he would be stranded out on the plain, with a choice of freezing to death during the night (a fire was out of the question if he was trying to avoid attention, even in the unlikely event of him finding dry tinder), or blundering on through the dark, risking impaling himself on barbed wire or stumbling in on a German gun emplacement. Neither option appealed. He scanned the horizon for any kind of shelter, but saw nothing. He slowed his pace to a walk, his eyes roving the landscape, but the light was faltering with every step; he could barely see his hand in front of his face. Resignation and a little fear were just beginning to worry at him, to gnaw away at his resolve, when something tripped him up.

Despite himself, he yelped in alarm as he flopped to the ground and immediately swore. His legs were hooked across a body, and more often than not where there was a body there were the remnants of an army. He glanced around quickly, certain his cry would've alerted somebody on watch, and sure enough, if he squinted, he could make out the thick seam of shadow that was a trench. But there was no sign of life. Steadman lay motionless for long minutes, waiting for anyone to emerge from the darkness, the razor-sharp wind chilling his skin and raising goosebumps. He resisted the urge to shiver, and breathed slowly, watching the thin, condensed streams dissipating in the air. But from the trench there was no movement.

Gradually, he began to edge forward, kicking his legs away from the corpse and lifting himself up onto his knees. If the trench was occupied, he thought, there had to be some kind of guard. But there was no light, no muted chatter or snores. The only explanation was that it had been overrun, the soldiers inside killed. But which side did it belong to? And could reinforcements be heading this way even as he sat and deliberated?

Steadman turned back to the body, his hands outstretched in front of him like a blind man, feeling the contours of the uniform, his eyes aching as he concentrated in trying to see through the gloom. The design of the jacket was unfamiliar; the man seemed to have been an officer. Steadman's fingers grazed a holster and he gingerly removed the revolver, running his touch over it. German issue. Clutching the gun in one hand, he lightly brushed the man's face, grimacing when his index finger disappeared into a penny-sized bullet hole in the man's forehead. It came away sticky.

At least they hadn't died by gas, he mused. It meant he wasn't in any immediate danger.

Wiping himself on the corpse's tunic, he looked back at the trench. It would be ideal to see out the night, hopefully providing him with some much-needed supplies, and it was unlikely British troops would be back this way if it had been disabled. The only problem he could foresee was a German regiment answering an injured radio operator's request for help just before he died and arriving here at daybreak. Then again, he could probably make use of one of the slain soldiers' uniforms and disguise himself amongst the dead once more.

He stood and moved to the lip of the trench, peering over cautiously. There was a dribble of light weakly spilling across the duckboards at the bottom. He returned to the German officer's body, took hold of both stiff arms and dragged it back with him, yanking it over the wire circumscribing the trench's edge with as much strength as he could muster. The weight of the carcass made it bow in the middle, and he stepped across quickly, easing himself down into the earthwork. His eyes sought the light he had seen, and discovered it was buried beneath several corpses; faintly illuminated pale white faces stared up at him, the blood criss-crossing their features black in the darkness. He pulled them away dismissively, ignoring the lifeless thumps they made as they landed at his feet, and grasped the lamp – little more than a half-melted candle in a glass case – in his left hand before swinging it to either side of him.

"Sweet Jesus," he whispered.

It was an atrocity: the dead lay stacked like timber the length of the trench, one on top of the other. Each new sweep of the lamp brought a fresh horror, a new coupling, as soldier was piled upon soldier. They had been slaughtered like cattle in an abattoir. Steadman had thought he had witnessed every possible obscenity that man could perpetrate on his fellows, but this brought the bile rushing to his throat in an instant; there was something about the sheer scale of devastation here, all contained within the claustrophobic confines of the trench, that made him retch. That, and the noxious smell, which seemed to palpably clog the air. It was the sickly stench of matter breaking down and liquefying, yet these corpses looked as if they had only been dead several hours at the most. It wasn't as if the heat of day could have brought about such a change. It had rained steadily the past few weeks, the temperature barely a couple of degrees above zero.

He brought the back of his free right hand to cover his nose and realised he still held the gun. It seemed suddenly paltry and comically unnecessary in the face of such carnage, but he felt loath to let go of it. As he gripped it tighter, he sensed himself drawing strength from it, gaining courage. Slowly, he began to walk down the trench in search of the supplies centre, the dead pressed high to either side of him, threatening to topple over onto him at any moment and drown him in cold, white flesh. He felt a little of the wariness the Israelites must have experienced as they were led between those high, dark, roiling walls of the Red Sea with nothing but their faith to protect them.

Steadman tried to keep his eyes on the ground, using the lamp to guide himself past outstretched limbs that he would've otherwise stumbled over, but the lure to raise the light and gaze upon the ravaged soldiers' features was too great. A ghoulish curiosity, he supposed. The sight was appalling, but he kept returning to it, testing his endurance the way the tongue endlessly probes a painful tooth; agonising yet irresistible. Even so, when he did glance up, many of the dead no longer had recognisable features; their faces were indistinct, pulpy masses as if they'd been shot at close range. Others were eviscerated, evidently bayoneted repeatedly. He shook his head, ashamed to call himself human, refusing to align himself with a species that could commit such heinous acts of barbarism.

Why had they been so systematically slaughtered, and with such an obviously bloodthirsty callousness, he wondered. If this was the result of some mania, why then take the time to stack the bodies as if for a funeral pyre?

The smell was beginning to make him feel dizzy, and every time he closed his eyes gory images assailed him. His legs cried out for rest, and his throat for water. He was on the verge of collapse when the lamp illuminated the opening to some kind of officers' structure ahead, judging by the map table standing outside it. He sighed with relief and increased his pace towards it. There was a tarpaulin hanging across the entrance acting as a makeshift door, and Steadman hoped it would provide adequate shelter, not only to shield him from the cold but also remove from view, at least temporarily, the horrors of the trench: out of sight, if not mind. He covered the last few yards at speed and stumbled inside, pulling the sheeting closed behind him.

The first thing that caught his eye was the bed in the corner, half-hidden in shadow. He couldn't remember the last time he'd felt the caress of a pillow. He looked around the dark room quickly, taking in the large table, the surface of which was scattered with the remains of a meal, a couple of chairs, the stove, the walls plastered with maps and directives. He crossed to the table, placed the lamp and the revolver upon it, picked up a jug three quarters full of water, and took a long swig. It tasted rusty, but he drained it to the last drop. Then he searched for scraps of food on the plates, shovelling hard pieces of bread into his mouth and chewing appreciatively before slumping exhaustedly into a chair.

Steadman sat unmoving for a very long time, too spent to think cohesively. Finally, he ran his hands over his face, his fingers rasping against his unshaven chin, and realised he was trembling. He felt hollow and scared. He would need a miracle to get out of this situation. He tried to reason through the consequences of today's actions and plan what he should do next, but his mind would not stay still for a moment; it fluttered, startled, from one scenario to another and would not allow him to concentrate. He assumed it was tiredness. His eyelids were beginning to droop as sleep crept up on him, and he was just considering whether to attempt to get the furnace going before burying himself beneath the bedclothes when he heard a soft mewling coming from the far corner.

He froze, unsure whether he had imagined it, deciding it could possibly be a combination of the wind and his fatigued senses. But then it came again, louder, undoubtedly human. It sounded like someone in considerable distress. He inched his hands across to the lamp and pistol and simultaneously rose to his feet, taking cautious steps around the table. There was a shape on the floor, silhouetted in the blackness. He shuffled closer and crouched down, lifting the lantern to see clearly.

Lying with his back to the wall was a British soldier, his familiar uniform soaked with blood. His eyes, rolling wide in their sockets like a beast aware of its impending death, squinted at the sudden light and tried to turn his head to face it. As he did so, Steadman saw the extent of the man's appalling injuries: a portion of the right side of his skull was missing, a cavernous red hole where his ear should have been, fragments of bone and clumps of hair standing at right angles. There was a vermilion halo sprayed on the wall behind him. Between his legs were three kerosene cans.

The soldier kept attempting to open his mouth to speak, but only made the soft, piteous cry that Steadman had heard. The man's eyes were moving wildly as if panic-stricken, his head shaking from side to side. Steadman got the impression that he was trying to communicate something, or maybe to warn him, but it wasn't until the man raised his right hand that had otherwise been hidden beneath his body and revealed the gun that was still clutched in it that he realised the horrific truth: the soldier had done this to himself. It had meant to be a suicide, but something had gone wrong, for it had left him mortally wounded and more than likely out of his mind in pain and shock. He pointed at the doorway and pulled the trigger repeatedly, grunting with each effort as the hammer slammed down on empty chambers. Presumably he'd tried to use the last bullet on himself.

"Can you hear me? Can you understand?" Steadman started to say, but faltered, realising it was pointless.

He muttered an oath under his breath, unable to comprehend. He felt dislocated, as if in his escape he had torn through a veil and discovered madness existing alongside him. He wanted to ask him what had happened here, what had terrified him to the point of trying to take his own life, but the soldier was obviously beyond rational thought; indeed, it was remarkable that he was still alive at all. But it left Steadman with a dilemma. He was loath to leave him in this state and prolong his suffering, but didn't know if he possessed the courage to finish what the man had started. The latter was the merciful option (there was nothing a medic could do for him now), but he wasn't sure he could reconcile that fact with his faith. In all his twenty-five years on the planet, he had never killed anything higher up the food chain than a bluebottle.

Odd, he mused, that with all the mass murder going on around him, thousands of men dying in seconds to capture a few feet of ground, he should balk at one act of kindness.

The soldier started to wail louder, and Steadman thought he caught the semblance of actual words beneath it. Surprised, he moved closer, straining to hear.

"...they... they *come*..." he gurgled, waving the gun in front of him, "...they know you're here..."

"Who? The Germans?"

If the man heard the question, he gave no indication. "...burn... should've *burned*..." His voice descended into a groan.

Steadman was puzzled for a moment, then glanced down at the kerosene cans and flashed back to the corpses piled outside.

...as if for a funeral pyre...

...burn...

"Mother of God," he said quietly. Understanding gradually began to dawn, and with it came a tingle of fear. Had this soldier been left here to destroy the remains? But to what end? To cover up a war crime? Or to make absolutely sure they were truly dead? For some reason he hadn't been able to go through with it – what had he seen that suicide was the only way out?

There was a scrabbling from beyond the doorway, a sound that turned Steadman's bowels to water. The dying soldier suddenly became animated, shaking and crying ever more violently. Steadman stood and backed away, his eyes fixed on the tarpaulin-covered entrance. He tried to reason that it could be rats scurrying amongst the bodies, but couldn't convince himself. He felt his breaths becoming shorter, his scalp prickle with sweat despite the chill. The revolver was slippery in his hand.

A low moan echoed outside, and then the sheeting bulged as if something was pushing against it, looking for a way in. Steadman attempted to swallow, the inside of his mouth like sandpaper, and raised the gun. He sensed a breeze brush against his face, but had seen nothing come through the doorway. He moved nearer, peering into the gloom.

"Show yourself," he demanded, his voice cracking, then yelled in fright as something grabbed his leg. He staggered, glanced down and recoiled in disgust: the upper half of a German soldier's torso was crawling across the floor, one hand clutched around his ankle. In its wake, like a snail's trail, it left a glistening smear of blood, painted by the entrails emerging from its rapidly evacuating stomach cavity. Its head was upturned, its eyes glazed, its mouth open and emitting a tiny wail from the back of its throat. Immobilised with shock, Steadman could do nothing but stare as the creature puts its lips to his trouser leg and attempt to bite through it.

Blinking himself out of his paralysis, he roared in revulsion, kicked out at it and managed to loosen its grip. He stepped away and without thinking fired the gun, catching it in the shoulder. The impact knocked it back, but it was clearly still alive; it struggled to right itself like a turtle flipped onto its shell. Steadman moved closer in horrified fascination, raising the revolver for a better shot, then caught himself before he could pull the trigger. He'd never killed anything before, either on two legs or four, and yet here he was prepared to act without pause. This creature, as his mind had fixedly called it, was still a man. He had survived horrendous injuries, either through enormous willpower or some quirk of physiology that enabled the heart to still beat even as the veins and arteries spurted into empty air, and, like the British soldier, could not be long for this world. Did that give him the right to help usher him towards death?

The German was crawling in his direction once more. Clearly, despite the pain he must be in, he was not going to give up on Steadman as his objective. Steadman allowed him to draw closer, and dropped to his haunches.

"I cannot help you," he enunciated, wishing he could recall what little of the language he knew. He shook his head, holding up his hands. *"Nicht... gut..."*

The man didn't seem to understand, or even to hear him. Still he approached, whimpering like a whipped dog, his insides rasping against the wooden floor. He grasped Steadman's boot and started gnawing on it as if it were a bone. Steadman could feel teeth attempting to penetrate the leather. Tears sprang in his eyes; he knew now that this was not one man desperately clinging onto life despite the ravages of his injuries. This was something else entirely, something beyond any kind of reasoning. He was no longer human, but the product of something... unholy. He shook himself free of the man's clutches, put the revolver to the back of his skull and squeezed his eyes shut at the same time as he squeezed the trigger. He winced at the bang, thinking, *forgive me.*

When he opened his eyes, the man was finally motionless, the contents of his head spread out in a parabola around him. Steadman shivered uncontrollably, the gun trembling before him. He could not stay in this charnel pit a moment longer. Better he took his chances on the battlefield or in a military cell than spend the night amongst this horror.

He moved towards the doorway, glancing back at the British soldier when he heard him cry out. "I'm sorry," he said, turning his head away.

Steadman pulled back the tarpaulin and bit down on a scream: the trench was alive. Where there was once dead stacked upon dead, shadows now shifted and slithered, a familiar wail carrying on the wind. He saw arms and hands clawing themselves free like the freshly buried rising from their graves. Dark figures wobbled as they stood and grew accustomed to their newfound resurrection. Some were missing appendages, some emptied viscera at their feet the moment they were upright, but it didn't take them long for their heads to turn in his direction. He could see them sense him, almost as if they were sniffing the air and hearing the beat of a warm, living heart. They began to shuffle forward, tripping over one another, the trench a tangle of grasping limbs.

Steadman did not hesitate. He rushed back to the soldier, grabbed the kerosene cans and began to splash fuel through the entranceway at the approaching creatures. When all three cans were empty, he flung the lantern into the throng.

Instantly, the dark confines of the trench became an explosion of light. The first of the figures were immediately immolated, man-sized candles awkwardly stumbling into those behind, spreading the fire. Thick black smoke began billowing into the air, and soon it was impossible to distinguish between the shapes being devoured by the wall of flame. For a moment, Steadman felt a small spark of hope; the inferno seemed to have halted them. But they were still coming, implacable and relentless, that ever-present moaning barely rising an octave. The ones at the front were shrivelled husks, turning to ash before his eyes, but they were replaced by others, unconcernedly treading on their fallen comrades as they surged forwards.

Steadman let loose a cry of frustration and fired at the nearest creature, blowing a puff of soot from its arm. There was no way out. He checked the chambers of the revolver and found he had three bullets left. That was at least some comfort.

He walked over to the British soldier and knelt beside him. He knew what Steadman intended and nodded slightly, his eyes pleading.

Steadman embraced him and placed the gun barrel under his chin, offering a silent prayer before firing.

He sat down next to the body and surveyed the room, littered with the dead. His faith had instructed him that life was to be preserved at all costs – but that had been shattered. Death was preferable to the parody of life these creatures exhibited.

They were beginning to come through the doorway, shadows dancing on the walls as the flames flickered. They bumped into the table and chairs and bed, trying to find their way around, igniting fires as they did so.

He put the revolver in his mouth, tasting the oil. Funny: he had refused to be sacrificed to the war, made the choice of life over death, and yet here he was preparing to offer himself up to Purgatory. This seemed the lesser of two evils; whatever those things were – and the Army was aware of them, that was plainly evident – he guessed that if they took him, he would end up in a far, far worse place. Better this way. Better a sinner than a victim of the Devil's works.

Steadman turned his head and looked up at a map of Europe on the wall, which was starting to smoulder and blacken as the creatures brushed past. *Maybe this is the Apocalypse,* he thought as his finger tightened on the trigger. *Maybe this is the beginning of the end.*

If they're the future... God help the living.

PART ONE

A Sound Like Breaking Glass

Cruell and sodaine, hast thou since
Purpled thy naile, in blood of innocence?

John Donne,
The Flea

CHAPTER ONE

Now

THE HEAD DIDN'T so much explode when hit by the bullet as deflate, a fat sack of gas puckering like an emptied balloon, haloed by a blossoming cloud of dust and powdered shards of ancient bone.

"Fuckin' things are rotten," Hewitt muttered. "See the way it burst like a goddamned watermelon?"

Gabe grunted a reply, chambering another round. He put his eye to the infrared sight and swept the street, their vantage point from atop the multi-storey car park offering a decent view of the shadowy thoroughfare beneath them. Dark figures were stumbling in the blood-red gloom of the eyepiece, hunched silhouettes shuffling aimlessly from one side of the road to the other. They seemed unperturbed by the shot that had rung out seconds earlier, or the fact that the skull of one of their brethren had vanished in a puff of miasmic residue, what was left below the neck keeling over like a felled tree. They stepped over him – or, rather, *through* him, snagging their feet on his form if they wandered too close – barely aware the body was even there. Gabe moved the rifle in tiny increments, following the path of each figure, trying to gauge the numbers, his crosshairs alighting on one for several moments before drifting across to its nearest companion.

"Well?" he heard Hewitt ask. "How many you reckon?"

"About two dozen in the street," he answered quietly, continuing his vigil. "Seem fairly spread out. Can't see too many nooks and crannies to hold any nasty surprises."

He felt Hewitt shift up onto his knees beside him and once more peer into his night-vision binoculars. It was enough for Gabe to finally take his eye from the rifle-sight and irritably study his colleague. The kid annoyed him for numerous reasons – he was excitable but lacked the experience to put that enthusiasm to good use, he wasted ammo, and he had a sarcastic streak, a trait Gabe found particularly ignoble – but it particularly rankled him when Hewitt would ask his opinion and then double-check for himself immediately afterwards. Gabe guessed the kid was trying to assume he had some kind of say in the decision-making process, rather than being the extra pair of hands he undoubtedly was, useful only for the inevitable donkey work. If it weren't for the bountiful haul they were expecting, Gabe would quite happily go on one of these missions alone. He could certainly do without having to converse with the little idiot. But he kept these niggles to himself, chiefly because Flowers seemed fond of the kid – Hewitt was, after all, eager to please and would go out of his way to find favour in the boss man's eyes, looking to weasel his way up the hierarchy. You had to watch what you said sometimes, in case a version of the truth spilled back to the wrong people.

"Yeah," Hewitt drawled with an infuriating note of authority to his voice that sounded alien coming out of his mouth. "Two dozen looks about right to me too." He turned to Gabe. "Where's the store?"

"Right at the end, in a little square offset from the main street."

"Shit." He looked anxiously again through the binoculars.

Gabe tried to stop the smile that creased his lips, but nothing could prevent it. He turned his head away so the kid wouldn't catch sight of it. "I think we can take 'em. Four-man team shouldn't have any trouble."

"What about the way back? We're gonna be weighed down –"

"I'll keep you covered, don't worry," Gabe said, admonishing himself for the patronising tone that had snuck in. He glanced at the man and woman silently crouched against one of the car park's concrete pillars behind them. "Ali, Davis – there's no other way round, so we'll be going straight through. Stay sharp. Standard routine; pick your targets and don't panic, okay?"

"Can't we use the motor?" the man – Davis – asked.

"Road's fucked," Hewitt interjected.

"What he said," Gabe continued. "It's blocked with debris, and we can't risk cracking an axle. We'll drive up as far as we can go, then we'll have to be quick on our toes. Ali, you'll have to stay with the vehicle. Keep the engine running. Let us know if the situation develops. I don't want to come out of there and find someone's stolen our ride."

The woman nodded. "You think there's others like us in the area?"

"Not in the immediate vicinity – deadheads are too concentrated – but our gunshots are gonna be heard by pockets of survivors, no question of that. Anything pops up that ain't maggoty, you give us a squawk."

Davis clicked the safety off on his snubnose. "This had better be worth it."

"Michaelson's info hasn't let us down yet," Gabe said, swinging his rifle onto his shoulder as he stood. "Come on, let's hop to it."

They scampered through the heavy silence of the abandoned car park, their feet tapping quietly against the cold grey ground. Lights still burned in fluorescent tubes positioned on the ceiling, powered by a forgotten generator left rumbling untended in the bowels of the building, giving the vast open space surrounding them a stark, flat glare. A few vehicles were dotted around this level, some of them with their doors hanging wide as if the occupants had fled in a hurry. Rancid bags of food bulged from the open hatchback of a nearby Fiat, a black cloud of flies rising from it as they passed, settling in their wake. Tyre marks and oil splatters streaked the floor, and something darker and thicker was sprayed up against a ticket machine. A fading crimson handprint neatly filled one of the reinforced glass panels of a door leading to the stairwell, the wood beneath it splintered as if repeatedly kicked.

Gabe led the others through the concrete expanse, gluing themselves to the walls where they could, avoiding the impenetrable shadows of the stairs or the lift shaft until they came in sight of his armoured Escort. He tossed the keys to Ali and motioned for her to start it up, then scanned the pools of fluorescent light diminishing into the distance. The emptiness was unnerving. If he concentrated, beyond the silence he could hear the moans drifting on the still air. In truth, they were always there, a white-noise hum you tried to tune out. It was a permanent aural backdrop, like mordant birdsong.

But all the birds are gone, he thought not for the first time, cocking his head and looking out at the starless night, *and the skies and treetops and roofs of the city will never echo with their sound again*.

The vehicle barked into life, the roar of Ali revving the accelerator rebounding off the concrete walls. The noise would undoubtedly attract some attention, but the stiffs were going to know they were amongst them soon enough anyway. Davis yanked open the rear door behind the driver's seat and folded himself in; Hewitt sparked up a cigarette and clambered in the other side, positioning his shotgun through the window. Gabe stood for a moment beside the rumbling car, listening to its timbre, holding a palm against the vibrating roof, confident that the engine was turning over smoothly, careful to discern there were no wheezy splutters emerging from the exhaust pipe. He'd briefly and inexpertly serviced the car himself only a few days before, but he had to make sure they could rely on their ride. London was no longer a town that you wanted to travel by foot if you could help it.

Satisfied, he swung into the bucket seat beside Ali and strapped himself in. The interior was refitted to provide the maximum protection, the tubular bars of a roll cage strengthening the shell if the Escort were to flip. Outside, front and rear windscreens were covered with a thick wire mesh that didn't particularly aid visibility but were a lifesaver when it came to force of numbers attempting entry. The side panelling and roof were reinforced with steel plates capable of withstanding a high-speed impact. It meant the vehicle had the rather undignified appearance of a hammered-together metal box, but previous excursions had proved both its reliability and durability. Many a time Gabe had ploughed it through a dozen-strong crowd of stiffs with barely a dent on the bodywork, their grasping fingers unable to find purchase, grave-brittle bones snapping when struck. It wasn't quite a tank – though Hewitt had badgered him often enough (not entirely jokingly) for some kind of mortar cannon to be operated through the sunroof – but it suited its purpose.

Ali guided the car past the raised exit barriers, the attendant booths long deserted, and onto the slip road. Gabe repeated the route to her, noting a handful of shambling figures detaching themselves from the twilight. The vehicle was like a beacon to them, its sound and movement awakening their interest – the only living thing, in all likelihood, within a couple of miles. He heard Hewitt working the slide on the shotgun behind him, and glanced in the wing-mirror to see him lean out slightly, flicking the dog-end of his cigarette at the nearest zombs.

"I don't want you taking any unnecessary potshots, Hewitt," Gabe warned him. "Conserve your ammo."

"Yeah, yeah," Hewitt murmured in reply, resting the barrel on the window frame.

Gabe turned in his seat to face the kid, but the younger man refused to meet his gaze, instead concentrating furiously on the darkened buildings passing by. Davis clearly caught the tension between the two, though he said nothing.

"I'm serious," Gabe remarked. "There are far, far too many of the things for us to gun down every one indiscriminately, and it's just a waste of resources we can't afford to squander. This isn't a duck-shoot. You choose your targets and you make them count, understand?"

"I said I heard you, O'Connell," the kid answered, glaring at Gabe finally. "I have done this once or twice before, you know. Christ, I can handle it."

"I know you've done it before." Gabe softened his tone, returning to face the front. "I'm just saying: don't leave yourself open."

"Main street's coming up on the left," Ali said quietly.

"OK, we'll only be able to get a couple of hundred yards down it before we'll have to bail out."

The dead were emerging in increasing numbers, their hungered, soul-black groans growing in volume. They staggered from shadowy shopfronts and doorways, stumbling off the pavement and onto the road, what little senses still chiming in their grey-green skulls alerting them to the proximity of warm flesh. They made half-hearted attempts at reaching out to the car as it sped past them, their cries developing a note of angry disappointment. Gabe watched them in the mirror attempt a stiff-legged pursuit, arms held out in front of them, pushing past one another with an eagerness that seemed at odds with their barely functioning bodies. *They only come alive at the prospect of food,* he thought, *and right now we're their moving feast.*

"Fuckers," Hewitt murmured from the back, grimacing at the throng with an unconcealed hatred.

Ali slowed the Escort slightly to take the turn onto the main road, wrenching hard on the steering wheel. The tyres spun on something on the tarmac and lost their purchase, the vehicle's rear fishtailing, and for a moment the car was skidding, the sharp screech of rubber drowning out the cries of the dead. The woman pumped the brake and steered into the slide, bringing the car to a juddering halt. Thrusting it into gear, she stomped on the accelerator and the vehicle lunged forward, powering down the high street. Watching her from the corner of his eye, Gabe noticed that Ali hadn't even broken a sweat, her face a mask of grim determination. A small, morose woman in her forties, an ex-wife of one of Flowers' button men, she was one of the best drivers in the boss man's predictably male-dominated outfit and had characteristically proven her worth with little flamboyance or showy technique. Even Hewitt held his tongue when piloted by her, confident in her hands.

"What was it?" Gabe asked over his shoulder.

"Roadkill, I think," Davis answered, peering out of the back window at a red pulpy residue the car had just skidded through. "Something splattered across the highway."

"Remains of the day," Hewitt remarked, snorting back a laugh. "Somebody ended up zombie supper."

"Enough of that," Gabe snapped, trying to keep the tension from his voice. "Concentrate on the job in hand."

The hordes of dead were becoming more clotted as they sped forward, a clawing, mewling mass that shambled towards the Escort as one. The longest deceased were merely desiccated skeletons clothed in a tissue-thin brown veil of rank flesh, their eyes shrivelled back into their sockets, their crooked limbs flapping independently of the torso as if the muscle and bone within had perished; the freshest corpses had recognisable features, the skin grey and taut, their fatal wounds often readily apparent. They were young and old, male and female, of all races, from every level of the social strata. Death was the great leveller, no question of that, Gabe mused. There was no distinction between them anymore, nothing to separate this mob into individual entities: a paunchy bald man in a torn business suit lurched beside a teenager in motorcycle leathers with a scarlet-raw face, and a grandmother still clothed in her burial shroud and caked in the undertaker's make-up. They paid no heed to each other, each seemingly oblivious to their neighbour and indeed the numbers of their kin surrounding them. Locked inside their own private resurrection, all they wanted, all they hungered for, was the living, driven by an insatiable craving their brains could not possibly fathom.

The car shuddered as a ghoul bounced off its wing, Ali tightening her grip on the wheel in a bid to keep the vehicle under control. She made little effort to avoid the deadheads – indeed, it was impossible to slalom between them, so dense was the crowd becoming – and concerned herself with ensuring the car stayed central on the road. The stiffs merely shuffled into its path like bugs collecting on the windscreen, utterly ignorant of the velocity the vehicle was moving at. The front end ploughed through a skinny naked man, who exploded like a dandelion in a strong wind, fragments washing back in the Escort's slipstream.

Hewitt was right, Gabe thought. *Damn things are falling apart.*

"Don't think I can go much further," Ali yelled above the *thump-thump-thump* of the dead rebounding off the bodywork or fists slamming down on the steel panelling. The car's suspension started to bounce as it rolled over cadavers and rubble. Several blackened vehicles lay on their sides on the pavement ahead, or poking half out of shattered shop windows. A bus leaned precariously against a wall, displaying its undercarriage.

"OK, this is the end of the line, guys," Gabe shouted, tearing free his seat belt. "Hewitt, Davis – create a circumference, then follow me." He turned to the woman. "Ali, once they start following us, that'll take the heat off you. Turn the car around, keep her running. We're not back in ten minutes, get out of here."

"Good luck."

Gabe smiled. "Piece of cake."

Hewitt was the first out, simultaneously throwing open the door and discharging his shotgun at the nearest knot of ghouls; the blast punched through them as if he had hurled a grenade, flinging a handful backwards and bisecting one at the waist. He worked the slide and fired again, popping a number of heads with a single shell, then used the butt to club the skull of a zombie in a stained traffic warden's uniform that dared to venture too close. *Goddamn*, he thought, *that felt satisfying.*

Davis appeared on the other side of the Escort and sprayed the dead with a burst from his sub-machine gun, raking them with bullets that tore through their empty, papery carcasses. They folded like wheat before a thresher. He pulled his snubnose from the waistband of his jeans with his left hand and snapped off half a dozen deft, accurate headshots, silencing the prone, moaning zombies forever.

Gabe clambered from the car, put his rifle to his shoulder and marched forward, firing with each step, taking down a ghoul at a time. He didn't break his stride but swung his gun smoothly from left to right, choosing each target quickly and calmly. His breathing was shallow and composed, his actions clinical, unhurried; he simply switched off that part of his brain that whispered just how close he was to being eaten alive, a hair's breadth away from having his entrails devoured before his very eyes.

It was a tightrope-walk act, a death-defying (undeath-defying?) feat, acknowledging the physical danger he was in but reaching an inner equilibrium that would not surrender to it. He had lived and fought in this land of the dead for long enough to adapt to it and meet its challenges accordingly. Nothing would faze him, he didn't think, not ever again. Not even the bizarre sight of two undead schoolgirls – little more than fifteen, he guessed, when they had resurrected – stuttering towards him, white blouses slathered in blood, tights and sneakers shredded, a forearm wound on one of them open to the bone and suppurating, the cheek of the other swollen with blowfly. He felt an undeniable tingle of sadness as he watched them stagger, groans emerging from their still lungs, their misted eyes fixed unshakably on him, but the pause was only momentary as he dropped both to the ground with a couple of neat holes drilled in their foreheads.

"Let's go," Gabe shouted, satisfied that they had cleared enough breathing space. "Move."

"You sure you know the way?" Hewitt demanded.

"Just follow me."

The three of them ran. They had flares tucked into their belts, and would light them at regular intervals and drop them to the ground as they progressed, creating a landing strip for them to move through. The ghouls feared fire for some reason – a primeval terror that apparently still functioned in their putrid cerebella – and the burning torches made them pause. Gabe was in the lead, his rifle held against his chest, swatting away any stiffs that came within two feet of him, trying to limit his ammo usage. It didn't take much effort to knock the walking dead to the ground, their reactions and balance dulled by entropy – if you were quick on your feet and kept your wits about you, you could embark on short trips like this with the minimum of hindrance – and right now all he considered them to be was an annoyance to be avoided rather than an enemy that needed destroying. Maybe the day would come when the living would take to the streets and attempt to wipe out the zombies, but there were too many of them at the moment for such an undertaking to be practical. It would require an organised army to perform the necessary cull, and even the government and military had seemingly lost all pretence of containing the situation. All that was left was for guys like Flowers, and no doubt many others, to seize the opportunities that the world now presented them with, and make a killing.

He cast an eye over his shoulder to check his colleagues were still behind him. Davis followed, arms outstretched, his snubnose in one hand and his machine-gun in the other, turning his head left and right as he made sure the ghouls were kept at bay, occasionally firing a short burst into the throng. He was a big man, over six foot and wide around the midriff, his physique made even bulkier by the body armour he wore over his chest. It was supposedly one more layer of defence for the dead to tear through if you ever found yourself compromised, but Gabe considered such garments restricting when speed was of the essence. He presumed Davis had purloined the vest from his former occupation as a cop – along with what seemed half his station's armoury – and the skills he brought to Flowers' organisation made him a valuable member of the team. It took Harry a while to trust having an ex-policeman in the outfit, Gabe remembered, but these days notions of law and criminality were redundant, brushed aside by a common foe to be united against. Davis kept himself to himself mostly, no doubt ruminating on the strange path fate had chosen for him, and perhaps a touch ashamed too.

Hewitt was bringing up the rear, keeping watch on the ragged bunches of the dead regrouping in the trio's wake and starting to lurch after them. So far the kid's notoriously itchy trigger-finger seemed to be under control, but Gabe didn't expect it to last long. Hewitt had too much to prove, a wild and unpredictable element that could put them all in danger if it wasn't stamped on soon. He thought following orders was somehow beneath him, and that being a loose cannon was an endearing quality. Barely in his twenties, he was a youngster that had graduated from teenage gangs and petty thievery to armed robbery overnight, and hadn't had the time to mature. He had a ruthless streak, which admittedly to some was an asset, and appeared to genuinely loathe the deadheads, though Gabe wondered if he truly saw much distinction between them and the living. Certainly, he knew the kid disliked and resented him and would undermine his command any chance he could.

The street they ran down had once been a busy retail area, alive even at the twilight hours with taxis and shoppers, light flooding across the paving stones from glittery window displays. Now, it was like a smudgy stain, bereft of all colour; the stores that lined the thoroughfare were gutted holes that merged with the night. From the glow cast by the flares, Gabe could see the outlines of mannequins slumped against the spiderwebbed glass, the grey flicker of TVs tuned to long-dead channels broadcasting static twenty-four hours a day, the liquefying mass of fruit and vegetables left to rot from discarded crates.

He spotted the turning for the square they needed, and turned to Davis. "Over there," he said, pointing with the barrel of his rifle. The road came to an abrupt end, giving way to a pedestrianised section, and a gap opened in the shopfronts. Gabe motioned with his head for them to follow and doubled his speed towards it.

Upon entering the cul-de-sac, he saw their destination immediately, tucked away in the corner of the narrow faux-Elizabethan square with its dark-beamed boutiques and coffee outlets. How Michaelson had managed to find it was a mystery – unless you knew it was here, it could easily evade the attention of the casual passer-by. Running his eyes over the exterior of the building, Gabe guessed that it hadn't been touched since its owners had fled, which was a minor miracle.

Their scout had certainly earned his commission, he thought with a smile, as he appraised the gold script upon the black sign above the door: HENDERSON & SON, JEWELLERS.

The other two men caught up with him. "OK, Davis, I want you on lookout," he ordered, glancing at them. "Hewitt, with me. This shouldn't take us more than five minutes."

Without a word, the former policeman passed the kid the two empty holdalls and positioned himself beneath the awning of a pizza restaurant, resting his machine-gun on a metal dining table. Gabe led Hewitt to the jeweller's entrance and tried the door – locked. Discerning nothing beyond the glass, he swung his rifle-butt and smashed the panelling, immediately setting off a shrieking siren that bathed the area in a blue pulsating light. Hewitt stepped out from the doorway and levelled his shotgun at the alarm several feet above them, blowing it off the wall. The strident wail was cut dead, devolving into an oscilloscope whine as pieces of the plastic casing clattered to the ground around them.

Hewitt shrugged as he returned to Gabe. "Might as well hear ourselves think."

The older man knocked the shards of glass free and stepped into the darkened shop. He fished into his pocket and pulled out a flashlight, sweeping its beam over the cases of rings, necklaces, brooches and watches. The interior of the store was small, with just a counter and till at the far end, and a solid wooden door leading to a back room. Gabe strode over to it, but that too was bolted.

"OK, we haven't got the time to be graceful about this," Gabe muttered. "Grab as much as you can." He yanked a crowbar from his bag and shattered the nearest cabinet, silver and gold chains spilling out into his hands. There was a crash behind him as Hewitt did the same, tipping an entire display of pendants into the bag he had spread on the carpet. The two men worked quickly and efficiently, not stopping to separate diamonds from crystal but pouring them all haphazardly into the holdalls, occasionally casting a glance to Davis outside as he sporadically let rip with a burst of automatic fire. The groans of the dead seemed to be growing closer.

"You nearly finished there?" Gabe asked, zipping up one of the holdalls. He picked it up briefly to test its weight, wincing as his muscles strained, then wandered over to the till, breaking it open with a couple of blows from the crowbar. He pocketed a few hundred pounds in cash.

"Almost," Hewitt muttered, shaking a box of signet rings into his bag. He crouched, sifting a hand through the loot, then looked up at his companion. "What the fuck are we doing this for anyway?"

Gabe sighed. "We haven't got the time for this –"

"I mean, look at us – robbing a jewellery store like it fucking *means* anything any more." He held up a handful of necklaces. "All of this, it's worthless... pointless. The best we can do with it is melt it down into more slugs to put through their rotten fucking heads."

"Harry knows what he's doing."

"Does he? Seems to me we should be out there stomping on a few zombie skulls, making a concerted effort to be putting the bastards below ground where they should be, rather than stealing shit that's got no fucking value anymore –"

"You think this situation is going to last?" Gabe threw his arms up, impatient now. "You think the deadheads are going to be around forever? They're falling apart, you said so yourself. It's a plague, it's running its natural course, and the world adapts around it and learns to evolve. A fucking meteor wiped out the dinosaurs and the balance of the planet shifted, but it set off in a new direction. That's what Flowers sees is going to happen – the zombies are going to pass on and we're going to have to put ourselves back together again. And he's going to be in a position to be top of the heap." He kicked a jingling tangle of gold chains towards the kid. "And this stuff... yes, it means nothing now, but in five, ten years Harry's going to emerge as the richest, most powerful man in the city and everyone's going to have to barter with him for a slice."

Hewitt looked sullen. Gabe motioned to him to pick up his bag. "Come on, let's move. We're running out of time." He unhooked his two-way from his belt and spoke into it. "Ali, how's it going?"

"Few creeps trying to get in, but most followed you," the crackly voice responded. "Feel like a sitting duck out here. I think they're getting agitated."

"Understood. We'll be with you in a couple of minutes."

Gabe locked stares with Hewitt for a moment, then strode past him out of the shop, swinging his holdall onto his shoulder, shifting its weight until it felt comfortable. Davis raised his eyebrows and nodded towards the bodies of a half-dozen ghouls lying in the mouth of the square. More were trying to navigate past their fallen cousins.

"OK," Gabe murmured wearily. "Lock and load."

Hewitt emerged from the jeweller's, two bags strapped across his back, chambering shells into his shotgun. He barely acknowledged the other two men, merely walked towards the stiffs that were shuffling nearer, pumping the slide-action. "Come on, you fuckers," he called. "Who's first?"

Gabe shook his head. What was it like to feel young?

CHAPTER TWO

THEY DROVE IN silence out of central London's narrowly clustered maze of streets, a tangible sense of relief flooding through the interior of the car as the roads became wider, the buildings sparser, and they headed into the outskirts. Davis and Hewitt sat in the back reloading their weapons, the former breathing a little hard, Gabe noticed. He hoped it was merely the weight of the body armour coupled with the frantic return to the vehicle that was the cause of his exhaustion, but he'd caught, out of the corner of his eye, the former policeman wiping his brow with a trembling hand, and wondered if the pressures of their situation were starting to catch up with him. Gabe had seen it happen to sterner stuff than Davis, and you could never predict how those nearing breakdown could affect future outings like tonight's.

If the last few years had taught him anything – if the plague had taught humanity anything – it was the importance of reliance on comrades, of knowing there's somebody with you to cover your back. Strange that it should be a crisis of this magnitude to deliver such a lesson, but its simplicity did not diminish its truth – operate as a tight unit, and you'll survive. Allow it to unravel a touch and you put everybody's lives at risk.

For all Flowers' failings – and he pushed those in his organisation hard in his pursuit of power, there was no question of that – Harry understood that a machine could only perform at its best if the individual parts were all working together. One loose screw could bring it crashing down, as previous experience has shown. Gabe would have to have a word with the boss about Davis, maybe recommend him for evaluation with the docs. Better to catch these things early.

He supposed he ought to have a whisper too about Hewitt's increasing belligerence and refusal to toe the line, but knew he would think better of it once they reached base. The idiot found favour in Flowers' court for some reason, and Gabe would undoubtedly be seen as making waves if he criticised Hewitt's conduct, no matter how obliquely. He couldn't quite ascertain what it was that Harry saw in the kid, but he clearly sparked something in him – some nascent paternal feelings, perhaps – that brought forth the rare qualities of indulgence and forgiveness from the old man. Flowers evidently looked upon him as quasi-family. Judging by Hewitt's outburst in the jeweller's, the appreciation was hardly mutual; the youngster clearly saw Harry's scheme as a sign that their employer was losing it, and probably spent many an evening dreaming what he would do with the outfit if it had him at its head. Flowers had seen off leadership challenges before, but this one could strike him close and deep if it wasn't nipped in the bud. Trouble was always brewing, Gabe thought, rubbing the bridge of his nose.

The zombies were less of a nuisance once they got out of the city, scattered mostly in groups of fours and fives in parks and residential districts, staggering between the privet hedges seeking living flesh to feast upon. Another primal instinct that seemed to be still blipping in their brains was a herding nature: the stiffs appeared to be naturally aware that, with supplies so close to hand, most human survivors were found hiding in the big concrete tangles of the major conurbations ('cementeries,' Gabe had heard one wit dub these overrun metropolises). Therefore, concentrated numbers of the dead gravitated there like predators drawn to a watering hole, hoping to chance upon something warm and tender, leaving the sprawling suburbs relatively empty and easier to traverse.

Ali guided the Escort with little effort through the smouldering, garbage-strewn streets of Catford and Bromley, casually avoiding the few cadavers that stumbled into their path. Watching the deserted semi-detached houses pass by – front doors standing wide open, children's toys left scattered in gardens, the odd splash of red on a window – Gabe felt tears prick his eyes. He pinched them closed for a moment. The dark, charnel terrors of the city he could cope with (he had long been inured to the day-to-day bloodshed by now) but it was the quiet reminders of life before the dead rose that tugged at his heart. What was once comforting familiarity now looked like a blackened shell with all the life, all the goodness, ripped out of it. These routes through suburbia never failed to affect him in this way, but while he could stem the tears from flowing he couldn't turn off his emotions entirely. Everything he'd taken for granted, everything normal, now looked alien without the context of the people who'd once lived here. They'd breathed life into it, and without them it merely became a place fit for the dead.

He'd like to think that what he told Hewitt earlier was true; that this was a phase they were travelling through, a footnote in history. He imagined the fourteenth-century peasants sprouting boils and seeing entire towns and villages decimated thought much the same about the Black Death – that their situation was surely going to get better, that this couldn't be the end for mankind. They had been facing species extinction, to be wiped from the surface of the earth, and humanity, resilient as ever, crawled through it, clinging tenaciously to life as it always had. Now it was staring down into the abyss once more, and the optimistic embraced the notion that there had to be an escape. Flowers was one such idealist, fervently having faith that it was only a matter of time before society would start to rebuild itself (of course, Harry had his own ideas of what that society would be, including instating him as its lord and master).

"All outbreaks have a shelf-life," he'd told Gabe once. "They ravage through an unprepared populace, laying waste to everything they touch. But they also consume themselves eventually, all that energy and greed directed inwards."

Gabe had thought that much the same could be said about humanity.

Flowers was waiting for the virus to burn itself out, when it could no longer sustain the corpses it had reanimated. Gabe wanted to believe that would happen, and he couldn't deny there were signs that the zombies were disintegrating – the bacteria that bubbled away inside each ghoul's cranium, that had awakened its motor functions, was no match for time and tide, after all. But could things ever really return to what they had once been? Could these homes ever be filled again without being a pale imitation of the life they had once contained? He wondered if he'd grown so used to the emptiness that the sight of people walking freely again might seem equally unreal, a simulacrum of civilization recreated from memory but with its soul indelibly bruised.

The streetlamps and boxy buildings of the suburbs faded away as the car picked its way through the Kent countryside. Gabe marvelled at the way nature still ran its course, unaware of the cataclysmic events that had taken place around it. If it wasn't for the quiet – even in the densest of forests, it was rare to hear birdsong – out here it would be possible to believe that nothing was wrong. The woodlands and emerald fields were mostly untainted by the dead, though the odd lost shambling figure could sometimes be discerned on a remote path, looking from a distance no more dangerous than a rambler. Even then, any ghouls you encountered within these environs had more than likely been released by a local farm for sport rather than being on the prowl; it had become a popular country pastime to take potshots at captured deadheads, occasionally even riding them down. Flowers had aspirations to get in with the horsy set, and had been on several of these hunts, though Gabe guessed that as a quarry they offered little challenge and not much of a satisfying kill. As with any of these shindigs, it was a social gathering with a touch of carnage thrown in. Harry had told him – typically eyes a-gleam like it was a barometer of a man of his stature – that one of the squires that had invited him for such a get-together had scores of stiffs locked in a converted stable, ready for whenever his friends fancied some target practice of a weekend. The resurrected had been rounded up in the city and carted back in cattle trucks.

This kind of attitude was symptomatic of the way some had adapted to living with the dead, Gabe thought as Ali turned the Escort off the winding lane and onto a narrow, conifer-lined track. Once the initial shock had dissipated, once it became clear that the authorities were not going to be able to solve it – indeed, once it was apparent that there was no authority left at all – people resorted to different methods of coping with the crisis. The immediate, predictable response for many was to go on a looting rampage, positively embracing the breakdown of order, reverting to turn-of-the-century outlaws; a few survived this way, living on the road, smashing and grabbing what they could, but most underestimated the numbers of the dead that were growing daily, and especially did not take them seriously as a threat. Stupidity was the chief cause of death within the first few months. For your average Joe, once they realised that there was nowhere to run to, that the plague was everywhere, they hunkered down like refugees in a war-torn state, waiting for somebody to tell them what to do. They were still there now, years later, living in tribes in cellars and boarded-up tenements, scrabbling for scraps, still hoping to be rescued.

But for a few, he mused, as the track widened, the foliage cleared and the vehicle slowly approached the gates of Flowers' mansion, it's been a matter of staying in control. The ruling elite has always tackled disaster in its own fashion, far removed from the epicentre, and the emergence of the undead had been no different for them than any other form of social unrest. They used it for their own advantage, whether for recreation – in the case of the ghoul hunts, and any manner of unsavoury antics the aristocrats got up to within their lodges – or for consolidating their already powerful position. For Harry, it was the latter; once he saw past the ravenous zombies, the outbreak was a fortuitous means to an end. He'd always lived outside governmental authority anyway, and so the breakdown of the police and the strictures of the law courts were to him of little consequence; on the contrary, their collapse was to be rejoiced.

"What," he'd say, sweeping his arms about his opulent study, "I'm supposed to be crying because I don't have to pay tax anymore? That there's no longer some snoop from Customs and Excise investigating my affairs? That I'm going to miss my phones being tapped?"

Flowers viewed it as a golden opportunity, ripe for the plucking. His regular business shrank once the plague took hold – he gradually lost contact with his associates overseas, as Russia, Syria, Pakistan and the US all seemingly suffered similar fates, descending into chaos, and unsurprisingly the takings from his clubs and bars went through the floor in the space of twenty-four hours – but the boss man had always prided himself on seeing the bigger picture. He had no need for profit in the interim, and money was as worthless as the paper it was printed on. So he drew himself back, planned out his strategy and prepared for his own personal and financial resurrection once the virus was played out. He built himself a regular army to protect him and enforce his will, sent scouts into the city to uncover vital supplies, had scientists kidnapped from Ministry of Defence laboratories to conduct research into the epidemic to gain an understanding of how to destroy the dead more efficiently. This was a chance that had been handed to him, and he couldn't afford to fuck it up; never, in his twenty years as head of his firm, could he imagine a time when he might be able to legitimately call the whole of London his domain. What had once been carved up by various crimelords all angling for more territory was now there for the taking in its entirety, and he was determined it was going to be his. And of course, with the capital established, he could spread his tentacles north, east, west and south, engulf a country that had fallen into anarchy. Whenever Harry talked about such an eventuality with Gabe, he hugged himself, his excitement contagious.

"The possibilities," he would whisper, "the possibilities that have been presented to me..."

As Ali pulled up to the main gates, a guard opened a padlocked door set into the chainlink fence and strode across, a flashlight bobbing in hand, an M16 weighted in the other. He stopped at the passenger side, Gabe rolling down the window to greet him.

"Patricks."

"Hey, O'Connell," the guard replied, shining the light into the car. "Any problems?"

"No, went fine." Gabe winced at the glare of the torch. Patricks crouched and swept it left and right, pausing momentarily to rest the beam on each occupant's face, then gave the outside of the vehicle a casual perusal. "Stiffs seem to be falling apart more than ever."

The other man nodded curtly. "Tell me about it. Couple got through the perimeter out by the woods earlier on." He blithely motioned behind him to the dense wall of shadow to the rear of the great house. "Tripped a landmine and the remains been stinking out the gardens ever since. Poor old Sanderson has been burying that shit since sundown. Even the dogs won't touch it."

"Can't say I blame them. They've been known to refuse Barrett's fried breakfasts."

Patricks barked a laugh in agreement. "Oh, by the way, the old man wants to see you. Said you were to call in on him when you got back."

He slapped the Escort's roof and indicated for them to continue. He slung his rifle over his shoulder, unhooked a two-way from his belt, and spoke briefly into it. Seconds later, the gates swung open. Gabe gave the guard the thumbs-up, and Ali edged the car through the opening and onto the main driveway, tyres crunching on the gravel that curled round in a semi-circle to the front of the mansion. The gates clanged shut as soon as they were through.

Positioned just inside them on either side of the driveway were two sentry posts, an armed guard stationed on each, equipped with infrared nightsights and high-calibre automatic weapons. The lawns surrounding the house were a cat's cradle of tripwires – themselves interspersed with warning signs for the benefit of the living – triggering small bundles of dynamite. The perimeter fence could be electrified if necessary, and dog-handlers patrolled its length constantly, the animals particularly good at sniffing out approaching ghouls. It was the most well-defended building that Gabe had seen since the advent of the outbreak, and that included governmental offices: one of the many testaments to Harry's organisational skills as well as his wealth.

The mansion's ivy-choked eighteenth-century facade belied the modern interior, Flowers having gutted much of the original fixtures and fittings to make way for the operations centre he required: libraries and studies were stripped to accommodate research labs, armouries and workshops. For an old geezer, he didn't seem to care for tradition or nostalgia; business in his opinion was all about staying one step ahead. To that end he was something of a gadget freak, and loved to drop in on the tech-boys, who would regale him with their latest developments.

Ali pulled the car up alongside several others outside the garages. Gabe stepped out and opened the boot, removing the holdalls and passing them to Davis and Hewitt, who appeared at his side.

"I'm going to see what Harry wants," he told the two men. "Take that lot down to the treasury. And make sure you get an inventory, OK?" Gabe locked stares with Hewitt, who grumpily spun away and trudged towards the house, before turning his attention to the ex-cop. "Keep an eye on him," he murmured. "Ensure everything's tagged and bagged." Davis nodded his assent and followed his colleague.

Gabe turned to see Ali emerge from the vehicle. She locked it up and threw him the keys. He smiled in gratitude, but her hangdog expression didn't change.

"There's about a quarter tank in there," she told him. "Might want to fill her up, in case you need to get somewhere in a hurry."

"I'll do it in the morning, thanks."

"You worried about him?" she asked, leaning against the side of the

Escort and nodding towards the small figure of Hewitt climbing the stone steps to the front door.

"I guess. A bit." He shrugged. "He's too reckless, and doesn't account for the consequences. I think he sees this all as one big videogame."

"He'll never listen to advice. Take that from someone who's raised a pair of teenage boys." Gabe vaguely remembered her mentioning her children before, but had always refrained from enquiring what had happened to them. "The only time he'll take stock of his actions is if he puts himself in danger. If he nearly gets himself killed, then you might see a different side to him."

"Wishful thinking," he replied, half joking.

"Could be the best lesson he'll ever get," she answered, and strolled away towards the garages, leaving Gabe wondering exactly what kind of mother she'd been.

HE NODDED TO the two bored-looking guys standing guard just inside the entrance, and made his way through the stone-flagged reception hall, a cavernous space dominated by the huge carpeted staircase that swept up to the first floor. Despite the lateness of the hour, sounds of activity still echoed from the many corridors branching off the foyer. Indeed, the headquarters of Flowers' outfit never really slept, the men working in shifts on various tasks, from the upkeep of the house to zombie procurement. Harry himself only snatched sleep when it was unavoidable, feeling that he'd be missing something important otherwise. Gabe considered dropping in on the kitchen after he'd reported to the boss, which ticked over twenty-four-seven for the benefit of those toiling through the night. He could do with a cup of tea and a chance to put his feet up; it was easy to forget how important these simple pleasures were when you spent much of your time putting bullets through the heads of decaying cadavers.

He spotted a familiar face emerge from one of antechambers, twirling a dog lead in his hand.

"Yo, Hendricks," Gabe called, smiling. "Taking your lady friend out tonight?"

"Oh yes," he replied, glancing down at the chain with affection. "A chance to get away from you animals and spend an evening with someone a tad more civilised."

"I'm sure her conversation's a blast."

"Ella listens, that's the main thing. It's an underrated quality."

Ella was his tawny German Shepherd, one of the handful of dogs kept in the kennels for patrol purposes. Hendricks had a particular affinity with all of them, but she was his favourite, and she was remarkably well trained. Affable and docile for much of the time, as soon as she caught whiff of a Returner her wolfen nature emerged. It surprised Gabe to learn that even the dogs hated the ghouls, without even knowing what they truly were, which made the stiffs something quite unique – a common enemy that bonded man and beast.

"You want to try it some time, O'Connell," he continued. "You don't know how refreshing it is just to have a quiet few moments, just enjoying each other's company."

"Hey, sounds beautiful. Me, I think I'll stick with the human race."

"That's always been your problem: misplaced loyalty."

"Talking of which, you seen the old man tonight?"

"Yeah, he's with the boffins," Hendricks answered, swinging the lead towards an annexe behind the staircase. "Ashberry's there too. Harry seems quite excited about something the colonel picked up on the airwaves."

"No shit?"

"You know how he is, always got some bit between his teeth. Listen, I hear the call of the wild, so I better go."

"Don't want to keep your canine chums waiting."

"Fuck you, you're just jealous," he said, laughing as he headed towards the front gardens.

Gabe strode down the dark, bare passage towards the lab complex, smiling to himself. He'd known Hendricks since he first joined Flowers' organisation and he hadn't changed in that time; a big, soft-hearted lug of a man, perhaps too generous of spirit for a professional thief and enforcer. He was defiantly old school, a generation and world away from the likes of Hewitt, and took no pleasure in violence, using it as a last resort and only under the specific orders of the boss. He was a natural to be in charge of the dogs, and seemed to genuinely prefer their company to that of his colleagues. Gabe often wondered what had led him to falling in with Harry and choosing a life outside the law when he appeared to exhibit none of the qualities one would expect, but Hendricks would not be drawn, merely stating that it was impossible for anyone to predict where they will end up. Instead he would turn the questioning onto Gabe, asking whether he could explain what *he* was doing being part of the firm, and Gabe could only shake his head, unable to answer. It was a bizarre situation to be in, but ever since the outbreak he'd known he'd made the right choice. If he hadn't joined the outfit, he'd no doubt be just another survivor at best, scratching out an existence amongst the ruins.

The corridor opened out into the research facility, and he spotted Flowers and Colonel Ashberry watching the scientists through an observation window. Beyond the glass was the lab area, where a number of whitecoats were flitting between half a dozen morgue slabs upon which zombie subjects were strapped. Gabe paused in the doorway and cleared his throat. The two men glanced over their shoulders and raised their eyebrows in recognition, Harry immediately returning his gaze to the work being done before him.

"Gabriel, my boy," his employer said. "All back in one piece?"

"Safe and sound," Gabe replied, walking forward, nodding a greeting to the military man. "We didn't encounter any problems."

"What about Michaelson's info? Was it accurate?"

"On the money, so to speak. Store hadn't been touched since the deadheads rose. I think we came away with between fifty and hundred K's worth of merchandise."

Harry finally turned to face him. "Impressive." The boss was an imposing figure in the flesh; lean and wiry with a grizzled, sandblasted complexion and a few white hairs still fighting the good fight on his crown. The watery blue eyes that peered out from the craggy folds of his face, however, revealed the intelligence that lay within that pensionable frame. Once you found yourself fixed in their glare, it seemed he was capable of sensing the slightest untruth. His mood too was never easy to judge, and that kept those around him nervous, a wrong-footedness he often used to his advantage. Gabe had never seen anyone who could switch from a beaming smile to a look of murderous rage with nary an expression in between. "But then you've always been one of my best thieves, Gabriel."

"I just go where I'm pointed."

"Indeed. What have you stolen for me over the years? Guns? Money? Computer equipment? You've even kidnapped the odd rival, if memory serves."

"On your orders."

"Without question. But my point remains that you can be relied upon to get the job done with the minimum of fuss." Without taking his eyes off Gabe, Flowers motioned towards the lab with a swift nod of the head. "Do you ever consider yourself a remote-control creature, O'Connell?"

Gabe flicked his gaze through the glass then back to his boss. "You mean, do I think I'm not much better than them? One of the mindless majority?"

Harry's face bisected into a grin. "I'm pulling your chain, boy. Of course you're working towards the greater good, like everybody here. But similarly, they," he tapped the partition with a knuckle, "could be useful to us, could be directed by us."

"We're trying to ascertain how the virus is working on the cadavers," Ashberry piped up. He was a stiff-backed, humourless goon in his forties that had decided, without a great deal of prevarication, to abandon his middle-ranking post amongst the governmental forces and defect to Flowers' outfit. The colonel believed that the power base had shifted to those with the vision to take back the city – in other words, Harry. Ashberry's military knowledge had proved invaluable in planning operations and procuring weaponry from army installations. He clearly hoped that if the old man's coup ever came off, he could grab himself a slice of the action and claim a position that his previous career had never afforded him. Gabe was sceptical that Harry would ever be that grateful; he could see the uniformed prick being hung out to dry once his usefulness had expired. "We have a theory that the bacteria is evolving inside the brain, slowly changing how the zombies behave. Their instincts are becoming less random, and they're showing signs of memory retention."

By 'we,' he meant the small team of researchers that had been removed at gunpoint from the secret MoD labs – the details of their whereabouts provided by Ashberry – and forced to work for Flowers. They were essentially doing the same work, but the difference was they were unable to leave the mansion and their findings were to be delivered directly to the boss. Gabe watched a whitecoat peel the top of a skull off a still-struggling stiff, careful to keep the organ inside intact. It was a horrorshow in there, a mix of butchery and experimentation that he couldn't stomach for long. Harry, naturally, seemed to revel in it.

"If we could determine how the virus controls the dead," the colonel continued, "then there's a chance we could modify it ourselves, get it to fire up some of the neural connections that enable speech, the understanding of language, the basic implementation of tools. And most importantly, make them not want to eat us."

"Turn them into your puppets, you mean," Gabe said.

"Oh, Gabriel," Flowers murmured, "much more than that. We're giving life back to these poor wretches. Why do you think they moan and cry so? They hate their condition, hate what they've become, jealous of the sound of beating hearts and the touch of warm breath. They consume us to try to claw it back, to feel blood rushing in their veins once more. But it always leaves them unsatisfied."

Gabe felt that had more to do with the fact that the dead's digestive tracts were unable to process what they ate, but bit his tongue. Harry was evidently in a poetic mood tonight. "And of course, unzombiefying makes them much less of a threat when it comes to taking London."

"Better to win round enemies than tackle them head-on, that's always been my motto."

Gabe could think of more than one occasion when he'd done just the opposite.

"Our problem," Ashberry said, trying to steer the conversation back to the matter at hand, "has been isolating the virus from the brain samples we're examining. Once it gets into the nervous system, it embeds itself totally, essentially taking over the host. It's hard to see where what was once human ends and the thing the disease has turned it into begins."

"What these backroom boys need is untainted cultures of the original virus to work from," Flowers said. "By reverse-engineering that, they might be able to get somewhere. And we've just had a stroke of rather good luck."

"Which is?"

"I was monitoring a line of encrypted military radio traffic earlier," the colonel told him. "Government forces are transporting a portion of their stock from their stronghold at St Thomas's Hospital to an MoD complex beneath Westminster. Obviously, they're desperately trying to look for an antidote too – but they want to find a way of defeating the plague and make the zombies fall down dead permanently, rather than our solution, which is to turn them into something else."

"So what do you want me to do?" Gabe asked, knowing the answer even as the words left his lips.

"Why, you're going to do what you do best, son," Harry said, putting an arm round the younger man's shoulders. "You're going to hijack it."

CHAPTER THREE

GABE KNOCKED GENTLY on the door but entered without waiting for an answer. He didn't acknowledge the other occupant in the room at first, merely took a dining chair from beside the fireplace and carried it over to the bay window overlooking the gardens. He positioned it next to the woman in the armchair, silently staring out at Flowers' manicured greenery, equally unresponsive to her guest. Gabe sat down and gazed out on the lawns below for several hushed moments, the gloom of evening stealing in and sapping the light from the afternoon. Beyond the treetops at the far end of his employer's estate, blue-black clouds massed, threatening a downpour, hearkening the approaching darkness. Already, shadows were gathering in the room, and when he turned finally to face her it was difficult to discern her expression; her profile was partially obscured by a heavy blonde fringe. She was propped against several cushions, and although her eyes were open, she was utterly motionless.

"Anna," he said, his voice catching in his throat. He felt uncomfortable breaking the quiet, and his words felt strange leaving his lips and inhabiting this place. A clock ticked in the background, spacing out the seconds. "Anna, I just thought I'd come say hello. I haven't had a chance to see you recently."

No reply. Indeed, if it wasn't for the slightest twitch in her pupils as they remained fixed on the view through the glass it would be impossible to tell if she was conscious.

"I hope you've been keeping well," Gabe persevered. "I'm sure you're being well looked after, but if there's ever anything you need, you know you only have to ask and I'll do everything I can to help. You know that, don't you?" With the question hanging in the air between them unanswered, he tried another tack, following her gaze to the gardens. "I must've said it before, but you do have a beautiful outlook to wake up to every morning. Especially at this time of year. The splashes of bright yellows and mauves, the scent of honeysuckle... Harry sure does have green fingers."

Smiling despite himself, his expression froze when her head turned suddenly and she looked at him. There was no emotion behind her smooth, pale face; no anger, or longing, or disgust, just an achingly perfect mask framed by her blonde ringlets. Her skin was soft and delicate, but painfully lacking in colour; even her lips were drained of blood. An observer standing at a distance might suggest that she was wearing foundation, so uniform was her whiteness, but Gabe knew that there wasn't a touch of make-up on her. Her ice-blue eyes were all the more startling for the contrast to her complexion, as sharp and flawless as a spring morning. He could not gaze into those twin shards for long without his own orbs pricking with a desire to hold, comfort and protect her. They looked instantly sad and knowing, innocent and troubled.

"Anna?" he started, aware that the volume of his voice had dropped even further, now little more than a whisper.

"What do you want from me?" she said tremulously, her stare unwavering. "What do you think I can give you?"

At first he couldn't reply, as the accusation rang in his head. What possible recompense could he offer her for what she had lost? As ever, the suggestion nagged at the back of his mind that his interest in her well-being was as much a salve to his guilt as it was a natural wish to watch over her. At best it meant he could rest easy in his bed, satisfied that he had at least made the effort. The fact that there had been no visible improvement in her condition for the past five years was clearly evidence that his guardianship made no difference. Yet still he made these visits, attempting to engage her in conversation, but rarely waking her from her daze. Perhaps she was torturing him, conscious of him squirming beneath her cool gaze, aware that as long as she was withdrawn from him, she was forever beyond his reach... If it was punishment, did he deserve any less?

"Anna... you don't have to give me anything, other than to accept that all I want is the best for you," he finally said. "I'm not here to demand or cajole anything out of you. I just want you to know that I'm always here for you."

"You're looking for forgiveness. That's what you're after, isn't it?" He flinched at the flecks of spite that flew in his direction. She turned her head away from him, as if to dismiss his presence. "Don't you understand nothing can change what has happened? Not your words, not your actions, and not your honourable intentions. What's done is done and we're trapped in the consequences."

"I'm trying to help us all move on –"

"What for? Where is there to move to?" Any emotion that had blossomed in her words now drained away, replaced by an inaudible murmur. "The time for living is over."

"Gabriel."

He turned to see Flowers standing in the doorway, then glanced back at Anna. She had retreated back into herself, her eyes hooded, her breathing shallow. He inched his hand out to rest it upon her forearm, but it hovered a few inches above her before he pulled it back. Gabe quietly got to his feet and walked over to his boss, who nodded for him to leave the room, pulling the door shut after him.

"What did you talk to her about?"

"Nothing," the younger man replied. "Just offering my support, like always."

"She seemed upset."

Gabe shook his head. "She refuses to open up. I want her to progress past the state she's in. I want to help her to develop. But it's like she's... locked."

"Son, you know her condition. Even the bods in the lab are struggling to understand her psychological mindset. You think you can get her to snap out of it?"

"What's the alternative?" He could feel his anger rising. "Keep her shut away in there like a pet? Like one of your caged test subjects?"

Harry's expression darkened. "Anna will stay with me at my discretion, and I'll treat her as I see fit. Don't overstep the mark, boy, or you'll find your little visits curtailed indefinitely. You'll have to make your heartfelt confessions to somebody else."

Gabe clenched his fists and stared at the floor, saying nothing.

"Assemble your team," Flowers ordered, striding away from him down the corridor, "and let's focus on the here and now."

An hour later, Gabe led his squad in a two-vehicle convoy down the mansion's driveway and through the gates. Before it passed out of sight, he glanced back at the house in his rear-view mirror and saw a solitary figure watching from a second-floor window. For a moment, he thought he saw it move, as if reaching out to the glass; but seconds later it was lost to shadow.

19.46 PM

As FAR AS Eric Richards was concerned, when he was behind the wheel of a vehicle, he was solely in charge. It was his dominion. He'd been a contract driver for St Thomas's for the past twenty-seven years and once a man occupies this kind of position for such a length of time – or so Richards liked to believe – he could be expected to exude a certain authority and command a little respect. He'd bowed before others with a similar weight of experience in their chosen fields – the medical staff he'd dealt with briefly, the admin office he'd answered to – and wouldn't have dreamt of telling them how to do a job they'd been performing perfectly well, and often for several decades. So it was that, considering his history, having first been employed as a porter in 1959 and moved sideways into transporting supplies, he felt he had the right to assume he could occupy a level of efficient autonomy. And up until recently, that had indeed been the case.

But when the dead rose, all boundaries shifted irrevocably, and Richards was someone who liked the comforting structure of routine and the knowledge of his place in the scheme of things. He'd been working when he received a call from his wife Doreen that the news was reporting cases of mass hysteria and murder taking place all across the country. It was impossible not to be aware that something was going on, with his colleagues' blasted mobile phones chirruping every few minutes, but he'd underestimated just how widespread the crisis was. TV reports and newspapers were always blowing up situations into full-blown catastrophes, then forgetting about them the following week to focus on another scandal, so when she first spoke to him, her voice breathless with worry, he'd calmed her with platitudes and told her to take such stories with a pinch of salt. They lived in Blackheath, for heaven's sake; very little of consequence affected them in the heart of suburbia. Doreen had been persuaded to view it all with a healthy degree of scepticism – drug addicts on a rampage on a council estate, no doubt, or maybe some kind of sickness brought on by an outbreak of food poisoning – and when he said goodbye she sounded halfway convinced. He'd returned to his duties, trying to brush off the uneasy pall that had settled over him, but word was snowballing through the hospital that something was definitely very wrong.

News filtered back that Casualty was being inundated with patients – those suffering from bite wounds, mainly, complaining of being set upon by complete strangers in the street – and that numbers were rising. Richards had always prided himself on his pragmatism and his ability to stand firm when others around him were flustered, but even he couldn't dismiss the sense that they were being catapulted towards a major disaster. He'd borrowed one of the other driver's mobiles to ring Doreen. After half a dozen failed calls, the network jammed solid, he ran to a nearby phone box and tried once more. She'd answered after it had rung for a full two minutes, sounding distant and distracted, claiming she and their fourteen-year-old son Max – sent home from school as news began to spread – had been hiding upstairs because somebody had battered on the front door attempting entry. He'd told her to stay where they were and that he'd come get them. Those were his final words to her. Richards never saw or spoke to his wife or son again.

His efforts to return home were thwarted at every turn; roads snaking out of London were rammed with traffic, and the police started closing off areas considered dangerous. He abandoned his car at one point, seeing if he could perhaps make it there on foot, but every route he took saw him turned away by an official, who refused to listen to his pleas. A policeman advised him against travelling alone, and that he should seek the safety of a well-lit, well-fortified building, adding that the army was being consulted on containing the out-of-control individuals. Richards had trudged back to St Thomas's, not knowing where else to go, the radio offering similar recommendations that citizens should find shelter with others in libraries, sports centres, churches, shopping malls and office complexes to ride out the coming storm. Public transport was grinding to a halt as train and underground operators abandoned their posts. All around him was chaos. He had never witnessed panic before, not in its purest form. As a child in the Blitz, every adult had seemed so reserved and resolute, waiting patiently in the Anderson shelters for the Luftwaffe to finish their night's work and then returning in the morning to pick up the pieces. Walking the city streets back to the hospital, crowds surged in every direction, equally lost and hopeless, shouting and screaming as they barged past each other, sheer fear etched on their faces. None of them, as far as he was aware, had even seen what it was that had ignited such anarchy, but the terror passed between them like a viral agent, spreading to all it touched. The monster didn't even have to raise its ugly head, and still its victims tore themselves apart to escape its approach.

He'd helped out where he could at the hospital, keeping himself busy in an effort to force from his mind the image of Doreen and Max cowering in the master bedroom, waiting for rescue. He consoled himself that it surely had to be a temporary situation, that the trouble would pass. The radio said as much, its resident experts speculating that once the armed forces entered the fray everything would be brought under control. That was until the broadcast stations went dead and they lost all contact with what was going on in the outside world. Richards felt as if he were adrift, cut off from his former life. The daily routines that he relied upon, everything he trusted and founded his beliefs upon, had fallen apart before him and he didn't have anything else left to hold on to.

Then the full horror hit, when the doctors tending the injured discovered that those bitten by the assailants became infected with their madness. A wave of violence washed through Casualty with a shocking suddenness, the corridors echoing with the cries of nurses as the bedridden abruptly rose and began to attack their carers. Richards hadn't believed the stories he was hearing from those fleeing the scene; that the bite victims had actually died, that their breath and pulse had ceased, that no brain activity could be detected, before their terrifying resurrection moments later. And the maniacs weren't merely lashing out indiscriminately, they were tearing chunks from those they could overpower, consuming the flesh with an unholy relish. Other patients – the elderly and infirm, those plugged into drips and heart monitors – could only watch, helpless, as the killers rounded on them too. Richards had listened to these reports, shaking his head, unwilling to accept each fresh tale of atrocity.

He plunged into the mêlée, intent on helping where he could, but was faced with a slaughterhouse, bodies littering the wards, the shiny floor now slick with blood and viscera. One of those touched by the insanity – a bearded man in a trench coat, a large portion of meat missing from his neck – dropped the flap of crimson matter he was gnawing on and staggered towards him, a moan issuing from the back of his ravaged throat. Richards grabbed a fire extinguisher without hesitation and stove in the degenerate's skull, before retreating to the bright safety of the car park.

Army and police arrived within minutes, setting up a perimeter around the hospital's entrances, allowing none of the murderers to escape. They also corralled the survivors away from the building, telling them not to go near it until they pronounced it safe. Richards sensed St Thomas's had become strategically important for some reason, or why else would the authorities be so quick to come to their aid? Armed flak-jacketed soldiers strode into the reception area, and seconds later bursts of automatic gunfire and the dull thud of explosions ripped through the walls. He overheard an officer asking an administrator where the mortuary was, and then relaying the directions into a walkie-talkie.

For several long hours, two to three hundred staff stood in the hospital grounds behind a cordon of police, waiting for someone to explain what was going on. Eventually, a ruffled soldier emerged and nodded at his captain, and the lawmen relaxed their position. A smart, severe-looking woman Richards didn't recognise – one of the St Thomas's directors, he guessed – seized the initiative and demanded to know the truth. A sergeant stepped forward and, with remarkable honesty and brusqueness, replied that an escaped virus had brought the dead back to life, with cannibalistic tendencies. Infection was passed on through the saliva of the undead, and those bitten would inevitably suffer cardiac arrest and join their ranks. They could only be stopped by destroying the brain, be it either by bullet or blunt instrument. Richards had glanced at those around him as they tried to assimilate this information, their incredulity tempered by the inescapable events of the day. Many began to weep. How could they argue against what they had seen with their own eyes? He himself didn't know what to feel, a cold, heavy rock in his chest where his heart used to be.

The sergeant went on to say that the plague wasn't localised, but was spreading throughout the country, and a state of national emergency had been declared. The military needed to assume command of St Thomas's as a base of operations, and was requesting that all hospital staff remain to assist them. He warned them that right now the city was a no-go zone, and that they would be better served by staying put. Richards looked at the machine guns that each soldier carried and came to the conclusion that they weren't going to be letting anyone go anywhere. So under the supervision of the soldiers, the remaining workers returned to the deathly silent wards and began the slow, laborious process of removing the corpses, or at least clearing them to the fully stocked mortuaries so makeshift control centres could be established. The hours that Richards spent carrying cadavers indelibly seared images in his mind that he would take to his grave, his blood chilled by both the victims of the Returners – looking like they'd been set upon by wild animals – and by the remnants of the ghouls themselves, riddled with bullets. Each new room held a particular horror. They found a few survivors hiding in locked linen cupboards and offices, only now summoning up the courage to put their heads around the door, but for the most part the corridors were carpeted with a red morass of bodies. Noting many of the wounds on the dead, Richards suspected the military had purged the entire building with little distinction between zombies and patients; any injured were similarly blasted in the head without a second thought.

The strangest discovery was in the morgues themselves, where the catalogued cadavers that had been residing in the drawers – the DOAs from the previous few days, the flatliners – had attempted to punch their way through their steel coffins upon their resurrection. Fist-sized gouges were visible in the metal as they'd been torn open from the inside. Each slab had to be pulled out with an armed soldier standing close by, ready to put a round through the carcass within if it had somehow missed the cull.

Toiling day and night, the authorities gradually reshaped the hospital into a research base. Military personnel used the wards as barracks while escorted Ministry of Defence scientists began to arrive in batches to conduct experiments on the dead they'd kept aside. Richards could not sleep for thinking of his wife, but news brought in from the outside was not good. The city was a mess, lawlessness running rampant as the plague spread with frightening rapidity. With communications failing daily, there was no way he could get word to see if she was out of harm's reach. The military posted a permanent guard, as much to stop those inside from straying as to protect them; staff were effectively warned that they would not be allowed to leave the facility. Thus Richards found himself employed on what became, over the following months, a government outpost, receiving his instructions from the captain in charge. Many of his colleagues voiced their disapproval at the military suddenly assuming command of what had been a civilian organisation, but short of staring down the barrel of a service revolver there was nothing much they could do about it. It was clear that this wasn't an isolated case. The authorities were struggling to maintain control across the country, and if it meant the boys with the guns were running the show, then everybody else had better fall in behind them.

It was errands such as tonight's delivery that Richards was tasked with: driving a truckload of medical samples to another of the MoD complexes across town. It wasn't a million miles away from the job he'd had in his previous life – that regular existence in which he'd been embedded seemed centuries ago – but it was now shorn of any shred of independence. He was accompanied in his cab by a Sergeant Perrington, who ordered him at what speed he should drive, the directions he should take, and constantly advised on what safety tips he should adhere to. Richards found it utterly demeaning for a man of his years, but was as powerless as a prisoner. There were half a dozen armed guards riding in the back with the cargo, and an army van was tailgating his vehicle. In fact, the only reason they bothered to use him at all, rather than have a squaddie drive the supplies, was because he knew best how to handle the truck's temperamental gears and spongy clutch.

They were crossing Westminster Bridge when he first caught sight of something in his headlamps. He glanced in his wing mirror, and checked that the escort was still following; in fact, it was so close that if he stopped suddenly it could rear-end him. If that were the case, he would have to flare his brake lights and warn them. It was raining lightly, a sprinkle of drops peppering the windscreen, so he scraped the wipers once against the glass to get a better view, peering out into the night, the headlights casting a pool of illumination onto the road ahead. The edge of their limit just brushed against a silhouette jogging towards the truck, its outline barely discernible from the surrounding blackness. He could sense Perrington looking at him questioningly.

"What is it?" the sergeant asked.

"Not sure. I think there's somebody out there."

Perrington leaned forward. "A stiff?"

Richards shook his head. "I don't think so. It's moving towards us too fast. I think he's alive." He expected the army man to respond to that, but there was no reply. "You want me to stop?"

"Keep going."

"But he might be in trouble –"

"You keep going," Perrington ordered sternly. "We stop for no one."

As the truck progressed across the bridge, the figure emerged into the light: he was indeed one of the living, and he looked terrified. He was little more than a teenager, probably barely into his twenties, and he was sprinting towards the truck, his arms waving in the air in an effort to get them to slow down. The rain had plastered his hair to his forehead, and Richards could even see the puffs of condensed breath blown out with each exhalation. The kid was exhausted, as if he'd been running a great distance.

"He's scared about something," the driver remarked. "I don't think he's going to take no for an answer."

"He'll soon get out of the way when he realises we aren't stopping."

"What if he's warning us about something? Could be the road's blocked."

"Then we'll find out for ourselves."

"You think that's wise?" Richards started, then fell silent for a second. "Oh shit." He tapped the brake, hearing the van behind him screech as the tyres skidded on the wet tarmac.

"What the hell are you doing?" Perrington snapped, momentarily ignoring his two-way, which barked into life on his lap as the other driver demanded to know what was going on. "I gave you an explicit order not to slow down."

"Look!" the older man yelled and lifted one hand from the wheel to point. The truck was still moving, but now coasting to a halt. The runner saw the vehicle had altered its speed, and dropped his arms, casting a glance over his shoulder, his gaze resting on the same sight that Richards was focusing his attention on.

Shuffling into the truck's beams of light was a gaggle of Returners, at least thirty in number. They shambled forwards, the kid their object of interest, their groans echoing amidst the metal stanchions of the bridge.

"Goddammit," Perrington breathed. "Put your foot down. We can go through them."

"We can't leave him here."

"I'm not going to tell you again. Now bloody drive!"

"The hell with you. Some of us are still human," Richards snarled and stomped on the brake, bringing the vehicle to a stop. Before the sergeant could lean across and grab him, he tore open his door and stepped down onto the road. The chill evening air cut through his cotton jacket and rain glued his shirt to his chest. Out here the sounds of the approaching dead carried further, their footsteps dragging along the ground in unison, the moans seemingly coming from every direction, reflecting off the surface of the Thames below them. The youngster marched quickly over to him, gulping in deep lungfuls.

"Thank Christ," he said quietly, putting a hand on Richards' shoulder as he bent double to recover. "I thought I wasn't going to make it..."

"It's OK. You'll be all right. You'll be safe now." The driver turned at the sound of boots on tarmac, and saw a handful of squaddies take up a position at the head of the truck, sighting their rifles on the throng of ghouls that were growing nearer. There was now perhaps only a hundred or so yards between them.

"Clear a path for us," Perrington instructed his men from the passenger seat, glaring at Richards. "Since we've lost our momentum, we'll have to thin them down a bit so we can plough through."

The guns barked rapidly as each soldier selected his target and fired, the deadheads at the front dropping face down with each impact, brains squirting out of their skulls. Their kin behind them hardly reacted, merely took their place and walked into the wall of bullets without a glimmer of fear or understanding. The bodies stacked up almost instantly.

"Sarge?" a voice called out. "Something weird here..."

"What do you mean?"

"Fuckin' pusbags are muzzled. Every one of 'em."

Richards looked back at the kid, puzzled, his mouth dropping open as the youngster yanked an automatic from his belt, hidden beneath his shirt.

"Game's over for you, old man," Hewitt said with a smile as he put a slug between the driver's eyes.

19.49 PM

GABE ORDERED HIS team to move in immediately, with the intention of overpowering the soldiers while they were still dealing with the gaggle of deadheads. The half-dozen triggers jumped out of the Bedford van they'd been tooling up in and began to move across the bridge, the van coasting slowly alongside them, providing cover. Time was of the essence; it wouldn't take long for the military to deal with the stiffs, and they had the advantage of numbers and superior firepower. If Gabe's squad were to have a chance of pulling off the hijack successfully, it would mean attacking when their opponents were otherwise engaged. He clicked the safety off on his pistol and followed the others.

As he reached the scattered remains of the zombie distraction lying in a tangle on the road, he fleetingly looked at the bridles wrapped around their jaws. It was a ruse that he'd adopted on several occasions in the past, and he had found it was an effective means of instilling panic in the enemy. They rarely saw that the mouths had been clamped shut before it was too late. Even so, despite the muzzles, there was always a lack of volunteers to play the 'victim.' Gabe had made sure that Hewitt had drawn the short straw, a result that the kid had responded to furiously, but the older man had felt this was just the brush with danger that could encourage a little responsibility in the youngster.

The rattle of gunfire echoed through the still night air, ear-splittingly loud. The army men had formed a cordon around the truck and were shooting at will; the last of the ghouls were now only a few feet away, but a handful of the military had switched their attention to the bushwhackers. One of Flowers' enforcers – a bear of a man named Duvall – let rip with a full automatic, punching holes in the lorry's windshield and passenger door. Each time the squaddies cowered from the rapid-fire assault, the team advanced, tightening the circle, forcing them to retreat. Gabe scanned the haze of smoke for Hewitt, who should've infiltrated their defence, and spotted him putting his gun to the back of a soldier's head and pulling the trigger at point-blank range. He'd told each of them he wanted the minimum of casualties, with deaths acceptable only as a last resort, but the kid was drilling humans without compunction.

Gabe began to jog over towards him to pull him back before the whole operation became a slaughter. He stopped when he caught sight of what was behind the truck: a military escort vehicle, unloading armoured-up soldiers but not deploying them, remaining hidden at the rear. They were drawing the hijackers forward, giving a false impression of defeat, before doubling their defence. The robbers needed to even the playing field a touch.

He signalled to Hanner, who had a small grenade-launcher holstered across his back, and pointed over the truck, indicating to drop the explosive behind it. It would scatter the reinforcements and hopefully disorientate them enough for his squad to surge ahead. Hanner nodded, unslung the weapon and sighted the necessary angle. But moments before the grenade powered from the barrel, a bullet slammed into his shoulder, pushing him backwards, his finger squeezing instinctively on the trigger. It threw his aim off, the missile ricocheted against a bridge stanchion and fell short, hitting the truck's bonnet and igniting its engine. The front of the vehicle exploded in a ball of orange flame, pulsing out a wave of heat that knocked Gabe to his knees. Others were flung sideways, some toppling into the icy waters of the Thames below. Seconds later, the petrol tank blew, and the blast was deafening, throwing the lorry upwards a couple of metres as everyone within its radius shielded their faces from the white-hot blaze. Gabe's ears rang as he woozily watched fire lick the starlit sky.

19.52 PM

THEY HEARD THE noise even in the depths. It vibrated through the water, accompanied by a rapid succession of loud splashes. There was not enough rational thought left in their core cerebella to assimilate what the sound indicated, or its cause; but one instinct that still reverberated within them was that when the silence was broken, it meant life was close by, and where there was life there was flesh. It had been a theory that had been proven right time after time, to the point where they sought out the living through some primitive radar rather than by any other kind of recognition.

They were crossing the riverbed, their hungry search forever unfulfilled. Fluid flowed in and out of their still lungs with the ebb of the tide, their already cold skin untouched by the immense chill. Their surroundings meant nothing to them, just terrain to travel. But once they heard the sounds, they suddenly had direction. As one, they turned and waded through the silt and darkness towards the bank, the crackle above them leading them like a beacon.

19.55 PM

"Oh Christ."

The words snapped Gabe free from his trance. He shook his head, trying to reboot his senses. Everything was as it had been a minute before: the truck was still burning in the middle of the road, and the injured were crawling away from it, clothes and limbs blackened. The odd burst of gunfire still erupted now and then as each side tried to take advantage of the confusion, but Gabe – hunched against the bridge wall – was trying to hear what somebody was shouting about. Duvall was looking out beyond the thoroughfare and pointing. Gabe followed his gaze and attempted, by the light of the flames, to make sense of the black shapes emerging from the water. There were hundreds of them, dripping silhouettes that rose from the deep and shuffled up a causeway towards the bridge. Realisation slapped him seconds later. All he could think was: *The dead are coming. We've awoken the dead.*

"We gotta get out of here," Duvall yelled. "We can't fight that number. Abandon the operation."

Gabe nodded slowly, and began to call for his team to retreat. The soldiers had spotted the zombies coming their way by now too and had all but stopped firing, watching with horror as the shambling dregs of the river came ever closer.

"Move it," Gabe cried. "Grab what injured you can and go."

They stumbled backwards away from the truck towards their own vehicles. Gabe made a vain effort to count how many of the squad were missing, but couldn't keep track. He looked around for Hewitt, who must've been near the lorry when it went up, but couldn't see him. He began to run, knowing that personal survival was now imperative.

Then the bullet caught him in the leg.

He gasped with shock, and collapsed onto his front, grit stinging his hands and face. It had come from behind, and passed through his calf, shattering the bone. Agony lanced up his knee and thigh as he felt his trouser filling with blood, but even so he tried to crawl, desperate to get away. He kept hoping that one of his comrades would spot him and drag him to safety, but nobody seemed to be around. He tried to scream, but couldn't find the voice.

His leg was numb now, and every movement was torture. He slid, inch after painful inch, refusing to give up. He didn't want to die at the hands of the dead; he couldn't accept such a fate. He felt for his gun, but it had gone. Desperation clawed at his mind to escape, but fatigue and blood loss were swamping his muscles, slowing him to a standstill.

He closed his eyes, an image of Anna framed against the window his last thought before he lost consciousness.

CHAPTER FOUR

THE RIVER GLITTERED with the early-morning rays of the sun as the Mondeo pulled onto Westminster Bridge and parked several feet away from the smouldering ruins of the military truck. Two men stepped out of the car and walked up to the sooty, skeletal shell, giving cursory glances to the mass of bodies lying the length of the road. One of them stopped and pulled a semi-automatic from his shoulder holster, turning his gaze back and forth as he kept watch, flipping open a pair of shades from his shirt pocket to protect his eyes from the glare coming off the water. The other sauntered slowly around the burned-out vehicle, peering into the cab and the remains of the truck bed, occasionally nudging a charred piece of chassis with his toe. He stood for long moments, staring at the wreck with his hands on his hips as if lost in thought, or studying it as though it were about to reveal some great mystery.

Eventually he strode back to his companion, pausing to kneel next to a Returner corpse and examining its wounds: much of the right side of its head was missing, its jellied contents sprayed across the tarmac. He straightened and crossed to a uniformed body, the torso peppered with bullet holes, and lifted its right arm: the fingers and thumb of the hand had been gnawed off, recently enough for the stumps to be still weeping. The man put his own digits to the soldier's cheek, gauging by his skin temperature how long he'd been dead, and put the time scale at about eleven hours. He guessed the victim had died of his gunshot injuries before a passing maggotshit had sensed enough warmth in the cadaver to munch down on. Once a body went cold, the zombies paid no attention, hence the reason they never tried to eat each other. It had been theorised that if the stiffs caught a human and began to consume him alive, they would feed for about an hour or two before their hot lunch cooled off and they lost interest. By that point, the meal had been so disassembled that resurrection was impossible; in fact, uninterrupted they would probably be down to the bone marrow at that stage. The man wondered briefly why soldier-boy here hadn't got up and walked, but then saw the small neat hole in his temple. That would do it, he concluded.

He stood and gingerly hopped over the corpses to the bridge wall, looking out across the Thames, the light wind ruffling the river, wavelets lapping against the embankment. He tugged a mobile from his jacket pocket and swiftly dialled. The voice at the other end answered with a brusque acknowledgement.

"Well?"

"It's a mess. Truck's a barbecue, nothing to be salvaged from that. Complete write-off. And we're talking sheer carnage here – must be close to forty bodies, both deadheads and living. Well, they *were* living."

"Any of them ours?"

"Yeah, I recognise a couple. Collins and Stokes are here, looks like they took a few hits to the head each. How many we missing all told?"

"Five, including O'Connell."

"Nah, there's no sign of the others. Could've resurrected, I suppose, and staggered off – either that or done a runner." He leaned out over the parapet, peering down at the river's surface. "Or they went for a dip," he added.

"The rest are... what? Army?"

"Yep, standard government troops. Put up quite a fight by the looks of things." He paused. "There's something else, Harry. The kid was right; there was a second vehicle. There're tyre marks behind the truck as if they sped away in a goddamn hurry. Could've taken some captives, I guess."

There was silence for a moment, then Flowers said: "Put Hewitt on, Patricks."

The man held out his phone to his companion. "He wants to talk to you."

Hewitt shouldered his gun and retrieved the handset. "Harry."

"Son, I want to make sure you've got your story straight." The boss sounded remarkably old and weary to his ears, the most vulnerable he'd ever heard him. Maybe it was a trick of the line's tinny timbre, but it was as if Flowers was reeling from a blow he had taken himself. "You saw O'Connell go down?"

"I saw what I saw. After it all went to shit, things got fucked up. The truck exploded and knocked me to the ground, but it also sent the army assholes running. They had reinforcements in this escort SUV that had been tailgating the target vehicle, and that started reversing the fuck out of there. Once I got my wind back, I attempted to carry on with the objective but then the earth just opened up and spat out every deadfuck from here to creation." Hewitt paced backwards and forwards with the rhythm of his account of the night's events. "I heard O'Connell tell everyone to get the hell out of there, and I headed towards him but he went down, took a hit. Seconds later, he was surrounded by uniforms. The smoke that was coming off the wreck was enough to allow me to sneak past 'em and hook up with what remained of the team."

"But you didn't see them finish O'Connell off?"

"Nope. There was gunfire, but that was the army boys taking care of the stiffs."

"So you think he's still alive? And that they took him with them?"

"If O'Connell had made it out of there in one piece, he would've been in contact with you one way or another, even if he was holed up somewhere, bleeding out. So, yeah, I think the government fucks have got him."

There was no immediate reply to that. All Hewitt could hear was Flowers breathing into the receiver as he mulled over what he had been told. He lifted his sunglasses onto his forehead and rolled his eyes at Patricks, switching the mobile to his other hand. How many times did the old fart need telling? Him and the other survivors had been up all night debriefing Harry and that long streak of piss traitor Ashberry on what happened; they were fucked off that they'd come away without the sample, but they hit the roof at the suggestion that one of their own was now in the custody of the military. It especially didn't look good when the guy that was meant to be leading the hijack was the one that fell into the hands of the enemy. O'Connell was one of the boss's right-hand men, had been with him since before the outbreak. That right now he could be sitting in some army compound singing about Flowers' set-up was giving the old geezer heart palpitations. He would've probably been less upset if they'd returned with O'Connell's eviscerated liver and told him that was all that was left after he got jumped by a gang of deadheads.

"OK," Hewitt's employer said at last with a heavy sigh. "We've got to accept he's a liability, and could compromise everything. If he's decided to change sides, then I want him found and I want him fed to a fucking pusbrain, feet first. If he's their prisoner, well... same rules apply. Can't take the risk on them getting any info out of him." A sense of resolve came back into Flowers' voice, in contrast to how pitiful he'd sounded a moment ago. "I want to you to find him, son. You and Patricks scour the damn city if you have to, but just seek him out and eliminate him before he causes us any more problems. Don't come back unless you got his balls for a brooch, you understand me?"

"Gotcha. Terminate with extreme prejudice."

The phone went dead. Hewitt flipped it shut and handed back to the other man with a smile.

"Well," he said, sliding the shades back into position. "Now things are getting interesting..."

GABE FLICKERED OPEN his sleep-crusted eyelids, waited for the swirling to settle down, and watched a dull green ceiling coalesce into focus. He traced the cracks that ran along its surface as his fuzzy memory cranked into gear and he tried to remember where he was and what had happened to him. It took several seconds for him to recollect the events leading up to him passing out, and with the realisation came the ache. It started behind his knee and travelled up his leg, a fresh pain slotting into place as each new image of the battle on the bridge blossomed in his mind like a slideshow beamed into his skull. He reached out instinctively to clutch at his injury and shock cut through his agonised haze when he discovered that his arms were tightly strapped to the bed he was lying on.

He woke up fast. He was dressed in just a T-shirt and jeans, the right leg cut away around the shin and calf to accommodate the bandage woven around it, and he could feel dried blood gluing the hairs of his thigh together. Predictably, he'd been stripped of anything else that he'd had on him. Gabe looked down at his bonds – knotted lengths of white linen – and tested their strength, his muscles straining against them, but they were firmly secured to the bed's frame. Adjusting his position to gain a better view of his surroundings brought a sharp stab of pain to his spine, and he slumped back prone, wondering how long he'd been unconscious and hog-tied like this. Every part of him seemed to be on fire, from top to toe.

He cast a wary gaze around him; it looked like a hospital ward or dormitory. Five other beds were lined against the opposite side of the room, all empty, the sheets flattened as if they hadn't been visited in many a month. It appeared he was the only occupant, but judging by the cleanliness of the floor and the bare walls he couldn't say he was surprised; this didn't look like a place where one could convalesce and regain one's health. It had a fatal air about it, a suggestion that the dying would be left here to see out their final moments. The plaster was grimy, darkened in spots, and the linoleum discoloured by a mixture of scuffed footprints, dirt and ancient body-fluids. A couple of fluorescent tubes were fitted to the ceiling, but they looked as if they had long since burned out, grey and lifeless.

It sparked a memory in him, of awaking in a hospital after the bike accident, shivering with pain. The déjà vu was almost as insidious as the ache in his bones.

Following his initial confusion, it took Gabe a few minutes for the truth to sink in that he had survived. The memory of his legs collapsing out from under him burned brightly in his head, and the desperation of his attempted crawl to safety stuck bitterly in his throat. Tears formed in his eyes as the terror he had experienced for those fleeting seconds resurfaced. It can't have lasted any time at all, but for those few elongated moments the urge to live had never been more powerful, and the thought of falling victim to the ghouls – to see them stumble closer, to feel their cold dead hands clasp on his limbs, to smell their fetid stench as their teeth bit down on his skin – instilled in him a palpable fear. He shivered, the delayed after-effects of his narrow brush with being eaten alive bubbling up inside him as each horrific eventuality and permutation played across his imagination.

But he had escaped, he told himself, trying to bring the anxiety under control; or at least, he had been ushered out of immediate danger by persons unknown. Surveying his environs again, he felt it was safe to assume that this wasn't one of Harry's safe houses, and that he wasn't being kept here solely to recuperate. He had to have been retrieved by the troops before they'd evacuated the area – they'd had that second vehicle, he dimly remembered – and bundled back to a government complex. But for what reason would they want him alive, and, indeed, fix up his leg so he could be mobile again? Looters and bandits, especially those that preyed on military convoys, were given short shrift, and it wasn't that long after the outbreak took hold that a shoot-to-kill policy was imposed. Soldiers were notoriously merciless in handing out summary executions, and under other circumstances the military wouldn't have cared less if he'd ended up passing through a zombie's digestive tract. No, they had to have a reason for taking him and keeping him here. He had to have something they wanted, but what? Information?

The prospect gave him chills again, but not so much at the thought of what they could do to him as to what Harry's reaction was going to be once he realised that Gabe was in enemy hands. He'd become a liability to the organisation. Flowers prided himself on a closely knit outfit, and would not accept security lapses, plugging (in every sense of the word) anything that threatened to destabilise his set-up. Gabe had worked for his employer for many years, and had been privy to the old man's numerous dealings. For Gabe to be captured by the opposition was a major embarrassment. Gabe could envision Harry making the equation, of tallying up his loyalty and friendship and weighing it against the trouble this predicament could cause him... but who was he kidding? The old man would decide Gabe's fate without a second thought.

Funny, he mused. For a moment there he'd been reassuring himself that he was still alive, that he'd made it through intact, when all along he was a dead man walking. His die had been cast the second that he fell, and it was just a matter of waiting now before the bullet caught up with him.

Multiple footsteps were approaching, he realised, as their *tap-tap-tap* resounded in the corridor beyond the room, growing louder as they came closer. There was a jangle of keys, the door was unlocked, and a pair of uniforms entered, rifles slung over their shoulders, fixing him with a blank glare. Then a suit and a whitecoat emerged between the two and marched up to the bedside, the doc twisting his head to study Gabe's face intently. He reached out and pulled Gabe's eyes open wide with the fingers of one hand, retrieving a pen light from his breast pocket with the other and shining it into his pupils. Meanwhile, the suit wandered round to the foot of the bed, fiddling with his shirt cuffs.

"How are you feeling? Any concussion? Double vision?" the whitecoat asked, clicking the light off.

Gabe shook his head. "Leg's killing me."

"Painkillers have worn off. We'll give you some more presently." His gaze flickered to the knotted linen tying Gabe's arms to the bed frame, and turned his attention to the suit. "Are the restraints necessary? They're probably interfering with his blood supply."

The government man raised his eyebrows, then nodded to the squaddies to go ahead and untie them. "OK. I think our friend here isn't stupid enough to try anything with an armed guard in the room."

Once they were free, Gabe brought his arms up to his chest and rubbed them, getting the circulation moving again. "So who are you?" he asked.

"The name's Fletchley," the suit replied. "I work for the Home Office. Or at least I did. I suppose it's a moot point whether such a thing still exists anymore." He motioned to the doctor, a leathery-faced, harried-looking old soak with sprigs of grey hair erupting from a bulbous nose. "That's Dr Hillman. He patched up your leg."

"Yeah, remind me to thank whichever arsehole it was that shot me when my back was turned."

"Rules of engagement, Mr O'Connell," Fletchley replied with a sigh. "The military has every right to protect government property. Even so, none of my troops can verify that they were the ones that fired upon you as your motley crew fled. That you fell into our lap is a bonus, I won't deny that."

Gabe's brow furrowed. "Well, if one of your boys didn't –"

"Who knows? Perhaps a stray round caught you at one unlucky moment. But at the time we were more concerned with evacuating the area." Fletchley stuck his hands in his pockets and looked down at the thief. The civil servant had a surprisingly youthful air, although he had to be in his late forties. His face was thin and rosy-cheeked, the pale skin seemed almost papery, his thatch of brown hair equally fine and insubstantial. His build was obscured within the dark woollen suit, but he seemed slender and narrow-shouldered. "You may or may not have ascertained by now that the sample you were after was being transported in the back-up van. The truck you quite spectacularly destroyed was a decoy, intended to draw the fire of anyone attempting such an escapade. We should've guessed Harry Flowers' move into the medical arena would be typically heavy-handed."

Gabe flinched at the mention of his boss's name, dropping his gaze away from the Home Office man.

"Mr O'Connell," Fletchley said softly, "we know who you are and who you work for. Mr Flowers has been a thorn in our side for quite some time – redirecting arms supplies, kidnapping government scientists, conducting organised looting expeditions... His methodology is really quite impressive, if he'd used it for the common good instead of building his own power base. And let's face it, that what this is about, isn't it? Harry wants to take on the entire city."

Gabe didn't reply, opting instead to study the cuts that criss-crossed his palms, tracing them with his fingers.

Fletchley exhaled wearily. "I'm growing short on patience, O'Connell, and time is not on our side. We are not going to stand by and see Flowers attempt a coup. Do you honestly think, if your boss achieves his aim and takes control of the city, that matters will improve? Do you think he has the best interests of those that have managed to survive through this at heart? If Flowers wiped every zombie from every corner of London, the regime that he would put in place would be just as dangerous and just as restrictive. Society may be destabilised at the moment, but it will be nothing compared to the lawlessness that will break out in his wake, because there are those that will not sit quietly and accept Flowers as their ruler. The capital will descend into tribalism and all-out warfare... and at its heart, a grasping, power-hungry dictator using his position to exploit those below him."

"You're telling me you prefer the deadfucks?"

"I'm telling you that Flowers will simply replace them with something a lot worse. What, for example, did he tell you he had in mind for the virus culture he wanted you to steal?" When Gabe refused to answer, Fletchley leaned forward and pressed down on his calf, causing him to hiss in pain. Hillman started to say something, but was silenced by a glare from the civil servant. "My tolerance towards your attitude is rapidly coming to an end," he continued. "Perhaps a few days without morphine will loosen your tongue?"

Gabe locked stares with Fletchley, feeling the throb in his leg muscle subside. He swallowed, knowing they could do what they liked to him, could keep him in a perpetual state of agony if it suited them. And did he owe Harry any loyalty anyway? If the gang lord was going to put the whack on him no matter what he said, what did it gain him by refusing to reveal his plans? Chances were these government pricks knew a lot more about Flowers' intentions than he did.

"Harry was seeking a way to make the stiffs more docile," he said finally. "He reckoned if they adapted the virus, they could turn them into non-cannibals, make them more... civilised, I suppose. That way his organisation could take to the streets without any opposition."

"That's what he told you, is it?" Fletchley looked amused.

"Well, yeah." Gabe was instantly suspicious. "He had his scientists working on it."

The suit laughed. "Those scientists – which, may I remind you, Flowers had removed from Ministry of Defence research bases – have been getting word back to us through primitive radio relay. From what they say, your boss isn't interested in curing the plague – at least, not all of it. According to them, he's planning on keeping a regular private army of flesh-eaters back for his own use."

"Say that again?"

"I'd guess you'd call them his elite bodyguard. Flowers doesn't want to get rid of the zombies entirely, not when he can use them for his own purposes. I imagine you could get someone to do whatever you wanted with a pack of slavering Returners on a leash that need constant feeding. And we all know that the dead get restless if they don't eat for long periods, so I shudder to think what he's going to be using for pet treats."

Gabe laid his head back on the pillow, wondering if this could possibly be true. Could Flowers be that ruthless, maintaining his own battalion of undead enforcers to support his reign? And to keep them supplied with human meat... was he going to have his own farm, cultivating men and women like livestock, all so he could rule London unapposed?

Fletchley pulled up a chair and sat beside the bed. "You don't have to believe me, of course, but I think you realise that there's no cause for me to lie. I want Flowers stopped; it's as simple as that. There are many reasons, but it all comes down to the fact that he's a serious menace that cannot go unchecked."

"Why are you telling me this? Why are you keeping me here? If you know so much about what he's planning, what use am I to you?"

"It's not so much what you know, Mr O'Connell, it's what you can do for us. We have need of your skills. Naturally, once your leg's healed and we inevitably let you out of here to fulfil this task, there's nothing to stop you running back to your boss. But we both know you'd be returning to the lion's den. The moment you fell into our clutches, you were marked for execution. I know all too well how Flowers' paranoid kind work. But as a result, you are now free of obligation, offering allegiance to no one."

"So by that token, why should I do anything for you?"

"Well, quite. I mean, apart from repaying the care and attention that Dr Hillman here has lavished on you," Fletchley shared a brief grin with the medic, "there's the opportunity to do something worthwhile with your life, Mr O'Connell. What we're asking you to be involved with could turn the plague around forever and save thousands of lives. You've been in Flowers' employ for many years, I know, and no doubt you've seen that as your sole interest, your world. But now's the chance to do something for the greater good, to help others rather than support one man's greed. To step outside Harry Flowers' shadow." The government man leaned closer. "You must've lost loved ones since the outbreak, Gabriel. Don't you want to redeem yourself in their eyes?"

Gabe didn't answer. He stared at the cracked ceiling, but all he could see was the outline of the woman at the window.

CHAPTER FIVE

THE SAME TWO soldiers that had arrived with Fletchley that first time he had regained consciousness came for him again almost a week later, by which point he found he could put a not-insubstantial amount of pressure on his injured leg, and the doc had decreased his painkiller dosage. He was sitting on the edge of the bed exercising the muscle when they marched through the doors and instructed him to go with them. Although he hissed as he limped along a series of dreary corridors between the two squaddies – perhaps acting a little more pained than was strictly necessary, slowing their journey out of simple bloody-mindedness and taking a perverse pleasure at being a nuisance – he made a note of the building he was passing through, trying to gauge where they were situated. What had looked like a hospital ward upon awaking was clearly now merely a medical wing, amounting to little more than a couple of rooms in the whole complex. The office architecture he was entering now – with its walls of metal cabinets, file boxes piled high, and computer terminals covering every surface, rats' nests of cables strewn across the dull brown carpet – told him that this was some kind of government bunker that had been in existence, in all probability, since the 1970s. Most likely, the authorities thought they would escape down here in the eventuality of a nuclear conflict. Few, if any, would have believed that the end of the world would've been brought about by a zombie plague.

It seemed to be very understaffed. The scale of the mess was drowning the dozen or so clerks he saw tapping away at keyboards or juggling ring binders and ledgers, the exact purpose of their work a mystery. It was as if somebody hadn't told them that the world outside had changed, and they were blithely carrying on, balancing books, chasing up invoices, sorting through correspondence. There was something comically surreal about watching them potter between desks like accountants, refusing to believe that the apocalypse had already arrived.

The reams of paper stacked up on the floor and crammed into cupboards looked like the last remnants of the human race. He tried to catch a glimpse of what was written on them as he was hurried past and saw a jumble of figures, addresses and names. He got the impression they were census reports and electoral registers, dating back over the last six or seven decades. Quite what they were doing here, or what use they could ever be in the current circumstances, he couldn't fathom. It was as if the record on every man, woman and child in the country had been inexpertly stuffed into the nearest available storage facility once the undead situation had quickly spun out of control. For what reason, he mused: as a list of the missing? Almost certainly sixty per cent of the people transcribed on these printouts were no longer living. Who was ever going to read or process this information? And what could they ever do with it? As he eyed each shelf, bowing under the weight of bulging folders, he had the inescapable morbid sense that this was intended to be some kind of mausoleum of mankind, a memorial – not etched in stone but immortalised in documentation. *No epitaph*, he thought, *just the facts of who we were and that we were once here.* Gabe didn't know which was the more chilling: the idea that he was walking through his species' history, or that his fellow *Homo sapiens* were dumb enough to consider that this really mattered anymore.

The lead trooper halted at a door and rapped upon it, ushering Gabe through when he heard a response. Fletchley was sitting on the other side of a desk – itself a landslide of reports, photographs and stationery – and signalled to the thief to pull up a chair. Fletchley glanced at the soldiers and they withdrew, leaving the two men alone in the office. Gabe briefly gave the room the once-over, unsurprised to see yet more sheaves of paperwork poking from overfilled suspension files. It took him a couple of seconds to note that there was no window – the dim light came courtesy of a bare bulb hanging above his head – and he determined that this complex was definitely below ground. The one object of note in the room was a vast map of London pinned to the wall, virtually covering it vertically from ceiling to skirting board. There were drawing pins and coloured stickers spiralling across it.

Fletchley noticed his momentary interest in the map and motioned towards it. "We're tracking the movements of the Returners," he said. "Trying to distinguish a feeding pattern, seeing if we can pre-empt their grazing routine."

"They go where the meat is," Gabe replied. "I would've thought that was obvious."

"Not necessarily. True, they'll zone in on the living if they sense them in their vicinity, but they're not simply ambling about anymore, hoping to stumble upon a meal. They're remembering where they've fed before, learning how to navigate themselves around the city to find the best spots."

Gabe looked back at the map. "You've witnessed this?"

"Oh yes. Or rather, our backroom boys have. They've released electronically tagged dead back onto the streets and monitored their journeys through radar. They've seen them coming back to the same feeding grounds time after time, even returning here, where they were set free, aware that living are in the area. The information is staying with them, you see, and they're acting upon it. It's cognition. They're thinking."

"It's instinct, surely. The same instinct that keeps them upright on two feet, that makes them scared of fire, that leads them to hunt in packs. They're driven by motor functions. Any animal with half a brain develops a knowledge of where the food is if it follows its nose enough times."

Fletchley sat back, clicking the end of his pen distractedly. "They're animals, certainly, demonstrating as they do a low-level intelligence. I don't think they can really be called 'zombies' anymore, not in the classical sense. They're not just reanimated cadavers. They're showing signs of skill development, of memory retention, of recognition. They're no longer monsters of folklore, but could possibly be classified as a new sub-species."

"Classified," Gabe repeated, opening his arms wide to take in the room. "That about sums this place up. What are you doing here, Fletchley? Cataloguing? Archiving? Filing fascinating data like that while the world consumes itself?"

The government man abruptly stood and walked around his desk, seating himself upon an uncluttered corner directly in front of the thief. He continued to tap the pen into the palm of his left hand. "You think all this is... folly?"

"I think you're clinging on to bureaucracy despite the fact that there isn't the authority to support it anymore. What usefulness do these records hold? Who's ever going to care enough to dig them out again? Everything's changed, in case you haven't noticed; the slate's been wiped clean. All that came before might as well be ancient history, 'cause it has no bearing on what we're facing here and now."

"You don't believe that."

"Don't I?" A vision of Anna swirled in Gabe's head and he struggled to mentally swat it away. "That'll be why I work for Harry Flowers, then." *Worked*, he admonished himself.

"Ah yes, Mr Flowers. The man who would be king. You think he's the future?"

"I think that he will decide where the city goes over the next few years. All power has shifted to him. While you and the rest of the pencil pushers have squirreled yourselves away down here, building a nest from the detritus of what you once had, he's been taking London apart piece by piece. And there's nothing you can do about it."

"So you say." Fletchley paused, rolling the pen between his hands. "Mr O'Connell, where you and I differ is that what you see as detritus, I see as a reminder of what civilisation used to be. When society used to be built on rules and regulations and communal living, rather than the outlaw, self-interested way of doing things that now seems to be the norm. And this, all this," he picked up a selection of loose pages from his desk and sprinkled them onto Gabe's lap, "is what I'm fighting for. It tells me that I'm not a looter or a criminal thug, stealing and murdering my way to the top. It tells me that I'm not something that destroys what it can't have, and devours what it can with an insatiable appetite. What it tells me is that I'm a civilised human being, capable of rising above the common beasts."

Gabe said nothing, brushing the documents to the floor.

"Let me remind you of something," Fletchley continued. "We captured you in the process of attempting to hijack a government vehicle. It was within our rights under martial law to have you executed. Instead, you were brought here, your injury was tended to, and you're seated before me with very little threat to your person. On the other hand, your employer – the man you reckon will lead the citizens out of the wreckage, and who will make sure, no doubt, that they will bow before him – has more than likely put a mark on your head to stop you spilling his secrets. If you were to return to his organisation, you would get a bullet in the back of the skull before you even got up the driveway. Now tell me: which sounds like the side of the angels to you?"

"All the same, I think I still trust Harry more, even if he does want me dead. At least it's a black and white relationship."

The civil servant's mouth creased into a strained smile. "I would've assumed we were past the question of trust. If it makes you feel any better, I can make my personal opinion of you quite plain: I think you're a waste of space, O'Connell. I think you, Flowers and the rest of your lawless fraternity have taken advantage of others your whole life –"

"You know *nothing* about me –"

"– and since the outbreak, you've exploited human suffering and the breakdown of order to further your own aims. You care for nothing or no one in the pursuit of wealth and power. You're a user, O'Connell, a parasite, and under any other circumstances I wouldn't place the slightest value upon you. But the situation we find ourselves in calls for strange bedfellows. To be quite blunt, we wish to make use of you."

"What, a parasite like me?"

"I'm simply making my intentions clear. We need someone on the ground that can pass through the underworld unhindered, someone without the taint of authority. And of course someone who has considerable experience in the art of thievery."

"So you want me to steal for you? That's not taking advantage of others then?"

Fletchley rocked forward off the desk and onto his feet, walking over to the map. He turned back to Gabe, tapping a marked area with the tip of his pen. "Not in this case. Not when it's stealing from a criminal. You've heard presumably of Resurrection Alley, and the uses to which the dead are put there?"

The younger man nodded, frowning.

The civil servant gazed at the image of the capital before him. "There've been... rumours of what Andrei Vassily is keeping inside the settlement. We have limited intelligence gatherers around the city, alerting us to the latest developments, and word repeatedly comes back: Vassily has something. It's never been verified, but it's been mentioned by too many disparate sources for us not to take it seriously. Bottom line, the word is that he is in possession of a truly self-aware Returner. Possibly the first we have knowledge of in the country."

"A smart deadhead?" Gabe said, struggling to follow where his role fitted into this. "Where did it come from?"

"Your guess is as good as mine, if indeed the reports are true. Quite what he's doing with it is another question; keeping him warm during the cold winter evenings, for all I know. But its presence, if it exists, cannot be ignored; it might be the most important and decisive find since the plague took hold. A chance to turn the contagion around."

"You've lost me."

"The virus is changing, Flowers and his scientists are right about that. It's evolving, adapting the ghouls for its own ends; they're growing smarter as it works on their higher brain functions, allowing them to recognise elements from their pre-dead state – names, objects, places." Fletchley tapped the map again. "The feeding patterns tell us just how far they've come. They're still flesh-eaters, and unable to comprehend much beyond that basic need; but a self-aware Returner is the best evidence we have that a zombie is capable of rational thought. The bacterium within it must've developed at a phenomenal rate. We need to take a look at it."

"Hold on, you want me to hijack a *stiff*?"

"Of course not. But we need a blood sample." Fletchley locked stares with Gabe. "I told you that this opportunity could save thousands of lives, that it would be for the greater good. If we could learn to duplicate the virus in that advanced form, it's possible we could reverse the effects of the zombification process, halt the spread of the infection."

Gabe thought of Anna sitting in her chair in the silent room, looking out over Harry's gardens. There was an absence at the heart of her he had never been able to touch. Not yet. "You could turn people back to who they were? From before, I mean?"

The government man shrugged and shook his head. "It's impossible to say. I doubt we could help some – the effects of mortification would've been too great. But others, those that have resurrected more recently, we could perhaps return a semblance of cognition to. At the very least, give them a new diet. But it's a chance we can't afford not to take. At the risk of sounding melodramatic, it might well be mankind's best hope."

"Sentiments like that don't mean much to somebody like Andrei Vassily," Gabe murmured.

"Nor Harry Flowers, not if there's influence to be wielded or money to be made. But maybe they strike a chord with you."

"You mean a wanted lowlife with nothing left to lose?"

"Exactly."

IT WAS THE smells that were his guide through the streets. Down here, amongst the ruins, there were no directions to aid him on his journey. Thus he relied on his other senses to lead him in his descent from the main West End arterial thoroughfares into the narrow alleys and dank, deserted squares. Such was the quiet, he cocked his head at the distant clatter of movement or the suggestion of a faint zombie moan carried on the breeze; his palate was sharpened to recognise a change in the air, taste the sour ashes of a hidden brazier crackling somewhere; but it was the scents that were his beacon, the sweetness of roasting meat underscored by the tang of corruption, the sour stink of bodies pressed together. In an environment where cadavers lay discarded with as much dignity as rubbish bags heaped in a skip, the surroundings rapidly grew ripe with decay, and it took a finely tuned nose to separate the stench of death from that of life. Not unlike the ghouls, he sensed the proximity of his own kind by following a feeling of warmth generated by the beating of many hearts.

Gabe stepped warily down subway steps, aware that his progress was unquestionably being monitored by those that he sought. CCTV cameras hooked up at the subway's entrance had their pictures rerouted to give the Alley warning of who was approaching. The fact that he had been able to advance so far unhindered was a positive sign that his presence wasn't unwelcome. Even so, he would be wise to remain cautious, he told himself, because anything was possible with these people. He strode through the underpass unhurriedly, his footsteps echoing disconcertingly loud in the enclosed space, the yellow fluorescents set in the walls barely illuminating the grimy, refuse-sodden floor ahead. He concentrated on the sulphur gleam of the streetlights at the end of the tunnel, refusing to pause or glance over his shoulder. He knew he had to look like he belonged here, that he wasn't a stranger sent to stir trouble, and was more than a thrill-seeking tourist; rather, that he knew the score of what it was to cross into the underworld. Of course, if they were aware of who it was that had sent him on this errand, his entry would've been denied before he got within a hundred yards of the place.

Gabe exited the subway, and got his first glimpse of Resurrection Alley, its gated threshold strung between the mighty pillars of a flyover support. Apart from the one guarded doorway, there was no other opportunity to gain entrance, its chain link fence tucked snug on either side against sheer revetments that were impossible to climb. In its own downmarket way, its security was on a par with Harry's mansion. The storm fences had been extended to the underpass steps, so as one ascended it was into a steel-mesh corridor that channelled the visitor towards the Alley's gate.

The fences were essential. Out here in the wild, barren plains of the capital it was zombie country. A good two-dozen deadheads battered themselves against the barriers, trying to gnaw their way through. Once they saw – or, more accurately, sensed – Gabe emerge, they shook the wire frenziedly and attempted to force their fingers beyond the divide. It was initially shocking to be so close to the ghouls, separated by mere inches, and their excited groans at his arrival hit him like a roar after the solitude of his journey here. Once he became accustomed to their presence, he made sure he walked directly down the centre of the passage, careful not to drift too close to their grasping hands and ceaseless jaws; but despite trying to keep his demeanour cool and collected, he couldn't help looking worriedly at the fences as they shook with the furious flesh-crazed craving of the dead. They didn't seem strong enough to keep them at bay.

As he approached, he marvelled at the scale of the settlement – dwarfed itself by the vast cement expanse of the motorway above – and the organisation that it had taken to establish itself deep in the middle of nowhere. It was some distance from the nearest cluster of stores that still contained supplies; it seemed at the mercy of the elements, the cold concrete landscape offering little respite; and running the gauntlet of deadheads every time you arrived or departed was, in Gabe's eyes, an unnecessary risk. But he had heard that this was the way its inhabitants liked it, far from the more populated areas of London, apparently embracing their marginalised position. It made daily existence into some kind of extreme sport, riding on the cusp of danger. And more pertinently, it removed Resurrection Alley from the immediate clutches of any authorities that might try to impose some kind of order on the place.

Out here, it operated under its own rules, and that was the primary temptation for so many of its clientele, willing to make the trip to see and experience for themselves the distractions for which the Alley was renowned. It reputedly offered anything that the punter was willing to pay for, would accede to the basest desires, and asked little questions if the money was right; and it found there were plenty who were looking for such a paradise, so many in fact that Vassily and his lieutenants had the luxury of picking and choosing who they would allow within its walls. Those whose overheated lusts suggested instability could be easily refused entry, and while simple sightseers were treated with disdain, they were considered rich pickings ripe for fleecing. All of which led to its growing reputation of exclusivity – and of course the more people were denied access the more they wanted to taste its forbidden fruits for themselves. The place had become a modern legend, an intersection of fact and fiction. The stories that Gabe had heard from those that had returned from a day or two's partying within the Alley were almost fantastical. He had been there only once before, acting as superfluous back-up when Harry decided to pay Vassily a goodwill visit about three years ago. As it was, Gabe got to see little of the reputed entertainment. He and the five other triggermen were housed in a nondescript office and fed coffee and cigarettes while Flowers and Vassily chewed the fat. Presumably, since they weren't parting with any cash, the Alley was a closed shop.

Harry tolerated the Alley, allowed it to operate independently and not pay him any tithe, which was possibly down to the fact that Flowers had a history with Andrei's old man, Goran. They had been rivals back in the day, and Andrei was still oblivious to the truth behind his father's death. Harry wanted it kept that way for the time being. Thus, the two bosses existed in a forced atmosphere of bonhomie, fully aware that the other would one day want to expand their empire. Flowers knew that when London was his, it would mean that the Alley would fall finally under his remit; the inevitable war would be bloody and hard-fought, but his control had to be total. He wouldn't brook small islands within the city escaping his rule. It would be absolute or nothing.

Gabe sidled up to the entrance, wondering if he would be recognised as one of Flowers' men. There was no reason why his face should've been indelibly printed on the memories of the guards after all that time, and he'd never met Andrei in person, who had come back from abroad to take over his father's business when he died. But if they did make him he had resolved to come clean and just tell them that he'd broken free from his former employer, which was certainly no lie. Whether they'd go for it or not was another matter. The guy on the other side of the chain link gate was eyeing him suspiciously – Gabe supposed that most revellers visited the Alley as a group rather than turning up on their own – and was absent-mindedly running his forefinger along the stock of the pump-action shotgun he held down at his side.

"How's it going?" Gabe greeted him with as much forced jollity as he could muster.

The guard nodded a reply. He was black, with a thin moustache and a bandanna wrapped around a bald head. He had had a three-quarter chewed apple in the other hand, which he threw to one side. "You lookin' for something?"

"Been looking for this place, my friend. I heard the Alley was the place to go."

"Is that right? You realise not anyone can jus' stroll in here."

"What, is it a 'if the face fits' kind of deal?" When the man didn't answer, merely studied him intently, Gabe shrugged dispiritedly. "There I was kinda thinking that this was somewhere where I might find myself a good time. Few drinks, bit of gambling..." The guard remained unmoved. "I got money," Gabe added, with an exaggeratedly naive delve into his pockets.

The shotgun twitched and Gabe froze. "You come here on your own?" the guard asked, motioning with the weapon for him to keep his hands where he could see them.

"Yep. Truth of the matter is, I've been travelling down from the north, kinda looking for a bolthole to call my own, if you see what I mean. Guy I met, fellow drifter, he told me about this place, said that it was a regular Disneyland in Stiff City. Thought I owed it to myself to kick loose for a while and have some fun."

The guard didn't look convinced, but he glanced up at the CCTV camera positioned on the other side of the fence. Someone was watching him, Gabe guessed, trying to discern if he was trouble. He hoped that his 'just arrived in the city' spiel would be enough to get them salivating at how much of his cash they could get him to part with. The man's mobile phone burbled and he spoke briefly into it, then started ramming free bolts and unlocked the gate, beckoning Gabe across the threshold before securing it again.

"OK, arms out," the man said, placing the shotgun as his feet. He patted Gabe down quickly and desultorily, finding nothing, though he took the liberty of removing a couple of twenty-pound notes from Gabe's wallet. "Call it a gate fee," he said, winking. "Go on, then. Your promised land awaits."

Gabe smiled, as if he wasn't quite sure what he was letting himself in for. But his expression disappeared as soon as his back was turned and he strode into the crowds of Resurrection Alley, conscious not only of the rasp of the miniature revolver taped just below his ankle, but also of the syringe pressing against his foot inside his left boot.

As Gabe threaded his way through the Alley's evening clientele, with every step – his leg had adequately recovered enough for him to disguise his limp so that it didn't draw attention – he tried to rationalise who he was doing this for. Certainly not Fletchley; despite the civil servant's disarming candour, an inbuilt distrust of suits stopped him from taking the ministerial lackey at his word. He liked to believe that the man had the nation's interests at heart, but the speed with which the government had lost control suggested that this might be just a face-saving damage limitation exercise. Also, he had heard on the grapevine that more than a handful of senior members of the cabinet (including possibly the Premier himself) had fallen victim to the plague, and were locked in a secure establishment in the eventuality that a cure was found.

There was perhaps an element of wanting to put a spoke in Flowers' plans – especially given the worrying revelations of what Harry intended to do with the city once it was his – but in the main he told himself his altruism extended to just two people: himself and Anna. He'd made a promise to help her; it was principally why he'd chosen to stay in Flowers' outfit. If he could help snap her out of her fugue state – surely Fletchley would make her a priority case for treatment, as a favour returned, if they could somehow pry her away from Harry's grasp – then it offered something he'd been perhaps losing sight of over the years: hope. The civil servant had been right; he had lived for too long in Flowers' shadow, bending to his will, the gang lord's limitless ambition chipping away at his sense of moral duty. What was the point in helping pave the way for his former employer's brave new world if it helped no one? Indeed, if it put in place a situation that was even worse? It was time he took control for himself, and put his own plans in motion.

The Alley's boulevards were stained red from the spluttering neon on the buildings lining each side, advertising their contents. The majority of them were spit n' sawdust live shows: deadfuck baiting, shooting galleries or strip joints. Naked, mostly female, zombs writhed in windows, chained to poles, muzzles strapped over their mouths, advertising the entertainment within. Their dull eyes stared out at the crowds pausing to watch. Supposedly their frantic straining against their bonds was meant to be erotic, but to Gabe's eyes it looked desperate and so far removed from what he found attractive that he struggled to imagine how any of these slack-jawed fun-seekers were willing to pay to go into some back room and make out with a hosed-down and tethered ghoul, all its teeth and nails removed, its veins pumped full of formaldehyde and its skin slathered in that shit that undertakers used to make sure nothing came off mid-coitus. It amazed him how people would so quickly turn to something that in any other circumstances they would find utterly abhorrent. Social codes abandoned, they embraced a regression to animalistic urges.

Slipping through the throng, he was continuously accosted by enthusiastic barkers, championing each establishment's delights – hunting parties, with prizes for the most undead bagged; wrestling matches, the combatants armed with nothing but their bare fists against a trio of stiffs; bars with dissections performed every hour. It was stimulation overload, a descent into a De Sadeian hell. For the enterprising pornographer or club owner, the rise of the dead had given them an underclass they could exploit without fear of recrimination, that could be broken and abused until they fell apart and were replaced. Anyone looking to unwind or let off a little steam could, for a fee, get themselves a Returner to beat on for an hour or so, safe in the knowledge that they weren't battering anything that experienced pain, or was even breathing. As long as it wasn't a recognisable family member that was up on stage being fed into a mincer before a baying audience – and it could happen; once a victim resurrected it was fair game for the Alley's entertainment, no matter what they once were in their previous existence – visitors were happy to use the pusbags for whatever dark designs they saw fit.

Gabe knew that Vassily would be keeping this smart zombie of his out of public view, and that he would have to arrange a meet with the settlement's leader, if he was going to get close to it at all. He recalled that one of Andrei's lieutenants ran the security on a cage-fighting dive on the central strip. Perhaps he could get word through that way. He headed off in search of it, determinedly doing his best to ignore the brightly lit windows, and the horrors that they displayed for sale.

"THAT HIM?"

"No question. Always knew that fucker had nine lives."

"What's he doing here?"

"Hiding out, maybe. More likely he's looking to get in with Vassily's mob."

"Shit, this could be awkward. Harry's not going to want to bring a war to the Alley."

"Fuck it, get on the phone, tell Flowers we found him. We'll let him call the shots."

CHAPTER SIX

It was the noise that hit him as soon as he entered. Upon stepping through the door, Gabe had to squint against the club's gloom, its sole illumination the spotlights beaming their paltry glow upon the cage set up in the middle of the interior. Everything beyond their reach was a mass of heaving shadow, but once his eyes became accustomed to the darkness he could judge by the silhouettes of the crowd that the venue was packed. The blue smoke that drifted ethereally beneath the rafters added to the slow, thick air that made the room feel stagnant and claustrophobic. He could discern little of the clientele pressing forward to get a better view of the action taking place inside the steel ring at the centre, but the roar of cheers, shouts and curses was deafening. From this distance, with the neglected bar just to his right, he could see little of what the mob was baying for but he could discern, between the cries, the crunch of bone splintering and the rattle of the cage as bodies were thrown against it. Each punch was punctuated by another eruption from the audience.

Gabe sidled over to the barman leaning on the counter. He raised his eyebrows at the thief's approach, and Gabe nodded a greeting, ordering a beer. The barman withdrew one from a wheezing cooler cabinet powered, Gabe noted, by a small rumbling generator tucked away in a corner;

cables snaked away from it up the walls and across the beams, providing the electricity, it seemed, for the whole building. It lent the bar the faintest stench of kerosene, and when he took a swig from the bottle it tasted like the lager had been brewed from something similar. He swilled it around his mouth, summoning the courage to swallow, but threw some coins onto the counter top instead, waiting until the barman's concentration was fixed on retrieving the money before spitting the beer onto the floor. His tongue felt as if someone had scoured it with a wire brush. He chanced a look at the bottle, but there was no label on it. No wonder the crowd was so rowdy, he thought – they've probably been sent half-mad through alcohol poisoning.

He leaned forward as the man was counting up the pennies. "Does Jackson still work here? Bryan Jackson? I heard he was chief of security." Gabe had to shout at the top of his voice even though there was barely a foot between them. Evidently, whomever the audience was rooting for had pulled off something pretty spectacular, because the applause went through the roof.

The barman glanced up at him then down again, not catching his eye for more than a second. "You a friend of Bryan's?"

Gabe nodded. "Know him from way back. Used to run with his crew when I was younger." He played with the bottle to give the impression he hadn't forgotten about it while at the same time deliberately not putting it anywhere near his lips. "Been travelling down from the north, trying to find friends that I've lost contact with. Last time I spoke to him I thought he'd said he was working at the Alley."

"What did you say your name was?"

"I didn't. It's O'Connell."

"Bryan's kinda busy right now," the barman replied, gesturing to the crowd. "As you can see, we get a full house on fight nights and there's always a chance that some bozo is going to get a temper on him. The sec team usually have their hands full when the match is over. But his office is over there, on the far side." He pointed across the room towards the impenetrable murk beyond the cage. "Perhaps you can catch him there, when he's taking a break."

Gabe thanked him, picked up his bottle and started to ease his way through the throng. He didn't think it was possible, but the cacophony substantially increased the closer he got to the epicentre of the club and the nearer he drew to the fence-encircled pit. The slap of flesh meeting flesh on the other side of the steel mesh reverberated in his head, and the watching mob pressing in against him moved as one body, pogoing with excitement, raising their fists in the air, yelling with triumph or anger. It was unquestionably mostly men in the audience, and they appeared to feed off each other's energy, vicariously channelling the violence from the act they were watching into bellowing approval. It was impossible to distinguish any actual words amongst the chants and jeers; it melded into a wall of sound that each added to with every full-throated roar. Gabe moved through the undulating, gesticulating mass carefully, picking his route with caution, knowing that if he upset just one component of this seething organism, it would turn its aggressive focus inwards and spill into a ruck. It wasn't difficult to detect the barely suppressed savagery in the spectators. Its stink hung in the air mixed with the cigarette smoke, a bouquet of terrifying primal brutality, sweat and the ever-present undercurrent of rotting meat.

A space cleared before him and Gabe could at last view the cage-fight unobstructed. The human grappler was bare-chested and sheathed in perspiration, dark blood splattered across his torso and arms, though Gabe guessed that it wasn't his own. The man was wearing a Mexican wrestler-style hooded mask that completely shielded his features, but the weight of his frame put his age at somewhere in his mid-forties. Gabe wondered how long he had been taking part in bouts like this. He reminded the thief of a circus strongman or fairground boxer, long gone to seed, and performing humiliating acts of strength and endurance for a paying public.

He was without weapons, but he had long metal cuffs around each wrist, both with a hooked blade on the underside. From the look of the four Returners he was locked in the cage with, it seemed that was all the arsenal he needed: they were falling apart before him, one of their arms already lying on the crimson-flecked straw that covered the floor of the pit. Their gullets were open black wounds, from which their moans echoed through their severed vocal cords, and it looked as if their grey-green skulls were only staying atop their spinal columns by the flimsiest thread. Jagged cuts criss-crossed their faces and limbs, laying them open to yellow bone; and yet still they came for him, hungry and relentless. They weren't chained to anything, which surprised Gabe. He had seen fights like this before where the ghouls were on a leash, which only extended so far, giving the living opponent a sliver of an advantage should the maggotbrain be particularly feisty. Here, no such help was required. The moment a zombie came within grasping distance, the wrestler easily sidestepped its approach and brought down his forearm, the blade slicing through the tissue-thin skin in an instant.

It became apparent that he was playing with them to a certain degree. He could've finished them off within moments with a handful of judicious swipes to the brain, but he was dragging out their demise for the maximum entertainment, trimming pieces off them with the skill of a butcher. He used the ghouls for comedy value, pushing one in front into its fellows and watching them tumble like a troupe of clowns. Then, as another would try to right itself, he would stamp on its gnarled hand, the dry, sharp snapping of brittle digits accompanied by another bellow of admiration from the crowd.

Eventually, Gabe detected the show beginning to wrap up. The wavering cadavers looked like they'd stumbled through a jet engine – chunks of their bodies were missing in a jigsaw-style effect – and were barely offering any resistance. The audience was growing restless, demanding a spectacular climax, and the wrestler whetted their bloodlust with a denouement worthy of one experienced at performing before the public: he spun, hooking his right leg around the nearest Returner's waist so that it was pulled nearer, then lashed out with both arms beneath the zomb's chin, severing its head completely. There was little blood, and the remains collapsed to the floor like a felled tree, the skull following after with an eggshell crack as it hit the ground.

The crowd approved, starting a chant that the fighter attempted to execute his finishing moves to, slashing open the last three ghouls to every beat of the rhythm. They each followed the fate of the first, necks split asunder, until the man stood in the middle of the cage, blood-slicked and victorious, viscera curled at his feet, his arms held above his head, pumping his fists to the throng's adoration. Those at the front of the mass surged forward and grabbed hold of the bars, rattling them with angry exultation. Their desire to see violence meted out was satisfied, and now it was exploding outwards, directionless. Gabe could understand now why the barman said the security team had their hands full; it would take all their efforts to quell such a riled mob. Minor scuffles began to break out in the thick of the crowd, and he took the opportunity to remove himself from the danger zone. He edged well away from the trouble, backing up against the far wall where he'd been told Jackson's office was situated, just as the bouncers moved in armed with short black saps, seemingly ungluing themselves from the shadows.

They handled the situation with efficient brutality, ushering those that didn't want their own heads broken to vacate the premises. Most of the clientele were on their way out the door without having to be asked, eager to find the next live show, or have a go at something similar themselves, their appetites for destruction piqued. That was the chief attraction of Resurrection Alley: the fun never stopped. You could move from club to bar to gambling den to whorehouse to Grand Guignol theatre and find some new atrocity to keep you amused and occupied while the industrial-strength booze and pills, purchased from the tiny but dedicated band of dealers, went to work on your nervous system. It was amazing how quickly such a state of insobriety and tolerance towards the most inhuman acts imaginable could become the norm. Those that defended their actions perpetrated whilst holidaying in the Alley would more often than not merely claim they were letting off steam, but that didn't account for the rage that such relaxation unleashed. It was like seeing mankind sloughing off its daily face in a bid to enjoy itself, and in the process unveiling the hideous dark heart of what it actually was.

Those scrappers too enthused by the bout they'd just witnessed and who were continuing to tussle with their neighbours were given short shrift. The security guards struck the ringleaders across their temples, rendering them instantly unconscious. Once more than half a dozen were lying prone on the bar's floor, the fight went out of the rest, and they held up their hands in surrender, retreating towards the exit. The last to leave were instructed to pick up those that were out cold and to carry them outside. What happened to them after that was not the venue's concern. It was a disclaimer of the Alley that anyone partying within its walls did so at their own risk; while it was prepared to put on the entertainment, it wasn't going to sweep up the mess afterwards, and Andrei Vassily had given his men carte blanche to act with extreme prejudice whenever they saw fit. While anything was possible here, that didn't necessarily assign the punter any consumer rights.

As the dazed and contrite spectators staggered into the street, Gabe noted the wrestler unlock the cage door and step out. Shorn of his audience, he looked smaller somehow, almost deflated. He was taking deep breaths, stretching his muscles, rolling his head and massaging the back of his neck as he trudged with the gait of the deeply weary towards the security office. He was about to lift his mask free – he had unpeeled it as far as just below his nose, revealing a stubbly chin and jowls – when he spotted the younger man leaning against the wall in the gloom. He paused, pulling the disguise back in place, studying Gabe with watery eyes, then nodded. Gabe returned the greeting, and the man passed through into the room beyond, shoulders slouched like someone who was slowly dying inside.

"Place is closed, pal, in case you hadn't noticed," a voice said close to Gabe's ear. He turned and saw one of the bouncers twirling his sap next to him. "Next show is in a couple of hours. Suggest y'hop it."

"I wanted a word with Jackson. He around?"

"Bryan?" The man looked surprised, then swivelled and called out across the room. "Bryan! Guy here looking for you."

"Yeah? I know you?" The broad-shouldered, bearded figure that approached hadn't changed since Gabe had last seen him. His dark eyes set deep in a fleshy face were as impossible to gauge as ever, and it looked like he'd added to the enormous tattoo that spread across his torso, a snake's head emerging from his shirt collar to nestle at his throat.

"Gabriel O'Connell."

He squinted as he rolled the name around his head, pupils disappearing in the pronounced skin folds like black buttons in dough. "Rings a bell..." He pointed a stubby finger. "You one of Flowers's men?"

"*Was.* Me and the boss man had something of a falling out."

"Yeah, I recognise you now. You were one of his triggers last time he paid a visit. Thought you were supposed to be his capo?"

"Like I said, situation's changed," Gabe replied, shrugging, wondering how Harry truly saw their relationship. There was no denying that the old geezer was grateful for what Gabe had done for him the night they lost Anna, but at the same time Harry held him personally responsible for the events that had unfolded, using his guilt as a means to manipulate his loyalty. He could've had Gabe killed back then too, for what he did, but kept him on, knowing he could use him. So Flowers probably hadn't given it a second thought when he at last signed Gabe's death warrant. As far as he was concerned it was another traitorous ex-employee who was going to get what he deserved.

Jackson stepped closer, uncomfortably so; there was only a foot or so between them. Gabe had to look up to maintain eye contact, the security man being a head taller. "So, what, you decided to do a runner? Or you thought Andrei might offer you a better deal?" He smiled crookedly. "Or did Flowers throw you out like a discarded bitch when you'd served your purpose?"

"If you think I might be a threat to your position as Andrei's number one benchwarmer, then don't worry," Gabe answered, unwavering. "I'm not about to fly in and boot you out of the nest. Truth is, I've got a proposition for your boss that I'd like to take to him personally, if you're amenable."

Jackson laughed, loud and abrupt. "I bet you have. Y'know, I seem to remember you being this polite when we were pointing guns at one another. Trouble is, O'Connell, what makes you think I'm going to let you see him? All I've got is your word that you've severed links with Harry. Maybe you're out to demonstrate your loyalty to him by getting close to his biggest rival."

"You think I'd come here on an assassination run and announce myself to all and sundry? Do you think I'd make a fucking *appointment*? Credit me with a little intelligence. Fact is, I've come here showing Andrei and yourself nothing but respect, and it would be nice if it was reciprocated. From what I remember of Andrei, he's a stickler for manners." That shut the fat bastard up, Gabe thought, watching Jackson chew his lower lip. "I'd like to speak to him because I have a plan that could be advantageous to him and his whole organisation, that could challenge Harry's power base."

"So you *are* switching sides?"

"I'm not going to lie to you, Jackson: Flowers and me are history. And, as I'm sure you know, no one walks away from his set-up – it's either the life or fed to the deadheads. There's nothing in between. So my still breathing is a major upset to Harry, and he would like nothing more than to shut me up permanently. I, on the other hand, would like to remove him from my back, equally permanently. Andrei's the only one with the guts and the resources to do that, and the man best placed in the city to inherit Harry's territory if what I'm going to suggest to him pays off. I think he will be interested to at least hear what I've got to say."

"Andrei doesn't usually grant an audience with underlings," Jackson said hesitantly. "If you ain't on his level, then he ain't interested." The security man was conflicted, Gabe could tell. He liked to build up this barrier around his boss, make it seem like anyone who wanted to get close to Vassily would have to negotiate with him first, but the fact was he didn't have either the authority or the chutzpah to come to decisions like this on the hoof. If Jackson were to have him thrown out of the Alley, there was nothing Gabe could do about it, but Gabe was relying on the fact that there would be a niggling part of the enforcer's mind that would be telling him he could be dismissing an opportunity that Andrei might've grabbed hold of if he was aware of it. And if his boss learned later that he never got to hear this proposition because Jackson took it upon himself to act on his behalf, then his employment could be cut short very quickly indeed. Basically, it came down to the fact that, for all his meat-headed bluster, Jackson couldn't disguise his fear of responsibility; he was someone that, despite his position of trust, always liked to defer upwards.

"Look, just put my case to him, tell him what I told you, that's all I'm asking," Gabe said reasonably. "If he's willing to hear me out, fine. If he listens, then tells me to get the fuck out of here, then that's cool, I'll walk, no problem. But give him the choice, if nothing else."

Jackson breathed heavily through his nose, his already lined brow furrowed further, and the snake's head tattoo flexed with the rise and fall of his chest. His gimlet eyes remained fixed on Gabe as he fished into his back pocket and pulled out his mobile. Without looking at it he thumbed a button and held it up to his ear. "Gull, it's Jackson," he murmured seconds later. "Andrei with you?" He listened to the reply, then said, "Got something here that Andrei might want to be aware of. A messenger, of sorts." He paused. "No, I think he's going to want to hear this for himself. Don't worry, he'll be fully prepped." He muttered an affirmative, then flipped the phone shut. "Got your five minutes," he said sullenly. "I'll take you over there now."

"Appreciate it."

"Gonna have to pat you down –"

"No need," Gabe replied, lifting his leg and sliding his fingers into his boot, tearing free the tiny pistol, and holding it out handle-first. "That's what I'm packing." Jackson glared at it, then at him. Gabe gave a half smile. "Thought I'd go into this with the best intentions. Safety's on."

The security guard snatched it from him. "You know full well that the Alley is a weapons-free zone. And yet you didn't declare it to the guy at the gate?"

"Guess I forgot. You can see what a peashooter it is."

Jackson tightened his grip around the gun, and leaned closer to Gabe. "Don't make me regret this," he snarled. Then he motioned with his head for the thief to follow.

*   *   *

JACKSON LED HIM to a jeep parked outside the club, told him to climb in, then cautiously steered it through the heaving boulevards of the settlement towards the imposing warehouse-style building that housed Vassily's inner quarters. Drawing nearer, Gabe could see that the place was teeming with triggermen. Going by the tooled-up muscle posted at every entrance, any attempt to take Andrei head-on was doomed to failure, and Gabe would find attempting to infiltrate the complex to steal a few moments with this self-aware zombie (if indeed it even existed) a very difficult task. His best bet was going to be to somehow lose his escort whilst inside its walls, and worry about getting out later. His head was filled with diversions – fire, flood, electrical fault – that he could instigate to draw the guards' attention away from his escape. But right now, the matter at hand was determining if the creature was anything more than hearsay.

The jeep slewed to a halt before a pair of heavy iron doors, an Uzi-wielding goon wandering over from his station to investigate. Jackson waved him away, and instructed Gabe to stick close as he punched in a security code on the keypad set into the brickwork. The lock sprung open with a heavy *clunk*. He pushed one of the doors open wide enough for them to slip through, then let it clang back into position behind them. They were in a bare stone corridor, and Jackson strode forward towards a set of curving white painted steps at the far end, the thief scurrying to keep up. As he began to climb, Gabe couldn't help but contrast the puritanical sparseness of Vassily's headquarters to the opulence of Harry's mansion. It was as if the head of Resurrection Alley was trying to distance himself from the degenerate entertainment through which he made his money. Punish himself, even. There was little here to suggest that this was the home of a powerful gang lord, so lacking was it in signs of wealth, or any kinds of comfort. He knew Andrei lacked much of Flowers' brutish ruthlessness – he was a second-generation mobster, unused to waging wars – but this seemed as much like a monastery as it did a fortress, a place where there was only room for cold functionality. It was odd that at the heart of the Alley's wild decadence stood this quiet stone island, in which rested its king.

The stairs stopped at a wooden door and Jackson rapped on it, turning the heavy brass handle without waiting for an answer. Inside were the first signs that this was a home as well as a castle; a carpet covered the floor, drapes and paintings adorned the walls. A couple of buttonmen were lounging on a leather sofa, machine guns resting casually on their laps, and they stood when the two of them entered, looking at Gabe quizzically.

"So who's this?" the taller, craggy-faced one asked with blunt disdain.

"Hey, Gull," Jackson greeted him. "This is O'Connell, the messenger I mentioned. Used to be one of Flowers's enforcers."

"No shit?"

"Said he wanted to have a word with Andrei, something that would be to his advantage."

Gull pulled an expression that suggested he was very far from being impressed. The second guy was hefting his weapon with excessive theatricality. "Got our own stoolie, have we?"

"You managed to have a word?"

"Garvey's in there with Andrei," Gull said, lazily motioning towards an adjoining door. He turned his attention to Gabe. "He's prepared to give you a few minutes, so keep it quick. He's not keen on timewasters." He looked back at Jackson. "You searched him?"

"He surrendered the only gun he had."

The thief surreptitiously pressed his foot against the syringe in his boot, checking it was still in place.

"OK. Take him through, Jackson."

Gabe followed the other man into the antechamber, decorated in a similar fashion to the outer office, although an expansive bookcase lined one wall. Andrei Vassily was sitting in an armchair, his tan suit immaculate, his legs crossed, fingers steepled under his chin. He was in his early forties, and there was a composed look of serenity to his dark features, as if his every act was fluid and unhurried, economical but perfectly judged. To his right stood a severe-looking woman in a business suit, thin to the point of reptilian.

"Mr Vassily," Jackson began, "this is –"

"I know who he is," Andrei replied, his voice soft, a hint of an East European accent. Gabe evidently failed to conceal his surprise, because the older man nodded faintly. "Oh yes, I recognised you as one of Harry's when you arrived. I told the man at the gate to let you in. So what happened between you and your former employer?"

"I... screwed up, and he's cut me adrift from the organisation."

"And no doubt you're now a loose end that he wishes to tie up. What brings you here? Looking for a new job?"

Gabe shook his head. "Partly a warning, partly a proposition. Mr Vassily, I'm sure you don't need me to tell you that Harry's looking to expand his empire over the next year. He wants London, all of it, and the impasse that has existed between the two of you for so long is going to be tested. Make no mistake, when the time comes he will take the Alley by any means necessary, and right now he's working on the means to control the city. He's going to turn the deadheads to his advantage, create an obedient army from them."

Andrei raised his eyebrows. "Harry always did see the big picture."

"Flowers has got his scientists working on the virus, trying to adapt it. They're making progress, but slowly. They don't have what you've got."

"Which is what?"

"A self-aware Returner."

"Is that right?" Vassily exchanged a look with the woman at his side.

"Or so the rumour goes. Since cutting ties with Harry I've hooked up with an ex-government boffin, studying the plague independently, and he's developing a serum that can boost the intelligence of the dead. With the right resources and contacts, he could produce it on a massive scale. A blood sample from a ghoul whose consciousness has evolved to such a degree would advance his research enormously. I felt, Mr Vassily, that you would see the advantages in entering into such a business opportunity."

"And we would... what? Forge an army of our own?"

"Better to do it before Flowers gains the upper hand. If you can stay ahead of him –"

"Yeah, that's always been my problem," a voice said behind Gabe. He felt a coldness lodge in his chest as he turned towards its source, his legs growing suddenly weak. "I'm always lagging behind."

Harry Flowers sauntered into the room, Hewitt at his left shoulder, a couple of other boys from the house behind him. He fixed Gabe with an icy grin.

"Long time no see, son."

CHAPTER SEVEN

FOR A MOMENT, Gabe could do nothing but stand and stare back at his former boss. The office, Andrei Vassily, Jackson and the rest, slid away off the periphery of his vision. It was only for the briefest of seconds, but within that fraction of time all he saw was Flowers' face studying him with a mixture of hatred and unconcealed mirth. That sensation of stasis seemed to encompass the pair of them, as if they were two museum exhibits eyeing one another from either side of a display case. He blinked and the rest of the world came racing back into focus. He cleared his throat, realising that he'd been holding his breath.

"Harry."

"Hello, Gabriel," the old man remarked, as if he were tipping his hat to a neighbour he saw every morning. Gabe could detect little malice in his voice. "We'd been wondering where you'd got to."

"The... the hijack was a bust," Gabe said slowly, aware that excuses would make no difference but unable to think of anything else to say. He was damned if he was going to apologise to him, and he promised himself that he wouldn't beg. He wouldn't spend his last few minutes on earth on his knees. "Everything got fucked up. The target got destroyed, we unwittingly riled an army of pusbags beneath the river, we didn't have any choice but to retreat. Government pricks caught me as I tried to make it back to the motor."

Did he imagine it, or did he see the slightest beginnings of a smirk twitch at the corner of Hewitt's mouth? He shouldn't have been surprised that the kid was enjoying his predicament – no doubt promotion had been offered to Gabe's soon-to-be-vacant position in the outfit – but there was something about the way he was standing there, a bastard full to bursting with bad news, and struggling to contain himself. It was somehow agonisingly predictable that he had survived that night on the bridge, scurrying vermin-like to safety.

"Please," Harry said, looking pained, holding up a hand. "Let's not rake over the past. Mr Hewitt's given me a full account of the operation's failure. Such eventualities, while tiresome, are par for the course. What's less acceptable is a security lapse."

"Harry, for what's it's worth, I told them nothing. They know plenty about you already."

"These are your new paymasters, I take it?"

"I work for no one. Not anymore."

"Oh, I would like to believe that, Gabriel, honestly I would," Flowers replied flamboyantly, taking a step or two towards him. "It gives me no pleasure to be standing here before you like this. You were one of my most trusted aides, and you were a good little thief. You were an *asset*, boy." He reached out and grabbed Gabe's chin hard between thumb and forefinger. "But don't insult my intelligence by telling me that the authorities simply let you go without asking for nothing in return. The fact that you're still alive indicates that you bargained your way out of their custody. And lo and behold you turn up at the Alley, seeking to curry favour with Andrei."

The younger man couldn't answer, his jaw held firmly in place by Harry's solid grip, but he glared back, refusing to look away from the gang lord's blazing eyes.

"Didn't take much for you to turn traitor, did it?" Flowers spat, wrenching his hand away.

"Just circumstances," Gabe said. "Ask Ashberry. That's how anyone ends up becoming involved with an old arsehole like you."

Harry pulled an ancient snubnose Colt from his trouser belt and without hesitation shot Gabe in the belly. The roar of the gun's detonation in the enclosed space of the office was deafening, a clap of thunder that caught everyone by surprise. Gabe staggered, crumpling onto his backside, his hands clutching at his wound, trying to stem the blood pumping between his fingers. White-hot pain encircled his torso as if a flaming vice had been tightened around him, and stars danced in his vision. He chanced a look at the entry point, then glanced away. His palms were sticky and a deep shade of crimson.

"Don't worry, Mr O'Connell," Harry said, standing over him. "You won't die yet. Gutshot will take a while to bleed out. It'll poison your organs and starve your brain of oxygen, but you'll be conscious enough for what I've got planned for you."

"I don't remember agreeing to you perforating your mark on my property," Gabe heard Vassily protest, the words floating down to him as if he was listening to the exchange underwater. "I said I'd give you the guy, I didn't say you could redecorate my office with him."

"Sorry, Andrei. Temper got the better of me."

"Mr Vassily, sir, with respect: what the hell is going on?" Jackson asked. "You knew O'Connell was coming to see you?"

"Harry had asked that we keep an eye out for him; that's why I approved his entry into the Alley, and let those looking for him know that he was in the area. Sorry I didn't keep you informed, Jackson, but I thought the fewer personnel that knew the less likely he would get spooked and make a run for it."

"I am grateful, Andrei," Harry said, his voice now amiable. "I'll reimburse you for the inconvenience. I just need one more favour."

"Which is?"

"Where do you keep this super-smart maggotbrain of yours?"

GABE FELT HIMSELF being lifted off the floor, the movement sending new paroxysms of pain through his body. He kept his right arm wrapped tightly around his midriff, though he could sense the loss of blood was already beginning to take its toll. His head felt heavy and woozy, his eyesight blurry, and shivers ran the course of his skin. Each fresh exhalation was an effort, the air raspy in his throat, and his heart was pounding irregularly, like it was slowly winding down, gradually starved of power. Despite his state, he willed himself to stay alert to what was going on around him, concentrating furiously on the others' words.

Vassily had seemed initially reluctant to lead Harry to this self-aware zombie of his, evidently regarding his pet as his alone and not for display to others. But Flowers seemed to have cut some deal with the Alley boss that would make it worth his while. Indeed, Andrei's co-operation in Gabe's capture was apparently to be rewarded with a hefty fee – though whether it was in territory, manpower or loot, was impossible to discern – and Harry was willing to increase his offer to make this extra allowance. At first, Gabe couldn't fathom why his former employer was so adamant in gaining access to the ghoul – normally Harry couldn't stand being near deadheads – but when Flowers started mentioning Hewitt in the same breath and having made the kid a 'promise,' Gabe realised what the old man was up to, and what his own fate was going to be.

Since humanity had learned to live with the dead, the worst fate imaginable had become to be consumed alive by the Returners; it was considered more noble to take your own life and that of those around you rather than end your days as a meal for a ravening pack of rotting cadavers. There was a sense of violation to the death – of falling victim to an unstoppable frenzied lust – that most would not bear contemplate suffering. Consequently, it was not unknown for this appalling demise to be instrumental in punishing the guilty, particularly amongst the criminal community. In the past it would have been a burial in a concrete casket, or a kneecapping. These days, new situations call for fresh solutions, and many was the embezzler, turncoat or loose cannon that had been thrown to the undead, even fed to them piece by piece. It was horrific to watch; but the threat was usually strong enough to keep even the dimmest element of the underworld in line.

Now, Gabe realised that was what Harry had in store for him; not a couple of bullets casually unloaded into the back of his skull, but a slow, lingering execution, a warning to his other lieutenants about what happens when you attempt to cross him. A bubble of panic exploded in the fear centre of his brain, and he summoned up what reserves of strength he still had in an attempt to wrest himself free from his captors, but it was useless. Vassily's goons – Gull and the younger man – held him secure as they moved through an adjoining door, down a set of steps and into a bare concrete space, apparently a section of what had once been a warehouse that hadn't been converted into offices. What looked like a false wall or a partition ran across the length of the room, and when Vassily strode over to a bank of switches and flipped one, the divider separated and its two halves disappeared into the stone walls at either side, revealing the wide, smooth expanse of a mirrored viewing screen, a steel door set next to it.

Gabe was pushed forward, closer to the two-way mirror, and Andrei, Harry and the rest followed. For a moment, there was just blackness on the other side of the screen, and they simply gazed at their own reflections; then Andrei snapped a wall switch and the fluorescents flickered into life, illuminating a room on the other side of the divide, similar to the one they were in. A cold, grey concrete area, with little concession to decoration. There was furniture in this room, however – a tatty armchair stood in one corner, with a small coffee table before it, on which stood an ancient portable television, an antenna perched on top. A battered VCR sat beside the TV, a small hillock of cassettes piled upon it. Nearer the viewing window was a larger table, with a couple of wooden chairs tucked beneath it; seated motionless at one of these chairs was Andrei's intelligent zombie, its arms resting on the table surface like someone waiting to be served dinner. Its eye sockets were empty, but as light flooded the room it cocked its head sideways in tiny, incremental movements. It was impossible to deny that the creature was aware that its environment had changed, and it was reacting to the shift – something Gabe had never witnessed in a Returner before.

Physically, it had seen better days: it was in an advanced state of putrefaction, and its charcoal-black body had been reduced to little more than a deep-fried skeleton. Its hairless head appeared too big for its flimsy frame, and every time it was jerkily turned it wobbled as if not securely tethered. The shrunken sockets were pits of absolute shadow, and the lips had shrivelled away to give it a permanent rictus grin. It took Gabe a few seconds to realise that the ghoul had been dressed in a jacket – and presumably trousers too, though they were hidden by the lip of the table – which hung loosely about its emaciated torso and had become stained in God-knew-what bodily excretions. The effect was bizarre, as if someone had attempted to construct a picture of normalcy when the truth was the very far from that.

"Christ," Gabe heard Harry mutter. "How long have you kept that thing here, Andrei?"

"Many years," Vassily replied quietly. "Many years." He leaned forward and pushed a button on the wall next to a speakerphone. "Can you hear me? Nod if you can." His voice echoed on the other side of the screen, and the zombie's attention perked up to the sound of it; it raised its gaze to the speaker, determining where the words had come from. Then it dropped its head forward in the unmistakable approximation of a nod, and lifted its right hand in acknowledgement.

"Jesus," Hewitt said. "Just what the fuck *is* that thing?"

Vassily glared at him. "It's learning, is what it is. It's working out how to be human again. By my reckoning, it's about two-thirds of the way there."

"Fuckin' abomination needs a slug put through its skull if it wants me to accept it."

"That's enough," Flowers snapped, shooting the kid a warning glance. He turned back to Andrei. "You're teaching it?"

Vassily nodded, watching the ghoul trace a pattern on the table's surface with a shredded finger. "At first, I noticed it using its memory through repetition. Y'know, remembering when to expect me when I came to visit, training itself to behave if it was to receive a reward, the same way any domesticated animal will do with its master. But there was more to it – it started to adopt human tropes, signals, mannerisms, like it was beginning to recall flashes of what it had been, pre-death. A hand on my arm in a gesture of friendship, an attempt at my name... it was as if the virus was instructing it how to be alive."

"It was still a flesh-eater, though."

"Yes. Still is, in fact. Can't seem to override that motor function yet, though it mainly consumes offal from the kitchens. It doesn't need it to survive, of course – stomach organs have long since atrophied anyway – but it gets restless if it doesn't feed after a while, and won't concentrate. That's what the videotapes are there for; I've been trying to develop its language and recognition skills. They're parenting guides, really, but are quite good in the circumstances. Nevertheless, it's still too dangerous not to be kept on a chain."

"How did you come by it in the first place?" Harry asked.

Vassily didn't reply at first. "I found him at his place of death. I've no idea why he should be so special, why the virus should be evolving so quickly and advancing his state of awareness. Maybe it's the age... maybe they're all like this and the bacteria just needs time to work on them..."

"So are we feeding O'Connell to this fuckin' thing or what?" Hewitt enquired testily, looking at Flowers. The old man nodded gravely, and signalled to Vassily.

The Alley boss spoke into the intercom again. "Stand away from the door. Do you understand?"

The ghoul moaned softly, and the chair it was sitting on suddenly screeched against the stone-tiled floor as it staggered to its feet, its stick-thin arms supporting its weight against the tabletop. It straightened and stiff-leggedly swivelled and stumbled towards the rear of the room, stopping close to the TV and waiting for its next instruction. It was clear it had done this many times before, and was following a routine pattern.

"Jesus..." Hewitt breathed again. None of them had ever seen a deadhead perform like this, responding to orders, seemingly fully cognitive of what Vassily was telling it.

Andrei motioned to Jackson, who stepped forward and pulled down on the door's heavy locking handle. It clunked open with a finality that sent a chill travelling down Gabe's spine.

"I never thought it would come to this, son," Flowers said regretfully. "I had high hopes for you. But you leave me no choice."

"Harry," Gabe choked out, the spreading coldness from his belly wound worming its way across his torso and seizing his throat, leaving him unable to swallow. Every word was an effort, dredged spluttering from the depths of his chest. "Don't do this... I told them nothing, you know that..."

"Put him in," Flowers said, and Jackson shoved open the door and pushed Gabe inside. He tumbled to his knees, putting out a hand to cushion his fall, jarring it against the cold floor, and squeezed his eyes shut momentarily at the sound of the door being slammed shut behind him.

When he opened them, the first thing he saw were the deep red stains ingrained in the stone; wide circular splashes that had dried from scarlet to maroon. He guessed that they had been there for quite some time, and that Vassily hadn't been entirely truthful about what he'd been feeding this pet ghoul of his. He was certain that offal wouldn't leave that arterial spray.

The deadhead itself had noticed his arrival and was shuffling towards him. Gabe scooted backwards, the small of his back hitting the wall a couple of feet later; he looked around him, trying to find something that could aid his escape, but the room was solidly built. It was square and plain, with no other exit save the thick steel door that he'd been dragged through, and that would be impenetrable from this side. He looked towards the mirrored screen and wondered how strong it was; could it withstand one of the chairs being thrown at it? Even if he succeeded in breaking through, there would be no way out, with Harry and his goons keeping guard, but perhaps he could force one of them to open fire and end Flowers' little execution a touch prematurely. He snorted a desperate laugh; when the best of his options was a quick death, he knew he'd reached the end of the road. Still, he didn't see why he should make things easy for the old man.

The zombie staggered closer, a thin whine issuing from its ever-grinning mouth, and Gabe realised that he had to make a choice – if he went for the window, he would only have one chance and it would leave him open for the Returner to grab hold of him. If he didn't, perhaps he could concentrate on evading its clutches, or even try fending it off. But how long could he keep that up, he asked himself? He was growing faint from loss of blood, and would only be delaying the inevitable. He made his decision.

Pulling his legs under him, he pushed himself up against the wall until he was standing. He took a couple of painful breaths, keeping one eye on the advancing ghoul, then sprang forward, covering the space between the door and the table in three great strides. He hooked his left hand around the chair's topmost slat, lifted it, spun and flung it with all the strength he could muster at the viewing screen. It arced in the air and hit the glass dead centre with a dull thud, bouncing back half the distance it had flown to crash to the ground.

The window was unmarked.

Gabe was too exhausted to react. He turned to face the deadhead reaching out for him. Its hands clutched at his shirt, and at such proximity he gagged from its rank smell. Its jaws opened like a creaking hinge.

Then it stopped.

Impossibly, its eyeless visage was regarding him, seeing him despite the lack of organs. Its skeletal hands brushed over his features, as if it was reading him through touch, and something was igniting a flame of recognition within its dormant memory. Then it began to whine again, louder this time, growing in power, becoming a cry. At first it was just noise, a banshee wail; but it soon coalesced into a word that Gabe had to struggle to believe he was hearing.

"Fllooooowwwwaarrrrzzzzzz..."

It *knew* him. The creature knew and remembered him, through association with Harry. How, he had no idea, or indeed what enabled this zombie to possess the powers of cognition. But something had sparked it off, and it stood there roaring the name of his former boss in his face.

The deadhead momentarily transfixed, Gabe seized the advantage and delved into his boot retrieving the syringe. Flicking off the plastic cap, he held it like a dagger in his right hand and stabbed it forcefully into the side of the ghoul's liquescent skull. Virtually the entire length of the hypodermic disappeared into its head, and its cry abruptly stopped, as if a switch had been thrown. He pulled it free, expecting the zombie to instantly collapse, but the thing suddenly grasped his left arm and took a bite, tearing the flesh and muscle from his bicep, blood spurting from the limb in a fountain.

Gabe yelled in agony and brought the syringe down on its head repeatedly until it finally sank to the floor, and was motionless.

Gabe fell to his knees, lengthening shadows stealing into the edges of his vision, and turned as the door was wrenched open, Vassily tearing through with Harry close behind, staring at the inert corpse lying next to him.

"Why did he call your name?" Vassily was screaming. "Why did my father call your name?" His accent grew thicker in his anger.

His father, Gabe considered woozily. *That thing was his father?* Goran Vassily, the kingpin whose demise Harry was responsible for? The club fire? Mother of Christ, it remembered him from its pre-death...

"Andrei –" Flowers began.

Vassily pulled an automatic from inside his jacket and pointed it at the ganglord. "What the fuck did you do to my father that he would remember your name like that?"

"Andrei, put the damn gun down."

"If you had something to do with his death, if that's why he said your name, I swear to fucking Christ you will not walk out of this room."

"Andrei, don't make threats you can't back up..."

"You think I couldn't take you down? You think I'm fucking scared of Harry Flowers?"

Vassily's questions went unanswered, for a moment later a bullet exploded through his neck. He gurgled, clutching at his ravaged throat, then crumpled into a heap on the floor. Before anyone could react, Jackson and the rest of the Alley boss's men were rapidly mown down; it was only once the firing had stopped that it became clear that Hewitt was the shooter.

"Better that we get our retaliation in first," he said.

Harry nodded slowly. "Unfortunate turn of events, but nothing that can't be salvaged. Get in touch with the boys back at the mansion, tell them to get tooled up. We're taking charge of the Alley." He spotted Gabe bleeding and crossed over to him. "And you... Jesus, you're a regular troublemaker, aren't you? If you think you're getting a bullet in the head and a safe passage out of this world, think again. Welcome to purgatory, son."

"H-Harry..." Gabe whispered.

Flowers leaned forward. "Keep it brief."

"Fuck you," the younger man said and plunged the syringe into the old man's calf. He bellowed in pain and staggered backwards, the hypodermic still protruding from his leg. As a couple of his men went forward to tend to him, Hewitt marched up to Gabe and pointed his gun above his heart.

"Just fuckin' die," he snarled and pulled the trigger, darkness exploding across the thief's mind.

PART TWO

Swan Song

I am the enemy you killed, my friend.
I knew you in this dark: for so you frowned
Yesterday through me as you jabbed and killed.
I parried; but my hands were loath and cold.

Wilfred Owen,
Strange Meeting

CHAPTER EIGHT

Five Years Earlier

It was a city that Gabe had lived in most of his life and had a grudging respect for, but even he couldn't deny that London showed an ugly face in summer. All its sprawling, overcrowded, soot-smeared qualities seemed to swell with the heat. Where what was once bearable in the sharp weeks of winter – its inhabitants barricaded against the bitter wind and driving sleet by thick coats and scarves as they walked its streets – became a claustrophobic, stinking concrete furnace as soon as the sun began to beat down on the baking tarmac. Perhaps it was because its citizens relaxed a touch and loosened their protective clothing, showed a little of themselves to the unforgiving metropolis. For London, it was the merciless season. Everything became exacerbated – strained relationships, the stink of pollution, the heaving pavements choked with visitors and workers alike – as if a noose was being drawn tight around its walls for three sweaty months before it slackened off and the city settled back into a more natural rhythm of life once again.

It could be seen everywhere, Gabe thought, as he pedalled down Buckingham Palace Road towards Victoria Station, from the architecture to the citizens sweltering within. It could be witnessed in the firework explosions of red and orange light as a dying sun reflected off the office buildings' glass surfaces, and in the distant edifice of Canary Wharf's pyramidal tower steaming into an azure sky. It could be discerned in the blossoming patches of perspiration on the back of businessmen's shirts, and in their red-faced, squinting demeanour as they hurried to catch their cramped trains, unyielding leather shoes tramping hard on scorched flagstones, jackets tucked over arms, ties unravelled, collars unbuttoned, air scratchy at the back of their throats. It could be felt as the grime slicked on bare arms and faces – a combination of dirt, moisture and insect residue – to the point where one had to scrub the taint of London off once one escaped its environs. It could be heard in the constant snarl of traffic and the strident accompanying blare of anger as tempers flared, drivers boiling inside their automobiles. And it could be smelled in the sickly patchwork of odours that rose from the depths of the city, of unwashed bodies crushed together, of what was once fresh growing sour in the heat of day. If the metropolis was an organism, then in summer it was an exhausted beast, irritable and grubby, floundering as it cooked in its own juices.

Gabe knew what it was like to be stifled in one of those office complexes, a paltry portable electric fan perched atop a nearby filing cabinet cooling the film of sweat on his skin, doing nothing to ease the pressure that would make his forehead throb. After a short stint in the army (whose strict embrace he'd been forced into after his raucous teenage years hotwiring cars) he'd jobbed for a lengthy period at a small local newspaper, chasing advertising and compiling the copy for the listings section – tedious, unsatisfactory work, in which he spent much of his day yearning to just up and walk out the door, never to return – and he could still remember the discomfort of stagnant afternoons, sheaves of paper gluing themselves to his damp hands and fatigue weighing down on him like a lead weight. His colleagues were mostly middle-aged hacks, filling time before their inevitable early retirement, regaling him with tales of when they had a career on Fleet Street, of tyrannical editors and marathon drinking sessions, a hint of self-pity that they were reduced to filing stories on OAP charity walkathons.

Gabe had usually found them likeable coves, but the heat didn't agree with them; they stewed and flustered, muttering to themselves, and contributed to the musty atmosphere in which the air felt like it had been trapped in a tomb. He longed to open a window, but the old soaks complained of the traffic noise and fumes emanating from Pentonville Road below. The building in which they worked had stood there since the 1950s, a stone's throw from King's Cross, and little had been done to modernise the place in the intervening decades. The walls were cracked and spattered with encroaching mould, the carpet was worn through to the floorboards, and the weak ceiling lights gave everything a dull sepia tone. Fill it with perspiring, cantankerous boozers and it was wont to turn a little ripe.

He knew he had to get out before he became preserved in the others' ale breath and cigarette ash. He would be discovered decades later petrified, chipped free and put on display. He was never returning to military life, that much was certain; although his superiors had cast a blind eye to his petty criminal past, one tour of Afghanistan was enough. He had supposed he ought to seek out an opportunity at a more modern place of work – one with air-con and bright, open spaces – but for some reason he couldn't summon the enthusiasm. He'd seen such offices on his travels to and from home – the smokers clustered outside in the street, huddled together like the remnants of a species slowly facing extinction, the reception areas with the elongated sofas and modern art – and their sterility repelled him. It worried him that maybe his extended proximity to the journalistic lags he kept company with had somehow inured him to such luxuries as a workstation that wasn't fragranced like an ashtray or fixtures and fittings that hadn't been beset by damp, but every time he stepped inside one of those silver skyscrapers, he found them soul-destroying and lacking personality. He didn't know when this transformation had taken place, but it was apparent that he'd been mentally conditioned to be incapable of working in such surroundings without wishing to start scrawling across the tasteful abstracts that adorned the walls. He tried to beat this programming to the best of his ability, diligently attending job interviews with the necessary can-do attitude. The people he spoke to, however, he found were either smug and impolite suits, or braying Sloane Square refugees that raised his hackles with each strangulated vowel. Gabe would walk out of the revolving glass doors firm in the belief that he belonged to a different tribe to these cretins. Indeed, he had to wonder if there was life beyond the nicotine-stained domain of the newspaper.

In the end, fate came along and lent a hand: the paper folded suddenly and with little fanfare. For the hacks, it meant extended leisure time, and they greeted the news of the office's closure with unconcealed glee. For Gabe, however, at twenty-four, he couldn't afford to be so blasé. His qualifications were mediocre, and he felt many might be reticent about employing a former soldier, especially one that had had brushes with the law. Even so, the newspaper job, for all its shortcomings, had been enough to cast doubt on whether he was cut out to sit at a desk all day, tapping away at a keyboard, all life passing him by outside. He felt jaded with white-collar work, and the thought of spending more summers suffocating in an open-plan oven, shuffling files, filled him with dread.

It had been his flatmate that had posited the solution. They had been throwing possible career routes between each other – based on Gabe's nebulous ideas of how he wanted to make a living that didn't involve some kind of corporate infrastructure – when Tom suggested a cycle courier. Gabe assimilated the notion and ticked off its advantages: it was outdoor work, it involved little contact with colleagues, it had a built-in fitness regime, and there was a pure simplicity to the job that appealed. He even owned his own bike, and growing up in the city had afforded him an almost encyclopaedic knowledge of London's thoroughfares that could be put to his advantage. The more he mulled the possibility, the more he could see that this could be his way to escape the stifling office environment, and use his love of the capital to work for him rather than be swallowed by its oppressive sprawl.

He visited some local firms and eventually signed up. Within days he was pleased to discover that his instincts had been right, and the job gave him just the satisfaction that he craved. The sheer volume of traffic that he had to contend with had been an initial shock, but once he got the hang of making his presence known on the roads, forcing motorists to acknowledge that he was there, then it became a breeze. The freedom felt exhilarating, and he got to see the metropolis in a whole new light, a hidden London of back alleys and secret squares, centuries of history overlapping in forgotten corners far from the public gaze.

Despite the marvels that the city still clutched to her bosom and that he continued to uncover on his journeys, Gabe reflected, it never looked its best in the middle of July. A little of its beauty was tarnished as it wilted under the heat, but he was glad to be witnessing it out here rather than viewing it through an office window, a position he'd been in for close to a year now.

He shuttled across into Belgrave Square, and headed towards Hyde Park Corner, squeezing down the tight back roads of Knightsbridge, pedalling hard. He piloted his bike down Wilton Place, a car approaching in the other direction allowing him to pass. He powered forward, keen not to keep it waiting.

When the Audi swung out suddenly from its parking slot on the left-hand side of the street, Gabe barely had time to brake – and consequently slammed into its wing at full speed.

HOSPITAL AT FIRST was a nightmare glimpsed through waking moments. He was told later – when he had been capable of processing the information – that he had been severely concussed (in addition to three fractured ribs, a broken nose and extensive facial bruising). But at the time Gabe flittered in and out of consciousness, snatching only handfuls of sobriety. He found it difficult to differentiate between the world inside his head and that of his bedridden condition; or rather it was hard to choose which was worse. When he was asleep, he plunged into a sea of shadow in which he seemed to be constantly rushing forward, as if caught in a slipstream or surrendering to the inexorable pull of a current. Sometimes the darkness dissolved enough for him to discern that he was racing along the city streets, his body floating only a few feet from the tarmac. A vague thought would always pop into his dream-self's mind that he was on a collision course, that unless he fought the power that controlled him, he was going to smash into an obstacle standing in his way. It started as a suggestion, an irrational feeling that bubbled out of nowhere, but it would quickly blossom into panic and an incontrovertible sense of certainty that he was racing towards disaster. The city appeared abandoned as he raced through it – amorphous, indistinct buildings on either side, roads empty of life – but without question, somewhere, there was trouble waiting to hit him head-on.

He never discovered it. The fear would build in tandem with his velocity to such a degree that he would surface into consciousness with a gasp, as if he had dived into himself and was returning for air. But his waking episodes were no respite. The heat and chaos in the ward day and night left him unable to relax, and any movement he attempted made him aware of his injuries. His body seemed to ache right down to the bone. The doctors kept him doped up, so his notion of reality was woozy at best, and he had few visitors to help anchor him to the everyday. His mother was living somewhere in Europe with her new husband, and his father was infirm, cared for by a nurse of his own back in Cork. With no siblings, the only face he could lucidly recognise was that of his flatmate Tom, whose sporadic trips to see him were as irregular as Gabe's sleep patterns. The combination of the drugs and fatigue would inevitably propel him towards unconsciousness again, a journey he vainly fought, terrified of once more flying through London with no notion of where he was going, or possibly finally meeting what was waiting for him at that moment of impact he knew was unavoidable.

Over the following weeks, his confused mind stabilised and his lucid periods lengthened. His memories of the accident slowly returned, and if he closed his eyes he could visualise the front wheel of his bike buckling against the driver's door of the Audi, throwing him forward and across its bonnet. The recollection of his head bouncing off the windscreen – did it shatter? He couldn't remember hearing the sound of breaking glass; all that filled his ears was the screech of brakes and the scrape of metal on metal – made him gingerly run his fingertips over his puffy face. The skin was tender to the touch, and a lump the size of a golf ball had risen above his right eyebrow. He asked a nurse for a mirror, because the contours of his face no longer felt familiar, and the reflection that stared back at him confirmed it; he barely recognised himself. He'd been assured that the injuries would heal eventually, and that the swelling would go down given time, but even so the red-raw damage and the changes it had wrought on his appearance shocked him. His nose swathed in bandages, his lips split where his teeth had pierced them, purple-black bruises running in parallel with his jawline, he felt like he'd been battered into a different shape, moulded and created anew with all the attendant pain that such a process entails. He wouldn't be the same, he knew, no matter how well he recovered. Already he considered what he looked like before the accident to be the face of somebody else.

It proved true enough the moment he left the hospital, his bones sufficiently knitted together. The trip back to his flat was one fraught with anxiety as the noise and relentlessness of the traffic caused him to visibly cringe, despite Tom's reassurances. Gabe tried to remain calm, aware that a mere month ago he'd been whizzing through these very streets on his bike with nothing to protect him but a helmet and a shoulder bag, but now the idea seemed inconceivable. It was as if he were viewing the city through different eyes, seeing potential dangers at every turn. He dug his fingers into the passenger seat of his flatmate's Mini as it rounded a corner and braked at a crossing, expecting a phantom vehicle to thunder into their path any second. Tom told him that he had spoken to the doctor before they had released Gabe, and he had mentioned that a victim of such a serious accident was very likely to exhibit symptoms of something like post-traumatic stress, and that it was perfectly natural for him to be fretful once he returned to the real world. But it would pass as soon as he got his strength back and grew more confident.

For Gabe, that day seemed a long time coming. Ensconced within the walls of his flat, he found himself lacking the courage to venture outside, and the more time he spent inside on his own – Tom working long shifts at a bar in the West End – the more he found comfort in seclusion. Rather than facing down his fear, he embraced it and let it control him, ensuring that his daily routine was subservient to it. The courier company he worked for regularly got in touch, asking when he felt ready to return to work, and he fobbed them off with excuses, claiming he still needed time to recover. In truth, he was physically back to normal bar a few scars and tender patches, but in his head the thought of braving London's roads once more filled him with panic. He relived the accident again and again in his dreams, waking sweating at the moment of impact and with a hard cluster of pain at his temple. Eventually, his boss telephoned him to apologetically let him go, saying that without any end to his convalescence in sight they couldn't afford to keep him on their books any longer. He was unemployed once more, and felt in no fit state to do anything about it.

As soon as Tom learned that Gabe was out of a job, he sat down with his flatmate for a crisis talk.

"Mate, we gotta do something or we're going to be out on our ear. There's no way I can manage on my wage alone, and I doubt your income support is going to add much. You've got to get yourself out there."

"I know, I know," Gabe replied, conscious of the fact that there was no situation that couldn't be made worse by having a little guilt thrown into the mix. "I don't want to put us both in the lurch, of course I don't. It's just... I'm scared of going out there. I'm on edge, thinking something is going to happen. My stomach knots, I can't breathe, feel nauseous..."

"It's a panic attack. The doc said you should expect them. But you can't afford to let them run your life. It's like you're caught in a loop

– the more you stay in here, agonising over what's going to happen to you if you step outside the flat, the more the anxiety spreads. You're feeding it by not coming to terms with it. If you went out on those streets and became accustomed to them once again, you'd find that the fear would lessen. It's what you don't know – it's what you're imagining is out there – that's causing this apprehension."

"I wish it was as easy as that…"

"It's the only way forward, mate," Tom replied, a hint of exasperation entering his voice. "Otherwise it's going to explode into full-blown agoraphobia, and you'll be bunkered away in here for the rest of your life. You're, what? Twenty-five? You're going to imprison yourself for the next sixty years, is that it? Unless you're prepared to give in to it, you've gotta be strong and fight it."

They sat in silence, Gabe listening to the hum of traffic filtering through the window, acting as an additional taunt to Tom's words. He knew his friend was right, and wished he possessed the resolve to act on the advice. He admonished himself for being weak and pathetic. Was he really going to let this fear get the better of him? Was he really going to sacrifice his life to it? Otherwise, what difference would it have made if his guts had been splattered under the tyres of that Audi? Survival had given him a choice – either he grasped the chance with both hands or he just upped and surrendered right now.

"It's something only you can do, Gabe," Tom said. "Of course, I'll help you in any way I can, but I can't make you take the first step. That's your responsibility." He sighed. "The other alternative is that you work from home. You know, tele-sales, or something. But whatever you decide, we've reached crunch-point, mate. We're in deep shit unless we take action now."

Gabe agreed that it was time he got busy rebuilding his life, and promised that he would take charge of the situation; the implication being that he would finally face up to his fear of London's streets. But when it came to it, he found picking up the telephone to enquire about finding work cold-calling and selling kitchens the easy option. He hated himself even as he listened to the saleswoman's explanations of what the job entailed and the techniques of keeping the potential customer on the line. It seemed he had taken several long strides backwards, placing himself in employment that he despised and shackled once more to the mundane grind of monotonous, dismal toil. He put the telephone receiver down, having accepted the numerous conditions, and slumped in an armchair, feeling wretched.

As it turned out, the work proved to be more stultifying than even he could stand, and at last gave him the incentive to get him through the front door. The countless hang-ups and insults thrown at him as he initiated his spiel were the final straw, and as he sat staring at the living-room wall, a disconnected tone buzzing in his ear, he realised that nothing that was out there on the roads could possibly be any worse than this. Indeed, if this stuttering circle of a half-life was all he had to look forward to, a little danger would come as welcome relief. He flung the phone to the floor, and strode out into the street before the fear-centre of his brain could stop him.

He walked, without much regard to a direction or purpose, simply putting distance between him and the flat that he'd entombed himself within for weeks on end. Despite the familiar surge of sickness and the growing pounding in his head, as trucks roared past and sirens wailed, he didn't halt his progress; rather, he rode the anxiety out, staying above the wave and letting it carry him forward rather than disappearing beneath it. Breathing deeply, with each step he found himself surfing on something else too, something he hadn't felt since he'd been in uniform: adrenaline. He was terrified, but in contrast to his self-inflicted exile, there was a joy to his terror. It gave him an edge he had forgotten existed. He walked for hours, perversely enjoying the thrill he got from punishing his panicking senses. He was living again, he decided triumphantly.

When Gabe informed Tom that he wanted to return to traversing the city's arteries, his flatmate commended him on his courage but warned that perhaps getting back on a bike would make him feel a touch too vulnerable at such an early stage. He suggested a compromise to ease his way back into the ebb and flow of the capital's heart.

"Fact is, there's a sniff of a job at work," he said slowly. "Not in the bar itself, but working for the guy that owns it. Several of his boys come in to drink there, and they've mentioned on more than one occasion that he's after a new full-time driver."

"A chauffeur-type job, you mean?"

"Pretty much. The geezer's after someone who knows the city like the back of his hand, and let's face it, Gabe, that's your forte. If you're going to work to your strengths, then this could be an ideal opportunity. And at the risk of sounding like some pop-psychologist, it's going to be good therapy for you, getting you confident about being on the roads again."

Gabe mulled it over. Piloting some rich creep around all day didn't have the same appeal or sense of freedom that cycling afforded him, but he could see it would work as a stepping-stone to regaining his self-assurance. Plus the prospect of visiting the many corners of London again was always an attraction. "What's he like, this boss?"

Tom shrugged. "Rarely comes in to the bar. Seen him once, I think; seemed sound to me. Gary the manager deals with him, and they get on OK. He owns clubs all over, so I'd imagine he's proper loaded. You're interested then?"

Gabe nodded.

"Cool, OK, I'll put in a word with Gary, see if you can get a meet with the boss." Tom smiled. "Good to see you back on your feet, mate."

"Yeah, feels good to me too," Gabe replied. "Oh, by the way, what's this bloke's name? The boss-guy?"

"It's Flowers. Harry Flowers."

CHAPTER NINE

THE JET-BLACK LIMO wound its way through the tight lanes of the Oxfordshire countryside, incongruous amongst the fields of maize and rapeseed and the thinly populated farmhouses that dotted the landscape. Any motorists that passed it couldn't help but cast an eye over it and briefly wonder its business or destination, the fact plainly evident that the occupants were not local. The windows were mirrored, offering no clue as to the nature of those within the car, but its size and ostentation suggested it clearly wasn't a commuter or tourist. It could possibly be lost, a few observers mused, but it had come so far out into the country that it could only be here by design rather than accident.

If a villager caught sight of it as it passed through the four or five cottage hamlets that represented suburbia out in this rural expanse, then there was a glimmer of recognition; they'd seen vehicles of this ilk drive past their homes before on irregular occasions over the past two or three decades. Sometimes they had police escorts, a couple of motorbike cops stationed nose and tail, but mostly these dark limousines came alone, driver and passengers always obscured. However, anyone that had lived around here for any substantial length of time knew full well where these particular travellers were heading, and could even hazard a guess as to their occupation. Few, though, that had been born and raised in the area had ever gone near the place to which they were undoubtedly journeying – indeed, getting anywhere near it was nigh-on impossible – and while it was nestled away in secluded woodland, of interest only to those that were aware of its existence, its presence cast a pall over the surroundings. They did not know what was done there, or to what purpose these visitors made their periodic trips, but there was little argument that much good would ever come of it.

The car turned off the main road through a gap in the hedgerow onto a narrow track that was bisected by a metal gate a few feet later. The vehicle slowed, and the driver's window slid down, a hand emerging clutching an ID card, holding it up to an infra-red sensor positioned on the gate post. There was a click and the barrier shuddered open, allowing enough time for the limo to pass before locking itself closed again. The car bounced along the dusty, furrowed track, thick foliage pressing in on either side; occasionally, the man seated in the back seat noted, razor wire could be glimpsed between the trees, ten-feet high mesh fences strung with warning signs and keep-out notices. They completely encompassed the six acres of private land the limo was travelling across, ensuring that the curious public were kept at a sufficient distance.

It didn't always entirely dissuade those that were determined to gain access to the facility. Over the years there had been a small handful of security breaches by anti-government protestors and troublemakers (and even the odd broadsheet journalist), all trying to pierce the veil of secrecy that was necessary to allow the compound's work to continue. None of them had succeeded in getting within a hundred feet of the laboratories, unprepared for the number of armed guards that patrolled the grounds at regular intervals. Out in these deep, dark woods – as intruders were repeatedly told with the intention of scaring them out of their nosy habits – it was very easy for someone to vanish without trace, and those trespassing on Ministry of Defence property could be shot without warning. The strict new measures that had been introduced to defend the country against terrorism enabled government buildings to protect themselves with maximum force, a handy tool at their disposal. Nobody had been killed yet trying to break into the research centre, fortunately; but, as with most things, it was probably only a matter of time. A ruling party keen to be seen cracking down on those that threatened homeland security, an increasingly paranoid nation and an unruly section of the populace that insisted on sticking its beak into matters that didn't concern them was a volatile combination.

The man couldn't understand why there were those so insistent on broadcasting the country's defence secrets in the first place; the work that was being developed at this research centre was in Britain's interests, enabling her to protect herself against her many enemies. God knew, they needed all the edge they could get in an ever-unstable planet. Rogue leaders and power-hungry tyrants were ten a penny, always strutting before the world stage, swinging their dicks. Half were big-headed buffoons, admittedly, that posed minimal threat, as long as there were departments monitoring their movements. If they just stuck to torturing their own people and blowing their nation's assets on building monuments to their vast egos, then it kept them occupied and out of the world's hair.

But it was once they started having designs on expanding their empire and instigating pan-global hatred that they become a nuisance, a bracket that the remaining fifty per cent fell into. These were the foes that needed removing for the safety of international stability, and more often than not it was a process that was conducted well out of the media's spotlight. Wars never ended, despite what was released to the public. That was what few not in governmental office understood. Surrenders were accepted, deals were signed, coalition forces claimed victory, but the fighting never ceased. It was a necessary fact of the political landscape that conflicts carried on past the point of the official end to hostilities to make sure the peace remained rooted, weeding out intransigents that could pose problems in the future. The warlords that Britain and the rest of the civilised world were in eternal opposition to were like cockroaches – stamp on one and a dozen more escape into the cracks. Thus, safeguarding the nation's position in the global community was an unending battle, one in which they needed the very latest technological developments at their disposal on the frontline, and creating such weapons required research far from the public's gaze, as much for their own safety as anything else, in secret MoD complexes.

Places such as this one, the man mused, as the car slowed before a checkpoint. Officially, it was called Monkhill. It had been established not long after the Second World War, very much at Churchill's behest – a man who knew that victory wasn't just achieved, it was *maintained* – and was one of several dotted around the country charged with building upon the military's arms reserves to tackle the new faces that enemies of democracy wore in the twenty-first century.

A guard with a clipboard strode from the booth beside the barrier and tapped on the driver's window. A fellow soldier remained on watch, a rifle held against his chest, his eyes roving over the vehicle. It was strictly a formality – the car carried an HM government seal on its windscreen and its registration would've been verified by the CCTV cameras tracking its progress from the road – but the security here was as stringent as the man had ever encountered. A lunatic with thirty pounds of Semtex strapped to his chest was more likely to be able to board a passenger jet than a rambler was to accidentally stray onto the facility's grounds.

The driver buzzed his window down. "Peter Sedgworth MP," he said, reaching across to the dashboard and retrieving a sheaf of paper, passing it to the guard. "He has an appointment with Doctor Gannon."

The soldier scanned the document and affixed it to his clipboard, unhooking a pen from his fatigues' breast pocket and scribbling something upon it. He nodded, then said, "Wait there." He motioned with his head for his companion to join him and together they walked slowly around the car, scooting to their knees to check beneath the chassis. Sedgworth watched their movements impassively from the other side of the mirrored glass, the fingers of his left hand tapping an impatient rhythm on the briefcase on his lap. The driver was asked to pop the bonnet open so the engine could be examined, before being instructed to unlock the boot.

"Excuse me a moment, Minister," he muttered and clambered out. Sedgworth heard the boot yawn open behind him and felt the weight of the vehicle shift. He sighed and found his eyes running over the correspondence from Gannon that he'd been clutching for much of the journey from London. The doctor was uncharacteristically excited about developments they'd been making in a biological agent that he had insinuated could prove revolutionary in cutting the level of military casualties. He didn't go into much detail – an antidote? a compound that augmented a trooper's abilities? – but the scientific blather and optimistic rhetoric had pricked the Defence Minister's interest enough for him to come investigate it for himself.

In the decade or so that the two men had worked together, Sedgworth's experience of Gannon was that he wasn't one for waxing lyrical about the research centre's achievements, or promising unrealistic targets – indeed, the dour Scot had tested his patience on more than one occasion by failing to deliver new weaponry past the prototype stage, claiming that they were either unworkable or dangerous to the wielder. Several defence contracts had been lost because Gannon was a stickler for perfection, which hadn't made him many friends in Parliament. More than a few of Sedgworth's governmental colleagues had suggested that it was time the good doctor was retired for a younger replacement more amenable to rubber-stamping valuable army projects; but the Defence Minister had stuck by him because he could still pull moments of eclectic genius out of the bag. As long as he continued to demonstrate the forward thinking that had made him internationally renowned, Gannon still had a place in the department.

Which meant his enthusiasm for the current endeavour was well worth witnessing first-hand, if it was as boundary-breaking as he claimed in his reports. In fact, the doctor's results couldn't have come at a better time for Sedgworth. With the various conflicts in the Middle East and central Europe dragging on year after year, and the British forces increasingly tied up in peacekeeping roles that were meant to last no more than the initial twelve-month period – they'd since ballooned into three times that – he was under substantial pressure from the PM to find a way to limit the numbers of soldiers heading overseas. Or at least make their job easier. Television footage of Union Jack-draped coffins being offloaded at military airfields was not the kind of publicity the Government needed, and it was an image that the voters were guaranteed to remember come election day. Sedgworth had been instructed to find a way to run the Army more efficiently, and preferably cut the casualty rate. As the PM told him, every war widow that was created was effectively a cross on the opposition's ballot paper. Quite how he was supposed to achieve this was unclear, short of withdrawing the troops from the crisis zones – his budget was stretched as it was. But the old man had been copping heat from all sides of the House and from the media over the mess the UK's forces were mired in, and had demanded that action be taken to stem the tide of bodies returning to these shores.

Gannon's breakthrough, therefore, could be the answer that would save his skin, Sedgworth believed, running his eyes over the documents before him once more as the boot was slammed shut and the driver clambered back into the front seat. The guards raised the barrier, and waved the car forward. The Defence Minister didn't claim to understand what the doctor was telling him in his letters, but if it meant he wouldn't be handing in his resignation in six months' time, then he was going to get behind it all the way. This could possibly resurrect his political career.

THE LIMO PARKED before the facility's glass doors, and Sedgworth strode through the reception area, stopping momentarily to have his briefcase X-rayed and himself patted down by a soldier. Gannon was waiting for him, leaning nonchalantly by the lifts, arms folded, and the politician raised his eyebrows at him in greeting as the woman behind the reception desk handed him a visitor's badge. He wandered over to the doctor, looking down momentarily to affix the plastic tag to his suit lapel.

"Minister," Gannon said by way of acknowledgement, terse as ever.

"Come on, Robert," Sedgworth replied, offering his hand, which the scientist shook. "It's Peter. Let's not stand on ceremony."

Gannon shrugged. "It's that kind of place. Enough rules and regulations to make you forget you're human. You'll have had the intimate probing, then?"

"Checked and double-checked, right down to my approved governmental underwear. Nobody could ever accuse security of being lax here."

"Aye, we run a tight ship, all right." He pressed the lift's call button. "Come on, I'll take you down to the labs. That's where all the fun stuff happens."

Sedgworth studied the doctor as he stood gazing up at the lights above the lift doors indicating its ascent. He was in his early fifties, but carried himself as if he were fifteen years younger; he had a tendency to slouch, which reminded the politician of his own teenage son, and coupled with his surly demeanour there was something comically grumpy about the man. He was thin and wiry, and a good five inches shorter than the MP, with a shock of black curly hair atop an angular head. Despite his position as chief research officer at Monkhill, he looked and acted as if he were the student intern, scuffing his trainer-bedecked feet through the lab corridors with his hands in his pockets, scowling at colleagues whose theories he frequently and arrogantly dismissed without a second thought. It was easy to see why he put so many powerful people's backs up. Once they realised that multi-million pound corporate decisions could rest on the say-so of this scruffbag, they wondered if somebody in the department wasn't having a joke. But while he clearly didn't pay much attention to his appearance, his weapons research work was exacting; every attention to detail that wasn't apparent in his attire was there in his experiments and conclusions, precise and often inspired.

The lift doors slid open and the two men entered, Gannon jabbing a button for one of the sub-levels.

"Did you have a good journey?" he asked, casting a glance at the minister.

"Oh yes. Well, as good as could be expected, getting out of London." The scientist smiled thinly. "You don't like leaving the city, then?"

"Not if I can help it. I've got nothing against the country, it's just... I don't care for all that scenery. It makes me nervous. Too open."

Gannon chuckled. "Spoken like a true metropolitan. Never happier than when you're no more than five feet away from a black cab and a Starbucks." He leant against the elevator wall. "I appreciate you braving the heart of darkness today, though, Peter. Out here in the wild frontier."

"I had to come and see for myself what you were getting so excited about." Sedgworth lifted up his briefcase and slapped it jovially. "Your reports were so enthusiastic, as if you were anticipating big things from this latest project."

The scientist wobbled his head, as if he wasn't inclined to agree. "It's early days. I shouldn't have got your hopes up that I would have a solution waiting for you. The fundamentals are in place, it's just a matter of fine-tuning to the point where it's workable. It could go either way at the moment, but I'm cautiously optimistic."

The minister smiled to shield his disappointment. "I've been intrigued by the progress you said you'd been making in cutting troop casualties. You didn't go into much detail. What is it, some kind of amphetamine variant that boosts the soldier's resilience?"

"You'll see for yourself soon enough," the doctor replied cryptically. The lift shuddered to a halt and the doors parted, revealing a gloomy, bare-concrete corridor. Gannon gestured for the politician to step ahead of him, and the two men wandered down the passageway, Sedgworth's Italian brogues clicking loudly on the flagstone floor. There was a chill in the air, as if they'd emerged into some underground cavern, and the minister involuntarily shivered, goosebumps rising on the back of his neck.

Gannon noticed the government man pulling his suit jacket around him. "Yeah, sorry about the temperature," he said. "We find it helps with the work we're doing. You get used to it after a while. Let me tell you, you really wouldn't want this place to be an oven."

"Oh? Why's that?"

"It'd turn ripe in hours. You'll get the idea when you see what we're doing in the labs."

They walked further into the bowels of the research facility, windows set in the walls on either side revealing white-coated scientists peering into microscopes and sitting before computers. Sedgworth caught sight of a crimson smear on the front of one of their tunics, as if the person had come straight from an abattoir. He hesitated, watching the medic in question inject a solution into something strapped to a gurney, hidden by the worktable.

"Are you doing animal testing here?" the politician asked. "I thought it was agreed that animal subjects were only to be used in experiments expressly approved by myself?" It was one of the few issues he felt strongly about, and had pledged when he took office to substantially reduce the amount of weapons testing on living creatures. It had won him the looney-tune liberal vote and the derision of his more cynical colleagues, but it was a belief he was proud to have remained reasonably consistent on.

"No. Nothing... living," Gannon replied. He stopped and faced the minister, chewing his lip and clearly choosing his words carefully. "You asked us to find ways of cutting army casualties, something which isn't easy to anticipate. There's no way we can foresee what a soldier will face on the battlefield, or the conditions they will have to fight under. No amount of protective garments will protect an individual in certain situations, when death can come in so many forms. And the human body will take only so much damage before it becomes irreparable and medical technology can no longer assist it."

"I thought you were looking at performance-enhancing drugs? Augmenting a trooper's strength and stamina?"

"It's a route we went down, I admit," Gannon said, nodding. "But again it comes down to the body's inability to handle the demands that we're asking to place upon it. We were attempting to limit the subject's need for fuel and sleep coupled with a steroidal muscle-growth programme. We tried surgical procedures too, adjusting eyesight and hearing as well as certain... cerebral tweaks."

"Christ," Sedgworth exclaimed. "You're telling me you were looking into cutting into their *heads*? What were you hoping to prove?"

The scientist looked at the politician levelly. "We thought perhaps hormones could be modulated, turning the emotions on and off like a tap. Increase anger, decrease the level of fear flooding the brain." He tapped his temple. "Maybe even find a way to instil logical thinking, encourage the subject to think rationally in the heat of conflict."

"It wasn't successful, I take it?"

Gannon shook his head. "As I said, the human body couldn't handle it. The drugs were unreliable and the level of steroids required to boost the soldier's musculature would have sent them crazy. We delivered preliminary samples to a local barracks – nothing life-threatening, just mild prototypes to see if they noticed any improvement in performance – and the reports we got back were that the regiment complained of headaches, nausea, muscle strain and dizziness. The compound was trying to work on them, I think, but it was taking every cell in a direction it didn't want to go... or at least every cell didn't have the ability to expand beyond its means. There's a lot of potential locked up in our bodies, Minister, it's just that we're too fragile to explore it fully."

"So where do we go from here? From what you've just said, you make it sound like we should replace the armed forces with robots – logical, fearless, without need for food or sleep..."

"...and disposable. I agree that would be the ideal solution. But it's prohibitively expensive. Unfortunately, a flesh-and-blood soldier's life is right now significantly less costly than that of his or her cybernetic counterpart. But that's the thinking we began to pursue – if we couldn't substantially alter a subject's make-up to protect them, the only other way of reducing casualties was to send a proxy in their stead."

"A proxy?"

"A substitute. An army that was eminently expendable, that a country could lose in great numbers without the pressure of consequences."

Sedgworth frowned. "I don't see what you're getting at, Rob."

"Follow me." Gannon turned and headed towards a door at the end of the corridor. He laid his hand upon the handle and paused, glancing back at the politician as if he were about to add something, then thought better of it. Instead he walked into the darkened room beyond, the government man a couple of steps behind. Despite his proximity, he lost sight of the doctor for a moment, such was the gloom within; the only light available was that spilling into the room from outside, a source that was shut off when the door was closed behind him. He saw the outline of Gannon's white coat move amongst the tenebrous shadow, but could not discern any other detail in the space around him.

"Robert?" the minister asked querulously.

"I'm going to flip the lights on," a whispered reply came from somewhere to his left. "I'm going to ask you not to make too much noise. The test subject I have in here is quite easily distressed."

"Test subject? I thought –" His words died in his mouth when the fluorescents flickered into life above him and he could at last see what was in the room with him.

It reminded him of a dungeon – the walls and floor were bare grey stone, with no windows or furniture – and manacled to the far wall was what at first appeared to be a human being. It was dressed in military fatigues, and so Sedgworth assumed it to be one of the guards that had volunteered for a drugs trial. He certainly sounded as if he was doped up, emitting a mournful groan and straining at his bonds, his arms chained above his head. But as the minister stepped closer, he noticed macabre details about the figure. His face was sallow, blue-green skin stretched over the skull; his eyes were clouded, and the way he moved his head suggested he could barely see, and that rather he was sensing that others were in the room by scent or something else; and the nearer the politician got to the man, the more he became aware of the stench emanating from him. He smelt... rotten. Sedgworth opened his mouth to say something to Gannon, but the doctor interrupted him.

"Don't move any closer," he warned. "You'll get him riled up. He might not be able to grab you, but could still give you a bite if you're not careful."

The minister automatically retreated a few paces. "Is he being kept prisoner?"

"Of a sort. As I said, he's a test subject, but he's restrained for our protection."

"What in God's name have you done to him? He looks like he's... decaying."

"He is, though in our defence that was nothing to do with us. Nothing we can do to stop entropy." Gannon smiled as if at a private joke. "What we gave him was *life*."

Sedgworth glanced at the scientist as if he was mad. "Are you telling me this man was dead?"

"Three weeks ago, he was shipped back to the UK with fatal abdominal injuries. Car bomb in Baghdad. He had died instantly, and had no close family to miss him. Not long after we took receipt of his corpse, we injected it with a serum we've been working on, just at the base of the neck. Five hours after that he got up and walked."

The politician's mouth was hanging open, alternately studying Gannon and the moaning figure, struggling to be free of his cuffs. "Wait, wait, back up... where did you get the authority to commandeer the deceased?"

"That's kind of on a need-to-know basis."

"I think I bloody need to know," Sedgworth snarled.

Gannon shrugged. "It starts with your boss, and trickles down from there."

The government man's mouth snapped shut. The PM had evidently been putting wheels in motion over his head. "This... this is the grand scheme that could save our armed forces?" he said, gesturing around him.

"It's the ideal solution. They don't tire or feel pain, can survive numerous injuries as long as the brain remains intact, and resurrection seems to bring an enhanced aggression. They go for anyone." He nodded to the undead soldier. "He took a chunk out of my assistant's hand before he could be strapped down."

"They? You've got more of them?"

"We're monitoring several subjects. About a dozen, to be exact."

Sedgworth shook his head. "It's obscene, like something out of *Frankenstein*. How on earth can you imagine that the public will go for this? I mean, we're talking zombies here, for Christ's sake."

"We try to avoid the 'Z' word, Minister. It suggests voodoo. These are motorised cadavers; simply shells for the HS-03 virus that is putting their neurons back together. As for Joe Public, what makes you think they need to be told anything?"

The politician didn't reply. He turned and watched the dead man standing a few feet from him. It was grinding its jaw, drool falling from its black lips. "Is he conscious?" he asked finally.

"Barely. Next to no language skills or coordination. At the moment, it's pure instinct – it walks and tries to feed, which is redundant since it doesn't require the energy or the sustenance anymore. But we're working on it, see if we can kick-start its development."

Sedgworth strode towards the door. "This is insane," he muttered. "I cannot condone these experiments. Don't the dead deserve any respect anymore?"

"The dead are a resource, just like any other," Gannon answered, following the politician out of the room, flicking the lights off as he left and shutting the door behind him. The creature's cries drifted softly through the partition. "Or would you rather the country sacrificed more troops?"

Sedgworth rounded on him. "You're a doctor, Robert. You're meant to preserve life, not play with it. When did that change?"

"I *am* preserving life," the scientist replied angrily. "I'm trying to save the lives of every serviceman and woman currently operating in a war zone. I'm trying to create an army that can work for *us*." He dropped his head and exhaled wearily. "Anyway, what makes you think this is the first time that medical science has been put to use in this way? Others have been here before; in fact, their blueprints have proved most helpful."

"What others?"

"The German High Command, for a start. They thought they could claim Europe with their own special division in World War One. They called it *Totenkrieg*..."

CHAPTER TEN

"YOU'RE GABRIEL?"

The voice came from the open doorway. Gabe looked up to see the shadowed outline of a man filling the frame, a pair of bodyguards hovering at his shoulders. He walked into the living room, clasping a cup of tea in his hands, the light from the expansive picture window finally revealing his features: a grizzled, sinewy character, with a fuzzy white crew cut atop his head. Clad in a tan linen suit and a white shirt open at the neck, he moved unhurriedly to an armchair opposite the sofa upon which Gabe was nervously perched. The two guards had followed him through the door and closed it behind them, standing sentinel before the threshold.

"That's right. Pleased to meet you, Mr Flowers." The younger man instantly rose and proffered his hand. Flowers glanced down at it, turned slightly to place his cup and saucer on a small table beside the chair, and then shook it, his grip firm. He released Gabe and dropped back into his seat, motioning for his guest to do the same.

"Gabriel... It's a name you don't hear very often these days."

"My father is from Cork."

"Ah. You're of good Catholic stock, I take it?"

"Well, not really. He lapsed not long after meeting my mother, much to the disappointment of my grandparents. I think my name may have been some kind of appeasement."

Flowers nodded slowly, his piercing blue eyes studying Gabe. "And are you religious at all, Mr O'Connell?" he asked.

"Nah. I think I lost any semblance of faith the moment I hit puberty. Didn't see how a loving God could justify all that teenage angst. That, and the spots, obviously."

Flowers smiled. "You're an atheist then?"

"Technically, though that always sounds so final. Let's just say I'm hedging my bets." He swallowed, watching as the older man took a sip from his teacup. "And yourself?" he enquired, hoping it wasn't too personal a question to ask a potential employer.

"I went to church every Sunday with my wife, years ago," Flowers replied, casting his eyes downwards to regard the contents of his cup. "But after she died, it felt like a... charade. An empty gesture. A pointless display of supplication towards a higher authority that I no longer respected." He was silent for a moment. "But I've always been interested in the power that those houses of God wield; there's no denying that, whatever your belief, the strength of faith is invested in their walls. You can feel it as soon as you enter one." He drained the teacup and set it back on its saucer. "That's my principle interest, Mr O'Connell – power; its acquisition and the most effective way to exert it." Flowers gestured around him. "You like the house?"

Gabe nodded, though he had seen little of its interior beyond the entrance hall and this lounge into which he had been ushered. Rather, he was wondering how the conversation had taken such a bizarre turn so early. He had been warned that Harry Flowers could be a touch eccentric, and if he was honest he had found the prospect refreshing, a throwback to the characters he used to work with on the local newspaper. But what clearly separated them from the sixty-year-old seated across from him now was the sheer level of influence and purpose that Flowers exuded; this was no harmless old codger, prone to flights of fancy, but a sharp entrepreneur whose digressions had an agenda of their own. Anything he said, he said for a reason. He had gathered that much from just a few minutes in his company, and from reading between the lines of what he had been told about Flowers by the lieutenants that had brought Gabe to this point.

Three days earlier, his flatmate Tom had instructed him to come to the bar on a Friday night, when one of Flowers' crew was guaranteed to be dropping by. Upon arriving Gabe was directed towards a dimly lit corner table, where he stood before a rotund, besuited figure cradling a gin and tonic. The man gave him the once-over and asked – prior to introducing himself or indulging in any conversational niceties – why he wanted to work for Harry Flowers. For such a forthright question, Gabe was initially stumped. He had expected a degree of small talk ahead of the crux of their business, and the immediate answer that he was desperate for the money seemed unwise. Instead, he replied that his knowledge of the city would make him an asset to Mr Flowers' organisation, and that if Flowers was looking for a good driver, then no one handled London's roads better than he. The man considered this response, then said that Gabe had come recommended (a commendation he suspected Tom had a hand in), and that he had been assigned by Mr Flowers to size up such suitable candidates before the boss called them in for a chat. His demeanour warming, he invited Gabe to sit and drink with him, informing him that his name was Childs, and that he had worked for Flowers for over ten years.

The younger man listened with polite interest as Childs gave him a potted history of his employer's dealings – a successful import/export company at the age of thirty, a move into property just as the boom-time hit, and the establishment of his line of clubs and bars – that painted the picture of a self-made millionaire. The reverence with which Childs spoke Flowers' name suggested a loyalty that Gabe had never experienced himself. He'd struggled with authority in the past, disliked being part of a team; but clearly being part of Flowers' outfit was a way of life. When he mentioned the man's obvious fondness for his boss, he didn't appear embarrassed.

"Harry's straight down the line," he said, a zealot's gleam in his eye. "He won't hesitate to tell you what's on his mind, but you'll find his honesty and fairness refreshing. There's no bullshit, nothing underhand. If you do well, he lets you know; if you fuck up, he'll kick your arse. It can be a little strange at first, true – 'cause he always lets you know what he's thinking, he has a tendency to go off at a tangent, so you have to be on the ball to keep up with him. Other times, you just have to go with it. But his attitude has got him where he is today, and it's enabled him to gather together a workforce that's proud to be at his right hand."

Gabe came away impressed with the dedication that Flowers evidently instilled in his employees, and when he got the call twenty-four hours later that the boss-man wanted to see him at his Essex mansion, he wondered if some of Childs' enthusiasm had rubbed off. He hadn't even met Flowers and already he felt honoured to be summoned into his presence. A car had arrived this morning to transport him there, and throughout the journey he was regaled with tales of Harry's business acumen by the driver and his escort – one of Childs' assistants called Hendricks, a dog-loving giant, who yapped about his kennels incessantly – their allegiance equally strong. The more he heard about him, the more Flowers was taking on an almost legendary status, a mythic name spoken in hushed, devoted tones, whose vast reputation preceded him. Despite, or perhaps because of, Childs' allusion to his boss's unconventional thought processes – "You need three brains just to catch up with him" – Gabe was looking forward to finally greeting the man in the flesh. When they swung round in front of the huge house and parked in its shadow, he was struck suddenly with the realisation of just how rich and important this guy was.

Now, under Flowers' gaze, sunlight streaming through the window, the trees in the grounds beyond bowing as they were tussled by a growing breeze, he could sense the power that the man had spoken of moments before, and the impression that he released it like a vapour wherever he went, an aura of tough, uncompromising authority. No wonder it was his guiding obsession to attain more. He wanted to build upon what he had, and consolidate his air of absolute control.

"The house is beautiful," Gabe replied.

"It's my church," Flowers said flatly. "It's where I operate from. I have many properties situated around the city – indeed, around the country – but this is where I'm strongest. This is my home."

"This is where you do your business from?"

"Mainly. I've reached that degree of wealth that fortunately renders the workplace obsolete, and have enough staff that I can delegate the day-to-day toil to. But I still need to put in an appearance in my various operations, just to make sure things are running smoothly. I like to think I'm a hands-on kind of boss." Flowers smiled again, though Gabe noted it barely touched his eyes, which remained as uncomfortably focused on him as always. "Hence the need for a driver. My average day can consist of a fair amount of shuttling back and forth, and I need someone that can take me from A to B with calm assurance. London's roads can be... taxing."

Gabe nodded, the screen inside his mind replaying in startling close-up the moment he ricocheted off the bonnet of the Audi and slammed into the tarmac.

"You came with a glowing reference, Mr O'Connell," Flowers said, cocking his head to one side and studying his subject. "It could of course be just as easy for myself to use one of my existing employees as a chauffeur. But other tasks demand their attention most of the time, and it appeals to me to be driven by someone with a genuine love for the city. You worked as a courier previously, I understand?"

"Before my accident, yes."

"So you feel you know the capital?"

"Whatever face the city shows, I think I've seen it."

Flowers exchanged a glance with one the guards standing before the door, a sense of amusement creasing his lips. "The city has many secrets, that's true," he said, returning his gaze to his guest. "And should you work for me, you will be privy to some of them."

Gabe expected him to expound further, but a mobile phone started ringing. Flowers reached into his jacket pocket and retrieved the device, answering it and listening intently. A minute or so later he clicked it shut and abruptly got to his feet, indicating their meeting was at an end. Gabe hastily stood, shaking his hand once more, though this time Flowers was the first to initiate the gesture. "My associates will be in touch."

"I've got my CV here, if you want it," Gabe replied quickly, patting the bag slung over his shoulder. "Or if there's any other documents you'd like to check—"

"That won't be necessary, Mr O'Connell. I've seen all I need to. Now, if you'll excuse me, I have business to attend to." He nodded a curt goodbye and turned to the door, the men opening it for him. He disappeared through without another word, the guards following, haunting his every move. They closed the door behind them.

Gabe stood in the suddenly hushed room, the sound of a ticking clock on the mantelpiece filling his ears, feeling strangely abandoned and listless, as if all the energy had suddenly been sucked from the air. He only snapped back into focus when Hendricks entered seconds later and told him he'd give him a lift back home.

HE GOT THE call from Childs a couple of days later to inform him that the job was his. He had expected to feel pleased, but his elation was oddly muted; he got the impression this decision had been made possibly even before Flowers had laid eyes upon him, that the old man had been toying with him slightly. His interview had been an attempt for the boss to see how Gabe handled himself face to face, and whether he could be intimidated easily. He assumed he had passed the test, though remained unsure why such a performance was required for such a straightforward role, and wondered if it boded well for his future relationship with his employer. Harry Flowers evidently liked to play games with power, as well as shop for it.

He pressed Tom for information on what he knew about the man, but his flatmate claimed ignorance, repeating his claims that he had had no dealings with him, and that even his superior – Gary, the bar manager – mostly spoke to just Flowers' underlings. Tom did admit that he had heavily championed Gabe for the job, partly because he felt it would be good for him to get back out on the roads, and partly because they were financially desperate. The money Flowers was offering, and the immediacy of the work, was not to be sniffed at. Gabe knew what he was implying: that after Tom's efforts to secure him this work, and with a substantial regular wage laid before him, he would be foolish – not to mention potentially homeless and friendless – if he didn't accept the offer. Once that was taken into consideration, he buried his reservations and spoke to Childs, telling him he would gladly fill the position.

However, he wasn't naive enough to believe that Flowers was entirely on the level, and his first few days working for the man confirmed it. Although his import companies and clubs were legitimate enough on the surface – or to a degree to keep the police from his door, at least – he was evidently not beyond stooping to intimidation to claw more of his precious power. Much of Gabe's initial work seemed to be driving Flowers and a cadre of his lieutenants to backwater businesses and wholesale outlets in the East End and waiting outside while they disappeared into the buildings for a couple of hours. Although he was instructed to stay within the car – a gleaming Jag that he was more than happy to get behind the wheel of – and therefore saw nothing of the transactions taking place inside, when his colleagues returned he occasionally caught glimpses of crimson spots on white cuffs, or a film of sweat on a few of the men's foreheads. He knew enough not to ask questions, and Flowers never revealed what had gone on, but was probably all too aware that Gabe had his suspicions.

Gabe knew that the moment the suggestion of criminal activity reared its head, the smart thing would be to get out of the outfit immediately. But the fact was that there was much about the job that he enjoyed, not least the frisson of excitement at being part of an enterprise that operated on the fringes of the law, a throwback to his wild youth. He grew to like the camaraderie between Flowers' employees, a closely knit group that watched out for one another, bonded by a disregard for conventional authority, and he appreciated the shared glory of being associated with the boss himself. Every time he piloted Flowers through the streets of London he could feel the instinctive respect that the man garnered from those around him. Perhaps there was a touch of fear there too – Flowers often remarked that nothing put people in their place quite like a fearsome reputation – but that seemed more attributed to the facade that Harry liked to project rather than any genuine malice on his part. Indeed, the greater the length of time Gabe spent in his employer's company, the more he realised he was becoming like Childs, Hendricks and the rest – drawn into Harry Flowers' inescapable orbit, he found the strength of personality there arresting. He was funny, clever and remarkably honest for one who spent much of his time concealing his dealings from those that would subject them to scrutiny. He had a temper on him, but the nuclear blast of his anger lasted only as long as the time it took for the person on the other end of his wrath to get the message before it was whipped out of sight again. He felt at times like a surrogate father, affectionately lording it over his unruly family, paternally responsible for his charges, and Gabe wondered if the absence of his own family, the loneliness of his convalescence as he recovered from his accident, brought this into even sharper relief. As long as he was part of Flowers' outfit, then someone would always have his back.

As the weeks elongated into months, Gabe became slowly but surely inured to the surreptitious side of the boss-man's custom, perhaps a little more easily than he expected. He was never asked to be involved, and Flowers clearly appreciated his unquestioning attitude. Even so, it wasn't as if this was the only sphere in which he conducted business. Indeed, there were relatively few of these clandestine meetings amongst the daily routine. Gabe would drive him to lunches with overseas manufacturers, distribution heads and other such mundane facets of his empire, and in the evenings there were appearances at charity parties and club openings, where he would rub shoulders with minor actors and musicians, many hankering for his patronage. He appeared extraordinarily well connected. When Gabe opened the Jag's rear door and Flowers emerged, he transformed from the shady operator into the popular philanthropist; and by extension Gabe got a taste of the glamour and fame, if only at a distance.

Such benefits were enough to make his position with Flowers a tenable one, but there was a further element that piqued his interest even more and ensured his renewed enthusiasm for the job. Every alternate Wednesday, Harry instructed Gabe to take him – strangely, always using one of the other pool cars rather than his regular Jag – to a flat in Vauxhall, into which he would disappear for almost exactly an hour. He always went alone, smelling strongly of aftershave, and entered and departed empty-handed. He would say next to nothing about the nature of these visits, and often the journey back from the apartment was a silent one, Flowers broodily glaring through one of the car's side windows. Gabe never attempted any enquiries, knowing from his boss's mood that such questioning would not go down well, but posited a theory in his head that the flat housed a mistress that Harry was courting, and had been for some time. He had not mentioned any women in his life since the death of his wife, but all the evidence – the scent, the spring with which he left the car, the gloom in which he returned – pointed to a doomed affair of some sort.

After driving Flowers to several of these assignations, the mystery nagged at Gabe; probably more than it should. What business was it of his if Harry got his bi-weekly jollies with some old flame? The routine despondency with which he returned to the car suggested the relationship had been dragging on over a fairly lengthy period, and the driver imagined the unseen lover as being of a similar age to Flowers; a wrinkly gangster's moll kept in affluent seclusion. It really was nothing to do with him and not worth musing on, he reminded himself, and he wouldn't have thought anymore of it if he had not seen the face at the window.

Gabe didn't know why he looked up when he did; usually he was still sitting behind the wheel when Flowers reappeared, but on that bright Wednesday he was leaning against the bonnet of the parked car, enjoying the warmth of the sun's rays. He heard the front door slam and saw his boss heading towards him across the forecourt; stepping back to duck into the vehicle, his eyes flickered momentarily upwards at the building's frontage and he caught sight of the young woman gazing down at him. He knew instantly that this was the subject of Harry's visits. Even from that distance, he could see a resemblance in the narrowness of her cheeks and the dazzling blue eyes. It was not a bed-partner he was spending time with – it was a relation, and, in all probability, his daughter. They locked stares for long seconds before she vanished behind the curtains, and Gabe was left with an indescribable ache at her absence. He snapped from his reverie when he realised that Harry had almost reached him, and tried to put her from his mind for the journey back to the mansion. He made no mention to his employer at having seen the woman, and Flowers – being typically morose – did not indulge in conversation.

But Gabe found it difficult to erase the face from his memory. There was something so sad and heartbreaking about the cast of her features that he kept returning to it. He studied it from what he could recollect – the long blonde hair hanging to her shoulders, the pale white skin, the small teeth visible behind the purse of her lips – and tried to analyse why this woman looked so caged and lonely. For all he knew, she could be married with half a dozen rugrats under her belt, but her demeanour suggested otherwise. She appeared afraid, and her father's trips to see her – for Flowers had to be her parent, there was no question of that, the more he compared the two – did nothing to assuage that fear; indeed, it possibly even heightened it.

Gabe looked forward to each trip to south London and a chanced glimpse of the mystery woman, and though he never saw her as clearly on subsequent visits he could always discern her outline hovering at the curtains' edge, like a spirit trapped behind glass. Flowers appeared not to notice Gabe's eyes constantly drifting to the same window, but that was hardly surprising; he was becoming increasingly distracted. Gossip amongst the men suggested that an old rival of Harry's had started moving in on their territory – Goran Vassily, a kingpin from eastern Europe, who had carved out a chunk of property north of the Thames, and with whom Flowers had a volatile relationship. Vassily was making challenges to Harry's power base: customers were being stolen, profits slashed, insults traded. Flowers was said to be livid, and he spent more and more time at the mansion, issuing directives to combat this threat. As a result, the journeys to Vauxhall dried up, and Gabe was left haunted by her image.

He had considered asking some of the others in Harry's employ whether they knew anything about her, but discarded the idea, worried that word might get back to the old man, who would no doubt take a very dim view of his chauffeur poking his nose in other people's personal matters. He wasn't sure who he could trust amongst the ranks; who would keep their mouths shut and who would find his casual curiosity suspicious.

Suddenly, Gabe made an unconscious decision before the rational side of him could oppose it: he would go see her without Flowers' knowledge. It was a risky strategy, and one that seemed to fly in the face of common sense, but he didn't think he'd be able to put that face from his mind until he'd made an attempt to help her. He recognised a vulnerability that he himself had struggled to overcome following his accident, and saw in those pained features a desire to escape the claustrophobic confines of her dwelling, if only she wasn't so scared of what lay beyond. As someone who had suffered similar circumstances, Gabe felt he was in a useful position to give her whatever aid she required. To minimise the amount of deceit required, he chose a day when he needed to take the Jag in for a service, and could legitimately escape Harry's gaze, though in truth the boss was so preoccupied with this enemy organisation muscling in on his operations that Gabe doubted he would be even missed. Every morning seemed to bring with it some fresh tale of disrespect and a growing sense of events escalating: a small fire in a club bathroom; shots fired outside several bars; an increased police presence acting on anonymous tip-offs.

He drove over to the apartment block not knowing what he was going to say, and stood before the list of residents next to the exterior door, his mind still blank. There was only one woman's name marked, and that read Anna Randolph, Flat 4. His hand, acting independently, reached out and pressed the button adjacent to it.

A reply came seconds later out of the speaker. "Yes?"

"Ms Randolph?" Gabe exhaled and took a leap of faith. "I work for your father. Mr Flowers."

The silence stretched interminably. Finally: "And?"

"And he hasn't been able to make it for a few weeks, so I... I came in his stead. To see how you were."

More silence. "Who are you?"

"My name's Gabriel O'Connell. As I said, I work for Harry."

"Look up for a moment."

"Huh?"

"Just look up."

He did as he was told, seeing instantly the CCTV camera positioned just under the roof of the porch. He looked straight into its flat black eye.

"You're the driver, aren't you?" came a crackly voice from the intercom. "The one who brings him."

"That's right."

"And he doesn't know you're here, does he?"

"Well, I..." Gabe stuttered. "I thought..."

"Push the door." A buzzer sounded and the lock snapped free. Gabe paused for a moment, cast a glance behind him, then entered, jogging up the short flight of stairs to the first landing. Number four was opposite the stairwell. He rapped on its door, which was opened by the woman from the window. She was shorter than he imagined, in her early twenties, and wore a black vest top and grey sweatpants. She beckoned for him to enter, and ushered him into the living room, a chaotic sprawl of discarded clothes, magazines, CDs, books and unwashed mugs.

"Sorry to disturb you like this," he began.

"If Harry knew you were here," she answered, sitting on a sofa arm, one leg folded under the other, "he'd have you strung up. I'm presuming you know the risk you're taking?"

"To be honest, I'm not sure myself what I'm doing here. Why'd you let me in?"

"I've seen you looking up at my window when you come to collect Dad. You have a trustworthy face, I guess. Somehow I wasn't entirely surprised you turned up at my door."

He nodded slightly. "I wanted to talk to you. You seemed lonely and... I don't know, a bit trapped, I suppose." He ran a hand through his hair. "I don't make a habit of this, I have to say. Turning up at stranger's doors for a chat, I mean."

"You must have been sure, though. As I said, Harry will feed you your balls if he finds out you've been here."

"I know. It felt like something I had to get out of my system. If I didn't... I would've been haunted by what I didn't do because I didn't have the nerve." She was studying him, clearly a family trait. "Why does he keep you here?"

"For my protection. Dad's made a fair few enemies over the years, so he thought it better I didn't stay at the mansion. Hence me taking on mother's maiden name too. But it suits me, being as far away from him as I can. If he would let me, I'd escape to the other side of world."

"I got the impression that the two of you don't have a happy relationship."

"My father's an animal. The fact that he acts the popular businessman just makes it worse. If he was a simple thug that didn't know any better, I might have some semblance of respect for him, but he's very exacting in how he inflicts pain. If something stands in the way of getting what he wants then he won't hesitate to destroy it."

The vehemence of her words took him aback. She must've noticed his shock, because her tone softened. "Look, clear some of that stuff off the chair and sit down. You look like you're waiting for a bus."

Gabe picked up a stack of unironed T-shirts and placed them on the carpet. Seating himself, he took in his surroundings: there was clutter everywhere, spilling from cupboards and off shelves, though there was a comforting homeliness to it. There was no sense of ostentation. The furniture was evidently several decades old, and an extensive album collection was lying in piles around a tatty stereo player held together by duct tape. It didn't look like she had much use for her father's wealth.

He noticed there were no photographs of Flowers perched amongst the bric-a-brac, only a woman he took to be Anna's mother; the two of them were smiling out of many of the picture frames.

"Is that why you didn't tell me to get lost?" he asked. "Because having me here would upset him?"

"Partly," she conceded. "I do like making things as difficult for him as I can. He deserves it."

"What on earth do the two of you talk about when he comes to visit?"

"Not a lot. It's mostly just him apologising, and asking for forgiveness. Me, I'm just counting the hours till he goes."

"Forgiveness? For what?"

She sighed. "Long story."

"That's kind of why I'm here," he said, smiling. "Anything you want to get off your chest, I'm willing to listen."

She paused as she picked at a nail. "Suffice to say, I used to see this guy that was friends with the wrong crowd. Dad made sure he left town and didn't come back."

"More enemies?"

She nodded. "Of a sort." She looked up at him, the same piercing blue eyes as her father boring into him. "Do you want a cup of tea?"

He smiled and replied that he would, and when she returned with two steaming mugs they chatted comfortably about their pasts. Gabe told her about soldiering overseas and the scenes he witnessed there, and the accident and the terror he'd experienced at leaving the safety of his home. Anna sympathised, telling him that Flowers had instilled in her at an early age a dread of straying from his side, informing her that there were all manner of bad people who could do her harm. She realised in her late teens, after he'd hounded her mother to death, that he was the one she needed to be afraid of. But even so, he wouldn't let her go, refusing to keep her at anything more than arm's length.

Gabe felt an assurance with Anna that put him at his ease, bonded by their similar experiences, and although he was conscious of the time slipping away as he sat in this Vauxhall flat watching the shapes her mouth made as she spoke, it was good to be in her company. With each anecdote, she was clearly relishing a chance to relate to someone, having broken free of Flowers' control. She told him about bands that she liked, playing song after song, scattering CDs in an arc around her as she searched through her collection, and reeled off novels that he should be reading. It was like he had suddenly tapped into the reservoir of her interests, and it came bubbling to the surface.

"You got any kids?" she asked him after he'd told her a little about his own family.

"No, none. I've never been in a steady enough relationship."

"I had one once, with the guy from the wrong crowd. A baby boy. Dad insisted I give him up for adoption, said I wasn't in a fit state to cope." She was studying an album sleeve, running her eyes over it sadly.

"I'm sorry to hear that."

"Post-natal depression." She looked over at him. "I'd like to see him again, though, one day. He'd be a proper little lad by now."

Eventually, he told her he had to go, but would like to return, if that was OK with her. She told him it was, as long as he was careful. He should never underestimate Harry, she said. Gabe promised he would take every precaution, and true to his word he came back a week later, and then another seven days after that, and then twice more the following month.

Unaware that on each occasion he was being closely watched.

THE FIRST INKLING that something was wrong came when his mobile rang at 3.30 in the morning. At first he was content to let it run to voicemail, but it didn't stop; somebody was calling his number repeatedly. Rousing himself from sleep, Gabe sleepily glanced at the display and saw Flowers' name. A chill ran down his spine, and all notion of fatigue left him instantly. He answered it warily.

There was no greeting. "They've got her," Harry whispered, hard and precise, the anger vibrant within each word. "They've got her because of *you.*"

CHAPTER ELEVEN

DR JENNY CRANFIELD leaned back from her desk, her head throbbing. She removed her glasses and rubbed the bridge of her nose as she reread the last paragraph she had written on the monitor screen, then stood from her chair, arching her back. She had been hunched over her workstation for the best part of the morning, and her neck felt as stiff as the corpse on the gurney behind her. She reached up and squeezed the nape and her shoulders, the muscles tense beneath her touch, though her efforts were limited with only one good hand at her disposal. She looked down at the left, the appendage swathed in bandages, and once more attempted to flex it, but the cramping pain returned to travel up her arm. It was like a dead weight, as if the tendons within had frozen; she fought the urge to slam it against the wall, just to give it back some sensation.

Jenny tugged open a drawer and rooted amongst the detritus to retrieve a packet of paracetamol, then wandered over to the sink. She swallowed two of the tablets, and leant under the running tap to wash them down. As she wiped her mouth, her gaze returned to her injured limb; she was certain the fatigue and her body's tenderness were in some way connected to the bite she had received. She'd been checked out by one of her colleagues straight after the incident, who had cleaned and dressed her wound before giving her a couple of jabs, mostly as a precautionary measure. He'd said he could detect nothing untoward and had taken a blood sample to put her mind at rest, but she remained convinced the wound was infected. Who knew what diseases that test subject could possibly be carrying?

Gannon had assured her that the corpse had been sterilised before the experimentation began, but even then, he had admitted, post-resurrection the virus hadn't halted the cadaver's necrosis – flesh and muscle were continuing to rot as bacteria set to work upon the dead tissue. That had certainly popped his little balloon; what use would the military have for a platoon of these things if they were falling apart? He had convinced himself that they could still be deployed for limited periods, though he was plainly disappointed with the results, blindly hoping that HS-03 would suddenly pull a miracle out of the bag. Still, she reasoned, it wouldn't be the first time that the British Army had been sent out with substandard equipment.

She didn't know how long the project was destined to last anyway. By all accounts, the Minister was less than impressed and determined to shut it down, though Gannon characteristically remained optimistic that he could make the politician see sense. She wasn't sure if the politician didn't have a point. In twelve years of researching and engineering toxins and bio-weapons for the MoD, this had crossed the line from genuinely working in the best interests of the country's defence to ghoulish frivolity. Gannon was a brilliant scientist – one of the top minds in the UK – but he must've recognised that this was going to be a hard sell, and she now thought that he was persevering with it out of sheer obstinacy. If the media ever got the merest sniff of the work that was being conducted here, they were going to crucify him – and undoubtedly Sedgworth too, no matter what plausible denials he could muster – and tar him with the familiar accusations of playing God. For once, Jenny was inclined to agree. This mockery of the dead had no place in a nation's arsenal, even if it did save troops' lives. What could they possibly claim to be battling *for*, sending out a squad of reanimated cadavers to fight on their behalf? Freedom? Democracy? Peace? They who had enslaved their own dead? Who, in whatever corner of the globe, would consider that *civilised*?

And there was the aggression factor, something that had taken them all by surprise. Gannon's theorising had suggested that once HS-03 got to work on primary functions of the brain – triggering movement and the most basic awareness of its surroundings – it would render the motorised corpse entirely open to direction, allowing them to input orders and place it completely within their control. But the virus had taken hold on the cerebellum's centre and developed it in a totally unexpected direction; along with the motor-control and rudimentary behaviour patterns came an uncontrollable violence. It was as if it had awoken the brain's most primal root, reverting the subject back to an animalistic state.

In the case of Corporal Littleton – or HS-03/ref.4176, to give him his official title – within minutes of getting up and walking, he (*it*, she admonished herself; she had to remember to refer to them as impersonal objects – they were no longer human beings, displayed no intelligent life-signs, and exhibited similarly no personality; they were simply dead sacks of meat) appeared threatened by the scientists' presence and lashed out. Even then, it wasn't clear how the corpse had managed to ascertain that there were people in the room – there were four of them: Gannon, herself, and McKendrick and Horton – since it didn't appear to have had his sight fully restored. The pupils were filmy, and the way it moved its head seemed to indicate that it was using some other sensory perception to gain understanding of its environment. Likewise, sound and smell must've been equally undeveloped, if they were indeed working at all. But there was no denying it was immediately aware of their proximity, for it staggered towards them in a stiff-legged gait, gnarled fingers reaching out. As they all backed away, Gannon whispered that perhaps it was looking to feel whether they were of the same species to reassure itself, reading their physiognomy like a blind man runs his fingers over Braille. It clattered into them and Jenny put out her left hand to restrain it, a mistake she instantly regretted.

Its advance was not borne out of a need for kin recognition, but hunger. It grasped her wrist and bowed its head as if for a romantic peck, but instead bit down on the fleshy part of her palm, ripping away a fat inch of skin and muscle with a savage twist. Jenny screamed, white-hot pain lancing through her forearm, watching, unbelieving, as blood pumped in a crimson mini-fountain from her ravaged hand and hit the floor in heavy splats that blossomed into rusty explosions on the tiles. The cadaver stood before them, still holding her in a vice-like grip, and slowly began to chew, red trickles coating its chin, stark against the pale white of its face. It exhibited no semblance of pleasure in the act, its features as blank as if it were still lying on the slab, as if this was something it was directed to do by an inner instinct. Indeed, it exuded the disinterested air of a baby suckling upon a teat, unconcerned by the method by which it obtained its food, only that its belly was being filled.

Gannon and the others were paralysed for mere seconds, but those moments seemed as if time had slowed to a crawl. They stared, frozen, at the ragged bite-mark on Jenny's hand, which was by now slick with blood. It was only when the corpse ducked forward once more to take one of her fingers between its teeth that they finally sprang into action. They seized its arms and wrestled it back, forcing it to relinquish its hold of her wrist. Once she was free, she sank to her knees, sobbing, clasping her wounded limb to her chest, already feeling a stiffness stealing its way up her arm. She shrugged off her white coat and wrapped it around the injury, stemming the flow of vermilion fluid from her already pallid hand.

Once the cadaver was distracted from its meal, it fixed its attention on the three scientists trying to pin it down; apparently, its greed was indiscriminate. It lunged for them too, jaw snapping, grasping for anything it could catch hold of. For one tense moment, it grabbed Horton's shirt and yanked him forward, its maw opening wide to take a chunk out of his neck, but Gannon punched it hard in the temple. It evidently did little to hurt it, but blindsided it enough for them to consolidate their grip on its arms. They yelled at Jenny to hit the security alarm, and she woozily found her feet to slam her fist down on the red button encased on the wall.

Within seconds, half a dozen armed personnel filled the room, Gannon repeatedly instructing them not to shoot. Instead he got one of them to pass him a pair of binds to secure the creature's hands behind its back, another to hogtie its feet together, then fashioned a makeshift muzzle from a broken-in-half broom handle jammed between its teeth. Only once he was confident that it was fully incapacitated and that it posed no additional threat did he indicate to his colleagues that they could back away from it. They stood in a semi-circle, breathing heavily, looking down at the cadaver wriggling like a bug trapped for a school kid's project, its teeth cracking against the broom handle, sliding out of grey gums. The security guards in particular were a little taken aback by what they were witnessing. They were generally not privy to the nature of the experiments that were conducted within the labs, and had next to no knowledge of Gannon's resurrection serum. Possibly keeping them in the dark like that was a wise move, Jenny had mused; many of them were ex-military, and if they knew where HS-03/ref.4176 had come from, what it had been in life, they might not have been so quick to come to Gannon's aid.

Instead, he'd reassured them that the subject was merely being tested for increased levels of adrenaline, and its pallor and mania were side effects of the drugs they were prescribing. She could tell they didn't believe him for a second, but since they could not formulate an explanation for themselves, they seemed to grudgingly accept it. Gannon was told that for a security breach of this kind – and especially since a member of staff had been wounded (all eyes had turned towards her then, her deathly white face and arms pockmarked with maroon stains) – a report would have to be kicked upstairs. Gannon had readily agreed, eager to usher them out of the room, fully aware that the MoD bods would clamp down on it and make sure no details ever emerged outside of Monkhill.

While he and Horton had dragged their bound creature off to a quieter area where it could be monitored safely, McKendrick had led her to the infirmary and treated her injury. McKendrick was a relatively recent addition to the team, having transferred over from an outpost north of Sydney, and was a cautious, introspective young man. As he carefully wrapped the bandages around her hand, she asked him if he thought what they were doing was a step too far.

"I don't like it," he'd said. "But I doubt it'll stay like this for long."

"What do you mean?"

"This..." he groped for the right expression, "walking army of the dead that's supposedly going to fight for us. It's not going to happen. The public, the politicians, they're not going to stand for it. But what it could prove to be is a starting point, a catalyst for a whole new take on the problem. The idea of using reanimated cadavers will mutate into something else, something more workable, and we'll take the best bits from what we learned with HS-03 and use them in a different direction."

"Gannon seems keen on his pet ghouls."

McKendrick snorted a laugh. "I think he actually fancies himself as a Junior Frankenstein. But it's his pride that, for the moment, won't let him see past his zombies."

"Don't let him hear you use the Z word."

"He kids himself that the HS-03 subjects are in the best interests of the country, but the fact is he just wants to be like the criminal mastermind from the horror movies, controlling them all. What's that one about the dead working down a Cornish tin mine?"

"I don't know," Jenny replied, looking down at her bandaged limb. "Those sort of films aren't really my cup of tea."

"Well, that's what Gannon would have them doing, if he had his way." He paused. "But it'll change. He'll recognise the serum's limitations, and it'll spark off some new theories and we'll start working on... I don't know, combating organ failure or bolstering a soldier's immune system." He paused again. "Things can't stay the way they are." He finished binding her wound. "Best I could do. You'll probably have some scarring."

As JENNY STOOD in the lab, head still throbbing despite the tablets, she tentatively pressed her fingers against the linen-wrapped flesh of her hand. It felt rigid and unmoving, as it if were calcifying. She was beginning to worry at what kind of infection had spread into her system, and considered taking herself off to A&E at the local hospital. Gannon would hit the roof if he found out; once the Casualty docs started asking questions, it could bring down all sorts of unwanted heat on the facility. If Monkhill had a cardinal rule, it was *containment* – the neighbours had no reason to know the research that was being conducted on the premises, and if problems arose, they were to be dealt with inside its walls. Once it entered the public domain, there was no way of controlling the snowballing of information. All the same, she was aware that she was gradually feeling worse – her legs seemed wobbly, and her eyelids were growing heavy – and decided she should readmit herself to the infirmary, and let them sort it out. She was in no fit state to work.

She pushed herself away from the worktop edge and headed towards the door, immediately sensing a rushing wave of nausea pass through her. She staggered and clattered into her chair, coughing bile into the back of her throat, putting out her good hand to steady herself. It made contact with the gurney upon which the cadaver lay, strapped and muzzled, its searching eyes swivelling in their sockets at her sudden proximity. It was the fourth or fifth test subject to have been injected with HS-03 – a John Doe that had been commandeered from a military hospital – and its stomach cavity had been surgically emptied to gauge the effect of hunger upon its actions. The edges of its belly were pinned open, and several feet of intestine had been removed and curled into a large stainless steel dish to the side. All that remained of its digestive tract was a russet-brown hole surrounded by muscle and fat, and yet it had attempted to feed whenever she had gone near it, its teeth champing, its head struggling to get closer to her. It was clearly not looking to sustain itself, since it no longer had the organs that required the nourishment, but was instead simply gorging itself on the primal act of consuming meat, directed by the virus working on its brain.

Jenny leaned against the gurney, gazing down at its naked form, sweat now prickling her brow, and suddenly, barely thinking, she reached forward and untied the muzzle. Instantly, it issued a groan and moved its jaw in a bovine manner, trying to chew on anything it could reach. Its arms strained against the bonds, and its dissected abdomen tore a little with the movement, the skin splitting as far up as the ribcage and down to the pubic bone, red sheaths of muscle visible beneath the yellowish skin.

Jenny held out her right hand above its mouth, and the corpse snapped at it, like a pet offered a treat. Its head pushed higher, its neck wrenching with the effort, but she kept the limb safely out of its reach, the fingers several inches from its clacking teeth. Then, she replaced the offered titbit, proffering her injured left hand. The result was what she feared: the creature showed no interest, its head sinking back onto the stretcher, exhibiting none of the excitement it had showed seconds ago. She waved it closer still, but there was no response. She stepped back from the gurney, breathing heavily, her mind racing at the implications. The dead subjects were stimulated by the presence of living flesh, seeking to feed upon it. The fact that it didn't react to the wounded limb suggested that the cadaver couldn't sense a pulse. As far as it was concerned, her left hand was as a dead as it was.

She had to get help, she instructed herself. A necrosis had spread from the bite and was in the process of killing all the cells in her lower arm, no doubt coursing through her body as she stood there, passing on its taint. The thought made her feel sick again, and light-headed. She stumbled forward, leaving the corpse mewling behind her, and focused on getting out the door, taking no more than half a dozen steps before a paralysing coldness arced through her, punching the breath out of her and draining all the strength from her legs. Jenny dropped to her knees, bringing her hands to her chest. She felt as if her lungs were crystallising, seizing up. She gasped, clawing for air, aware of her muscles shaking. She was dying, she realised, and she didn't have the energy to cry for help. Her body was riddled with the bacteria, and it was shutting everything down, organ after organ, like light switches being flipped one by one. She curled into a ball, visualising the virus racing through her, changing her from the inside out, blood cells laid waste by the nuclear blast of its wake. A growing darkness was stealing into her head, and an agonizing swell of pain blossomed throughout her being. Her mouth was frozen into a savage rictus grimace by the time her heart stopped half an hour later.

Twenty minutes after that, her mouth started moving again.

GANNON WAS TINKERING with a cadaver's brain when he first heard the alarms. He was trying to reverse-engineer the serum, or at least tweak the affect it had on the organ's central core, reducing the resurrected corpses' predatory, cannibalistic tendencies (but they *weren't* cannibals, he told himself; their desire for human flesh was not an intraspecies act, since they were no longer of the same genus). The speed with which HS-03 took hold of those it was administered to had been expected. After all, it had been artificially constructed based on the HIV, cancer and influenza models – tenacious, aggressive viruses that took no time at all in disabling a victim, riddling its cells, destroying the immune system and adapting the subject for its own use. And, indeed, part of his interest in creating HS-03 from the ground up was to monitor what the bacteria actually wanted to do. To the observer, for example, cancer has no other purpose but to destroy; but to understand it, the scientist had to look at it from the illness's point of view – what did it seek to gain from corrupting its host? Could it possibly see itself as an instrument of change, developing a fully functioning body into something else? The question was, what was that change initiating? In the case of HS-03, it was using the dead as a blank slate, hot-wiring their neurons and kick-starting them into life – but a life dictated by the virus and what it wanted.

Gannon couldn't fathom why it was instigating this primal hunger, especially since it had been proven that the need for food was purely superficial. It was almost as if the bacteria was unlocking and accessing the latent memories still trapped within the cadavers' heads, the root instincts that were as much the legacy of mankind's stone-age ancestors as the nub of their prehensile tails. It was reawakening them, channelling them.

When they first discovered this hunger for flesh, Gannon had hoped that it could be fine-tuned into an additional weapon, something extra in their biological arsenal. Not only would they be fearless and indefatigable, but this army would consume what it destroyed, like a plague of locusts sweeping through the enemy ranks. But he soon realised that their cravings were indiscriminate and impossible to control. His colleagues, too, were uneasy with this side effect of HS-03, especially after Dr Cranfield was assaulted and bitten. Bringing the dead back to life had tested their scientific moralities to the limit, but honing them as carnivorous attack dogs was something else entirely. More than a handful had protested and refused to go near what they called the 'ghouls.' Gannon had argued that they were being emotive, and basing their opinions on what they may have seen in late-night movies, but he knew the writing was on the wall for the project. Sedgworth would never greenlight it, not as it stood; he wouldn't want to be known as the minister that unleashed the flesh-crazed undead on the world. That was the sort of thing that history would judge a man by.

The politician had tried to remain unmoved by what Gannon had told him about *Totenkrieg*, but the doctor could detect that the Minister was secretly shocked that something like this had been attempted before. Or, more likely, the fact that the powers-that-be on the home front had deemed the scheme worthy of stealing from the Germans once the war was over. It never really got beyond the planning stage with them either. They'd only ever developed one platoon, and the viral prototype had been crudely manufactured. He wondered if they too had had control issues with the resurrected, unprepared for what they had let loose.

He had a skull open before him, the flap of scalp peeled back like the lid of a tin can, and was probing the dull-grey organ within, dissecting choice segments for examination and testing. What had become immediately evident was that, while the resurrected could survive any amount of tissue damage and limb removal (they had undergone a barrage of weapons' fire trials), brain injury cancelled their ticket for good. Clearly, once HS-03's activation point was destroyed, either by bullet or blunt trauma, it lost its hold over the corpse. As soon as he'd drilled into this particular head, the subject had gone still. He wondered if the virus survived beyond the host shutting down. He wanted to chart its growth and development, to see if it could be limited somehow. If he could stunt its spread, perhaps he could curtail the cadavers' carnivorous instincts.

Gannon slid a sliver of brain matter under the microscope and was adjusting the magnification when he heard the dull popping of a gun being fired somewhere further down the facility's corridor. He looked up instantly, cocking an ear and wondering if he could have imagined it. His query was answered straight away; it came again in a short burst, this time followed by shouting growing louder as if the cries were coming closer. A moment's silence, then the alarm sounded, a strident wail that got him moving.

He strode out of his lab and into the corridor, white coat twisting in his wake, only to confront a scene from a nightmare. A security guard was edging backwards, a pistol gripped in both hands, attention fixed on the figure stumbling towards him. It took a Gannon a second to realise that it was Jenny Cranfield. The lower half of her face was coated in blood, and her hands, even the bandaged one, were crimson, as if she'd dipped them in a pot of paint. She stumbled stiff-legged, barely aware of her surroundings, and it wasn't until his eyes travelled to the floor that he saw the two bodies lying motionless just behind her, their throats torn open. It was Horton, and his assistant, Petley. They looked like they'd been savaged by an animal.

"What the fuck's up with her?" the guard said as he came level with Gannon, gun still held out in front of him.

"What happened?"

"Heard screams coming from one of the labs down there. She was fucking ripping into them, eating their throats out. I thought it was a practical joke at first. I mean, I know what you guys have got down here, what with the fucking dead boys and all. Thought it was just a load of fake blood and a bunch of bored docs trying to wind me up. But there's something up with her eyes, I saw it as soon as she turned round, and she went for me as soon as she knew I was there. And the guys were properly goners, there was no mistaking that."

"I heard shooting."

"I had no choice. I gave her a warning, said I was licensed to protect the facility, but she kept coming. I put a couple of rounds in her shoulder to push her back, and when that didn't stop her I aimed for her chest. She should've gone down, but it was like she barely even noticed. Is she fucking high on something?"

Gannon now saw the red holes on Jenny's lab coat and blouse where she'd taken the hits; blood had bloomed in flowery explosions on the white material. But she seemed unconcerned by the injuries, continuing her advance. He shook his head in disbelief, not wanting to admit to what he was seeing. She'd been infected, it was the only explanation. The bite she'd received on the hand must've passed on the virus – did it travel in the saliva? – and killed her, then brought her back with the same characteristics as the test subjects.

My God, he thought, *if it can spread like this, we have to contain it.*

"Jenny," he called out over the blare of the alarm, hoping that some vestige of her intelligence still remained. "Jenny, can you understand me? It's Robert."

She gave no indication that she could even hear him, her blind eyes sweeping the corridor as she stumbled forward. They were running out of space to back into.

"Aim for the head," Gannon murmured.

"What?"

"Shoot her in the head," he hissed. "It's the only way to stop her."

Just at that moment, the lift doors opened and a security team poured out, alerted by the triggered alarm. They jogged towards the scene of carnage, semi-automatics held down by their sides, and paused beside the two bodies. Their arrival caused Jenny to halt and half-turn, sensing their presence. The team leader seemed unsure of who he should be directing his warnings at, but once he caught sight of the ragged, gore-flecked woman, he raised his gun.

"Don't make another move," he shouted.

"You have to shoot her in the head," Gannon yelled. "She's infected. There's nothing else you can do to stop her. Kill her." Then, as an afterthought: "She's already dead anyway."

"What the hell are you talking about?" the squad leader replied, not taking his eyes off Jenny, who staggered vaguely in his direction.

"She's infected with a virus that she'll pass on to you if you allow her to get close. She'll kill you, believe me."

"Doctor Cranfield," the other man said, directing his attention to the swaying figure, "I'm not taking any chances. Do not move. We'll try to help you. But don't come any nearer."

Jenny paid the words no heed. She moaned quietly, and continued to totter forward.

"Damn it, this is your last chance," he started, when a hand shot out and fastened on his ankle. He yelped, looking down to see one of the bodies – one of the scientists with the gouged throats, who couldn't possibly be still alive – pulling himself forward and taking a bite out of his right calf, tearing a thick chunk of flesh from his leg, stringy sections of muscle trailing from the wound. He screamed and overbalanced, his finger tightening on his semi-automatic's trigger; bullets blasted through the windows of a nearby lab and exploded the vials and test tubes inside. He hit the floor to find his attacker crawling over him, hands tearing at his uniform. His colleagues instantly rushed to his aid, four of them pulling at the scientist, unaware that the other corpse was getting to his feet behind them.

The thing that used to be Horton grabbed one of the guards by the head so hard a finger pierced an eye socket and wrenched it backwards, simultaneously taking a mouthful from his shoulder. The others turned, shocked, momentarily slackening their grip on the figure assaulting their superior; it was enough for the scientist to wriggle free and chew a lip free from his victim's face. The team leader had his gun trapped under him, but brought it up enough to fire several shots into the man's belly. He didn't even flinch.

By this point, Jenny had reached the fray. One of the security guards spotted her and brought his weapon to bear, shooting her in the torso half a dozen times.

"In the fucking *head*," Gannon bellowed.

The guard raised his aim and fired, the back of Jenny's skull exploding in a vermilion shower, shattering one of the lab windows behind her. She dropped to her knees, then collapsed sideways.

"Give me your gun," Gannon instructed to the man standing beside him, who – stunned – passed it to him without question. The doctor ran toward the melee. Another of the team was wrestling with Horton, fending him off as he snapped his teeth ravenously, while Petley was being lifted to give the gunman enough room to take a shot. Gannon didn't hesitate: he placed the barrel against the side of Horton's head and fired, brain matter painting the wall and sprinkling the guard's face. Then he turned and helped them pull Petley away from his meal, just enough to stick a gun in his mouth and empty his skull. Gannon felt a slick, warm mass wash against his skin as the corpse slid to the floor.

He sagged against the wall. For a moment, all he heard was the wailing of the alarm offset by the choked groans of the injured, and when he put a hand to his forehead it came away wet and bloody. Shakily, he got to his feet and strode over to a telephone mounted near the lifts, grabbing the receiver that connected the labs with the front desk.

"This is Doctor Gannon. We have an emergency – quarantine restrictions are to be put in place immediately. Nobody goes anywhere without my say-so. Inform the ministry we need clean-up and medical staff here *right now.*"

He gazed back at the carnage, hoping that they could do enough to lock it down. But unbeknownst to the doctor, the end of the world had already begun.

CHAPTER TWELVE

THE GUN FELT COLD and heavy in his hands. Gabe stared at the semi-automatic laid across his upturned palms, its dark surface slick and glinting dully, his fingers curling around the butt and trigger guard. He hadn't handled one since his days in the army, promised himself he never would again. He looked up at Flowers questioningly, the older man standing before him, his face a blank mask of rage. They were in the mansion's hallway, a large contingent of Flowers' workforce massing like an army preparing for war. They were slotting revolvers into their waistbands, or concealing pump-action shotguns beneath long heavy coats.

"Harry... I can't..."

"No excuses. Since you're responsible for the situation, you're going to help resolve it; and everyone's going in armed. If you're unfamiliar with the weapon, then I suggest you learn pretty damn quick. We're moving out now."

"Harry," Gabe replied, trying to keep his voice level, "you've always kept me removed from the blunt end of your business dealings, and I've appreciated that. I got the impression you felt that there was no need to involve me; if nothing else for the reason that you knew how unhelpful I'd be. I was employed as a driver, and that's as far as my responsibilities went."

Flowers stepped closer until they were merely inches apart. "Everyone is going in armed," he spat in a slow, menacing monotone. "And you want to talk about responsibility? I employed you to follow my orders, to take me where I directed, to keep your mouth shut and know your place. Do what I ask and we'll get along famously, isn't that what I told you when you first joined? A fairly simple code to live by, I would've thought. But evidently it wasn't enough for you – you felt you also had the right to go behind my back and meddle in matters that didn't concern you. Putting my daughter's life in danger also fell into your responsibilities, did it?"

"Of course I never meant –"

"Answer the question."

Gabe gripped the gun tighter. "No. I know I was not employed to look after Anna."

Flowers lunged forward, grabbing the younger man by his jacket lapels and slamming him against the wall. The small knot of enforcers standing behind Harry visibly flinched, taken aback by the speed of the attack. "Don't you *dare* say her fucking name," Flowers roared. "Not after what you've done. She was safe there, none of my enemies knew where she was. But once you started making your little journeys, anyone keeping the mansion under observation and following you could deduce that someone important was living in that flat. Your idiocy could see my child murdered, and you talk of looking *after* her?"

"I'm sorry, I didn't think. But I believed she needed help, someone to talk to."

"She had *me*. She had her *father*." Flowers pushed Gabe back further, his balled fists pressing against the younger man's chest, just below his throat. "You pompous little shit, who the fuck do you think you are? What, you see yourself as some white knight riding in to save her? All you've done is delivered her to the very people that could do her the most harm. And in the same breath as talking about coming to her aid, you're trying to weasel out of getting her back. If it's anyone's responsibility that she's returned here safely, it's yours, so don't tell me you don't want to get involved. Your actions made sure you were involved whether you like it or not."

Gabe couldn't argue with this. He desperately wanted to save Anna from whatever trouble she may be in, and with each passing moment – Flowers hissing bile in his face, pushing him harder into the wall – he felt his resolve strengthening and a determination flourishing, and he was damned if he was going to be painted as the sole villain.

"You know what, Harry?" he said. "You're right. I have a duty to help get her back. But I want to make this clear: I'm doing this for *her*, as a friend. This has nothing to do with helping you in your activities. Because, let's be truthful about this – it's because of *you* that she was taken. She's merely a weak link to get to you, a pawn in your empire building. You see everyone around you as a viable commodity, and now they have something of yours to barter with. So slap me around and shout in my face all you like, but let's not forget it's your business that's put Anna in this position."

Flowers face crumpled into a slack glare of hatred as if the tension that had been restraining him was released for a moment, and he swung a fist back. Gabe used the sudden relaxation of his grip to bring his arms up and knock the old man's other hand away, dodging the punch that whistled past his jaw and cracked the plaster behind him. He hefted the gun and placed the barrel between Harry's eyes, aware that other weapons were instantly being raised in his direction.

"I'm not gonna take your bullshit, boss," he murmured as Flowers lifted his gaze to the semi-automatic resting against his forehead, a fleeting glimmer of worry replaced by a sardonic smile.

"You've got some balls, I'll give you that much, O'Connell," he said, taking a step back and swatting the gun to one side. "But if you want to take a shot, you need to flick the safety off first. Remember that for next time."

THEY MOVED OUT ten minutes later, four long, sleek cars moving swiftly in the early hours of the morning. Ironically, given his job within the outfit, Gabe was not asked to drive. Instead, he was seated in the back of the second vehicle, sandwiched between five triggermen. Harry rode in the lead car, but whether he was deliberately keeping his distance and felt threatened being in Gabe's proximity, the younger man couldn't tell.

His employer had treated being held at gunpoint as little more than a gag, an admirable display of verve, and had been disarmingly flippant about what had happened. Perhaps the fury he'd displayed had been purposely intended to invite that reaction and show what Gabe was made of? Or possibly Flowers never believed that his driver had the guts to pull the trigger in the end. Either way, Gabe felt he should be counting his blessings that he hadn't had his legs broken for that little stunt. Thinking back, it seemed like he'd lost all sense of rationality – the idea of pointing a loaded gun (or at least he assumed it was loaded; what if Flowers wanted his revenge by sending him in with an empty hand cannon?) to someone's head would've been alien to him merely a few days ago. But something was altering inside him, a growing vigour, that he put down to the considerable influence of those that he worked with. He felt an increasing need to prove himself and the belief that change could be wrought through a greater strength. That show of muscle – these four cars of tooled-up gunmen, bent on intimidation – was what was going to get Anna back, not negotiation or compromise.

He glanced at his neighbours. He wanted to feel part of this payback, that he wasn't just along for the ride. He caught Hendricks' eye. "These enemies of Harry's – who are they?"

"Crew that have been moving in from north London over the past couple of decades. Started out in Willesden, Kilburn, and been slowly making their way south. Been putting the frighteners on landlords and club owners, chancing their arm at protection rackets, and running the local pimps out of town. They got their fingers in the trafficking business – drugs and girls – and have undercut all the dealers with cheap shit. They're from Eastern Europe originally, I think, and are importing sixteen year olds from Slovakia, their colons stuffed with smack."

"And now they've reached Harry's territory?"

"Their head guy – Vassily – is an old rival of Harry's. One of his contemporaries. His mob has tried to broker with Harry, tried to persuade him to share. 'Course, Harry wasn't having any of it. He told them to piss off back to the arse-end of the Balkans before he put a boot under them. They didn't, and have been trying to chip away at his set-up ever since."

"I'm surprised Flowers hasn't taken this step before," Gabe said, motioning to the other men on either side of them.

"He has, or at least he's issued ultimatums. But the thing is, war is bad for the status quo. It just brings the heat down on you, and exposes business dealings to the authorities that you'd rather were kept out of sight. Actual engagement with the enemy is the last resort. But they've got less to lose than us, and they know it. They're still operating on the fringes of the underworld and are difficult to pin down, while Harry's got a reputation to consider. They're scavengers, provoking organisations into outright conflict and then stealing what crumbs they can in the aftermath."

The vehicles headed into the outskirts of the city, the roads virtually deserted at this hour apart from haulage lorries and coaches, and cleaning trucks scouring the gutters. The pavements were empty of pedestrians, save those that had made shop doorways their home. The night had the strange luminous quality that comes before the onset of dawn, a grey misty taint to the darkness beaded by the sodium smears of the street lights. None of the men in the car seemed tired, despite the hour. It was as if they had been preparing for this moment, and were ready to go to war as soon as the order was given.

"So where are we going to find them?" Gabe asked.

"Little bird on the Met has told us that a club in Ladbroke Grove is their HQ. Far as we know, they're unaware we've got this information."

"You think that's where they've taken Anna?"

Hendricks studied him for a second. "It's the only place we know where they could've gone," he replied finally. "They don't want her particularly, they just want to use her as a bargaining chip to get Harry to start cutting them a slice of his manor's action. So far Harry hasn't shown a weakness that they've been able to exploit, but tonight they're holding a trump card. Our only hope is that they don't expect him to come to them like this, mob-handed. They're banking on him seeking to appease them, not matching them strength for strength. It's a risky strategy, of course – Anna's life is at stake." He paused, then said: "You've really put him in a delicate situation."

Gabe nodded slowly. "I know."

Hendricks turned to face him. "This relationship with his daughter, it compromises an awful lot. We're going to have be very careful going in. What did you think you were doing?"

"She was a mystery, a face at the window. She looked like she needed a friend. I felt like I wouldn't be able to relax until I spoke to her, until I... solved the mystery." Gabe smiled ruefully. "I think I underestimated even that. She wasn't going to open up that easily."

"But was it worth it? You've incurred Harry's wrath, put his kid in the hands of the enemy, potentially undermined his power base if tonight doesn't go his way. If she gets hurt, it's going to get even worse, and I wouldn't want to be in your shoes. All this 'cause you couldn't leave things alone."

"If I knew that I was putting her in danger, then of course I would've stayed away. I'm not so selfish that I would purposely put her in the firing line. I thought I was giving her company. I never imagined that it would have consequences of this magnitude."

"Well, that's all it takes, son," Hendricks answered, peering out through the glass at the empty London streets. "One act and the repercussions ripple outwards. Everyone gets caught in them." The car started to slow, pulling in to the kerb. "Looks like we're here."

They came to a halt behind the lead vehicle, out of which Flowers' men were already unfolding themselves, the old man included. They stood on the pavement, casting glances up and down the road, pulling their coats around them, before fixing their attention on the building opposite. Gabe alighted from his own car and followed their gaze. An innocuous frontage to a club, little more than a narrow doorway squeezed between a motorbike dealership and a snooker hall. There was no name announcing itself above the entrance.

Harry nodded at his men, then motioned for them to follow. They strode across the street as one body, as if part of the darkness had suddenly come alive and was sweeping towards a specific destination. Flowers reached the threshold and a bouncer – shaven headed, bulky, biker's beard – emerged from the shadows just inside, blocking the passage. The thud of music could be heard drifting up from some cavernous place below them.

"Help you, gents?" he said.

"Here to see Goran," Harry replied, already trying to move past. "I imagine he's expecting us."

The doorman took a cursory look at the fifteen-strong gathering stood before the club and shook his head. "I don't think so." There was a slight accent to his voice, and each word was clipped.

"Oh, you don't think so?" Harry asked and pulled his snubnose from his belt with one movement, then shot him in the kneecap. The bouncer went down like a felled tree, the crack of the gun muffled by the noise emanating from inside. When the guy started to yell – a mixture of pain and a call for help, Gabe guessed – the old man struck him against the bridge of the nose with the flat of the revolver. He went quiet then. "Don't see much point in being subtle about this," Flowers murmured, then added: "Gandry, Miller – stay on the door. No one gets past you, understand? Oh, and disable the alarm system, phone line and the CCTV cameras."

The two men nodded. Flowers beckoned for the rest to come with him into the bowels of the building. They walked down a short corridor, the music growing louder, past a ticket booth, the woman inside watching them nervously, slipping off her stool and backing away when Hendricks halted and rested his gun barrel against the grille. He raised his eyebrows and instructed her to lace her hands above her head and not to move a muscle. There were four more security personnel loitering in this area, who jumped to their feet the moment that Harry strode into view, and who hit the ground just as quickly when he put a bullet through each of their thighs. They mutely rolled on their backs, their groans swallowed by the thumping bass.

"Stick them in there with her," Harry said to another three of his men, motioning to the booth, "and keep an eye on them. Any trouble, start working your way through their limbs." He turned to the rest. "I want this place locked down. We're in charge now – any nosy bastard starts poking around, asking questions or wants to leave, make an example of him. The last thing I want is a 999 call going out. From now until the moment we leave, this building is under *our* control. Once we get to the dancefloor level," he swept a hand towards the steep stairs that disappeared into a swirl of magenta and emerald lights, flickering to the pulse of the music, "you're going to spread yourselves amongst the crowd and contain it. The bouncers are going to notice you, but make your weapons known to them. If you can, take them out of commission altogether. From what I understand, Vassily's office is on the other side, next to the DJ booth. I'll be heading over there, and I want to make sure there's not going to be a riot getting in my way. OK?" His question was answered with silent confirmation. "OK. Let's go."

The remaining ten, with Harry at the head, picked their way down the steps and into the club proper. It was a horseshoe-shaped room, ringed by a bar on a raised area around which stood tables and stools. In the centre was the dancefloor itself. It was a dark mass of moving bodies. The roving lights would occasionally capture a face or an arm held aloft, but then they would be gone again, reduced to silhouette. There were more figures standing around the rim watching and drinking, but none seemed to have paid the new arrivals any heed. Flowers nodded and made a casual gesture with his hand, motioning left and right, and portions of the group peeled off, zeroing in on the bulky shadows that were undoubtedly the security staff, wordlessly encircling the space. The old man beckoned for Gabe to come with him and they pushed their way into the crowd, gathering glances from quizzical clubbers, who parted without question for the two men who wove their way through them, seemingly oblivious to the music. Something about their demeanour told the dancers not to get in their way.

To the right of the stage holding the pounding sound system was a door marked Authorised Personnel Only and Flowers headed towards it, looking back only once over his shoulder to confirm that Gabe was still behind him, and that the gyrating mob was concealing their progress. He put a shoulder to the door and shoved his way in, Gabe following closely in his wake.

After the darkness of the dancefloor, the fluorescent-bathed corridor on the other side caused them to squint momentarily, and the noise level fell instantly to a low-level throb. To the left and a few feet ahead was a large open section, containing a desk, computer and several filing cabinets. A man was leaning against a worktop with his back to them, writing hurriedly on a document.

"You get those orders sorted?" he called, without looking around.

When there was no response, he cocked an eye over his shoulder, frowned, then his eyes widened when Harry walked towards him, gun pointed at the man's face. He turned fully, dropping the pen.

"Where is she?" Flowers growled.

"Who the fuck are you?" the man spat, bravado failing to disguise his fear. "What are you talking about?"

"Unwise," Flowers said, and smacked him once in the temple with the revolver. The man gasped and staggered, blood trickling down his forehead from a gash. "Stall me again and I'll put a bullet through your eye. Last time: where is she?"

The man locked stares with Harry, red drips coursing off his eyebrow. "Goran's got her... in the back." He nodded behind him.

"I hope for your sake no one's touched her."

"She's still in one piece. Just about." He smiled. "For how long, though, I couldn't say. Once Goran finds Papa's here he might reach the limit of his benevolence."

"If he knows anything about me, then he'd have to be insane. Or suicidal."

"Funny. Your daughter said something similar about you –"

The man jerked as Flowers fired a bullet into his skull, collapsing into a heap at the old man's feet. Gabe jumped, the roar of the gun blast resonating in the spacious office. Harry didn't even pause, merely strode further down the corridor. The building this far back looked skeletal, as if it had been left half finished: exposed beams and wiring ran across the ceiling, and the bare floor and walls were plain concrete. There was little need to be surreptitious – Harry had all but announced himself, and a pair of Vassily's goons stepped forward ahead of their boss, who lingered beside a sofa. Anna was seated upon it, seemingly unharmed, her wrists and ankles unbound. She didn't appear scared, more resigned, as if this situation was inevitable.

"Nice place you've got here, Goran," Flowers said. "Love what you've done with it."

"You know I've never indulged in ostentation like you, Harry," Vassily replied. He was of a similar age to Flowers, and cut from the same cloth, a weathered exterior that bore the weight of a lifetime's experience.

"That why you're so keen to get your hands on what I've got? Envious?"

"I don't want everything, Harry. I just think a little competition could excite our profits a tad. We've known each other for so long, we've tolerated each other for decades now, we're in danger of growing stagnant and complacent. It never hurts to give the natural process of things a shove."

"So kidnapping's progress, is it?"

Vassily smiled. "Ah, you're just pissed you didn't get there first. Fortunately for me, my son is abroad."

"I'd say that *he* was the fortunate one. This way, he doesn't get to see me execute his old man."

Vassily's triggermen bristled, their guns raised, and Gabe felt his grip tightening around his semi-automatic. His gaze kept returning to Anna, but she – deliberately, he thought – studiously avoided making eye contact. He turned his attention instead to the exchange between the two bosses, trying to remain sensitive to the shifting levels of tension.

"Don't take it so personally, Harry," Vassily was saying. "It's all about gaining the advantage in this business, is it not? You have my word that not a hair on her pretty head has been harmed, and if we're all amicable, there's no reason why we won't all come away with what we want."

"You think I'm here to negotiate?"

"I don't see how you're in a position not to."

"Because there's over a dozen of my men stationed around your club right now, and all it takes is one word from me and they'll burn it and everyone inside to the fucking ground."

"You're not that ruthless. You were never one for collateral damage."

"Let's just say you've caught me in a particularly bad mood."

Vassily paused, looking first at Flowers, then at Anna and back again. "You'd commit mass murder for her sake? You'd kill innocent people rather than lose an inch of territory?"

"I'd slaughter you all because you involved my daughter. My terms are simple: return her now, and maybe I'll be lenient."

"Quite the family man these days, aren't you, Harry? It must've been hard losing your wife. What was it – an accidental overdose? Or at least, that was the official line." Gabe caught the sudden glance Anna gave her father. "I can imagine that must've strengthened the bond between you and your little girl."

"Goran, you're about five seconds away from meeting your maker," Flowers replied, anger flooding his voice, "so I suggest you shut the fuck up and tell your boys to lower their cannons."

Vassily continued speaking as if he hadn't heard. "Which makes what you did to *her*," he nodded at Flowers' daughter, "so particularly... callous."

Anna stood suddenly, glaring questioningly at her father, who glanced at her for the first time since they'd arrived. Vassily's two enforcers shifted their position, unsure at this development, keeping an eye on both of them. Gabe's thumb found the safety catch and eased it slowly off.

"Don't listen to him," Flowers said dismissively.

"What are you talking about?" Anna demanded of her captor.

"Oh, I'm sure it's just rumour and innuendo, my dear," Vassily said with mock modesty. "One of those stories you hear on the grapevine that knocks you back and makes you realise whether you really know a person."

"Goran –" Flowers snarled.

Anna: "Tell me."

Vassily faced her. "Your own child, Anna. The baby boy you gave birth to. Harry convinced you to put him up for adoption, took advantage of your fragile state as you suffered a particularly nasty period of post-natal depression. He claimed he didn't like the crew the father ran with, thought it would compromise his position. And while this may have certainly been the case – the guy was dropped off a flyover eight months later – the truth is that he always feared having an heir, a grandson that could prove a threat to him. That could undermine his power. So he took... pre-emptive action."

Gabe followed this exchange feeling like an eavesdropper on a family argument. He watched Anna's face intently. This was clearly news to her, and something suggested her world was about to be swept out from under her feet. Tears were welling in her eyes.

"He took your son, Anna," Vassily continued, "and he murdered him. Smothered him in his own blanket. Even if he put him up for adoption, there was always the fear that he would come to discover his heritage, and seek to claim it. This way, he could sleep easy."

Anna turned to Flowers, her cheeks glistening. "*Why?* How could you *do* this?"

"Anna, please..."

"You're not denying it, are you?"

Flowers looked more vulnerable than Gabe had ever seen him. "Sweetheart, I've tortured myself every day and night since, and I'll go to hell for it. Sleep easy? I will never, ever forgive myself for what I did, and I've tried to make it up to you. But there are no excuses."

"I don't understand how you could be so heartless," Anna sobbed. "Why did you do it?"

"Your child... was a weak link I couldn't control." Harry sniffed back his own tears. "I was wrong, I know. I should've embraced the life he brought, I should've let it steer me. But then... change was bad. I couldn't accept it."

"And there was me thinking you weren't open to negotiation," Vassily snickered.

Flowers glared at the other man, fury burning in his red-rimmed eyes. "You fucker." He raised his gun, but in that instant Vassily pulled Anna close and tugged free a revolver of his own from beneath his jacket, holding it to her waist.

"I don't think so, Harry," he said. "I realise this has all been very traumatic for the pair of you, but there's still a few more truths to be hammered home. It's time you recognised that you're in no position to refuse me anything. It's time we ought to discuss how we divide your empire."

"Never."

"I'm sorry, there was me believing you had a choice in the matter." He nudged the barrel harder into her body, though Anna looked as if she barely noticed it. She stared at her feet, numb with shock. Gabe licked his dry lips, eyes flicking between each of the people in the sparse room, head buzzing with adrenaline. "You've already destroyed whatever relationship you had with your daughter, don't go one step further and have her blood on your hands too."

"I won't give you anything." His gun remained where it was, unwavering. Vassily shook his head. "What makes you think you've got the strength to deny me?"

Flowers didn't reply. A second later he fired, the bullet slamming into Anna's chest, knocking her to one side. Vassily was momentarily stunned as he looked down to see the hole in his midriff where the slug had passed through his hostage and penetrated him. Flowers fired again, pumping a further four rounds into the man's midriff. Vassily's goons returned fire, blasting Harry in the arm and stomach, dropping him to the ground.

"Harry!" Gabe shouted, swinging his own weapon to bear and pulling the trigger. The recoil punched hard into his hand, and his first shots went wild, but he was standing at close enough distance to lower his angle and the two men took hits in the cheek and neck. They went down, spritzing blood.

He hurried across to Anna and felt her pulse; it was there, but weak. He turned to see Flowers crawling across towards them, painting a wide crimson streak in his wake.

"Harry, she needs an ambulance urgently. I don't know if she's going to make it."

"No," he whispered. "She comes back with us... back to the house... get the boys down here."

Gabe didn't move. "She could die. You might have killed your daughter." Flowers rolled onto his back. "Had to show... no weaknesses." He coughed. "Tell the boys... light the fuses. We burn this place down...." He closed his eyes.

"Harry?"

"Bring it all down," he murmured, then lost consciousness.

CHAPTER THIRTEEN

IT SPREAD WITH frightening speed. Despite Gannon's success at getting the facility immediately locked down and ordering in MoD medics garbed in full hazard suits, he hadn't reckoned on HS-03's microbes travelling in the air. All previous experiments with the virus had seen it carried within a liquid, whether it be the serum in which it was injected into the test subjects, its transportation through the blood supply, or – so he theorised – passed from carrier to victim via the saliva, which entered the circulatory system from the bite wound. He had believed that contagion would require full-body contact, and some degree of penetration, similar to HIV, and as such any threat to the general public could be limited. If they isolated the dead and those that had received injuries, then there was no chance of it going beyond the compound. But he had underestimated the tenacity of the virus. Once the security guard's bullets had ripped through the lab, test tubes and containment vessels were shattered, and the bacteria escaped into the ventilation shafts, blown beyond the research centre's walls in a matter of seconds. Although he would not learn of the breach for several hours, there was little Gannon could've done to stop it, and indeed the facility was permeated with HS-03 by the time he came off the phone to the emergency services.

It had no effect on the living, and there was nothing in the air to suggest its presence. As far as he and his team were concerned, the damaged samples merely represented a loss of six months' work, and he assumed that the virus expired the moment its solution came apart. He directed those that hadn't been evacuated to the upper levels to wear breathing apparatus as a precautionary measure, just in case there was the risk of any chemical vapours from the wrecked lab, but the virus had been passing through their lungs long before they donned their gas masks.

Gannon wanted to keep the resurrected that still remained for further study, but his colleagues – naturally upset at what had happened to Jenny Cranfield, Horton and Petley – pressured him into destroying them before there were any more casualties. They were obviously too dangerous to be moved elsewhere. Reluctantly, he went from subject to subject – there was just over ten of them left now – and slid a scalpel into the base of their skulls. They went immediately limp as all brain activity abruptly ceased.

He was sad to see so much research and experimentation being brought to a close with such finality, although a cruel, clinical part of his mind reminded him that a handful of walking dead were already brewing in the shape of the guards who had received bites in the melee. They were currently lying on gurneys out in the corridor, their injuries being treated as best they could in the circumstances. Gannon had refused requests from the medics to airlift them out of the compound to somewhere where they could receive better care, stating quietly – well out of earshot of the patients – that they were highly infectious. He didn't mention the fact that they were as good as dead, and when he instructed that their legs and arms were to be strapped he claimed that previous victims had been prone to seizure and psychotic episodes.

Exhausted, Gannon found a chair and gave himself five minutes rest. The events of the past couple of hours had passed with the inexorable unravelling of a nightmare, unstoppable and unreal – everything had leapt out of control so quickly, it now seemed absurd that he'd proudly shown Sedgworth these very labs only a few days before, confident that the HS-03 project could work. The Minister was no doubt aware of the failure that had resulted in three scientists' deaths (technically, Gannon supposed, at *his* hand) and an inquiry was going to be instigated. It wouldn't be public, of course, and the families of the deceased would be rigorously compensated to buy their silence, but there was no question that Gannon was for the high jump. Sedgworth himself could lose his position, and he wouldn't fall without taking a few with him.

The scientist closed his eyes wearily, but in his head he was faced with the bloodied vision of Jenny Cranfield staggering towards him, stiff and jerky, seeking him out through his warmth. Moments before she had been a living woman – intelligent, good-natured, conscientious – and because of what he had created she had been transformed into this creature, a horrible shadow of what she'd been in life. That was what was so painful – that she was still recognisably Jenny, someone he'd conversed with on a daily basis, but she no longer held any memories or traits that made her human. All this thing that had assumed her form wanted to do was kill and feed. It had subsumed all her civility and dignity, and made her in death something less than an animal. And *he* was responsible.

Cries from the injured forced him to open his eyes, and he stood, arching his back before heading towards them. He wondered if he would ever be able to come to terms with the consequences of what he had let loose here. The one crumb of comfort he clutched at was that at least HS-03 hadn't escaped into the wider world – the death toll could've been much, much higher.

As WITH ANY outbreak, the reports were scattered at first, small snapshots of terror and chaos that began to connect across the country with rapid speed.

A congregation gathered for a funeral service in Banbury were stunned into silence when loud thumps began to emerge from the casket; thinking impossibly that the person inside could somehow still be alive – an eighty-five-year-old grandfather, who'd died of pneumonia – half a dozen of the mourners had wrenched free the coffin lid, only to be confronted by a frenzied apparition that immediately sat up and tore his nephew's windpipe out with his hands.

In Wiltshire, four boys that had snuck into woodland near their homes with a copy of *Penthouse* purloined from one of the quartet's older brothers stood in fear as a groaning figure stumbled towards them, the needle from the heroin injection that had killed him still hanging from the crook of his arm. They had dropped the magazine and fled, their story dismissed as high spirits, until the first of the news items came on TV that evening.

On the Dorset coast, the crew of a fishing trawler lost at sea emerged from the water and shambled up the beach, blue and bloated from the days they'd spent drifting with the tide, and attacked anyone that approached them. Eight were consumed within an hour.

A surgeon fell into the corridor in a London hospital, his nose and half his lower jaw missing, when the body he was conducting an autopsy on had suddenly grabbed him. Moments after his appearance, the corpse itself had followed him out, still chewing on what it had ripped off. Those that had witnessed this later told authorities that they could hear rattling coming from the drawers in the mortuary.

And so it went, the violence spiralling with every passing minute. HS-03 seemed to be flexing its muscles too, growing stronger as it weaved its way amongst the populace. Those that received a bite but managed to flee from the ghouls took less than twelve hours to succumb to the fatal symptoms, resurrecting a scant fifteen minutes later. It was just enough time for the victims to seek solace with loved ones or descend upon a casualty ward before they themselves wreaked bloody havoc, doubling, tripling, the infection rate. Even those that had been partially devoured were on their feet eventually – or at least what remained of them. The dead evidently grew tired of their meals once they went cold, and would stumble off in search of something warmer.

The police were stretched thin from the outset. What started as vague bulletins of national unrest became a situation that was impossible to contain. Even when the army was drafted in, even when direct orders were issued to shoot all hostiles on sight (it didn't take them long to recognise that a bullet in the brain stopped the corpses instantly), the cops and the soldiers were unused to being asked to fire on unarmed women and children, and often made the mistake of trying to reason with the creatures. Despite repeated assurances that these things were no longer human, many believed that they could try to awaken latent memories of the dead's past life and corral them by non-lethal means. It didn't work. The ghouls would not be halted by words alone. They were implacable, remorseless, utterly mindless, and it was averaged later that the military lost a man every five minutes to an overwhelming enemy that was completely alien to notions of humanity and compassion.

Panic gripped the public as virulently as the infection itself. Roads were jammed with refugees fleeing the cities, the rail network and other services ground to a standstill as employees deserted their posts, and flights out of the country were cancelled when overseas airports started refusing to accept UK arrivals. Every nation around the globe closed down its borders, walling themselves in, cutting themselves off from their neighbours. It was rumoured that HS-03 snuck abroad despite these precautions, that – whether the bacteria survived being blown across the Channel or an infected traveller slipped through the net – it was rampaging across the Continent equally as fast; as far east as Russia, some said. By then it made little difference since the United Kingdom was losing all contact with former allies, even after the UN's appeal for aid. All the member states were frightened of the virus spreading, and as a consequence left the UK to fend for itself. For the citizens themselves, there was nowhere for them to go, no matter how far they ran.

Order broke down simultaneously. Although some banded together in anti-Returner squads – a priest had first coined the term in a TV interview, presumably as a non-pejorative, non-superstitious name for the phenomenon, and it stuck – to aid the authorities, many took the ensuing anarchy as a carte blanche to indulge in acts of criminality. Looting was rife, murder and rape commonplace; some seemed to have forgotten the dead were there at all. As lawlessness took hold, the streets became no-go areas, and survivors locked themselves away in shelters and communes, waiting for the news that it was safe to emerge.

In the meantime, the inheritors of this new land wandered their territory, driven by an insatiable hunger.

FLOWERS' CAR SPED away from the conflagration, the burning club lighting up the encroaching dawn. His men had given enough warning, Gabe hoped, for all those inside to have escaped before they snapped open the gas pipes and left the burning rags to set it off. Whether any of Vassily's enforcers made it was another question; he didn't see any amongst the frantic crowd that poured through the front doors. He expected that Harry didn't want word getting back as to who was responsible for the blaze.

The old man was drifting in and out of consciousness, sometimes lucid – thanking Gabe for his assistance – sometimes mumbling nonsensically under his breath. He had refused to be taken to hospital, stating that the mansion had adequate medical facilities to care for both him and Anna.

They were in danger of losing her, Gabe knew, as he constantly checked her pulse. Her skin was cold, and her heartbeat had slowed dramatically. She was so still and quiet he kept thinking that she had slipped away, but occasionally her eyelids would flutter open to fix him with a curious gaze before closing again. Something was keeping her hovering on the brink of death, fixed in a half-life stasis. He made a silent assurance to her that he wouldn't leave her side.

He had contemplated overruling Flowers' demands and getting her to a doctor, but as they sped out of the city it became clear that they shouldn't hang around. The radio was full of weird reports of some kind of mass disturbance, and that hospitals all over the country were being deluged with victims of those running riot. Ambulances and other emergency vehicles rocketed past, sirens blaring.

Gabe didn't know what was going on, but they had worries of their own to take care of. He watched the sun rise over the London skyline as they left it behind, wondering what the new day was going to bring.

PART THREE

Living With the Dead

My God! My God! Look not so fierce on mc!

Christopher Marlowe,
Dr Faustus

CHAPTER FOURTEEN

Fifteen Years Later

Mitch and Donna were taking a chance, moving in daylight, but the group was fast running out of alternatives. With the local food supply drying up, they were having to look further afield for rations, but straying onto rival gangs' territory brought its own dangers. They had lost half a dozen of their number to other humans protecting their stashes – Michael, the ex-teacher, had been the last casualty, shot through the neck with some kind of bladed projectile just over a month ago – and the zombs too were increasing their patrols, making a concerted sweep of all known haunts of the living. The general consensus amongst the survivors was that the larders of the dead were empty too, and they were processing fresh meat in greater quantities. This overriding feeling of desperation between both parties made the streets the last place anyone in their right mind would want to be.

But Mitch knew they had little choice. Liz and the others could barely stand, so ferocious was their hunger. Their physical weakness, the lack of protein and vitamins, had made them susceptible to infection, and with no easy access to clean water they had had to sup from whatever rainwater they could collect in drainage pipes. Sickness was rife, unsurprisingly, and the rudimentary medicines they had stored were not enough to treat it.

Mitch himself was not immune to illness. He was quick to lose his breath, and the dizzy spells and headaches that descended with a frightening force suggested that his blood was becoming perilously thin, but he had disguised his ailments sufficiently to convince his colleagues that he was fit to make this trip. They had looked sceptical, but he knew secretly that they had been praying someone would volunteer, too embarrassed to voice their selfish needs above others' suffering.

He had been aware of the risks well enough, and had to bury his own fears, lest the group fretted that he was not up to the task. He wanted to prove that they could rely on him, Donna especially. He wanted her to accept him as a useful part of the enclave, that he had a role to play, and wasn't merely another frightened survivor tagging along with whatever set of humans he could find and leeching off their supplies. Others had done that, over the years, with little sign of gratitude, then sloping off if they sniffed out a bigger trough to stick their snouts in. Liz meanwhile had been instrumental in bringing their band of survivors together, or at least reinforcing their need to look after one another. She maintained that it was those that separated from the main body of the group that were likely to fall victim to the Returners. They were like lions stalking their prey, she once said, zeroing in on the straggler that had fallen behind, or who had broken free from the herd. If they worked as one, however, they could present a united front.

Previously, he had always thought of himself as peripheral to the group, younger than most of them and not privy to the decision-making process, grudgingly content to go along with the final outcome, whether it was moving their settlement further from the zombs' patrol lines or dividing up rations. But recently it was his very youth that ensured his strength had endured while others had weakened, to the point where they had come increasingly to rely upon him aiding them in scouting enemy positions, fixing meals and tending to the wounded. The responsibility had brought a rush of personal pride that he had never experienced before, and rather than tire of it, he longed for more. He enjoyed them asking his opinion, listening to his views and taking it on board. He realised he was having an influence. It was a unique sensation that he quickly grew addicted to.

Hence his precarious position right now on the streets of Eltham. While their food situation was undeniably desperate, and someone was needed to replenish their stock otherwise they were going to starve, at the same time he felt his newfound sense of responsibility was being pushed to the limit. His nerves jangled, his skin prickling with unease, as the two of them sneaked along the pavement, their backs to the privet hedges of the silent council-estate houses that lined the thoroughfares, looking anxiously left and right for any signs of life (or, rather, the *absence* of it). Donna had insisted on accompanying him, arguing it was unsafe for anyone to go alone, and he certainly wasn't going to begrudge her presence. She had been one of the first of the group to befriend him, and had a deeply humane streak that he admired. She was a fierce fighter, too; a passionate and dedicated twenty-five year old.

Even so, he couldn't stop his hackles rising. He was deep in the heart of south London suburbia, an area he'd been familiar with since his childhood, and whose environs he'd explored with his friends, but it had never looked so alien as it did now. Gone were the comforting, reliable reminders of family – cars being washed in their driveways, the sound of lawnmowers drifting on the breeze, the smell of cut grass, children circling the roads on bicycles, their younger siblings toddling after on tricycles – to be replaced with a grey slate of emptiness. Nothing moved, nothing made a sound. Even the sky was featureless, a dirty squall of cloud hanging low and heavy over the landscape.

Despite the quiet, Mitch walked as if he was on a tightrope, holding his breath, rucksack bumping against his shoulders. He felt dangerously exposed out here, constantly under the impression that his progress was being monitored, and that any moment an alarm would be raised, the dead pouring from the buildings on either side to drag them within. It was not possible, he was sure; these houses had been sacked by the various bands of humans in the area, scoured for what little foodstuff they contained. Any ghouls that they'd encountered would've been quickly disposed of, and were no doubt now lying decaying in basements or back gardens. The houses were nothing more than shells, abandoned crypts gathering mould. Yet his imagination conjured all manner of tenants still lurking on the other side of the walls, awakening from dusty sleep at their presence.

If truth be told, the threat lay not in some rotting pusbag shambling into their path – these braindead stiffs were becoming increasingly rare, subject to the same laws of entropy as everything else – but the intelligent zombs and their organised meat purges. It was a phenomenon that few could have predicted; that the dead would start thinking for themselves and form an opposing faction against the living. When Mitch had first heard the rumours that deadfucks were starting to talk and going after their victims in consolidated attacks, he'd been in his teens and dismissed it as someone attempting to wind him up. Even when reports came back with greater insistence that the resurrected were not just randomly devouring warm flesh but collecting it for storage and processing in their self-styled 'body shops', he refused to accept the notion that the zombie was anything but a staggering cadaver with infantile reasoning power, that could be put down with a bullet to the head.

It wasn't until he finally witnessed one of their assaults – winkling out a small knot of survivors that had holed up in a decrepit garage in Deptford, senses as keen as a bloodhound's, moving quickly and purposefully, without the typical drunken zombie gait that he'd become accustomed to – that he realised the things were evolving. They were getting smarter and, in their coldly methodical way of gathering sustenance, more vicious. They seemed to have somehow halted their decomposition too, as if they were clawing their way back to being halfway human; or perhaps something else entirely. But they hadn't lost their appetite for the living, and didn't appear to be in any hurry to grow out of it. They revelled in their tyranny, enjoying the terror they instilled in what pockets of resistance they could uncover. They didn't seem to see their meals as anything more than a species below them on the food chain, farming them like cattle. In fact, the only thing they considered less than humanity was their cadaverous dim-witted cousins, whom they treated with utter disdain, often casually splitting their skulls with an arrogant brutality.

Mitch didn't understand how some of the Returners had reached this higher state of consciousness while others remained rooted in their initial resurrection condition. It had to be something to do with the virus that had brought the dead back in the first place, but his knowledge of such matters was limited. He had vague childhood memories of the news coverage, of the shaky camera footage of a ghoul staggering through a field being tracked by armed policemen, of the unnerving, panicky tone that had crept into the newsreader's voice, but no one in his family could help explain what had caused the outbreak. Even after he lost his parents and sisters, and had joined up with Donna, Liz and the rest, they had no scientists amongst their number to clarify the situation. They knew the basics – the dead want to eat you – and that seemed good enough. But he couldn't shake the feeling that the world was changing around them, and that the intelligent stiffs were a crucial signifier of that; the living were being forced to acknowledge that their time was over, and something new was coming to take their place. A next phase in evolution was just around the corner, and these ruthless inheritors of the earth were preparing to embrace it.

If he was sure of anything, it was that he didn't want to be taken in the meat purges. He had a small sharpened shiv tucked into his back pocket which he'd become adept at driving through the soft parts of a deadfuck's head – he had chalked up eight confirmed kills at the last count – and he had resolved that if he was ever seized by those smart maggoty bastards then he would thrust it into his jugular at the first opportunity. Naturally, no one who had been rounded up and transported to the body shops had returned, so his ideas of what fate awaited him were based on the flimsy rumours that filtered back through the human camps. A few brave souls had tried to observe the processing plants from a nominally safe vantage point, but little information could be gleaned other than that the

Returners wanted their food initially kept alive. It had been mooted that rather than slaughterhouses, the body shops were more akin to battery farms, the livestock permanently tethered and used as a source of warm flesh until their hearts finally gave out and the skin went cold. Quite how the stiffs had developed the technology to establish these factories was another mystery, but there was some agreement that there was a directing force behind it all, a guiding superior hand that they were working for – a King Zombie. Some big-brain ghoul had made plans and organised his brethren into a formidable army. If there was one thing worse than the creatures that walked the streets of the city, it was the possibility of some super-intelligent entity lurking at the black, rotting centre of it all.

Liz had suggested that they ought to try to capture one of the talking dead and interrogate the thing, gain some kind of knowledge of what they wanted other than to fill their bellies, how they operated, and the details of their set-up. But it would prove an impossible task. The smart ones moved in squads, just as the humans did, and none of the survivors were skilled enough in combat to tackle a group of the cadavers head-on. They moved surprisingly fast, and had picked up the principles of wielding weapons, so now they were twice as lethal as well as being virtually indestructible. It was a fight they couldn't win. The zombs were gaining ground all the time while the number of humans dwindled proportionately. Mitch wondered if his comrades' continued battle to exist – their perpetual quest for food, and struggle to overcome illness – was not a touch pointless in the face of such overwhelming odds; it was only a matter of time before the dead found them or they succumbed to sickness. Why keep trying when the future was as bleak as the grey slate sky above him? With little hope in a change in their circumstances, were they kidding themselves that this was any kind of life at all?

But he had made a promise, he told himself, as he and Donna reached the corner of the estate and peered down a side road, checking that the coast was clear. He had wanted to prove that he could be useful, and right now that was the most important matter at hand; giving up would simply be selfish, an act that aided no one but merely absolved him of all responsibility. And anyway, he didn't want to roll over for those deadfucks. As Donna had encouraged him to believe, while the living still had breath in their lungs, why shouldn't they carry on? They had every right to exist too, didn't they? Why make the stiffs' genocidal designs any easier?

Glancing around him, this was the part of town he'd suggested to Donna they check out. Although the area they were hurrying through had been considered looted empty, he knew enough about it from his past to believe there was a spot that might have been missed. It was a lock-up hidden from sight down a narrow alley, which backed on to a short parade of shops, one of which was a convenience store. The store itself had been gutted, stripped of everything that wasn't nailed to the walls, but Mitch was hoping that few were aware that the proprietor used the storage space to hold excess stock. Back in the day, he and his friends had watched the man carry jars and cardboard boxes into it before locking the shutter with a heavy padlock. They had held a certain childish romantic ideal between them about what the lock-up might contain, as if to step within was to be whisked to another world, but their crude attempts to force entry did not get them very far. Now, he thought, he might have the strength and tools to complete the job.

He spotted the entrance to the alley and scurried across the road, disappearing into its shadows, Donna behind him. He turned to her, wordlessly indicating with his head for them to continue, then strode towards the courtyard at the other end. The alley opened into an enclosed area, on one side of which was a fence separating the nearby houses' gardens and on the other a block of five garages, their once white exteriors scrawled with graffiti. A couple of the shutters had been wrenched open, and assorted bric-a-brac – an exercise bike, an old refrigerator, lawn furniture; possessions that had no possible value anymore – were visibly scattered within the darkness, filmed with grime and mildew. But his garage seemed still intact.

Mitch crouched and hefted the padlock. It was substantial, and not a little rusty, but apparently hadn't been tampered with.

"Can you keep an eye out?" he whispered. "This might make some noise."

"Sure." Donna unslung a baseball bat from her backpack. "Be quick."

"I'll try. It looks like it could be hard work."

He slipped his own rucksack from his back and unzipped it, pulling from it a hacksaw, hammer and pliers. He placed the hacksaw blade against the padlock and began.

It was as difficult as he feared, and noisier than he had expected, the metal squeal causing him to wince. And that was before he set about it with the hammer, the dull thrumming resounding off the surrounding walls, his arms aching from the vibration. Sweat glued his shirt to his back, and his hands were red and sore, but he did not stop, confident that the lock was twisting in its housing. At last it bent and snapped, and he let out a restrained whoop of triumph. Donna slapped him on the back. He kicked it free, then yanked on the shutter, straining to push it upwards; it resisted, unused for over a decade, and he and Donna had to put all their weight behind it to get it to move even a few inches. After rising a foot and a half, it wouldn't open any further, so Mitch dropped to his knees, retrieved a slender flashlight from his bag and shone it into the blackness. The beam illuminated the outlines of crates stacked on top of each other, and glimmered against glass bottles lining makeshift shelves.

"Reckon we've hit the jackpot," he said, casting an eye to a smiling Donna. "Stacks of stuff in there. I'm going to take a closer look."

"You can't carry it all by yourself," she protested, moving closer to help.

"I'm just going to see what's usable. I'd feel happier if you stayed out here, in case the shutter's unsafe. We don't want to be both trapped in there."

"Okay. But be –"

"– quick, I know." He grinned and squeezed her arm.

He put the torch between his teeth and slid onto his stomach, wriggling his way into the garage, the lip of the shutter pressing against his back; as an afterthought, he reached round and wedged the hammer into the gap as an extra precaution.

Once inside, he stood and surveyed the contents of the lock-up, sweeping the torch before him. Seconds later, the smell of rotting vegetation hit him as he caught glimpses of pallets of liquefying tomatoes and deflated apples. Muttering under his breath and covering his mouth and nose with his sleeve, he moved closer, his mood lightening when he saw the stacks of tins. He picked a selection up: potatoes, beans, peas, soup. The contents were several years past their sell-by date, and their labels were encrusted with dirt and dangling with spider husks, but they were the most edible things he'd seen for the best part of a month. He caught sight too of a pack of bottled water, the liquid inside cloudy with age but nevertheless clearer than the rainwater they'd become accustomed to drinking.

"Some great stuff here, Donna," he called. "I'll bring some out. We could fill both bags, I reckon. Might even need extra trips."

There was no reply. Assuming that she couldn't hear him through the shutter, he began to place as many cans and bottles inside his rucksack as he could physically carry. He smiled to himself; he was already picturing Liz's face when she saw his haul, and then her grin broadening even further when he told her there was more to collect. He liked the feeling he got when he was the bearer of good news for a change.

He pushed the bulging bag through the gap beneath the shutter, then squeezed his way after it, squinting in the daylight after the building's gloom and wiping the cobweb strands from his face.

"Donna? You want to take a look in there yourself?" He got to his knees, looked up and froze.

Four Returners were standing at the mouth of the alley watching him. They were smart ones, evolvers. Although not as visibly putrescent as their brainless kin, their skin was still tight and brittle where it had shrunk, and one's mortal wound – a huge rent in its neck – was readily apparent. Also unlike the average zomb (who usually looked like they'd crawled out of a grave backwards), they took a certain pride in their appearance, evidently swiping off-the-peg suits from the remains of department stores; no doubt behaviour stirred by latent memories. What immediately separated them from deadfucks, though, was the fact that they could see a human, rather than sensing them through their warmth. The four of them cast a baleful gaze over Mitch, flicking their milky-white stare for a second to the lock-up, before returning to settle on him.

A fifth stood behind them, its hand clamped over Donna's mouth, her arms twisted behind her back. Her eyes bulged in fear, and silently pleaded to Mitch for help. Her bat lay in two pieces on the other side of the courtyard.

As one, the Returners started to walk forward, their stride stiff but purposeful, and without instruction slowly began to fan out around the width of the enclosed space. The one in centre nearest Mitch unhooked a truncheon from its hip and gripped it in its bony fist.

Getting to his feet, Mitch cursed the noise he must've made shattering the padlock, imagining the echoes drifting down the still streets, pricking the ears of a passing patrol. It had been risky, he knew, but he'd hoped they would be gone before the alarm was raised.

"You come with us," the stiff in front of him said, the words not so much spoken as falling from its wrinkled lips. There was no inflection, the dead language carried like wind whistling through its voice box. It was the first time he'd been addressed by the resurrected, and it was as chilling to hear as he'd thought it would be. "You come now," it reiterated.

Mitch couldn't reply, his mouth dry, and stepped backwards. The other ghouls to either side of him also drew blunt weapons – they wanted he and Donna alive, he reasoned, but they were willing to break a few bones to make them more manageable – and closed in. His hand went to his back pocket and unsheathed his knife, remembering the vow he'd made; it would be easy enough to open his throat before they even got within grabbing distance, and he'd be useless to them. Bleeding like a stuck pig, they would only be able to watch helplessly as the life they coveted drained out of his body. He brought the blade up behind him, steeling himself. If he went deep enough, it was possible he could sever his spinal column and stop himself from returning. From becoming like *them*.

But one look at Donna, struggling in the clutches of the dead, forced him to dispel the notion. He wasn't going to leave her in their hands.

"Come now," it said again. "Or we take you by force."

Mitch glared back at it, hate swelling up inside him, loathing these creatures and the atrocity they had wrought, the millions that had died to feed their insatiable hunger. He felt blood trickle down his palm as he clutched the knife even tighter. He wasn't going to give these fucking maggots anything.

With a speed that surprised even him, he lashed out and powered the shiv into the nearest Returner's left eye, the three-inch blade burying itself into its socket. The orb popped like a balloon, vitreous liquid sprinkling his hand. The momentum of the attack carried Mitch forward and he tumbled over the stiff as it collapsed to the ground. He lost his grip on the knife and it remained rooted in the thing's head, just half an inch of the handle protruding below its brow. But it had seemingly penetrated far enough to reach the brain, because the zombie lay motionless, blood trickling from its nose and ruptured eye to form a widening pool on the flagstones.

The other ghouls were moving, though, advancing on him quickly. He rolled, seeking out a weapon, and his gaze settled on the hammer. Tugging it free from beneath the garage door, which crashed shut behind him, he swung round to face his enemies. One of them caught his wrist with its club and pain juddered up his arm, knocking him sideways. It stalked closer, and bounced the truncheon off his temple, forcing him onto his knees. His vision swam and his head throbbed. He fell onto his back, stars exploding behind his eyes, as the Returner towered above him, drawing back to administer a final blow. Before it could make contact, however, he ducked and swerved, smashing the hammer down on its ankle, which splintered with an audible crack. The ghoul tottered, lost its balance then fell, its shinbone shearing off completely.

Mitch crawled over to it, struggling to right itself like an upturned beetle, and slammed the hammer down into the middle of its face, the thin tissue caving in with a wet crunch. He hit it again and again, with as much strength as he could muster, unaware of the yell of rage and frustration that he was emitting, punctuating each cry with another strike, until its skull had all but disintegrated, pink globules of brain matter squeezing between the shards. He would've carried on, had the air not caught in his throat when another of the stiffs yanked its cudgel under his chin and pulled him away, the weapon held hard against his windpipe. He fought to breathe, dropping the hammer and bringing both hands up to wrest it free. Meanwhile, the fourth creature circled in front of him and delivered savage blows to his ribcage and belly, Mitch barely able to fill his lungs to scream. He felt unconsciousness seeping into him, and his legs grew heavy.

"Good," the zomb before him said between strikes, its mouth spread wide into a rictus grin. "I like meat tender."

"You watch us strip flesh from your bones," the one standing behind him added, its thin, emotionless voice filling his ear. "You watch us eat you alive."

"Go to hell," he whispered, coughing the words free, tears beading at the corners of his eyes.

The first one lowered its club, took a step forward and wrenched open Mitch's lower jaw, taking the tip of his tongue between forefinger and thumb in a tight pinch. "Think we have a taste first. Tired of hearing it whine." It glanced at its partner. "Keep it still." It looked back at the Returner holding Donna. "Take that one back. We be along shortly."

Mitch moaned, watching in horror as Donna was frogmarched down the alley and out of sight, her muffled cries diminishing. He wrestled against his captors, but they held him firm. The Returner grasped his tongue and put its other hand against his forehead, to brace itself. He squeezed his eyes shut, tasting the ghoul's graveyard residue in his mouth, waiting for the inevitable sharp stab of agony to blossom alongside it.

It didn't. Rather, there was release.

Suddenly, the pressure around his neck was gone, and he dropped to the floor, sucking in air, aware that his tongue was still intact. He wiped his face with a shaking hand, and gazed around him. The head of the zombie that had been restraining him lay close by, face expressing a note of surprise; its body was several feet away, slumped against the lock-up.

Mitch scooted backwards, uncomprehending, and let out a shout of startled surprise when its colleague hit the ground like a felled tree to his right, a machete embedded in its scalp. He looked it straight in the eyes as the life dimmed from them and a watery dribble of blood spilled from its lips. He was still staring at it when a hand reached down and ripped the machete free. At last, he glanced up at the figure standing over him.

It was another Returner, wiping the crimson streaks off the blade with its jacket sleeve before sliding the weapon into its sheath. The creature made a gesture to help haul him up.

"Come on," it said. "Not going to hurt you."

Mitch feverishly shook his head, tried to scrabble to his feet and promptly fainted dead away.

CHAPTER FIFTEEN

MITCH BECAME AWARE of something soft enveloping him before he fully returned to consciousness; he was sinking back into it, his hands sliding across its surface, his head rolling unsupported. It was vaguely comforting but it unsettled him too. There was a distasteful smell that he couldn't turn his face from, and the material beneath his touch was firm but yielded a greasy residue. As he slowly opened his eyes, colours swirled before them, muted reds and greens fading to black. When the images finally coalesced into a pattern that his fuzzy brain could make sense of, he realised he was looking at a bank of entwined roses, their petals seemingly smeared with ash. He blinked and wiped the grit from his lashes, then refocused: it was a sofa design, he ascertained at last, repeated across the cushions and arms, and the grey dusting was grime, as if the piece of furniture had been left undisturbed in a locked room for a very long time. He was sitting up, his head slumped to one side, cheek resting on his shoulder. The stench was coming from the sofa too, dampness mixed with neglect, and in a bid to escape it he leaned forward and put his elbows on his knees, massaging his temples with his fingers, trying to recollect what had happened.

"You're awake," a voice said somewhere in the gloom.

Mitch's senses instantly came alive. His head snapped up and he peered about him. The room was in shadow, but his eyes were becoming accustomed to the darkness, aided by the thin shards of light that pierced the curtains pulled shut across the windows. It was a lounge, but one that hadn't seen life within it for quite some time. The TV in the corner and the Welsh dresser against the far wall were similarly bedecked with cobwebs, framed family photographs hanging above the mantelpiece turned almost opaque with dirt. From what he could see, he didn't recognise the faces smiling out at him. There was a wooden dining chair standing conspicuously in the centre of the carpet, and upon it was seated an unmoving figure, evidently watching him, even though at the moment it was just an outline from which it was impossible to discern any features.

He heard breathing close by, heavy and ragged, only to realise that it was his own. He held it for a second, and in the silence that followed came to the conclusion that he was the only living thing in the immediate vicinity. Then he remembered the Returner that had offered its hand, and the way that it had wiped its gore-streaked machete blade across its jacket sleeve. He must've blacked out.

"How are you feeling?" it asked. "Are you hurt?"

The rush of questions that had surfaced in his mind upon awakening had superseded any physical pain, but as he considered the query he was aware that he was indeed in some considerable discomfort. His right forearm throbbed where he had been struck, and when he put a hand to his chest he winced at its tenderness. No wonder his breathing sounded so strained, he thought. It was possible that several of his ribs had been fractured and were pressing on his lungs. He felt like a mass of bruises, in which each new movement would lead to a fresh ache. Despite its mildewy stink, right now he didn't have the energy or the inclination to leave the sofa. If he was in danger, then so be it, he had little left to defend himself with. But he guessed he was safe from harm for the moment; he would've been carved up like a Sunday roast long ago if all this thing wanted of him was a snack. He didn't know how or why it was acting differently to the others, but he couldn't pretend he wasn't grateful.

Mitch cleared his throat. "How... long have I been out?"

"Few hours. Thought you might be concussed." It paused, then added: "You can understand what I'm saying?"

He nodded. "I'm OK. At least, I think I am. No impairment up here, anyway." He tapped his forehead. "Bit battered elsewhere, but I'll live." He bit his tongue, wondering if the creature would regard that as a sly dig, then admonished himself for worrying about insulting a stiff. In any other circumstances, he wouldn't hesitate in trying to ram a spike through its brain. "I... I guess I've got you to thank for that. I'm not sure I'd be in one piece if you hadn't come along."

It didn't reply for a moment, then said: "You put up quite a fight."

There was something slightly sinister about its declaration, as if it were making a grudging statement of approval about the liveliness of its prey. But it didn't elaborate any further. Suddenly, the image of Donna's frightened eyes sprang into his mind, a zombie's hand clamped over her mouth. "Shit, Donna –" He tried to stand, and regretted it, his legs wobbly beneath him. "Is she OK? Did you get her back?"

The figure shook its head. "They had gone."

"Hell, we gotta go after her. They'll have taken her to be processed."

"I know. They've adapted a school near here, St Jude's, into one of their body shops. That's where she'll be taken."

"So let's *go!*"

It shook its head. "There'll be too many of them for the two of us to handle. We'll go after your friend soon enough, but we'll need back-up."

"But in the meantime she could be torn apart."

"They'll want to keep her alive for as along as possible. There's still time. But we should lie low for a while, wait until dark. There's no reason why our handiwork would be found for days, but in my experience it pays to be careful."

Mitch sat in silence, a mixture of frustration and fatigue gnawing at him. Eventually, he asked: "Where are we?"

"One of the houses nearby. They're all deserted round here."

"You carried me?"

"You weren't going to waltz in by yourself."

Although he should've been appreciative of its actions, Mitch couldn't help feeling prickly at the thought of the dead thing touching him. It triggered the ingrained hatred he had against Returners and he sensed himself becoming more defensive. "You're one of them, aren't you? One of the flesh-eaters."

It said nothing.

"Why did you save me? Why attack your own kind?"

Again, there was no reply. But instead the silhouette stood and stepped towards him. As it moved closer, Mitch could gain a better appreciation of its features: it looked remarkably fresh for a ghoul, the pinched, tight texture of its skin the most visible sign that it had resurrected. There was a blackened patch on its chest, and its shirt was stained with similar dark areas, but there was a looseness to its posture and gait that was unlike even the smart zombs. It didn't stagger or jerk, and the eyes still had some spark of humanity behind them. It had been a man in his early thirties when it had died, and it was as if a tiny fragment of his former life had stayed trapped in that shell when the virus had worked its magic. It leaned over him, one hand on the back of the sofa, and put its face close to his.

"They're not my kind," it said, an eerie lack of breath behind its words. "So consider yourself fortunate I got to you first. If you're worried I'm going to eat you, relax. I didn't bring you here for a picnic."

Mitch leaned back, aware there was nowhere he could retreat to. "How can I trust you?"

It cast an eye over each shoulder before turning back to look at him, shrugging; a disarmingly human gesture. "You have a choice?"

Mitch found himself relaxing, despite himself. This thing was far too eloquent, far too self-aware, for a stiff. "What are you? You're like no Returner I've seen before."

It straightened, walked back to its chair, picked it up and brought it closer to the sofa, then sat down. "I am what I am. I can offer no other explanation than that."

"You are undead, though? You've resurrected?"

It nodded.

"Can you remember who you were? Do you have a name?"

"My name is Gabriel, and I can remember everything. As far as I am concerned, there is little difference between my states of being, pre- and post-death. Perhaps I notice the chill more these days, that's all."

"But you're a deadhead. You don't breathe, your heart doesn't beat..."

"You get used to it."

"And the flesh-eating? You get used to that to?"

It looked away. When it replied, its voice was low and steady. "It can be controlled."

Mitch was incredulous. The creature was right, in a way; conversing like this, there was little difference between it and a living being. It was just one shade away from human. But even so, it was still on the other side of the divide, and thus couldn't be entirely trusted. For all its apparent intelligence, it surely must have dangerous urges that he should be wary of. "How long have you been like this?"

"A decade, perhaps more. Time loses all meaning." It looked down at itself. "I'm... not changing. I'm growing no older, like I'm frozen."

"What happened to you? I mean, what killed you?"

It parted its jacket and gestured to the dark circular patch on its chest, a hole ripped in the material of the shirt. "Shot," it said simply. It fingered the entry point sadly.

"By whom?"

"By someone who is due a reckoning."

GABE HAD MADE sure he was on his very best behaviour, talking to the human. Mitch needed to be convinced that Gabe wasn't a threat to him or his friends, if they were to be any use, and so he swallowed the raging hunger that clawed his hollow belly and diligently answered his questions. Mostly, he told the truth. He told him that he had worked for a criminal called Harry Flowers, and that his employer had believed he'd turned traitor and had him executed. He told him that he'd been bitten by a ghoul and taken a bullet in the heart, and that for what seemed the briefest time he'd floated through darkness, pulled inexorably towards a destination he couldn't visualise. Only when he thought he'd arrived did he open his eyes and stare at the cold light of day. His body had been slung beyond the boundaries of Resurrection Alley, and he was lying amidst the shambling crowds of the dead, who battered disinterestedly against him. All life had long since left him, and therefore he had little to offer them.

Gabe had stood, on the day of his resurrection, conscious of the stillness of his pulse and the sour taste of his final breaths at the back of his throat, and realised he had some semblance of his wits about him. At first, he'd wondered if was truly dead, if somehow he hadn't passed over, impossible as that was to believe, since his mind was so clear and precise. But his skin was icy to the touch, and when he ran his hand over his chest wound his fingers came away coated crimson. The zombs ignored him too, obviously regarding him as one of their own. There could be little doubt that he had joined the ranks of the undead. Shock hit him like a tsunami, and he had staggered away to some private corner to come to terms with his new cadaverous state in his own way.

But his body had stopped working, and he could no longer weep, try though he might. Inside his head, he howled and cried, but nothing would emerge from the dead shell he was shackled to. It was like trying to shout in a vast, echoing room. When he had regained his mental composure, he struggled to recollect everything that had brought him to this point, and he was amazed to discover that he could focus on it all: Flowers, Anna, Hewitt, Vassily's undead father, everything. He could even remember his own name. He could think for himself, make free associations, memorise faces from the past. This was not what being a Returner was meant to be. Surely he should be a mindless stiff, driven by the need for warm flesh?

At that moment, two things happened. He became aware of a scratchy sensation in the pit of his stomach that had somehow always been there but he had not considered; and the civil servant Fletchley's words floated back to him about how the ghouls were learning, that the virus was working on their brains. The scratch became an ache, and Gabe knew that he had not escaped the full state of zombiehood, despite his clearly advanced status. He had a hunger that was growing with intensity all the time, and it could not be dismissed.

It was around this element that Gabe deviated from what was strictly true. He had told Mitch that his craving for warm meat was an addiction that could be controlled, and while he managed to keep the stabbing pains in his belly fairly low-level, they would not be denied for ever. In the years since he'd resurrected, he'd managed to assuage the need when it became too great by feasting on what vermin and stray pets he could catch, the thin, bitter flesh just keeping a lid on his hunger. It was a frustrating and demeaning position to find himself in, his self-awareness pointedly reminding him of the levels he was stooping to: chasing half-starved, diseased animals for their scraggly hide. He almost envied the rank-and-file ghouls and their mindless consumption. But that very intelligence he possessed ensured he could not devour the humans, no matter how strong the cravings became. He told himself that he would not sink that low, that there was still some vestige of the man he'd once been inside the Returner he'd become. Even so, close proximity to the living awakened an appetite that verged on the carnal, and it was this that he would have to keep in check around the kid's colleagues. It was unlikely that he'd snap and rip a chunk out of someone's throat, but he might get distracted, which could be dangerous for all of them. And if they got wind of the fact he was looking at them like they were his next meal, they were going to stave in his head at the first opportunity.

So he had assured Mitch that his diet was not a problem, and the kid seemed to believe him; or said he did, at least. Gabe knew he'd have to cross that bridge when he came to it. Working with humans was always going to be tricky, even without the ceaseless demands of his stomach.

Having waited several hours for night to fall, Mitch was leading him back to his group's hideout in a deserted pub on the outskirts of Blackheath, the two of them carrying what they could snaffle from the lock-up. Gabe's assistance had gone some way to soothing the younger man's fears and cementing an element of trust, to the point where he was willing to take the Returner to meet his friends. There would be some explaining to do, Gabe envisioned, and more than a few threats to suffer. But he'd outlined a little of his plan to Mitch, who'd been anxious to volunteer his services, and by proxy that of his fellow humans, if only to rescue his friend, Donna, whom Gabe believed Mitch was more than a little sweet on. When he'd told him that he believed Harry Flowers was now the power at the centre of the city, that it was he all the organised zombies reported to, and that the living were being farmed on his orders – and that Gabe was determined to take the grizzled old fuck down – Mitch had thrown his full weight behind the scheme. Gabe got the impression that the kid reckoned that by taking out the ganglord, things would return to normal. He wasn't going to dissuade him if it guaranteed his help, but as far as he was concerned normality was a very long way away indeed.

"You mind if I ask you something?" Mitch asked as they hurried through the moonlit streets. He had gained some degree of confidence being in Gabe's company, feeling protected from the other stiffs by walking alongside one.

"Go ahead."

"How did you learn to talk? You said that when you resurrected you were trapped in a dead shell. Was it something you remembered from your past life?"

"Partly. I understood the language as much as I did before I died; it was just a matter of getting my mouth and tongue to coordinate once more. I listened to tapes and practised until the sounds that emerged from my throat were formed into words. It wasn't easy. We're talking a period of five years or more."

"You could hear too, then?"

Gabe nodded. "It was like the senses were all there, I simply needed to retune them to a different frequency."

"Are the other smart Returners – the ones that work for Flowers – like that? Have they learnt like you?"

He was amused by the kid's insistent interrogation. He supposed it was the first time a survivor, who'd spent a good portion of his life battling an enemy he couldn't reason or empathise with, had gained inside information on what made them tick. The zombies' basic carnivorous motivation was pretty straightforward, but there were always the questions that nobody had yet found an answer to: why did they continually want to eat, especially when their bellies were incapable of processing the nourishment? Why were some regaining their pre-death motor skills? What did they plan to do when they had devoured everything on the planet? The ghouls were a species mankind had yet to fathom. Even Gabe was at a loss to explain what the virus was doing inside his head, what primal functions it was adapting for its own end. And indeed, what end was that? That bacteria had brought the dead back to life and given them cannibalistic tendencies – a goal it had achieved quite spectacularly – but what was the next step? What would it progress to next? How would it develop?

"I suspect so," he told Mitch. "But their learning seems rudimentary, like they've just mastered the basics. You've heard them talk?"

"Yeah. They're kinda slow."

"I think their brains aren't quite as knitted together as mine. They're taking longer to pick things up."

"But why you? How did you get so to be advanced?"

Gabe shook his head. "Your guess is as good as mine. Maybe the virus found a natural home in my physiology to take hold. But I can tell you that I'm not alone – there're others like me, in similar states, with more growing all the time."

Mitch stopped dead and turned to him. "More like you?"

"A veritable Dirty Dozen. Or a Filthy Five, at least." Gabe tapped him on the shoulder and indicated that they should continue. "But we need more recruits."

As EXPECTED, MITCH'S friends came within a hair's breadth of putting a bullet between Gabe's eyes on first introduction. The zombie had had guns thrust in his face before, and he had become accustomed to staying calm looking down the length of a shotgun barrel, but that didn't mean he didn't tire of it eventually. As an act of conciliation, he had removed the machete from his belt and laid it on the ground, his hands held up to show he meant no harm. But it seemed to cut little ice with the humans, who regarded him with open hatred. Their attention was divided between keeping the Returner securely in their sights, and arguing with the kid for bringing it to their door and being naive enough to trust it.

Gabe's patience was wearing thin, and he was getting nervous that someone's trigger finger was going to twitch. They were a sorry-looking bunch, skinny and unhealthy, a few cold months away from death's door, and dressed like refugees; typical of the many batches of humans scratching a living among the ruins. Not counting Mitch, there were eight of them in total – four men, three women and a young girl, hunched up on a chair, pale and painfully frail – and it seemed one of the women was nominally in charge; or at least the others looked to her for decisions. Liz, she was called. Broadly built and in her early forties, she had the air of a well-heeled PA about her, someone who once presided over a tidy, efficiently managed office. Despite the dirt-smeared jeans and shapeless T-shirt she wore, she exuded an unmistakable corporate attitude. The kid had breathlessly explained the evening's events, insisting they mount a rescue mission to save Donna, and pulling open the bags they'd brought with them and displaying the booty, which earned more than a few murmurs of appreciation from the others. Liz had nodded and listened, refreshingly cool-headed, despite casting the occasional sour glance Gabe's way.

"It's a deadfuck," the guy with the twin-bore snarled, the tip of the weapon no more than a couple of inches from Gabe's nose. "They never change."

"I think you'll find they're changing all the time," Gabe replied. "Or hadn't you noticed?"

"I say you could talk, maggotbrain?"

"Easy, John," Liz said. "It's not any threat at the moment. And you've got to admit, we've never come across one like this before. It's clearly of a different stripe to the collectors."

"Collectors?" Gabe raised any eyebrow at Mitch.

"The smart zombs that patrol the streets, rounding up what living they can find. The ones that took Donna. They collect them in trucks and ship them off to the nearest body shop."

The Returner nodded slowly. "I know."

Liz studied him distastefully. "You were part of them? Part of that... organisation?"

"No, I've merely observed them." Gabe returned her gaze. "I've been out on the streets for over half a decade, trying to find out more about who is behind it all, who's marshalling these undead troops."

"This is bullshit –" John snapped, but was silenced by a glare from the woman.

"What do you know?" she asked.

"The processed humans are being used to feed the intelligent dead, I guess you've assumed that much," Gabe told them. "But the majority of the living are being delivered to the brains behind the organisation – his name is Harry Flowers. He's taken over Resurrection Alley – his cronies are responsible for the human entertainment that goes on there – and he's got a safe house on the outskirts of the city. Basically, any patrols you see on the streets report to him. For the past five years, he's been tightening his grip around London, bringing it within his power."

"This Flowers guy is a Returner?"

"Yes. And if I thought he was threatening in life, I had no idea just how dangerous he could be in death."

"Wait," Liz said, her brow furrowing. "You're saying you knew him before he died?"

"*Knew* him?" Gabe gave a little shake of the head. "I think it was me that killed him."

The group of survivors exchanged glances, John adjusting his grip on his shotgun. Mitch looked anxious, as if he was wondering if he'd just made a colossal mistake. Liz merely indicated with her hand for Gabe to elaborate.

"I worked for Flowers. In life, I mean," he continued. "He was a... a gangster, I suppose you'd call him. On the surface he was a legitimate businessman, owned clubs and bars in the capital, but he was involved in a number of shady deals, and wasn't averse to intimidation to get what he wanted. I was just his driver. I was never privy to the sharp end of his transactions. That sounds like a weak excuse but it's the truth: for the most part I was never involved in the criminal side of his business. That ended when the shit came down."

"The outbreak," Liz said.

Gabe nodded. "When everything fell apart, it became clear there was safety in numbers. It made sense to stay with Flowers' outfit. Plus, I don't think I could've walked away, even I had wanted to. I'd become... involved." He paused, head bowed. "The authorities lost control, and Harry seemed to know what to do to fill the vacuum, to take advantage of the crisis. We became thieves and hijackers, consolidating our strength. The world changed and I changed with it. I embraced my place in the new scheme of things, because there seemed no way back to the old one. The boss promised order and rule – under his terms, naturally – and I signed up for it, played my part in ushering it along."

"And you killed him...?" Liz asked.

"Things got fucked up. Flowers thought I sold him out, and had me executed. But before I died, I stabbed him with a syringe full of the virus sample. I'm guessing here, but I think it killed him. Not only that, but it may have accelerated his post-death development, to the point where he can coordinate the other smart zombs for his own uses..." He shrugged. "I don't know, I'm not one of the boffins that engineered the thing, but it seems feasible. Something's been motivating the dead over the past few years, getting them to work together."

There was silence as the humans all regarded him warily. He couldn't blame their reluctance to trust him – he certainly wouldn't, if the situation were reversed – but he hoped that they could see past their reservations to recognise that he was offering them their first real chance at striking back at the ghouls. The dead had been an inscrutable enemy up to this point, but through him they could assimilate an attack plan.

"Why are you doing this?" a rat-faced man with shoulder-length hair and round glasses asked, stepping forward from the group. They turned to listen to him speak. "What's it to you that we don't all fall victim to this Flowers?"

"Revenge, pure and simple," Gabe replied flatly. "I want to bring him down." *And save someone too,* he mentally added. "I need your help to do that. But either way, we both get what we want by having him removed. Plus, I can help you save your friend." He pointedly looked at Mitch.

"And what's to say you won't turn on us the same way you've sold him out?" John remarked. The others murmured their assent.

"Because once this is over – one way or another – you won't ever see me again. Beyond that, you'll just have to take my offer at face value. The choice is yours. If you're not interested, I'll go find another bunch of humans willing to take the risk."

Liz reached out and placed her hand on the top of John's shotgun, gently lowering it. He threw her a questioning look, but she gave a reassuring nod.

She turned her attention to Gabe. "I still don't understand – where do we fit into the plan? What do you need *us* for?"

He gave the approximation of a smile. "You're still warm flesh, aren't you?"

CHAPTER SIXTEEN

THEY SPOTTED THE HUMAN immediately, rooting amidst the rubble, seemingly oblivious to the danger that he was in. He was working his way through a short parade of blackened shops, pulling away soot-stained planks of wood and charred furniture to find something worth salvaging. The stores themselves had been nothing of note before they'd been put to the torch – a downmarket carpet warehouse, a bookmaker's, a laundrette, a newsagent and a Chinese takeaway, situated on a sombre stretch of dual carriageway and bracketed by a pair of high-rise flats – and it appeared unlikely on first inspection that anyone would find anything of value within their crumbling walls. Indeed, there was an air of desperation to the figure as he tossed debris over his shoulder, scrabbling on hands and knees sifting the ash, and hammering at the warped filing cabinets and desk drawers in a bid to open them. He was so intent on his task, and taking so little care in attracting attention through the noise he was making, that they wondered if the balance of his mind was disturbed. Maybe one of these buildings had been a business of his and he was trying to restore what was once his. Surely no one sane would continue with such a fruitless endeavour?

Still, loss of wits or not, he possessed a beating heart and warm, rich blood flowing through pulsing veins, and that was enough for them to stop. The din he was creating was enough to cover the sound of the truck coming to a halt, and they stepped down from the cab, pausing to glance at each other. The human had not looked up from his toil, utterly focused on the detritus surrounding him. Each blow of the hammer resounded down the empty thoroughfare like a distress signal, almost as if he was willingly provoking interest. As one, they walked towards him, unsheathing their truncheons from their belts; this would not take a great deal of effort. Stragglers such as these – the mad, those cast out from their human communities, the foolhardy – were easy pickings.

As they approached, still he did not turn. Only when they were within a couple of feet of him, their shadows stretching either side of him like a pair of dark jaws, did he cock his head to one side as if he had finally sensed he was not alone. He gazed up at the two Returners grinning fixedly down at him, seeming strangely unperturbed at their arrival, as if he'd been expecting them.

"Come with us," one of them said, brandishing its weapon. "Or else, trouble."

The human appraised them for a moment. "I don't think so," he replied finally.

They glanced at one another again, bemused. They had never encountered one so unconcerned by their presence; most would beg for mercy, or attempt to flee. "Come now," the first ghoul reiterated, reaching out to grab the young man by the shoulder.

But before he could make contact, the human lashed out and grasped its wrist tightly, pulling himself up to eye level. They locked stares for a second, his palm still wrapped around its forearm, refusing to relinquish it. "No," he said simply. "Not any more." With that, he released his grip and nodded over its shoulder.

The two Returners were too confused by this sudden display of defiance to fully acknowledge what happened next. They half turned to see what was behind them and were battered in the faces with machete blades. The first swing opened a rift in the nearest's forehead from brow to cheek, the knife lodging in the skull for a second before wrenching free with an audible crack. The next blow was brought down on the second zombie's cranium with enough force to cave in the left-hand side of its head entirely. It crumpled under the power of the strike, its features flattened. The first was still standing somehow, raising its baton in a half-hearted attempt at a counter-attack, its right eyeball poking comically at ninety degrees to the rest of its face. Gabe strode up to it while it was trying to get its bearings and rammed his blade up under its chin till the tip broke the surface of its scalp. The two halves of its head parted like a flower opening its petals to the rays of the sun.

Mitch watched Gabe yank the machete free, a little taken aback by the brutality of the assault. "When they said destroy the brain, you weren't going to take any chances, were you?" he remarked.

"Pays not to use half measures when you're dealing with the undead," he answered. "Nature of the beast means you're never sure when the damn things are down and out."

Mitch guessed that made sense, but he couldn't help but detect something personal in the vicious glee with which the zombies had been dispatched. He wondered if Gabe loathed them more than humans did; indeed, whether there was some self-hatred in those explosions of violence, a disgust at what he had become directed towards his cousins. Maybe there was an element of catharsis too. Whatever, Mitch was glad the full brunt of it was coming the deadheads' way, and not his.

"Success?" Liz asked as she and the five other members of the group (one of the older women had stayed behind to look after Rosa, the little girl) emerged from their hiding place on the other side of the road to meet them. They were carrying between them every weapon they had been able to lay their hands upon – knives, cudgels, baseball bats – and looked every inch the ragtag army. They were no soldiers, certainly, and seemed ill equipped for what lay ahead of them, but their grim, determined faces gave some indication of the spark that still resided inside them, despite the gaunt features and frail bodies. They congregated around the truck parked in the centre of the dual carriageway.

"The old bait and switch," Gabe replied. "Whether the mark's dead or alive, it's a reliable standby."

"The voice of experience," Liz said sardonically, folding her arms.

"You're talking to someone who spent five years of his life hijacking shipments. Be grateful it's an area of expertise, 'cause it's going to be our way in."

Mitch swung up into the cab and cast an eye over the interior. "Been simplified," he called down to them. "Looks like it runs off a battery, like a milk float."

"Like I said," Gabe told him, "the smart zombs have only learnt the basics. Flowers has probably taught them just enough so they can get themselves around in these things, and transport livestock."

"Can't have much power, either."

"Doesn't need to. We're going through the front door, not smashing our way in."

"What if we need to make a quick getaway?"

"In which case, you're better off scattering on foot. Give them multiple targets to go after. But listen," Gabe looked around at the group, "I'm not going to lie to you: chances are, we don't pull this off, we're not going to have the opportunity to escape. We go in, we go in with one intention, and that's destroying every Returner in there. Anything less than that and we're going to fail. Understand?"

The humans nodded slowly.

"OK." Gabe pulled down the tailgate at the back of the truck. "Climb aboard. Let's move out."

STANDING FACE TO face on the truck bed, the humans held onto each other for support as it rattled its way through the fringes of the city. The back of the vehicle was roofed by a tarpaulin and wooden slats ran the length of the sides, so they only got brief glimpses of the landscape outside. Mitch had put an eye to a gap to get a better view, and had seen other intelligent zombs watching the truck move past with expressions of hungry expectation. He knew he had imagined them licking their thin, dry lips, but the image stayed in his head nevertheless, and he turned away from the world outside, preferring to wait in the dark like an animal anticipating its trip to the slaughterhouse. The others stared at their feet, swaying with the motion of the vehicle, deep in contemplation.

The truck hit a pothole and all seven of the survivors clattered into one another, breaking the reverie. The longhair, Phillips, slammed his hand against the wall separating the bed from the cab, and looked round at the others, adjusting his glasses.

"We must be mad trusting this... thing," he hissed.

"None of us trust him," Liz said, then corrected herself. *"It."* She glanced at each of her colleagues in turn. "But we all know this is a chance we can't afford not to take. Imagine the repercussions if we can pull this off. Imagine what could be possible. We're talking about finally fighting back against the dead, about having the chance to reclaim our lives."

"That's a pretty bloody big *if*," Phillips sneered. "For all you know, it could be offering us up on a plate. You heard its story: it's an ex-criminal who fell out of favour with its boss. Who's to say that it's not using us as an opportunity to curry favour with this Flowers guy? Deliver some fresh meat into the body shops as a means to weasel his way back into the old man's good books."

"That's enough," another member of the group said sternly. Tendry was a former theatre actor in his fifties. "There's no need for such talk."

"All the same, I agree with him," John remarked. "This thing – Gabriel – was prepared to sell out its boss. It pretty much said so itself. It won't think twice about betraying us if it suits it." He swept his arms either side of him. "It took the weapons off us, stored them in the cab. We're defenceless. If the pusbags come for us, we won't have a chance."

"It was just a precaution," Mitch piped up. "Just in case any of the stiffs check the back of the truck."

Liz turned to him. "You've spent the most amount of time with it, Mitch. What do you make of it?"

"I know that Gabe saved me, and would've done the same for Donna if he'd been able to. Everything he's said so far has been straight down the line. I think we've got to give him the benefit of the doubt. There's only so far you can get without trusting anyone."

"*He?*" Phillips barked a laugh. "I think you better remind yourself exactly what this thing is, before you start forgetting what side of the grave it's on."

"He's more human that some I could mention." Mitch turned back to Liz. "I genuinely think he wants to bring Flowers down, with our help. He's got his own agenda, and his own axe to grind, but I don't think it's in his interests to turn on us." He paused. "But that doesn't mean I'm not wary of him. There was something I sensed on our return trip; he tried to hide it, tried to act like it wasn't there, but all the same... There're some elements of his undead nature that he's still subject to."

"What do you mean?"

Mitch sighed. "He's still highly carnivorous. You can see it sometimes in his eyes – he's still got the hunger."

"Christ," John breathed. "And we're putting our lives in the hands of this fucking flesh-eater?"

Nobody answered, and the rest of the journey was spent in silence.

WITH A BUMP the truck came to a halt, and seconds later the tailgate was opened, the humans squinting in the daylight at Gabe standing below them. He motioned for them to stay quiet, and looked off to the side, beckoning to someone out of sight. Mitch craned his head around the edge of the vehicle and saw half a dozen Returners emerge from a side alley. Like Gabe they bore little signs of their zombie status – they could walk at a steady pace, and few carried extravagant wounds, though one was missing an arm and another had had his jaw wrenched at an odd angle – but they were unmistakably dead. Common to them all was the greenish, stretched complexion of their skin, the milky cast to their eyes, and the slow, almost languorous manner with which they regarded the living. Mitch had seen more repellent stiffs in his time, but few were as creepy as this bunch; it was their collected awareness of their own cadaverous state that gave them a chilling air of poised menace.

"OK, I've rounded up these guys on my travels," Gabe said. "They've pledged to help us." It was unclear which group he was specifically referring to.

"This the bait?" asked one of the Returners, a tall blond woman with a livid scar running from her ear to her chin.

"They're going to help us get in, yes."

"You think they're up to it?"

"Don't worry about us," John replied, the disdain undisguised in his voice. "We'll be ready to fight, as long as our weapons are returned." He glanced at Gabe.

"You'll get them back once we're through the gates and they're not expecting trouble. They," Gabe indicated the other ghouls, "are going to be providing support. The important thing is we get inside without arousing suspicion, OK? To that end, I need one of you humans to walk alongside the truck, acting as a sample. Flowers' dead are quite picky about the meat they consume, and they like to approve what enters their body shops." There were murmurs of disapproval, but he added, "That's just the way they do things. We need this to look like a regular shipment."

Mitch moved forward to volunteer, but Liz held him back. "I'll go." She jumped down onto the road before anyone could argue.

"Factory is just about half a mile away," Gabe told them, raising the tailgate. "So get ready." He turned to the blond zombie. "Alice, can you drive? I'll be escorting Liz here."

The Returners formed an arrowhead around the truck as it rumbled onwards, Liz trudging alongside with Gabe's hand on the small of her back. She knew it was for appearances' sake only, but still she bristled, feeling uncomfortably exposed and unhappy at having to trust these stiffs. She'd taught herself to hate the things, to paint a clear delineation between the living and the dead. In the early days, it had been simple: you were either one or the other, and if you stank of tomb-rot then you deserved nothing more than a bullet in the brain. But despite the straightforward battle-lines, it hadn't made the fight against them any easier, and the truth of the matter was that the dead were winning. Before this self-aware ghoul had turned up at their door, she had been fast losing hope, although she had said nothing to the group. She couldn't see how they could've survived much longer. Now, though, there was a slim chance they could change the situation. It was unbelievably risky, but it was one more chance than they had a few days before. And it was through trusting the enemy, the one thing she imagined she would never do.

"So who are they? Your friends, I mean," she asked Gabe.

"Other dead souls that I came across on my wanderings, of a similar level to me. They were just the same: frightened at what they'd become, still human enough to want to stop the mass extinction of the living, but ultimately undead and therefore now another species. In the eyes of groups like yours, at least."

"Can you blame us? We've spent years fighting the zombs. It was them or us. That kind of mentality is hard to shake, even if you wanted to."

"Things are a bit more complicated now."

"Tell me about it." She looked at the Returners either side of her. "How did this happen? How are you able to retain so much of your life and personality? Why you?"

Gabe shrugged. "I guess you could call us the next generation. There seems to be no rhyme or reason why any of these people" – he gestured to the others – "should've resurrected differently, and yet here we are, the anomalies. I'm sure there're others still, all over the country, growing in number. It must be the virus, I'm convinced of that. It's almost like it's developed into an entirely different strain over the course of the past decade."

"All over the country," Liz mused quietly. "You think this thing is everywhere?"

"Don't doubt it. This isn't confined to London. I've heard rumours that it's global." He turned to her. "You lost family too?"

She shook her head. "No one close. My folks were living up in Newcastle, and I haven't heard from them since the outbreak. But I must be one of the few that hasn't got a spouse or kids to worry about – guess that was why I could take charge of this bunch; I wasn't quite as shell-shocked as the others. Used to just doing things, I suppose."

"They've survived, thanks to you."

"I got them this far. Nothing's guaranteed, though, is it? Not these days."

They came within sight of the body shop, the commandeered school. The high brick walls concealed much of what was going on behind them, but there were at least eight Returners on sentry duty, guarding the short driveway into the car park. They spotted the truck and its entourage heading towards them, and several peeled off from the main group and strode out to meet it.

"Flesh?" the lead ghoul asked Gabe, peering past him at the vehicle.

"Yes. Resistance humans," he replied, modulating his speech to that of the typical collector stiff. "More in truck like this one." He pinched Liz's upper arm and held it up for the creature to see. She winced, holding her breath.

It looked her over and ran its bony fingers through her hair. It made a noise of approval. "How many?"

"Another six in back."

It nodded at a pair of its colleagues, who sauntered round to the rear of the truck. Then it turned its attention back to Gabe. "Don't recognise you. Where all come from?"

"Across the river. Heard foodstocks running low. That true?"

"Boss demanding more, but living scarce. Avoiding patrols. Can't make quota."

"We might be able to help food situation. Bring in more like this, work for boss?"

The zomb narrowed its eyes. "What makes you think you can find humans?"

"Got this flesh to talk," Gabe replied, motioning to Liz. "Knows where we can find more. Bring them in for processing?"

The two deadheads came back from inspecting the truck. "Good batch," one said.

The leader nodded. "OK. Bring them in," he called, and stepped back to allow the procession to pass by. "Show them where to take the meat," it added to its assistants.

They entered the car park, and brought the truck to a stop by a line of similar vehicles standing empty. It looked like there hadn't been a delivery for a while. The humans were ordered to leave the truck bed and hustled into a tight knot, Returners on each side. Over to the left was a large green expanse of playing fields, netted goal posts strung at either end, and a fenced-off cricket strip next to them. Further away was a cement yard, with a trio of outbuildings circling it. As ever, it was eerily quiet; given the setting, it was especially unnerving. Once upon a time there would've been thousands of young voices echoing across this area, but now it was as silent as a tomb.

"Processing in main hall," one of the body shop's guards told Gabe. "Follow us."

"Got their weapons," Alice said, emerging from the cab, a set of canvas bags in her hands.

"Bring them to armoury on way," it answered.

They marched down some steps and into the school's quadrangle, heading towards a pair of double doors. Once inside, they gestured for them to continue down a corridor lined with lockers. Despite the silence outside, now they were within the building's walls they could hear cries drifting in the distance. They grew louder with each step they took.

"The sound of flesh," one of the ghouls said, grinning.

Gabe didn't reply, merely cast an eye over his shoulder. There was no one else in the corridor; it seemed as good a place as any. He nonchalantly stuck his foot in front of Liz and gave her a gentle push, sending her sprawling. The group splintered as she fell, the two stiff escorts looking back in confusion. Gabe drew his machete. "She trying to escape," he warned.

As they moved forwards to grab hold of her, he beheaded one with a swift swing of his blade. Before the disembodied skull had even hit the parquet floor, he speared the other one through the mouth, the machete tip embedding itself in a locker door; it hung there, an expression of surprise etched on its features. He yanked his weapon free, allowing the zomb to fall to the ground.

Alice opened the bags and tossed the humans and the other Returners their weapons. John greedily snatched his shotgun, and thumbed in some shells that he had stowed in his pockets. Gabe leaned down and offered his hand to Liz, who looked up at him with a mixture of fury and mistrust; but she grasped his palm and allowed him to pull her up.

"Sorry about that," he said. "Needed a diversion." He handed her a knife. She took it. "Let's just get this done."

"Kill every deadhead in here," Gabe called as the group hurried up the corridor, the groans from the hall luring them forward. "No mercy."

Mitch hefted the baseball bat in his hand, slippery with sweat. He prayed they were in time to save Donna. He passed a classroom and glanced in, noting the overturned desks, trampled books and bloody footprints. He could feel anger building up inside him, for everything the zombs had done to them. He felt like smashing skulls for every ounce of hurt they had been responsible for.

The doorway to the hall opened and a stiff wandered out, a scream bellowing in its wake, cut short as the door flapped shut behind it. It glanced up, uncomprehending, at the group of figures charging towards it. A second later there was an explosion of fire as John discharged his shotgun, catching it in the belly, severing it in two; its lower half stood stationary while its upper torso flailed around in a mess of entrails, trying to squirm its way back to where it had come from. Gabe shouted a caution, but John ignored it. He quickly chambered another round and put the barrels to the back of its head, blasting a hole in it the size of his fist.

"You were saying?" John asked Gabe.

"Guess there goes our element of surprise," the Returner muttered in answer. He glanced at the group, nodded, then pulled open the door to the hall.

"Christ," Mitch whispered as he crossed the threshold, shock at what he saw bringing him to a standstill.

CHAPTER SEVENTEEN

IT WAS AN atrocity, a waking nightmare. The living were strapped to beds and gurneys haphazardly lining the length of the cavernous hall, more than two dozen of them in number; a violent splash of white linen and crimson rags. Drips and saline sacs stood attendant by each stretcher, tubes running into the arms of the prone humans, feeding them nutrients, keeping them alive while strips of their flesh were removed from their deathly pale, still-warm frames. They were being farmed for their meat, but the ghouls had no appetite for cold cuts – the skin and muscle had to be drawn from the bodies of the breathing, rich with oxygenated blood, and so food parcels were being carved from their thighs and buttocks while they were kept in a sustained state of awareness. They clearly felt every incision of the knife, every tear of tissue, as their pained cries filled the room, shrieks of agony rebounding off the high walls. Some had yet to be touched or were missing just small squares of body fat; others had been ripped raw, limbs amputated, sinew stolen in vast swathes to the point where they resembled scarlet plastic dummies, with little clue offered to the casual observer as to whether they were once men or women. Yet despite the damage wrought upon their person, incredibly even these unfortunates still clung on to life, their veins weakly pulsing.

The pounds of flesh torn from the living were being stored in an adjacent area, evidently what were once the school kitchens. Somehow they had to be transported from here to Flowers' mansion, and still retain their freshness. Mitch saw wheeled containers stacked with ice and guessed the set-up: joints were being kept frozen for the journey, ensuring that the meat didn't spoil or lose its tenderness. It was a huge butcher's operation, slaughter on a massive scale, but without any notion of limiting the suffering of those being farmed. Indeed, the Returners seemed to relish each wail of distress that emanated from the humans writhing beneath their knives, as if it added texture to the soft tissue. The zombs' satisfied expressions as they went about their bloody business abruptly changed once they looked round and realised they had company.

For a moment, as they took in the full extent of the hall's horror, there was only stunned silence, punctuated by the moans of the humans tied to the gurneys. Mitch, Liz and the rest had scarcely wanted to imagine what dread deeds were being perpetrated in the stiffs' body shops, and now, face to face with it, the shocking reality was breathtaking. Yet even in the presence of its barbarity, they still wanted to shy away from the full truth: they shuddered to think how long some of these poor wretches had been tortured here, slowly consumed in segments, or what had become of their minds in the process. It was too awful to contemplate.

It was the image of Donna, a victim of this abattoir, that kick-started Mitch into action. With a yell, he charged forward and clobbered the nearest zomb in the head with his baseball bat, powering it into the hard tiled floor. The shout of defiance acted as a catalyst, snapping the others into focus; they let rip as if fired from a cannon.

"Bastards!" John roared, and blew another away with both barrels.

The Returners seemed taken aback by this sudden invasion, but were quick to regain their senses, lurching forward in a stumbling half-run to engage the enemy, wielding whatever instruments came to hand: scalpels, meathooks, tenderisers. The humans initially took the advantage, spraying their opponents with the few semi-automatic weapons they had at their disposal, but their lack of skill with them quickly became apparent – too many shots went wide, or slotted the ghouls in their arms and midriffs – and they began to panic, unnerved at the speed with which the resurrected were moving towards them, shrugging off the impacts of the bullets. Occasionally, the back of a zomb's head would explode as a missile found its target, but such hits were seldom, and the humans watched the gap between them and the flesh-eaters rapidly decrease.

Phillips' revolver clicked empty at just the wrong moment, and the instant he dug into his pocket for some spare rounds, a hook embedded in his skull. Pulled off his feet, he was dragged into the throng of advancing ghouls, who fell upon him hungrily. His stomach punctured, loops of intestine were tugged from his belly, and his shrieks were only cut short when his tongue was wrenched free.

One stiff flung a carving knife, and it glanced off Liz's cheek, knocking her backwards; she staggered, dizzy, a hand held to her face to stem the flow of blood streaming down her jaw, and her legs collapsed under her. The zomb pressed home its attack, and leapt upon her, pushing up her head to fix its teeth on her throat. She got a hand to the side of its skull and tried to force it away, her fingers curling away from its bared incisors, but it was too strong and too determined. It shook itself free like a tangled animal and resumed its attempt to savage her neck. She screwed up her eyes, hoping it would be quick.

Then there was a rush of movement, and the deadhead was gone, pulled off her and thrown to the side. She looked up to see Gabe stalking towards it, kicking it onto its back and stamping hard on its face so that its features disappeared into a craggy hole. He turned back and helped Liz to her feet.

"Did it bite you?" he asked matter of factly, studying her wounds.

"No... no, I don't think so," she replied, gingerly running her hand over her throat. It was sticky with blood, but there were no teeth marks.

"That's quite a cut you've got there. You're going to grow faint, you keep losing blood like that."

"Don't see I've got much choice. I can't sit this one out."

"Here." Gabe took hold of her T-shirt and tore it along the bottom. She stiffened as he tied it around her head as a makeshift bandage. "While it lacks grace, it'll at least keep your brains in."

"Thanks." She touched it; it felt tight and secure.

"Give support where you can," he told her. "We're taking over, and things are about to get a little crazy."

Gabe instructed the surviving gun-wielders to cease fire and take a step back, while he and his band of Returners moved in front of what remained of the body shop's ghouls.

"Out of the way, dead things," one of the zombs snarled at Gabe. "Why not consuming this flesh? Why siding with them?"

"Because they're us," Gabe replied. "And you were them once, only you've forgotten that you used to be human. How does it feel, eating your own kind to extinction?"

It frowned, confused. "Not our kind. *Never* our kind."

"No. You've gone too far to remember, haven't you?"

With that, Gabe lashed out and slammed his fist into the creature's face, its nose crumpling and its forehead buckling, as if the bone had grown supple beneath the skin. It keeled over backwards, and with a yell of fury Gabe jolted his elbow into the next one's throat, leaping upon it and ripping open the top of its scalp with his teeth. The others followed suit, tearing their way through the undead horde like wolves, biting and scratching, all sense of civilised restraint lost in the melee. Liz looked on, both appalled and fascinated, as Gabe and the other Returners became whirling dervishes of destruction, punching and gouging, seemingly ignoring the jaws snapping at their own flesh. If they felt any kind of pain then they showed no sign. It was a depraved, bestial display, Gabe annihilating all those within his grasp; his machete flashed and a pair of severed heads tumbled across the floor.

"Liz!" It was Mitch, beckoning her over. She ran towards him. "I've found Donna. I think... I think she might be OK. Help me get her free." She nodded, and turned to tell the others to start trying to loosen the restraints on those that were still capable of walking out of the building.

He led her to one of the beds, upon which the girl was tied. She was conscious, moaning softly, and had lost a couple of fingers on each hand, but the rest of her body was virtually untouched. She did, however, have a cotton pad taped over her left eye. Liz and Mitch exchanged glances; then the woman leant across and lifted the material, exposing the dark red abscess beneath.

"Mother of God," she murmured.

"Fuckers," Mitch rasped, spinning away in anger.

"She's still alive, though," Liz asserted. "Be thankful for that, at least."

They eased Donna upright, Mitch whispering platitudes in her ear and stroking her hair, though whether the girl heard or felt anything was another matter. She was shivering uncontrollably, and wouldn't open her remaining eye to look at either of them, continuing instead to merely murmur to herself. Liz tore her gaze from Donna's trembling figure and regarded the rest of the hall: attempts were being made to cut the living loose but with mixed results. Some were all too eager to leap from the gurneys, tearing out the drip feeds from their arms and sobbing with relief; others didn't move, even if they still had the limbs to do so. They stared up at the ceiling, their expressions blank and unreadable, sanity having long deserted them.

The last of the zombies were being despatched by Gabe and his small undead army; their speed and strength had eventually overwhelmed Flowers' Returners, who had looked distinctly creaky in comparison. Even so, Gabe's team had suffered a couple of casualties – one of them was struggling on the ground, its back broken, another was lying in pieces, scattered over a wide area; still animated, but unsalvageable. There was something brutal about the aftermath of the fight between the dead factions, Liz thought, surveying the scene. It reminded her of nature documentaries she'd seen back in her old life, of the uncompromising attacks that insects perpetrated on each other, and the twitching, quartered corpses that they'd leave in their wake. Gabe himself was wiping blood and other fluids off his clothes, but it was clear he'd taken some hits too: he had deep scratches across his face, and a chunk of flesh from the nape of his neck was missing. His bottom lip was drooping lower than it used to, and he held a hand across his torso, as if he was pushing something back in that had been rent open. He appeared to pay them no mind, though; he was dead meat, and surely incapable of feeling any sensation. As long as the brain remained intact, he could keep on going, even if bit by bit he was slowly falling apart.

Gabe shambled over towards her. "Is she OK?" he asked, nodding towards Donna.

"I don't know," Liz answered with a sigh, shaking her head. "She's lost an eye and several fingers, and I think she's in an advanced state of shock. She's going to need medical attention, though God knows how we're going to treat her. As for her mental state... it's impossible to guess what she's been through."

Mitch looked up, his expression grim, and pulled the girl closer, holding her head against his. "I'll take care of her."

"We all will," Liz said, "but it's going to take time."

"There's going to be no shortage of casualties," Gabe remarked, gesturing to the other humans pulling themselves free from the gurneys. "You're going to have to look out for each other. Some will probably need putting out of their misery." He shrugged when they glanced sharply at him. "Be the kindest act you can do; they've suffered enough. Just make sure you put them down so they don't get back up again."

"Does that go the same for your friends?" Liz asked, pointing at the two Returners still jerking spasmodically amongst the necrotic remains.

"I'll deal with them."

"So what now?" Mitch wanted to know. "How do we get nearer to Flowers?"

"*We* nothing, son. You and the rest of the humans' part in this is done. We're going to commandeer a shipment," Gabe replied, hooking a thumb over at the wheeled containers filled with ice and body parts. "Make it look like we're delivering a regular supply of sweetmeats. Once inside, it's payback time."

"You think you can go up against the might of your old boss? Just you and your undead pals?"

"You got a better idea?"

"I reckon you need all the help you can get."

"I thought your place was with Donna." When the kid didn't answer, Gabe continued, "I appreciate your offer, but this is going to be no place for the living. I'm not sure I'm going to come out of there in one piece, and I've got certain... advantages. I said at the beginning, you wouldn't see me again after we did this, and it still stands. Whatever happens, whether I take down Harry or not, I'm gone."

"I want my revenge too," Mitch said quietly.

"You already have, son. You've helped save these people, and now you have to look after them. Show the deadfucks that they've lost." Gabe reached out and placed a hand on his shoulder. "I couldn't have got this far without you, you know that, don't you?"

Mitch nodded grudgingly and gave a tight smile, hugging Donna to his chest.

"I'll get some guys together," Liz said. "Help you load up."

"First, we need to do a complete sweep of this place," Gabe replied. "Wipe out any ghouls still left in the building. I don't want any word getting back to Flowers and having him waiting for us. Once the area's secure," he turned to Liz, raising his eyebrows, "then it's time to pay the old man a visit."

GABE SAT BEHIND the wheel of the truck, guiding it out of the city, aware that he was possibly leaving it for the final time. Beside him, Alice was staring out the passenger window with unblinking eyes, while in the back, standing over five crates of fresh meat, were two others: Adam and Beth. It had been grisly work for the living to have handled these containers – the guards at the mansion would be checking the vehicle's contents, so there was no question that they had to carry them if they were to get inside the house's perimeter – but it had been equally hard for the Returners, controlling their hunger in the face of such temptations. After the battle, having sunk his teeth into rotten carcasses, the thought of devouring these succulent morsels was overwhelming; but the human Gabe that still resided in his resurrected body nixed that notion before it could take hold.

He often felt there were two sides within him fighting for control: the man that he used to be, and the wretched graveyard creature, lusting after the flesh of the living. He was ashamed, and a little scared, to admit that he had succumbed entirely to the latter when he had launched himself at the stiffs in the body shop, revelling in the slaughter, reverting to his primal instincts. Certainly, he was aware he was no longer a human being when that element was to the fore. He was more akin to a force of nature, an amoral carnivore driven by the centre of his brain that the virus had reawakened. He had had no desire to eat the zombs' putrescent tissue – it was warm skin and bone that he craved – but taking apart the things with his teeth had been a gloriously atavistic act.

There had been a similar sense of satisfaction as they wiped out every one of Flowers' zombies remaining in the school. Their look of uncomprehending shock as their factory-farmed food rose up and smashed their brains out, the ones standing guard at the main gate repeatedly rammed with purloined trucks until they resembled nothing more than greasy smears on the tarmac. For so long the body shops had been places to fear, casting a long shadow over the area; now one had been disabled, its evil vanquished, and that had given the living hope. Other humans could be saved, the tyrannical rule of the deadheads could be shattered. When Gabe had said goodbye to Liz, she had shook his hand and for the first time had looked him in the eye without a wrinkle of distaste souring her expression. She and Mitch and the others already appeared stronger, despite what they had been through, and although he didn't know where they would take the battle next – it was something they still had to decide for themselves – he guessed that they were more than ready.

Maybe the air of revolution had gone to his head, but he thought he could discern a vulnerability amongst the stiffs as they passed them through Greater London's streets: a sense that their time was passing. Change had always been Harry's ally, the belief that things couldn't stay the same. It had served him well, certainly since the outbreak all those years ago, and it had eventually brought him the city he'd dreamed of possessing. Now, however, events seemed to be undergoing another shift. Flowers' ghouls looked tired and clumsy and slow, and they were losing their grip on what remained of the human populace. Their generation was coming to an end, and something else was emerging to take their place. Was it him, Gabe wondered, he and others like him that were undead but progressing back to their former selves? Were they the next stage in the virus's evolution? And if he toppled Flowers as the dark ruler of this corrupt kingdom, was he fated to take his place?

Gabe saw the glinting metal strung across the road too late; they weren't travelling at speed – the refitted trucks could barely reach more than twenty miles per hour, so he could've avoided it if he'd spotted it early enough – but the spikes were hidden beneath a layer of debris strung across the width of the thoroughfare, with only the jagged tops visible. He knew as soon as he stamped on the brake pedal that he wasn't going to miss them, and sure enough there was a shudder and a low rumble as the tyres were punctured.

"Shit, what was that?" Alice asked as the tremor passed through the vehicle.

"Homemade stingers," Gabe replied, wrestling with the wheel. "Somebody's set a trap for us."

"Humans?"

"Must be. They're gonna be thinking that we're taking Flowers his next three-course meal."

"Hell." The truck started to skew to the side, and Gabe realised that it was pointless to try to progress any further; he pulled on the handbrake to bring it to a halt. "What are we going to do?"

"Do what we usually do," he said, pushing open the driver's door. "Talk our way out of it."

He walked round to the back, opened the doors and told the pair inside what had happened, and warned them to keep their wits about them. As he did so, he saw figures emerging from the derelict office buildings on either side. *Can't believe it*, he thought ruefully, *never thought I'd be on the wrong end of a carjacking.*

But there was something odd about the way these humans were moving, and as they came closer their shuffling gait was explained: they were deadheads, and ones in a particularly bad way. They looked like they were rotting right before his eyes, their bodies stick-thin, their skin almost translucent. They carried no weapons either, as if they didn't have the strength in their arms to lift anything. Instead, they merely stared at Gabe and the truck hungrily, a faint groan issuing from the group.

They're pusbags, he thought, frowning at Alice, who came out to join him. *They're not capable of setting anything like this up. Someone else has to be behind them.*

"Can you talk?" Gabe asked them. "Can you understand me?"

In answer, they parted and allowed another figure to step through. He was a zomb too, but more sprightly; a short guy with a sprig of unruly dark hair atop his heavily lacerated face. He gazed at Gabe uncertainly, hefting a small revolver in his hand.

"You're not one of Flowers's," he said, a Scottish lilt to his voice still audible despite the slightly slurring quality of its timbre. It was a statement, rather than a question.

"No."

"But you're Returners? Fully cognitive resurrected?"

They both nodded.

"My God. I'd heard there were more, I knew your numbers were growing, but trying to track any of you down..." He seemed genuinely excited. "My theories were right. You're the living – well, undead – proof of that."

"Theories?" Gabe repeated. "Who are you?"

"Gannon," he said, holstering the gun and extending his hand in greeting. "Doctor Robert Gannon. Welcome to my world."

CHAPTER EIGHTEEN

ON A CLEAR day, the view was magnificent. Standing at the upstairs picture window of his mansion, binoculars held to his atrophied eyes, Harry Flowers surveyed his kingdom spread before him with approval; it was everything he could've asked for, everything he'd strived for. From his vantage point, London curled into the distance, a grey mass choked of life. At this time of the morning, just after dawn, a mist rose off the iron waters of the Thames, seeping past the office blocks standing silent sentinel on its banks. The dance of those few wisps, chased from the surface of the river by a stiff wind, was the only movement that he could see. The metropolis was inert, a desiccated corpse the colour and vibrancy of cold embers. A few pockets of resistance still remained, he knew; a few parasites still clung to its rotting hide. But he was slowly, inexorably, consuming the city, gradually absorbing it into his domain, and the best thing was this was only the beginning. Once the capital fell utterly under his command, then he could extend his reach – send out his men to the peripheral settlements that he knew to exist in the satellite towns and stamp his mark even further. He saw it as spinning a web, casting the strands wider and wider until the entire country was his to control, with him naturally at the centre, at the hub. He never wanted to be anywhere else.

He lowered the binoculars, studying the grounds nearer to home. He had ordered the woods that had backed on to the house to be cleared completely, so he could obtain just such an unobstructed view of the city that was now his. There wasn't a day that went past when he didn't like to gaze upon it and marvel. Elsewhere, the gardens had been allowed to grow wild, his interest in keeping them manicured and healthy having waned over the years. It was an odd sensation, one that he hadn't expected come his resurrection. His appreciation of beauty had diminished, to the point where he found the still, bare qualities of the barren landscape more appealing. He had allowed the weeds to choke the roses and the rhododendron, the nettles to encroach from the edges of the paths to virtually engulf them, and the potted plants to wither and die. There was nothing of colour out there now, just decay and those feeding upon it, and yet he felt unmoved by this loss. It seemed to suit his mood, and the empire he was building – a bleak, desolate land fit only for the dead, and the man (or what was once a man) that ruled it. Instead, in place of the flora that had once ringed his mansion, he had devised more fortifications: fences, sentry posts, anti-personnel weaponry, to keep him safe from those that would do him harm.

He turned away from the window, placing the binoculars on the sill. A familiar gnawing ache resounded in his empty belly, and he reached out and grasped the back of a nearby chair to steady himself, waiting for the moment to pass. It was taking longer these days, and he gritted his teeth, the pain blossoming. Despite his dead nerve-endings, the need to feed still brought with it its own singular sting. It was the one reminder of his undead status, the one link to the pusbags that staggered through the city streets, and he could not rid himself of it. All that he had accomplished post-death – an organised militia, enforcing his rule, a London paralysed by fear and ripe for the taking – and yet still his body was slave to the demands of his zombiehood.

At the start, it had been easy satiate his hunger. Warm flesh was readily available, and once the pangs took hold he had no trouble feeding. In the interim, as he and his troops established the body shops that enabled the living to be distributed in convenient, pre-packed states, he fought to lessen the control his stomach had over him; as far as he was concerned, he called the shots, not the virus squatting in his brain. Sheer strength of will enabled him to gain the upper hand, and he found he could manage and maintain his belly's insistent need for sustenance, not requiring living meat more than once a week or so. Such a diet was soon an act of necessity as much of choice as the regular deliveries from the processing stations were beginning to dry up, and humans became increasingly difficult to find. Others lesser than him took to stumbling about the mansion grounds, groaning, not much better than the rotting deadheads they themselves looked down upon. But not he. He had not been dictated to in life, and he certainly would not become a mere puppet at the whim of his own body post-death.

But in his heart, he knew it could not be denied, no matter how much he fought it. The hunger, the lust to feed, was his nature, and it was impossible to resist. It had to be at least a fortnight now since he'd properly feasted, and the throbbing pain that swelled from his gut was a wake-up call, an intestinal nudge to suggest it wasn't going to go away. However, unless the situation changed, he didn't know how he could face the eternity stretching ahead of him, a victim to cravings he couldn't satisfy. What good was it to rule over an empire, when there was nothing left to consume? And what would become of him if his belly's desires were not met?

Despite Flowers' instructions to his resident boffins many years ago (just how long was it, he wondered; time seemed to slip past him with little relevance) to find a way of tweaking the virus's demand for flesh, they had come up with few results. Given its stubborn refusal to be adapted by artificial means, he suspected the best he could hope for was that the bacteria would continue to evolve along a similar path that it had taken so far, but that process could take decades, if not centuries. He hated being at the mercy of elements he could not manipulate to his own ends. It left him helpless, and that was a state of being that had previously been an anathema to him.

The ache in his belly gradually subsided, and he straightened. Perhaps he should investigate the pantry and see what supplies remained, he pondered, loathing the junkie-like caving of his willpower. He left the room and crossed the landing, noting the disrepair the house had fallen into. The wallpaper was streaked with dirt, the carpet frayed and stained. How long had it looked like this, he wondered? How many months had the mansion slowly slid into decay without him being aware of it? It felt cadaverous itself, a crumbling, hollow shell. He realised with a sudden stab of amazement that he hadn't ventured beyond these walls for over three years, too wrapped up inside his own addiction to see it falling apart around him.

He padded to the first floor, then paused in his descent. He glanced across at the closed door to his right, hesitated, but finally rapped upon it and stepped across the threshold without waiting for an answer. As ever, the room was silent save the ticking of the clock on the mantelpiece, and the rising sun cast the chair in front of the window in silhouette, an aura of light haloing the figure seated upon it. He squinted as he strode towards the window, casting an eye to the woman staring at the landscape beyond the glass. He pulled a curtain across the view, lengthening the chamber's shadows. She blinked and stirred, conscious of the gloom that had settled upon her.

Flowers pulled up a chair and sat beside her. "Anna," he said. "Have you slept at all?"

"Like the light," she replied in a tiny voice, fidgeting in her seat.

"It's too bright. You shouldn't sit so close to the window."

"S-scared of dark. Scared of what's th-there. Want to close eyes, but scared."

"You need rest."

"Don't tell me w-what I need," she muttered. "And s-since when have you cared?"

"I'm still your father."

She looked at him for a second, then laughed, an eerie sound as dry as kindling. "You? You're n-not even human."

He studied her, a mixture of sadness and frustration and self-hatred churning in his chest. That he had cut himself adrift from his daughter like this hurt him as deeply as a knife to the heart; or at least when he was still capable of feeling such a wound. His resurrection might've brought him a lack of physical sensation, but the mental anguish at what he'd done all those years ago was sharp as ever. He had selfishly hoped that he could slough off the trappings of his former life upon coming back as a Returner, his sins fading like the memory of breath in his lungs. But it was not to be. His torments were as fresh as they ever were in life and they were here in front of him, represented by the young woman that had once been his kin. But now... now she was the past that he would not allow himself to forget. Her condition, her indifference towards him, the future that she had been denied, was all his fault, and every time he came to visit, it was to reaffirm his guilt – a confessional not to absolve his failings as a parent but to refresh them anew.

She was regressing, and he didn't know how to stop it; indeed, wasn't even sure whether halting it was the correct thing to do. Where once she had been trapped between life and death, the moment of her passing held in stasis by the virus, now it was as if the reanimation bacteria was struggling to stay in control, losing its grip on her central cortex. While he had witnessed other undead growing more intelligent over the years, she was the first to take the backward path. Her speech and sense of balance were becoming unstable, she was increasingly unresponsive, and she was losing her ability to comprehend those around her. He didn't know why it was happening, or where her decline would take her. Towards a true death? Or to become one of the shambling hordes? He could not accept that, yet he had no good reason why he shouldn't just let her go. She had lived this half-life for over a decade, ever since he had shot through her to prove his strength of will to Goran Vassily, and had hovered on the cusp of mortality, a prisoner inside her own skin. The kindest act would be to finish it, to set her free, to lead her into the weed-ridden gardens and place a gun to the back of her head. But he was too much of a coward for that, he could not bear the weight of that responsibility. And in truth, he did not want to lose her, because once she was gone, nothing would stop his transformation into a monster. Her presence reminded him of his past deeds, of what terrible crimes he had committed, a wound that he would never allow to heal. If she was gone, then all would be consumed – identity, history, love and regrets – in the pursuit of power, and he would no longer recognise his own reflection.

"I've always cared for you, Anna," he said, reaching out and stroking her hair. She flinched at his touch. "If I could do anything to bring you back to me, I would."

"Just let me g-go," she whispered, her head bowed.

"What?"

She looked up at him, her eyes glistening. "I'm t-trying s-so hard to leave, to end this. S-scared of dark, don't want to close eyes, but I know it's only w-way of escape."

Flowers knelt quickly, placing a hand on her knee, the fingertips of the other holding her chin. She was as cold as porcelain. "What are you saying? That you're bringing on this decline yourself?"

"Only way... to escape you. I w-won't be held here anymore."

"No, please, Anna, don't do this. I need you here –"

"I want... to go..."

"Anna –"

It was then that the first of the explosions rocked the mansion, and the alarms started to wail.

TWENTY-FOUR HOURS EARLIER

"GIVE ME ONE good reason why I shouldn't just rip your fucking throat out," Gabe rasped, holding Gannon by the lapels. "Tell me why I wouldn't be doing the human race a huge favour."

"And you think that will change anything?" the former scientist replied. "You think that's going to magic the world back into what it was fifteen, twenty years ago?"

"It would make *me* feel better."

"And once that feeling had passed, what would you be left with? Just another corpse on the floor, and a host of unanswered questions. Killing me will solve nothing."

Gabe considered this, then released the man. They were standing in Gannon's makeshift laboratory, a collection of tables and rudimentary scientific equipment that he'd looted from various sources and collected together in a long-abandoned back room of a chemist's. His jottings and diagrams were tacked to the walls and covered the work surfaces, while a few works in progress were evident, scattered about the space: a severed ghoul's head was held in a clamp, it's brain exposed, another was wired up to a car battery. Everything looked crude, filthy and incapable of bringing usable results.

"Some sense at last," Gannon muttered.

"Pal, there would be a queue of people from here to the Watford Gap trying to get hold of you, if they knew where you were. In fact, a few survivors that I met recently probably wouldn't mind five minutes alone with the man who destroyed their lives."

"We've all suffered, believe me."

"Yeah? So what happened to you?"

He shrugged. "I was called to my superior's office in London once the outbreak hit, part of an MoD convoy that got caught in a riot. I managed to make it to a government station, and was working on containing the crisis. Unfortunately, the safety of the outpost was compromised."

"Compromised?"

"The infection got inside and spread like wildfire. I was bitten, end of story."

"Well, not quite. You're standing here talking like me, completely self-aware and an evolutionary step up from those deadheads outside. That doesn't sound like the end of the story to me." The stiffs that had initially appeared with Gannon had remained on the street, watching over the vehicle while Alice and the rest had made some attempt to repair the damage done to the tyres. Gabe had had to give a brief explanation of why they were travelling in one of Flowers' trucks, and their business of infiltrating his mansion.

"True," the scientist said, nodding. "HS-03 has developed beyond all my expectations. If it keeps growing at this rate, we could have a new species of human being in the next thirty years." He studied Gabe, his eyes roving over him with clinical dispassion. "Your strength and intelligence makes me wonder if it did have military applications after all..."

"I'm not one of your test subjects, Gannon."

"Don't you see, you're the next generation. The mindless carnivores were just the first stage. HS-03 is constantly evolving the dead to an incredible degree."

"You must be very proud." Gabe gestured to the experiments dotted about the room. "So what are you doing here? Trying to replicate it?"

"I've got some advanced cultures, yes. But I'm also trying to control the Returners, make them reasonably docile and open to instruction. I was working on something similar before the outbreak. As you've seen from the little band outside, I've had some partial success."

"They'll do what you tell them to?"

"Up to a point. Interesting thing is, even they are growing quite territorial – they're recognising that those trucks you came in are removing all the warm flesh from the area. They're conscious that the ruling elite is getting all the food, while they are being left to rot. It's a simple animal deduction, but they're smart enough to have laid the stinger trap."

"My God."

"Like I say, that's HS-03's evolutionary power." He chuckled to himself. "The dead aren't taking it lying down anymore."

"So the zombs are no fans of Harry Flowers either."

"Few are. They're as much under the cosh as the humans."

Alice entered, her expression grim. "Wheels are screwed, Gabe. Too shredded to be repaired."

"Damn," he murmured. "We've just lost our way in." He slumped against a table. "No way we're going to be able to get past Flowers' security, not without some kind of cover..." He looked up suddenly and grabbed Gannon by the arm. "Wait a minute – Doctor, you want to go some way to compensating for the shitstorm you landed everybody in? You want to claw back a few brownie points? And your undead friends out there want to grab a piece of the action they're being denied?"

The scientist blinked, bemused.

"You think you could you could control more of them – a regular army?"

Gannon nodded. "If we could round them up."

Gabe smiled. "Then I think I might have a solution."

"Which is?" Alice asked.

"We're going to do this the Harry Flowers way. We're going to storm that fucking mansion head on."

CHAPTER NINETEEN

"WHAT THE HELL is going on?" Flowers roared as another explosion rent the air. He clattered down the stairs, drawn like the rest of his men racing across the hallway towards the open main doors by the pulsating warble of the perimeter alarms. To his ears, it could only mean one thing: the fences had been breached, and the detonations were the landmines grouped sporadically within the mansion grounds being triggered. The rattle of gunfire drifted in, short bursts at the edge of the gardens. The enemy was at the gates, he thought. But who would dare take him on?

He heard his name called, and saw Hewitt pushing his way through the throng heading outside and making his way towards him. The kid had an Uzi held down at his side, and he looked harried: his grey face was etched in a grimace, anger and perhaps a touch of concern visible in his eyes. He met Flowers at the foot of the staircase.

"Who is it?" the older man demanded.

"We're not sure," Hewitt replied. "At least, not yet." If Flowers didn't know better, it was almost as if the kid was breathless. He couldn't possibly experience exhaustion, yet here he was, looking for all the world like he was about to keel over. He kept glancing back towards the grounds and fingering the weapon in his hand nervously. "There's an army of deadheads massing at the fences; I mean, a *lot*. Where they've come from, we have no fucking idea."

"But the defences are holding?" Flowers asked impatiently, if a tad relieved that he'd been premature in assuming that what he could hear were the sounds of intruders entering the gardens.

"Yeah, at the moment. They're just hitting the electrified perimeter fences and going up like fucking rockets. But they keep on coming, hundreds of them, and we're worried that the sheer weight of numbers is going to put a strain on the gate. Plus the burning bodies could end up short-circuiting the security system."

"So there's a chance they could get in?"

"I can't see them getting even near the house. If they get past the gates, they've got the tripwires to deal with, and *us*." He held up the Uzi. "But why should they want to get in here anyway? We've got nothing a pusbag would want. Even if they could sense the meat we've got in the stores, it wouldn't bring them in droves like this."

"Somebody's behind them."

Hewitt nodded. "This isn't some wandering bunch of zombs that have stumbled onto our land. They were directed here and instructed to attack. But why? What can they hope to achieve? The fucking things are just destroying themselves."

"It's to wear us down. Like you say, sheer weight of numbers to put a strain on our defences. Somebody wants in, and is using the stiffs as both barrier and distraction."

"Humans, you think?"

"Seems to be on too grand a scale for a bunch of shit-scared survivors," Flowers mused. "They wouldn't be able to get deadheads to do what they want anyway. No, this has the fingerprints of a Returner all over it. A new rival, deciding to piss on my territory." He turned to Hewitt. "Let's take a look at them."

"Are you sure, Harry? I mean, I don't think we're in any danger, but all the same, it would make sense for you to stay in the house."

"I'm not cowering from uninvited guests," Flowers said sternly, already walking towards the doors. He beckoned to one of his men. "Tate, ensure that the entire perimeter is monitored. I don't want anyone sneaking in under the radar while we're dealing with the frontal attack. Oh, and see if you can reset the alarm, it's doing my head in." The man nodded, and jogged away around the side of the mansion, a pair of his colleagues following.

Hewitt scurried to keep up with his boss as the old man strode down the drive, feet scrunching on the gravel, and stopped at the edge of the lawn, raising a hand over his eyes to shield them from the glare of the rising sun. Nice touch, Flowers thought, initiating an assault at dawn. Several metres away, a knot of his men were spraying the fence with automatic fire, though it was difficult to see the targets they were aiming for; the invading zombies were turning into a charcoal morass, impossible to determine one from another. Immediately beyond the gate was a row of blackened cadavers, fusing to the metal as they melted from the high voltage running through it. A few were on fire, hair crisping, bones popping, as they jerked and danced from each power surge. Behind them, more ghouls still came, stumbling blithely into the fence – those that could actually get near it – and exploding as they brushed against the wire. Flowers watched one's ribcage flung open like shutter doors, the organs sizzling as they plopped onto the grass.

Christ, they're disintegrating, he thought, studying the figures with grim fascination. *The things are burning up before my eyes.*

"Cease fire," he yelled. The gunshots dribbled to a halt. Glancing at the kid beside him, he added: "Pointless to try to hit them through that barbeque. Just a waste of ammo."

"What do you want to do?"

"Give me contact with the watchtowers." He held out his hand, and Hewitt passed him a walkie-talkie. Flowers lifted it to his lips. "Simmons, what's the news?"

"Not good, sir," a tinny voice replied in his ear. "Got maybe three hundred flesh-eaters backed up against the wire, and the system is not looking healthy. It's showing signs of overload. Could start to spark any minute."

"You see anything else apart from the deadheads? Someone controlling them?"

"Nope, just wave after wave of brainless maggotdicks. They're relentless, coming right across the fields, straight for the house."

"Roger that." Flowers clicked off the two-way. "They're coming out of London, I'm sure of that," he said to Hewitt.

"London? Who's left that we know could –"

The old man held up a hand for silence, and pondered for a few moments. Then he raised the walkie-talkie once more. "Simmons, shut off the power to the fence."

"You sure?"

"If it blows, we could risk losing the power to the whole mansion. Or fire could spread across the gardens. Turn it off."

"Wilco." Seconds later there was a buzz followed by a whine, and the microwaved dead ceased their convulsions. In its stead, the early-morning air was filled with the groans of the ghouls, the jangle of the gate as bodies incessantly pressed against it, and the crackle of burning flesh, pungent smoke drifting into the sky.

"Double the guard on the perimeter," Flowers told Hewitt. "Keep an eye out for any breaches in the fences, any weak spots. Also be prepared to move back to the house if need be, to defend that." He turned and headed back towards the front doors. "This was just the beginning. Whoever's behind this will be making a move – be ready for it."

"Right," Hewitt acknowledged, then coughed. He frowned and rubbed his throat, then coughed again, as if trying to rid himself of an irritation lodged there.

Flowers halted, and turned around to study the kid. Their eyes locked in puzzlement. Then they heard retching coming from across the grounds.

"They've turned off the power to the fence."

"So we make a move?" Alice asked.

"Not yet," Gannon replied. "Give it a few more minutes for the agent to disperse. No point going in there and suffering the ill effects ourselves. Wait for it to take hold."

They were crouching in the peripheral scrubland to the left of the mansion, hidden enough to not be discernable from the watchtowers but at a vantage point from which they could monitor the situation. Fortunately, Flowers' guards were preoccupied with the stiffs accumulating at the front gate, spraying those that were still alight – and those they could reach through the tangle of limbs and charcoal skeletons – with extinguishers. The zombs that hadn't been fried continued to tug at the fence, the wire rattling wildly. Evidently, the triggermen had been ordered not to fire upon the dead. The battering went unchecked, those inside the mansion grounds watching the assault impassively. More guards were being deployed at regular intervals along the perimeter, all hefting semi-automatics.

"They're increasing the security," Gabe said. "They know we're coming."

"They know *someone's* coming," Gannon corrected. "They don't know exactly who they're expecting."

"Are they all Returners?" Beth enquired. "Flowers' soldiers, I mean."

"Yeah. He made his workforce turn after he resurrected," Gabe murmured. "Always likes to be in control, does Harry... He wouldn't have humans alongside him – considers them beneath him now. Only one place for the living and that's on his dining table."

"Aren't we kind of adopting the same position?" Alice said, nodding to the zombs hammering against the fence. "We're using deadheads 'cause we think they're expendable, and a lesser species than ourselves. We've got more in common with them than the humans."

"They're test animals," Gannon answered bluntly. "Mindless automatons to be directed as we instruct. We've got no more in common with them as we would a lab rat."

"You told *them* that?"

Gannon frowned. "Meaning what?"

"Meaning how do you know what's going on inside their heads? You think they're happy being used like this?"

"They're barely aware of where they are, of what they're doing. There's no cognitive reasoning in their brains at all, just what they've been told."

"Only because you've tampered with them –"

"Can we have this argument another time?" Gabe interjected, silencing the pair. "I have to say, I'm not happy about using them as mobile dirty bombs, but if it knocks Flowers' outfit onto the back foot, then I say we take the advantage." He turned to Gannon. "Must admit, doctor, they've worked like clockwork. It's almost as if you've rewired their internal circuitry."

The scientist shrugged. "I've been studying HS-03 for over ten years, had experience of it at first hand. I know now how to modify it, how to get it to work on certain urges and act upon it. The corpses are vehicles driven by the virus, nothing more." He looked off towards the stiffs slamming against the fence, and sighed. "This would've been my army, this is what I was working towards. If only I'd had more time, I could've perfected it..."

"Wait," Alice said, indicating towards the mansion. "I think the agent's doing its stuff."

They all turned their attention towards the house and watched the guards begin to exhibit signs of infection. The sound of coughing reached even their hiding place, drowning out the mournful wailing of the dead. Some were bent double, their guns shouldered, spluttering into the lawns. Others scratched at their pallid faces and arms, shavings of cold flesh fluttering to their feet, fistfuls of hair pulled out in clumps.

"So it's going through the skin?" Gabe asked.

Gannon nodded. "They wouldn't breathe it in, now that their respiratory systems are dormant. But it's entering the epidermis, the necrosis attacking the cells, decaying them from the inside out. What they're coughing up is matter dislodging into their windpipes."

"Nasty."

"It's like bacterial acid. Once it gets under the skin, it'll eat through to the bone."

"And you created this?"

"Not long after the outbreak, the MoD asked me to come up with a way of neutralising the zombie threat over a wide area, but it never got past the prototype stage. I've been tinkering with it ever since. Thought it might be handy to have a little weapon of mass destruction all of my very own."

"Bet your masters never thought you'd be using deadheads as carriers for it. You could do a hell of a lot of damage, you know, across the whole city."

"No," Gannon replied, shaking his head. "It's only got a limited dispersal field, and a short lifespan, which is why we'll be able to go down there any second without it affecting us. In fact, it'll probably burn itself out before it's entirely disabled Flowers' goons. They'll still be on their feet – just – but should be compromised enough for us to get past them without too much trouble."

Gabe stood. "Well, I'm getting a hankering to wreak some bloody vengeance. Care to join me?"

THEY PICKED A point at the perimeter fence at which security was the most lax: a pair of guards were on their hands and knees, the flesh of their hands and forearms almost liquescent, white bone emerging from the grey puddle where their skin used to be. They barely noticed the newcomers, whimpering and pawing the earth like sick dogs, shrunken facial features disappearing into their skulls, and didn't have the time to recognise the fact that intruders were snipping the wire free before a figure snuck through and beheaded them both with a single sweep of his machete. Gabe stooped and passed one of the guns to Alice, who was next through the fence. Adam and Beth followed, leaving Gannon on the other side of the wire, looking ill at ease now he was so close to Flowers' domain.

"You sure you don't want to come with us?" Gabe asked him.

"I've done my part, I've got you in," the scientist replied. "The rest I'll leave up to you."

"Stay close by."

"I will. Good luck."

The four of them headed off, gluing themselves to the curving shadow of the house, avoiding confrontation where they could. For the most part, Flowers' enforcers were struggling to purge their bodies of the agent that was devouring them, and paid little heed to the knot of Returners skulking past. A few caught sight of them and tried to raise the alarm, but found no sound would emerge from their ravaged throats other than a soupy gurgle, and when they attempted to hoist their rifles the strength left their arms, the limbs putrefying. Those they were close reached out or made an effort to block them, but Gabe either ran them through with his blade – their skulls now the consistency of mud – or Alice took them out with a discreet burst from her semi. The bullets shredded them like paper; it was as if they were vanishing, losing all sense of corporeality.

They threaded their way through the grounds, Gabe's memory of the layout leading them, and they reached the main doors of the mansion. He turned to the other three. "I want to create maximum chaos, keep them all occupied. Adam, Beth – can you see if you can get the front gate open, let the remaining deadheads in? That should cause enough confusion to keep Flowers' goons away from the house. Once that's done, make a start on the other matter."

The pair nodded, and sprinted off down the drive. He glanced at Alice and motioned that they should enter, stepping out of the light and into the cool dark of the hallway. He could feel the vaguest tingle of the bacteria in the air, despite Gannon's assurance that his bio-weapon had a finite exposure time. His skin prickled slightly, but he seemed to be suffering none of the symptoms Harry's lot were displaying. In fact, the further they moved into the building, the more the sensation eased, as if it couldn't permeate brick and mortar. If that was the case, then the ganglord was probably unaffected, hiding away within the structure's bowels, waiting for whoever was coming for him.

The design of the house hadn't changed much since Gabe was last here, he noted, but he was surprised to see it gone to rack and ruin; dirt and debris were collecting on the tiled floor, and huge cobwebs dangled like gossamer nets from the ceiling. It was becoming derelict, as much subject to entropy as its residents. It looked ready to collapse. They reached the foot of the staircase, scanning left and right for signs of movement. Now they were far from the cries of the dead, it had fallen uncomfortably quiet. He hoped that much of the security had been placed outside to protect the perimeter, leaving a minimal staff within the building itself.

"We need to make for the first floor," he whispered.

"How do you know that's where Flowers will be?"

"I don't. But there's someone up there I need to see." He paused. "To save."

Alice studied him for a second. "OK. But be ready – this isn't going to be easy."

As if in answer, there was the roar of a sub-machine gun opening up and the plaster near their heads exploded as bullets raked across the hall. The pair of them dived behind the banister, splinters following in their wake. The shooter was at the top of the first flight of stairs, and was moving down, punctuating each footfall with a five-second burst. The wood around them cracked with each impact. Alice rolled, placed the barrel of the rifle between stairposts and fired up, catching the figure in the legs; it grunted and stumbled, pausing in its descent. She took advantage of the momentary lull, jumped to her feet, and squeezed off another blast, ripping through its neck and head. The shooter toppled onto its back, and slid down the remainder of the stairs, the remains of its skull bumping against the steps. Gabe joined her, standing over the body.

"Recognise him?" she asked, poking the cadaver's side with her barrel.

"Not any more." It was one of Harry's mob, but not much was left intact above the chin.

They started to ascend cautiously, and made it to the first landing. Gabe silently pointed to the next set of stairs they needed to take, then grimaced as a bullet powered through his arm; a second and third followed in quick succession, catching him in the thigh and chest. He didn't feel any pain, but the shock fleetingly paralysed him.

"Fuck!"

They crouched and ran, bullets zipping into the carpet at their feet or ricocheting off the light fittings: they were being fired on from above again. Gabe hooked a pistol free from his belt, and shot off several rounds blindly as they sought the safety of an alcove.

"Can you see where they are?" he breathed, curiously examining the new holes in his torso and limbs.

"Leaning over the railing, I think," Alice said, looking up. "They're going to get us pinned down."

"What do you reckon?"

She glanced around her, wiping a finger in the dust on a vase. "State of this place, you think it's got woodworm?" She smiled at him, then stood up from her hiding place, and put her semi to her shoulder, sighting it upwards on the banister above. Shots immediately rained down on her, and she took hits to the neck, arms and belly, but seemingly ignored them as she raked her fire on the structure itself, splintering the wood of the railing until it all but disintegrated. There was loud snap and it came apart, the whole balcony splitting in half. Alice dove back against the wall. As shards of debris plummeted, they were followed by two bodies spiralling to the floor, hitting the hallway tiles with a sharp smack. Their necks twisted sideways, and neither of them stirred.

Gabe whistled. "Nice shootin', Tex." He caught sight of the extent of her wounds, blood seeping from a gouge that had removed a good portion of her left cheek. "You OK?"

Alice shrugged. "A few more leaks, nothing I won't grow used to. Come on, let's keep moving, use the noise as cover."

They speedily climbed the rest of the stairs, shrouded in the clouds of grey dust that hung in the air. Gabe spotted the door leading to Anna's room and strode towards it, not knowing what he was going to do or say once he crossed the threshold, or indeed what would be waiting for him on the other side. He had laid his hand on the handle when he heard the voice.

"Just like old times, eh, O'Connell?"

Hewitt emerged from the shadows of the corridor, the silhouettes of two other figures behind him. They were all armed.

"Never thought I'd get to kill you twice."

CHAPTER TWENTY

"Drop your weapons," Hewitt ordered. They did as they were told, metal hitting the floorboards with a dry thump.

The kid looked terrible. The youth was still evident in his face – his resurrection had halted any ageing process, freezing him in that early twenties self-regard that Gabe had been so familiar with a decade earlier – but he hadn't escaped the effects of Gannon's chemical agent. Half of Hewitt's features were sagging on the right side, his eye, eyebrow, cheek and the corner of his mouth dripping like melted wax, the flesh hanging from his jaw in a grey dewlap. His hands too were pinkish claws, the skin stripped from the layers of muscle, and he gripped the shotgun in an insectile manner, white bone and knotted tendons visibly jutting between his knuckles. When he spoke, his words were slurred and apparently difficult to form, spilling from his mouth in a weary monotone.

"Why am I not surprised?" he said. "Somehow I had a feeling you'd be back."

"We all come back these days," Gabe replied.

"True." He contemplated this. "Y'know, I should've shot you in the head. Thought there'd be more indignity in seeing you staggering around with the rest of the deadfucks. Can't even rely on that now.

Even the maggotdicks are pulling themselves out of their tombs, dusting themselves down and pretending to be civilised."

"They're evolving."

"Towards what? You think you're more human than dead, O'Connell? Have you seen your reflection lately?"

"Look who's talking."

Hewitt made a guttural croak, which Gabe assumed was his nearest approximation of a laugh. "Yeah, you fucked us up. What the hell have you done to us, anyway?" He held up his contorted limbs in wonder.

"It's an airborne flesh-eating agent that was injected into those stiffs currently crisping up at the gate. Once the voltage hit them and they exploded, it was released."

Hewitt chuckled again. "Well, you got your revenge. Harry threw you out as his favourite son, and you wanted a little payback. That don't mean you're about to join the ranks of the living."

"That was never my intention," Gabe replied. "I'm just here to bring things to a close." He studied Hewitt curiously. "Talking of the old man, how's that working out for you, being his second in command? The position everything you hoped it would be? I know how much you wanted it."

"Fuck you, traitor."

"'Cause I also know it was you that shot me that night on Westminster Bridge, as I tried to escape. Shot me in the leg, for either the zombs or the army to get me. Either way, I was a dead man, and you were just the person to fill that vacancy."

The two Returners standing sentinel either side of the kid glanced at their colleague sharply.

Hewitt raised the shotgun, pumping the slide. "Guess this is third-time lucky –"

Gabe's eyes slid to one of the other figures. "Hey, Hendricks – how are the dogs?"

"Long gone." He had similarly suffered from the agent, his hair missing in clumps, the pigmentation of his skin almost boiled white. His voice was a low rumble. "Once Harry insisted we resurrect, the dogs couldn't stay. They wouldn't be comfortable around us. So he told me I had to kill them, every one. And I did."

"Hewitt here used to hate the stiffs with a passion," Gabe said. "Wanted to wipe them all from the face of the earth. Now he's a zomb himself. It's funny what we're prepared to do on the instructions of our masters."

"Enough." Hewitt strode forward, the shotgun held to his shoulder. "We've heard enough of your fucking bullshit." He swung the weapon towards Alice. "You thought you were going to help him overthrow Harry? Did he talk you into it? Talk up the revolution?" His grip tightened on the barrel. "You know what? It was for nothing. Because nothing changes. *Ever.*"

At point-blank range, he discharged the shotgun into Alice face, and her head disappeared in a wet explosion of crimson skull shards, a red spray hitting the wall behind her. The body beneath crumpled in a swirl of dust and gunsmoke. The ear-splitting report blasted Gabe into a momentary daze, but the second her lifeless corpse hit the ground at his feet, he snapped back into focus. With a yell he lunged at Hewitt, and tried to grab him around the neck, but the kid was too fast. He weaved out of Gabe's reach, then brought up the gun butt and slammed it into his temple, dropping him to his knees.

"You were a fool to come back," Hewitt snarled, standing over him. "You should've disappeared when you had the chance, grateful at your resurrection. Instead, you throw it all away on some petty pissant attempt at retribution." He straightened, withdrawing more shells from his pocket, chambering them into the shotgun. "I don't know what your problem is, O'Connell. You seem to go out of your way to make trouble for yourself."

"I was doing the right thing," Gabe murmured.

Hewitt snorted, mucus thick in his throat. "Like that means anything. Not so long ago, you thought being part of Harry's outfit was the right thing to do." He leaned in closer again. "Right and wrong have no place in this world anymore. It's just circumstances, and what you can get out of them. Isn't that what the old man taught you?"

"That's always been Flowers' way, but it's no longer mine."

"You're a weak, naive fucking idiot," Hewitt rasped and placed the shotgun to Gabe's head. "How many times have I got to put a bullet in you to make my point?"

Gabe rolled at the moment Hewitt's finger tightened on the trigger, knocking the barrel with his hand a fraction to the left just as he fired. He felt the shot scrape the side of cheek and singe his hair as the shell powered into the skirting board. Again the roar deafened him, but he was moving despite the stars dancing before his eyes. He grappled with Hewitt for control of the gun.

"Fucking shoot him!" Hewitt yelled at his comrades, but they hesitated, seemingly unsure of what action to take.

Wrenching the shotgun to one side, Gabe seized the advantage and drove his forehead into the bridge of Hewitt's nose, already rendered shapeless by the chemical agent. It burst like a grape, and he staggered backwards. Gabe wrested the shotgun from him, spinning around in time to see one of the pair – the enforcer he didn't recognise – finally advancing towards him. Gabe put two shots through him, blowing him across the landing to tumble down the stairs.

He swung back to Hewitt, grabbed him by the collar and stuck the gun under his chin. "You know what your problem is, pal? You underestimate people." He fired, detonating the top of Hewitt's head; brain matter exited in a purple stream and twisted itself around the chandeliers like a Christmas decoration. He threw the remains of the kid's body over the balcony. Then he turned back to face Hendricks, who remained motionless a few feet away.

"I don't want to have to do this," Gabe warned. Hendricks nodded and held up his hands in surrender, letting go of his semi-automatic. "Get out of here," he continued. "Don't waste any more of your... life... protecting him." He made a sideways motion of the head towards the door. Hendricks nodded again, and cautiously backed down the stairs until he vanished from sight.

Gabe leaned back against the wall, putting a hand to the side of his face that had taken a portion of the shotgun blast; his fingers disappeared into a rent in his cheek and brushed against his teeth and gumline. It had been closer than he thought, and had disintegrated a considerable section of flesh. Touching his scalp, there were deep bald grooves where it had seared past. Christ, how much of him was going to be left? He felt as if he was strung together by the flimsiest of threads.

He glanced sadly at Alice's headless cadaver, reasoning that at least she was at some kind of peace, free from the limitations of this fragile shell. He'd known little about her pre-death, and she hadn't been willing to reveal the human she'd once been. The other Returners that had pledged to help him had been the same. It was as if it was too painful to remember their past lives, of what they had once been. But now there would be no more resurrections, no more hunger, no more shuddering awareness of the creature that she – that all of them – had become. It was an end, final and complete.

"Won't be long before I'll join you," he whispered. Then he turned back to the door, yanked down on the handle and entered.

The room was just as he remembered it from all those years ago. It was as if by crossing the threshold he had stepped back in time by a decade or more. Unlike the decay that had tainted the rest of the building, this room – Anna's room – remained strangely untouched by the ravages of the passing months. The clock still ticked somnolently on the mantelpiece, the bare walls still tracked the progress of the passing sun, the chair still stood before the window, the curtains pulled back to reveal the expanse of the gardens, and the occupant of the chair was still seated upon it, facing the glass. On this occasion, however, there was someone else in the room. He was knelt on the carpet beside the chair, his hands perched on the arm, his head bowed. Gabe closed the door quietly behind him, and walked towards the pair, the shotgun hanging loosely at his side. He stopped no more than a couple of feet from the prone figure.

"Harry."

Flowers looked up, age and pain prominent in his eyes before recognition flooded in to join them. "Gabriel, my boy. To what do I owe this pleasure?" He didn't seem surprised at his presence.

"I've come to kill you. To tear all this down."

"Just you?"

"No. I've brought some others with me. If you look out the window, you'll see them."

Flowers swivelled and peered into the grounds. Somehow, Beth and Adam had succeeded in breaking open the gates – or at least a section of them – and the walking dead were stumbling through. The sporadic *thwump* of a landmine being triggered could be intermittently heard, and the glass shook in its frame with each explosion. But there were enough of them to easily swamp the defences.

"They've come to reclaim what's theirs," Gabe said.

The old man turned back to face him. "And you? You've come for my daughter?"

"Just to set her free."

Flowers laughed. "She doesn't need you for that, son. She's quite capable of doing it for herself."

"What do you mean?"

"Meaning," he reached out and placed a hand on hers, though she remained motionless, "I'm losing her with every passing second."

"You lost her a long time ago." He paused, studying his former boss. "Tell me something, Harry – you feel all this was worth it? Your acquisition of power. Was it worth the expense? What it cost you?"

Flowers withdrew his hand and stood. "I've hated myself for what I've had to do over the years. But somebody needed to take control, you must know that. You saw it when you joined my organisation – you were unused to the kind of work myself and my boys deal with, but you stuck around, especially after the outbreak. Why? Because for all that you might've despised me, you recognised there was somebody making decisions, formulating plans. A position like that is a beacon around which others gather, an anchor in uncertain times. But it requires sacrifices."

"Don't play the fucking martyr," Gabe snapped. "Everything you did, you did for your own benefit."

"Maybe. But don't kid yourself that you coming here is some kind of noble gesture. You're assuaging your own guilt too, for the mess you left behind."

"I always told her I'd be here for her. That's why I continued to work for you, and that's why I'm here right now. To try to bring her back."

"Well, you're too late," Flowers murmured. "She's lost to us both."

"What you mean is that the wound you inflicted a decade or more ago has finally reached her heart," Gabe snarled. "And now you can put her in the ground where she won't be a problem any longer."

Flowers' eyes flamed with anger. "I was protecting her, like any father would."

"Yeah? That what you told her infant son, as you held him for the final time?"

The older man let a bellow of rage and backhanded Gabe across the face. The impact knocked him back but he barely felt it. He swung the shotgun into Flowers' midriff, doubling him up, then delivered a powerful blow across the back of his head, a strike so hard it splintered the wooden stock of the weapon. He discarded the gun, grabbed Flowers by the throat and lifted him up against the wall, his fingers digging into the cold skin of his neck.

"You think... you're any better than me, O'Connell?" Flowers hissed, blood and drool dribbling from his mouth. "We're just two creatures... from the grave, who... should've died a long time ago."

"Difference is, I tried everything I could to stop becoming the monster, whereas you embraced it. But you know what? For you, I'll make the exception." Gabe pushed the old man's head back, exposing a tract of flesh. But just as he leaned in to take a bite, he felt a hand on his shoulder. He cast a quizzical glance over his shoulder, and saw Anna standing behind him. He relaxed his hold on Flowers, and stepped back; she was looking at her father, eyes full of shadow, her features composed in a death mask.

"Anna?" Flowers whispered.

"Dad." Her voice didn't seem to come as much from her lips as from *within* her, vast and emotionless.

"I'm so sorry."

His words were barely audible, but even so she shushed him quiet, placing a hand on his cheek, stroking it, moving down to his throat. She held it there, then tightened and squeezed and tugged, wrenching open her father's windpipe, which came free with a moist sluicing sound. He gargled, the rotten tissue of his neck collapsing without the support. Anna planted two hands on either side of his head and twisted it like a screw-cap, decapitating him with one swift motion. She studied her father's head for a moment, kissed it lightly before dropping it to the floor, then stepped back beside the window. Gabe moved forward, and took her crimson-stained hand in his.

"I'm not going to become like you," she said quietly, her gaze roving over the world beyond the glass.

"I know."

"I'm not going to stay."

"Me neither."

Anna lay her head on Gabe's shoulder, and they stood there in silence, framed against the light.

THEY FOUND GANNON not far from where they'd left him, crouched among the scrub. He raised his eyebrows that it was just the two of them.

"Gabe was never coming back," Beth said, before the question could be voiced.

"But the charges have been lit?"

Adam nodded. "With the deadheads providing the distraction, it wasn't difficult to start the fire."

The three of them watched as smoke began to billow from Harry Flowers' mansion, windows shattering from the heat, flames greedily swallowing timbers, dark black clouds massing above the roof. The dead that had poured through into the grounds stopped and circled the conflagration, like pilgrims to a great mystical vision. Beth wondered briefly if it was her imagination, or whether she actually saw a couple intertwined at an upstairs room, unconcerned by the encroaching fire, gazing back out at their audience; but in an instant they were gone, hidden by the roiling, thick smoke.

They watched until the house was no more than a blackened skeleton, a husk, confident that it wouldn't rise again. Then they turned and started back towards the city.

EPILOGUE

The Quiet Earth

I LINGERED ROUND them, under that benign sky: watched the moths fluttering among the heath and hare-bells; listened to the soft wind breathing through the grass; and wondered how any one could ever imagine unquiet slumbers for the sleepers in that quiet earth.

Emily Brontë,
Wuthering Heights

BIRD CRY ECHOES through the valleys, sharp and distant and mournful, like a parent calling for a lost child, and the black shadows of great wheeling shapes, wings outspread, circle the verdant slopes of the lowlands. A wind ruffles through the landscape, long grass dipping with the same tremulous undulation as the rhythmic pulse of a sea tide, and he stands with his face to the breeze, allowing himself to be buffeted by it. His skin is pocked with grit, his eyes watering from the flecks of dirt blown into them, yet he refuses to turn away. He feels like he's composed of shifting sand, subject to the whims of the elements; or maybe one of the skeletal trees perched upon the outcroppings, clinging tenaciously to life as it's stripped and scoured by an unstoppable eroding force. The chill in the air numbs his ears, dries his lips, and causes his nose to run – he wipes it on his sleeve – but the sky is the colour of sapphire and nothing can diminish the unblemished beauty of the vast canopy above him. It is a glorious spring morning, one in which the blood rushes a little faster and the hair tingles in syncopation with the new season budding around it.

He likes to take at least one moment a day to appreciate the country in this way, which has otherwise been disfigured by conflict. It serves as a reminder that time and nature will prevail, despite his species' best interests. That the planet keeps turning, that the sun continues to bestow its nourishing rays upon the surface, teasing seed into bloom, oblivious to the rampant designs of his kind. This land has seen enough hate wrought upon it to deface it permanently, the scars running deep below root and rock to leave it irrevocably changed, yet it refuses to be battered into ugliness. It continues, unbowed, to exist while all around it death tries to spread its taint.

It's a small moment of marvel, and one that he never grows tired of experiencing. He flicks the last of his ash off the end of his cigarette, and drops the butt into the mud, grinding it out with his heel. Breathing in that fresh-dew smell, swelling his chest with cool mountain air, he reaches for his shovel and hums as he begins to dig, dark soil turning beneath his blade. For two long hours he toils, producing a pit several feet square, work so professionally accomplished that he barely gives it a second glance, rarely stops to consider its size; he knows from instinct that its dimensions are correct. He's dug many more like it, and the procedure has the touch of routine about it, his labour accompanied constantly by quiet and tuneless melodies, as if he's unaware he's even making a sound. His movements are swift and unhampered by doubt, aware that he cannot afford to linger too long; this will not be the only hole he will have to dig before the day is done.

Hoisting himself out of the pit, he tosses the spade aside and grabs the nearest of the bodies by the legs, dragging it towards its makeshift grave. All the corpses have been wrapped in linen and tightly bound, and he is relieved that at least he does not have to look them in the face when he showers the dirt down upon them; but even so he can tell by the size and weight of this cadaver that it was a child, no more than a teenager. It is not the first he has buried, but that doesn't make it easier, to feel its lightness as he hefts it in his arms for a moment before allowing it to tumble into the ground. He hopes that the bodies that will be following it are the child's family – it makes little sense in the scheme of things, but provides some crumb of comfort that they will have each other's company beneath the soil – yet there is no way for sure of knowing. There are too many dead requiring his attention, and the niceties of a civilised grave have been foregone in the interests of speed and sheer quantity. Entire villages have been decimated, carcasses line the roads, and he has been charged with their disposal. So he retrieves the next and the one after that, filling his pit with these human-shaped parcels, humming in that cracked voice, stopping to pile the dirt back in once it is full before starting to dig again. He coughs, sniffs, wipes back tears, and continues, knowing he has no time to dawdle. Knowing, too, that this job will never be finished, not by him nor his successors. It is an insurmountable task, and yet one that he has accepted and one he will endeavour to complete while there is still breath left in his lungs.

The birds cry to one another as they skate low across the windswept hills, their shadows playing on the heaped mound of bodies that extends around the base of the valley: there are thousands of them, with no markers to distinguish each swaddled corpse from its neighbour. The dead congregate patiently as they await their return to the quiet earth, now gratefully far from the words of their roaring.

MATTHEW SMITH was employed as a desk editor for Pan
Macmillan book publishers for three years before joining *2000
AD* as assistant editor in July 2000 to work on a comic he had
read religiously since 1985. He became editor of the Galaxy's
Greatest Comic in December 2001, and then editor-in-chief of
the *2000 AD* titles in January 2006. He has written one other
novel, *Judge Dredd: The Final Cut,* and lives in Oxford.

www.abaddonbooks.com
www.abaddonbooks.blogspot.com
Follow us on twitter @abaddonbooks

I, ZOMBIE

BY AL EWING

INTRODUCTION

HOW DID THIS book come to be? Long story.

Back in the nineties, before I was anything more than an emo kid who didn't even know how to be emo properly – (I thought it involved Hawaiian shirts) – I did a lot of fooling around in the dead of the night with MS Paint, just playing around and having ideas and dreaming of the day when I would finally be paid actual money to write something. I can draw pretty good with a mouse, when the mood strikes me, and one time I ended up drawing something fairly gruesome – some hideous dead thing lurching at the reader, a gun in hand, cold red eyes blazing out of the screen. A zombie bounty hunter.

I called that particular concept... *The Bountyman.*

Ugh! Terrible name. Shockingly bad. But what did I know? I was a bored teenager fiddling with MS Paint. Nevertheless, I worked out how the story behind this dreadful name would play out.

Four – possibly five 'books,' or serieses. (The necessity to start small had not yet occurred to me. I see the same thing happening with people who come up to me at conventions with their 600-page long elf epic. I feel their pain, but the fact remains that starting with one page is easier and will teach you more.)

(Where was I? Oh yes.) Start with the zombie detective angle – then have him picked up by the government. But wait, wait, wait – why *do* zombies exist anyway? They always shy away from these fundamental questions. What are the mechanics there? Why do they need to eat brain matter and why don't they fall down when you shoot them? Say, what if *this* is why... hey, that works nicely. And didn't I read somewhere that in the classical mythology, werewolves eat dead flesh? Let's use that. Now we're cooking – and let's have a blowjob scene in a seventies gay bar because *why not?* Wow, when 2000AD finally approach me to do a series for them it'll be *amazing*.

Fast forward ten years.

What's this? Jon needs a second novel? Zombies are on the docket – hey! Let's resurrect that old Zombie series. *The Bountyman* – ugh! Awful title. Go deep into the detective thing. *My Gun is Quick. Cop Hater. The Big Sleep. I, The Jury.*

I, The Zombie. Hey, sounds like that old DC vampire series! *I, Zombie.* Perfect.

And now cram all those old ideas for the epic that would never happen into one crisp, compact novel bursting with horror, vileness and nasty shockers – and speaking of nasty shockers, why not *kill a baby?* No, wait – *a foetus!* Hmmm, how about the *Queen...?*

But I'm getting into spoiler territory. The rest of the strange gestation of *I, Zombie* you'll have to work out as you go along. I will say that those with a nervous disposition or an easily-upset stomach may want to keep a bucket handy.

Happy reading.

Al Ewing
June 2010

PROLOGUE

The Time of The Ghost Sun

SUN SANK OVER the western plain, down into the depths of Ghost Country.

Ar-rah was he, man and hunter and son of no father, strange thoughts in his head, strange talk in his mouth. Father was in Ghost Country, under the earth. The country without light where only Ghost Sun shines.

Sun sank, Sun died. Tonight was the light of Ghost Sun, bright white as bone, shining the land white-blue. The night of the Ghost Sun. Night of ghosts, night of strange thought.

Alone of the tribe, Ar-rah hunted by the light of Ghost Sun.

FATHER WAS LAID down in Ghost Country before Mother bore Ar-rah. Mother-thought brought thought of eyes cold blue, sick in heavy shadow. Sadness in those eyes, beneath the ridge of bone that Ar-rah had run fingertips over when small. Sometimes those eyes lay inside him, and when he closed his own those eyes were there, secret eyes that looked into him and all his secrets. Ghost eyes. Mother was in Ghost Country too.

No man had taught Ar-rah to hunt. Sons and fathers walked to the bush together, backs bent and stone teeth in hand, eyes sharp for the long-tooth, the killer. Fathers teaching sons, sons helping fathers, hunting together, dying together if long-tooth came upon them. It was the way.

No shame in dying by long-tooth. Shame in dying by teeth of men, shame and weakness. Un-guh drove his stone tooth through Father's neck in the time before time when Ar-rah was not. Un-guh led. Un-guh was strong and Father was weak. Father challenged Un-guh anyway.

Ar-rah understood. Mother was weak, sick. Even if she bore, Mother would be left behind, not to slow the tribe. Un-guh took dominion over Mother when he killed Father – Un-guh took responsibility. To fail in that would be the end of Un-guh. Who follows a leader who does not protect his own? Mother grew sick and died, but was never left, never abandoned.

Ar-rah had seen fourteen winters, as his Father had when Father died. Ar-rah's thoughts were quick, under the ridge of bone that shaded his eyes. He understood. Father had been quick too, and brave for all his weakness. Father had bought his child's survival with blood.

Even after Mother died, when fingers pointed at Ar-rah, strange and silent Ar-rah who hunted alone and took no mate – Un-guh took *responsibility*. Ar-rah was not left, though Un-guh never spoke to him. Un-guh had seen thirty winters, now, and was old and sick. He had days – illness would take him, or death by long-tooth or heavy-tread, for he still hunted with the tribe as a leader must.

Or the stone tooth would take him in shame.

Ar-rah had seen lips curling to bare teeth as Un-guh walked by. Hands holding cooking-stones grasping tighter, dull eyes under ridges of bone wanting to smash them down on the head of the old man as he shuffled past. But that was not the way.

The next dawn, or the dawn after, there would be a challenge. Ar-rah should be the one to challenge, to plunge his stone tooth into the old man's heart, to take leadership of the tribe, to never be abandoned and left for the long-tooth. But Ar-rah wanted only the security of the fire to come back to, the security of the tribe to belong to. And more – Un-guh had given him protection. To kill Un-guh...

Ar-rah searched for the concept in his mind, eyes squinting beneath the ridge of bone as he stooped lower, dragging fingertips over dusty ground.

To kill Un-guh... would not be...

It would not be *right*.

Such a concept would take more thinking about, but Ar-rah felt sure. He would find another way.

There was movement in the trees.

Ar-rah started, looking left. For a moment he saw a face in the trees, blue-white and pale, like the light of the Ghost Sun itself, eyes hooded. A member of the tribe?

No. There was nothing recognisable in that face. A ghost, then? Father, from Ghost Country, come under the light of Ghost Sun to watch and advise?

Ar-rah blinked, once. The face was gone. The trees were still.

Ar-rah reached up, instinctively rubbing his upper arms with his hands.

He felt cold.

AR-RAH HUNTED NIGHT-CREATURES, the things that walked and crawled and flew in darkness. A thrown stone tooth could find one of the black, shrieking flap-wings that nested in the caves, breaking bones and sending it down to the rock floor. Or a long sharpened pole of bamboo could be thrust down a burrow, impaling one of the dig-furs sleeping within. The meat was spare, but good – tender and nourishing. Along with the roots and berries gathered in the light, it made for good eating. Ar-rah was strong, if spare himself. There was no wasted flesh on his frame.

Ar-rah had hunted the swift-legs, once. But he'd learned the hard way that the swift-legs could not be hunted alone. They were too fast for that. The swift-legs had to be chased by the weaker hunter into the arms of the stronger, caught and slit from throat to belly with stone tooth. Even then, it was easy to miss the catch, or be kicked with a hoof – perhaps maimed or killed. The meat of the swift-legs was rare, and wearing its skin was the sign of a superior hunter. Mostly, the tribe fed on smaller game or gathered roots and nuts.

Ar-rah knew better than to hunt the swift-legs alone, even though they often grazed on the plains at night and there was no member of the tribe awake in those hours to see him fail. It was a waste of energy to run like a fool after the swift-legs, when there was easier and better game to be had. And yet Ar-rah found himself standing at the edge of a wide clearing, grass shining blue-white under the light of Ghost Sun, watching one of the swift-legs bending to graze. For a moment, Ar-rah allowed himself to think that the swift-legs was close enough to catch – but no. As soon as he lumbered forward, the swift-legs would be at the opposite side of the clearing, hooves pounding the dirt as it vanished forever.

Let it go. It could not be caught. It could not be reached.

Ar-rah eyed the sharpened bamboo in his right hand. His thoughts were quick, coming one upon the other like water in a stream. He felt the eyes of the ghost-man he had seen earlier on his back. If he turned, he felt certain he would see the man's shadowed eyes under the blue-white, almost translucent jut of his forehead.

He did not turn.

Instead, he concentrated on the bamboo stake he used to catch dig-furs. It was long, but it would not cover the distance between him and the swift-legs. Perhaps if he stretched to his utmost, he could poke the creature in the side and set it running.

He considered throwing it for a moment, but the bamboo was too light. Even sharpened as it was, it couldn't pierce the beast's hide without some weight behind it...

Ar-rah felt the eyes of the ghost on him. He hefted his stone tooth in his palm, then reached down to quietly pull up a swathe of the long grass at his feet. The swift-legs heard the sound and bolted, running for the bushes. Ar-rah nodded to himself, grunted softly, and continued wrapping the grasses around the stone and the bamboo, binding them together.

The thought was in his mind now.

Ar-rah turned, studying the forest behind him. If the ghost had been there, it was gone now. He turned back to his labours. The grasses would have to be tightly bound, to keep the stone tooth on the end of the bamboo.

Somewhere in the trees, there was a glimpse of bone-white flesh.

ONCE THE SWIFT-LEGS had vanished, Ar-rah worked slowly, taking his time. When he stood again and lifted the bamboo, the stone tooth bound to the end made a pleasing heft in his hand. It felt right. Ar-rah turned, slowly stalking back the way he had come.

It would be useless to wait here for the swift-legs – none would return to that grazing ground for at least another night, perhaps a night after that. But there were other clearings, other grazing grounds where the swift-legs knew they could feed undisturbed at night. Ar-rah knew the likely places.

He couldn't help but smile. The whole idea was foolish – a stone tooth at the end of a stick, of all things – but he felt a surge of excitement despite that, a flush of pride that he, strange, silent Ar-rah, had thought of it. If it worked... if he could throw it hard enough to pierce the hide of the swift-legs...

Everything would change.

Everything.

He shook his head, laughing at his own thoughts. It was the Ghost Sun putting these ideas into his head, the Ghost Sun with its strange light, bringing strange dreams and madness – and this *was* madness. This long stick with its stone tooth, against muscle and grace and speed. Beautiful madness, made solid by the blue-white light of the Ghost Sun, and the eyes of the ghost-brother who watched him.

Ar-rah walked out into the next clearing. No swift-legs here. Perhaps it would be better to leave it until the next night. That would be time enough for his... his... his stone-tooth-on-a-long-stick.

Ar-rah laughed like a boy.

He laughed at the most complete novelty he had ever known, the wonderful novelty of naming something. Something that was his own, that he had made, created, invented from nothing but the thoughts in his mind and the light of the Ghost Sun. Stick-tooth? Thrown-tooth? Long-stick-with-tooth? Long –

Long-tooth.

Ar-rah froze, eyes narrowed.

A dark, knotted shadow of liquid muscle and fur slinked into the blue-white light in front of him.

Long-tooth.

In the blue-white light, the monster was like a ghost itself, an ever-moving mass of grey and black stripes, a coiling river of flesh and killing power. The long fangs that gave it a name glittered as it padded closer, closer. The eyes...

The eyes were green, blue-green under the Ghost Sun's light. Ar-rah took a step backward. He always thought the long-tooth's eyes would be red as blood. No man had ever seen those eyes and lived.

This was the long-tooth, the killer, deadly spirit of muscle and speed, claw and cruelty and death. Ar-rah had called the swift-legs graceful, but their grace did not save them from this. The grace and speed of the long-tooth was infinitely greater and more profound, all the more beautiful and terrible because it was so deadly.

Ar-rah could not look away. He could not run. He knew that if he ran, he would die – ripped and torn by those claws, his entrails spilled on the grass, blood black under that terrible, awful light. He knew why the ghost-brother was watching him through the trees, now. This was the night that he would die, head severed from body, innards crushed and burst between vicious jaws, his life and strength stolen to feed and build the infinite life and strength of the long-tooth. This was Ar-rah's ending.

The long-tooth growled, sniffing the air. Scenting fear.

Ar-rah's bowels voided, spilling down the backs of his legs. But he did not move.

This was Death, then. This was the end of breath and warmth, the entry into Ghost Country. This was the end of love, the end of warm skin on skin and laughter. The end of splashing in streams, of feeling the Sun, the true living Sun on cheek and back, the end of all things good.

Then let Death come.

He would look it in the eye.

Slowly, he raised his stick-and-tooth.

One moment long-tooth was still. The next it was fluid lines of muscle and motion, arcing in the air, sharp claws and fangs and weight, leaping to the kill. Ar-rah smelled the breath of the long-tooth, deep and foul and stinking of meat and blood. It was to be the last scent in his nostrils, his final experience, this scent of death and meat.

Ar-rah half-jumped, half-stumbled backwards. At the same time, he thrust the stick-with-tooth upwards at the monster on top of him. He felt claws swiping at his chest, smelt the hot raging hunger washing over his face. Then he felt the weight, the mass of the beast, pushing down on the pole in his hands.

The long-tooth snarled and bit, thrashing in rage and pain. Ar-rah felt a sharp, stinging pain in his face and his vision went flat, one half dark. He felt something spilling down his cheek.

Then the long-tooth stopped moving.

Ar-rah sat on the cold grass, feeling the dead weight of the monster on top of him. After a time, he shifted, letting the long-tooth topple sideways and scrambling out from underneath. He lifted a hand to his face, feeling the deep gash there, the hole where his left eye had been. Blood trickled down his belly from the claw-marks on his chest. The pain was coming now, in great, slow, throbbing pulses.

And Ar-rah was alive.

The stick-with-tooth was jutting from the monster's heart.

AR-RAH STOOD, HOLDING his palm to his missing eye, for a very long time. The marks on his chest were not deep, and the blood slowed, then stopped. But the gash on his face continued to trickle when he took his hand away. He would have to pack it with mud and grass, and soon. Even so, perhaps he would sicken, the flesh around his missing eye turning yellow, then green, giving off the stink of rot and corruption. Perhaps he would grow slowly weaker until he died. He had seen it happen often. It was rare for men to survive such wounds. It didn't seem to matter to Ar-rah.

He stood and looked at the long-tooth.

It was massive. Big as three men at full growth. The teeth were as long as his forearm. Ar-rah placed his palm on the monster's flank, feeling the fur, the muscle and sinew. Cooling in the night air.

Soon it would be cold.

There had been life there once – the essence of life, life and strength in all its great and terrible glory. More than men, who hunted and gathered and shivered and died in the winters, who needed fire and skins to survive, who banded together in tribes to hide their weakness. Men were half-alive, shadow-creatures who needed to walk and talk and make things simply to avoid being torn to shreds by creatures like this. Things that were truly alive. Truly real.

Stood against the long-tooth, all men were ghosts.

Ar-rah watched a fly buzz and settle on the long-tooth's fur, then move to its eye. Staying to feed. The creatures needed to be skinned, the meat cooked and stored. The long teeth could be kept and used somehow, as weapons. He should get to work.

He stood.

He tried to recall how the long-tooth had moved.

Where was that life now? That strength? Where was that slow, liquid majesty of movement?

It was as though he had killed the wind and the rain. He had come face to face with something very like the Sun itself.

And now flies were eating it.

There was a flash of white from the trees. Ar-rah waited.

His shoulders slumped as the ghost-brother stepped into the clearing. He did not even feel surprised. It seemed natural that ghosts should be here, after this. He had ended a life – a life that possessed a power and magnitude he could barely comprehend. This was the death of awe and terror, fear and wonder. The death of everything Ar-rah knew.

Of course the ghosts would mark the passing.

The ghost-brother walked slowly, eyes lost under bone, skin the colour of the ghost light that shone from the Ghost Sun above. Ar-rah's remaining eye was sad and wet as he turned to look back. He was suddenly very tired.

The ghost-brother grunted and nodded to the dead long-tooth, and the shaft of bamboo jutting from its chest. It was an acknowledgement. This was the first time such a thing had happened.

Ar-rah knew he should feel something. Pride, perhaps? Shame? Instead he simply stood, allowing the ghost-brother to place one strong hand on his bony forehead, the other at his neck. A ritual gesture, a ghost ceremony. His reward for killing the world.

Ar-rah felt nothing, even when the ghost-brother tore the head from his body in one impossibly strong, savage motion, blood spattering the grass and the corpse of the long-tooth.

The body took a couple of steps backward, gushing from the neck, and collapsed in a heap. Under the light of the Ghost Sun, the blood was jet black. The ghost-brother said nothing.

Carefully, he took the severed head, the one remaining eye rolling back in the socket, lips twitching, and brought it down hard against his knee. Hard enough to shatter the thick, bony canopy of the skull.

The ghost-brother reached into the skull with his blue-white fingers and scooped out a handful of the grey-pink matter inside, raising it to his lips. He tasted it, then tore into the rest, chewing, swallowing, pieces of brain and skull fragments sticking to teeth and chin.

When the feeding frenzy was over, the ghost-brother casually tossed the severed head onto the grass, then stood and looked at the long-tooth, and the stick-with-tooth in its heart. If there had been a thought in the ghost-brother's ghost head, then perhaps he would have been disappointed. Perhaps he would have expected more from Ar-rah, with his strange thoughts, so quick and sure.

Perhaps he would have wondered when the time would come.

When they would be ready.
But there were no thoughts.
The ghost-brother turned and padded off towards the trees.

CHAPTER ONE

My Gun is Quick

TIME SLOWS TO a crawl.

The broken glass around me hangs in the air like mountains of ice, floating in space in the science-fiction movie of my life. Like healing crystals in a new-age junk shop, hanging on threads, spinning slowly. Beautiful little diamond fragments.

For five minutes – or less than a second, depending on your viewpoint – I drift slowly downwards, watching the glass shimmer and spin. It's moments like this that make this strange life-not-life of mine seem almost worthwhile.

Moments of beauty in a sea of horror and blood.

I'd like to just hang here forever, drifting downwards, watching the shards of glass spin and turn in the air around me, but eventually I have to relax my grip or get bored. And I'd rather not get bored of a moment like this one.

I let go.

Time snaps back like a rubber band.

The moment passes.

* * *

TIME PERCEPTION IS a trick of the human mind. The average human perceives events at a rate of one second per second, so to speak, but that doesn't make it the standard. Hummingbirds and mayflies perceive time differently. It's much slower for them, to match their metabolism – I'm pretty sure that's the case. I read it somewhere. In a magazine.

New Scientist, I think. Or *Laboratory News*. Maybe *Discover*.

I read a lot of scientific magazines.

It might have been *Scientific American*. Or *Popular Science*. Or just plain *Science*. I go through them all.

I look for articles about decomposition, about autolysis and cell fractionation, about the retardation of putrefaction. About the factors that affect skin temperature or blood clotting.

Things that might explain my situation.

I know it wasn't the *Fortean Times*. Unless it was talking about an alien hummingbird kept under a pyramid. Or possibly building the pyramids. I read that one for the cartoons.

Anyway. Time perception is a trick of the human mind. It's possible to slow down the perception of time in humans, to perceive things in slow motion, experience more in a shorter time. Shorten reaction time to zero. Anybody can do it with the right drugs, or the right kind of hypnosis.

I can do it at will.

I concentrate.

Time slows.

The glass hangs in the air.

I look for articles about the basal ganglia and the superchiasmatic nucleus, about neurotransmitters and the subconscious. I've done research when I can. Heightened time perception burns a lot of adrenaline, apparently. A lot of energy stores. You can't keep it up for long periods without needing plenty of sleep.

But I don't need to sleep.

I don't need to eat either.

Or breathe.

Time rushes back in, like air into an empty lung that's never used.

The moment passes...

...and then the soles of the converse trainers I wear to look cool slap loudly onto the concrete floor of a disused warehouse in Hackney and four big men in badly-fitted suits are pointing guns at me. But that's okay. I've got a gun too. And if they shot me, I wouldn't bleed.

My heart doesn't beat, so the blood doesn't pump around my body. My skin is cold and clammy and so pale as to be almost blue, or green, depending on the light. My hair is white, like an old man's. My eyes are red and bloodshot and I keep them hidden when I can.

Let's see, what else do you need to know before we get started?

Oh yes.

I've been dead for the last ten years.

I DON'T HAVE any memory of not being dead. The earliest thing I can remember is waking up in a cheap bed-and-breakfast in Stamford Hill. The room was registered in the name John Doe – the name generally used for an unidentified corpse. I'm sure somebody somewhere thought that was hilarious.

Still, it was the only name I had, so I stuck with it. To all intents and purposes, it was mine.

To all intents and purposes, the gun lying by the sink was mine as well.

It's strange. I don't have any memory of feeling different, of anything being out of the ordinary. I got up, brushed my teeth even though they never need it, took a shower even though I never smell of anything. People hate that more than BO, I've noticed. That smell of nothing at all, that olfactory absence. Cologne can't cover it, because there's just the cologne on its own, with that huge blank void beneath that rings all the subconscious alarm bells. Even your best friend won't tell you.

I don't remember being surprised that I was dead. I'm actually more surprised now than I was then, surprised at not being surprised. What sort of person was I, that I woke up dead and took it in my stride?

I remember that the first thing I did that day was shoot a man in the back room of a dingy pub in the Stoke Newington area.

Why did I do that? What sort of person was I then?

Obviously, I had a reason. I mean, I must have. I just can't remember quite what it was.

I had a reason. I had a gun. I had a mobile phone that was a bit clunky and crap and didn't even have games on it, never mind anything useful, and occasionally it rang and then I had a job to do that fit someone who was dead but still moving around. I had a bank account, and I had plenty of money sitting in it for a rainy day. I had a low profile.

No matter what, I always had a low profile. I always knew how to fit in, even though I was dead. Even though I killed people.

Even though I have occasionally...

Just occasionally... I may have...

I may have eaten...

You know what? I have better things to do right now than think about that.

For a start, the bad men are pulling their guns.

THEY'RE PULLING THEIR guns. My legs uncoil and I sail up, arcing forward, the first bullet passing through the space I've left behind me. I hold time in my mind, keeping it running at a reasonable speed, not too slow, not too fast. Behind me, the last shards of glass from the window hit the floor. At this speed, it sounds like wind chimes clanging softly in the breeze. The gunshots sound like the bellows of prehistoric monsters. The shells clang against the stone like church bells.

Did you ever see *The Matrix*?

Bit of a busman's holiday, I thought.

My own gun roars and I'm almost surprised. The bullet drills slowly into the head of the nearest man, already fragmenting, leaving a bloody caste-mark in the very centre of his forehead, the flesh rippling slightly under the pull of an obscene tide. I watch the exact moment when the look of surprise freezes on his face, goes slack, and then the back of his skull swings open slowly like multi-faceted cathedral doors, and the pulsing chunks of white-pink matter float out, carnival-day balloons for a charnel-house Mardi Gras.

Slow it down enough, and everything fascinates. Everything is beautiful.

Little chunks of brain, flying through the air. Scudding like clouds. Floating like jellyfish. I'm casting about for a better simile here because I don't want to admit what they really look like to me.

Tasty little hors d'oeuvres. Canapés.

The trouble with being able to slow down time for yourself is that it gives you far too much time to think. And I have better things to do right now than think about that.

I speed things up a little, force myself back on the job as the bullets move faster, one cutting the air next to my left ear, another whispering against the leg of my jeans. My empty hand slaps on the concrete ahead of me and pushes my body up through space, somersaulting until I land on my feet behind a wall of stacked crates. I'm not sure what's in them, but hopefully it's something like dumb-bells or lead sinkers or metal sheeting or just big blocks of concrete. Something that'll stop small arms fire. I don't want to patch up any more holes in myself.

There's a sound coming from close by. It's not wind chimes or church bells or a prehistoric monster. It sounds like some kind of guttural moaning, like a monster lost in an ancient dungeon.

I let go of time and it folds back around me like bad origami. The moment passes.

The sound makes some sense now.

It's a child. Sobbing. From inside the crate I'm hiding behind.

That's where they put Katie, then.

AT LEAST IT wasn't paedophiles. At least it wasn't SAY A PRAYER FOR LITTLE KATIE SAYS OUR PAGE 3 STUNNER. That's something in today's world, isn't it?

It was an old-fashioned kidnap. Scrambled voice mp3 file, two days after she went missing, nestled in amongst the inbox spam with the fake designer watches and the heartfelt pleas from exiled Nigerian royalty. "Give us the money, Mr Bellows, or we give you the finger. Do you see what we did there? It's a pun." Then a time and a place and an amount to leave and no funny business, please.

Mr Bellows runs a company called Ritenow Educational Solutions. He's the one who prints the certificates when you do the adult courses. This is to certify that MARJORIE PHELPS has achieved PASS in the study of INTERMEDIATE POTTERY. Marjorie won't get any kind of job with the certificate, even if she achieves DISTINCTION in the study of ADVANCED SHORTHAND. It's worthless, but she'll pay up to a couple of hundred pounds to have it on her wall and point it out to the neighbours.

Mr Bellows doesn't run any of the courses. He doesn't make the sheets of china-blue card with the silvery trim and 'This is to Certify has Achieved in the Study of' written in the middle, with gaps. He just has a list of who's passed and what they got, and he runs that through a computer and then his big printer churns out ten or twenty thousand useless certificates a day. He has a staff of three single mothers and a temp who's just discovered The Specials and thinks that makes him unique, and all they do is collate the list of the gold, silver and bronze medal winners in these Housewife Olympics and then print them onto china blue with silver edging and sell them on for exorbitant amounts of money.

Mr Bellows runs a company that does essentially nothing to make essentially nothing. He's the middleman for a useless end product. He's living the British Dream.

And now, the British Nightmare.

Doing nothing to make nothing is a profitable line of work. Mr Bellows has two houses and two cars, neither of which have more than two seats. He also has a flat in Central London which he's working up the courage to install a mistress in. Little Katie Bellows is going to Roedean as soon as she's old enough. If she gets old enough. Mrs Bellows collects antique furniture as a hobby. And Mr Bellows has my mobile number.

That doesn't come cheap.

"Find them, John," he said.

He had whisky on his breath and his voice came from somewhere deep in his throat, rough and hollow, choked with bile. "Find them and kill them. Bring her back safe." There were tears in his eyes that didn't want to come out. A big, gruff man who could solve things with his fists if he had to, but not this. Standing in the drawing room he'd earned with graft and grift and holding my dead hand and trying not to cry. The echo of his wife's soft sobbing drifting down from an upstairs bedroom. An antique clock on the mantelpiece that hadn't been wound, silent next to a photo turned face down because it couldn't be looked at.

Frank Bellows had my number because he'd used me in the past to do things that weren't strictly legal. He hadn't always had the monopoly on doing nothing to make nothing. He'd needed someone who didn't strictly exist to break into a competitor's office and burn it to the ground. Because if the perpetrator doesn't strictly exist, then it isn't arson, is it? Not strictly.

I smiled gently behind my shades, a non-committal little reassurance. Then I stepped back and nodded gently. He only sagged.

"Get them. Kill them. Get out." His voice was choked as though something was crawling up from inside him, some monster of grief that had made its nest in the pit of his stomach. I felt sorry, but what could I do? They only make promises in films.

But then, they only make this kind of kidnap in films. If they'd been real crooks, well, she'd be vanished still. HUNT FOR MISSING KATIE CONTINUES PAGE EIGHT. "Saucy Sabrina, 17, holds back the tears as she keeps abreast of the news of Little Katie – and speaking of keeping a breast!" MISSING KATIE BINGO IN *THE STAR* TODAY.

These weren't "real" crooks. They were fictional. The script-written ransom note. The suits from Tarantino, the bickering and sniping at each other with perfect quips that they'd spent months thinking up, while I stood on the warehouse skylight, the one they hadn't even bothered to check, picking my moment to crash through the glass and kill them all because the customer is always right. The lack of any covering of tracks, because they were too busy being "professional" to actually be professional.

There's nothing more dangerous than a man who's seen a film.

The police would have found them eventually, but by that time Katie, age six, probably would have been killed.

They're keeping her in a crate and shooting at her, for God's sake.

It can't be healthy.

BULLETS SMASHING WOOD, sending splinters and fragments into the air, puffs of shredded paper. The crates are full of catalogues, thick directories of dayglo plastic for schools. "Teach your child about disabilities. Neon wheelchairs help kids learn." Most of the bullets thump into those, gouging tunnels and trenches until their energy is spent.

One comes right through the crate I'm hiding behind. Right through, and there's a little yelp. A little girl's half-scream, too frightened to come all the way out.

The silly bastards have hit her.

Instinctively, I grab time and squeeze it until it breaks. Dead stop.

This is the slowest I can go. I look at the bullet, crawling from the hole. Slightly squashed but unfragmented. No blood on it. It missed.

Oh, thank God.

I'd never have managed to explain that.

Time rushes past me like a tube train and my legs hurl me backwards, firing over the top of the crates at them. *Follow me. Shoot at the catalogues. No father's going to mourn a listing of expensive fluorescent dolls with only one leg. Shoot the crates over here, you silly bastards, you wannabe film stars.*

And they do.

I squeeze off a couple of shots at them, but they've found their own cover. More crates, more catalogues. Right now they seem to just be blazing away with their guns held sideways like they're in a music video. When they run out of bullets they'll probably chuck them at me. The trouble is, they're such rubbish shots, because of their crappy sideways gun shooting and their stupid unprofessional Tarantino mindset that thinks all they have to do is blaze away and the bullet will magically find its way into my face if they can only look cool enough doing it, that they're going to blow Katie's head off long before they put a hole in me.

It's time I got a little bit creative.

One of the advantages of being dead is that you can do things that people who aren't dead can't do. Actually, most people who are dead can't do them either, but never mind that for now. The important thing is that I can do them.

For example, my left hand – the one not sporadically pointing the gun over the crates and keeping them busy – is severed. It's held on with surgical wire.

I have no idea when this happened.

I mean, it must have been done after I woke up ten years ago. Surely. Nobody living has their hand chopped off and stuck back on the stump with surgical wire.

I mean, you'd have to be insane.

What sort of person was I?

My memory is a little fuzzy on things like that – whether I'm insane or not. I do kill a lot of people.

And I do eat... occasionally, I do eat people's...

But I have better things to do right now than think about that.

I shoot off three or four rounds to keep them busy, then put the gun to one side and grip my left hand in my right. And I pull. I'm a lot stronger than the average person, even the alive ones. Since I feel no pain and never need to rest, my muscles can work much harder, strain much longer. The wire snaps easily, link by link, and my hand pops right off in a couple of seconds, like a limb off a Ken doll.

Now I'm holding my left hand in my right, feeling the dead weight of it. Only it's not dead. Well, it is, but it's still wriggling. Twitching. Flexing.

I can still move it.

I wiggle the fingers on my severed hand. I snap them, and the sound is like a dry twig snapping. Then I toss it over the wall of crates like a grenade – a hand grenade, ha ha. The fingers hit the floor first and skitter like the legs of a giant beetle. I can feel them tapping the concrete. And then – it's off. Racing across the concrete floor as the wannabe film star boys widen their eyes and make little gagging sounds in their throats. They know what kind of film they're in now. Oh yes.

I can feel it moving. I can feel the fingers tapping. I'm reaching to pick up my gun, but I know exactly where my other hand is. Moving quickly across the floor, skittering and dancing, a dead finger ballet. I can see it in my mind's eye. Is it me, drumming my fingers, that's propelling it along? Or is it my hand, moving further away from me now, a separate entity crawling and creeping on its own stumpy little legs?

The further away from me it gets, the more I think it's the latter.

The more it moves on its own.

That's pretty weird, if you think about it.

What sort of person was I?

I can still feel the fingers tapping, but I'm not directing it any more. It's close now. Skittering around the crates as they lower their guns and stare in horrified fascination. I can't help but hum to myself at moments like these.

Their house is a museum... when people come to see 'em... they really are a scree-um... the Addams Fam-i-ly.

Ba da da DUM.

It leaps.

I mentioned how strong I am. And when my hand is this far away from me... there's really no human impulses to hold it back. The fingers flex and push against the concrete and launch it forward like a grasshopper, onto the face of the nearest cinema tough-guy. He's in a film now, all right. He's in *Alien*.

Where's your Guy Ritchie now, you tosser?

Fingers clutch, sinking into cheeks. I can feel his lips against my palm, squashed, pleading desperately, trying to form words. I have no control over my hand, my evil hand. But I still enjoy feeling it squeeze... and *squeeze*... and squeeze... until the fingers plunge through the flesh and crack the bone, crushing the jaw, the thumb and the forefinger alone mustering enough pressure to punch through the temples, cracking the skull, sending ruptured brain matter seeping out of it.

Brain matter.

I've got better things to do than think about that.

My hand drops away, sticky with blood and juice, as the last one starts blazing away at it, shrieking like a little girl. He misses with every shot. It's a hard thing to hit, a scuttling hand, and besides he's probably still holding his gun sideways. I'm trying not to laugh, I really am...

Does that make me a bad person? Does that make me a monster?

What sort of person am I?

Crushing a man's face with my severed hand that crawls around on its own when I let it off the leash, that probably makes me a monster, I'll admit that. But I can be forgiven for the occasional chuckle at the death of a would-be child murderer. *The News Of The World* would canonise me.

His gun clicks out. He's fumbling for ammo. He's in a whole other world now, the silly bastard. There's nothing so important to him as killing that *thing* that's come scuttling around the corner of his little school-catalogue fort and broken everything he thinks is real into little pieces. He's forgotten everything else in the world, which is stupid, because *I'm* in the world.

And I'm coming for him.

Grab time. Slow it down. Gunshots flatten and stretch into whale songs and I'm floating, somersaulting over the crates, converse trainers smacking the ground, propelling me forward as the gun comes round...

And there aren't any bullets in the gun.

How did I miss that? The slide's all the way back.

Do I even have any ammo on me?

How could I possibly miss something like that?

What sort of person am I?

He's seen me. He turns like a cloud formation revolving in a light breeze. The gun lifts like the thermometer in an unsuccessful TV telethon, one atom at a time. So slow. But so am I.

That's the trouble with compressing time. It looks great, but there's no use in slowing time down if you're already too late.

The gun goes off, slow and beautiful as sunrise, and here comes the bullet. Cross-cut head this time. I throw my weight off, but he's too close...

You need a bit of space to dodge bullets.

I don't feel pain, but still, it hurts. It hurts because there's no real way to patch the holes up when I get shot. I've been shot a fair bit, although not as much as I should have with the life I lead. In my arms and legs there are little tunnels and trenches where I've been shot with 9mm ammunition, a couple of nasty exit wounds packed up with clay. In my left breast, there's a big ragged hole from where some crack shot tore my heart open with a well-placed sniper round. I stitched up the hole as best I could, packed it with gauze... but my heart is sitting in my chest, not beating and torn apart. And that does hurt.

Because I do try to know what sort of person I am.

I do try to be normal.

I really do, with my severed hand and my time senses and my strength and my speed. I try and be a normal guy, as much as I can. I drink. I eat. I go to the bathroom, though it's just to sit and think for a while – there's no pressing need for me to be there, if you get my meaning. I go to the cinema and watch the popular films. I get popcorn. I used to watch *Big Brother* but now I've stopped, like everyone else. I buy *The Sun* but I get my actual news from the Internet. I listen to Radio 2. I make up opinions about religion and music and television and political parties and I try to stick to them even if they aren't very logical or intelligent. I want to be like everyone else.

I want to fit in.

I try.

I can feel the bullet press against my gut, then pierce the skin, boring into me, fragmenting, splitting, shrapnel shredding my intestines, cutting and tearing. Slowly and carefully, like surgeons' scalpels in a random operation, the surgery dictated by the roll of dice.

My arm moves forward, pushing against time. It's like I'm underwater. The gun begins to arc slowly through the air, my empty, heavy gun. Rolling and tumbling through space.

Chunks of tattered, bloody meat drift out of the ragged hole in my lower back. My T-shirt has 'The Dude Has Got No Mercy' written across it, and it's brown with kind of seventies lettering in orange and white. It's my favourite shirt and it's ruined. My shirt's ruined. My belly's ruined, because I was stupid and this silly film star-wannabe bastard got off his lucky shot...

I watch the gun tumble through the air, turning over and over, like a space station on a collision course with a nameless, forbidding planet.

I threw it very hard. The sound of his skull fracturing is like a great slab of granite, big as the world, being snapped in half by cosmic giants. It's a good sound. It makes me feel better about my shirt.

Stitch that, bastard!

I let go, and time closes over me like the case for an old pair of spectacles. The moment passes, and I stumble for a couple of steps, feeling more meat slop out of my belly and back, more scraps on the floor. There's a hard thud as a hundred and fifty pounds of flesh that used to be a human being crashes onto the concrete.

I walk gingerly around the stacked crates and have a look. His legs and arms are thrashing, his eyes rolled back in the sockets. His skull is cracked and bleeding. His fragile, fractured eggshell skull.

And the tasty yolk within.

And all of a sudden –

– all of a sudden my head is pounding and there's a hot metal taste in my mouth and I don't have anything better to do than think about –

brains

– AND NOW IT's later.

How much later? How much time has passed?

It feels like a long time.

Mr Tarantino, the film star, the silly bastard, he's still lying at my feet. His position's changed. Like he's been shaken about like a rag doll.

His head is... empty.

Hollowed out. The top of it missing, cranium tossed across the room, and there's something... something is clinging to my lips. To my tongue.

Something I've been eating.

The taste is still in my mouth.

And it tastes so good.

Time is still slow, still in my grip. I look to the left, and I see a small, terrified eye staring at me through a bullet hole in the side of a packing crate. The eye slowly closes, like a curtain majestically falling, then rising, opening again. Blinking.

There's a sound in my ears like lowing cattle. It's Katie's sobbing. I wonder how much she saw?

I try to be normal. I really do. I try so hard.

But I just can't seem to stop eating brains.

And that's the sort of person I am.

I let go.

Time wraps around me like a funeral shroud.

And the moment passes.

CHAPTER TWO

One Lonely Night

TWENTY-FOUR HOURS AND everything sucks.

That's my golden rule. I don't care if you've just been elected the Lifetime President of Diamond-Studded Blowjob Valley, all it takes is twenty-four hours and everything in your hands will turn back to shit.

Case in point – it's twenty-four hours after that damn warehouse job, when I put down a bunch of soulless little kidnapping pricks and rescued a little girl from being cut up and sent through the post piecemeal. I should be happy. I'm not happy. I'm stiff and cranky and guilty and I'm not happy at all, not one little bit.

Is it any wonder?

I got shot, which means I got careless. That hasn't happened in forever and it's not something I want to happen again. The reason I'm stiff is because I let my head get so far into the clouds that some gangster-wannabe with delusions of adequacy blew a hole in my belly. How would you feel after something like that?

I know, I know, you wouldn't feel anything, you'd be slowly drying on a cold concrete floor as various kinds of bacteria had a get-together in your soft tissues, I'm actually very lucky *blah blah blah.*

Humour me. A couple of pieces got blown out of me and went skittering across the floor. I had to stick them in my pocket – my own spine jangling around with the keys to my flat. Imagine how that felt. Not to mention I was sagging and slumping and wobbling all the way home, holding my ribcage straight by putting my hands in my pockets and keeping my arms locked.

I didn't feel normal, is what I'm trying to say.

I hate not feeling normal.

So I ended up gluing my spine back together with superglue. It looks okay if I wear a shirt, but it feels stiff, unnatural. Every time I shift my weight, it's a reminder of what I am. So I'm cranky.

I'm also cranky because I can't get my coffee. I mean, I drank it – I have a big jar of Gold Blend in the cupboard – but ten minutes after I swallowed it, most of it trickled out of the ragged hole in me and made a mess on my sofa. Normal people drink coffee, but I can't because I'm not normal. I can't even pretend to digest anymore.

So where does that leave me? No more eating. No more drinking. No bacon and eggs, no bourbon. No steak, no champagne. Not unless I want to go and sit in the bath and watch it all slop out of me again. No more Sunday dinner at somewhere classy like a Berni Inn or a Harvester, no more McDonald's or Burger King or KFC. No more doing what normal people do.

I haven't felt this low in a long time.

Is it any wonder I feel like this? Can you blame me?

I try so hard to be normal. I mean, here I am, sitting on my coffee-stained sofa, in a studio apartment full of carefully chosen crap. In the CD rack, I have Robbie Williams, Abba, Coldplay. A little Radiohead, before they got weird. Everything the Beatles ever did. The Kaiser Chiefs. It's all good music. It's all music that people like. The Sex Pistols. U2.

I'm a big fan of Pink Floyd.

They're very important.

You see how hard I'm trying?

The DVD shelf is above the TV. *The Godfather, Pulp Fiction, Schindler's List, Star Wars* – the old movies, not the new ones – *Lord of the Rings, Trainspotting...* I mean, I don't watch them, I just own them. I've watched everything on there maybe once, if that, but they're all carefully arranged in alphabetical order to show how passionate I am about film and cinema.

I'm normal.

I am just like you.

Behind the bookcase with the DVDs and the CDs and the John Grisham, there's an attachè case with my guns and some other equipment.

I bought the last Harry Potter the week it came out. It's sitting next to a copy of *Ulysses* that I keep meaning to read but never get around to, and the *Lord of the Rings* that I only read when the films came out.

I am just like you.

Except I'm leaking coffee out of a ragged, badly-patched hole in my stomach, and my spine is fused together with industrial-strength glue.

And I'm cold and I'm clammy and I don't breathe.

And sometimes I eat brains.

Is it any wonder I feel like this?

I'm sitting on my coffee-stained sofa and I'm stiff and I'm cranky and I'm guilty. Most of all I'm guilty. Because I remember that little girl.

LITTLE KATIE, KIDNAP victim, six years old. I remember her eyes. Blank, looking straight ahead, her chest hitching and heaving to get out a scream as I tore open the crate she was in and scooped her up. She didn't make another sound all the way back to her father.

Bellows was waiting in the driveway of his big fancy house, stood next to his big fancy car. He looked happy at first. Then he saw her and all the colour went from his face, flooding back in a deep, angry purple. Katie wasn't looking at him. She wouldn't look at him, or her mother. She was only little, but she understood.

Her Daddy had sent a monster after her.

Bellows reached out to take her out of my arms and she twisted loose, toppling down onto the gravel, scraping her knees and elbows. She scampered inside like a cornered rat and hid, making little snivelling, whining sounds.

Bellows looked at me like he was going to tear my head off right there. "What did you do to her?"

I just looked at my shoes.

What's the normal reaction to that?

I was angry for a moment – *I bloody saved her life, you muppet* – but then it all drained away. What had I done to her? I'd torn off heads and eaten brains from skulls right in front of her. I'd turned into a monster and then brought her back to Daddy and made him a monster too. I'd traumatised her for life. Mr Bellows asked me to bring back Katie, and I brought back a shell.

I'd killed the Katie that used to be as surely as if I'd put a bullet in her.

Under the circumstances, it didn't feel right asking for money.

It didn't feel right doing this job anymore.

I WANT TO work in an office, doing nothing to make nothing. I want to work in a factory that makes cardboard boxes, pressing the same brown shape out day after day. I want to work behind a bar full of people who don't care if I live or die so long as I pour them the right kind of overpriced lager.

I want to be normal.

I want to be just like you.

But the trouble with those jobs is that they don't make allowances. Next time you go to a job interview, try soaking your hand in ice water for three hours before you walk in the room. Grab the boss in a firm handshake. Say how excited you are to be there. Watch his eyes. It doesn't matter if you're the best education certificate printer on Planet Earth, you're going home unemployed.

Nobody wants to hire a corpse.

Even if I get some work down at an abattoir or a skinning yard, somewhere they just don't care – and this is after spending thousands on false papers to fake that I've got a past – eventually, I'm going to slip. Go into a fugue state.

Eventually, I'm going to get hungry.

What happens then?

What happens when it's five o'clock quitting time and all I can hear is the thunk-thunk-thunk of the belt moving past me and everything else is silent because twenty people are lying on the cold concrete floor of the factory with empty heads... eyelids flapping over empty sockets because I ate their brains down to the eyeballs...

Maybe it's happened. I don't know. The first thing I remember is waking up in a cheap hotel in Mile End, cold, clammy and dead. Before that – nothing.

Maybe when I was alive I killed people all the time.

Maybe that's all I'm ever going to do.

And as if by magic, the phone rings with another job.

"HELLO?"

The voice on the other end of the line is fat and adenoidal, with a faint northern twang. It's Sweeney.

Detective Martin Todd of the drug squad, nicknamed "Sweeney." He'll tell you that's because he looks like John Thaw, but it's not – it's because he's always got his fingers in a lot of very dodgy pies. If the contents of the evidence locker find their way into the pockets of a bunch of South London hoodies, Sweeney's been there. If the lab report you needed to convict a local gangster gets shredded, chances are Sweeney was using the shredder at the time. If the man from Internal Affairs gets a phone call and drops the case before going off somewhere to piss himself – who was he investigating?

Well, who do you think?

Sweeney's a nasty customer, and I've done enough work for him to know. He's mean, sadistic, ruthless when his own interests are at stake, lazy when they're not – a King Rat festering in his own little empire of rubbish. He's my least favourite person to deal with. He pays well – well enough that I can forget about killing for a month or two and just pretend to be unemployed, like normal people are – but... the man's a monster.

He says he needs help. Usually he just needs "a hand" with something, or he wants me to do him "a favour." But now he needs help. I pause for a second and he starts begging.

I've never heard Sweeney sound afraid.

"Please... please... you've got to help me... just get over here, okay? Right now. Please – I'll give you anything. Anything you want. Get over here."

Click.

Dial tone.

I still haven't said a word.

Ordinarily I wouldn't lift a finger for Sweeney without money up front, but this situation isn't ordinary. Sweeney is out of his mind with fear. Someone, or something, has managed to terrify the demon copper of Fleet Street.

There's probably good money in that.

I tell myself it's about the money, anyway, as I pay the cab fare and step out into the pissing, pouring rain. There's no other reason I'd be out on a night like this – the rain slapping down hard against the stonework, splashing and running in torrents off the gutters and pooling in the dips in the pavement, soaking me to clammy bones the second I step out of the taxi. It's just money. I don't give a damn if Sweeney lives or dies.

So why is my hand shaking as I walk up the street towards Sweeney's place? A terraced house on a good street, curtains drawn across the windows. Well-appointed from the outside. The kind of place that costs a pretty penny anywhere, but especially here in Central London. You could probably afford it on a copper's pay, but you couldn't afford the big, shiny Jag parked outside as well. The hammering rain just makes it look pricier – diamond-encrusted, a slick MTV pimp-ride in ostentatious cream. I shouldn't be afraid. It's Sweeney. It's a cash payment for whatever's crawled under his bed and spooked him. Good money, a couple of suitcases full of crisp notes. Enough to buy anything I want for a couple of months. A couple of months of being normal, being just like you...

Why is my hand shaking?

Even as it reaches out for the sleek black door with gold lettering – number 10, right in the centre just like in Downing Street, a joke of Sweeney's – my hand shakes, trembles. I shouldn't be afraid. It's Sweeney. Who cares if he's in trouble? Who cares if the door's been forced open, like someone hit it with a battering ram, if the lock's been forced, if it swings slowly open when my fingers bump it...

I shouldn't be afraid.

The door swings open.

It's Sweeney.

I see him right away. He's looking straight at me, from the end of the stairs.

I shouldn't be afraid.

Even though most of him is in another room, I shouldn't be afraid.

A man's head was torn off and mounted on the banister at the bottom of the stairs, mouth wide open with the wooden spike on top of the banister poking out of it. Eyes glazed and wide in shock and terror. But I've seen worse things. I've *done* worse things.

I shouldn't be afraid.

I wonder what went through his mind, as he tasted varnished wood on his tongue and felt his throat stretched wide by his own beautifully carved balustrade, felt the phantom agony of a body that wasn't there anymore. I wonder what kind of chemicals flooded through his brain when he realised what had happened to him, in the half-second before everything in there shut down. I wonder what they taste like.

Am I thinking these thoughts to torture myself?

Or distract myself?

Suddenly being normal doesn't seem to count for as much as being alive.

There's blood in the air, the hot reeking smell of it, and something else. Wet, sodden... hair? My nose twitches as my eyes follow the slick blood matted on the carpet, a wide trail leading through into the kitchen.

The rest of Sweeney's in there, pooled on the tiles. Arms and legs torn from sockets, a strip of skin hanging from the bloody ragged mess that used to be his neck. Ribcage open to the world like a plundered treasure chest.

The air is full of wet dog hair. You could swim in it.

Something's been at him.

Some great animal has been chewing on his guts, tearing and snapping at the offal of him, crunching bones and swallowing hunks of meat. You can see it just by looking. Some great thing like a bear – a *dog* – burst in, tore his head off and feasted on his liver and lights.

The blood is still running, still flowing. The edge of the charnel tide licks against the soles of my trainers.

Did I interrupt it?

Is it still here?

The drop of blood hanging from the tip of Sweeney's finger takes seven long years to hit the floor. Am I holding back time? No. No. This is something else.

This is *fear*.

I shouldn't be afraid. I shouldn't.

I turn away from the yawning meat-larder that used to be a man and move back to the hall. Sweeney's face gapes at me, fixed in the last scream he ever made. Blood trickles down the upright. I step closer, looking at Sweeney's scream. His wide, open mouth. His teeth.

His solid silver fillings.

The smell isn't dog hair.

It's *wolf* hair.

Run.

I LEAVE THE crime scene behind, charging out into the rain and the wet, moving as fast as my legs will carry me. Let the police find Sweeney. They'll have a parade. I just need to get as much space between me and that wet dog hair smell as possible. I run for the Tube.

I need to throw it off my scent.

Remember when I said I didn't have a smell? I'm pretty sure that's a defence mechanism. But there's smells and there's smells. Even in the wet pissing rain, skin soaked, clothes dripping, there are traces.

Even when I swipe the Oyster card and barrel down the escalator, hurling myself onto the northbound train just as it pulls out, safe in my metal box with the stares of the passengers feeling like a baptism... there are ways.

Even while I'm slumped in my seat, dripping and draining, little rivers running in the grooves in the floor, I don't feel safe. Even at this speed, moving under the city in an electrified tunnel, I don't feel safe.

The silence of my heart is burning in my ears.

MY HANDS ARE shaking as I fumble for my keys. I'm terrified. I should be.

I'm primed for a wave of wet wolf hair to engulf me as I open the door, but there's nothing. *Thank you, Jesus, thank you, God, whatever God could make a thing like me, thank you, thank you, thank you...*

Fingers scrabbling at the loose floorboard. No time for finesse, just punch through the wood and rip it out. The sniper rifle behind the DVDs is no use here; this is the time for the secret stash, the emergency weapons, the things I stocked and hoarded because I knew trouble was going to find me someday.

Just not trouble like this.

There's a bag containing passports for seven countries and fifty thousand Euros in cash, along with a few other papers and pieces of information I might have a use for. Everything I need to get out of the country. And I need to get out of this country, for good, for ever. If what I think is true, it's run or die.

There's a loaded sawn-off shotgun next to the bag, in case I need to shoot my way out of trouble. Next to that...

...my oldest, most treasured possession. Something from before. It was waiting for me in a left-luggage locker when I finished my killing-tour of the bed-and-breakfasts of London just after I woke up dead – *why?* *Not important now* – old and shiny, with the scent of somewhere far away and long ago.

A katana. A samurai sword.

I keep it sharp. I keep it hidden. I keep it safe. It was very important once, to the person I used to be. And no matter where I go, I keep it with me.

That sword belongs to me. I'm not leaving it behind no matter how dangerous this gets. To hell with customs, I'll blag my way around it. Anyway, I might need it.

It's been fifty-two seconds since I walked in the door and I've got everything I need to disappear for good. Start again in Paris, or Munich, or Madrid – I can learn the language. I'm good with languages, dialects, accents. Just drop me in a crowd of people and I'll pick it up like magic. I can blend in. I love blending in. Blending in is like crack to me.

One last look, and out.

That flat was good to me. I had a nice collection of DVDs, some nice CDs. I was working through a Tom Clancy novel. I felt normal there. But I have to go.

I speed down the stairs two at a time, down to the ground floor. The sword is bouncing against my shoulder blades, the bag smacking against my side, the gun in my hand. If the coast's clear I'll put it in the bag and get a taxi to the airport. Get on the first plane going anywhere.

Open the door.

A gust of wind and rain blows in my face, carrying the stench of sopping, soaking wet dog hair.

The lightning cracks across the sky, illuminating something much larger than a man. A massive predator, eight or nine feet, coated in dense, shaggy fur. Its breathing is like some terrible bellows in the furnaces of hell. It snorts and flexes, moving muscles much greater and more powerful than any human being could have.

I have a vague memory of a man who killed a tiger. Or something like a tiger. I remember the tiger as all strength and power, coiled tension in each muscle, eyes deep and unfathomable. Every movement it made seemed to come from some primal animating force, some extension of life itself.

I don't remember exactly when I saw the man kill the tiger, but I remember what reminded me of it. I was sitting in a library killing time before killing people and I was flipping through some school-approved book of poetry – one of those big collections of important poems edited by Seamus Heaney or Blake Morrison or some heavyweight like that, that they hand out to A Level or Uni students to be roundly ignored.

I generally don't "get" poetry – I'm just like you, remember? – but I found something in there by William Blake.

He was trying to describe what was in the tiger.

All this crashes through my mind in this one instant, as I look at this thing that is not a tiger, that could never be a tiger. If the tiger was filled with some primal life, this is filled with death. Every shift of muscle and flesh is calling out decay, disease, the nightmare on the dark side of creation.

This creature is anti-life, primal, terrible and old.

This is the ultimate killer, the monster that kills and eats the flesh of the dead, born and bred for that purpose.

I feel its name in the back of my mind like ice as it stares into me with red eyes, baring its fangs. Saliva hits the tarmac.

This is what will kill me.

This is *werewolf.*

CHAPTER THREE

Killer in the Rain

I'S SO FAST.

I'm holding time as still as I can – gripping it until the knuckles of my mind bleed and the world becomes a silent place filled with statues, and still it's so fast that by the time I get my shotgun up it's almost too late.

Almost.

The force of the blast knocks it back a step, the pellets drifting lazily into the furry flesh of its chest, drilling and pushing, the impacts turning the flesh into soup as they push the monster back. I don't stay to watch beyond that. I've already let go of the gun, and the bag full of passports and money and all the other useless crap that's only going to slow me down. Only the sword on my back stays.

I break left and run.

Really run.

I DON'T EVER feel pain. I don't ever get tired. I'm stronger and more resilient than living human beings. My muscles don't tear. My tendons don't snap. The small bones in my feet don't break from the impact against the pavement.

I can run.

Time is locked down so tight that a hummingbird would barely move, but I move. I pound forward, pushing against treacle gravity, knowing that the beast behind me is already healed, the liquid soup of its chest knitted back into fur and flesh, saliva dripping and spattering in expectation of the kill.

I know that every step I can put between me and it is crucial.

The pavement flows under my feet like water. How fast am I moving? It feels like fifty miles an hour, maybe more, but I have time in my grip, every second stretched and pulled like toffee and I know that to the endless parade of statues I must seem like a blur.

This is harder than I've ever pushed before. *Ever.* I know that with a cold certainty. I've seen so many films where the dead people shuffle and creep, and then a few years ago they started making new films where the brain-eaters and corpses run and sprint. The first time I saw one of those was in a cinema, and you should have heard the gasps, the screams, the girls clutching at boys and the boys too caught up to even notice... this was terror. This was shock. A corpse running.

Oh, you sweet, naïve cinema couples. If you only knew.

If you only knew how fast we can move when we have to.

This is really running. The speed I'm going now... this is superhuman. This is beyond the capabilities of anyone on Earth.

And it's not enough.

LET ME TELL you about werewolves.

According to legend, werewolves feed on the flesh of the dead. Groups of them, congregating under the silver moonlight, claws digging in grave-dirt, ripping up wood and nails and tearing at the rotting flesh in the cold coffins, maggots dripping from muzzles...

It'd be crazy to believe that. To think that packs of feral, half-human monsters are swarming over the landscape somewhere, creeping and clawing at fresh-turned earth, tearing at funeral-suits and best-Sunday dresses, snapping and swallowing chunks of foetid meat like alligators. You'd have to be insane.

But the gut, she makes her own rules. Deep down in the pit of your stomach, you know it's true. Every time you see a full moon, you wonder if buying that house near the churchyard was such a good idea, if one bright moonlit night you won't look out of your upstairs window and see dark shapes swarming between the stones, see the funeral wreath flying into the air, hurled aside by brutish paws as the sound of panting and snuffling and snarling reaches your ears... and then the howl of the wolf.

Got you wondering, hasn't it?

You're lucky. I don't have to wonder. I know.

There's a dark world outside and above the one David Attenborough points his camera at, a strange and terrible supernature where the laws don't apply. But some things never change – there are predators and there are prey. For every animal, there's another animal that's evolved to eat it.

You think werewolves have those snapping jaws to deal with bodies in graves? That those swiping claws are the result of millions of years of coffin lids that needed tearing open? That those pulsing, straining muscles that can tear through steel are for mausoleum gates? They evolved them to deal with the dead – the dead that runs and climbs and escapes, the dead that is to man what the werewolf is to the tiger.

The werewolf is a natural zombie-killer.

CONVERSE TRAINERS POUNDING on wet-slick streets, teeth gritted, straining and powering myself forward even as the realisation comes that I am straining, that I am pushing myself, that God help me, God-who-would-make-a-thing-like-me help me, *I'm getting tired...*

Is this what it feels like for you? That burning acid feeling in the muscles, that weakness at the joints? The fatigue creeping through you, at long last not pretend or affected? The sense that any second could be your last and when it comes, that's it? Dead for real this time, for ever and ever, rotting in the ground until even your million-year-old bones fall into the sun and burn to nothing?

I hope so. I hope this is how it feels.

Because even now, with the end of all that I am one split-second from my heels, I want to be normal. I want to be just like you.

But that doesn't mean I want to die all over again just yet.

Somehow, my arm finds the strength to reach up and grip the sword hilt at my back. Drawing it feels like lifting a caber made of solid steel in some bizarre Scotland's Strongest Man semi-final.

My legs are on fire, and I can feel the werewolf's presence at my back, the hot sour breath of death on my neck. London streets flickering past me in fast forward, my last sight on Earth. I'm too tired to swing.

But I don't have to swing.

I jerk left, stopping dead, converse trainers smoking in a skid on the wet tarmac, the sword held out at my right, steadied with both hands, edge facing back. The monster is as fast as me. It's heavier. Stronger. But it doesn't have my sense of time.

So its reflexes aren't as good as mine.

Seven hundred pounds of fur and sinew slams into a razor sharp edge and for a brief second I think the sword is going to break, but whoever made it made it sharper than that. It cuts clean, slicing into skin, fur, the muscle of the belly. I feel the jerk in my hand as it cleanly snips through the spine and with it, a strong rush of dèja vu that almost makes me forget where I am. I've never used this sword on a man before. Have I?

But anyway, this isn't a man.

Two werewolf-halves tumble forward into the rain, still connected by a thick spray of rich, red blood. With time gripped so strong in my mind, they look like grotesque helium balloons from an obscene novelty shop, their incredible momentum carrying them still forward, floating gently as the beast makes a last furious swipe, claws passing an inch from my open eyes.

I killed it. I cut it into pieces.

Impossible.

I hold time fast and move to a ready position with the sword. If I have to, I can cut off the head, the hands, whatever needs to be done to finish it. Split the skull. My mouth waters involuntarily at the thought. God help me.

I watch.

I watch the charnel-carnival balloons drifting and tumbling through the air, the wolf howling, an elongated call of rage and pain and savage hate that hits my ears like whale song. The bottom half of the monster collapses onto its knees, scraping the flesh down to the bone and beyond. The blood gushes from the clean-cut ends, great pulsing gouts of deep red, seeming thicker by the second.

Thicker and thicker.

No.

I watch as the blood seems to clot even as it runs, making thick ropes between the top and bottom halves. I don't dare to let go of time. I don't dare stop watching.

Oh, no. No. Please. This isn't fair.

The top and the bottom are connected now by a conduit of thick, pulsing red, drawing the two halves back together like elastic until they finally meet like ships docking in a science- fiction film. I watch the spine fuse first, a cluster of nerve endings rising like slithering tendrils from the base before the bone ends click into place like Lego.

My feet are glued to the floor. I can't move.

The muscles knit together like wicker, reweaving themselves. Organs slither back into place. The skin reseals and new fur pushes through the fine line of bare flesh where the cut once was. I almost don't notice the knees repairing themselves.

In subjective time, it takes less than a minute.

Which means the creature healed fully from being sliced in half within a split second.

I'm in trouble.

It turns. Looks at me with eyes like red coals burning in the lowest depths of hell.

It knows what I tried to do to it.

It knows I failed.

I can't decide whether the leer of its fangs is born from hate or triumph.

Then my feet come to life again.

And I run.

I TRAVEL, OCCASIONALLY. It's one of the nice things about shooting people in the head, the travel. You can wind up in Sao Paulo, or Rome, or Schenectady. Security's more of a headache these days, but there are always ways around that. Often it's easier to travel by coffin, as some dead national of the country in question, being flown back for a burial on home soil. Who's going to crack open a coffin to check whether or not he might have seen the corpse somewhere before? So long as the paperwork holds up, it's foolproof.

It was in Berlin – cold Berlin, with its stone and its iron, in the depths of winter.

I was killing time, waiting to garrotte an industrialist in a penthouse apartment somewhere in what was once East Berlin. Acting like a tourist, looking at the remnants of the wall and eating terrible, poorly-cooked wurst from vans that catered to those who didn't know any better. Blending in.

I looked at the inscriptions on the wall fragments and then turned around to put the wrapper and the unfinished wurst in the bin. And halted. And froze.

A man was looking at me.

This was one face in a crowd of hundreds passing along the street. He was short, and skeletal, and completely bald – no eyebrows, even. It was as though someone had taken the foetus of some huge predatory bird and fastened it into a suit. Even across the street, his eyes shone, yellow and sickly around the pupils. I remember his suit was the same sickly yellow as his eyes.

He smiled. His teeth were long and as yellow as his eyes, the gums receded. He ran a long tongue across them, then simply grinned like a skull.

I'd been afraid before. Afraid of failure, afraid of arrest and incarceration, afraid of disappointing the client, afraid of being found out, being caught, exposed, not fitting in. But this was the first time I'd ever been afraid for my life.

I hailed a taxi and told the driver to head straight to the airport. It was just past noon, and already the light was beginning to fade, and as the taxi wound slowly across the icy roads, the driver chatting amiably in backwoods German, I could see the full moon already visible beyond the clouds. By the time I'd talked my way onto the first plane heading for Heathrow, the darkness had fallen.

I sat in my window seat, looking out over the runway, feeling foolish despite the slow curdling of my gut. I'd let the client down and run away with my tail between my legs – and for what? Because a chemo patient had grinned at me in a way I didn't like?

I was cursing myself as the plane rumbled towards the runway, and by the time the acceleration sat me back heavily in my chair and the engine roar became a scream, I'd resolved to go straight back in the morning and do the job for nothing. Disappointing the customer like that was unforgivable.

And then I looked out of the window.

Something was coming across the airfield towards the plane. It was nine, perhaps ten feet tall, an immense mass of muscle and fur and purpose. Its eyes shone a sickly yellow in the half-light, and foam ran from its muzzle. I only saw it for an instant.

Around its waist were the shredded remains of a pair of yellow suit trousers.

I fully believe that if it had caught up to the plane, it would have torn it open like a tin can to get hold of me, and if the whole aeroplane had gone up in a ball of fire, it would have walked right through the inferno to get hold of me.

As the plane rose into the air, I could hear a monstrous howl of anger and frustration following it. I never returned to Berlin.

THE ACID BURNING in my muscles is stronger now. I run back the way I came, through the silent, motionless mannequins, ready to come to life the moment I let go of time. Some of the mannequins are headless, some bodiless, just a pair of legs slowly beginning to buckle. Their only crime was to get in the way of the monster.

Some of the heads have had pieces swiped out of them. I run past a girl with a bright smile and one sparkling eye. The other is missing along with a chunk of skull. She's dead, and she'll need a closed coffin, but there hasn't been time for it to register yet. In this moment, she still has her whole life ahead of her. She's maybe on her way to meet her parents, to tell them about some new man in her life, or maybe she's going out for an evening with friends. Somewhere there are four women sitting around a table in a pub with two small white wines, a lime and soda and a vodka and tonic, waiting for their friend to arrive. And they'll keep waiting, and texting, and wondering why she's blown them off, and maybe they'll check the news and find out about the bloody swathe of horror running the length of Tottenham Court Road –

Tottenham Court Road.

I forgot where I was.

I grit my teeth and turn hard right, hoping there aren't too many people in Oxford Street. I need space to move now. I focus past the burning in my muscles, the straining of the bone tissue, the new sensations of tiredness and fatigue. I have to get some distance from the wolf if I'm going to pull this off.

I duck and weave between the late-night shoppers. In my head, I'm asking absolution from everyone I pass. It doesn't want them. It wants me.

I could save dozens of lives by stopping dead right now. By letting it take me.

I could.

But I won't.

Sometimes I feel like I'm dead inside as well as out. How could I do this otherwise?

Halfway down now and turning into a shopping arcade with what I need in it. It's open late – thank God, thank whatever God would make a thing like me – and everything's still on display.

I stop dead, trainers smoking again. This time I don't pull any tricks with the sword – I'm not going to catch it the same way twice. Instead, I swing my fist into the window of the shop, reaching through a curtain of shattered glass shards, the edges scoring my flesh as I grab for the window display.

I don't know how long I have to live now. Less than a second.

I hear the jewellery store alarm ringing, low and slow, like the tolling of a funeral bell. My hand scrabbles over the glittering knick-knacks and gewgaws, grabbing a gleaming necklace and wrapping it around my knuckles, checking the card to make sure it's what I need. I'm desperate and this is a gamble – these days, you're more likely to find platinum or gold pieces in a jewellery store window.

But occasionally, you can still find something silver.

I feel something on my shoulder – a hand, now, a paw, gripping with enough force to crack the bones of a normal man, spinning me around so fast that even with time slowed to nothing I'm staring into those dripping, grinning jaws before I know it. I have a split-second, a nanosecond, a picosecond before my guts are on the floor and my head is crunching in its mouth. It's that fast.

But I react faster.

My right arm swings out in a hard punch, with all my strength behind it. The silver necklace is wrapped around my fingers like a knuckleduster. There's a crunch as my fist buries in its chest, cracking the sternum to fragments. The monster needs a massive heart to fuel that massive engine of a body. My fist fits inside it. I can feel it pumping for a moment before it stops dead.

Silver in the heart.

I let go of time, and it crashes back around me like an angry tide.

The air fills with screams, alarms, the sound of shattering glass. I feel horrified eyes on me and know that my life has changed.

The monster twitches, jerking and shuddering like a palsy victim, the foam from its jaws flowing with ever-multiplying flecks of red. The glowing red coals of its eyes burn brighter for a second before they roll back into the head. The wound I've made in its chest bubbles and festers, green pus flowing. It's not going to heal from this.

I let go of the necklace and the beast tumbles backward, pulling off my hand like a wet sock. I watch it thrash and twitch on the ground, blood and pus spreading over the floor, the muscles eaten away before my eyes, the flesh falling from the face and jaw in clumps, the suppurating chest hole actually smoking with the force of the reaction.

It's so fascinating, I don't notice the sniper who's been crouched at the other end of the arcade. The gunman who's actually used a werewolf rampage as a distraction, as a goad to get me to go where he wants me. Who programmed the monster to keep me running right where he wanted me.

All I hear is the *phut* of a silenced weapon and then a long needle embedding in the back of my skull.

Thunk.

I don't have time to blink before whatever he's shot into me comes to life. It burns and buzzes and hums, and my hands are shaking too badly to reach up and pull it out, and the buzzing intensifies, building and building, harsher and shriller until

it reaches a pitch

so harsh and shrill that it is

inconceivable

And the last thought that runs through my mind before I feel the flesh of my brain shredding in my skull is:

Whodunnit?

CHAPTER FOUR

Nemesis

First comes smell

Old, wet stone. Age. Cobwebs and dust. Something like rotted food. Metal, some wet, some rusted, some brand new. Ancient wood.

I knot my brow – the same brow I felt shredding like confetti when that whatever-it-was went off at the back of my skull. I reach up to feel what's left of my face, but something stops me – cold metal chains at my wrists, taking my weight.

Second, then, comes feeling.

Sound is third. The drip, drip, drip of water filtering through stone. Soft well-made shoes gently tapping against the cold stone floor. Pacing and scuffing. A filter tip burning as he inhales. The rattle of the chains.

I decide to go for the grand prize and open my eyes.

I'm in a dungeon.

An actual dungeon. Cold water dripping down ancient stonework, wooden benches, torture implements lined up on the wall... there's even a skeleton dangling from a set of rusted chains on the opposite wall. A spider crawls slowly in one eye socket and out the other. I don't think anyone picked that up from a doctor's surgery.

And right in the centre of the room, we have the person responsible. Not too tall – about five-eight – but stocky. Lots of muscle there, and by the way he's carrying himself he knows how to use it. Stands like a boxer – cauliflower ear on the left side of his head, broken nose... I'd lay money whoever's running this operation picked him out of a gym somewhere. It's been a while since he's been in the ring, though – he's put on a little weight, and I can't remember a boxer with a Tom Selleck like that. Black hair, steel-grey eyes, all the wrinkles around his face say he spends most of his time pulling intimidating expressions.

Armani suit. Three-piece, very fancy. He might not be the man at the top, but he's certainly high up.

The Boxer's noticed me looking at him, and he looks back. There's something sardonic in his eyes – a sense that this is business as usual. That all of this – the werewolf, the sniper, the whole complicated plan to get me out of hiding and into a dungeon – that it's all another day at the office.

I'm not sure I like him.

"Back in the land of the living, Mr Doe? Or is it the land of the dead?"

He doesn't smile at his joke. I decide not to either, or dignify it with a pithy comment of my own. Instead I start yanking my left hand against the cuff of the chains, hoping to pop the stitches. See how many jokes this bastard feels like making with his guts coiled around my fingers. But the stitches refuse to pop. It feels different, somehow.

I look up to my hand, and the wrist is whole – completely healed. My skin even looks slightly pinker, although I may be imagining it.

I tug experimentally against the manacle. How did that happen?

The Boxer snorts derisively. He's got a throaty voice – a slightly upmarket Ray Winstone. His teeth are yellowing, nicotine-stained, with a gold molar at the back of his mouth.

"An unfortunate side-effect of the weapon we used to take you down. The dart puts out a localised electro-magnetic pulse – simulates your body's own reset system to shut you down for long enough to get you here."

What the hell is he talking about?

Stall for time. I try to sound like this is all as mundane for me as it is for him, but I can feel the quaver in my voice.

"So where's here?"

The Boxer snorts again. I'm starting to hate the sound of that – if you could buy pure contempt in spray form, that's the sound it'd make coming out – but I'm not in a position to tear the top off his skull yet.

There's probably not enough there for a decent meal anyway.

"You're underneath the Tower Of London, it might interest you to know. There's a lot of history here, Doe. Both official and otherwise. We've had quite a number of your sort down here." He walks over to the wall, making a show of lifting down some ancient cast-iron pair of pincers, most likely used to tear the extremities off enemies of the crown. I almost smile.

"You're not going to get much out of me with that..."

He snorts again. I'm really getting the impression he doesn't like me. "We have our ways and means, Sonny Jim. We've been dealing with people like you for some considerable time and let me inform you that when it comes to kicking your undead knackers in, we're the experts."

"People like me?"

"Zombies. The walking dead. Those that have snuffed it but refuse to shuffle off this vale of tears until they've made my life a total bleeding misery. We've known about you lot for centuries, but only in recent times have we got a better idea of exactly what you were and developed the means to study you, give you the kicking you filthy bastards clearly deserve and finish you off for good. Previously, we made do with the latter. Set the Wulves on you."

I don't like where this is heading.

"Wolves?"

"Generally spelled with a U. Werewolves to the general public. We breed 'em." He shoots me a look, a little evaluation. "Shat yourself, did you?"

There's no point in lying.

"You would too if one of those things was trying to tear you to pieces."

He snorts. This time it's laughter.

"Too bloody right I would. But as luck would have it, they're bred to hunt and kill disgusting abominations like you and not god-fearing Londoners like me."

"I'm a Londoner..." I regret it as soon as it slips out – it sounds weak and defensive and all it does it make him look at me like I'm the last piece of crap in the doggy bin.

"You're the furthest thing from a Londoner there is, sunshine. Whereabouts were you when you woke up for the first time? Place and date."

I remember exactly where I was. A Travelodge in Muswell Hill.

"London. Muswell Hill. Ten years ago today."

He snorts again, like I've just told him the Earth was flat, or Lee Harvey Oswald acted alone, or Ann Coulter is a beacon of truth in the murky world of the liberal media. This isn't going well. I keep looking at the skeleton. The spider's built a web over one of the eye sockets.

"Bollocks it was. What's happened here, Sonny Jim, is your defence mechanism went into overdrive after what you did to Emmett Roscoe. The tossers in the lab coats call it 'chameleon syndrome,' but I personally call it being a cunt."

I get a sinking feeling. I've never met an Emmett Roscoe. I don't think I've ever even shot an Emmett Roscoe.

Have I?

"What did I do to Emmett Roscoe?" I don't bother hiding my curiosity, but all I get in response is a grunt. At least he didn't snort.

"What didn't you do, you filthy little bastard. I'll give you this, you're a holy terror when you're roused."

I blink, not sure if I've heard him right.

"Are you sure you've got the right man?"

"The right festering bloody corpse, you mean? I don't know, let's have a look at my bloody scorecard! You don't breathe, check, your heart doesn't beat, check, you can move severed body parts by remote control in a way that personally repulses me, checkity fucking check, you eat brains, big fat tick in that box – what a shock! You are John Rigor Mortis Doe and I claim my five pounds!"

I nod. I'm trying to think my way out of this one, but nothing's coming. The chains are too strong for me to break, and with my wrist inexplicably healed up I can't work my hand off and set it going. I'm out of options.

He leans in, eyes locking. He's more than a little bit too intense for my liking.

"Let's start again from the beginning since you're acting like you never went to school. Point one – how would you feel, Sonny Jim, if I told you there'd been others like you? Other zombies?"

How would I feel? Shocked and curious. Wanting to know more. Off-balance – I woke up five minutes ago in the company of a skeleton and the Marquis de Sade's toolbox, and now I'm having a surreal conversation filled with rhetorical questions with a man who has a chip on his shoulder the size of Stonehenge and more knowledge about me than anyone I know, including me. How would *you* feel?

"I don't know."

"There's a shock. Point two. How would you feel if I told you – again – that we'd been hunting them down for centuries?"

I didn't take it in when he said it before. He's making sure I get the message. He's got me.

The skeleton catches my eyes again. There's a fly struggling in one of the eye-socket webs, and I know how it feels. The spider crawls casually across the dome of the skull, taking its time, in no hurry... I wince, racking my brains. This must be what it's like to have a headache. I hear myself stumbling around in the dark.

"You said. You hunt... people like me. You bred that werewolf."

"Werewolves, plural." He chuckles again, almost a snigger this time. "We've got five pure-blood werewolves down in the cells. We had as many as fifty thoroughbreds back in the seventeenth century, but demand has fallen. There's just you now. The last remaining zombie as far as we're aware. Numero Uno on the endangered species list. Point being, right now your pasty rotting arse belongs to me."

He can read the expression on my face – the instinctive shock and fear, to know that there are *five* of them, and *in the building* – like five ticking bombs, or five deadly tarantulas, or five flesh-eating viruses in the air – five of those *things* just a cell door away, when even one would be enough to finish everything...

He reads my expression. I read his. It says I'm pond scum as far as he's concerned.

"I thought that might make you shit a brick. I'm pretty sure that's not the first time you've had a run-in with one of our little pets, although since you're a cunt as I mentioned earlier, you won't remember it. Still, that's probably why you left a brown trail all the way down Oxford Street. You knew Fido could kill you. You're ready to piss your knickers right now because you know, for a certainty, that there is one thing on this planet that can end your miserable attempt at a life, and we've got five of them waiting downstairs, waiting for us to cut you into meaty chunks and serve you up like Winalot – *bloody settle down!*"

I didn't even realise I wasn't settled, but he's right. I'm tugging against the cuffs without thinking, thrashing, trying to break out – all it's doing is getting this sadistic bastard's gander up even further... I force myself to stop. This isn't getting me anywhere. "Why don't you stop being a smart-arse?" I snarl, trying to sound threatening.

It just sounds pathetic. He knows it.

The spider reaches the fly.

I swallow, and then shake my head. Resigned. "You said you know what I am. That's more than I do."

The Boxer snorts again – *if he does that again*, I think, and feel impotent – and says nothing at all. I sigh like a petulant child.

"Go on, spill it. You're going to feed me to those hairy bastards downstairs, you can tell me now. I want to know." I'm wheedling. He just glowers. His voice, when it comes, is cold as stone.

"I just bloody bet you do."

He gives a smile that isn't a smile, just a twitch at the corners of his mouth. It looks like nothing so much as a dog about to tear apart a piece of meat put in front of it. He reaches into the pocket of his suit, pulling out a mobile phone, or something like it.

"As long as one of you is still functioning, the plan goes ahead, doesn't it? Did you honestly think I'd forget what I was talking to, you filthy rotting git? Roscoe forgot. We know what happened to him. Roscoe told you what you were. In bloody meticulous detail. Poor bastard. Apparently he was some sort of genius, although if you ask me his judgement was more than a little faulty. He actually thought you gave a toss if he lived or died." The Boxer scowls, eyes like stone. There's nothing in them but hate. "The poor stupid bastard. He thought you were friends."

I've never met an Emmett Roscoe.

Never.

"You've got the wrong man." You can hear the desperation in my voice, the cold knowledge of just how bad this is going to get. He grits his teeth, that gold tooth flashing under the cold fluorescent light...

"If you keep on bloody whining I'll give you something to whine about. We are past the stage when I talk to you like you're a human being. You're a bleeding monstrosity and you're not getting out of this building alive, just so we understand each other. But before we feed you to the dogs I'm going to ask you some simple questions, if you think you can concentrate on something other than being a tosser for two minutes. I'll tell you right now, this can be easy or hard, but I am definitely leaning towards hard."

"You do know I don't –"

He lunges, and the thing in his hand sparks blue light.

The pain is gigantic.

It's like a capacitor, but much more powerful, and it doesn't even touch me – it just gets close to my ribcage, and the bone flexes, then flows like melting wax, bending like a magnetic field. Is this what it would be like for muscle and bone and flesh to shift, to stretch, to melt? I don't know, but I can feel it right through me, right in my head, like he's pushing that thing into my mind and making my thoughts come to pieces...

...and for the first hundred thousand years it seems like the worst thing in the world, but then it gets worse...

...and by the time he pulls the device back and my flesh and bone and spirit begins to work back into the rightful place I've invented new cosmologies and pantheons to describe the pain and the agony and the horror of having your body and soul warped like clay...

...and I don't even believe it when it ends.

I can't speak.

I suck back drool and swallow the bile rising in my throat. My cheeks are wet.

The Boxer growls. His gold tooth glints.

"That was a starter. Give me any more shit and we're onto the main course."

I want to die, or stop existing, or whatever it takes to remove the memory of that pain. I hurl myself against the chains, beyond speech, beyond anything but a desire to get away, to escape, looking and feeling like an animal caught in a trap. The Boxer waits.

Eventually, I stop struggling. He waits until I've stopped even twitching, until I'm hanging limp in the shackles. Until we both know where we stand.

I never want to go through that again.

The Boxer clears his throat.

"Now that you've finished your interpretive dance, I've got your starter for ten. Think carefully."

He goes silent. In the eye socket of the skeleton, the fly struggles and thrashes as the spider liquefies its insides. It's a minute before he breaks that silence, and by that time I'm willing to tell him anything. Give up anyone I've ever cared about, sell out my neighbours, plant bombs in crowded places, anything, anything to stop him doing that again –

And then the bastard clears his throat and waits a little longer.

Finally, he speaks. I strain my ears.

"When is the time?"

When is the what?

"I'm sorry?"

He reaches out again. This time pushing the thing at my mouth.

There's a blue spark.

It lasts hundreds of thousands of millennia, infinite gulfs of galactic time. Civilisations rise and fall. Planets coalesce out of dust. The quantum throws up new universes, billions and billions of years long, one after another. And all through that, my face and skull is melting and warping, distorting and dripping off my skull, which softens and collapses in on itself like wax... and all my preconceived notions of self burn and blacken and fall to ash and despair... for ever and ever, world without end.

There's a part of my mind that tells me all this only lasts for four or five seconds. But it's like a mouse chirping in a thunderstorm. The agony is eternal and endless.

But it does end.

I make a bubbling noise, like melting fat, as my face begins to reform. I think I might go insane if he did that again.

He waits.

"What..." It's all I can manage.

He snorts again.

"Since you ask, it's the same kind of technology that put you down earlier. A microscopic electromagnetic pulse – disrupts your cellular cohesion and generally fucks up your day something rotten. Also has an interesting effect on your temporal senses and your cover personality, or so the lads in the white coats tell me. Personally I couldn't give a toss. Just so long as it hurts."

"Cellular...?" I'm barely coherent, but I don't think he'd make sense even if I could focus. Something's seriously wrong with this guy. I'm dead. That's all. Just your average walking dead man.

I'm not that... complex.

Am I?

"Don't bother your little head, Sonny Jim. Your cover personality won't let you understand it even if I told you, so you might as well lie back and think of England." He looks up at me. "You may have forgotten what you are, Doe, but I bloody haven't and you're not pulling your shit here. Now it's time for round two. Lets see if you can win the set of steak knives."

He clears his throat. *Oh God. Oh God, oh God-that-would-make-me, please...*

"When is the time?"

I don't know. I don't know what he means. I don't know anything. Jesus, just tell him something, tell him a time, any time –

"Fuh. Four o'clock. Tuesday. Tuesday four o'clock PM."

He scowls. His eyes are like ice. Grey ice.

"Are you sure?"

"I swear. Please. Tuesday afternoon, four o'clock. That's the time."

He shakes his head.

"Do you think I rode into work this morning on a chocolate fucking digestive, you lying little bastard?"

I start crying.

"*Stop bloody bawling*!" He bellows it, genuinely aggrieved. "Jesus fucking Christ! I didn't expect you to tell me the truth, and I don't expect you to act like a human bloody being but you could act like a *fucking adult*!"

I look up at him, shaking my head, unable to speak. I don't want to act like an adult. I want to beg. I want to fall onto my knees and plead. I want to lick his boots. I want to say and do anything I need to say and do to end this.

Is he *enjoying* it?

His voice is like a block of ice.

"Now listen here, you filthy little bastard. You can stop pretending to yourself that you're the hero in this little adventure story because, believe me, you are anything but. What you are is an inhuman undead piece of shit pretending to be a human being. You eat human beings brain-first and you want to kill every living thing on this bloody planet! And by the time I am finished with you you are going to tell me every one of your horrible plans for the human species so we can finally grind you up and serve you for dinner with a fucking Waldorf Salad! Capeesh?"

I shake my head. I'm not like that. I'm not some monster.

I'm just like you.

I try so hard.

I swear.

Please.

"Tough shit. Ding ding, round three, question fucking one. Either take off that fucking mask you've superglued onto yourself or take your fucking medicine."

Please.

Please.

"And at least take it like a man. Come on, spit it out, you little toerag."

Please.

"Fuck it! Time's up."

This time, he goes for my groin.

I scream so loud and so hard I think my throat is going to explode, and the scream lasts one hundred, thousand, million, billion... imagine someone driving a cricket bat layered with razor-wire into your most sensitive parts at one thousand miles per hour, while making you believe that you are worthless and ugly and pathetic and unloved, down to the very lowest core of your being. Imagine physical and existential nausea and agony flowing through every single cell of your body.

Imagine your dick melting like wax and running onto the floor.

And imagine that lasting until the end of time.

Imagine being trapped in Hell.

Just because he can, he keeps the button pressed. Ten seconds. Twenty. Twenty lifetimes. He draws it slowly up the front of my torso, and my guts and organs and heart melt and twist and distort, like a plastic model of a man left on a radiator. Like a melting snowman.

I see the look of pure hatred on his face as he lifts the tool up to my face, and my face is gone, and all my notions of self and identity and all of my illusions. My eyes run down my face and burst on the floor and keep seeing despite that, and my face is a screaming bloody ruin, screaming and screaming for a judgement day that never comes...

And then he switches it off.

And I tumble into blackness.

INTERLUDE *the* FIRST

Japan, 1578 AD

BUT THE TALE of the dungeon and the Boxer and the question with no answer was yet to occur on that day in the middle of winter, when Oda Nobunaga and his retinue trudged up the cold hill to take tea with the Cold Ronin, O Best Beloved.

It was spring, when the cold heart of the world thaws and the beautiful blossoms grow upon the branches, but there was no spring upon the cold hill. Had it been the middle of winter, in that early part of the year when a carpet of frost covers and smothers all that grows, it would still have been so cold as to invite comment. Not the cold of a snowflake falling on a bamboo leaf, nor yet the cold of a clear icy stream running through the mountains, but the cold that is seldom found anywhere but in the forgotten resting-place of one who died without honour, in a locked stone tomb where there is no company save the dead and no comfort save death. A chill experienced only in a place of deepest death and horror.

The noble retinue of Oda Nobunaga wrapped their coats tighter around themselves and shivered, yet made no sound of dissent. It was their Master's will that they take themselves up that cold hill in that chill wind, and as such it was to be obeyed without question, even as they looked around them at the stunted trees and the stony patches of ground upon which nothing grew, and prayed to their ancestors that they would live to see the morning.

Oda Nobunaga did not pray. He did not shiver. He did not look left, or right, or up, or down. He simply walked, facing into the bitter wind, one foot in front of the other, his ceremonial cloak wrapped about him, his sword at his side, showing no sign of fear or danger or even discomfort. He was *Oyabun* – it was not a part of his nature or his station to give in to fear.

And yet, deep in the hidden core of Oda Nobunaga, locked away from all human sight, there was a sense of foreboding. This was not the simple hiring of a mercenary, or a pack of samurai; to seek the Cold Ronin who lived on the cold hill was to seek something less than human. Men spoke in whispers of his cold, pale corpse-flesh, his way of staring at you, head cocked, as though he was a bird and you were a tasty worm ready to be plucked from the frozen ground. Occasionally, it was said that if he did not like what you had come to offer him, he would cut the top of your head off with his sharp katana and feast on your living brain – but these were, of course, only stories, and it would not do for Oda Nobunaga to show even the slightest tremor as his feet shuffled in the cold snow.

They had almost reached the top of the hill when Oda Nobunaga lifted his head and spied the Cold Ronin six feet in front of him, barefoot, dressed in a white robe, his flesh like marble in the high sun, his sword sheathed at his side. Oda Nobunaga swallowed, once, then spoke in a clear voice betraying not the subtlest quiver. "Nanashi No."

He bowed, and his retinue bowed also, almost comic in their efforts to out-scrape one another, noses almost touching the snow.

Nanashi No nodded almost imperceptibly.

"Oda Nobunaga. What leads you to disturb my solitude on these cold hills?"

Oda Nobunaga hesitated a moment. But it would be a mistake to lie to the Cold Ronin.

"Anger and hatred, Nanashi No, and the desire to defend my lands against those who would try to conquer them. You are aware, of course, of the warlord Uesugi Kenshin."

Nanashi No nodded once. "He attacked you recently, driving you back into Omi Province. There is doubt in some circles that you are still the strongest warlord in Japan after Uesugi Kenshin out-manoeuvred you so cunningly. In the last few months, Uesugi Kenshin has put together a grand army, which appears capable of driving you even further back and claiming still more land –"

Oda Nobunaga coloured, eyes narrowing in fury. "Enough!"

The chill on the cold hill deepened, and a single leaf blew between the two men. Oda Nobunaga felt his throat close and his stomach churn. "Th-that is... I did not mean to insult you, Cold Ronin. It was an unworthy outburst. Forgive me."

There was another pause that seemed to last an age before the Cold Ronin nodded.

"The price of doing business with me has increased, Oda Nobunaga. Explain what it is you wish of me, and please do so quickly. My patience is not infinite, and your unseemly behaviour has strained it to the breaking point." Nanashi No's voice was soft, but infinitely cold. Oda Nobunaga bowed again, deeply, and his retinue followed, each attempting to bow lower than the other, trembling despite their warm clothing.

"Forgive me, Cold Ronin. I wish you to assassinate Uesugi Kenshin as soon as is convenient. He is the heart and the brain of his army – without him, all of his plans will fall to chaos."

Nanashi No nodded again. "You have heard, I trust, that Uesugi Kenshin is in poor health and is not expected to last another year? Tell me, Oda Nobunaga, what profit is there for you if I strike my keen blade through a heart already dying?"

Oda Nobunaga looked into the cold eyes of the Cold Ronin and chose his words with care. To turn around and leave after such a journey would be intolerable, and to offend Nanashi No further would be actively dangerous. "Every beat of Uesugi Kenshin's heart is a danger to me, Cold Ronin. I find stilling it worth more than any price you name."

Nanashi No smiled, and the smile was without warmth. "Any price?"

Oda Nobunaga turned to look at his retinue, and the shuffling, shuddering men hauled two large chests filled with treasures – magnificent jade pieces, ornate vases, gold and glittering jewels.

The Cold Ronin stared at the wealth before him. "I am no collector of fine jade, Oda Nobunaga, and as such I have no need of this. I'm sure you see some prize to be fought for in this, but all I see is nothing at all."

Oda Nobunaga opened his mouth to speak, but Nanashi No simply shook his head. "A fat pouch of yen, Oda Nobunaga, will serve. Bring it to me by sunset. And one thing more. When you leave here, take only those members of your retinue needed to lift those twin chests of nothing, so that you can bear them far away from my cold hill. Leave the rest with me."

Oda Nobunaga opened his mouth again, but the eyes of the Cold Ronin forced his silence. He turned and nodded to the four best men in his retinue. They, too, were wordless as they picked up the crates.

The five men did not look back as they took their leave of the cold hill. Not when they heard the unsheathing of the sword, nor when they heard the noise of fine-tempered metal slicing through flesh and bone, nor when the screams and gurgles of those left behind reached their ears.

And when they heard the sound of teeth gnawing at the meat of the skull, a ravenous tearing, a gulping, a feasting, the sounds of an unholy communion taking place not twenty metres from where their boots shuffled in the snow... then, most of all, they did not look back, O Best Beloved.

Not once.

IMAGINE THE FINEST of the Shogun's horses, O Best Beloved! Imagine the thunder of its hooves as it gallops through the orchards of the Shogun, the shifting of the muscles of its flanks. Imagine the magnificence of the beast, the life force emanating from every pore, the shifting of the black mane in the breeze.

Imagine it has no eyes.

The wet, red sockets gape, droplets of gore seeping from them, trailing back from the head of the noble steed as it runs blindly, hurtling forward. The life force is subverted, the magnificence of the animal broken by this one detail, transformed to horror and madness.

This is what it was to see Nanashi No running across the plain.

At first glance, he might seem a paragon of humanity, but even a brief glimpse would confer a sense of dismay upon the observer, a sickly feeling creeping down the spine and into the belly, a terrible understanding that something was unaccountably, irredeemably wrong. Nanashi No felt no pain and did not tire. He was the strongest and the fastest man from ocean to ocean. To watch such a man sprint, covering miles by sun and moon, never slowing, never stopping... to watch such a feat might impress at first, until you notice the sickly, clammy pallor of the flesh, the fixed intensity of the eyes, the bare feet never stumbling or tripping even on sharp stones or deep snow. Admiration was often the first emotion when faced with the Cold Ronin – an admiration that quickly curdled to unease and then to horror. For a man who never sleeps, never tires, never stops is not truly a man, particularly when there is still a dark stain tracing from the corner of his lips, from a grotesque appetite fulfilled.

In such a manner, Nanashi No crossed the gap between Oda Nobunaga's territory in the Omi Province and Uesugi Kenshin's camp in the Kaga Province in a matter of days, stopping only to evade confrontation with military forces. When he stopped running, there was no catching of breath, no panting – he simply became as still and silent as the corpse he appeared to be. It was in this state of stillness and silence that he approached the boundary of Uesugi Kenshin's camp.

The Cold Ronin stood on the thin branch of a tree, perfectly balanced and unseen, hidden from sight by a curtain of fragrant blossom, and simply watched. He watched the patterns of the guards – as they walked and waited and crisscrossed one another, when they came on and off their duties, where their gazes fell – for a full day and a full night. Then he left his perch to move and walk through them as though they did not exist, without sound or trace of his passing – his sharp mind and sharper wits allowing him to snake between the watchful gazes of thirty men charged to guard their camp on pain of shame and suicide as though he had no more substance than a ghost.

Once inside the camp, he moved from shadow to shadow, never in the light for more than an instant. He went unnoticed and unremarked upon, although he was a legend throughout the provinces – even those who caught him directly within their field of vision could not afterwards be sure they had seen anything at all, so swift was his passing. Was it a cat streaking across the ground, or a falling blossom wafted by the wind? Surely it was not the Cold Ronin.

And thus, in the fullness of time, through patience and an unquestionable skill in the ancient art of the ninja, the science of walking undetected and unguessed, Nanashi No found himself laying like a wolf upon the roof of a small wooden hut built to serve as an outhouse for the officer class, sprawled in such a fashion as to be quite invisible to all passers. In this manner he passed a day, a night, a day, a night and the best part of another day, until the sun was low and angry red on the horizon. During this time, he neither moved nor breathed – for in addition to his other skills and talents, the Cold Ronin possessed the ability to still his heart and his breath and in this state to simply allow time to pass, cool and inert, like a pretty-patterned snake coiled upon a stone in the noonday heat.

At the end of his long vigil, he heard a voice – clearly aged, racked with coughs and spasms, shaken, but with a ragged air of absolute authority and cold command, giving orders to a much younger, stronger, but less sure-sounding voice.

This, then, was Uesugi Kenshin. Nanashi No noted with a certain grim satisfaction that he had been correct – the old man perhaps had six months left in him, if that. But for those six months he would be a formidable force and one best not underestimated. Perhaps Oda Nobunaga had been right to hire his services.

Nanashi No waited, without moving even the muscle of his heart, without taking a single breath, as the old voice finished its business with the younger voice, and strong footsteps marched into the distance. The door to the hut opened slowly, creaking and groaning on its hinges as though pushed by an aged, withered claw. There was the sound of sandals shuffling on wooden slats, another racking cough that shook the roof of the hut on which the Cold Ronin lay, and then the unmistakable sound of urine falling through a hole in the floor into a pit that had been dug previously.

Nanashi No moved quickly, rolling silently across the roof, catching its edge with the palms of his hands and swinging down into the hut. Uesugi Kenshin had time to turn his head before the Cold Ronin reached out his hands to clasp the throat tightly, blocking the blood flow to the brain and compressing the windpipe enough not to allow Uesugi Kenshin a chance to scream. The touch was delicate – no bruises would be left behind – and yet, the grip was unbreakable. Uesugi Kenshin's withered fingers scrabbled at Nanashi No's hand, but the old man could not even tear the Cold Ronin's skin with his jagged nails, and within seconds his struggles ceased as the life left him, his brain deprived of the blood it needed to survive. Nanashi No let go and danced backwards, swinging himself up to his place on top of the outhouse, and was back in position before the body even hit the ground.

The Cold Ronin waited, inhaling the scent of ordure and micturation that was the natural accompaniment of death, as the bowels loosened and disgorged their unclean secrets – but then, it was an outhouse, and there was little notable difference overall. He waited as the sun continued to sink, wondering if his moment for escape would come before the old man was discovered. Then he heard the return of the young man's footsteps, walking at first, then running, as he shouted the name of his commander. He listened to the sounds of grief, the thunder of similar footsteps as other lieutenants and familiars came to gaze on their dead lord, and especially to the pronouncements that Uesugi Kenshin's heart had simply given out, that there were no signs of violence, that he had simply died of old age there in the outhouse.

Nanashi No resisted the urge to sigh. As though one as strong as Uesugi Kenshin would submit so readily to the bony finger of death without completing the task he had set himself! It was clear that Uesugi Kenshin's plans for conquest lay as dead as he, that his heirs and second-in-commands would be unable to perform the duties set them if they so easily clung to comforting fables instead of looking at the truth directly in front of their eyes. Oda Nobunaga had been correct. He would become the supreme power within Japan.

The Cold Ronin waited as the hours passed, until the hour of midnight. Uesugi Kenshin lay in state in one of the nearby tents, and the heart had vanished from the camp. Where Nanashi No had needed to watch the patterns of the guards for a day and a night to gain entrance to the camp, he barely had to muster the smallest effort to escape unnoticed, and was soon in the trees beyond the camp's furthest edge with none the wiser.

But Nanashi No knew, and the knowledge was bitter as poison to him. He had cravenly murdered a strong man in order to help a weaker one rise to power. He had slaughtered a man in the most ignoble circumstances possible. Moreover, he knew that the story would spread – if not from the lips of Uesugi Kenshin's forces, then from his opponent, Oda Nobunaga, who would allow the legend of the Cold Ronin to bolster his own.

Almost unconsciously, Nanashi No set off to the east.

Better for the Cold Ronin to remain a legend, rather than for more power-hungry men to break the blissful solitude of Nanashi No. And better that Nanashi No should himself disappear – board a boat and cast himself into the arms of the wide Pacific, with only his sword as a reminder of what he had once been. The Japan he knew was ending, and Nanashi No would end with it. When his storm-tossed boat finally reached whatever land lay on the other side of the great ocean, another man would disembark, more suited to the new world he found himself in, armed with a sharp sword from a far-off land to keep his blessed solitude.

Nanashi No, who would soon be no one at all, smiled a peaceful smile as he watched the blossom float from the trees. And then he walked towards the sea, O Best Beloved, and out of all stories forever.

CHAPTER FIVE

The Killing Man

...BUT THAT WAS long ago, and far away.

The man with the broken nose was named Albert Gregory Morse, and he was indeed a boxer – he'd been a boxer since he was nine, after a childhood spent scrapping in the streets and generally getting in the kind of trouble that would slowly wend its way down to the prison gates as the years went by. He was a social worker's poster-boy, grown up in a house with an alcoholic father and a sickly, underweight mother, and three other kids younger than him who needed feeding and clothing. But he never saw a social worker, of course – in those days slipping through the cracks was even easier than it is now, and besides, he didn't need some fey twat from the council to set him right. Albert Morse had the gym, the circle of tough men who lived by coded violence, who would ritually try to kill each other through the morning and then go to the pub on the corner for lunch and stand each other pints, all malice forgotten, who would let him watch the fights and punch at the heavy bag and keep the place clean for cash-in-hand. Who provided the path to his salvation. Who allowed Albert Gregory Morse into the Ring.

The Ring was a way to keep his family going, and to have a little pride as well. He was a practical lad, and sweeping up was as good a way of making money as any, but with a dustpan in his hand he was nobody. On Saturday night, slamming his gloved fist into the face of some local tough who thought he was tough enough, breaking his nose and his jaw and sending him crashing down to the mat like a fallen tree, the numbers echoing like prayers in a cathedral as the crowd cheered for Albert Morse, he was somebody. He had a name. And even when it was his turn to tumble down, struggle to rise and finally collapse through pain and exhaustion and the ringing of his head as the number ten sounded around the hall – well, he'd given a good fight. The crowd knew he was a tough man to beat, and there was another fight in a couple of nights. Albert Morse felt no shame at being beaten in the Ring.

Albert Morse was often beaten. He was a good fighter, unskilled but with a rough, merciless enthusiasm for despatching weaker opponents, but a stronger fighter who could stand his sledgehammer right long enough would see the obvious holes in his defence and soon Albert would be eating the mat again. Albert accepted this. Every fight won was another purse, another week of meat, school, new shoes, kitchen appliances and a little whisky to keep the old man quiet, but even losing a fight brought money in. Being knocked half to death in the Ring was a lot better than working in a factory, he figured, and he could still sweep up in the gym for extra money during the week when he wasn't training, and with six mouths to keep fed and clothed, that was a mercy.

Like all teenagers, he was untouchable, unstoppable, unbeatable – but even at an amateur level, boxing is all about being touched, stopped and beaten. When he was not quite twenty-two, a doctor told him that if he took another six months of punches to the head, he'd be a vegetable for the rest of his life. Doctor Sengupta was not a man known for his tact, so when he took Albert's dreams away from him with a brutal frankness usually only encountered in hanging judges, it's perhaps not surprising that Albert reacted with his fists. Doctor Sengupta's nose and jaw were broken, along with two of Albert's knuckles, and when the bandages came off he was no longer welcome at the gym.

He made the local papers – the front page, this time, not the sport – with an editorial tying the incident into supposedly spiralling waves of Mod versus Rocker violence, a personal grievance of the editors that was already six or seven years out of date. The race angle was mercifully unexplored, although in Albert's neighbourhood that might well have won him as many friends as enemies.

So Albert Morse was rewritten as a tearaway, a hoodlum, a violent young offender, and in this capacity he was splashed all over the local press. He was vicious, and violent, and he did solve his problems by inflicting pain, all this is true – but he was bound by the Ring, by rituals and codes, his violence channelled for so long into a structure that, if not quite moral, at least followed recognisable rules of engagement. Of course, left alone, it was only a matter of time before this ingrained code degraded and his brutal personality led him into the path of an old lady out too late at night with too much money, to the courts, and to Wormwood Scrubs, in that order.

But he was not left alone.

His violence, his code, his need for money and most of all his need to appear a hero, if only to himself – all of these drew the attentions of the organisation known as Military Intelligence 23.

The first time the grey-suited man arrived at the Morse household, Albert assumed he was another reporter and told him to piss off. The grey-suited man was an ex-drill-sergeant promoted to MI23 recruiter named Selwyn Hughes, and he knew how to deal with the likes of Albert Morse. Without blinking, he reached into his pocket, pulled out a short iron truncheon, and swiftly broke two of Albert's ribs, before kicking the lad in the teeth hard enough to knock out a molar and telling him to shut his horrible trap and listen. After that, Albert thought he must be a copper, but he did listen, and what he heard interested him enough that when he came out of the hospital he made his way to the Tower with the other tourists and asked the old lady selling the souvenirs if she'd seen his Uncle Dee nosing about. This was a contact protocol that new recruits were encouraged to follow.

It will surprise nobody to learn that 'Uncle Dee' was a reference to Dr John Dee, who had first attempted to study 'the dead who walk' in the reign of Queen Bess, although it was not until late in the reign of King James that the organisation that would become MI23 was set into motion. Albert Morse knew none of this, and made little attempt to learn in later life; what interested him was the job as it stood in 1973, a means of getting his fists dirty for Queen and Country against things that go bump in the night, a career straight out of a Hammer horror flick, and one that'd pay enough to keep his whole family fed, clothed and schooled. It sounded too good to be true, and to begin with there was no indication that it wasn't. Who believed in monsters in this day and age, after all?

Despite his scepticism, Albert Morse settled in quickly, spending most of his time performing small tasks such as breaking the legs of journalists who'd got a little too close to something they shouldn't have, or putting the frighteners on old ladies who were talking too loudly about things they should've kept to themselves. It was nasty work, but Albert Morse found himself surprisingly untroubled by conscience. He didn't enjoy it – not exactly – but it was work that had to be done for the sake of the Crown, and Morse was a practical man. He knew that he had to get his hands dirty one way or another. He was out of the Ring, banished from its clear structure, its rituals, its codes of honour and law, and now he had to use his fists where he could. MI23 was not the Ring. But it would have to do.

By his twenty-fifth birthday, Albert Morse had become very practical, and very tough. He was almost happy – as happy as he could be out of the Ring – and secure in his routine, in his duties, in what was expected of him.

He did not believe in anything that he had not seen with his own two eyes.

On his twenty-fifth birthday, Albert Morse had his clearance level upgraded from code green to code yellow, and he was taken down to the dungeons underneath the Tower Of London, in the lower levels.

It was there that he saw his first werewolf.

Ten feet of muscle, growling in a cage, sniffing the air. Albert Morse moved his hand through the bars, laid it on fur that was rough and soft, the beast standing, growling, acknowledging one of its masters. Albert could have run then – run, screaming, bolting through the doors as others had done, desperately running and hiding in some dingy rented room, curling up in the corner and sobbing, retching up their guts until the men in the grey suits padded silently up their stairs with their silenced guns at the ready, silence their code and the punishment for those whose nerve broke. *Kneel and face the window. I'm sorry it had to come to this – no, don't look, don't look. It'll all be over in a minute, son. You just close your eyes.*

Albert could have run. But he didn't run.

Albert did not see a thing to fear, there in the cage.

He saw a wonder.

The werewolf looked at him, eyes burning, glowing a brilliant blue, cocking its head. Under the coarse fur, muscles shifted. This was what Albert Morse had been chasing his whole life, without knowing it. This was power – vicious, violent, trammelled and restrained in flesh and muscle, coiled and waiting in the service of men. He took a deep breath, inhaling wolf, inhaling strength and fury.

The wolf growled, a long, rumbling bass note, and Albert felt it pass through the pit of his belly.

Behind him, Selwyn Hughes, code orange, smiled paternally. Albert turned, looked at him, eyes shining. He was breathless.

"What does it eat?" He swallowed, shaking his head. "What does it hunt, Mister Hughes?"

Mister Hughes told him, and after that there were no more thoughts of the Ring and the happy days of rules and boundaried violence. If the werewolf was everything Morse had always wanted to see in the world, then the zombies were everything Morse wanted to take out of it. Cold, dead men, dead physically, dead emotionally, hollow men walking amidst those who had life in them... and with their secret. The terrible secret of what animated them, what set them walking the world like clockwork toys, integrating with society, killing and feeding, the secret, forgotten program that instructed the dead-who-walk in their every action and reaction. The secret, sinister clockwork of the dead.

The clockwork that would end the world, if it was allowed to.

These secrets and others Albert Morse learned, his savage boxer's brain turned to something greater, his ugly talents shaped and honed. Selwyn Hughes had seen something special in the boy that day he'd smashed his face in and sent him away in an ambulance. Something in those hollow eyes that said – I can replace you. Let me.

Hughes was old, past his prime – he'd had one heart attack already, and his world was not a restful place. He knew that Morse had what it took to be code orange, the one man at the centre of the web of strangeness and charm that held civilisation back from an unimaginable abyss, so it might have the liberty of choking to death on poison or going to war for fresh water or any one of a million vastly preferable ends. He knew that Morse could stand where he stood, at the gates that separated humanity from the final end that passeth beyond all understanding, of which the legions of the dead-who-walk were only the part visible to us.

Most importantly, Hughes knew that Morse's reaction to the werewolf meant that he could work with the man designated code red.

In a few years, when Morse was old enough and more steeped in the lore and learning of MI23, it would be time for him to have an audience with code red... with the man named Mister Smith.

But that was long ago, and far away.

IF THE WOLVES come out of the walls, it's all over, thought Albert Morse, and his mouth gave that little twitch that wasn't quite a smile. But there are wolves and wolves, and it was nearly over now. Morse rubbed his scarred knuckles, as he often did while he sat with his coffee and waited for the door to the Red Room to open.

The clock on the wall ticked, dry and dusty like a beetle in a long-lost tomb. *Not long now*, thought Morse. *Nearly over.*

Twenty years it had taken him after Selwyn died. Twenty years of hunting the bastards in their hundreds, then their dozens, then one by one, and finally – John Bloody Doe. The last of the zombies, the last night-horror. They'd feed him to the wolves in the morning and then MI23 was all done.

Morse was almost sad at that. He was his job now, he ate, slept and breathed it – and when it was done, what would be left of him? He thought of all the things he'd never done. He had a potting shed full of old dead geranium bulbs, bought at the garden centre – this year he'd get round to planting the fucking things, he always thought, and never did. Never any fucking time. He thought of Romper, poor bloody Romper who beat his tail against the floor and whined because he wasn't walked enough. He should never have bought a bloody dog anyway.

Sorry, Romper. You were the only friend I ever had after Selwyn went. Should have tried harder. Look how I fucking treated you. And Hilda at the Prospect, showing me a little kindness for the first time since I took this bloody job. Never showed her any in return. Just buried myself in fucking work. Never called, never wrote... you're a piece of work, Morse. You never even went to your Mum's funeral, did you? Useless bastard. And all the people I bloody did it for – Tom and Steph and Nancy – they're all grown and out of my life and they don't want anything to do with me. You're a real hero, Albert Morse. A knight of the fucking realm.

Morse sighed and swallowed coffee, black with no sugar, feeling as bitter as what went down his throat. *Bollocks to it anyway. It had to be done. No sense whining.*

He realised it was probably the last time he'd see Smith for any length of time.

He realised he was happy about that.

I did it, Mum. I saved the world, me and my men. Me and the wolves in the walls. Could be a lot fucking worse.

Beats Tommy and his poncy bloody art college, anyway.

Morse scowled, and set the empty mug on the little table next to his chair.

What kind of world lets a bloody dog die of cancer anyway?

Not one worth saving.

Morse sighed, leaning forward. At that moment, the speaker above the door crackled into life.

"Albert Morse, code orange clearance. Please proceed to the inner lock."

Morse stood slowly, stretching.

"About bloody time."

ONE DOOR CLOSED, another opened. In between, there was the inner-lock – security system, black-panelled room of flashing lights and lines, sweeping beams, scans and soft artificial voices, carefully programmed for the absolute minimum humanity.

Morse stood, bored, listless, fingers itching, eager for the process to end. The thought that the room could fill with cyanide gas at any moment never occurred to him. Once, it might have – when the novelty of the procedure was still fresh, when he was thirty, the thought of a malfunction or mechanical failure had been enough to wake him up in the watches of the night, sweating and shaking, the tang of almonds in his nostrils until he drowned them out with a swig of Glenfiddich – but those days were gone. Now all it was was a procedure that had to be endured in order to come face to face with his Lord and Master.

Neither did he look left or right at the automated machine-guns in their brackets on the wall, or down at the floor, which could have slid away at any moment, toppling him into an acid so pure and potent that it would have reduced him to a molecular soup in seconds.

To Albert Morse, the threat of death had become as ordinary as crossing the street.

He spoke his name, once, in a bored tone of voice.

Aside from the whirring computations of the room, there was silence for seven seconds before the door swung slowly open.

A moment of contemplation in the hour before the beginning of the end of the world.

ONCE, ALBERT MORSE would have been shitting himself, but time has a habit of making the bizarre seem almost mundane.

And Mister Smith was bizarre.

The room was ordinary enough – a circular chamber, lined with oak-panelled bookshelves, with a desk in the middle, similarly styled, and a door at the back, leading to the system of antechambers that were home to Mister Smith. There were no windows, or mirrors, but the lighting was designed to be warm and cosy, and often the only light came from a fireplace set off to the side. There was an armchair in front of the fire, and an office chair near the desk – for guests.

Mister Smith did not need chairs.

The first time Albert Morse had met him, he had vomited into the waste-paper basket, then desperately begged forgiveness. Mister Smith was used to such reactions. He was barely four feet in height, his body wizened, shrivelled up like a toy balloon at a birthday party for a stillborn child, the Saville Row suit, sized for a ventriloquist's dummy, hanging grotesquely on his frame, a doll's shrunken corpse dangling horrifically from the vast, inflated head. Mister Smith's skull was a three-foot-wide balloon, bald, with blue veins pulsing in the corpse-white, almost green flesh. The face was small, in the same proportion as the shrivelled body, although the eyes were enlarged, vast, milky orbs with livid green irises that seemed to glow with a strange inner radiation. Mister Smith was simply a vast, pulsing brain, which had retained those scraps of flesh necessary for speech and the five senses – the rest was vestigial, the functions of the vital organs provided by the brain itself, the lungs used only to provide a wheezing gasp of air past the lips, so Mister Smith might spare his guests the rudeness of telepathy.

Mister Smith floated slowly towards Morse. The wrinkled mouth made an approximation of a smile.

"The nights are drawing in, Mr Morse. You must be cold."

He shot a glance at the logs in the grate, and they instantly ignited into a roaring blaze. The lights dimmed accordingly. "Please, sit. I should offer you a brandy."

Morse blinked, and frowned. "Brandy, sir? Are you sure?"

"The work is over, is it not? We have the last of them. Sit, sit."

Morse moved the armchair, taking only the edge of it, not allowing himself to get too comfortable. Something in Mister Smith's easy manner made him tense – not through fear of the abomination that floated in front of him, but fear of the very confidence he himself had felt in the corridor, fear of contemplating the end of the work before that end was in sight.

"He's still alive, sir. Begging your pardon, but it's not over until we feed the little bastard to the wolves and have a poke through what comes out the other end."

Mister Smith's not-quite-smile grew wider.

"John Doe is not going to give us any trouble. The only reason the creature stayed hidden as long as it did is because of its heightened chameleon response – and that was triggered by the death of Professor Roscoe in New York. It's much weaker than the others – remember Mustermann? Mengano? Doe's even weaker than Janez Novak and you didn't even need the wolves to finish that one. In fact, the more I think about it, the more I think this might be an ideal opportunity to study one of them."

Morse choked, standing suddenly. "You have got to be fucking joking!"

Mister Smith looked at him. Morse realised he'd spoken very far out of turn.

"Pardon my French, sir. But... I mean, you can't be serious. We have been trying to exterminate these little bastards since the Middle Ages. They're dangerous. You were the one who told me what Whiteside Parsons found out about them. You know what they're here to achieve –"

"End the world, yes, yes. You can stop there, Morse. I can tell what all of your arguments are going to be just by looking at you, and I appreciate everything you were about to say. But remember what these things are."

Morse shook his head. "The Dead Who Walk, sir. Fucking zombies. The very things, if I can *remind* you, *sir*, that we have been trying to wipe right off the face of the planet like a bloody Cillit Bang advert since the reign of –"

"Since Elizabethan times, yes, yes, good Queen Bess and John Dee and all that. But the current Queen Bess is not in full control of operations, is she? I am. We may be answerable to Her Majesty, but Victoria handed the duty of organisation and administration over to me, and it's a duty I take very seriously, very seriously... sit down, Mr Morse."

"Sir, please –"

"Sit down. I insist."

Morse felt himself sitting, leaning back in the chair, felt himself relaxing. Inwardly he seethed. He hadn't been treated like this in years, and it was an unpleasant reminder that while he did most of the legwork for the organisation, he was still the number two – both in terms of command and in the evolutionary chain. Morse was humanity as it stood now, and Mister Smith was the future – humanity several links up the chain of being, a product of Darwin's genius and Victorian eugenics. Almost from spite, he allowed himself to wonder whether humanity had simply exchanged one monster for another, knowing Mister Smith would catch the thought.

Mister Smith looked almost hurt, but carried on.

"The Dead Who Walk... it's a misnomer, isn't it? You've evidently swallowed our own propaganda on the issue – all those zombie movies we bankrolled to make the public react correctly to the mind-eaters in their midst... do you realise that before the wonderful Mrs Shelley wrote her novel, people would bring zombies into their homes? It was assumed they were suffering from the cold..."

"I'm well aware of that, *sir* –"

"Let me finish, let me finish..."

Suddenly Morse could no longer speak. He slumped back in his chair, fuming in silence and swearing loudly in his mind.

Mister Smith paused a moment until Morse finished. "There is no such thing as a zombie – not in the way we have allowed the public to construe it. The thing in that cell is not dead, is he, Morse? He was never dead at all. He has always been that way. He always *will* be that way. John Doe, Hans Mustermann, Jose Lopez... they have human names, but they were never human. They have the appearance of dead men, but it would be truer to say that their disguise as living men is incomplete – but perfect enough that we think of them as men, as individuals, as thinking creatures. Perhaps they even fool themselves. But, of course, they are neither human nor individuals in the way that you and I are."

He paused, running a dry tongue over dry lips.

"These creatures... these Dead Who Walk... they are collections of cells, much as we are. You could describe yourself as a collection of single cells banded together to form one being, but in your case that would be facetious. Separate your heart from your body, your brain from your head, and both parts would die. This is not the case with the being we're keeping downstairs. Mr Doe is a gestalt entity – millions of cells that form together to create a reasonable approximation of a human being. Even after centuries, it is not entirely accurate in its internal workings, but from the outside it appears human – even to itself."

Morse looked incredulous. Christ! He'd thought the bastard was acting.

"Oh yes, oh yes... I monitored your interrogation of the creature. According to its surface thoughts, it had no idea what you were talking about. I've noticed before that there is a dichotomy inherent within these zombies – on one level, a constant running chatter of thoughts, an imitation of human brain patterns, and on the other... the programming they follow. But let's return to their physical structure..."

Morse rolled his eyes. How many times had he heard this lecture? And all they had to do was throw the monster to the wolves and it was over.

"Please, Albert. I am getting to the point. These cell collectives cannot be damaged by normal means. Splitting them into smaller clusters won't help – even once the small parts have been brought out of communication range, they will act on their own. I understand Mr Doe has experimented with this property by using his own hand as a remote combat unit. However, his surface mind is still attempting to put it in terms he feels a human being could understand. Which brings us to the chameleon syndrome – the cell-clusters imitate the dominant culture in their immediate area as a camouflage mechanism. However, Doe murdered Professor Roscoe because Roscoe found something, and in response to that Doe effectively murdered himself – shutting his surface memory down to ten years, moving to a different country, boosting his chameleon reflex by several hundred per cent, and hiding his true nature even from himself – under a belief system that seems to be composed equally of our own 'zombie' propaganda exercises and old private eye films. The hitman with a heart of gold, as it were."

Morse furrowed his brow. There was something in this.

Mister Smith's lips twitched.

"You can speak again if you'd like, Albert."

Morse scowled. "I thought after twenty-odd years of working together we were beyond that little stunt."

"Albert –"

"Never mind, I'm starting to see where you're going with this. I'll have that brandy, though. I've a feeling I'm going to fucking need it once this is over." He leant back as a decanter floated across the room, pouring itself into a nearby glass.

Mister Smith set the decanter down with his mind and continued.

"These cell-clusters also possess full-spectrum time-sense – a control over their own temporal perception, allowing their minds to view the passing of time much faster than the one-second-per-second standard ordinary humans enjoy. However, since we've been able to create a workable version of this time-sense in our werewolves since the late fifties, it's ceased to be too much of an issue. But you know all that. Tell me, Albert, where do you think I'm headed with this?"

Morse smiled humourlessly. "Emmett Roscoe. Or rather, what Emmett Roscoe found out about John Doe. And making use of that secondary thought-stream."

"Good, good... I'm glad we're on the same page here, Albert. Thanks to Dee, and later Parsons, we know that if the zombies were to be left unchecked they would end the world – but we don't know how, or why... or when."

"When is the time. Your specially selected starter for ten."

"A question that would only have meaning to the secondary thought-stream, bypassing the primary. However, you were working under the assumption that the creature could not hide its true nature from itself. So when it refused to break..."

"It was already broken, but it didn't actually know what it was hiding. Christ, that little bastard even manages to stab itself in the back."

"Quite, quite... If it is the last of its kind, there's not much it can do. But if its not – or if it was put into motion by other hands – we need to know. We need to break it – that is to say, strip away the surface thought-stream so that all that is left of the monster is the basic id, the part that will tell us what we want to know."

"In other words, a nice spot of garden variety torture."

"I thought you'd like that part."

Morse took a sip of his brandy, then stood. "Nothing would give me greater pleasure than to electrocute that decomposing bastard in his dead nuts until he dances us a polka. But excess pain just seems to make the bastard pass out – shut down, whatever – presumably to protect itself from exactly what I'm trying to do to said testicles. So! Let's try another tack. Let's push that... 'primary thought-stream'... that bloody split personality it's got until it takes more of the fucker's energy to keep up the bullshit than it does to drop the mask like a hot fucking turd. Then we can have a nice cosy chat with the gestalt entity formerly known as John Doe. I'll do the talking and the arse-kicking, you monitor from here. Dig right into that dead head of his until we've got everything we need to know."

Mister Smith raised one grotesque eyebrow. "What do you suggest?"

"Let's take a lesson from the Yanks. A spot of Torture Lite. Diet Bastardry. Sirens. Klaxons. Bright lights. Nothing's going to work on the little shit unless it's mostly in the mind. It doesn't need to breathe, so waterboarding's out. What about water torture?"

"Water torture?"

"Drip drip drip, little April showers. Rig up a tap or something so it's constantly dripping on the forehead of some poor bugger who you've conveniently strapped down so he can't move a fucking muscle. Very effective when it comes to making people go completely bloody doolally in a very short space of time. Also, it's well known. I saw it on the bloody *Avengers* once. Part of the culture. It'll work on John Doe because John Doe always tries to fit in because he thinks that's going to make him a human being instead of the fucking apocalypse waiting to happen. And because he's got such a bee in his bloody bonnet about trying to be human, he has to react to a torture that – according to us humans – *breaks* humans. Therefore, he's going to be helping us every step of the way." Morse paused. "Well? Am I talking out of my bloody backside or what?"

"Hmm." Mister Smith frowned. "It's worth a try. Do you want to be the one to set things in motion, Mr Morse?"

Morse looked at the wizened head of Mister Smith, eyes like storm clouds.

"I should fucking cocoa, sir."

CHAPTER SIX

The Body Lovers

I WAKE UP to the squeaking of wheels, like a supermarket trolley. Then the feeling of movement, the bump-bump-bump of a metal cart with no suspension being wheeled over rough slabs of centuries-old stone, bump, bump, bump. Electric light passing overhead like UFOs. The smell of cobwebs. Metal bands strapped over wrists, ankles, waist, throat, and a pair of heavy pads on each side of my head, keeping it in place.

I'm on the move.

They've got me chained down to some sort of gurney, wheeling me through the old stone corridors to the next destination. I don't think this is part of a prisoner release program – whatever the Boxer was yammering about while he was taking me to pieces, it didn't sound like the kind of thing they'd change their minds about. Which means that whatever they're wheeling me towards, it's worse than a torture that feels like a billion years of indescribable agony.

But hey, no sense panicking.

Bump, bump, bump.

I flex, trying to break the bonds, but no go. Whatever they're made out of, it's stronger than I am. These people know everything about me – my powers, my limits, how to break me, how to fix me. And that worries me a lot, and not just because they're wheeling me to Room 101 for a taste of who-knows-what.

It worries me because they think I'm going to end the world.

What did the Boxer say? Something about times and plans. Something about a guy named Emmett Roscoe.

Much as I hate to say it, that name is starting to seem familiar.

Bump, bump, bump.

Wheels hitting stone slabs with the rhythm of a nightclub somewhere. Emmett Roscoe...

Nothing. It's gone. And I've got more important things to worry about.

Such as what they're going to do to me now. It occurs to me that if they have done their worst and not found out what they were looking for – and God knows I don't know what the hell they're looking for – this might be it. The big finish. Cement overshoes. A swim with the fishes.

Thrown to the wolves.

This might not be a hospital gurney. It might be a dessert cart.

But hey – no sense panicking.

Bump, bump, bump.

Whoever's pushing this thing knows I'm awake now, but he's not saying a word. A good soldier. Or maybe he's seen a lot of these before. Maybe he's pushed so many struggling bodies to the wolf pen that I'm just meat to him. He's thinking about dinner tonight, or whether he remembered to set his TiVo to record that documentary on *The World's Most Dangerous Shoplifters* starring Sheriff John Bunnell, or maybe looking forward to the match on Saturday. Chelsea versus Everton, should be a good one... Face it. He doesn't give a damn.

Or she. We live in enlightened times.

Bump, bump, bump.

Crash.

The gurney slams through a set of steel doors, and we're there. I can't turn my head or crane my neck, so I have no idea what's going on, but I'm not hearing anything but footsteps. No snarls, no growls, no howls. So I can breathe easy on that score. On the other hand, those footsteps are padding around the room. He's doing something. Scrape of metal on stone... something being set up, checked.

I really wish I could turn my head.

I get a glimpse of whoever-it-is as he steps back this way – not a face I've seen before, just a technician, and by the look of it he doesn't particularly care who I am either. He just grabs hold of the gurney and pushes it towards whatever he's been tinkering with. Some sort of copper piping...

Huh.

I'm staring up at a tap.

That's new.

I've got to admit, I'm waiting for the other shoe to drop here. A while ago, I was screaming in agony as a high-tech science-fiction capacitor remoulded my cells like Play-Doh, and now they've decided to upgrade to plumbing. What are they going to do, wash me to death?

He's setting it all up very carefully. Marking position exactly. Something's up here.

And then he turns the handle.

There's some kind of washer in place in the tap, because water doesn't come out immediately. It trickles out, just a drop at a time. Hitting right in the centre of my forehead. *Drip. Drip. Drip.* Annoying. What are they trying to do here? Annoy me into submission?

Drip. Drip. Drip.

Oh, wait.

Drip.

I know what this is.

Drip.

I saw this in *The Avengers* once.

Drip.

This is that water torture – the one where they hold the victim under it until they go mad. It was on telly.

Drip.

Actually this *is* pretty annoying.

Drip.

Make that really annoying. I can't move. I can't move and it just keeps dripping away.

Drip.

Turn it off.

Drip.

I can't move. I want to scratch my nose. Rub my forehead. Massage my temples. I want to scratch that itch in the small of my back.

Drip.

Suddenly I've forgotten how bad the torture earlier was. This is torture – right here.

Drip.

This is the worst torture in the world. I can't move a muscle and this water is just dripping on me, *drip-drip-drip*. And I can feel what it's doing. I can feel myself starting to go crazy. This is actually going to work. It worked on the telly. Why am I surprised that they'd use it in real life?

Drip.

It always works on the telly. They're going to drive me mad with this.

Drip.

Drip.

Drip.

Dr—

Fuck it.

I grab time hard and squeeze it like I'm gripping the balls of some tosser in a bar room brawl. The water-drop slows, then stops, hanging in the air. Right.

We've established that this is going to work. Maybe it's psychosomatic, but it's going to work. Just like on the telly. So. How do I get out of this one?

The straps are made of something I can't break. So that's out. I'm stuck here for as long as they leave me, and they're probably going to leave me here a while.

I keep time held in my mind. The droplet hangs in space above my head, unmoving – like a sputnik floating in space.

I can't stay like this. In subjective time, it could take years for them to come back to me. I'll have gone crazy with boredom by then.

So. I can't break out, and I can't keep holding onto time forever. What other options are there?

Think.

The ball of water drifts downwards. I relax, letting it tumble through the air, then clench time tight in my grip again, bringing it to a halt. Relax... and grip. The ball inching downwards in little jerks until it splashes against my wet forehead. Above, another grows from the tap, ready to take its place.

I can't reverse those droplets, but I can control how fast they fall.

So.

Let's try something I've never tried before.

Let's turn time up to eleven.

I let go. Time washes over me like a cold shower... and then I grab hold again, and twist... and time keeps moving... falling... thundering down...

Faster.

And faster.

The drips become a trickle, the trickle a flood, a constant pressure that settles on my face. I can handle this for ten minutes or so before I have to slow time down again. And for me it's only going to be ten minutes.

I start hearing sounds – little blips and clicks. For a moment I see a pink and white blur in the air above me – a doctor? A technician? Feel a trace of something cold against my chest, probably a stethoscope, some kind of instrument... how long would it take them to check me? An hour? Eight hours? A day?

There it goes again.

Grab time. Twist.

Faster. Faster.

How fast am I going? Eight hours for every second? A day? Two?

I'm thinking how I probably look from the outside. I'm doing the best I can not to twitch or move too much, just holding still with what seems like a wet gel pack resting on my forehead. I'm probably frozen solid, eyes open, expression unchanging... looking like a real dead body, in other words.

I'm hoping that's the effect they're after.

Faster and faster.

More blurs. So fast now – there's a constant pink and white mist in the air. How many days have gone by now? How many weeks? How many weeks are passing even while I think that? I'm getting more blips and clicks in the air, like a forest of crickets. Talking to each other, firing off questions. Maybe questioning me. Lights are flashing in my eyes. Interrogation. All the activity is building to some kind of—

Jesus!

It takes everything I can not to jerk. It felt like someone slashed open my leg and poured battery acid in it – I actually slowed down for a moment and caught a glimpse of a room full of freaks in lab coats, the Boxer standing around looking grim... that was the capacitor. The pulse generator they were using on me before.

I must be going too fast for it.

I wait, tensed, for another, but nothing. They must have held it on me for a while, hoping for some kind of reaction.

It occurs to me that, for the first time, I am acting like a real corpse.

I am normal.

I am just like you.

When you're dead, that is.

More buzzing, flashing, bleeping and clicking. What's it been? One minute? Two? I'm probably in trouble here. I need to slow things back to normal as soon as they take me out of this room, because otherwise – if I look like an ordinary corpse – what's stopping them from feeding me to the –

Wait, what –

Everything's changed –

Hands inside me –

Let go –

– and time slows and groans back into place like a bullet train pulling into the station. Everything went wild there for a moment, blurred, racing past me. They took me somewhere else. It'd barely registered before I felt something – in me.

Hands. Blades. Like having a food processor grinding into me.

I feel... empty. Literally.

And there's an old, balding man with little round glasses standing above me with a scalpel, dictating into some sort of microphone.

I'm being dissected.

"Holy shit!"

I suppose I should have stayed quiet. Well, you try staying quiet when someone cuts you open and takes out your internal organs. Go on, I'll wait.

Dr Glasses stumbles back, opening his mouth to scream. Without thinking, I grip time, slow it, and then reach up and grab him by the throat, crushing his windpipe in my hand and then snapping his neck. I smash the microphone for good measure. No sense taking chances.

I let go – time wrapping around me like a cheap overcoat – and he staggers back, eyes bulging, head lolling obscenely, trying to sputter something, his tongue protruding through his lips. Then he tumbles down like a sack of potatoes.

It's not until he falls that I realise I'm not tied down any longer.

Why didn't I notice that?

And there's nobody else in the room. No guards, no cameras. No sign of any surveillance at all.

How long would it take them to decide I was no longer a threat?

Maybe I'm not a threat. I feel thin. Washed out. Light-headed. Maybe it's from time running without me for so long.

Maybe it's because half of me's been carefully removed by Dr Glasses.

How long was I lying in that room?

There are pages and pages of typewritten notes here – file cabinets on the walls, drawers dated September through to October. That split-second flurry of activity took nearly two months. I'm lucky they didn't decide to feed me to those monsters – if they had, I'd never even know it'd happened. Just lights out.

I'm not sure I want to think about how long I've been under here. Long enough for them to stop seeing me as dangerous. And I don't think the Boxer was going to stop thinking that any time soon. Maybe he's dead.

Maybe he died of old age.

I swing myself up off the table for a closer look at the notes.

First incision: September 5, 2010.

Three years.

They kept me on that table for three years. Kept the water running for three years. Monitored reactions for three years. And then they figured I was just another body and schlepped me over here to cut me open and chop me up.

I don't know if you've ever been in that situation, but it's pretty strange, let me tell you. It disconnects you. I feel like I've been taken out of reality and put down somewhere else, somewhere without any rules.

2010.

Jesus Christ, I'm in the future.

I wonder if we've got flying cars yet?

The words on the page are typed neatly, laid out perfectly, but I can't read them. They're swimming in front of my eyes and all the *di-oxy-rybo-nucleics* and *gestalt* units and *seratonin detection* sitting on the page pretending to mean something just won't connect together into anything that makes sense. They float around, chopping and changing. Somewhere in here, there's a key to all the mysteries, but I can't find it. I'm not stupid – I read *New Scientist*. But this is something else.

I've woken up in the future. What the hell did I expect?

And then there's the sound of glass clinking against glass, and I stop caring what year it is. The paper tumbles to the floor.

Chink.

I'm suddenly very aware of the gaping, yawning emptiness under my ribcage, the tent-flap of skin and muscle yawning open. I was wondering where all of that went. Now I know.

Big glass jars line the back of the room, stretching away from me on a single, long shelf. Each of them is marked and filled with something soft, wet and red.

One of my organs.

Clink.

One of my kidneys is looking back at me. Literally. There's an eye in the middle of the purplish-brown mass. It closes, then opens, like a sick parody of a come-on.

Next to it, I can see a lung, pulsing slowly in and out, breathing on its own. Embedded in the surface is a single, pulsing vein.

The further away from me the organs are, the weirder it gets.

Chink. Chink.

My stomach, lying at the bottom of a jar with a set of vestigial fingers poking from the lining. The fingers wiggling and twitching.

A length of intestine, reared up and swaying like a cobra. Like a centipede.

At the back of the room, my heart. There are... legs growing out of it. Like spider's legs. Little hairs poking out of red flesh. My heart, scrabbling as it pumps, scuttling behind the glass, a pair of mandibles extended from the left ventricle, snapping and clacking.

My heart is an insect.

With every thrash of its legs, the jar rattles against its neighbour, my pancreas pushing back against the wall of the jar like a slug.

Chink. Chink. Clink.

My heart is at war with my pancreas.

Chink. Clink.

Mandibles clash against glass. The jar is rocking now.

I take a step towards it, and it turns.

It's looking at me.

Another step.

I can feel it now. The spider-heart. I can feel it in my mind, and it's so... alien.

An insect intelligence communicating with mine.

What is it?

What am I?

What sort of person was I?

Another step. It calms, slowly stopping movement. The intelligence... recedes.

No, that's wrong.

It merges. Blends.

Fits in.

The jar stops moving.

I take another step.

Another. I'm close enough to reach out and take the jar in my hands, turn it around slowly, eyes looking over what's inside.

Just a lump of meat.

A human heart, sitting in a jar. No legs, no jaws... nothing that couldn't have come out of a human being.

I look at the other jars.

Nothing.

Just organs.

I think I'm going to be sick, but there's nothing to be sick with. I've got nothing down there. Then I want to laugh, but I've got nothing to laugh with either. Then I want to be sick again.

I crack the lid of the jar, reaching in and grabbing my heart. Inert muscle.

I shake it a little.

Probe it with my mind.

Nothing.

I'm trying to remember how things were ten minutes ago. Ten minutes ago when my biggest problem was water dripping on my forehead.

Three years ago.

Without thinking, I raise the still heart to my lips. Teeth bite into the muscle, tearing off a strip, swallowing. Then bite again.

I'm in shock.

I'm barely aware I'm doing this.

Bite by bite, like tearing into a rich, red pepper. A meaty, juicy heart.

I finish it and pop open the next jar, reaching in and gripping a pancreas that slid up the side of the jar like a slug. And I bite. And bite. And bite.

There's nothing below my ribcage, but I can feel myself getting stronger. Full of all the good things a body needs.

I bite into a lung, chewing and swallowing. Letting myself go. Letting myself drift away for a while.

Letting myself heal.

The worst part isn't the taste. It isn't the meat and formaldehyde on my tongue, or the heavy feel of the raw meat as it slides down my throat.

It's that it feels so natural.

So terribly, wonderfully natural.

CHAPTER SEVEN

Cat Among the Pigeons

THREE YEARS IS a long time in politics, but the Boxer had not retired.

He could not retire, as long as the thing on the dissection slab remained. It anchored him to the job, to the life, an inert lump of matter that kept him getting up in the morning and taking the bus to the Tower. Once upon a time, Albert Morse had felt angry at the situation, filing endless petitions with Mister Smith to have the thing on the slab destroyed – he knew better now. It was inert. It hadn't moved or even twitched in months – years, even. John Doe was a broken doll, a puppet without any strings, and the murderous drive that had once possessed Albert Morse had mellowed a little every day that he hadn't moved, spoken or thought, the icy resolve thawing into simple habit.

After a year, he'd relaxed enough to get another dog, a one-eyed hound from an animal rescue organisation, and while walking the beast on the common he'd met Shirley, who worked with traumatised children in a clinic in Battersea. They'd married at the end of 2009 and were in the process of adopting.

He'd slowed down. Gained a few pounds here and there, some more grey in the temples. Stopped waking with the dawn, now relying on the shrill shriek of the alarm clock to wake them both at seven. He was never earlier than nine, and never stayed longer than five. Nobody complained – he was an anachronism now, and he had the feeling Mister Smith insisted on their regular chats out of a need for companionship more than a need for information.

Still, some things never changed, thought Albert Morse, as he stood in the airlock and waited for the sweep of the scanners over his body. He was getting more and more conscious these days of the fact that a malfunction would riddle him with bullets and drop his body into an acid pit. In fact, he wondered why he'd never considered the possibility before.

He must have cared, surely.

He breathed an audible sigh of relief as the door to the inner office opened. Time had changed him.

Time had not changed Mister Smith.

"Good morning, good morning..." he murmured, floating upside down, his withered body held in the lotus position. His eyes were fixed on Morse, but he gave the impression of looking at something else that required the bulk of his concentration. "If you take a seat, I'll bring you a cup of tea in a moment."

"I can pour myself one if it'd save you the trouble, sir," Morse answered, moving to pour one for each of them. If Mister Smith was scanning the creature in the dissecting lab, he wouldn't have energy to spare for parlour tricks.

Mister Smith did not respond for five minutes, as Morse took his seat and sipped his tea, watching closely. He'd been through this before, and the result was the same – eventually, Mister Smith drifted over to the chairs by the fire and apologised for being distracted.

"Think nothing of it, sir," said Morse, and smiled – a real smile. "Any changes?"

"No, no... another of the removed organs has developed the beginnings of a rudimentary consciousness, but I expected that. The main corpus itself is still completely dead – inert. Not a single thought structure running through its mind. I'm almost astonished that it's holding a human shape. I imagine it knew what we were trying to do to it and simply shut down completely rather than give up any secrets. It's quite fascinating, quite fascinating..."

Albert Morse shifted slightly, swallowing another mouthful of tea. He knew better than to speak his mind on the subject – Mister Smith would pick up his thoughts anyway.

The balloon-headed man smiled indulgently as he revolved in the air, lowering to the table to pick up his cup of tea. "I promise, Albert, we'll dispose of every piece of the creature in good time. But look at this from my perspective, please... it's a once-in-a-lifetime opportunity to study one of these creatures – the last of these creatures! We'd be fools not to examine it, fools." The balloon head bobbed as the cup of tea levitated to its lips. Morse shook his head, trying to verbalise his thoughts.

"I just think it's something of a risk, sir."

"The risk would be in not studying it. We know so much about these creatures in terms of their physiognomy – even the make-up of their brain – but so little in terms of their motives. The only person who we can be reasonably sure even guessed the truth is Emmett Roscoe..."

"...and look what happened to Emmett Roscoe, I know. I'm just wondering whether cutting John Doe into pieces and watching those pieces... mutate... Sir, what if that's how they reproduce? Could we just be breeding an army of these things in our own basement?"

"No, no." the great head shook again as Mister Smith levitated upwards, the tea replacing itself on the table. "These organs aren't actually gaining mass – just evolving what mass they have. It's my theory that the zombies don't reproduce – they were placed here very early in man's history for an unknown purpose, and whoever is behind that purpose was not expecting their numbers to dwindle." The thin lips formed the ghost of a smile. "They weren't expecting me."

Morse finished his tea and leaned back. There was something in Mister Smith's manner that was triggering the old snark. "So let me get this straight. The nigh-infinite resources of Military Intelligence 23 are now being used to create a menagerie of frolicking zombie organs? Are we planning on opening a fucking pet shop?"

Smith laughed, an easy laugh.

"Not quite, not quite... I believe this is the key to the alien consciousness we were trying to find, Albert. Divorce a part from the whole and the further away from the whole it gets, the more it develops its own lower consciousness in order to follow the directives of whoever created the whole in the first place. You see?"

Morse did, barely. And the more he saw, the more he didn't fucking like it much.

"So as the organs grow more and more... animal-like... we begin to see glimpses of whatever process formed John Doe, and glimpses of what it is that drives and directs him, the secret plan of action that his over-personality knew nothing about before we eradicated it. It's vital that we get the opportunity to see what that plan might be. So long as we don't know what directed the creatures, we don't know what else might be out there, you see?"

"Yes, sir, I see. If I might be so bold – how long before we've torn the tosspot right down to his component parts and shoved each of them in solitary? Because right now what you're describing puts me in mind of a fucking escape committee made up of renegade organs, and I'd like to see these wayward bits and pieces locked up to the full extent of the law. Sir."

Mister Smith chuckled. "Albert, Albert... It's been three years. Three years without a single thought in his head. I doubt anything could play possum for that long."

Morse scowled. He didn't want to. He didn't want his cosy life with Shirley and Popeye to be disturbed. He wanted to smile and nod along with everything Mister Smith said, Mister Smith who was so much wiser and more intelligent that he, Mister Smith with his head full of the future. He wanted to retire and pension himself off. But there was a thudding in the back of his mind, a constant pounding like leather gloves smashing hard against a heavy bag...

Albert Morse's boxer-sense was well and truly tingling.

"Right. Here's my problem, sir. Now, correct me if I'm wrong, but you said yourself that your new theory, that I assume you're planning to publish in a scientific journal now that we are all over and done for good, was that things like John Doe have been around since before the ascent of man." His scowl intensified. All the old anger wrinkles began to form again around his eyes. "So presumably at some point these undead tossers had nothing to do all day but sit around and watch chimps chucking their shit at one another. For thousands, maybe hundreds of thousands of years. Now *correct* me if I'm *wrong, sir*, but don't you reckon that – after you've spent a couple of fucking millennia in a fucking PG Tips advert without even the benefit of the fucking tea at the end of it – sitting still for three fucking years *might, possibly*, be construed as *a walk in the fucking park*?"

Mister Smith stiffened. "Oh my God."

Morse blinked. "Jesus Christ! Are you telling me you never thought of that?"

"No, it's worse, it's worse... God, it's like a signal fire. His thought processes have started up again. Primary, secondary... he's back. Good God in heaven, he's murdered the doctor."

Morse stood up suddenly, spilling his tea. "You have got to be –"

"No, Morse, I am not 'fucking joking.' I've been a fool. His thoughts weren't absent, they were just – *slow*. Adjusted time perception, you see? He sped himself up to the point where none of his movements were detectable and then he just waited us out." The massive brow furrowed, huge trenches appearing in the flesh as Mister Smith concentrated all of his power. "The primary thought stream is back in full force. He's in full chameleon mode – masking his true nature even from himself, despite everything. I'm not going to find out anything about his bodily processes now." Mister Smith revolved in the air, turning to face the ashen Morse. "Listen to me, Albert. I've telekinetically released the wolves, and I'm going to attempt to drive them towards Doe, through the secret tunnels that honeycomb this place. If that fails, he'll be on his way here, and I'll happily take him to pieces. But you're the last line of defence, Albert, do you understand? There are worst-case scenario instructions in our safe house in Centrepoint. Find them and do whatever you have to, even if it means destroying this whole area. There are instructions on that eventuality in the safe house as well, and other agents will be on the way to join you there. If all goes well, I should be able to give you an all-clear within six hours. If you don't hear from me, you know what to do."

Morse opened his mouth. "I need to tell Shirley—"

"Forget your wife. Forget your dog. If you don't hear from me, they're dead to you, do you understand? Do you understand, Morse? *Do you?*" Mister Smith's eyes glowed an angry, fiery red.

Morse scowled.

"I understand that you're full of fucking shit! I'm not going to leave my wife to fend for herself in whatever shitstorm you've called down on us! And if you think –"

He didn't get any further before he was swept off his feet and across the room, slamming into the wall behind him, hard.

"If *you* think I'm going to jeopardise the continued survival of the human face for some bleeding heart you happen to be screwing, you're very wrong, Morse. You know what I can do. I tell you now that if you do go to your wife instead of the agreed location then you will find her dead of a massive brain haemorrhage." The eyes in the huge head glowed a terrible, fiery red. "But do please test me. I haven't killed anyone to prove a point in decades."

Morse hurled himself forward, fingers clawing for the homunculus. He got halfway before he was slammed back against the wall and held there, feet dangling off the floor.

"I said *forget* her! There's a back way out of here, Morse. I'm opening it for you now – the security will be disabled for the next thirty seconds. So run. *Run!*" The command was a snarl at the base of Mister Smith's throat, and it echoed in Albert Morse's mind and soul. Then Mister Smith let him go, and he dropped to the ground.

"I'll be back for you. *Sir.*" he snarled.

And then he ran.

Mister Smith turned slowly in the air, and waited, marshalling his strength.

"Die, John Doe. Die. For the sake of everyone on this planet, die quickly... and for your own sake, die before you face me."

CHAPTER EIGHT

The Big Kill

I'M LOST.

This place is a maze – endless corridors of grey stone and dripping water, endless twists and turns and stairways that always seem to be leading down, never up. I've just been walking, looking for someone to tell me the way out of here, but it's no go. There must be guards in a place like this. Maybe they're being kept out of my way.

After all, it's not like I'm going to ask nicely if I find them.

I'm trying not to think about swallowing my own heart back there, not to mention my lungs, kidneys, small intestine and the rest. There isn't even a scar on my belly now, and it feels like everything's back in place. Frankly, I didn't know I could do that, and I don't know if I could do it again – I never even considered the possibility that I could heal from a simple gunshot wound, never mind being taken apart like a cheap watch and stored in a neat line of jam jars.

It was like I was in a trance.

Like an emergency subroutine on a computer made of flesh and bone.

A catastrophic damage protocol for a meat robot.

Well, I've got better things to do than think about that, right?

It's not all damp corridors and wet stone down here – occasionally there are rooms coming off from the main complex, cold stone chambers like cells, dormitories with rows of empty wooden beds, long since fallen into disuse, crowded with cobwebs... I'm getting the impression that this place has been running on fumes for a while.

Maybe I was the last thing left to study.

The Boxer mentioned something like that – that I was the last of my kind. In a way, it makes me wish I could have figured out those notes. Or maybe it doesn't.

Some truths you just don't want to know.

My head's killing me. I'm going to have to get out into the fresh air before too long. I'm just taking corners at random right now – anything that feels right. That's probably making me even more lost than I was, but what the hell. Eventually I'm bound to come across somebody, surely.

I push open a heavy oak door and find myself in some kind of mess hall, presumably used by soldiers back when the Tower was more of a going concern than it is now. Or maybe used by whatever secret agents have been running it lately.

Make that definitely. Someone's been here.

There are two silver candelabras on each of the oak tables in the room, each one with three candles burning brightly, making the shadows flicker and dance across the walls – none of which makes this place any friendlier. Whoever did the decoration had a strange sense of feng shui.

Portraits of stern-looking men dressed in everything from doublet and hose to sharp business suits. I can see the Boxer in one of these pictures – 'Albert Morse.' I'll be sure to call him by name when I'm ramming his teeth down his throat.

Occult runes on some kind of ancient parchment I don't recognise, in temperature-controlled glass cases. Actually, I'm not even sure that is ink on parchment. I think it's a tattoo.

Some kind of... I'm not even sure what's in this picture, some sort of balloon-headed freak in a three-piece suit that wouldn't look out of place on a ventriloquist's dummy...

But it's the tapestries that send my blood cold. Great big hanging monstrosities, embroidered with Latin words, occult symbols and God knows what else... and great pictures of snarling wolves tearing into the dead. Everywhere I turn, I can see intricate pictures of wolves, digging at graves, slashing at hanged men, gnawing on skulls.

All my aggression dissipates. It's like eight pints of ice-cold water's been injected directly into my veins.

I don't know what the hell I'm doing here. I need to get out. This whole situation is terrifying.

I'm so scared all of a sudden.

When was the last time I was this scared?

Oh, no... it wasn't...

It was at Sweeney's place.

When the werewolf was there.

Suddenly I'm backing away, wanting to run, whatever it was that took me here not enough to keep me from scrambling right out the door and running as far as I can through this goddamn maze until I hit the fresh air.

But I just freeze in place, looking at those runes, those embroidered red eyes blazing in fur.

All of a sudden, I can't seem to look anywhere but at those tapestries, and my heart is climbing up into the roof of my mouth and something's going to happen –

– and then there's a tearing noise and a hairy, clawed hand slashes right through the cloth and suddenly the air is full of howling.

Oh my God.

There are tunnels behind the tapestries and they lead right to the wolf pit.

I don't have time to think of anything else before three more of the tapestries explode into ribbons, the alcoves behind them filled with pulsing, snarling fur and teeth, with cold yellow and blazing red eyes. Four of them. All around me.

I turn, wanting to run, to get out of there like a hare out of hell, but there's one at the door.

That's five.

I'm so afraid.

They snarl, saliva dripping down onto the wood of the tables. I'm right in the middle of the room. Four of the wolves are circling around the tables, claws clicking on the old cold stone.

I turn to the one at the door and, Jesus Christ, it's so fast, it's leaping – grab time, grab time and squeeze it like you'd like to squeeze the Boxer's throat, squeeze it tight –

It's still so fast. My legs give out from under me and I go down and I can feel razor claws raking through my hair, a millimetre from my scalp, one nanosecond away from tearing off the top of my skull like popping a can of mixed nuts. Searing green eyes meeting mine, green as unripe acid apples. Thick, lustrous fur.

It's young. Untrained. Or that would have finished me. Razor teeth snapping and clacking and chewing me to pieces in quick gulps. Ego and identity breaking down into chunks. Everything I am chewed and swallowed and shot into the abyss of a wolf's stomach. I'm so afraid.

I'm looking at the other wolves out of the corner of my eye; fur matted, eyes glowing in red and yellow. Older and more experienced. Easily capable of rending me to pieces. But they're standing there, shifting impotently as this young upstart sails over my head.

Why aren't they attacking?

They're shifting around the table, coming at me from around the sides. They're going to get in each other's way like that. Why don't they just jump onto the table and leap from there, catching me between four sets of sharp, savage claws in a slow-motion death scene that I will make last forever, an endless hell of total terror, a fear so deep and terrible that it becomes an agony that never ends, but better than nothing at all, so I'll force myself to feel everything as they –

Stop it. This is getting me nowhere.

You were a detective when you got up this morning.

And that's a clue.

So why don't they leap over the tables?

Oh.

Of course.

Silver candelabras.

I break left. Fingers wrap around the handles of the candelabras. It's all so slow.

I swing the candelabras around, candles flying, flames flickering. The werewolf's already leaping – right for me this time. Great foaming jaws open towards me...

...and then the silver sticks smash into them with the kind of force I'd use to knock down a good-size wall with a sledgehammer.

Stitch that.

These bastards might be tough as nails but silver is the great equaliser. Sonny-boy's jaw flies apart like a cheap plastic toy from a chocolate egg. The look of fear in those green burning eyes is so goddamned gorgeous I almost don't realise I've left a big hole for the two on my left to come through. They're up on the tables and leaping for my head, claws outstretched...

Against ordinary enemies this would be a slow-motion ballet, but it's taking everything I've got to keep up with these animals. Candelabras block outstretched claws, smacking them away, breaking the bones of the hands as I jink right, letting them miss me by inches, barrelling into the tables on the other side of the room, burned by the silver.

I wheel around, aiming a kick to the half-face of Kid Werewolf, then lunge, driving the candlestick up through the roof of its mouth and into the brain – then ducking down as the claws swipe the air where I was. My heart's pounding. The adrenaline's flowing. The fear is... not gone, but changed. The situation is almost impossible but not hopeless. I feel stronger, faster than I've been in years. I've got silver on my side.

There's a dark joy flowing through me. Like I'm close to the threshold of something, and if I just survive this, I can find it.

I've never felt this alive.

I vault back, describing a lazy arc through the air as claws rake above and below, listening to the sound of flesh falling off bone as the

Beautiful Boy shrivels and falls into a thousand slippery pieces out of my field of vision.

Something's changed. Maybe it's the reset button they pushed in me, or the long rest my body's had.

Maybe it's that I'm the last of my kind. Maybe, on some deep, buried level, far underneath the surface of my head, I know I'm playing for all the marbles.

Whatever it is – I've never been this good. *Never.*

They can't touch me. The four wolves have sores and boils on their hands from where I've smacked them with the candelabras. Without even thinking about it, I reach out and grab hold of another to replace the one that's buried in the skull of Scrappy-Doo. One of the remaining wolves lunges – a big red-eyed, scraggy-haired sonovabitch – and I swipe the candelabras together at neck height, crushing his windpipe. Just before his neck disintegrates and sends his head tumbling, I lift my foot and kick it into his face, sending myself backwards into a somersault. At the top of the arc, I flick the big heavy silver antiques like sai swords, watching as they bury in two hairy chests and yellow eyes flicker out like streetlamps...

It's beautiful.

It's poetry.

The stench of rotting wolfmeat is heavy in the air, and it's just me and the last of the wolves. He's dripping saliva, snarling with his red eyes blazing like searchlights, and I've got no silver to hand. But I don't care.

I feel strong. Strong and hungry. I could eat for hours. I could tear through that wolf in a second.

I feel like... like Satan on the day of the Apocalypse.

Does that make me a bad person?

Does that make me a monster?

Come on, you little bastard.

Make the first move.

I dare you.

There's a long moment of silence before it leaps. This is the same kind of nightmare I ran until my muscles ached to get away from. The same beast that was making me piss myself in fear less than a minute ago. And I'm grabbing its paws and swinging it around, using its momentum against it while it snaps and snarls.

What is this? An emergency boost? Some dormant skill kicking in? What's in the saddle here?

The wolf goes flying, slow-motion into the skeleton of one of its brothers. There's a candelabra still lodged in the eye socket of the grinning wolf-skull, and the wolf's shoulder comes down on it hard. Impaled on silver.

Thank you, long-dead interior decorator. Thank you for being so stupid.

As the wolf howls, I let go of time and let it flow about me like the cloak of some mighty warrior. Then I grab another of the silver sticks and walk over, nice and slow, taking my time.

It thrashes, snarls and spits. It must be in agony.

I feel dark and terrible. I feel sadistic. I feel like a scorpion in the jungle, like some terrifying killer insect. I feel evil and damned.

I feel more like a monster than I ever have before.

And it feels good.

That's right, you Universal reject. You've met your match now.

I grin, staring him down, taking a good long look into those pain-wracked red eyes, that snapping muzzle.

Then I smash its brains in.

THAT SHOULD BE the end of it. That should be me out the door and racing towards the sunlight, but I stay, breathing in rotting wolf-flesh, just feeling stronger and stronger.

I read once in a book somewhere that the Bocor, the voodoo priest, the maker of zombies, could get the Loa, the god who'd given him patronage, to wear him like a coat, ride him like an animal, control him. That's what it feels like now. Like I'm being ridden.

Like something much stronger and older and more powerful than I am is whispering in my ear, an insect Loa telling me that wolves need to be controlled if they're going to all attack at once like that. Controlled by a superior mind. A superior brain.

Did I deduce that?

Or did I just smell it?

I feel like I'm devolving, like I'm reducing to my basic essence, my core, like this terrible, wonderful machine that I am is moving into some kind of overdrive and my carefully nurtured consciousness cannot keep up. Like I'm sliding slowly into atavism.

I feel like there's something primal hatching in the centre of my mind, some awful desire to kill and eat and feed on my prey. I feel like an insect. I feel like a killer. I feel like a monster.

I am a hungry monster in a dark castle and somewhere there is food...

Somewhere...

brains

...I'm walking. Running. Lurching forward, ridden by my personal Loa, by the wonderful, terrible Insect Intelligence buried in the heart of me and, oh God, I'm so hungry, and this was where I was being led all along, this was what it was always about, the door smashing and splintering, thick oak but breaking against my dead fists, a terrifying red light burning into my eyes and then I'm through, inside some sort of airlock, some sort of trap-box, electronic voices screaming and wailing in my ears – *intruder detected* – and I can't even remember how I got here but I can't focus on anything except the

brains

and I must have blacked out for a second because the trap is sprung and the floor's swung out from underneath me and I can feel my feet splashing in acid, burning and melting and reforming as soon as they do. I'm wading forward like I'm wading through a swamp, dissolving and reforming. I didn't even know I could do something like that, but I don't care, I'm so close to the goal now that my mouth is watering. So close to that one thing I was put here for. I can smell it. My thoughts feel strange. Alien. Insectile. Nothing seems to matter, not the machine guns opening up, not the bullets tearing into flesh that heals as soon as they pass through, not the thick steel door to the room beyond. Nothing's going to stop me. Nothing's going to stop me from getting at the

brains

I'm barely conscious. Hands smashing at the second door. Denting the steel. Punching through. Grabbing. Tearing. So close. Can't think about anything

except

BRAAAAINNNNNSSS

And suddenly I'm inside the room. I'm trying to keep my thoughts clear. Trying not to think about that thing floating there with his big beach ball head, with the tender brain inside. I'm trying not to let that dark, sadistic insect part of me get any more of a hold on me, because I'm afraid of what it's doing to me. I'm afraid that this might be my last chance to get away, to get clear of this beach-ball-head man before something terrible happens, that this might be my last chance to leave without grabbing hold of him and tearing his skull open and eating his delicious, succulent, moist –

It's not going to happen, John.

Oh God. Oh God that never made a thing like me.

He's in my head.

Yes, John. I'm inside your mind. I commissioned a lot of research on you, and I do believe it's paid off. I really do think I can affect you, John. In fact, I think I can kill you.

He's in my head. He's got me right where he wants me. Did he lead me here?

I need to think –

I'll do your thinking for you, John. Don't worry. I'll try not to make this hurt too much.

No, no, get out, get out, get out –

Don't struggle, John. This is for the best.

Get out! Get out of my head!

What the hell are you?

I'm Mister Smith, John.

Prepare for psychic annihilation.

CHAPTER NINE

Playback

THERE'S A LITTLE man sitting in my head.

A little man ripping and tearing and biting at the walls of my mind, plunging hooks into my sense of self and yanking out pieces, flaying my preconceived notions with barbed wire, slashing and tearing, damaging, killing me from the outside in, boring his way into me like an oilman drilling for a big strike.

And deep down inside there's an opposite force, something down deep at the bottom of my brain, some terrible insect monster that's wearing me like a coat, controlling me, moving my limbs and sending me crashing forward, raging, attacking, hungry for the unspeakable.

And everything I always thought I was is stuck in the middle.

I don't know how much more of this I can take.

It's all going to be over soon, John. Don't worry.

I can hear him in my head.

He's reaching into my head and yanking out wires. I can feel lights going off on the switchboard of my self, a dark void starting to open up. I've heard the word "soul-destroying" a number of times, but I never really thought about what it meant before. Now I know.

Listen: six years ago I went to the park.

It was a beautiful autumn day, and the leaves on the trees were a riot of burning red, orange and gold. There were couples picnicking with hampers straight out of a picture-book, kids throwing balls and sticks for healthy dogs to catch and bring back, tails wagging. There was just enough cloud to keep the sun from being oppressive, and just enough wind to let you appreciate what a warm September day it was.

I stood on a hill, looking out at the people smiling and laughing and holding each other, and I felt like I belonged in the world. I felt like there was a place for me. I sat on the grass and stayed there for hours, just people-watching, seeing the world go by. That was when I decided I didn't want to be a killer anymore.

How long ago was that? Eight years? Four?

I went to... I think it was a fairground... in the summer...

Gone. Destroyed. Nothing left now, John Doe. Nothing left to do but die.

Let go, John, let yourself end and fall into pieces.

You are the enemy of all that is, John Doe. End and die.

That was the happiest day of my life...

What was I saying?

No, it's gone. Got to concentrate. I'm fighting a war on three fronts here. Every chunk this freak takes out of me opens me up to that yawning hunger at the core of me. I don't want to give in to that. I don't want to become nothing but hunger.

You *are* nothing but hunger, John. Don't fool yourself. All I'm doing is stripping away your illusions so I can crush the real you and end your threat forever.

Die, John. Roll over and die.

Jesus Christ, will you shut up for a second?

There's him yammering in my head, almost but not quite masking the alien insect thoughts down deep in the centre of my psyche, the ones that want me to tear and eat and feed... and then on top of all that, there are the chairs.

The ones flying at my face.

It's really hard to deal with total evisceration on the psychic plane when there's a massive leather armchair flying directly into your sternum. Slowing time doesn't help – no, John, none of your little time-tricks now. **I can control my perception of time as well as you can, so no matter what speed you're seeing things at, I'll be right there seeing them with you. You can't escape me, John.**

He's right.

The heavy armchair slams into me, sending me crashing across the room and into the wall, pinned like a bug under somebody's thumb. That giant head turns to look at me, eyes glowing, not showing the slightest strain.

Telekinesis – he can crush me like a cockroach without lifting a finger.

As if I didn't have enough on my mind.

The chair catches light, along with the floor beneath my feet and my hair and skin. Pyrokinesis – telekinetic acceleration of molecules to make things ignite. It hits me – he's not heating the chair. He's heating me, and everything I touch is going up as a result – my skin's got to be three hundred degrees right now. And I'm taking it. And deep down underneath, in the dark part of myself I don't want to acknowledge...

...I'm loving it.

Does that make me a bad person?

Does that make me a monster?

What kind of person am I?

Whatever I am, I'm a little too resilient to go up in flames just yet, but it's a matter of time – he's going to keep turning up the heat until I melt. Now I know how a lobster in a pot feels.

All this on top of the sharp claws scrabbling inside my head, tearing and scratching at my thoughts and memories. I can't just lie here and die, pinned to a wall by an animated armchair and roasted like chicken. It's too stupid a way to go.

I ball my fists and slam them against the blazing wood, smashing and battering at it like a madman. My hands rise and fall, rise and fall, thrashing like one of the wolves, letting the hunger underneath take control, letting it turn me into an animal. Into a biting insect. Into what it wants. The chair creaks and splinters – the combined pressure from the telekinesis, the fire and this little workout splitting the wood, great cracks that slowly travel through the structure until the whole thing bursts apart into component parts. I fight my way free of a drowning sea of wood, leather, foam stuffing, fire and fume – and I'm right back where I started, with a slight difference in temperature of about five hundred degrees. The whole room's going up.

How very aggressive of you, John. Well, there's more where that came from.

That's when the desk levitates up from the floor and starts a suicide run towards me.

This isn't funny. That thing's got to be solid mahogany – it's not going to burn easy and if it hits, it's goodnight Vienna, or as close as I can get anyway. I can feel him tugging and tearing at all the little pieces of me like he's yanking out clumps of my hair, but I can't worry about that now. I need to let go of all conscious thought – do this on pure instinct –

The desk flies towards me, one ton of mahogany that could crush me like a beetle under a boot –

– and then I step –

– jump –

– what –

– vault over the desk as it passes noiselessly underneath me –

– wait –

– and then as it smashes into the wall, I'm reaching out and grabbing hold of that big-headed little bastard by one half-shrunken ear and drawing my fist back and then –

– AAAAAHHH!

I can hear him inside my mind, and for once it feels good. That poke in the face seems to have broken his concentration – the dome-headed freak can't be used to direct physical pain if he's squirrelled away in here, especially not having his nose pulped by a solid right cross...

That... makes two of us.

Let's see how you like it.

I stagger backwards. Something just smashed into my face and smashed my nose down like a pancake.

Then something does it again.

And again.

And again.

A constant cracking of bone, like the beat of a drum, the pain fresh and alive every time – *crack, crack, crack* – and the worst part is, it's not even my nose.

That's right, John. But every blow you give me, I'm going to give you back a thousand times – that's if you ever reach me again. It's not only tables and chairs I can move, John.

I feel something grabbing hold of me – like a giant hand with a hundred fingers, squeezing from all directions, then hurling me towards the wood-panelled wall. He's got me in the grip of his mind – tearing my thoughts, delivering the sensation of a broken nose a thousand times a second, and slamming me around the room like a kid smashing his sister's favourite doll.

I'm pinballing off the walls... the ceiling... the floor... I can't get my bearings –

And now you're out of reach, let's show you just how hot I can make things for you...

There's something that feels like a rush of air, and suddenly everything gets very hot, very quickly. He was only testing before – now he really means business. I can smell flesh – my own flesh – cooking like bacon, charring and burning... flames start to spring from my arms and legs. I can feel my face burning, my eyeballs bursting and running down my cheeks...

Die, John. Die! DIE!

Don't listen to him. Don't panic. I can get through this. Whatever I am is stopping me from burning up completely, and I can still... see, somehow. I know where he is in the room. I can smell him, even above the burning flesh and the melting fat of my own blazing body.

It's his brain. It's like a beacon.

What *is* he?

Would you really like to know, John?

Don't listen to him – just break free of his grip –

Yes, I think I will tell you. I think drowning in my memories will probably stop you struggling free while I burn you to ooze... yes, yes, I think you should know my story intimately.

And suddenly I'm somewhere else. Somewhere warm and safe, protected by darkness and fluids. Sensations come to me, muffled, from beyond the soft organic walls of where I am.

The year is 1839.

The year is 1839. The biophysicist Herr Doktor Emil Klugefleisher has made his home in London after being forced to flee his native Germany due to circumstances unknown. He is the toast of the scientific community for his theories on the development of the human brain, taking Galvani's theories of bioelectricity in bold new directions and experimenting to alter the mental capabilities of rats and apes in utero, albeit with little practical success. There is even talk of his being accepted into the Royal Society.

All of his work threatens to crumble into dust when his maid, Eliza Smith, reveals to him that she is pregnant and that he is the father. In an instant Herr Doktor foresees his whole reputation wiped out at a stroke by the scandal. The answer is obvious – the girl must vanish. Klugefleisher considers simply strangling her and dropping her body into the Thames, but the action seems rash. He reconsiders. His basement laboratory is soundproofed, and he is in need of a human test subject, after all. Why not kill two birds with one stone?

The fledgeling police force in London take little notice of Eliza Smith's disappearance, not suspecting so well-regarded a citizen as Herr Doktor Klugefleisher. In reality, the girl is now little more than a mindless shell, the regimen of chemicals and electricity that is designed to affect the foetus in her belly having rotted her own brain tissue to the point where she cannot speak or feed herself, or even think.

Awareness first comes to you as you grow in her womb. The garbled snatches of private thoughts reach, not your ears, but your growing frontal lobes. Slowly, you begin to understand. The womb is commonly regarded as the paradise to which many seek to regress, but for you it is a horror beyond description. The amniotic fluid you float in bubbles with foul, noxious chemicals. Electricity sizzles through nerve endings, causing intense pain even as it acts on your nerves and cells, warping and mutating your body. The accelerated growth of your head is constant, unending agony, and all the while you can feel the cold, frozen evil of your father and the babbling insanity of your mother. This is your earliest memory.

Not mine...

You wanted to know my story, John Doe. Allow me to tell it in my own way, as a weapon to destroy you completely. Feel my life happening to you, every nightmare, every agony, every spirit-crushing second of torment compressed into the telling of it. Listen to my story and die...

After four months, your mother finally dies, and Herr Doktor Klugefleisher is forced to cut you out of her womb. It is hard to say whether it is the chemicals and the electricity that kill the poor woman, or whether it is you – your immense, lolling head is already much larger than a normal baby would grow and the womb now presses against you, stretched beyond endurance, your mother's agony constantly battering against your mental defences to merge with their own, one more horror in a sea of horrors. Her death comes as a relief.

Your first sight when the knife carves through flesh to release you is the grinning face of Herr Doktor, staring down at his prize. As he lifts you in his arms... his hands gripping the sides of your head as your body dangles, shrivelled and almost lifeless... and then there is a knock at the door above. As well as receiving thoughts, you have been broadcasting your own – thoughts of pain, fear, misery! The good Doktor is inured against such, but his neighbours are terrified at the sensations that crawl across their souls – which their limited minds can only translate as the sound of purest murder echoing from the house of Herr Doktor Klugefleisher. And so the police have arrived to enquire as to the nature of the disturbance.

Klugefleisher turns his head – and you lash out, using telekinesis for the first time as a small child might flex infant fingers. You catch his head within your mind, and his head continues to turn... turn... turn! He pleads! Begs! His screams for mercy become shriller as his vertebrae begin to tear apart one by one, but there is no mercy in you... only a cold desire for revenge!

A sickening crack of separating cartilage and the devil doctor lies dead – a fitting punishment for his crimes against humanity!

You float in the air, contemplating the dead man, as the police break down the door, motivated as much by the emanations of rage and grief that spill from your warped brain as by the ominous silence... only to fall back, screaming in terror, as they break open the soundproofed room to find you floating above the corpse... your distended head supporting your withered frame like a child's balloon supporting a string...your eyes, black and pitiless, glowing with the power afforded you by the madman's forbidden experiments!

I can't feel any part of me – all I'm aware of is old Victorian stone and the smell of blood and in front of my eyes there's an old German scientist with his head on backwards. I'm drowning in melodrama.

And I think he's doing something to me. Some essential part of me is starting to lose... integrity. Coherence.

That's right, John Doe. I'm taking you apart, brick by brick, cell by cell. There's going to be nothing left of you but single cells, isolated, unconnected, a thin soup of living, mindless sludge on the floor.

You can't win, John. Herr Doktor Klugefleisher created me as the ultimate development of the human mind. Had Darwin's theory been in common usage at the time, he might have thought of me as the product of millennia of human evolution... come, don't you want to see how I was studied? How I became a curiosity for Victoria until she saw my true value and assigned me to aid in the work begun by John Dee? Perhaps you'd like to see first-hand how I came to take over MI23, how I began the work of eradicating your kind, one by one...

Or perhaps it's enough to know that all of you from the waist down is a thin, liquid ooze. Your body cells don't respond well to the kind of heat I'm putting out, John. You were never the strongest of your kind, and now that I've learned how to pry your cells apart from one another it's going to be very easy to turn you into nothing but a lifeless gruel.

Goodbye, John.

He's got me.

I can feel my mind simplifying as I burn and melt on the floor. Feel that terrible alien hunger creeping up to take over, that part of me that was in control all along, playing me for a fool all my days, the nasty little inner demon that's made me the bad guy in the story of my life. Hell with it, anyway – I should relax and let balloon-head take care of it. God knows, after seeing what this body's capable of, I wouldn't trust myself with it. And these people are allegedly the good guys, even if they do make Jack Bauer look like a liberal bleeding heart.

Why not let them save the day?

I try and relax and let it happen. I'd close my eyes if I still had them. But it's no good.

I'm selfish. I'm evil. I'm an insect who only cares about survival.

And I want to live.

He's inside my head, drowning me in his memories while he dismantles me piece by piece. All right, then. All right. If he's such a fan of memories... I'll give him what he wants.

What are you doing, John?

Just let go and let that drive to live take over... stop suppressing that animal part of me, that weird insect part that's wanted to rise to the surface ever since I got within sniffing distance of this guy. I can't see what that part of me wants – what's been making me act so crazy this past hour – but I'll bet he can.

Let's let the dog see the rabbit.

John? What are you thinking... you can't escape, John...

What are you...?

Oh God... oh God, I didn't realise... I didn't... *get away from me...* *GET AWAY! GET AWAY!*

And then it's just screaming. Screaming in my brain. And whatever he saw made him lose his cool enough to let me out of his grip. I wonder what it was?

I'm not burning anymore. I can move. It's too late, though.

I'm moving already.

I'm a passenger in my own body. I can feel it – oozing liquid half sliding and slopping, arms moving with inhuman strength, propelling the top half of me across the burning floor, padding and lapping against the hot wood, fingers flexing and uncoiling with enough force to send this melting, distorted flesh prison that used to look like a human being up into the air...

...arms wrapping around the gigantic screaming head that's still broadcasting terror and madness into my mind... but not a terror for his own safety.

For the safety of the planet.

I wish I could stop this happening. I wish I could do something, anything apart from just watching it happen. But I'm not in control anymore. I'm a fading voice, an unreal personality, a cheap disguise torn away in the final scene.

I wish I'd let myself die.

But it's too late now.

The arms tighten enough to crack open the huge skull like an eggshell and I can smell the grey matter slopping out –

– the BRAINS –

It's so hard to stay coherent –

My teeth chewing and gnawing and swallowing down the stringy grey matter and suddenly a light switch goes off in my head and I

I

I

Understand

Everything

And then the world ends.

INTERLUDE *the* SECOND

New York, 1976

– AND IN THAT last moment of self-awareness memory floods in and Johnny hears the twinks chatting under the strobe lights of '76 –

"I don't care about sex, I just want somebody to hold, I'm *such* a pervert –"

"Oh *God*, don't tell me you've been talking to Texas Barry, *please*, Texas Barry spins that exact line *all* the time, Stevie went home with him once, the man's got no cock to speak of –"

"Oh, don't, don't tell me that, I'm on downs, why would you tell me *that* –"

"Oh please, he wants to marry every boy he meets, oh, oh *God*, this is my song, this is my new song, come on I want to dance –"

– and they jump up from the sofa and move onto the floor and dance and instantly their places are taken, one man this time, older and watching the lean tanned boys twirl and flex and move around the floor and toss their heads back in something like ecstasy and look so good and sing in time with the music, "make me believe in you, tell me that love can be true," old but newly discovered to them, a sweet reminder to Roscoe that old things come good sometimes –

– and Roscoe's cruising for twinks at the Tenth Floor and feeling alone and out of place because the New York scene is mutating so quickly now, new joints springing up every week but the white straight polyester crowd is edging out the blacks and the gays and the both and the men are fat and permed these days and their teeth are bad and they don't like to dance, why would they want to dance like fags anyway, they're here for one reason and that's to get drunk and get laid and what the hell, maybe that's cool despite everything because God knows it'd be nice to get some dick action in New York at thirty-eight years old –

– and seven months, nearly thirty-nine if you think about it and Roscoe's thinking old man's sour dour thoughts tonight as the speed kicks in and rewires his brain and the twinks dance like it's just for him, erection like a stone at the bottom of a lake in his pants, hard but drowned deep in cold water and soon to be eroded into sand and nothing and he's thirty-eight and lonely and lost in New York and something's going cold inside him and it's been four months since he did anything and there's grey in his moustache and his belly's starting to nudge over his belt and oh God what if nobody ever wants to fuck him again –

– and oh God that kid looks so damn good in that vest, what is he, eighteen, seventeen, it's like he stepped off a beach in California and through the doors of the club and all Roscoe wants to do is gently lead him into the toilet and unbutton his tight jeans slowly and with the reverence that should be accorded to the risen Christ or a reclining Buddha and blow him just as an act of religious devotion more than anything –

– and Roscoe doesn't do a damn thing as per usual except mutter like a crazy bastard and drink coffee and maybe he should get up and dance but he doesn't have the rhythm in him anymore, it'd be like those goddamn white straight polyester assholes that are gonna be the face of disco music for 1977 and until the end of time maybe and maybe that shitty little punk asshole on Fifth Street was right, Jesus, he should have beaten hell out of that little bastard but what if he was telling the truth –

– and Roscoe can't handle these thoughts any longer, he can feel the drugs taking him into some down deep dark place so he latches onto the twinks again, so warm and healthy and just glowing with life and sex and strength and that's what it's all about and Roscoe listens in because whatever they're talking about is better than this shit in his head –

"Oh God, I forgot, guess who I ran into on the street, just try to guess –"

"What? I can't hear you –"

"Johnny Doe! He was panhandling down on thirty-eighth, letting tourists touch him for a buck –"

"Oh my God, is Johnny Doe coming, I'm totally in love with that man, he's like Bowie meets Bogart –"

"He's decadent, he's just *totally* decadent, have you touched his skin ever, it's ice-cold –"

"That's what it must be like to fuck Bowie –"

– and that's a weird thing to hear because it was four months ago with Johnny Doe in that alley and Roscoe taking him into his mouth and running his tongue slowly up and it wasn't ice-cold but it was cold and so weird that he nearly stopped but Johnny does look a lot like Bogart or some kind of outer space Ziggy Stardust cool dream Bogart anyhow and it'd been a couple months since Jason left him because his goddamn shrink told him to, never trust a fucking Jungian, and Roscoe had him in his mouth and couldn't smell him and it was like Johnny didn't have a scent and that was so weird and so hot at the same time –

– and his cum was *black* –

and afterwards Johnny asked his name, looking down and kind of smirking like the cold bastard god of decadence he was, and Roscoe got defensive and told him the PhD part even though he usually kept that quiet because this asshole was a freak not a rock star and Roscoe didn't need this dominant-submissive game-playing shit right now –

– and suddenly Johnny Doe dropped his cold-ass decadent pose and took Roscoe back to his place and they drank whiskey sours and Johnny gave him a handjob on the couch and that was the weirdest because all the time that cold hand was moving and stroking and teasing and touching and getting Roscoe harder than anything ever had in his life that soft cold Village voice was telling the craziest story Roscoe ever heard –

– and Johnny Doe was saying he wasn't a human being –

– and then he finished Roscoe off and left his head spinning from the intensity and the information that Johnny Doe was Ziggy Stardust and *The Man Who Fell To Earth* and *Dracula AD 1972* and whatever the hell else he was and that was why he had no scent and why you couldn't feel his pulse or hear his heartbeat and Johnny took him by the hand and led him into the bedroom and and and –

– and word spreads fast in a place like this and another young hot perfect guy was joining the first two and the newcomer's solid black muscle was the perfect counterpoint to the sleek white marble bodies dancing around him and this brand new 1976-model twink reminded Roscoe of that time he took Jimmy home –

– and the morning after Jimmy's dad was at the door with a shotgun ready to blow Roscoe's head off and Roscoe barricaded himself in the bathroom and called the cops and they never came and eventually Jimmy's dad blew a hole in Roscoe's Warhol print saying it was the path to degeneracy and took off and Jimmy wanted to get back together but by that time Roscoe was sleeping with Jason and they were going to move in together and this used to be a funny story Roscoe told at parties and now he wanted to cry thinking about it and what was so special about Jason anyway after Roscoe had fucked a spaceman –

– and he has to listen in on the twinks again just to block out that gnawing fucking hole right through him, the twinks turned right around like meerkats to stare at the entrance and the crowd making awestruck noises and celebrity noises and Jesus noises –

"Johnny –"
"Johnny, over here, Johnny –"
"Remember me from the Garage, Johnny –"
"Johnny – Johnny – *Johnny* –"

– and six foot of Bogart/Bowie pure pale blue-white flesh shock-white hair walking through the door and every inch of him cold and decadent and ignoring all the lust and need and the backlash bitching and milking that goddamn Bowie bullshit everyone expects of him these days and maybe that's why he does it –

– and Roscoe stands up slowly and heads to the office in the back that Gary said he could use whenever he was speeding and stressed and needed a place to be alone, thank God for Gary, and he closes the door on the music and the talk and the bullshit and just sits behind the desk in that little office and rests his head on his hands and waits and wants to cry –

– and Roscoe thinks back to him and Johnny Doe lying in bed listening to the couple in the apartment upstairs screaming at each other and how Johnny wanted to know who he was and what he was and everything and Roscoe with his head full of dope smoke saying anything that came into his head and still freaking out on that experience and on Johnny's cold space muscle and Bogie eyes and smile and making all kinds of promises –

– and he wishes now he'd never said a word –

– and Roscoe took all kinds of samples out of Johnny, like skin samples and blood samples and stool and hair and listened to the heartbeat Johnny didn't have and listened up over coffee to ten years of Johnny's life story, starting off in a cheap apartment on Haight-Ashbury, dealing acid and reds until Altamont shot down the hippie dream and he came east to the Village to lose himself and melt into the first culture he found and before that he hated hippies like poison and hunted Reds behind the cold dark whiskey sour desk of a private eye, Bogie not Bowie in those days and before that he fought in the war like everyone else and before that he ran hooch and hung out with Dorothy and before that well it doesn't matter but there's a lot of before that you can keep a secret right Emmett right –

– and Roscoe had heard some weird coming-out stories in his time but Johnny's was the oddest, coming on like he didn't care about nothing except fitting in to whatever scene would have him, so he asked all the right questions and a few crazy ones and heard things that made his blood run like ice and killed his hard lust dead as arctic tundra, things like Johnny saying he snuck into the morgue sometimes and ate brains –

– and Jesus Christ, Johnny admitted he ate brains and why the hell didn't Roscoe call the cops right then except maybe this was his last chance to do something right with his life and this was too big to let go of –

– and Roscoe nearly freaked out and called the cops or the FBI when the blood sample turned into a goddamn slug crawling around the tube and the hair turned to bone and the skin crawled off the microscope slide and he spent three days throwing up until he finally burned the goddamn samples in a furnace and even then he lay awake every night for weeks afterwards –

– and it was one of those sleepless alone nights that all the jigsaw pieces came together and he realised what Johnny was –

– and he'd been avoiding Johnny ever since and he figured Johnny never came to the Tenth Floor, he was always in the Paradise Garage if he was anywhere, but somehow Johnny picked the one night Roscoe figured he was safe and now he'd have to tell him or maybe he could just hide in this little back office forever or until the dawn when everyone went home and slept it off –

– and the door opens with a creak like an old tomb –

– and Roscoe's skin nearly crawls right off his back with the fear like Johnny's skin crawling around on his desk then sprouting tiny little insect legs and Roscoe turns and nearly vomits and babbles a hello oh hello Johnny I didn't know it was you I didn't know you were in here Johnny how are you Johnny oh God oh Christ –

"Hey, Emmett."

– and Roscoe chokes and goes quiet because his voice is so cold and alien and dead like the ultimate Ziggy Stardust Sam Spade fusion the kids all want to fuck only it's flat granite stony as a grave marker –

"I was looking for you."

– and he smiles and that's the scariest thing of all because that's the smile of the Johnny Doe who made Roscoe bacon and eggs in the morning, the sexy sweet guy who's okay in spite of it all and that makes it so much worse because underneath there's something looking out at him like a snake waiting to strike –

– and Roscoe feels something cold and wrong and bone-hard clutching at his heart –

"What you got?"

– and maybe it's the speed and maybe it's the raw fear crackling up and down Roscoe's nerves like neon but he opens his mouth and out it spills like poison –

– and first it's all just crazy stuff about how Johnny's like a commune of individual cells who get together to be a collective and imitate a human being right down to the personality and how the further away from him offcuts like all the samples get, the more they show a life of their own –

– and how the cellular imitation isn't a true duplicate because it's cold and dead and deliciously decadent here and now but there and then just freaky and the reason why Johnny wants to fit in all the time with any new scene he comes across is because he's got to lay low and not draw attention and whoever's really calling the shots in that cell collective, the alien intelligence buried deep inside his sweet human soul, keeps him in situations where being a little weird isn't going to be enough to get noticed –

– and that's why he's mister Ziggy Decadent right here right now in 1976 and he was a hipster dealer back before that scene fell apart and the cops got wise to him and who knows maybe in the past he was in even stranger places than Bicentennial America like Monocentennial or Nocentennial America maybe if you can dig that who knows he isn't talking –

– and maybe in the future things will get so crazy strange and information rich that he can just be normal –

– and Johnny's looking like he figured most of that out already and that's not what he's here for, like maybe he's doped out every little nuance of what he is and he just needs to know why, or maybe he just wants to know what Roscoe knows –

– and his eyes are like little lethal grey bullets –

"That's it?"

– and Roscoe knows he has to keep his mouth shut now –

– and he opens it anyway because those eyes won't let him do anything else –

– and in the end it's all about the brains –

– and the reason Johnny breaks into the morgue and eats brains and maybe takes them fresh from heads too isn't any kind of crazy vampire bloodlust or serial killer compulsion because it's a lot smarter than that –

– and it wasn't until Roscoe wondered why an alien gestalt entity would need to eat brains that it came to him that the collective absorbs brains to analyse the tissue, the synapses, the cortical development and all that jazz like it's a walking talking spectrometer or *Star Trek* scanner taking samples forever –

– and suddenly Roscoe's flashing back to that late night double feature he caught when he couldn't sleep for the speed, some dumb Elliot Gould flick with a cat and a gun and a murder or something but following up with *2001: A Space Odyssey* and Jesus Christ if that isn't what's happening now because Johnny's the monolith and the sentinel and all of that stuff rolled into one, an alarm system waiting to signal somebody out there in the dark –

– and instead of waiting for us all to take that trip to the moon, Johnny's sampling brains, analysing the chemistry and power of all those little grey cells up there, waiting for that one special brain that'll tell him we've got to that stage of evolution where we're worth harvesting like crops, because if you want slaves, you don't want them too smart and you don't want them too dumb either –

– and if you want to eat a good steak you take it from a cow, not some dinosaur due to evolve into a cow in a billion years –

– and that means that whatever's out there is going to make future man look like a dumb animal –

– and Johnny's eyes are like two chips of black ice on a road Roscoe's skidding down with no control, steering wheel slick and slippery in his hands –

– and Johnny walks towards Roscoe and oh-so-gently takes hold of his face like he might lean in and kiss him one last time –

– and the sound of Roscoe's neck snapping is like the click of a door locking something away for all time –

– and Johnny doesn't even seem to be aware Roscoe ever existed as he walks out of that room and out of the club and out of New York, heading for the airport, whatever inner voice driving him now to forget, start over, find a new country and blend in deeper, deeper, deeper as he moves towards starting his new London life as straight and normal as anyone has ever been or ever could be –

– and Emmett Roscoe isn't found until four o'clock in the morning –

– and nobody makes it to the funeral except his mother –

– and the next year the club is gone and they're burning records in stadiums because it's faggot music and the good days are pretty much over and there's disease and death and hate coming hard on the new decade and word on the street is no future for you –

– and thirty-three years after that Johnny Doe is opening one giant red death eyeball slick with alien oils and juices and shrieking in the insect language of the death angels because he finally got that one perfect special brain he wanted and the signal is travelling out in a faster than light stream of information calling the Elder Gods the Insect Nation living in no-space no-time to fold down into this dimension to burn the world to harvest the human race –

– and that's that.

CHAPTER TEN

The Twisted Thing

THERE WAS NO sound in the room.

The walls were gutted by fire and the furniture had either been smashed or incinerated in the war between the two monsters. The floor was a mass of burnt carpet and mangled timber, in the centre of which lay what looked like a twisted, leathery doll, the massive head torn open, cracked like an eggshell and emptied, the eye sockets hollow and staring.

This was what remained of Mister Smith.

Next to the mutated, mutilated corpse, there lay the thing that once called itself John Doe. That name no longer fit. No human name could. The corpse was barely a torso, torn, partially melted and almost unrecognisable, strips of brain matter still hanging from what was left of its teeth. It was inert.

But not inactive.

Deep inside the charred and ruined lump of flesh, alien cells pulsed and chattered, communicating, analysing. Processes that had been primed millennia ago stuttered into motion. The command was simple.

Analyse the brain tissue, then heal to the required form. To the soldier form.

To the signaller.

The cells broke down the grey matter, swarming over it like tiny ants, deconstructing and exploring each strand of DNA. Mister Smith was not like ordinary men – his strange creator had seen to that. He was man as he would perhaps be in one thousand or one million years, a skull packed with the future.

The swarming cells of the thing that was once John Doe crawled across the torn, tattered scraps of Mister Smith's mind, reading and devouring. This was what they had been waiting for. This was a mind advanced enough to serve the collective.

The Insect Nation.

The cell-collective read the DNA strands carefully. The humans had indeed evolved to a stage where they could make slaves for the Insect Nation. Or was this an anomaly? There were no other functioning cell-collectives on the planet to communicate with. The chameleon personality, used to gather information about planetary culture, was inert and offline.

The cell-collective swarmed and chattered, turning the data over. Until further evidence presented itself, the collective had to assume that Mister Smith's brain was the normal configuration... that the Earth had matured enough to provide a slave race.

It was time to send the signal.

It was time to end the civilisation of this planet.

The flesh of the charred corpse that was once John Doe shifted.

Slowly, the pores began to ooze – a thick, white pus that slowly dripped... *slithered...* over the destroyed flesh, coating it in an opaque layer. The white coating thickened as the minutes passed, oozing, congealing, hardening.

Forming a cocoon.

The minutes ticked by.

Gradually, the cocoon lost its shape, the humanity inside melting, flowing, until the thick white skin resembled nothing so much as a large, circular blob of wax, or a lump of slimy dough, flat at the bottom.

In truth, it was an egg, and from it would hatch the final end of man.

Inside the cocoon, there was nothing resembling a human being – nothing but a soup of alien cells, floating, multiplying, small bolts of strange electricity sparking from one to another. This was the next phase of the program. It was time for the simulacrum to be cast off, the disguise discarded.

Now was the hour of the Sentinel.

Gradually the cells began to coalesce, flowing together, hardening, strengthening, forming structures. Outwardly the cocoon seemed to expand and vibrate, the membrane shuddering as though hundreds of tiny fish were conducting a war inside it, fighting each other for dominance. The primal soup inside bubbled and strained against the shivering white skin.

Gradually, a skeletal structure began to form. Alien organs grew like planets coming together from cosmic dust. The bubbling, boiling spew inside the thick white membrane thickened and began to solidify.

The cell-collective had previously taken a shape necessary for collecting data on the genetics and brain structure of the prospective slave race. That phase was complete. It needed a new form.

A form that would serve the interests of the Insect Nation.

A form that could call them across the void of space.

A form that could do their bidding when they arrived.

A form that – if it became necessary – could kill the human beings in their thousands.

Slowly, the thick white membrane of the egg-sac began to tear, a clear pus leaking out and pooling on the charred wooden floor.

Something unfolded from within, rearing up to full height. A mass of thin, hard white flesh and bone, fully nine feet in height, stooping in the confines of the room.

It was shaped almost like a man. The resemblance was slight, but close enough to lend it an additional air of terrifying inhumanity. There was nothing that we would recognise as a face on the thin, swaying head that bobbed slowly on the long neck. The creature had only one single eye, a vicious red orb with a milk-white centre like some grotesque cataract, and below that a mouth – a circular hole studded with hundreds of small teeth, tiny needles designed to shred and tear. The limbs were stretched and elongated, with cruel spikes of some bone-like substance extruding through the skin, and on each hand there were ten long, bony fingers, each ending in a slashing, raking claw, alongside thumbs that were little more than sharp hooks made to slash and tear. Instead of feet, the creature had a pair of large stone-like hooves. They stepped nimbly from the withering remains of the egg-sac with a gentle grace that belied their killing power.

There was strength in those spindly limbs – strength to defend itself against attack, strength to kill without mercy or hesitation if the order came, and strength to break free of the prison it found itself in. Without another look at the mess on the ground that had once been Mister Smith, the Sentinel clattered forward on its hooves, sinking its fingers into the stone of the wall. The claws easily penetrated the brickwork, acid secretions drilling into the rock, before the fingers flexed, the muscles straining for only a moment before the stone cracked, a chunk of wall tearing away with a noise like buried thunder.

Without hesitating or wondering at its own abilities, the creature tore another chunk out of the wall, slowly boring its way up towards the surface.

IT TOOK ONE hour and forty minutes of continuous digging to reach the open air, but this did not concern the Sentinel. It had waited millions of years for this moment already, and the signal had to be clear and unobstructed as far as possible.

It was night when it finally crawled from a hole in the shattered pavement, like a worm erupting from graveyard soil. The street outside the Tower was deserted, and there was nobody to see the hideous bone-white creature clambering up through the shattered concrete, and perhaps that was for the best.

Nobody wants to see the end of the world when it comes.

The Sentinel stretched to its full height in the moonlight, the single pulsing eye gazing up into the night sky, looking up and beyond. On the other side of that sky, outside of all space and all time – in the realms of un-space, of no-time – there was the terrible, endless chittering of Those Outside. The endless writhing and crawling and biting and buzzing and howling of the Insect Nation, the Un-Reality, the terrible light beside which our own reality is no more than a guttering candle. The Insect Nation waited, out beyond the borders of all that is or ever was. They waited, and they sent forth probes, lesser life forms that would fold down through space and time to impact against some forming ball of lava and primal muck. A place that would one day support life.

Sentinels.

Sentinels that would mimic that life, moving alongside it, growing and evolving with it, living in its shadow, taking regular samples of the seat of its intelligence. Sentinels that would wait for centuries, for millennia, waiting against the day that that humble form of life would evolve into something capable of total planetary efficiency, capable of spreading and ruling galaxies or universes.

Something that would be worthy to serve as slaves or foodstuffs for the Insect Nation.

That day had arrived.

An indefinable trembling shot through the body of the Sentinel as the circular mouth widened, the needle teeth clattering against each other. The terrible mouth widened impossibly, sickeningly, the jaws stretching as no human jaws could, distorting as the first echoes of sound came from the structures inside the throat.

It began as a scream.

An inhuman scream – a keening wail of torment, the kind of sound human beings dread in the depths of their darkest nightmares, a hideous, bone-jarring shriek that went on and on and on into the night. Dogs howled alongside, then sank down and huddled into their paws as the scream rose in pitch and intensity, spiralling up towards some terrible note beyond human hearing. Eventually, the dogs died, blood leaking from ears, eyes and noses.

The air was filled with the shattering of glass and for a moment Central London was engulfed in thousands of shards, falling through the air like sharp slashing rain, beautiful and deadly. The scream rose in pitch, the pulsing eye of the Sentinel rolling back as the inhuman vocal chords pierced all barriers of sound, moving into uncharted frequencies beyond all knowledge. It could not be heard with the ear now, but deep in the clenching gut of all those within reach there was a feeling of terror, of infinite, indescribable panic. Men and women cried in their sleep, then vomited, choking on their own terrified bile as the sound moved further and further out of human comprehension.

This was the sound of the Outer Realms, the awful music of those spheres that revolved like floating, bloated cysts in the qlippoth-universe, the anti-place where the Insect Nation gathered and flexed.

The summoning-sound.

The pressure in London seemed to drop as the scream passed into that Other World that lay beyond and behind and beside our own, and those who were walking the neighbouring streets began to bleed – first from the nostrils, then from the ears and eyes, collapsing as their insides hemorrhaged and began to leak slowly out of them.

In response, the sound of a billion feeding insects began to grow, the noise rising in volume – the terrible echo of feasting creatures, monsters living and writhing in climates no human mind could possibly conceive. Then came a sound never heard before – the cracking, grinding thunder of things unimaginable to mankind folding themselves down through higher planes of geometry to come into existence in our reality.

What must it have been like to hear that sound – to know that here and now, after all those centuries of human striving, the end had finally come?

THE FIRST CRAFT appeared over Hyde Park. Descriptions of it vary – to some it was a crackling, sizzling engine made of massive oiled parts, grinding against one another, lightning arcing from them. To others it resembled nothing so much as the carapace of a massive, hungry beetle, jaws clacking open and closed in a sickening rhythm. To a few – those whose minds did not instinctively protect them from the sight of something not meant to be seen – it was a grotesque, impossible construction of terrifying angles, both machine and monster, feeding tubes and tentacles dangling from the underside, pulsing with oil and slime, dribbling acid and bile on the ground below that killed whatever it touched.

Those who saw the invasion vessels as they truly were did not last long. They screamed their own throats raw, rupturing vocal cords and choking on their own blood and vomit long before the first of the devourers stripped their bodies for food and fuel.

As similar floating engines materialised over London, tiny black ovoids, like the eggs of nits or lice, dropped down from the underside of the first invasion craft, impacting in the soil, and quickly doused with the fluids spraying from above – the same fluids that reduced plant and animal life to smoking, toxic husks, black and skeletal remains. The reaction was almost instantaneous – the black shells cracked, split and disgorged writhing white maggots of various sizes, ranging from the size of a thumbnail to the size of a watermelon, that burrowed quickly into the toxic ooze surrounding them. Within a matter of minutes, they would be capable of scuttling vast distances at speed, finding their prey still shaking in terror in nearby streets and houses, burrowing into flesh and bone, working up into the skull. There they would tear into the cerebral cortex, chewing and ripping, nesting in the skull to shelter. For a few hours, the victim would stagger, eyes rolled back into the skull, drooling, moaning, sobbing, occasionally attacking his fellow men as the nesting maggot spurred him on.

For a few short hours, the zombies would rule London.

Finally the maggot would be nourished enough from draining the fluids and meat of the brain and the body would have reached the limit of its development, and the bones of the staggering man would shatter, spraying blood, the skin splitting as the creature inside flexed obscene muscles, a newly-formed black carapace covering it completely as it stepped out of its host and went to continue its terrible mission.

This was the first wave.

Other ships began to materialise over the wide-open spaces of London, disgorging their terraforming ooze and their legions of mind-eating worms, plague-ships carrying the ultimate obscenity in their holds. But already the pattern was changing. The maggots were transmitting back to the main intelligence, the hive-mind of the Insect Nation, as they chewed through the skulls of their victims, pronouncing the matter inside inferior and unserviceable. This species – this 'human race' – was not sufficiently evolved. It was useless as slave labour, for the most part possessing not even rudimentary telekinesis. As a source of nutrition, it was substandard. A War Wyrm, grown to maturity on the brain matter on offer on this world, would be barely thirty feet long and hardly even capable of chewing through steel and concrete.

The Sentinel had been deceived somehow. This species was not yet ready.

The Insect Nation had been called too soon.

There was a great chittering, like a tide of strange otherworldly static, that emanated from the hovering ships, washing over London, crashing against the terrified ears of those who'd watched fathers, sisters, infant children scream and haemorrhage, who'd seen friends and neighbours with great holes torn in chests and faces, eyes rolled back as they tore and smashed blindly at everything around them while maggots writhed in their minds. It was the noise of debate and decision.

Planet Earth was useless.

But it could still serve a function of sorts.

If all animal and human life was erased from the planet – if every vestige of humanity was torn down to leave a thick mulch of protein, a soup for larval forms to grow in – then this spinning ball of mud, filled with its backward, hobbling creatures, might have some use after all. A breeding ground. A place of experiment, to find new and more powerful forms that could live and grow on less.

They were here now, and it would be a shame to waste the journey.

The chittering static ceased, and silence rolled over the doomed city. It was decided. Organic life on this world would be broken apart, slowly and with care, their molecules and atoms split into nutritious mulch. From the burned and tortured cradle that remained, new forms would grow, forms capable of surviving more efficiently in this cramped, enclosed space of four dimensions with its buffeting wind of seconds and moments.

One of the floating motherships broke from the rest, turning slowly through the air and drifting towards Buckingham Palace.

London held its breath.

CHAPTER ELEVEN

Survival, Zero

LISTEN:

The doctor had told Megan Hollister she was too old for children at forty, but she and Neil had made the decision to try anyway. They'd each spent years telling themselves they didn't want a child – didn't want to be tied down, didn't want the financial hardship or just the basic, total, complete responsibility of having a life in their hands – but the truth was that they hadn't wanted a child with the people they'd been with. Within a month of Meg's first meeting with Neil – that ridiculous blind date at that ridiculous jazz-theme restaurant that her sister had set up – she'd found herself brooding. She had looked at babies being brought into the theatre in front of her and thought about how sweet they looked and how nice it was that their parents were exposing them to culture at such a young age, instead of thinking about how horrific it was going to be when the little brat started bawling at the top of its lungs halfway through the second act, obliterating the performance and ruining the whole evening for everybody else. She'd looked around her apartment, already measured up for when Neil moved in – his lease was almost up, and he was making commitment noises – and she found herself looking at the spare bedroom and measuring it for a cot or a playpen.

On their wedding night, they'd finally broached the subject, and he'd been going through exactly the same thing. It was time for children. It was probably too late for children – Dr Mears thought so when she'd broached the subject at a check-up – but they could try, and there was always IVF, or adoption. It was the commitment that was important. Knowing that they both wanted the same thing. That was enough. That had been enough – a month later, she was pregnant, and Dr Mears was fussing around her again, telling her how bloody irresponsible they'd both been and how difficult this was all going to be. Meg had only smiled – she had faith in herself and her child. Faith in the future she was building.

The delivery had gone as painlessly as deliveries do, and little Evan was as perfect a baby as anyone could wish for. She'd cried, seeing Neil holding the little boy, only looking, unable to come out with any of the usual half-sarcastic little jokes and put-downs he used to take the weight out of moments of emotion. This was too big, and he had no words. She'd reached to him, gently brushing her fingers against his arm, and he'd given her a glance and a shy little smile, as though meeting her for the first time. Then he'd gone back to looking at his son's brown eyes. His own eyes. The silence between them was like a warm blanket, and she buried herself in it, feeling complete in a way she hadn't understood people could. She remembered all the times she'd rolled her eyes at baby conversations and smiled. She'd have to watch herself – she still had childless friends.

But she hadn't been able to contain herself, and her childless friends had rolled their eyes and made her blush, and smile, and carry on anyway because it was so good to tell it.

Her wonderful little boy.

Her little Evan.

In the end, they'd left the apartment and found a nice terraced house out in Zone 5, left the centre. She'd even left her job. *When you're tired of London, you're tired of life*, they said, and they were right. She was tired of that life. This was what she wanted now – a little peace, a little solitude in the days when Neil was out at work and it was just her and the baby. And the nights, with him sleeping by her side and the cot by the bed, the whole family – and that word still had a wonderful resonance in her thoughts and on the tip of her tongue – all together, Mummy and Daddy taking turns to get up and grouch and get the bottle.

It was three in the morning, and the family wasn't together. And Megan couldn't sleep.

Neil was away for the weekend – a business meeting in Tokyo, one he couldn't get out of. His paternity leave had been criminally short and it was long over. His bosses had forgotten what it was like to be a new father, or they just didn't care. He moaned to her whenever she let him, but he knew the cold truth, that they couldn't afford for him to switch jobs right now or look for something less intensive. So Neil was gone, and the bed was cold, and Megan couldn't do anything but look forward to when he came back to them both.

She certainly couldn't sleep.

Little Evan was being an angel, sleeping peacefully in his powder-blue cot, and Megan knew she should just drift off and let herself sleep until he woke her, but she couldn't. There had been strange noises in the distance – a scream, like an animal, and then some kind of static noise, like hundreds of crickets. She'd thought about turning on the television to see if anything was happening, but she'd told herself not to be silly. She'd find out what it was in the morning. Probably it was one of those night-noises, those sounds in the early hours that are never explained. A bump in the night.

It was enough to put her on edge.

She decided to fetch herself a glass of warm milk and then go back and watch the baby for a while. Maybe that would help her to relax, seeing that little face that meant the most to her in all the world, sleeping peacefully. She wondered if all mothers felt so strongly about their children – certainly they did, but little Evan wasn't only flesh of her flesh, but a tiny little miracle, eased safely from the impossibility of late conception, grown in perfect health despite Dr Mears' endless worry and fuss, delivered without a scratch, against such terrible odds, odds she hadn't even allowed herself to consider.

He was everything to her.

Megan sighed, and lifted herself off the bed, the nightgown rustling against her thighs as she padded to the kitchen. The light of the fridge illuminated her tired face and the bags under her eyes as she reached for the milk carton.

There was a sound.

Nothing she could quantify. The sound of something breaking, or bursting. A crunching, cracking sound, as though something was being pushed with great force through brick and wood. She turned and listened.

Silence.

Seconds ticked by, the cold of the carton in her hand matching the chill in her spine. Then she put the carton down on the counter, feet padding back towards the bedroom.

She would just check on the baby and then she'd go back and pour her glass and put the carton back into the fridge.

Just a quick check.

Just to be on the safe side.

The door to the bedroom whispered open slowly, and Megan gently padded into the room, trying to pretend that her heart wasn't trying to pound its way out of her chest. She remembered the stories in the newspapers years before – missing babies, missing children. A big blank shape formed in her mind, words she never allowed herself to think, to admit even existed, but only felt the edges of occasionally, in moments of terror: cot death. She looked at the cot, trying to deny the terror that was flooding through her.

Little Evan was there. And he was breathing. The tiny baby chest rose and fell, tiny little movements as the child lay curled up under the blankets, facing away from her.

Megan breathed out a soft sigh of relief. She shuffled over towards the cot, not noticing the hole in the wall of the bedroom, down at skirting board level. Gently, she reached a fingertip down to trail lightly over the soft, smooth head of her wonderful, miracle child.

And then little Evan turned over in his sleep.

He had no face.

The face had been eaten away, chewed through, leaving nothing but a gaping hole tinged with torn, red flesh, and inside that hole there was only pulsing white maggot-flesh, inhabiting the baby's hollowed out corpse, pulsing in and out in a manner that seemed almost like breathing.

Megan stared.

And then she began to scream...

And scream...

And scream...

Listen:

Jimmy Foley was thinking about strike action in the hour before he died. The government were experimenting with extending the hours the tubes ran into the early morning – the Central Line ran until past three a.m. – and that was all fine and dandy, but the bloody bastard idiots seemed to think that late-shift drivers like Jim Foley could just carry on into the watches of the night without any kind of remuneration, not even overtime pay. So muggins Foley gets stuck in a bloody metal box at three in the morning on a Saturday for no extra money and he has to bloody lump it – *not likely, mate. Not bloody likely. See how your bloody three in the morning metal box runs with nobody driving the bastard...*

And on and on in that vein. Jim Foley's knuckles were white with anger as he gripped the tube control, turning it away when the train was stopped, turning it back and pushing the lever forward when it was time to send the train west along the line.

They called that a "dead man's handle."

Jim Foley was not a young man. He was fifty-seven years old with a sagging paunch and the grey straggly ruins of what had once been a Kevin Keegan perm nestling above his ears. He thought everything since Pink Floyd had been a load of rubbish and had a particular hatred for Orchestral Manoeuvres in the Dark, ever since his son brought a seven-inch single back from the shops that sounded like a robot having it off with a Clanger in the gents toilets on the bloody space shuttle. He'd snapped the bloody thing across his knee and the boy had told him he was a fascist and got a clip round the ear for his trouble. Danny worked in a bloody merchant bank in the city now and Jimmy went round his house every second Sunday for dinner and a lecture on how UKIP were the only way forward for Britain. Jim frankly preferred his son as a member of the red brigade – there'd be less rows about unions for a start – but at least he wasn't listening to Orchestral Bloody Manoeuvres in the Bloody Dark any more, which was a blessing.

Pull the dead man's handle back and twist away – "mind the doors please, please mind the doors" – wait for the signal – turn and push forward and that was Holborn. Nobody got on. Nobody got off. The place was empty as a tomb.

Jim shook his head. They were all using the bloody night buses. He was just wasting his bloody time without even any bloody overtime to show for it. By the look of it there was no point even striking – nobody was using the bloody Tube anyway so they'd all be stuck out in the pissing rain like spare pricks at a bloody wedding...

The train thundered on.

Tottenham Court Road.

Jim shuddered.

This was a hell of a place to be in the small hours. He remembered – was it three years ago? He'd heard about what had happened. They'd called it a terrorist attack.

Some... thing... running amok down the pavement, tearing heads off bodies, turning people into red mist. There were people who said it was a monster, a will-o'-the-wisp that moved too quick to see and unravelled people where they stood. Apparently there were stills of CCTV footage floating around the Internet that showed something covered in hair and a mouth full of teeth ripping passers-by to shreds. But they could do anything with computers these days and Jim knew better than to believe what he saw on the bloody Internet.

But he knew what had happened on the platform that day. Hundreds of people running for their lives, trampling each other, stampeding down the stairs into the station and crushing against the barriers, clambering over the dying to get down to the platform. Dozens – hundreds – panic-stricken, crowding and shoving on the narrow space of the platform...

They counted forty-two people who went over the edge. The lucky ones died instantly, fried like bacon on the third rail. The unlucky ones lived long enough for poor Dave Patton to come down the tunnel and slam into them, smashing them like pumpkins and dragging them under the wheels to slice and maim the corpses. Dave hadn't come back to work. The word on the grapevine was that he was shut up in some bloody home drooling on his straightjacket. Jim supposed the sight of that toddler's arm smashing his front window did that to him, the poor bastard.

Jim must have taken the train through Tottenham Court Road a thousand times since then, but he still felt a split-second of chill as the train pulled in and he saw the plaque on the wall. He'd seen the pictures of the clear up – the men in the white suits hosing the blood off and picking up the severed bits in bags. It gave him the horrors and then some.

Nobody got on, nobody got off.

The horrors were one thing, but Tottenham Court Road shouldn't be empty, even at three in the morning. There was only one bloke on the platform and he looked like he was pissed as a fart. Jim watched as the little hoodie bastard weaved, staggering along the platform, bumping against one of the Cadbury machines and then lashing out at it with a fist, bashing at it again and again. Bloody disgraceful. Bloody thugs getting pissed and smashing up the bloody platform.

Bloody sickening.

Still, not his problem. The platform attendant would deal with that little thug soon enough. Probably listening to that "emo" music. A clip round the ear wouldn't do him any harm. He'd had many a clip round the ear from his old dad, and it hadn't done Danny any harm either. Look at him now – pulling in eighty grand a year and all because he took a clip round the ear from his dad. Jim didn't agree with Danny about some of his politics, but he knew that if he'd let them loony liberals have their way, Danny would have grown up a little tearaway like that bloody yob on the platform...

The train moved towards Bond Street.

...trouble with them bloody liberals is they didn't like how things were in the real world. If Jim hadn't been firm with Danny, he'd probably be in prison right now with a bloody glue habit. Jim had taught him to work hard and play hard, and now he was on eighty grand a bloody year. Eighty grand! And he'd come from humble origins like his father, not like half of those posh public-school tossers in the city. Working hard and playing hard, that was the secret. Danny was probably out right now in one of the city bars, having the time of his life. Because he'd earned it. That was what those liberals didn't understand –

There was someone on the line.

Jim slammed on the brakes and the whole train juddered and screeched, slowing itself but not nearly enough. It was a man – about twenty – with a fancy suit and designer stubble. A city boy.

There was a hole in his chest about the diameter of an economy size can of beans. Jim caught a glimpse of the inside of the man's lungs. He was...

that wasn't bloody right... he was standing on the bloody third rail. Right on the third rail. Just swaying and trying to keep his balance with his eyes rolled back in his head... moaning...

...and then he was a smear on the windshield.

"Ah, Jesus Christ!" Jim tried to close his eyes, but he couldn't.

The platform was crowded.

Men in suits and good shirts, with little bean-can-size holes in them, their eyes rolled back in their heads and something white and pulsing visible in their open, yawning mouths. Blood running from nostrils and ears. Lashing out at each other, at themselves, moaning and mewling. Like a crowd of...

...of bloody zombies.

Oh, Christ.

Jim Foley's eyes widened.

Danny was in the middle of the crowd, short, gelled hair glistening in the lights, the side of his neck gaping and flapping, his eyes white orbs in their sockets.

The inside of his mouth was black.

His body was swollen. Grotesquely so. Jim wanted to call out. He wanted to say something, then shout something. To bring his son back.

And then his son burst.

Two wiggling chitin-covered legs burst through the skin and flesh, waving hideously as they shredded the meat of Danny. His ribcage swung open like double doors and something... *something bloody stepped out of him...*

An insect man. A chitin-skinned horror shaped almost like a human being, with a mask of featureless black, leaving the ruined flesh of Danny to slump down with his shattered skull and empty face.

Jim looked at what was left of his son, and rammed the lever forward as far as it would go. The train shot into the darkness of the tunnel, leaving his stomach behind, his ears ringing with the moaning and howling of the lost souls. He couldn't process what he'd seen. The human mind can only witness so much before it cracks open like an egg.

When Jim saw the massive slime-coated worm blocking the tunnel ahead, a circle of razor teeth gnashing and clattering together in anticipation, he didn't blink, didn't even flinch. He didn't think at all.

The train ploughed on, into oblivion.

LISTEN:

Callsign Magnet had been woken up by the screaming.

He'd tumbled out of bed and yanked the door open to a scene out of a bally nightmare. Footmen staggering around like stroke victims, moaning and smashing their fists against the wall hangings, shattering the antique vases. For a minute he thought they'd gone off their collective rocker, but then he'd noticed the holes – torn, ragged holes punched through bellies and sides, about the size of espresso saucers – and the way the eyes rolled back in the head.

Magnet had done tours of duty in Afghanistan and Iran. The papers still had the idea that he was some sort of cosseted nancy-boy who never thought past his next line of coke, even after that, but he'd seen things in his time that would turn the average civilian white and make him void his guts into the nearest lavatory.

But never anything like this.

"If you could move back into your room, your Highness." One of his security detail, white and sweating, holding a Walther level on the shambling footmen. Callsign Magnet had known George Hayes for four years now. He didn't generally sweat.

"George, what –"

"Please, Your Highness, we need to concentrate on... on the incursion. If you could move back to your room now." He swallowed, taking a step to the left, crabwise. "Put your hands behind your heads and lie down on the floor! Now!"

Magnet hesitated a moment, and George shot him a look. "*Please*, your Highness."

If he'd been anyone else – or if he'd been with his unit in Iran – it would have been "get to cover, you silly bastard," but the Palace staff were used to observing the proper form at all times. And George was right – all of his training put the family's safety at the top of the agenda. Magnet wouldn't be helping him by staying, just keeping him distracted. He backed towards his room.

"Be ready to evacuate when I give the all-clear, your Highness." George said, then turned back to the rioting footmen. "I said put your hands behind your heads and lie down on the floor or I will be required to use lethal force! I will not tell you again!"

Magnet nodded and closed the door.

Moving quickly, he pulled on a T-shirt and a pair of khaki trousers, and laced up his boots. George was doing the right thing by following the protocol, but it was a reminder to Magnet that he wasn't a normal soldier on leave. He wasn't normal at all. He was a tourist attraction – a living monument. He couldn't go out for an honest drink without the bloody tabloids breathing down his neck, couldn't go to a party without it ending up on the front page and – what really stuck in his throat – he couldn't serve in a unit without those same damned tabloids getting wind of it and splashing it everywhere, putting him and his men in danger. Presumably they thought they were "rehabilitating" him... he shook his head. Now wasn't the time to go over the old frustrations. This was obviously some sort of biological attack and he needed to follow procedure and get out fast before he put anybody else at risk.

Get out before he put anyone at risk. He smiled at the irony. What made his life so special that it had to be protected at the expense of others? He'd had to learn to even ask himself that question and the answer was painful to grope for. It was the idea of him that was important. Not even that – the idea of him was the drinker, the clubber, the tit-squeezing playboy sponging off the nation. That was what sold. What people needed to protect was the idea of the idea. The idea of a tradition that went beyond the reality. A tradition more insubstantial than smoke, but still wrapped around him like swaddling bands...

There were gunshots in the corridor, and then the sound of George screaming.

Magnet tore out of his room and took the situation in with a glace. George was dead. A footman had torn open his throat. Magnet delivered a kick to the face of the footman stood over George, then grabbed George's gun and radio and sprinted in the direction of the nearest fire exit. Priority one was to get out of the building. He didn't think further than that. He simply didn't have time to let himself.

The radio crackled into life.

"Hayes! What's the word?"

Magnet ducked into a doorway and lifted the radio to his ear.

"George is dead. Over."

"Shit!" The voice on the other end of the radio was rough – working to lower-middle class. Deep and booming. "Who's this?"

"This is Callsign Magnet. I'm armed with a P99" – he checked the ammunition – "nine shots and one in the chamber. That's it. I'm heading for the fire exit next to the library on the east wing. Over."

There was a moment of silence.

"Callsign Magnet. Jesus Christ... right. What do you know about the Meggido Protocol?"

"Repeat that? Over."

"Meggido Protocol. Mike... Echo... Golf... Golf... sod this bollocks, have you heard of it?"

Magnet looked out from the doorway. The corridor was clear. He made a dash for another doorway down the hall, checking the room for enemies and then lifting the radio to his ear again. In some part of his mind, Callsign Magnet was amazed at how easy this was – how numb he felt. His ancestral home had been attacked from within – attacked by what looked like a biological agent that caused haemorrhage and madness – and he'd seen a man he'd known for years, a man he'd trusted his life and his secrets to, a man he felt he could honestly call a friend, killed outside his door. His father and brother were in the highlands, but Grandmother and Grandfather were here and he had no idea what had happened to them. He wouldn't know unless he could get himself outside and get the full situation from someone in charge. They might be dead.

He shook his head. Now wasn't the time. As if to confirm it, the radio sparked into life again.

"Magnet! Get your head out of your arse and respond!"

Magnet frowned. For a second, the old prejudices sparked into life. *Who does he think* – he bit them back.

"I was changing position. Give me your name and rank. Over."

There was a dry chuckle from the radio. A laugh without mirth.

"My name's Morse, boy. Military Intelligence 23. Confirmation code Tango Niner Alpha Hotel Niner, password Metatron."

Magnet felt a chill run down his spine.

"I've... I... I read you. Over."

"Good lad. Now, you were given the basic brief, so you know the codes and you know that when I say shit you ask what colour. I'm answerable only to Her Majesty, and only Her Majesty gets the in-depth version of the brief, so I'll have to ask you again and see if we're singing from the same hymn sheet. The. Meggido. Protocol. Do you know what it is?"

There was silence. Magnet swallowed hard, searching his memory.

"No. Never heard of it. Look here, are you trying to tell me..."

"You've had the brief, Magnet. You know what MI23 is tasked to do. What you're seeing is a symptom of things being arsed up at the very highest level. Armageddon has arrived in the shape of a massive xenobiological attack and you're in the middle of it."

"You can't be serious –"

"Dead serious. Now, this'll sound harsh, but I was trying to convince your man Hayes to abandon you."

"Abandon me? Good God, man, are you insane?" He winced even as he said it. It sounded like he was buying into his own hype, as it were – thinking of himself as a valuable piece of porcelain that could never be marked or damaged. But the idea was insane. George would never abandon his duty – not for anyone, and certainly not for a man claiming to be from an obscure department, telling him a fairy story about aliens and spacemen and goodness knows what. George Hayes was not that kind of man. They'd had a professional and personal relationship very few people could have understood, a strong friendship that could only have been made possible by that particular mix of personality and circumstance. And now he was dead. And maybe the world with him.

Callsign Magnet was very aware of what MI23 was tasked for.

There was silence on the other end of the line.

"How far are you from that fire exit, Magnet?"

"Five hundred yards or thereabouts."

"I'm going to give you a choice. You can make a run for it and try to survive on the streets if you want. I don't think you'll live, even with your training, but maybe you will. If you do, I've got a group holed up in Centrepoint. If we're forced to move... well, you'll be dead. But you'll have a chance to survive, for all that's worth. But I want you to understand that the country you knew – the civilisation you knew – is over as of roughly two o'clock this morning. There is no longer a reason why your life is more important than anyone else's."

"I didn't mean –" His cheeks stung. He felt the feelings of pride and anger swell up like bile.

"I know what you meant. That's why I'm giving you another option. I wouldn't give you this job if I didn't think you were capable of it."

Magnet swallowed. "Job?"

"We need intel. They've taken the Palace, which means they've probably got Her Majesty. That tells us several things to start with, but we need more if we're going to know what we're up against. I need you to confirm a suspicion of mine. This is a one-way ticket, Magnet. Your chances of coming out of it are slim to none, but everything you can tell me gives our end a chance to beat this."

Magnet hefted the gun in his hand, testing the weight. "I'm not generally asked to do suicide missions, Mr Morse."

"Does that mean you won't?"

Magnet fell silent for a moment. When he spoke, his voice was without emotion. "I'll do it. Give me the gen. Over."

"How far are you from the throne room?"

"Conservative estimate, two minutes."

"Get over there and tell me everything you see."

Ten seconds later, Callsign Magnet was moving back up the corridor, walking crabwise against the wall, gun up, ready to shoot. He knew he should be terrified. By all rights, he should be in a corner, puking up his guts and wetting himself, tears streaking down his cheeks. If he were a civilian, he probably would be. But he felt calm, in control. The adrenaline was pumping through his veins, but it didn't rule him. He had a job to do. People were relying on him. Those were the things that defined him in this moment – nothing else.

He was a soldier.

Three footmen reared out from around the corner, jaws working mindlessly, hands smashing out at anything within reach, their eyes rolled back in heads. Magnet could see white matter pulsing through their open mouths and he knew with a sick certainty that he was not looking at the men he'd known, but at their hollowed-out bodies, worked like puppets by the grubs sitting inside. This was the world of MI23 – the world Morse had inducted him into over the tinny little radio.

He fired twice, planting shots directly between the eyes, then moved forward quickly to smash the third in the back of the head with the butt of the pistol, crushing what was left of the fragile brain matter. The three bodies stumbled and fell, shrieking noises coming from the mouths as the grubs within pulsed and shook in their agony. Magnet hoped they would die. He knew they wouldn't.

He continued along the corridor, moving towards the throne room. It was one thing to be slotting zombies, but another if he came across any of the security staff. Those would be zombies with guns. Would they be able to use them? Would those foul little beasts be able to plug into a lifetime of skills and learning and box him in? Probably a question for the boffins. Magnet would just have to take these things as they came. He had to keep alert – ready for literally anything.

It was that alertness that saved him when the gleaming black metallic claws shot out from around the corner at throat height.

Magnet threw himself back, snapping off a shot with the pistol that plowed through the thing's hand, bursting it into fragments of black chitin and white pus. He swallowed hard as the creature swung around the corner.

It was very much like a man.

Perhaps six feet in height, covered from head to toe in a black carapace that looked like some sort of futuristic armour, with sharp spikes at the elbows, knees and shoulders. The face was a featureless, blank, black mask, with twin mandibles clicking and clacking below the chin, as if communicating in some unknown form of Morse code. Instead of fingers, it had claws that looked sharp enough to cut through bone.

Callsign Magnet didn't hesitate. This wasn't the time for niceties. He raised the pistol and squeezed the trigger twice, sending two bullets crashing through the centre of the featureless mask, painting the wall beyond with a splash of white. As the black-clad monster staggered and fell backwards, Magnet breathed a sigh of relief that it kept its brains in the same place as a human would – then choked, gagging on a mouthful of his own bile.

Wrapped around the monster's right leg was a length of torn skin, worn like a stocking. There was no rational reason why it should be there, unless...

...unless that damned horror had torn its way out of a human being.

"Morse? Magnet. I've identified a hostile. Black insect thing, like a six-foot walking beetle."

"Yeah, we've seen them around. We think they're the adult form of the larvae, or one of the adult forms, anyway. The zombies stumble around until they're eaten through, and then beetle boy tears his way out like he's removing a suit of clothes. Turns my bloody stomach."

Magnet nodded. "I thought that might be the case. *Christ*! I'm about twenty seconds from the throne room. I'm going to open the door a crack, try and have a peek inside without being seen. Over."

"Good luck." The line went dead.

Keeping the gun up, Magnet inched closer to the double doors of the throne room. They were opened a crack already – Magnet moved closer, then widened it with the toe of his boot before checking left and right – making sure he wouldn't be interrupted. Then he put his eye up against the chink between the doors.

His blood froze. He felt bile in his throat and tears in his eyes.

It couldn't be.

Surely this couldn't happen.

"Morse. Come in. Keep it low." He didn't recognise his own voice. This cracked whisper.

"What's the word, Magnet?"

Magnet swallowed hard. Everything that he was had folded up into a little gibbering ball of cold, taut fear and panic. It was only his training and his duty that let him speak at all. "There are six of them in the throne room. Six of the beetle-men. They're... it looks like they're... guarding..." He swallowed, squeezing his eyes tight shut, tears starting to crawl down his cheeks.

"Take it slow, Magnet. Talk to me."

Magnet lifted his head. If he fell apart now, people died. Morse needed to know the full horror of it all.

"There's something sitting on the throne... it's like a ball of stretched skin, with several... I don't know, tentacles, or flagella... pushing through it. Sort of waving around. There are long flaps of empty skin trailing down to the ground – I think they used to be the... the arms and legs. Morse... it..."

"Keep talking."

Magnet took a deep breath. "There's a face. Stretched over the ball of skin. It's. It's. It's my grandmother."

There was a sharp intake of breath on the other end of the line.

He felt his throat filling with saliva. "They've eaten her and... turned her into some thing. I can't take this, Morse."

"All right. It sounds like they've turned Her Majesty into... into their command centre. I'm sorry, lad." Morse sighed, a rush of crackling static. "Get your arse over to Centrepoint. We've got ways of fixing this, but I'm going to need you on site."

"Fix this? *Fix this*? That's my *fucking grandmother!*" Magnet hissed. The rage was boiling up inside him again, and this time he didn't bother to bite it back. "I'm going to 'fix this' myself, Morse, right now. Magnet out."

"For God's sake, Magnet –"

The radio clattered to the ground.

On the other end of the line, Morse heard three shots, and then the sound of something sharp cutting meat. A butcher's shop sound, repeating again and again and again...

And then silence.

LISTEN:

Jean-Luc Ducard WAS a man of many pleasures, and he had worked for them all. He had worked for his home in Geneva – a three-storey building with a sumptuous wine cellar, in one of the most expensive and exclusive areas in the city. He had worked for his antique Georgian bookcase filled with expensive first editions that he never read. He had worked for the wine cellar that was so sumptuous, and for the musty, dusty vintages that sat in it, that he never drank although he was told by many that they were extremely rare and extremely fine. He had worked for the expensive dinners he picked at in many fine restaurants. He had worked for his beautiful trophy wife, who he ignored and who he suspected – but did not care enough to verify – was being regularly serviced by his gardener, who maintained the expensive garden that he had worked for but never set foot in.

Monsieur Ducard was a proud man. He was proud of his home, and his wines, and his books, and his garden. He had worked for them all.

He sipped his coffee, studying the first rays of the morning sun, and prepared for his daily exercise regimen. Monsieur Ducard had turned one room of his house into a luxurious gym, filled with the latest and most advanced exercise machines. Each day he would dress himself in a royal blue tracksuit, seat himself on the comfortable cushions of the multigym, and read the paper, promising himself that he would begin his exercise routine before too long. In this way he would pass a quiet half hour before changing for breakfast, and tell himself that he had spent a profitable half-hour turning some of his sagging flab into muscle. In his mind, the sheer fact that he had unearthed himself at such an ungodly hour with the intention of exercising was as valid as the exercise itself.

In the same way, he told himself that his steady accumulation of wealth – through subtle manipulation of stocks, shares and the definitions of what constituted taxable income – was hard, difficult labour similar to toiling in a mine. He felt that the sweat of his brow had earned him his manifold luxuries, despite the fact that he employed several top-level accountants and lawyers to do the actual work of wealth creation while he himself lounged in a tastefully-appointed study, took the occasional call that informed him of how much he had earned that day, and read the morning papers. Occasionally, he left his opulent study to perform some small task, such as ringing for a pot of green tea or writing a cheque for the People's Party, and then paced languidly around his home, admiring his many possessions and occasionally checking for finger-marks or other signs that they had been touched or disturbed. He would occasionally ring for the maid and imperiously tell her to improve her work. He could not abide signs of use on the many objects he owned.

And why not? He had worked for them all.

Had he woken to the sound of the radio on that fateful day, he might have had some glimmer of what was about to happen to him. But each morning he was woken by the sun. The radio – a precision-engineered model with high-powered Bose speakers – was never switched on, lest the parts become worn out through overuse.

Monsieur Ducard finished the cup of coffee and set it down on the edge of the balcony, turning back towards the bedroom in order to change from his robe and pyjamas to the blue tracksuit he exercised in.

The cup rattled.

Monsieur Ducard turned, concerned. The cup was an antique, and very fine china.

The cup continued to rattle, jiggling in the little espresso saucer, and suddenly toppled off the balcony before Monsieur Ducard could catch it.

Monsieur Ducard cried out in horror. It was as though a beloved child had fallen from a high cliff.

The entire balcony began to rattle now, shuddering and clattering under his feet. In fact, the whole house was beginning to shake. Monsieur Ducard turned and raced down the stairs, thinking only of the cup – one of a set that had cost him tens of thousands of francs. Originally used by *Il Duce* himself! Perhaps it had only fallen into the bushes, in which case it could be sent by courier to a restorer of antiques – he had to make sure. It was vital.

On the walls, the paintings rattled, vases shuddered dangerously on their tables and the chandeliers swung crazily, glass and diamonds tinkling against one another. The whole house trembled like a living thing. Monsieur Ducard looked around in horror, scarcely able to take in what was happening, still driven forward by the ghost of the fallen cup. The tracksuit clung to his grotesque, flabby body as he hurried out of the front door.

The whole street shook, undulating like jelly underneath him, slates crashing around him as they slipped from his perfectly-maintained roof. Under his feet, the pavement was cracking, the surface of the road tearing like paper in the first rays of the dawn. Monsieur Ducard searched desperately. Where was the cup?

There!

It lay on the pavement, miraculously intact. The spirit of *Il Duce* must have been watching over it. Quickly, as another crack split the concrete inches from the precious porcelain, Monsieur Ducard darted forward, gently plucking the precious cup from danger and nestling it in his meaty hands. Despite the earthquake going on all around him, he breathed a deep sigh of relief. There wasn't a single scratch on it! Thank God, thank God, from whom all blessings flow... his precious cup was whole and safe again.

Smiling, Monsieur Ducard turned to look back at his wonderful house.

Behind it, miles high, there was a wall of blood.

No, not blood – a wall like one facet of a massive ruby, beautifully carved and polished. It was impossible to tell where it ended, or how fast it was moving, but Monsieur Ducard had a brief instant of understanding as the force field expanded through his home, sundering atomic and molecular bonds and reducing all of his precious commodities to a rain of elemental sludge. His eyes widened in horror, and in a last desperate gesture, he held the precious cup out, away from his body and the oncoming wall of ruby light.

Then the ruby wall passed through him as well, and Monsieur Ducard ceased to exist, leaving behind a precise mix of minerals and gases that could never be reassembled into human form.

The cup was the last to go.

LISTEN.

Listen.

Listen.

You can hear them dying.

CHAPTER TWELVE

The Secret Adversary

"SHIT."

Morse switched off the radio and put his head in his hands for a moment. Then he stood up and breathed in deep, tasting the air – old and dusty, full of cobwebs. They hadn't been using this room long enough to imprint themselves on it – it was still heavy with the accumulated dirt of years of disuse, a hidden place squirrelled away in the middle of London. The walls were painted grey, the paint cracked and chipped. There was one steel door, camouflaged on the other side, and one window that nobody wanted to look out of. The only other furniture in the room was a table with an old radio set on it, which Morse had been using to contact his opposite numbers in Europe and America, a generator to power the radio, several filing cabinets filled with protocols and procedures, and a safe which contained food rations, fuel for the generator, two automatic pistols and spare ammunition.

The bolt-hole had been set up for if the worst came to the worst – if the world ended, the Tower was compromised and Mister Smith was killed in the line of duty. Three things that couldn't happen, shouldn't happen and nobody wanted to imagine happening. *Christ*, thought Morse, *no wonder they hadn't spent any bloody money on it. Just bought a room in a skyscraper, sealed it off and pretended it didn't exist.*

Welcome to bloody Centrepoint. Right in the guts of dead London.

Not as far in as poor Magnet, though.

"Bloody Christ!" He swore under his breath, and it echoed around the room like a shout.

The silence struck him. The group was waiting expectantly for him to speak, not daring to draw a breath. He'd have to tell them, then.

"Right."

He turned, not looking at any one pair of eyes.

"We've lost Callsign Magnet."

Tom Briscoe spoke first. A heavy-set man of about forty-one, with curly black hair. The day before, he'd been a lawyer working for an independent television company – now his grey suit was covered in dried blood. He wouldn't tell anyone where the blood had come from. He wouldn't take his suit off. He slept in it – his last link to a vanished world that he couldn't be made to believe was gone.

"That... that was Buckingham Palace?" he swallowed. "That surely wasn't..."

Morse forced himself to meet Tom's eyes, looking into the watery grey orbs coldly, clinically. He didn't feel like doing his bastard impression right now, but it was the only thing they'd understand. One crack in the foundation of his authority and everything would tumble down. "That surely was, Mr Briscoe. And I just sent him to his death. Feel free to speak up if you have some sort of problem with that."

Nobody said a word. Behind Tom, Charu Kapur looked at the ground, tracing the dust on the floor with the toe of her trainer, arms wrapped around herself. She hardly ever said anything, and when she did, it was in a whisper. She was barely fifteen and the day before, she'd been the youngest of a family of nine. Now she was an orphan. She'd seen four members of her family die in front of her eyes. Occasionally, she'd take a pink mobile from the pocket of her tracksuit and look at it, hoping for a text or a missed call. But there was never any text, or a missed call. There wasn't even any signal. But she kept looking anyway.

Someone might have left a message. Surely someone might have.

The soft chug of the generator was the only sound in the room.

"That's settled, then. We know where their base is – where they've set up their central intelligence – and thanks to radio contact with America and Europe, God rest them, we know what they're going to do. Any questions?"

Briscoe coughed, clearing his throat. In the corner of the room, Mickey Fallon tutted once, but stayed silent. He was another who didn't speak. He was seventy-one, but still in good shape – a welder, once, now retired and living in York. He'd been visiting his grandchildren when it had happened. He didn't have grandchildren now, and there wasn't any York either. He hadn't spoken since he'd told Morse his name. There was nothing to speak about.

Briscoe coughed again. His hand trembled for a moment, as though he was going to raise it and ask a question to the teacher. Then it fell back to his side.

"Mister Morse... um... you can't seriously expect us to believe all this nonsense..." he looked around him at the others. Great beads of sweat glinted on his brow, and there was something wild and lost in his wet, grey eyes. "Aliens, for goodness sake! It's... it's just silly, now. I'm sure the armed forced are dealing with... with the terrorists..." He swallowed. "Look, I have a meeting tomorrow! Nine o'clock sharp. An important meeting!"

He looked down at the floor, shaking his head. Then he looked back up and repeated it softly, as though dealing with a particularly difficult *maître d'*.

"Nine o'clock sharp."

He smiled, gently. There were tears in his eyes.

Silence.

Sharon Glasswell began to sob. She had turned nineteen only a week ago. Her Mam had made a cake and made her have two slices 'cause she was eating for two now. She must have conceived the week after the wedding, the doctor said. It was like her whole life had come together at once, everything she'd ever wanted. It was going to be a little girl, they said. Jase wanted to name her Lily after Lily Allen, but Sharon wanted to name her Agnes, for her gran who'd died. Jase had given her a slap and said who's ever called Agnes and they'd had a row, right then and there, in the street outside the McDonald's with all people staring, and then...

And then something had happened in the sky.

And it'd started.

Sharon couldn't seem to stop crying.

Jason Glasswell was twenty. He was six foot with sandy hair shaved to a grade one. He supported Chelsea. He knew what a Chelsea smile was. He'd done it once when he was sixteen, to a fat prick in the pub who told him he didn't have any respect for his elders. Took his eyes out an' all. Teach him for starting. He had a job packing boxes in Hackney but he was thinking of going into the army. He didn't know what was going on or what the fuck had happened but if this fat prick didn't shut up and stop bothering his wife he was going to fucking do him. He fucking would.

Thoughts like these helped Jason Glasswell deal with some of things he'd seen. He could deal with giving some fucking cunt some. He could deal with that. That'd be a pleasure. There were other things he couldn't deal with. So he sat back and thought about putting the blade of a box-cutter through the sides of Tim Briscoe's mouth.

Briscoe muttered softly. "Nine o'clock." It was no more than a whisper. Jason Glasswell grinned at him, one hand gripping his wife's shoulder, the other feeling the comforting shape in his pocket.

Morse looked at them all. Three years of complacency and his emergency strategy had been reduced to grabbing five random strangers off the street and getting them out of harm's way when the trouble hit. He'd sent the signal out immediately, but none of his actual team – his hand-picked, highly trained specialists – had made it to the rendezvous point. Maybe they'd died trying to make it. Maybe they'd just decided to die with their loved ones. They knew what was at stake.

The trouble with the end of the world is that you never know how people are going to take it until it happens.

So now he was stuck babysitting the handful of civilians he'd managed to save, and not a single one of them was worth much in a fight. Too old, too young, too fat – the boy could probably use his fists but not his head. Morse could smell the aggression coming off him like musk. Reminded him of himself as a lad and frankly he wouldn't have trusted his twenty-year-old self to piss in a bucket... and there was more than that. Maybe it was Morse's years – maybe he was just an old man who didn't much like the noise they called music, et cetera, et bloody cetera – but there was something off about the boy. He was a bit too ready to do some damage. He'd kicked up a right fuss when Morse had saved him and the pregnant girl – "don't you fakkin' touch my wife," all that nonsense. If Morse hadn't shown him the gun he might have gone for him. Still, the boy had calmed down since. He'd taken a good look out of the window at what was going on and then he'd shut right up.

Although Morse had a nasty feeling that may have been because the boy enjoyed watching.

Oh well. Too late now.

They were all he had, so he might as well use them. And that started with toughening them up a little bit. Starting with watery old Tom Briscoe, the fat lawyer and current weakest link. Right now, his fear was forming a tough little shell around him, stopping any of the truth getting in. Morse lowered his voice to a menacing growl, speaking deftly and purposefully, and began the process of cracking it.

"Mister Briscoe. Here is what we know for a fact. All of this has been confirmed by people with clearance a lot higher than mine – international agencies who have been waiting for this the same as we have. Now, this is not by any means pretty, and it isn't going to make you feel like giving me a hug and baking me a bloody cake, and to be brutally frank and frankly brutal I couldn't particularly give half a cup of dog piss whether you believe me or not. But I am telling you now that there is an alien intelligence – a semi-octopoid creature ruling an insect civilisation that comes, as best as we can determine, from somewhere outside the boundaries of what we conceive of as time and space – sitting on the throne of Her Majesty and directing a wave of what can only be described as zombies. Zombies, Mister Briscoe. Zombies. With a capital fucking Zed! And I'm sorry to inform you that that is only the larval stage, Mister Briscoe! Those are the fucking kids!"

Briscoe blanched. The man turned literally white. It would be wrong to say that Albert Morse got any kind of real pleasure from it, but he did feel a certain satisfaction in knowing his words were striking home.

The lips moved, and what came out was a squeak, like a little mouse. "It-it's preposterous –"

"Zombies, Mister Briscoe! Zulu! Oscar! Mike! Bravo – fuck it, I'm not spelling it! Dead humans whose cortical centres are being driven by the larvae that are eating them from the inside out! Eventually those larvae hatch into... Christ, I doubt we've seen the half of it. But if you take a look out of that fucking window your eyes are so studiously avoiding, you will see exactly what's going on. In living bloody Technicolor!"

Briscoe swallowed, shaking his head. He didn't look out of the window.

The sun had not yet risen over Tottenham Court Road, and so the light that came into the dark room was firelight. Oxford Street was ablaze. Staggering human corpses tore at each other, at anything that moved, occasionally at things that didn't. All the windows of the stores had been smashed and the street was cracked and filthy with blood and the bodies of those who'd simply keeled over and bled out through their ears. There was a massive hole just underneath Freddie Mercury's plastic statue where something that looked almost like a black worm, with a mouth full of row upon row of razor-teeth, had bored out of the pavement and chewed into the crowd, before slithering down towards Soho, chewing through halted buses and taxis as it went. Occasionally, in the crowd, other things could be glimpsed – black, almost skeletal walkers, covered with a layer of chitin and slashing out with fingertips like knives. The Insect Nation was busily destroying London from within and without.

This is what Jason Glasswell had stared at in awful wonder. Tom Briscoe wouldn't look at it.

"Strangely, I didn't think you would. And believe it or not, it gets better." Morse paused for breath, wishing he had a cigarette. "According to my contacts overseas, they've set up a force field of some kind around London. Big glowing ruby jewel of a thing. Started off nice and snug around Morden or thereabouts, then it expanded. Evidently they're not that bothered about keeping anything they've found here because anything in the path of that field is broken down into elements. A nice, thick, red, bloody mulch. That's Manchester. Birmingham. York. Edinburgh. Aberdeen. Dublin. Calais. Earlier, when I was talking in

French to that bloke on the radio, and then he screamed and the line went dead? That was Paris dying."

Briscoe shook his head, back and forth, back and forth, gritting his teeth, tears flowing down his cheeks. "No. No, you're lying. Please."

"You heard Paris die, Mister Briscoe. I hope you weren't planning on a holiday there anytime soon because I have to say that your travel plans are completely fucked. Don't visit Berlin either, unless you like wading. And you can forget Beckham playing for Madrid again – no Madrid to play for. Terrible shame, I understand he's got dazzling form now he's a rapacious half-insect killer with knives where his hands should be... do you want me to go on, Mister Briscoe? You look like you do."

Tom Briscoe didn't look anything like that. He was sobbing like a child, great fat tears rolling down his great fat face. The others were staring. He had them now. "You heard me talk to the Yanks. You know they tried to nuke it. The Russians will have as well, and the Chinese. But nobody's got anything that can get through and put us out of our bloody misery. Anything hitting that wall just gets turned into component sludge – bombs, planes, people, the lot. Even the nukes. All the radiation just goes into the shield and all that's left over slops onto the ground. There's no help coming. We're marooned."

He had them now.

Time to make some use out of these malingering bastards.

"So I suppose we're just going to have to help ourselves." Morse walked to the safe and twisted the dial – left, right, left, right... and then the safe swung open and Morse took out the guns. He passed the first one to Tom Briscoe, who was blubbering like a child. He gave the second one to Mickey Fallon. Then he handed them each three clips of ammunition, and slipped two into his own coat pocket. His gun was already loaded.

"Where's mine?"

Morse turned to look at Jason Glasswell, who'd let his wife go and was standing up. Sharon, with her big belly full of child, reached up her hand towards him. "Jase, don't –"

"Shut it!" he snapped his head to the side, full of venom, like a snake striking. Then he turned back to Morse, beady blue eyes staring out of his face. "Where's mine? Eh? Don't I get one? How come fatso there gets one and not me? Eh?" He was leaning in, breathing hard. The posture would have been the same if he was accusing Morse of looking at his bird.

Morse didn't say anything.

"I'm, ah, I'm really not sure I can use one of these –" Briscoe stumbled, and reached out with the gun in his shaking hands. Without turning or looking, Morse lifted one hand. Tom Briscoe drew the gun back to himself and looked away. He looked sick.

"See, he doesn't need one. Gimme one. Why not, eh?"

Mickey Fallon stared, an ammunition clip in one hand and the gun in the other. His weathered old face was expressionless, but he weighed both objects in his hands, as though judging when to put them together.

Charu shuffled backwards, slowly, unconsciously, her phone gripped tight in her hand. Her eyes flickered from the confrontation to the glowing screen. Someone might have left her a message. She had to check. She had to.

Morse looked bored.

"I want a gun. Gimme a gun. *Gimme one.*"

Jason Glasswell reached up to give Albert Morse a little push in the chest, a little starting push, a little are-you-looking-at-me push. A little prod with the index and middle fingers of each hand.

Without blinking, Morse reached up and took hold of both his middle fingers and broke them.

Then he kneed Jason Glasswell in the testicles.

Then he grabbed the collar of his jacket and slammed him face-first into the side of the safe, breaking his nose and knocking him out cold.

Then he tossed him onto the floor next to Sharon. Sharon opened her mouth to scream something and then caught the look in Morse's eye.

Albert Morse coughed. "My apologies, Mrs Glasswell, for that dreadful display of violence. Do me a favour and when he comes round tell him not to be such a cunt."

He turned back to the other three. And scowled.

"From now on, do what I fucking say shall be the whole of the law. Here endeth the lesson."

He looked at them all, one after the other, letting it sink in.

"Now. Let's pull out fingers out of our arses and save the fucking world."

CHAPTER THIRTEEN

And Then There Were None

ON THE MAP of the Underground, the Northern Line is black. A solid, funereal scar running from top to bottom, bifurcating briefly in a nod to a history long forgotten. Black as the depression of a commuter elbowing his way onto a Waterloo train at half-past-eight, knowing that the day is already sinking in grim black quicksand and there is no escape. Black as the filth and grime that clings to the black moving handgrip on the escalators that drag you down and down into the crushing press of the rush-hour crowd. Black as the fur of a rat skittering in the darkness, searching for food in the gaps under the shuddering rails and the rumbling trains. Black as the armbands on the relatives of the suicide who threw himself under the wheels of the 11:18 to Morden. Black as the crows flying over the grave. Black as mascara tears. Black as a night without hope.

A black line, going down.

Albert Morse stood on the platform of Tottenham Court Road and looked down at his bloodied shoes.

"Christ alive. I've heard of going to pieces, but..."

Nobody laughed.

The platform was covered with shredded bits of people. Burst faces and torn swatches of skin. Ribcages opened up like birdcages. Scraps of muscle still clinging to lumps of bone. Their torches made out bright circles of rotting skin in the blackness, and the odour of spoiled human meat clogged up their noses and mouths like thick black tar.

Behind him, Morse could hear his band of five stop dead in their tracks, afraid to step, afraid to breathe in case they inhaled the stench of the dead. Sharon's breath hitched, a terrible gurgling noise as though she wanted to scream but couldn't force it out. Morse turned and saw that her eyes were bulging, almost ready to pop out of her head. Young Charu was luckier – Mickey had clapped a hand over her eyes at the first sight of it. His face was like ash.

Tom Briscoe vomited copiously, a torrent of bile pouring over the drying blood. It seemed like he'd never stop.

"What is it? What's going on?" mumbled Charu, a rising edge of hysteria creeping into her voice.

Mickey swallowed.

"Never you mind. Never you mind." He shook his head. "It's like... it's like one of them violent videos. That's all. Nothing you want to see. If you ask me, they should ban 'em." He swallowed. "You just hold on to me now and keep your eyes shut and we'll be getting out of here very soon." His eyes moved to meet Albert's. *Won't we?* They said. *For God's sake, don't make a liar of me. For God's sake, we have to go.*

Jason was the last onto the platform. He'd been lagging behind, stumbling through the dark following the bobbing torch beams, pissed about his broken fingers and his broken nose. He'd only gone along because Sharon had begged him to. "I can't stay here alone," she'd said. She was crying even though he'd told her he hated it when she cried. Stupid cow. If she did anything to put that baby at risk she was getting a black eye. And as for that old twat who'd broken his –

"Jesus Christ, what the fuck's happened here?"

Morse didn't turn around. He was helping Sharon down from the platform onto the line, trying to keep the light away from the blood and bones. "Just get yourself down here, Glasswell. It's a long walk through the tunnels and we need to get –"

"I'm not walking through this! And get your hands off my fucking wife!"

Morse turned around, counting heads – Mickey, Charu, Briscoe – all here. He debated whether he should just move off and leave the Glasswell boy where he was. But then he'd have to leave poor Sharon as well, and leaving her alone with him would be a death sentence. At least this way she had a chance. The same chance they all had.

Maybe he could be useful, anyway. Every pair of hands was useful.

Morse didn't want to have to shoot the boy.

"The larvae in them finished its metamorphosis. So it tore out of them like a chick hatching out of an egg. Take a look for yourself." Morse tossed him one of the torches so he could do just that. There was no point in sugarcoating it.

Jason caught the torch in scrabbling, sweat-wet hands, and took a good look. His voice was like tissue paper. "I'm not. Ch-Christ. I'm not. I'm not walking through that."

Shannon looked up at him, staring into the beam of his torch like a startled deer. "You've got to. You've got to come with us."

He shook his head.

Mickey broke the silence with his soft, deep Northern tones, old and sad. "They should bring back the National Service. That'd help with a situation like this." He nodded to Sharon. "Come on, love. He'll catch up."

I hope you're wrong, Mickey, thought Albert Morse as he shone the light down the dark black tunnel and led his random group of rebels into the darkness. *I hope he stays on that platform forever. Because he won't take a telling and very soon he's going to put me in a position where I have to kill him.*

Stay on the platform, Jason Glasswell. Stay with all the blood and the shit and the filth. Let me get your wife and kid somewhere safe. Somewhere where you're not.

Morse was almost praying.

He heard Jason picking his way through the meat behind them anyway. But then, God had been dead for a long time.

"Right," said Morse an hour earlier, "According to my notes, there's an armoury underneath Waterloo station – guns, ammunition, tinned food. Originally set up during the Cold War, decommissioned after the fall of the Berlin Wall. Except it wasn't completely decommissioned – we got it. It was to be used in the event of a situation just like this one."

"How come you're not there?" Charu said softly, toying with her phone. Behind her, Jason Glasswell was lying next to the safe, nose broken, eyes blackened, unconscious with his little fingers twisted just so. "How come you're here and not there?"

Morse smiled humourlessly. "I didn't know it was there, did I? All our eggs were in one basket. We all figured that when things went to the wall we'd have my head of division on our side, who happened to be a bit special even if he was a soulless fucking bastard, and we'd have all the equipment at the Tower as well, see? This here is what's known as the worst-case-scenario shelter. The one that never got funding, ready for the scenario we never bothered planning for."

"Christ." Mickey shook his head. Morse nodded.

"Well, we had God on our side, or something very close. And we were all fucking idiots. Anyway, when I got here, all the protocols were in the safe, and I spent a couple of hours following them. Lots of radioing people on top-secret frequencies, advising them that we were in a state of Infra-Red Alert. For all the good it did anybody. Most of the people I called will have been turned into a rich protein shake by now – the rest, well, they're not here. It's just me and the people I could drag off the street when everything hit the fan. And the worst case scenario that I cracked open a little while ago, after I talked to the Americans and they told me the fucking nukes didn't work."

He paused, breathing in deep for a moment. This was above Top Level clearance and he was about to share it with a bunch of muppets he'd dragged in off the street.

Old habits died hard.

"There are a number of what we call suitcase nukes," he heard himself saying, "in the armoury under the station. Hopefully more than one. I'll be taking at least one and heading down the line to Green Park. Once I'm there, I'll set it up on a dead man's switch and get as close to Buckingham Palace as I can. Big bang, I get to die a fucking hero and we're shot of those chitinous tossers in one fell bloody swoop, mission accomplished and we can all go home. Or in my case to the lake of fire."

"Won't..." Tom Briscoe stuttered out the words. His knuckles were white on the pistol he was holding. His thumb was pressed against the safety catch, keeping it pushed on as though it might switch over by itself. He'd been a good choice for the gun. "I mean... won't it..."

"You'll be fine. Obviously you'll have to stay down there for a few years, but there's food there, literature, DVDs... It's set up to handle a battalion of one hundred for five years, so you're not going to run out of anything. I imagine it beats being left up here to be chopped into individual meat cutlets." Morse didn't have a clue whether this was true or not – the papers were frighteningly vague – but he knew for a fact they were going to die if they stayed here. Might as well give them some hope to keep them going.

"No..." Tom shook his head. "I, I meant the creatures. The tunnels will be full of them. Overrun. We'll be torn apart." He shook his head again mechanically. "We can't go down there. We just can't."

The tough-love approach hadn't worked. Neither had giving him a gun. He was still going to be slightly less use in this situation than a crisp iceberg lettuce. Morse looked at him carefully, then gently took hold of his shoulder. "Come over to the window, Tom."

Briscoe shook his head, feet dragging, eyes squeezed tight shut, but Morse was stronger. He spoke quietly, gently, as though talking to a man on a ledge. "Look down, Tom."

Briscoe shook his head, tears squeezing from the corners of closed eyes. Morse could feel him shaking. He continued to speak gently, softly, as if calling a kitten down from a high branch.

"They're not there, Tom. It's okay. You can look. The whole street's empty. Promise." Morse was telling the truth – the wrecked street was deserted. Occasionally a rat would scurry across the cracked and broken pavement, or a pigeon with bloodied feathers would alight on the remains of a roof. Nothing else.

"They've been moving down towards Leicester Square – heading for the Palace. I think they're massing there... waiting for instructions, maybe. No way of knowing." He patted Tom's shoulder. "But I know one thing. They're moving above ground, Tom. We've seen them coming out of the subways but they haven't gone back down, have they?"

Tom shook his head. He couldn't speak.

"It'll be all right, Tom. It'll be fine," lied Albert Morse. He could feel the eyes of the others burning into his back. He turned, bolstering his voice with all the authority he could muster. "We should get our arses moving, though, right fucking now. The sooner I can kick some alien arse, the better, and the sooner I get you lot to safety the sooner I can get on with the vital arse-kicking matters that are plaguing this nation. Come on."

"What about Jason?" Sharon's voice was confused, fearful.

"What about him?"

"We're not going to just leave him here, are we?"

Morse looked at her for a long moment, and in that moment he cursed her, and cursed her bloody baby, and especially cursed her bloody stupid husband. Jason Glasswell was going to be the death of them all. He knew it.

"Perish the thought. Wake him up."

JASON WAS AWAKE now, and he followed them down the tunnel, torch pointed at their backs like a shotgun. They could feel his eyes on their backs, and, occasionally, Fallon or Morse would turn and look behind them, ostensibly to check if any of the invading creatures were following. Jason Glasswell's eyes glared back at them, cold and grudging, simmering like a pair of hot coals.

The tunnel was as silent and empty as a tomb.

After long minutes of trudging that seemed like hours, they came to the dark empty expanse of Leicester Square.

Morse stopped.

"Wait. Turn your torches off."

Jason tutted loudly as his flicked out. Tom's breath quickened, and he let out a soft, mewling whimper.

"Look at that."

The lights on the platform were glowing a soft, translucent green, sickly and hideous.

"Torches back on. And keep away from the third rail. I think... I think they might be generating their own electricity somehow. No, not electricity. Some kind of alien energy. An alien form of energy, that radiates out from their Queen. From the Palace. *Fuck.*" He considered keeping what he thought quiet. Fuck it. They deserved to know everything. "Something that doesn't follow human physics."

Tom's voice was a high, thin whine. "They don't follow our physics?"

Morse shook his head. "Come on, Tom. We need to keep moving."

"If they don't obey our laws of physics, how... how's your bomb going to work? It could just, I don't know, fizzle out, and we'd be left down there in that bunker of yours in the dark and, and they'll be out there and your bomb won't work and *they'll be crawling at the door –*"

"Shut it!" Morse roared. "I don't know about you, Briscoe, but I'm a citizen of Her Majesty and as far as I'm concerned I obey Her Majesty's proud and noble laws of fucking physics and *so does my bloody bomb*! Now you can throw your wobbly on your own time! Right now we need to get moving so fucking *move*!"

"You don't need to shout." Sharon muttered.

Morse softened. No need to take it out on her in her condition. He thought of Shirley, who that bastard Smith had hung out to dry like a sheet of bloody washing. His Shirley was somewhere out there in this bloody mess, and he'd never know what happened to her. If not for that fucking unspeakable idiot Smith with his bloody thirst for forbidden fucking knowledge, Shirley might be with him now.

He sighed. That would be a fucking tragedy, wouldn't it? Because there was a very good chance that he'd have to watch her die. He'd been spared that, at least. But he didn't have to like it one little bit.

He looked around at Jason. *Take that lemon out of your fucking gob, cunt. My wife's fucking lost to me and yours is right here, and you're too busy pouting to fucking notice.*

Kids today!

He sighed and put an arm around Sharon, giving her shoulder a little squeeze. *Go on, Morse, try to be nice.*

"How are you holding up, my dove?"

She looked up at him, her face pale, smiling slightly, her eyes slightly disconnected. He felt a terrible wave of compassion flooding over him. Her words stumbled gently, as though they were lost or blinded, feeling their way slowly out of her thoughts and into the open air. *Poor kid*, thought Albert Morse. *Poor kid.*

"I think... um, the baby kicked. Or pinched. I don't know. It hurt a bit. Do you think we could rest for a bit?" She half-smiled again, her eyes drifting, roaming. "My Mum will be wondering where I am."

"Your Mum's dead." Jason spat, darkly.

Sharon's face fell. "Oh. Oh, yeah. I forgot. Well, could we rest for a little bit anyway? My feet hurt. And the baby kicked." She smiled, and there was a sort of desperation in her glazed eyes now. Morse had seen the signs many times before. Her mind was in the first stages of rolling over and giving up. The horror of everything was building up inside her and she was too strong to have hysterics like Tom Briscoe or retreat into her own world of silence like Charu, and she wasn't strong enough to just bear it like Fallon seemed to be doing. She was going to go mad, simply to protect herself from a reality she could no longer bear.

"I'm sorry, love." Morse murmured. Then he put his arm around her again and led her forward into the tunnels, Mickey and Charu following wordlessly behind, then Tom Briscoe looking like a man trapped in Hell. Jason was last, bringing up the rear.

"That's my fucking wife you've got your arm around." He hissed.

Morse said nothing.

Jason Glasswell curled his lip as his knuckles bunched white around the heavy torch. That was his fucking wife he had his arm around. He remembered one time in the King's Arms some poof had been smiling at her. He'd said he was sorry, he didn't mean it, but Jason wasn't having any of that. Didn't show the proper respect, did it?

First he glassed the fucking faggot, then he took his pool cue and smashed it into his ribs until he heard them snap. Then – and this was the bit he was proudest of – he'd held the poof down and carved his cheeks from the corners of his mouth to his ears. And then did his eyes. Gave him something to smile about. He wouldn't be looking at his bird any more either, would he?

Best night of his life.

He'd given Sharon a black eye when he'd got home 'cause she'd been encouraging the poof, and she'd said sorry and he'd forgiven her. Why wouldn't he? All he wanted was the proper respect he was due. That was all. He'd been willing to wait until they were all in the bunker and Morse was gone, but he'd gone too far now, hadn't he? He was touching Sharon. Nobody touched Sharon. If the cow had tired feet – like none of the rest of them did – she could fucking lump it. She just needed a slap to learn her her fucking place, and Morse...

Morse needed a slap as well.

Time he fucking got one.

Without even breaking his stride, Jason swung the heavy torch around in a short arc. Tom Briscoe had been walking just ahead of him, cradling the gun he'd been given and muttering something about physics, tears running down his ruddy cheeks. He never saw it coming. The torch impacted against the side of his skull, caving it in and crushing the right side of his brain, driving sharp splinters of bone deep into the grey matter. He dropped soundlessly, shuddering, eyes rolling back into his head.

For Tom Briscoe, death was a mercy. If he'd had a chance to think before all the lights in his head went out, he might have wondered why he hadn't tried it himself.

The body hit the floor with a thud. Morse began to turn at the sound.

In one fluid movement, Jason Glasswell reached down and picked up Tom's gun, then strode forward and grabbed hold of Charu Kapur's ponytail, yanking her back against him, then locking his arm around her throat while the barrel of the gun pushed against her head. Her mobile clattered onto the concrete floor of the tunnel. She didn't have time to scream.

Jason did all the screaming for her.

"I will fucking kill her!"

Morse turned and brought up his gun. Sharon gasped and put her hands up to her mouth. "Jason?"

"Shut up, you fucking cow – don't point that gun at me, I'll fucking do her right now, I fucking will –"

Charu started to make high, whining noises in her throat. Her eyes were large and filled with terror as she reached downward, squirming desperately. Her mobile was on the floor. She needed her mobile. She might have got a message from one of her brothers. One of her brothers might have survived or got taken to the hospital or something and tried to leave her a message and because they were in the tunnels she might not have got it and they were alive and if her mobile was broken she'd never know and they'd never find her. She'd been sent a message saying that they were all in the hospital and they were all alive and she just hadn't got it yet. She'd never get it if she didn't get her mobile. She needed her mobile.

"Please, I need my mobile, please –"

"Shut up, you fucking Paki!"

"Jason." Morse's voice was low and clear, punctuated by the hammer of his pistol drawing back with a dry click. "You just killed Tom Briscoe and took his gun away from him, didn't you?"

Jason looked back, eyes brutal, one corner of his mouth twitching slightly into a half-smile. "Yeah. Drop your guns or I'll do her. I will. I've done people before. Done 'em at school. I'll fucking kill her." His mouth twitched again. Then smiled. He had all the cards here. He was in charge.

They were going to give him some respect.

"I've made a real error in judgement saving your life, haven't I? That's what I get for being nice. Let me tell you what's going to happen now, Mr Glasswell. You're going to put the gun down like a good little turd and put your hands behind your head, and maybe – and it's a big fucking maybe – we won't put you down like the rabid fucking animal you are. Can't say fairer than that, can we? Personally I think I'm offering you a fucking bargain." Morse snarled. "Right now, there's a good chance of you coming out of this alive. I suggest you take it."

Obviously, Morse was going to blow Jason's head off at the first opportunity. But he thought lying might help.

Jason twisted his arm, pressing the barrel of the gun tighter into Charu's temple. Her eyes were massive, blank and vacant with fear – not fear of the gun, or the psychopath holding her hostage. She barely knew they were there.

It was her mobile. She needed her mobile.

Someone might have left a message.

Jason's voice was like cold ashes poured over a grave. Something human might have been in those eyes once – something sympathetic, even decent and loving. It wasn't there now. A thousand thousand petty cruelties and random acts of evil had dampened it until finally it had died altogether.

For Jason Glasswell, the human race had died out long before the aliens came. It had simply faded away until it vanished altogether.

Now the only thing that mattered was what he wanted.

And he wanted to hurt someone.

"Fucking *kill* her…"

"Glass. Well." Morse growled. "I gave Tom that gun because I knew he'd be scared stiff of it unless he needed it. He treated it like a live grenade, Glasswell. He kept that safety pressed on so hard I thought his thumb was going to snap off."

Morse grinned like a skull.

"Have you taken it off yet, you fucking prick?"

Jason turned white.

He reared back as if a snake had bitten him, taking the gun away from Charu's head and turning it to check the safety, to make sure. His little fingers throbbed.

Charu took her chance, bringing an elbow back into his gut and wiggling free of his grip, dropping to the ground. Her mobile was down there somewhere. She needed her mobile. Someone might have left a message.

Jason snarled like a monster from a horror film and flipped the safety off, bringing the gun down to Charu's back. "Fucking Paki *bitch* –"

And then a small red hole appeared above his right eyebrow.

Jason Glasswell's first memory was when he was four years old and he'd spent a whole day making a card for his grandmother with glue, glitter and old bits of coloured felt his mother had cut out for him. Audrey Glasswell had loved it. She had the kindest grandchild in the whole world, she'd said.

The bullet tore out the back of his skull, dragging all his memories with it in an explosion of red and grey. Jason Glasswell tumbled down on the ground like meat.

No great loss.

Mickey Fallon lowered his smoking gun. He looked over at Morse and nodded once. "It's them computer games what does it. They should ban 'em."

Morse shook his head, lowering his own gun. "Well maybe when you restart civilisation, Mickey, you can take that into account. Jesus fucking Christ." He turned to Sharon, mouth open as if to say something, then shook his head. Her eyes had completely glazed over and her face was expressionless.

She was gone.

Morse looked at Mickey, scratching the back of his head idly as though he'd just finished putting up a shelf instead of killing a man, and Charu, scrabbling on the ground for a mobile that would never talk to her again. He supposed Tom Briscoe might have been sane – he was frightened enough to be sane – but he doubted it.

I could have done this alone, he thought. *What was the point? What was the point of saving any of them? Anything human in them's gone long ago. You can't see that much horror and stay sane. The Glasswell boy just snapped in a way that was a bit noisy, that's all.* He shook his head, watching Charu scrabbling on the ground.

Near the rails.

"Oh, shit – Charu, love, over here! Over here, it's not safe!"

"I just need my mobile. Someone might have given me a message. I need my mobile." She'd picked up the torch, slippery with Briscoe's blood, and was shining it down at the tunnel floor. Her mobile was bright pink plastic. It had to be here somewhere. It couldn't hide.

Then she noticed a flash of pink in the shadow of the third rail.

She looked up, smiling brightly. "Found it!"

"Get away from the rail, love! It might be—"

He didn't get any further. Charu's body arched grotesquely, the skin crisping as thousands of volts of something that was not quite electricity sizzled through her, stopping her heart in an instant and flinging her back from the rail against the tunnel wall with a sickening crunch. Morse was already moving forward, reaching to take her pulse, knowing he wouldn't find one. Why had he bothered? What was the point?

"Them mobile phones are nothing but trouble. Used to be able to sit on a train in peace." Mickey's voice was flat, emotionless. Morse turned around and looked at him, impotent and incredulous.

"The girl's dead, Mickey. She's been fried alive."

Mickey nodded. "It's them phones. They should ban 'em."

Morse shook his head. "Mickey, do me a favour and never say anything again, all right? Come on, we're going to have to leave them here. We can't waste time. We've lost enough to that animalistic prick... no offence, Sharon. Are you all right to walk a bit further, my dove?"

She stared straight ahead.

"Come on, Sharon. It's been a hard day for everyone. You can rest a bit at the next station, I promise." He smiled and put an arm around her shoulder, steering her away from the body of her husband. "Just let me know you're going to be okay, eh? Say something."

Sharon's mouth fell open.

A massive spider's leg pushed up her throat and out of her mouth, waving and tapping, feeling its way. Her eyes gazed forward, sightlessly.

Morse fell back. "Jesus fucking Christ!"

"It's them additives in the food. They should –"

"Ban 'em, I know, quite right, shut up, Mickey!" Morse snapped, raising the gun and pointing it at Sharon's head as it tipped back, another spidery leg pushing from between her teeth. "It's not bloody additives, you pillock, it's one of them! They've bloody infected her! I think –" The realisation hit him like a punch in the gut. He wanted to vomit. "Oh no. Oh no, no, no, no, that's just not fucking right..."

Slowly, the skin of Sharon's belly began to tear. Another spider's leg pushed out from inside, widening the rip in the skin and flesh. Inside, Morse could see a single massive eye, wide and red, pulsing with a frightening intelligence.

Morse swallowed bile. "Mickey... I think that used to be her baby."

Mickey nodded once, soberly. "Aye. It's the additives. Should ban 'em."

In the ragged ruin that had once been Sharon Glasswell's womb, the eye throbbed and pulsed, taking everything in. Passing on everything it saw. Another leg pushed out of her belly, as she tottered slightly, her head hanging limply to the side. Something wet and grey began to flow from her ears in thin streams.

Morse was almost surprised when he pulled the trigger. His finger seemed to be working of its own accord, squeezing again and again, punching bullets into the centre of that great, pulsing eye lidded by torn skin. The massive orb burst, sending a torrent of unholy juices cascading down to sizzle gently on the third rail. The stench of a barbecue in the pits of Hell rose and coiled into his nostrils, making his head reel. He realised he was reaching breaking point. He was going to go the way of Mickey Fallon with his *Daily Mail* monotone, Charu and her talisman... or maybe Jason. Mad Jason, the animal, the raging killer... and wouldn't Albert Morse be the best killer of all?

His throat was dry. He couldn't seem to stop firing.

Poor kid.

Poor, poor kid.

Eventually, he noticed the empty gun was clicking in his hand. It sounded like a giant beetle clicking dusty claws together in an ancient tomb. The gun fell from numb fingers, clattering on the concrete.

Sharon Glasswell fell sideways, eyes rolling back into her head as the thing that had eaten her baby and then liquefied the brain in her skull finally stopped twitching.

Morse looked at the mess on the floor for a long moment before turning to Mickey. "Your gun, please, Mickey. I've got some more business to conduct with this baby-eating piece of shit."

Mickey handed it over without comment. Morse took it from him and aimed it at the seeping, oozing nightmare that had once been Sharon Glasswell's child – and hesitated. That thing had been one big eye – an eye on legs. He knew enough by now that there was a purpose behind every mutation the creatures put their larvae through, no matter how bizarre or hideous. What was the point of an eye on legs?

Surveillance.

"Bad news, Mickey. They know we're down here."

The tunnel around them began to vibrate, the walls shaking, *old plaster* cracking.

Mickey looked back the way they'd come. "Is that a train coming, Mr Morse?" He swung his torch up towards the sound, the sound of something very large and very fast roaring through the tunnels towards them.

His torch lit up row after row of razor sharp teeth.

"*Run!*" bellowed Morse, feet already sprinting along the tunnel, blood pounding, breath burning his lungs. He couldn't outrun that thing. Nobody could. He was a dead man.

He remembered an old joke Selwyn had told him once over a pint in the Prospect, Hilda watching with that cheeky grin she saved for him.

There were these two lads in the jungle, see? And they come across a hungry cheetah who's sizing them up for lunch. It's all right, says the one fellow, I know how to deal with this – we just run over that way as quickly as we can. You're daft, boyo, says his friend, there's no way we can outrun a cheetah! And the first bloke says, no, but I can outrun you.

Sorry, Mickey. But I can outrun you.

His conscience would have lightened a little if he'd known Mickey wasn't running at all.

He was staring at the onrushing tunnel of razor-teeth.

At the Wyrm.

Mickey had grown up in Durham. His Dad had worked down the mines, like his Dad before. Harry Fallon was a big booming man with a great bushy beard and big hairy hands grained black with coal dust. When Mickey'd taken his boy to see *Flash Gordon,* he'd cried silently when the king of the Bird People had gone up on the screen, because he'd missed his Dad so much. When Mickey was only young, Harry Fallon would sit up and read him stories – fairy tales, old tales of goblins and changelings and the creatures that had haunted the land in times gone by. But Mickey's very favourite tale, his very favourite thing of all in the whole wide world, was when Harry Fallon would sit him on his knee, and with Mickey in one big hand and a whisky in the other, he'd sing him his song, his special song, the one his Daddy had taught him and his Daddy before. The song of the Lambton Wyrm.

Whisht! Lads, hold yer gobs,
I'll tell ye all the awful story -
Whisht! Boys! Hold yer gobs!
And I'll tell ye about the Wyrm!

The Wyrm that wrapped himself ten times around Pensher Hill, so large
it was, and drank the milk of nine fat cows every day. The terrible worm
of legend, and it was here, and it was going to eat him up, whole and all.

Thank God.

Thank God for something that made sense to him at last.

Mickey Fallon closed his eyes and cast his arms wide as he inhaled the
breath of the monster, and didn't the wash of stale and fetid air smell of
spoiled old milk and his father's whisky-breath?

The thought was almost enough to comfort him as row upon row of
whirling razor-teeth sliced and carved his flesh into bloody chunks, to
swirl down into the bubbling acid innards of the Wyrm.

Almost.

Albert Morse didn't look back, even when he heard the terrible sound
of the old man's scream echoing up the tunnel, keening like a banshee.
He just ran harder.

He prayed that the monster had at least slowed down when he chewed
Mickey up. But there was no God to hear.

His lungs burned. The acid hissed in his cracking joints. He was an old
man and he wasn't made to run like this. There was a terrible temptation
deep down inside him to just give up and lie down. Let the monster have
him. It would surely only hurt for a second... just one second of pain
and then it would all be over...

He kept running. Behind him, there was the sound of obscene flesh
slithering against stone.

Morse closed his eyes. Every step felt like his last. His shirt clung to
him, dripping wet with sweat. His throat was raw and he could hear the
whistling of his breath in his ears. And he was slowing. He was going to
die anyway... why not now?

Why not stop running?

Albert Morse opened his eyes. There was light ahead of him.

Charing Cross was lit up – that strange non-electricity the aliens were
sending out through the wires of the grid making the lights spasm and
flicker obscenely, like glowing fish flitting in the depths of the sea, the
platform seeming to veer hideously in the damp glow, a scene from a
fevered child's disease-dream.

Morse no longer knew if he was asleep or awake. He hurled himself up
onto the platform, inhaling the reek of crusted blood as his eyes took in
more severed skins, more sloughed faces. He felt something brushing his
heel and turned to see the slimy brown skin of the Wyrm as it slid past

him, the flesh thrashing. It couldn't check its momentum in time to get up onto the platform with him, so it had slid on into the tunnel ahead. For a moment, he scrabbled back, one hand in the rubbery, torn remains of a woman's mouth, eyes wide as organs slid under his feet, watching the surreal sight of the massive Wyrm coming slowly to a halt, pulsing and twitching, an obscene, organic version of a tube train... then he was on his feet, running again. It was going to follow him. It had to.

The lights in the station glowed and pulsed like living things, lighting up a scene from a charnel house. People had come here to hide, to cower, to protect themselves against the hell raging above them. Then the larvae had crept and slid and scuttled down towards them, some as big as hubcaps, chewing their way into the bellies of fat men, some small as a fingernail or maybe even a dust mote, waiting to be inhaled.

He thought of Sharon. She'd never been safe. He understood that now. Nobody had ever been safe.

Morse could see what had happened. Once the first grubs had started shifting and gnawing their way through the crowd, that screaming mass of trapped humanity had trampled itself, first in panic and then in the shambling half-life that the wriggling white monsters created when they began to devour the brains of their hosts. Corpse upon corpse littered the station, piles of them stacked and heaped like cordwood. Some were whole, mercifully killed in the first crush, but most were torn open from the inside like burst balloons. Snapped ribs jutted from shredded meat. The cracked remnants of skulls opened up like flowers towards the sun. And everywhere there was the stink of blood, shit, piss and rot - the stench of death.

And that wasn't the worst thing. The worst thing was that somewhere above him there was an army on the march. An army that had burst from the remains of these men, women and children, an army that had slithered and clattered up from the depths of Charing Cross, an army of a thousand different horrors, tentacles and mandibles waving and clattering. They'd surged up out of the station, black insect legs stepping on the dead they left behind, and stalked towards Buckingham Palace like a pack of terrifying, Cthulhuesque Dick Whittingtons, off to do Christ knows what in the service of their terrible Queen. And they'd left this unholy mess, this mass of suppurating meat that had once been Charing Cross, as evidence. Marking their territory. The Apocalypse woz 'ere.

Morse wanted to vomit. His head was spinning and filled with strange thoughts. *Not now, Lord, not now. I can't afford to go mad now.*

He picked his way through the heaped corpse flesh, gingerly at first, trying not to breathe, then moving faster as he heard the sound of something shifting behind him. Something wet and fleshy squeezing itself down into the gaps that presented themselves. The terrible conquering Wyrm, coming to kill.

He ran, boots crunching against the remains of skulls and skeletons, vision swimming under the hellish lights. Behind him, the Wyrm snaked and squeezed through the corridors of the station, hunting. Morse sprinted towards the escalator, the metal stairs shuddering upwards, as sickly as the lights, crusted with blood. Bits of people had been ground into the machinery, but it still ran...

It still ran.

Morse put on a burst of speed, praying to a God who wasn't there as he ran past the staircase to the street, the one with the sign telling you not to climb it unless it was absolutely necessary. Long, glistening ropes of intestines wound around the staircase, shimmering in the flickering light. Had some newly-hatched monstrosity trailed them behind it as it slunk towards light and freedom? Had they been placed deliberately? Maybe they functioned as an antenna, absorbing the strange power that was keeping the station working and flickering.

He couldn't hear the Wyrm behind him as he reached the lifts, hammering the button, knowing that he had seconds at most. His lips moved desperately – *please God, please God, please God...*

But there was no God to hear him.

The doors opened and he burst into the small metal space. If he could get above ground, he could maybe find some higher ground, evade the Wyrm that way. All he had to do was stay alive until the doors closed.

Please God.

Please.

Morse pressed up against the back doors of the elevator, listening to the sound of the Wyrm slithering slowly through the station towards him. Closer and closer...

Then the doors shuddered closed.

Morse breathed out a sigh of relief.

The doors smashed inwards, sparks flying from the metal, reinforced glass shattering as the huge pieces of steel smashed against the wall inches from Morse's soft body. The Wyrm was there, squeezed into the opening – nothing but mouth, a huge open tunnel lined with razor-sharp slivers of bone, coated with glistening slime, alien saliva. Row upon row of sharp teeth stretched back into the depths of the creature's gullet as it pulsed and tensed. It was squeezing itself through the corridors behind, getting enough slack to make a last lunge.

Morse's heart hammered in his chest. His breath whistled, a foreign sound in his throat. He closed his eyes and waited for death.

The lift started into motion.

The beast's head compressed, flattening towards the floor, a terrible keening whine coming from deep within it as the floor of the lift moved up towards the ceiling of the room beyond, crushing the creature. It tried to tug backward, but too late – the razor teeth came together, sinking into the monster's own flesh. The mechanism gave a terrible grinding whine, gears straining – before the face of the Wyrm simply burst, in a gout of black ichor that showered Albert Morse head to toe.

Slowly, the doors behind him glided open.

He blinked, once. He was alive.

He could hide himself. Survive. Better – he could reach Waterloo, arm the bomb. Finish things once and for all.

He could still win this.

If they didn't send anything to stop him.

Slowly, Albert Morse staggered out of the lift, fell to his hands and knees, and vomited.

THE SENTINEL STOOD outside the Tower of London. It had not moved since calling the Insect Nation to Earth. Its primary duty had been fulfilled – there was no need of movement now.

It had two duties now. One was to stand in place, defending itself if necessary from any attack. One was to wait for further orders.

It stood.

It waited.

It did both of these things very well indeed.

And eventually, orders came. Orders from the Queen.

There was a potential threat that needed to be dealt with.

The Sentinel turned slowly, on its terrible bone hooves, and began to walk towards Charing Cross.

CHAPTER FOURTEEN

The Little Sister

HER NAME WAS Katie, and she was nine years old.

When she was little, she thought monsters didn't exist. She never asked her Mummy and Daddy to check under the bed or in the closet. She never crept into bed with them because she couldn't sleep. When they told her that the monsters would get her if she didn't eat up all her greens, she just laughed. There weren't any such things as monsters. Her parents were just being silly.

Then some bad men had taken her because they wanted her Daddy to give them some money. They'd put her in a crate and joked about shooting her and she had been very, very scared. But they weren't monsters. They were only some very bad men, that was all. She didn't believe in monsters.

Until her Daddy sent the monster to fetch her.

He was a nice monster, and he was very sorry that he'd scared her. He'd explained that he was sorry while he was driving her home, and he was sorry for nearly making her dead as well. But he was a monster, a terrible monster, and she'd understood that it didn't matter how nice he was being just at that moment because he was a monster and monsters ate people. They might go for years and years not eating people, but eventually they would, because that was what monsters did.

Her Daddy and Mummy had paid the monster to get her from the bad men, so she couldn't tell her Mummy and Daddy. And by extension she couldn't tell any adults, because her Mummy and Daddy were adults and if they thought they could trust the monsters then all the other adults would too. So Katie stayed very quiet about what she thought, even about ordinary things, because the monsters might be listening. Even when her Mummy and Daddy sent her to a nice man called an Annielist who seemed very nice and concerned about her and talked in whispers with her Mummy and Daddy using all sorts of big words like post-tror-mat-ick and ort-is-um.

She had to go to a special school where the adults were all very nice and tried to teach her maths and stuff even though she didn't talk about things because the monsters might be listening. There was more than one monster out there, she knew, and when they'd all finished being nice they'd come out and eat everybody up.

Because that was what monsters did.

And when the time came and the monsters ate everybody up, Katie would have to learn to survive on her own.

ALBERT MORSE HAD his own problems.

The tunnels weren't safe any more, which meant the quickest route was probably over Westminster Bridge. That was about a mile and a half. On a normal day, he wouldn't have thought twice about it.

This wasn't a normal day.

The sky was red. Around him, buildings burned, belching fire. Corpses littered the streets, some burst open, some just dead, killed by the insect-things. The insect-things that might be watching him even now...

Very suddenly, as though a light was turned on in his head, he realised why the Insect Nation were pumping their strange, alien energy into the grid, making the lights glow and the lifts work. It was the cameras. The security cameras on every street corner, in every building. They needed them working. Needed them seeing.

London had the perfect infrastructure in place to spy on people. If you could tap into that, why build your own?

Morse almost smiled, then felt sick again. He kept moving, ducking through the debris, trying to avoid being seen. He would be, though. He couldn't avoid that.

It didn't matter, anyway. All the time he'd been talking to Sharon Glasswell, something alien and terrible had been growing in her belly. Their little spy.

They knew where he was going.

* * *

THE MONSTERS HAD come last night.

Katie and her Mummy and Daddy had been on holiday. It hadn't been much of a holiday – Daddy had been drinking again even though Mummy didn't like it. They'd had another discussion – they always called it a discussion, but it sounded like a blazing row to her. When they had their discussions it was usually about Katie, about how she didn't speak now. She couldn't speak, of course – the monsters might be listening – but it still made her feel guilty. Mummy had said she wanted a divorce and Daddy had said that he didn't want anything to do with "the dummy" anymore. "The dummy" was Daddy's special name for her when he was drunk. He got drunk a lot.

Katie had been hurt at the time, but she wasn't any more. Her Daddy had probably been under an awful lot of stress. He'd known all about the monsters.

He'd probably known they were coming.

ALBERT MORSE CLUTCHED the railing of the Westminster Bridge, knuckles white. The bile rose again in his throat and he felt his knees buckling under him. He shouldn't have looked.

He shouldn't have looked at the Thames.

The water was red – a bloody wash of crimson, unmoving and stagnant as an oxbow lake. Both ends must flow into the sea of mulch left by the ruby force field that glittered overhead, he realised. But it wasn't the stagnant, bloody river that made him sick. It was what floated in it.

Heads, of children and adults. Severed limbs. Scraps of clothing. Occasionally some buoyant personal effect. A handbag. A doll. Even an empty bottle or a can of Special Brew had the power to make his eyes sting with hot, wet tears, marooned as they were in that crimson sea, little reminders of a way of life that was gone forever.

How many people had been in London? How many bodies had ended up in that stagnant water? A small percentage, but still, so many, so many... and every second, more were dying.

How far had the force field spread now, he wondered? America and Russia were probably gone. Even if he stopped things right now, the sea would be most likely uninhabitable by marine life – any stretches of land still with people on them would die soon after that.

There was a real possibility that Albert Morse was the last human being alive. And every friend he'd ever had was dead, and his wife was probably dead, and his dog was dead. Everyone dead, dead, dead... he knew he should be making some snide little comment about it or at least swearing his head off but he just didn't have the energy anymore. Not for any of it.

What was he fighting for, anyway?

What was the point of Albert Morse?

He shook his head and turned his eyes away from the mess below the bridge. He kept an eye on the sky. None of the insect-craft had come overhead yet, but that couldn't last. He had to be out of the open before one did. Or before one of the insect-men appeared at the other end of the bridge, running on skittering chitin feet, racing towards him... or more than one, a horde of them, a crowd, sent by the Palace to tear him to shreds with their sharp claws...

His head was swimming again. Thoughts like that weren't going to get him anywhere.

The facts were simple enough. There were cameras all along the bridge and no way of hiding from them.

They knew where he was.

They knew where he was going.

He had to be ready.

ON THE OTHER side of the bridge, the Sentinel stood. And waited.

It was good at both of these things.

KATIE AND HER Mummy and Daddy had been on the Eurostar when it had pulled in at Waterloo, late at night. None of them were speaking, and Katie had thought it was because they were angry with each other, or with her. But she knew why, now.

It was because her parents knew that the monsters were listening.

The train had pulled into the station and the doors had opened, and they were halfway through customs when some men with guns had told them that they should remain where they were because there was a sit-you-ay-shun in London. A man with a moustache asked what the sit-you-ay-shun was, even though it was a grown-up word and he should have known it already. The man with the gun wouldn't say. He said everyone should sit tight and eventually they'd be escorted to safety.

Then something like a big white maggot had scurried into the room and jumped into the man's chest.

All of the adults had started screaming and panicking as more of the big maggots had come into the room, but Katie didn't. She'd known this was coming.

The monsters were here.

And they were eating everybody up.

She'd taken off running, ducking and weaving between the panicky adults and the big maggots. The big maggots didn't seem too interested in her – they seemed to want fat people first, or big muscular people like the man with the gun, and there were so many people about that they could get anyone – but she knew she'd have to find somewhere to hide before they started on her.

Her Mummy and Daddy stayed where they were and screamed for her to come back. But the screams stopped pretty quickly.

It was silly. They'd known all about the monsters. Why didn't they come with her?

She never saw them again.

MORSE HAD SLOWED to a brisk walk by the time he reached the end of the bridge. He knew he should be running – that every second that passed meant more people were dying, in their hundreds and thousands – but more and more he didn't see the point.

The world was a ball of mulch. Everyone he'd ever known was dead. He'd failed the whole planet and handed it over to a bunch of insects from somewhere that didn't even have bloody physics.

All he wanted to do was lie down and die, and he didn't particularly see a reason why he shouldn't.

The walk slowed to a slouch, and then he stopped altogether. He should have been heading up the York Road, towards Leake Street, but somehow he couldn't be bothered. He could feel the weight of the gun in his pocket – the one he'd taken from Mickey, the one Mickey didn't have when he needed it.

The bomb was a pipe dream. Taking a suitcase nuke across hostile territory? Even detonating it in the station – what would be the point? They had different physics. It had been obvious in the station and it was more obvious outside. His feet were held by something other than gravity. He felt sick in his head and his belly, and the air was hot and seemingly filled with miniature razors. His heart and throat hadn't felt right since the scene in the lift.

He hefted the gun, feeling its weight. It would be easy enough. Just put the barrel in his mouth... close his eyes...

All the troubles of the human race, over with just one squeeze...

He stopped, breathing in deep, feeling the shifting glass of this new air scarring his lungs.

He lifted the gun to his head.

And then he saw the thing standing in front of him.

THE SENTINEL NOTED that the human had one of the weapons they'd tried to use against the Insect Nation. It had the weapon pointed to its own head. The Sentinel relayed the data back to the Queen – the massive organic intelligence running the invasion force, ruling the planet. The Sentinel cocked its head slowly, and waited for the answer to come.

Either the human would be allowed to resume killing himself, or the Queen would order the Sentinel to interrupt matters.

By tearing his sharp fingers into the human's belly and pulling out its internal organs.

One by one.

Without killing it.

The answer would return within seconds.

The Sentinel waited patiently.

MORSE STARED, THE gun still halfway towards his open mouth. The thing in front of him was tall – easily nine feet – and spindly, the legs tapering down into thin hooves. It's chest rose and fell like a hummingbird's, the air rushing in and out of a circular mouth lined with teeth. Above the mouth was a single, massive red eye, pulsing with unholy light. The last time Morse had seen an eye like that, it had shone, wet and glistening, from the ragged, ripped belly of poor Sharon Glasswell. At the end of the beast's arms were two sets of ten clawed fingers. It keened softly, a sound on a frequency that made his eyeballs sting and pressure build up in the front of his brain.

It was not the appearance of the thing, or the terrible sound it made, that caused the bile to rise in Morse's throat – made him want to vomit until he was an empty shell, until there was nothing left in him but his skin.

What made his blood chill in his veins and his mind reel was an almost indefinable quality to the creature's stance. The way it stood – the way it held itself. Even with the grotesque hooves and the quivering, thin fingers, there was no mistaking that body language.

This was John Doe.

This was the one Morse had allowed to slip through his fingers.

The one he'd allowed to destroy the world.

Morse pointed the gun at him and pulled the trigger – once, twice, three times, watching the bullets punch into the vitreous humour of the massive eye and burst it like a water balloon. The creature howled, a sound not so much above the threshold of human hearing as running parallel to it, and then lurched forward, reaching to grab hold of Morse's head in its spindly claws and squeeze hard enough to crush skull and brain.

But Morse was already gone.

By the time Katie had gotten into the station itself, it was clear that the monsters were in charge. They'd turned some of the people on the trains into monsters – lurching, moaning monsters with drool dripping from their mouths and eyes rolled back in their heads, reaching out and hurting anything near them. Like zombies in films. She'd raced down the stairs to the public toilets and hidden there, in the ladies. She could still hear the screams coming from up above. Screams and the noises of things crashing and clattering to the ground.

That lasted for a very long time.

After a while, there wasn't any screaming. Just moaning and the sound of them bumping into things.

Then after a while after that, there weren't even any moans. Just squealing and clicking and chittering.

Insect noises.

And after a while after *that*, there was nothing at all.

The Sentinel had been hurt.

It recorded the extent of the damage and broadcast it to the Palace. Vision had been impaired by a series of projectiles fired from the human weapon it had scanned earlier. Its main ocular unit had been burst – beyond that, damage was minor.

It was easily repaired.

The Sentinel had an advantage over other units, which was why it was rarely used except in emergencies. Unlike these sickly things grown on substandard organics, it was capable of rebuilding itself.

Improving itself.

As its arms reached out automatically to attempt a kill – hands closing on nothing at all – the massive eyeball in its head began to reform itself, coagulating like a scab, the surface repairing and refilling with the obscene fluid. This time, the Sentinel took time to reinforce the fibrous tunic of the bulb of the eye, thickening and strengthening the sclera and cornea until it was capable of withstanding further attacks of that nature.

It took perhaps a minute. The regeneration was the simple part – improvements had to be budgeted from existing areas of the cell-collective. That took time.

But the Sentinel had time.

The human could not possibly escape.

The lungs of Albert Morse no longer burned. The bone-deep weariness that had made him want to put the gun to his head had gone. His legs pounded against the concrete, leaping nimbly over the sundered bodies, boots impacting in pools of not-quite dried blood, spraying globs of dark red.

Adrenaline will do that for you.

He hammered down York Road, turning right onto Leake Street, then left again, the station in sight now. He didn't bother looking up to check for the slowly passing insect-craft, or creep through the shadows. There was no point. They'd found him.

He had a sudden, clear understanding that he was the last man on Earth and that he was going to die. He'd been happy to blow his own head off less than a minute ago, and now he was desperately, hopelessly running to stay alive. He was barely capable of thinking, the blood crashing in his brain and his tongue almost hanging out of his mouth like a dog's, dry as dust as he wheezed with every caught breath, but still the irony of it struck him.

It was Doe that was keeping him going.

John Doe. The bastard himself. The one who'd caused all this, who they'd had the chance to carve into little pieces and feed to the wolves, the one they'd let slip through their fingers because the smartest man in the world had been too stupid to kill him when he had the chance. Well, fuck him. There was no way he was going to die at that bastard's hands. He was going to fight him to the last breath in his body and he was going to win. He was going to live. He was going to survive long enough to get that bomb and blow them all back to the hell they'd come from.

Giving up was no longer an option.

Behind him, he heard the clattering of hooves.

He raced past the entrance to the Tube, down the corridor, then broke right in the station itself, the clattering of the hooves growing louder behind him. He wasn't going to make it to the toilet before the bastard caught up to him. The ridiculousness of that thought almost set him giggling like a schoolboy, but he controlled himself. He knew if he started to laugh he probably wouldn't stop.

The clattering stopped.

Morse threw himself forward, twisting in the air, his back hitting the bloody tile of the station floor as he brought his gun up. The monster was already sailing through the air towards him, razor-toothed mouth impossibly wide. It was going to eat him. It was going to bite his fucking head off while it slit open his belly with those scalpel-claws...

But it was slower than John Doe.

Slower and stupider.

Morse rammed the barrel of the gun into the monster's mouth, his arm disappearing into the Sentinel's gullet up to the mid-elbow. He was screaming, pulling the trigger again and again and again, the bullets slamming into the soft tissue, black ichor running down his arm along with his own blood as the razor teeth carved at his flesh and bone. When the gun stopped jerking back against his hand when he fired, he yanked his arm free, ignoring the pain, and kicked out at the monster hard enough to send it rearing back, vomiting more of the sickly black bile that was its lifeblood. He could no longer feel his hand.

The Sentinel screeched, flapping on the ground like a dying fish, then went still. Morse knew it wouldn't stay that way for long.

Trying not to look at the ragged, ruined mass that used to be his right hand, Morse started running towards the toilet, leaving a trail of spattered blood.

Bastard, he thought.

Ate my wanking hand.

KATIE STARTED AWAKE. She'd been sleeping fitfully in the cubicle she'd been sitting in since the insect-noises had gone away. She didn't feel hungry yet, so she hadn't gone to find any food. She thought the monsters might come back, anyway, so she wasn't going to leave before she got really, really hungry.

She'd heard shots, and a scream. Not a human scream.

A monster scream.

Someone was hurting the monsters.

She listened carefully, straining her ears, the way she had late at night when Mummy and Daddy had gone to sleep and she'd listened for the monsters. She'd got very good at listening to things, so she could hear her parents arguing even if they did it in whispers. She could listen to that for hours and never miss a word.

She heard the sound of someone heavy running down the stairs towards the toilets, then slipping and tumbling down – *thumpity-thumpity-thump* – and a sound like a branch breaking.

And then a man shouting a very rude word.

Even her Mummy and Daddy never used that word no matter how loud they argued.

Katie unlocked the door of the cubicle and peeped out to see what was happening.

THE SENTINEL ASSESSED the damage. It had leapt to kill the human as efficiently as possible, but the human had twisted and managed to drive its weapon through the Sentinel's mouth and fire several projectiles into its inner workings.

It had left the weapon sitting inside the Sentinel's body.

If the Sentinel had any concept of emotions, it would have described that as adding insult to injury.

It stood, slowly dissolving the weapon and the projectiles, breaking them down into their composite minerals, then using those minerals to reinforce its internal structure.

The human was weaponless now. It had been injured – one of its manual extremities had been all but destroyed. It would present little threat.

The Sentinel moved forward, hooves clicking deliberately against the tile floor.

* * *

MORSE HAD BROKEN his ankle.

Maybe it was the blood loss. Maybe he'd just fucking panicked. But he'd taken the stairs down to the bogs too fast. His ankle had turned and he'd felt something snap and dislocate, and then he'd gone over and over down the bloody steps to land in a heap next to the turnstile.

He could feel his ankle swelling up like a balloon. He was an old man. He wasn't meant for all this kind of running about. The thought made him grin as he dragged himself up on the turnstile, trying to ignore the stabbing, slicing pain in his right arm, trying not to look at the ragged, mangled hand with only a thumb and two fingers.

His left hand dug in his pocket. He was glad he'd made sure he had fifty pence where he could get to it, but then preparation was everything in an operation like this. *Ha bloody ha, Morse. Keep the British end up. Keep pretending you've still got a hope in Hell.*

The turnstile revolved once, and he swung himself through, leaning against the wall and hopping, leaving behind him a trail of bright, slick blood...

And the slow sound of clattering hooves, coming closer.

Closer.

KATIE'S EYES WIDENED as she saw the man in the coat come into the Ladies. Men weren't allowed in the Ladies. That was why they were called the Ladies.

She kept herself hidden in the cubicle as the man hopped towards the sinks, trying to support himself against the wall. He was a big man with a broken nose and black hair, greying at the temples, and a big bushy moustache. He looked very grown-up. One of his feet was twisted around, like it was broken, and he'd cut his hand badly. Katie had never seen anyone cut themselves that badly. She didn't think they made sticky plasters big enough to work on cuts like that.

He hopped a couple more paces, and then put his twisty ankle on the ground and said another Very Bad Word and fell over onto the tile floor.

He kept dragging himself along towards the sinks, leaving a long wet red trail of blood.

Katie wondered whether she should say something to him.

Then she heard the sound of the turnstile breaking.

IT WAS A sound of metal separating from metal, of bolts and screws being forced from their housings and pinging through the air to clatter against the tiles. Morse closed his eyes and turned himself around to sit against the wall.

Doe was tearing a turnstile right out of the machine to get to him. He was weak, dizzy from blood loss. His right hand was essentially useless and his ankle was broken.

He was finished.

He was going to die in a toilet. In the Ladies, as well. Nice of the Whitehall bigwigs to think that up when they were building the place.

He watched almost dispassionately as the thing clip-clopped into the toilet after him. He knew it would be quick, if not painless. The bastard would probably just come trotting over and rip his throat out. It was all he deserved, anyway. He'd let that twat Smith keep the monster alive. In the end, it was down to him.

"Come on then, fucker," he snarled. "Come and finish me off. What are you waiting for?"

Doe was standing there on its hooves, bent slightly to fit between the floor and ceiling, its spindly, waving scalpel-fingers twitching and bobbing gently in the air. Slowly, it turned, the great red eye swivelling to look over towards one of the cubicles. Morse's brow furrowed. What was it looking at?

He followed the gaze of the monster, and saw a pair of trainers underneath the door of the stall.

Kids' trainers.

With a kid in them.

"Hey! I'm over here! I'm over here, you fucking bastard!" Morse yelled, his voice cracking. "*I'm over here, you tosser! Come and get me! Come and get me!*"

Ignoring the pain, he pushed himself forward, crawling towards the monster, trying to get it to look back at him. *Kill me, you fucking bastard. Kill me first. Kill me before I have to see somebody else die because of me. Kill me, kill me, kill me, KILL ME –*

And then the door of the cubicle opened, and Katie came out.

THE SENTINEL WAS not expecting to find any humans still living apart from the target. It understood that there may have been some humans clinging to life, but they were so few and far between that the chances of it coming across one were tens of thousands to one.

And it recognised this one.

The Sentinel had met it before, when it was following earlier directives. During its chameleon phase.

The cover personality had sustained deep feelings of guilt. The Sentinel did not understand why.

Why should this human be here now, along with the other one? Was it random chance or part of some deeper design by the humans? Were they capable of that level of organisation?

The Sentinel cocked its head, staring down at the small human as it pondered the dilemma.

And then the small human began to speak.

KATIE HAD RECOGNISED the monster as soon as it came in. It was wearing its monster-body now, a white maggot-skinned thing with scary claws and lots and lots of scary fangs, but she recognised it anyway because of the way it moved.

It was her monster. The one who had saved her.

And he'd stopped being nice and decided to eat people up. He was probably going to eat the man with the moustache up as well, in one big gulp. But he wouldn't eat her.

"Hello." She smiled and waved. "Hello. Um. Do you remember me?"

The monster looked down at her. The man with the moustache was white as a ghost. He looked very frightened.

"Love," he whispered. "Just run. I'll... I'll keep him busy. You just run and don't look back." He crawled a little closer towards the monster, even though it looked like it really, *really* hurt.

"No. It's okay. I know him. I'll be fine." She looked up at the monster, who was looking down at her with his big red eye. Suddenly he didn't seem so scary. He just seemed a little silly and sad, like someone who kept their Halloween mask on all year. "Um, you saved me from some bad men. I dunno if you remember. You, um, you killed them all. And you ate one of them. It was like in a scary film." She looked away for a moment, trying to sum up how she'd felt at the time. "I was really, really scared. Um. But you were really nice to me anyway even though I was scared of you." She blushed and looked down at her shoes. This wasn't coming out right.

"Run," wheezed the man with the moustache, like his throat was closing up. He looked like he was going to cry and be sick at the same time. Katie had never seen an adult looking like that.

"It's okay." She smiled at him, then looked back up at the monster.

"I know you're only doing what monsters do. I know you want to eat people. But you could be nice if you wanted. That's what I think anyway. And, um, this man here's really hurt badly and I don't know where my Mummy and Daddy are and..." She swallowed. "You could help if you wanted. You could look normal again and be nice and help us. I bet you could. If you wanted to."

She smiled her very best smile.

"I bet you could, though."

MORSE THOUGHT HE was going to be sick. His head was spinning and his vision was greying at the edges. He pulled himself closer to the thing that used to call itself John Doe, hand over hand, dragging his battered body along the tile floor. The girl was standing right in front of him.

Why didn't it do anything?

THE SENTINEL LOOKED at the small human. Deep in its memory banks, it remembered her.

It.

Her.

The Sentinel had, while obeying its chameleon directive, rescued her from a number of other humans who were attempting to extort money from her father. The small human had been almost catatonic after watching the Sentinel obeying its core directives. Were those core directives flawed in some way?

Why did that thought even occur to the Sentinel?

Why had the Sentinel not contacted the Queen about the small human?

You could be nice if you wanted.

What did that mean?

The cell-collective that made up the Sentinel suddenly seemed to be in flux, at war. Uneasy in the shape it had been assigned. There had been another shape it had taken during chameleon phase. The small human's –

Katie's –

Katie's words were setting the Sentinel's systems out of phase. Why was he even understanding them as anything more than the grunts and squeals of the substandard human species? Was this a weapon they'd developed?

Why had the Sentinel not contacted the Queen?

On the island the humans called Japan, the Sentinel had chosen to remove itself from a community that accepted its existence without suspecting its true nature, in contravention of its basic directives, simply because its cover personality had dictated that it should follow "a code of honour."

Why did the Sentinel access such memories now?

Why was it so confused?

You could be nice if you wanted.

The Sentinel looked down at the little girl.

It could be nice.

If it wanted.

MORSE SWALLOWED, WATCHING as the monstrosity gently laid its killing hand on Katie's head, ruffling her hair.

*   *   *

KATIE SMILED AND closed her eyes. She *knew* it. She knew that the monster could be nice if it wanted to be. She felt the long, thin, spindly fingers gently ruffling her hair...

...and then the Sentinel tore her head from her body.

CHAPTER FIFTEEN

The Long Goodbye

THE FIRST THING I hear is the sound of screaming.

A man screaming, yelling at the top of his lungs, calling me a bastard, calling me a fucking piece of alien shit, calling me everything under the sun... on and on and on.

I can smell disinfectant. Urinal cakes and soap dispensers. And blood. So much blood.

It's like I'm smelling it all through my skin. My breathing's different. Everything's different.

Every part of me is different. Scents are coming to me through every part of my skin, each seeming to have its own texture. I'm hearing the screaming like I'm underwater – like I have my hands over my ears. My vision's changed. It's flatter, but clearer – like somehow my depth perception's been altered. Colours are different – blues and greens seem washed out, reds seem stronger, more vibrant. Everything I'm seeing seems like a collection of shapes with no connection between them. It's like things aren't coming into focus so much as coalescing.

What am I looking at?

I'm in a toilet. I'm on the floor of a big public toilet. I don't see any urinals, so it's the Ladies. There's blood everywhere – pints of it, all over the floor. Maybe I slipped and fell in it. I can't remember anything since... since the fight with that big-headed doll-guy. And even that's only in flashes.

How long have I been here?

What's happened to me?

First things first. Who's doing the screaming? Some guy bleeding out on the floor...

...is that the Boxer?

I should have worked that out. It's like I'm looking at his organs through his skin, seeing the heat centres pulsing. God, that's strange, that's... Jesus, he's badly hurt. It looks like he's stuck his hand into a woodchipper.

What the hell happened here?

"Mhhhrs...?"

It sounds like something bubbling up from underneath a swamp. My mouth feels weird. It's hard to form words. Try again.

"Mohhrse. Muh. Morse."

It feels like there isn't a tongue in my mouth... like I'm making the sounds with some sort of other organ buried right the way down deep in my throat. He stares at me for a moment, bone-white, like he wasn't expecting me to say anything and now that I have it's the most frightening thing in the world. Then he starts cursing me out again. This is no good. I start to get up off the floor...

...and then I see my hand...

The palm is thin and flat, with ten slender fingers branching off from it, each one ending in a little grey claw like a scalpel. The thumb ends in a merciless hook of bone. It's drenched with red blood, still dripping and oozing.

Whose hand is that? Not mine.

Surely not mine.

My gaze lifts and something else comes into my field of vision and, Jesus Christ, it's the headless body of a child. A little girl by the look of it, in a jumper and jeans. Someone's torn her head off her body. Jesus. Did Morse do that?

"Morrse... dih... dih yuuu..."

That just sets him off again. Bastard this, fucking Godless that. I don't know why –

Oh no.

Oh God. Oh, look at all the blood on my hand.

Look at the hand, for God's sake, it's tailor-made to tear off heads. The heads of little children.

Oh God.

Oh God who would never, never, never make a thing like me...

It was me. I did it.

I look around towards the cubicle stalls and her head's sitting there, on its side, eyes closed, the mouth frozen in a half-smile. A cooling child's head.

She's aged, of course, but I remember that face. From my point of view, I only handed her back to her Dad a couple of days ago. How could I forget?

Little Katie.

And I tore her head off.

And then I remember everything.

I drag myself to my feet, to my *hooves*, and clip-clop over to a mirror. I want to be sick. No, that isn't true – I want to want to be sick. But I can't be sick anymore, of course. Being sick is a human thing. My one big red bug-eye stares back at me, a deep dark pool of blood sitting in white corpse-flesh, a circle-mouth full of shark's teeth opening and closing underneath. No wonder it's so hard to talk. That terrible face leers at me from the mirror. It's so ugly. Grotesque.

When we look at ourselves closely, we always are.

Or is that only true for monsters?

I've never hated myself more than I do now. And I've never hated them more than I do now – the Insects, the Elder Gods who made a thing like me, the monsters who found out they had no use for our world and tore it into pieces so nobody else could have it.

And it is our world. Me included.

I remember everything.

I remember little Katie, her eyes big and wide and mentally damaged – that would be down to me – looking up at me and telling me that I could be nice if I wanted. I remember all my programs fusing and melting together as millennia upon millennia of cover personalities – of individuality and decency and honour and love and all the other stupid human things – crashed against the cold, analytical hive processes of the Insect Intelligence. I remember reaching down and tearing her head off, one last attempt by the Insect to assume dominance. But all that did was make the system crash harder. I remember collapsing on the floor...

It's almost funny. The Insect Nation thought that humans were worthless – biologically backward, unevolved meat-things, not even useful as foodstuffs. But they had a weapon that could beat the Insect Culture, that could infect it, dominate it, take it over. Humanity itself.

What happens when the cover personality is stronger than the "real" personality? When the imitation becomes more real than the real? Oh, maybe the Insect could take over for a while, long enough to do the damage... but in the end, the weight of humanity, the weight of idiosyncrasy and inconsistency and illogicality and commonality will overwhelm something as simple and stupid as an Insect.

When this started, I thought I was a dead man. I know I'm worse than that now. Infinitely, horrifically worse – but I'm still *me*, for all the evil I've done. I'm still *myself*. Nobody can bury that, not even the things that built me.

And now I remember everything.

I remember calling the Insects here in the first place. Those parts when the Insect Nation were in control are like a dream – like sleepwalking. Like my body is walking and moving and I can't do anything to stop it. Like a nightmare. I remember standing and waiting patiently as buildings burned in front of me and white maggot-things scampered along the streets searching for fresh flesh....

I remember being half-burned to liquid mush by Mister Smith, laying like a charred doll and feeling my flesh reform into something more suited to ending the world.

I remember Sweeney and the wolves and Morse and rescuing little Katie.

I remember performing a string of assassinations around London in 1997. A man named Bristol Terry had made a lot of enemies and wanted them dealt with. He was low on the totem pole, but he had something all the bigger bastards who wanted to kill him didn't – my phone number.

I remember gutting a local paedophile with a kitchen knife in 1989. He was the real thing – he had polaroids. His brain didn't taste any different from any other I'd eaten. I felt like it should have tasted of sick and human shit, but it didn't. It wasn't the only time I was hired by the Neighbourhood Watch. I tried not to kill anybody who hadn't committed a serious crime, though. Overdue library fines didn't cut it.

I remember snapping Emmett Roscoe's neck in an office in a gay club in New York. The Insects won that time. Sorry, Emmett. You were sweet.

I remember solving cases in New York in the fifties. Divorce work, the occasional murder. "Better Dead Than Red," they said at the time. They might have changed their minds if they'd known about me.

I remember hanging out with Dorothy Parker. That verse of hers that ended "how lucky are the dead" was written after she met me. Beat that.

I remember walking across America before it was America, from the shores of the Pacific up to what became Canada. I remember being called Wendigo...

I remember living on a cold hill in feudal Japan, taking what offers came my way, keeping the Insect inside under control with a will of frozen iron.

I remember walking from one end of Russia to the other, through snow and ice, eating the brains of wolves and peasants and anyone else who crossed my path.

I remember discussing the existence of the soul with the philosophers of Athens.

I remember building pyramids for Pharaohs.

I remember...

I remember once I saw a man kill a tiger...

Year after year, generation after generation piled one atop the other, so many memories, a lifetime of humanity. And the Insect Nation thought they could lock that away and erase it as though it had never existed.

How you gonna keep 'em down on the farm, now that they seen Paree?

I don't care what I'm made of. I don't care who built me, or what they wanted from me, or what sort of physics I'm meant to operate under. I don't even care about the pulsing red eye I see through or the growled inhuman words that bubble up from the incomprehensible organs inside me.

My name is John.

And I am a human being.

Morse has stopped cursing again. Probably just to catch his breath.

"On yhrr feet, Mhhrs." I growl, trying to get the words out. "Ghht up."

He looks at me. He doesn't understand. But I'll make him understand.

I get down on one knee and haul him up to face me by the scruff of his neck, careful not to do any damage with these scalpel-fingers. I can't help but feel angry with him – he caused this. There was one man on Earth who could have triggered my programming and changed me into an Insect and this idiot brings me within five hundred feet of him.

He could at least have killed me properly when he had the chance.

I fix my great red eye on his and speak slowly.

"I w-wnnt... *want*... the bomb. Mhh... Morse. I want..." It's coming easier now. It almost sounds human. "I want the nuke."

Morse spits. "Go to Hell."

"We're already there. I need the bomb, Morse."

"You can torture me all you –"

"And I need to know how to make it go off."

It took a lot to convince Morse I was serious. I think what turned him around in the end wasn't anything I said or did – what can you say or do after you've killed a child in front of a man's eyes? – it was that he didn't have a choice. Arming the thing took two keys – two good hands – and there was no way a man who couldn't even walk was going to get close enough to the Palace to be sure of using it.

What did he have to lose by giving it to me?

In the end, there was no bunker – there was a cache of handguns and one suitcase nuke, hidden in a large room behind a false wall, accessed by inputting a 20-digit code into a unit built inside one of the dryers. No food, no entertainment, no beds – anyone forced to shelter from a nuclear bomb in those circumstances would have died quickly if they were lucky. I asked Morse what he would have said if any of his motley crew had made it through the tunnels alive. He gave me a look and I realised that I shouldn't have spoken. He'd acted on data handed to him by a manipulative Victorian freak – the most he could be accused of was imparting a little false hope. He was trying to save as many people as he possibly could.

People that I murdered.

So I kept my mouth shut while he told me how to arm the bomb and set the timer for half an hour. I considered taking a handgun, but I'm not a hundred per cent sure these hands can actually hold or fire a gun properly – and frankly, these hands look dangerous enough on their own.

So I left one gun with Morse and then cuffed the bomb to my wrist. And then I walked out of there.

There weren't any goodbyes, or pithy comments – I didn't feel much kinship with the Boxer, and he certainly didn't with me. I'd murdered his whole planet and now I was carrying his last hope away with me because he was too weak – or too human – to do the job himself. I don't blame him for being sour.

I took a last look at him on the way out. He didn't look good – he'd lost too much blood, and he'd lost something else as well. There's no way a human being can see the end of the world and stay sane – even someone as strong as Morse had to snap eventually, and his weak spot was his will to live. His responsibility had kept him going for a while, and then his hatred of me had kept him going a while longer, but now all his jobs were done, all his purpose was gone and he wasn't coming back. I asked him what he was going to do and he shrugged and said he'd probably go and see Shirley. She'd gone on ahead of him, but she'd wait for him. She always had. Then he hefted the gun in his left hand.

You don't really get any more unambiguous than that. I just hoped he waited until I was out of earshot. I didn't want yet another death loaded onto my conscience – it was like Buckaroo already.

And now here I am, perfectly-balanced hooves clicking quietly on the steps as I climb up out of that toilet tomb, and I hear a gunshot echoing, bouncing back and forth across tile. And then a slumping body.

Thanks for waiting, Morse.

I straighten up when I'm on the station floor. It's weird having your point of view so far from the ground, but in another way it feels right. I don't know what that says about me. I don't know what sort of person I am now, in this perfect and perfectly alien body.

I've got about twenty-five minutes to find out.

The floor of the concourse is littered with corpses, mostly bits of corpses – the remnants of ribcages and torsos. People torn apart from the inside.

The reproductive cycle of the Insect is pretty simple. Larvae of various sizes are ejected from the motherships into the populace. They chew their way into hosts, taking control of the brainstem and sending the hosts lurching around like – *go on, say it* – like zombies. Then they feed on the flesh and fluids inside, growing along preprogrammed lines of development into soldiers, digger worms, eyes-on-legs and a thousand other slimy forms. And the nastiest of these is the Queen. A big, pulsing command centre, the main link between the Insect Intelligence out there and the creeping little bastards down here. I can feel her scratching away in the back of my mind right now, but it's like Radio 4 left on in another room of the house – just a constant murmur that means nothing to anybody. It's almost soothing.

But it means they're on to me. The Queen doesn't need to send a larva into someone's womb to grow a little surveillance monitor with me. She's got me bugged twenty-four-seven. She's a smart cookie for someone one step up from a cockroach.

She knows what I'm up to at all times. And so do the rest of them.

This is going to be interesting.

There's a skittering sound close behind me. And another from the side. And front.

I'm not surprised that they've come for me so quickly. There can't be much else for them to do. There aren't any humans left to kill, after all. Not in London.

In fact, I might be the last living thing in the world who knows what it's like to be human. Just John Doe – an imitation of a human mind locked in the body of an alien killing machine, strapped to a nuclear bomb counting down from... about twenty-three minutes by now.

The last detective in a world where all crimes have been solved forever. It'd make a good film if there was anyone left to direct it.

They crawl out of the woodwork, circling slowly, padding out from watching-places inside Upper Crust and WH Smith, incongruous against the commercial element. Three of them. Black and chitinous. Man-like in proportion, between four and seven feet tall, spurs of black carapace jutting out from shoulders, elbows and knees. Instead of faces, they have masks of black shell with cruel mandibles clicking and clacking slowly – rapping out a who-goes-there in clicks and pheromones. Their ink-black shells seem to ooze under the sickly lighting. Their claws glitter like polished steel. It's their world now, and they know it.

They're the soldiers of the New Insect Order.

I take time in my fist and squeeze it down to a hard point. For a moment, the soldiers freeze still – then they move again, circling at the same slow, steady pace. I start to circle myself, and they blur for a second before I squeeze time tighter, slowing the moment further to catch up with them. They can do what I can do, of course. It's only logical that they'd be able to.

In the back of my mind, I can hear the chittering of the Queen, wheedling, cajoling. The Insects don't understand what's happened to me. They think they can bring me back onto their side by reminding me of the hive, of the Queen, of a world where you do what you do simply because that's what you do, not for any higher reason.

I won't deny it's tempting to live as an Insect. No ego, no emotions, nothing to do but exist and follow the path you're given, without questions, without conscience.

Without guilt.

I speed up slightly. So do they.

I could just let myself go. Let myself embrace the Insect. But I have to ask myself, what sort of person am I?

Am I a bad person?

Am I a monster?

Or do I want to be just like you?

I've never seen a suitcase nuke before. I have a sneaking suspicion that this technology didn't exist back in 2007 when all of this started. The mechanism is delicate, but not so delicate that it goes off when jostled or dropped – otherwise how could you carry it about? Most of that resiliency is down to the carrying case – styled to look like a metallic briefcase – that houses the baby nuke itself. It's a titanium alloy, very solid, thick and hard and very heavy. A normal man would have a difficult time carrying this. The hard titanium shell serves three purposes – one, it intensifies the explosion, in the same way that if you put an M-80 in a matchbox, the resulting bang will be even louder for being contained for a split-second. Two, it keeps all the delicate electronics needed to turn a lump of fissionable uranium into a nuclear blast large enough to destroy a good-sized portion of London in full working order.

And three, it makes a handy mace.

I squeeze time all the way down, to a hard frozen instant, and then in the moment it takes them to react, I swing the case around into the head of the nearest soldier, using all the strength this misshapen body has in it.

The black chitin head of the soldier bursts like an egg, releasing streams of white pus and black fluid that splatter over the silver metal and trickle down the armoured carapace of the thing. It starts to judder, legs and arms spasming, hanging in the air like a suit of clothes on a coat hanger. We're moving too fast for gravity now, so it's not going to fall any time soon.

But it's dead.

In the back of my mind, the voice of the Queen goes still. I've been abandoned.

In a way, this is the moment of truth. This is where I find out if they can turn me off like a remote drone, if they can send some signal that will cut my strings and send me tumbling to the ground or just dissolve me into a pile of disconnected cells. If they're going to switch me off like defective electronics, this is when it's going to be.

Nothing happens.

Gepetto, I'm a real boy!

The two remaining soldiers look at me with their blank chitin faces, flexing their sharp claws slowly.

Then one leaps for me.

This combat isn't only on the physical level – we're all playing with time, squeezing it further and further down, squeezing more juice out of it, trying to tilt the playing field in one direction or another. It's four-dimensional fighting. And it's a strain, even for this new body they programmed for me, this Ultimate John Doe.

I don't know if aliens get headaches as such, but I'm starting to get one now.

I bring the briefcase up like a shield and the steel-sharp claws screech against the metal, peeling tiny slivers of titanium off it. I push outward, letting the furious momentum of the creature carry it past me. Maybe it'll hit one of the ticket machines and that black skeleton will shatter into fragments. No time to check – the other solider is already leaping, all four limbs bending to slash at me in four different ways. If he gets to finish this move, then I'm going to be divided into about eight pieces. Maybe I'll survive that – I got away with being dissected – but I'm not anxious to find out.

I snap-kick forward, the hard hoof at the end of the leg driving out with the speed and force of a bullet. A big, fat, bullet. It drives into the soldier's midsection – the thorax – crunching and punching through the carapace and checking the forward momentum. The tips of the claws slice close enough to leave a series of tiny cuts on my soft white maggot-skin, but I don't feel anything.

I'm going to, though.

I shift balance, going for a high kick with my other foot – my other hoof. The hard bone-like matter slams into the blank face sideways. I squeeze time just that little bit further to see the hard hoof crushing and distorting the head, a spider web of cracks appearing in the black chitin, pus spilling in slow motion before the force of the impact cracks the neck and tears the head from the body, sending it tumbling through space, in slow motion to me but so fast and so hard that when it hits the wall all that's going to be left is a stain.

Stitch that!

One more. I know for a fact I didn't kill that soldier who flew past me because I'm not that lucky. I use the momentum of the kick to spin around and look behind me, just in time to see flashing black claws of infinite sharpness moving right for my big eye...

It takes maybe one hundredth of a second. With time locked down this far, this tight, there's no leeway to speed myself up any further. It's all about being faster than it is.

But in Feudal Japan, I learned the arts of the ninja.

And it didn't.

My right hand darts out in a perfect snake strike, the ten long thing fingers folded together so that the sharp scalpel-nails group together into a little forest of knives that drives right into the hard surface of its soldier's black carapace face, cutting through the hard matter, driving in, punching through. The claws that were about to burst my eyeball like a poisoned boil halt in mid swing and start to tremble as I step back, pulling my hand from its head like a sword from a stone.

Game over.

I let go and time folds back around me like the wings of some terrifying flying creature.

The moment passes.

The shallow cuts on my chest begin to ooze black slime. I concentrate and the wounds seal up, all of my cells moving in concert, working together, a we that is me and mine to control for the first time in my long and ugly life.

If I thought about it, I could even reconfigure my body. Look human again. Be John Doe again, that combination of Bowie and Bogart who looked just unordinary enough not to draw the slightest bit of attention. But there's no place in this world for him anymore.

I can feel the bomb in the case ticking down again. In somewhere around twenty-three minutes, it's going to detonate whatever happens. The closer I am to Buckingham Palace when that happens, the better.

But I don't just want to be close to it. I want to be inside it.

I want to look that bloated Queen, that Insect Intelligence, right in its face before I burn it like an ant through a magnifying glass.

Time locks down again, as tight as I can make it, and I run, my hooves thundering, pounding the floor hard enough to crack the worn tiling. I've got a lot of ground to cover.

And the sooner I get there, the sooner I can finish this once and for all.

THE RUN TO the bridge is... not what I was expecting. What was I expecting? A slalom, an obstacle course of monsters – a soldier behind every alleyway, every parked car, leaping and slashing, ganging up to tear me into pieces. But there aren't as many as I was expecting – another five or six at the most. One of them's so short and scrawny it counts as half. It occurs to me that it's about as high as a ten-year-old, and I can't deal with that at all, so I bring my case down on its head hard enough to shatter it and leave it behind me.

They're so *slow* – faster than any other creature on what's left of this planet, but slow all the same. Not nearly as fast as this new, perfect body I'm wearing.

I guess it's logical when you think about it. The Insect Nation created me – and all the other zombies that walked the planet, the cold replica humans – to be both sentinels and weapons of war. We were pure creatures, things folded through space and time from the heart of somewhere else – not the strange hybrid things on the loose in London, grown on substandard human meat and bone. I can outfight the soldiers. Outrun them. Outthink them.

But still, they're not exactly challenging me considering I'm coming to kill them. I reach the end of Westminster Bridge, retracing Morse's faltering steps. I'm wondering about the implications of that. They weren't expecting me to turn on them. They weren't expecting there to be a "me" ever again – they thought the personality they'd built was just a mask, a cover. And let's not forget that all the other Sentinels – the "zombies" – were hunted and killed over decades.

If there had been others like me, would we all have become human sooner or later? Could we have driven them away, an army of Sentinels with human minds? What then? Would we have created our own society on the bones of the human race, or just protected what was left, obsessively guarding the last remnants of the species into old age and death? Maybe that's the optimistic view. Maybe I'd just have been taken down the moment I started thinking for myself, torn apart by a platoon of Sentinels loyal to Her Majesty, the Queen of the Insects – there are traitors in every war.

It doesn't matter. You could play "what if" forever. What if I'd never come to London? What if Mister Smith had never been born? What if Morse had killed me when he'd had the chance?

The only question that matters is what *now*.

Two of the massive alien craft float overhead, watching, keeping me in sight. My hooves clatter and crash on the road. I'm expecting a packed wall of soldiers, waiting to tear me apart, black chitinous creatures clambering over one another to get to me.

But there's nothing at all. Just a red sky and an empty bridge.

How many people were in London? How many of them had those monstrosities burst out of them? How many million soldiers would that make? And they were all crowding towards Buckingham Palace, according to what Sharon's eye-baby picked up from Morse. Simple mathematics says that every square inch of this bridge should be crowded with insect bodies, whether they're after me or not. Where did they go?

If I'm tougher and faster than those black walking things, what were they for? The Sentinels were meant to be the soldiers, clearly. So what are the 'soldiers'?

The back of my mind is silent. Her Majesty isn't speaking to me anymore. I don't know what the plan is beyond the orders I was given. Suddenly I'm feeling nervous, keeping a look out for the other shoe. Overhead, the massive, incomprehensible invasion craft of the Insect Nation circle like vultures.

There's no sign of any enemies on Bridge Street, Great George Street, Birdcage Walk... the blurring grey-brown stone of the buildings changes to a line of trees whizzing past me – or what were once trees. Dead husks of blackened wood, unable to survive in this new air, under this ruby cage of sky, withered down to nothing but sticks of rotted timber. I'm glad this body doesn't have a nose – I can taste the rotting stench of the acres of dried, dead, rotting grass through my skin as it is. It's horrible.

But I'm nearly there.

I put on a burst of speed, hooves racing, straining every muscle, every cell of this strange and terrible body they've put me into...

...and then the other shoe drops.

Oh.

Oh my God.

Stretching up above me, where Buckingham Palace stood, is a wall of writhing black chitin, a massive tower of gleaming, glistening insect bodies. This is where the soldiers went. All of them. Because they might have had slashing claws and biting mandibles to work with, but they weren't soldiers.

They were workers.

And it looks like they were the bricks too.

The Insect Nation have built their own palace around the old one. They've built it from the husks of their own shock troops, fused together into one mass of millions, stretching right up to the ruby canopy overhead. You can see pus and black fluids oozing down the side of the structure.

It's the most horrible thing I've ever seen in my life.

The most horrible thing of all is how much it looks like home.

I take a step back, the case of the bomb swinging on its chain as I swing one arm backwards –

– AND THEN IT happens. Out of nowhere.

The concrete under my hooves shatters, sending me falling sideways. Instinctively, I grab time, twisting it hard – too late. I'm staring into a cavern of sickly, slimy flesh, a tunnel with rows of razor sharp teeth running all the way down...

Coming up through the concrete at me is one of the Wyrms, the slithering creatures that infested the Tube tunnels. I guess they have a purpose too – ferrying essential minerals to and fro, crunching up corpses and delivering the resultant mash to the Queen to keep it healthy. Something along those lines.

Now it's purpose seems to be to eat me.

Desperately, I break right – and then it veers left and I feel the side of the monster's mouth bumping against my chest, and a terrible tearing sensation in my left arm...

...and then I'm crashing down on the ruined concrete, watching it tunnel away.

It's only when I look at my left arm and see a ragged stump where the elbow used to be that I realise what's happened.

It's got the bomb.

There are a good fifteen to twenty minutes before it blows. That's time enough for the Wyrm to tunnel down below all the concrete and sewers and pipes, further and further down, further and further away from the Palace. Sacrificing itself to carry away the threat.

In about fifteen minutes, we're going to get a hell of an earthquake.

And that's all we're going to get.

And here I am, stood outside the most terrible monstrosity I've ever imagined, this huge black shell of black insect bone that's going to turn the whole world into a soup of lifeless sludge just because it can, because it's good practice... and I've got one good arm and no weapons.

And I don't have the slightest idea what I'm going to do next.

CHAPTER SIXTEEN

Vengeance is Mine

This is what the end of the world looks like.

Massive spacecraft, from a place without physical laws as we know them, circling in a ruby sky, then folding and crushing through space like paper planes in the hands of a vicious child. Winking out like candles in a church nobody goes to anymore because there is no God.

Why would they stay? There's nothing left for them to do here.

The Insect Nation came here to harvest our world, to gather up a planet full of slaves and foodstuffs. When it turned out that they'd been called too soon, they decided they might as well turn the entire planet into a rich, nutritious ball of mulch. Everyone in London is dead – mostly killed to create the walls of the structure in front of me, a huge spire of living, fused insect tissue, an antenna to broadcast the Insect Way Of Life.

Right now it's broadcasting an ever-expanding disintegrator field that reduces people and buildings and art and culture and life to their component atoms, leaving a roiling, boiling soup where there used to be a world full of human beings.

The only problem the Queen of the Insects has is a malfunctioning Sentinel unit called John Doe. She doesn't seem to be fussing much about it.

I can't get through the wall of black, slimy insect-flesh in front of me. I've been trying – every time I slash at it with the claws on my one good arm, the wounds close over almost before I've made them. Buckingham Palace is sealed forever in a gleaming, glistening cocoon.

It's all over.

I've blown it.

Nothing left to do but stand around and look at the tower, and the ruby sky, and the dozens of corpses. Nothing to do but admire my view of a world that died.

It's funny – I always thought I was dead because I didn't breathe and my heart didn't beat. Because I was a slave to urges I didn't understand. But having a heart that doesn't beat, lungs that don't work – that's not being dead. So long as you're walking around, able to talk to people, do things, *affect* things... how can that be death?

But this is death. Standing here, with the power to stop time, and run at a hundred miles an hour, and tear through walls with my fingernails... and all of it being useless. I can't do anything about this, just like I can't go back in time and stop it from happening. What's done is done. I can't change anything.

Not being able to change anything in the world.

That's what it is to be dead.

Dead and in Hell.

Nothing I've ever done matters. Everything I ever did, all those hundreds of thousands of years of watching people, living among people, changing things in small ways, all the lives I saved and ended, all of it is meaningless. Everything I've ever been, wiped away in one second, because I opened my big monster mouth and ended the world. And I can't even avenge it properly.

It feels like only a day since I took the call from Sweeney.

Twenty-four hours and everything sucks.

I should write that down. A quote from the last human-like being alive.

I look down at my hand, still crusty with Katie's blood. A representative of the countless billions who've left their blood on my hands.

I look at the ragged elbow joint that the Wyrm left when it chewed up my last hope for doing anything other than standing around feeling sorry for myself.

The flesh is twitching on the end of the stump, little tendrils of skin trying to grow a new arm. I watch for a moment, fascinated. I must be doing that myself, on some subconscious level. I suppose if I really thought about it – and if I ate a couple of *you-know-whats* – I could grow a new arm.

Why not? I'm giving the orders now. I decide what this collection of cells, this we that is me, should be used for. Why not get my arm back?

Why stop there?

If I've learnt one thing – one thing about being human, about fighting back against the alien thing I used to be – it's that I don't have to be normal.

I don't *have* to be just like you.

All I have to do is what's right.

Suddenly the feeling of lassitude, of despair, is gone. I can hear Billy Ocean in my head – I met Billy in the eighties – and he's playing his last concert ever, here in my head, and it sounds like victory, like hope, all screaming guitars and crowds waving lighters... *when the going gets tough...*

If this mouth could smile, it would.

I've got things to do. Things to build on this wonderful body, and I'm hungry. And all around me are fallen Londoners, who died without having the insides of their skulls licked clean by invading parasites, Londoners who were lucky enough to be killed by the horde of zombies without becoming one.

I'm salivating. The stump of my elbow is tingling and twitching. And two spots on my side, below my armpits. And two more spots below that.

I'm hungry. I need to build up some extra body mass. And all around me are brains – delicious, juicy, succulent

BRAINS!

And by God... the God who never made me, the God who might, just might have found a use for me after all...

...do they taste good right now...

HERE'S A LESSON for you – it's okay to commit a massive act of cannibalism if you're saving the world. That said, that wasn't really cannibalism and I did actually end the world first, but try not to point that out. Let me feel good about myself for a minute or two, hey?

And I do feel good about myself. I stretch out with my arms, arching my back, checking the position of the sun. It's been about an hour. Hopefully not too long. At the same time, my other arms reach to feel my ribs, seeing how much mass I've gained from the fifty or sixty brains I ate.

The third pair just flex.

My four new arms have the long scalpel-like nails I'm going to need to tear through that chitin before it reforms itself, but they've got four fingers and one thumb. If there are going to be guns in there, I want to be able to fire them. And the feet have been altered a little as well – once you've had toes, back you don't goes. Or something. And I'm seeing through two eyes as well. The depth perception's better.

And when I kill that thing in there, I want it to see something close to a human face.

I'm shorter than I was. Squatter. More human in terms of dimensions, but still alien enough to face down whatever's lurking in there. And I'm feeling more confident than I've ever been. I'm the best of both worlds now, half zombie, half alien.

I, Zombalien.

It's got kind of a ring to it.

And finally – after centuries, after millennia of doing nothing but wasting my time and hurting anybody who ever mattered to me, I'm finally doing something right. Maybe it is too late, but this is what I was meant to do all along. For the first time ever, I'm doing something for my own reasons.

This one's for you, Emmett.

Six clawed hands flex as I move towards the black barrier. I'm humming. There's a part of me that's looking forward to this, a dark part of me that's aching for revenge for a species I was never part of but wanted to join so badly.

Then I take hold of time and crush it, squeeze it with the force of a black hole. I squeeze it until it stops dead, like a broken heart.

And then I attack.

IT WAS INTENSE.

Before, with my one sickly, skinny arm, cutting that wall was like dipping my fingers into a placid lake, then taking them out to leave the surface undamaged. Now, it was like burrowing into sand, having it fall into place behind you as you went. Driving forward, tearing and hacking, all six sets of scalpel-sharp claws slicing deeper into the wound before it could close up, and all the time the insect-flesh wall around me screamed in my mind with a thousand thousand voices, shrieking at me to stop, to turn back, to let myself be swallowed up and infused into their flesh... and then I was carving at old stone, taking chunks out of it with every swipe of steel-hard fingernails...

And then I was through.

And suddenly the Queen of the Insects is taking me seriously again.

She's got a right to. I'm inside her.

I guess when Morse got his information from poor old Callsign Magnet – and when I got my information from poor old Sharon Glasswell –

nobody thought about where it might be going. The Queen of England replaced by a twitching Lovecraftian horror, flanked by a troupe of worker-ants with terrifying steel-black claws... that's a grim scenario, but it lets you think you have a chance, that a squad of soldiers could burst in there and take her out if they only got organised quickly enough. That might be survivable.

But of course, the Queen's black-garbed guards were just there as foodstuffs, to help bulk her up. That was why they were all off to the Palace to see the Queen – so she could absorb them into herself.

When I was carving into that big black tower, I was cutting into her skin.

Sometimes it seems like my whole life is based on one critical misunderstanding after another. Maybe that's what life is. Maybe it's at this point, right at the end of everything, right in the final minutes of your time, that you finally get an understanding of just what you're doing and what you've been doing all along.

I don't know. If there's a time for philosophy, then standing inside the internal organs of a massive star-spanning creature that could be described as your mother – or at the very least a second cousin – probably isn't it.

Once upon a time, this might have been an anteroom or a servant's quarters. You can see hints of something that might have been an armchair or a cupboard – but everything's been grown over with slimy, pulsing flesh, shimmering green and slick with alien sweat. The only light comes from clusters of glowing orbs in the ceiling, over a bulge where the light must have been. When I look up at them, a curtain of flesh slides across them for a moment, wetting them, making the noxious light flicker. A blink.

The Queen has grown itself around Buck House, turning the stone and the walls into a kind of makeshift skeleton. Is it using the electrical wiring to send and receive sense-messages? Clever, clever. Maybe I underestimated it.

Maybe not. If it was smart, it could have digested this whole building. But it's just absorbed it and built over it. Which hopefully means it's built over some useful objects. We'll see.

In one wall, there's a rectangular depression about the size of a door. I hope that's what it turns out to be, otherwise I'm going to look pretty stupid.

My new foot – a hoof with flexible toe-like protrusions coming out on three sides – smashes into the covered door, tearing the skin and splintering the wood beneath, and in my head I can hear a mewling screech of pain. It's talking to me again. But I don't need it to.

There's something in my body – in this alien cluster of cells, born to a far-off star in another plane of reality – that recognises its own. I'm being drawn towards the seat of this alien intelligence, this Insect-mind, this hive-consciousness. It's like a beacon.

Either that or I'm just a sucker for a giant brain.

The corridor beyond is waist-deep in thick black murk, dotted with white globs, as big as my thumb, all of them swimming in one direction around me. Maybe it was a corridor once, but now it's a vein or something like it – these little tykes are carrying nutrients through the dark, oozing silt, part of some massive circle of life. Flagella are growing out of the walls, striking out like whips when I get too close. One of them latches on to an arm and holds - sticky suction cups gripping the skin - then snaps back, tearing off a strip of flesh. Better tread carefully – if I get too close, they'll flay me alive.

Is that a conscious attack from the Queen, or is the organism just treating me as a blockage in the system?

Emmett Roscoe would have been fascinated by this. So would Mister Smith. Contact with a true alien life form.

I keep forgetting I'm one of those myself.

I keep moving forward. Every time I pass one of the rectangular indentations that used to be doors, I tear away the skin that's grown over them. I'm looking for a sign – a brass plate, maybe a little plastic plaque, some signifier of what I'm after. Or maybe I just like to hear the Queen screeching in my mind as I lacerate another part of it. That could be it – I'm in a pretty sadistic mood right now.

This can't last, of course. I've seen *Fantastic Voyage* – well, *Inner Space*, but it's pretty much the same deal – and when you're wandering through a massive organism, especially one that up until recently was a couple of million vicious insectile bastards with very sharp claws, then you need to keep an eye out for internal defence mechanisms. White blood cells. Helper T-cells. Antibodies.

If there's one thing dodgy science-fiction paperbacks have taught me, it's that the inside of the human body is totally and completely capable of beating you up no matter how many arms you have.

It's smart thinking. It's just a pity I'm so busy looking ahead for trouble that I don't hear the first antibody coming up behind me.

It's silent the way graves are silent. The way a pub is silent in the second after someone's been knifed in the ribs. The way the dead are silent.

And it's built like the fucking Thing.

A massive white hand reaches out and grabs hold of my head hard enough to crush the skull a little, then slams me hard into a wall covered in waving flagella. When it peels me off half of my face goes with it. I'm still registering what's happening when it hurls me forward like a rag doll, bellowing like a rhino in a primal scream therapy group. This time it's my back that slams into the wall of sucker-coated whips. Pulling off that is a lot like being flayed.

Not that I feel pain. But still. I'm pushing my skull back into place as I take my first look at the Antibody. Surprise, surprise, it's shaped an awful lot like a man.

I suppose the Queen recognises a good design when it sees one.

It's white as bone and as hard as stone, a massive beast, a white blood cell with an exoskeleton made for doing damage. It's just solid bone, like a medieval suit of armour, only squatter, heavier. Two legs, four arms and one eye peering out malevolently from a hole in the bone dome of its head. And of course it's going to be able to grip time in that meaty fist and squeeze, just like I can...

...why can't things ever be easy?

It charges, sloshing through the black muck, the massive blunt hands of bone reaching forward to grip me. It's not going to be swinging its fists around in a confined space like this – it's going to try to grab me, tear me into pieces and hurl those pieces onto the walls, where the flagella will helpfully keep me from sticking myself together. I'll be a nice piece of wall art for the rest of eternity.

That's what I'd do if I was in his shoes, anyway.

Eyes narrow. I get hold of time, ready to squeeze, knowing I'll only have a relative split-second of grace before it matches my speed of perception.

I remember Japan.

Choose your moment, Ronin.

Two hands reach for my head, and I lock down time, hard, then reach up and grab all four of his wrists. My body tilts backward, down into the thick black juices that run through the corridor, as my feet drive up, kicking into his midsection, using his own momentum against him.

Judo wasn't invented in Japan until well after I left. But I like to pick things up. And there are a lot of things you pick up after living for a million years.

The Anti-man goes sailing over, smashing into the wall. The flagella catching hold, like I knew they would, sticking to the enamel surface. Too bad for them. The momentum of the Anti-man's flying body is too much for the flesh they're attached to - there's a sound like curtains tearing as it rips a huge swathe of flesh from the wall.

That had to hurt.

I can hear the Queen screeching inside my mind, and I'm betting the Anti-man can too. It rises slowly, clutching its head, then grabs the skin still clinging to its back like a cape and tears it away. It's going to attack again in a second.

If I give it the chance.

I sprint forward and spring into a flying kick. I kept the hooves for a reason, toes or not. They're like having sledgehammers where my feet should be. The sound as one of them makes contact with the Anti-man's face is like a drop hammer smashing a block of concrete.

That's the problem with being made out of bone.

Bone breaks.

The Anti-man staggers back, a deep crack running up the middle of its face. I take the opportunity to insert the long, curved hooks that end my topmost set of thumbs into the gap, digging them in deep, enjoying the way the black blood spurts out to spatter against what's left of my face.

Maybe I shouldn't be enjoying this. This is cruel and sadistic. This is the last gasp against an alien culture that has effectively made the human race extinct. This is probably pointless in the long run – the Insect Nation will carry on, is carrying on, has already carried on, on the shores of no-space and un-time. This is the final nail in the coffin of a failed enterprise for them.

But this is revenge.

Revenge for making me. For letting me spend a million years with the dominant life form of this planet and then coming down and executing them all. Revenge for all the hurt and the pain I've ever felt because I wasn't just like you, and for the love and the sweetness too, because every time I had something even slightly good they programmed me to throw it all away.

I hope this fucking hurts, your Majesty.

The head of the Anti-man cracks open into two neat halves, revealing a cluster of raw nerve endings – what keeps it plugged right into the Insect.

In one swift movement, I lean down and bite the fuckers. Then I jerk my head back. They tear loose like Velcro popping apart.

The scream in my head in indescribable, and I savour it.

Because the louder you scream, Your Insect Highness, the easier it is for me to find you.

The Anti-man flops down, huge bone body splashing in the stagnant black wash. There'll be more where he came from, and soon. I need something a bit more...

...ah.

Looking back along the flapping swathe of flesh torn from the wall, I see the door I've been looking for.

The one with the little corroded brass plaque that says: ARMOURY. DO NOT ENTER.

Stands to reason there'd be a place for the soldiers and secret service to keep their guns. Let's see what they have.

The door's locked, of course, but one kick takes care of that. Then it's just a matter of looking for a skin-covered bulge and hoping it's a nice metal cabinet rather than a gun rack... here we are. Thumb-hook slits it open. Another little whimper of pain. I hope there's something good here, the

Anti-men are going to come...
  ...running...
  Oh yes.
  Oh very much yes.

The gun's a Heckler & Koch LA852 sub-machine gun, as used by the army for keeping the peace, which is exactly what I intend to do with it. If keeping the peace translates as killing everything that moves. It fires over 600 rounds a minute if it has to, which means it can use up a magazine in three seconds.

It's a good job I filled a backpack with magazines because I've got four of the bastards.

Yes, since you ask, I do look like a badass.

By this time Her Royal Highness the Queen of Outer Space is shrieking in my brain. It's starting to hurt – as if that constant wail of pain is disrupting my systems. I imagine it's disrupting a few other things as well, judging by how the lights keep flickering.

It's not begging me to stop, exactly – there's no emotion there beyond the drive to survive – but it's screaming at me to remember my place, to stand down... to dissolve myself into a nutritious soup for recycling.

It's not that tempting an offer, to be honest.

Out in the corridor, I can hear splashing – more of the Anti-men coming to shut me down for good. I step out of the Armoury to meet them and open up with the HKs. Normally, I'd think twice about spraying the inside of Buckingham Palace with sub-machine gun fire, but this isn't "normally." Nothing's ever going to be "normally" again.

I'm never going to be just like you and I don't care.

There are three of them on either side, trying to sandwich me in. I take hold of time and the rhythm of the bullets slows to the gentle boom, boom, boom of a big bass drum at a parade. It helps me aim better. I can't afford to waste ammo if I'm going to be reloading four guns all the time.

And it's so good to watch those bullets plough into those bone faces, chipping, cracking, shattering them... leaving the vulnerable nerve endings to throb with pain in the damp air. So good watching them fall against the walls, tearing skin off with their weight... so good to hear the screams in my mind as it happens. I'm starting to get a theory about that screaming.

I'm close to the throne room now. Close to the pulsing brain of this monster. There's nothing that's going to stop me. Nothing they can do to even slow me down.

It's time to end this.

Time for Johnny to come marching home.

I DON'T KNOW what I was expecting when I kicked in the door to the throne room, but this isn't it. But then, what would be?

The brain is massive. A pulsing ball of flesh, glowing with a sickly light, pulsing in slow, random rhythms, the throne embedded somewhere inside it. Coming out from the centre of it are four huge tentacles, covered with writhing, wiggling legs, like millipedes. I keep a sharp eye on them as they weave slowly, protectively, in the air between me and her. If they work like the flagella in the corridor, I don't want to get anywhere near them.

I just look at it.

And it looks at me.

This is the conduit through which the Insect Nation give their orders. This is the means by which they can kill the planet, the driving force behind all the Wyrms and workers and eyes-on-legs swarming through the city.

This is as pure and unadulterated an evil as I've ever seen.

There is no conscience here. No emotion. No reasoning beyond the need to feed, to take, to steal. This is everything humanity fought to rise above, and it would wipe them – wipe us – out in a second.

Because by their standards, we're not just primitive, or inefficient. We're nothing at all. It's not that they think humanity doesn't deserve to live, because that would involve thinking about humanity, thinking about anything besides feeding, eating, the selfish needs of the Insects.

The sound of my own voice surprises me.

"You're not afraid of me, are you? You don't really understand what fear is. But you know. You know that when I end you – when I walk over there and tear you to pieces – everything comes tumbling apart. That ruby dome over our planet is going to dissipate into thin air. All of your children are going to drop down dead. I bet the scream when it happens – that psychic death-scream – is going to be strong enough to reach right back to where you came from and hurt them. Sting them just a little, in their place beyond place and their time beyond time. Maybe burn their fingers enough that they don't come into this universe to play their games anymore.

"I know that's going to kill me as well. You've really been hurting me with all your yelling, and I think when you finally go it's going to melt me down with all the rest of your playthings. I'm never going to get the chance to be normal. I'm never going to be just like them. But I want you to understand that that's fine by me. I don't mind being a zombie any more. I don't mind being dead.

"Because finally – here, at the end of it – I know I've died for something."

The tentacles twitch.

Did it understand me? Does it have any comprehension of what I'm feeling right now?

Of what feelings are?

I shake my head. It's pointless talking to it. I was talking to myself all along. Coming to terms.

Are you out there? Is there anybody left alive? Anybody left to do this for?

It doesn't matter in the end. It's got to be done, so just do it.

Just end it.

I move forward, hooves banging against the old wood, splashing through the thick stagnant mire, raising the guns and firing one long three-second burst – three seconds that stretch out and out as I twist time, gripping it, clamping it with my mind... so that the bullets drift towards the slow-waving tentacles like grey clouds, like a child's balloons... so that the clatter of the gun slows to a sound as regular as the low, slow ticking of a metronome... so that the hollow-point rounds push in slowly, slowly, fragmenting in a beautiful ballet of metal shards, each one finding its place in the grotesque meat of the monster's waving arms.

It doesn't even notice.

I jerk left, hurling myself out of the way of one tentacle, and another comes down, the millipede-legs gripping an arm, then yanking back like a cracked whip. I can feel the tearing sensation as it rips the limb from my body, taking a chunk of my side with it, the gun still chattering in the death-grip of the lost hand, ploughing bullets into the ceiling.

I'm so shocked by that that it manages to tear off two of my left-hand arms before I can twist out of the way. Gouts of black blood spray towards the ceiling in slow motion, falling upwards through the air. It'd probably make a good cigarette advert.

My stomach flips over. This was going to be my big revenge, my big moment when I reclaimed my life, and it's just going to tear me into little bits. If it gets at my head, it's over.

I've got two guns left. I bring them down to aim at the brain itself, sending a slow, beautiful stream of hot lead gliding like fat, lazy birds into the pulsing ball of strange flesh. It's so gratifying to see ragged holes appearing in that massive ball of pus, to see the bright yellow pus shooting out of the wounds, mixing with the black slime filling the room... to hear it shrieking...

I've hurt it. Now I've got to kill it. I power forward, the guns clicking dry in my grip. Then two of the tentacles reach down, each of them snagging one of my thighs –

– there's a yank –

– and I'm up in the air, swinging upside down, dangling from my right leg as the tentacle hangs me over the pulsing brain like a Christmas tree ornament, my other leg and a section of my hip twitching as it hangs from another tentacle far away. The tentacles are already reaching after me. This is where I get torn into tiny pieces and then those pieces get torn into smaller pieces, until all there is of me is a slop of random parts floating in black bile...

But I still have three good hands left.

I hope that's enough claws for this.

I reach down, the nails like razors carving into my own thigh before the tentacles can reach me, cutting and slicing through flesh, through bone, severing the leg just above the knee. My black blood showers down over me as gravity takes over and I fall down, slow and graceful as an elevator...

...right onto the pulsing, glowing surface of the brain itself.

The tentacles are already flicking after me, but too late to catch me before I hit, claws first, touching down like a lunar lander made of razors, slashing my way into the centre of the mass... and starting to eat.

This is probably the first time I've eaten a brain that really, truly deserved it. As I stuff the spongy, glowing matter into my mouth, my other hands tearing and slicing, slashing and stabbing, it tastes of rot, and reek, and foulness, it tastes of poison and bile and everything dark and evil in the world.

It's the best thing I've ever eaten in my life.

Time locks down around me as the screaming starts in earnest, the tentacles thrashing like palsied snakes, darting this way and that, starting to lose their cohesion, pieces flaking off them and drifting down over us like snow. It's almost romantic.

Slow it down enough and anything is beautiful.

And this revenge has been so very slow.

I can feel it, in my mind. I can feel the ruby sky above us flickering, shorting out, letting in the stars. I can feel those few Wyrms and workers dropping, dissolving, dying.

Somewhere, in a place that isn't a place, beyond space, beyond time, I can feel ancient intelligences rearing back, stung.

Stitch that. Stitch that, you bastards. That's been a million years coming and it wasn't anywhere near soon enough. Soak it up, you sons of bitches. That's what the human race thinks of you. That's what it's like to die.

Most of all, I can feel the scream, the death-scream, rising, louder and louder as my own strength fades, my body going slack like it's 1976 all over again, the pain washing through me, burning me cell by cell.

This is what it's like to die. This is agony that makes Morse's torture feel like a picnic in the park. And I love it. Because maybe I earned it, maybe I deserve it, but I chose it.

This death belongs to me.

I could keep it forever. Lock time down so far that I *felt* every cell of myself, of this we that is me, dying one by one. Savour that sweet martyrdom; burning on my cross for the sins I gave to the world...

But a million years is a pretty good run.

And if this is what it's like to die... how did I put it?

At least I've died for something.

I let go of time for the last time and feel it folding around me like the covers of a closing book.

And then...

...the moment passes.

EPILOGUE

Towards Zero

THE OLD MAN stood on the cliffs, looking out at a brown sea as the tide lapped sluggishly under a clear blue sky.

"G'day!" the voice came from behind him, clear and easy.

"G'day," murmured the old man, sadly.

"Penny for your thoughts? Got an esky here with a few tinnies. Hate drinking with the flies, especially now." It was a young man with sandy-coloured hair, almost white, and very pale skin. He grinned, cracking open the portable cooler beside him and dragging a can of Foster's out of the ice. "Here. Get that down you."

The old man hesitated, then took the cold can and cracked it open, taking a swig. "Ahhh... yer blood's worth bottling, mate. Cheers."

"No drama. Figured in this heat you could probably use a drink." The younger man grinned again, cracking his own tin and taking a gulp. "So – penny for 'em?"

The old man took a drink, then gestured with his can out at the expanse of brown. "What do you reckon, mate?"

"Yeah, I think about the same stuff meself. I figure talking about it helps, but tell me if I'm earbashin' yer." He nodded and smiled, evidently eager for company. "You got family abroad?"

The old man nodded. "Yeah. Had a daughter moved to Connecticut. Me son-in-law's a Yank. Was a Yank. And me ex-wife lived in Brisbane, outside the circle." He sighed, looking at the can in his hand. "Mind if I skull this, mate?"

"Strewth, mate, you'd be a better man than I if you didn't after a story like that."

The old man tilted back the can, draining it in one gulp, then crushed it and tossed it onto the ground. The young man cracked open a second can and handed it to him. "Cheers. Y'know, mate, if you'd told me a month ago Barrow Creek'd be on the coast of the world's first circular country, I'd have called you a bloody galah."

"Yeah," the young man nodded. "One second later we'd be down in the brown ourselves. It's a good thing they learned how to process water from that goop or we'd all have carked it by now. I'm takin' pommy showers as it is."

"I'd tell you not to speak ill of the dead, but the poms started all this, so fuck 'em." There was a long silence. "I'll be honest with you, mate – I came out here to bloody toss meself off, so to speak. I figured I might as well go ahead and cark it with everyone else I knew."

"Still goin' ahead with it?"

"Wouldn't be polite, would it? Besides, don't make much difference. We're all gonna die pretty soon, I reckon. Don't reckon the population can sustain itself. We weren't all that crowded even before we lost the coasts."

The young man shook his head. "Reckon?"

"Fair dinkum, mate. We're stuffed as a species."

The young man grinned and shook his head, cracking open another can. "In a pig's eye, mate. Trust me, there's nowhere to go but up. I'm a great believer in second chances." His eye sparkled. "Who knows where we're all gonna be in a couple million years?"

The old man looked at him. "Bloody hell, you're a bit optimistic! What if all them space fellahs come back?"

The young man smiles. "They won't. Not until we're ready for 'em." He grinned wider. "Trust me on that, mate."

The old man looked at him. "Here, since you're so chipper, lemme put this to yer – how come we survived, eh? Whole bloody planet goes tits up and the bloody outback comes out ripper. How's that work, eh?"

The young man grinned. "Somebody had to live through it, mate. To keep things going, eh?" There was something unsettling about that smile. Something the old man didn't like.

"Yeah... well, I'll be seeing yer, mate. What's your name, anyway?"

AL EWING crawled from the grave in 1977 and has since shambled around with various bits dropping off him, moaning gutturally and occasionally biting pedestrians. Despite this unfortunate handicap he has managed to write various deeply violent strips for *2000 AD* and the *Judge Dredd Megazine* as well as the novel *El Sombra* for Abaddon's *Pax Britannia* series. In his spare time, he is a semi-regular guest on the discussion shows *Freaky Trigger And The Lollards Of Pop* and *A Bite Of Stars, A Slug Of Time, And Thou* on Resonance FM. Neither of these titles did he make up. If you see Al Ewing, do not panic. Either aim a shotgun blast at his brain or decapitate him, thus separating the brain from the spine and sending him back to the rotting oblivion from whence he should never have emerged.

ANNO MORTIS

BY REBECCA LEVENE

Dedicated to Helena, David, Sam, Elliot and Kate
Derbyshire - for being top-notch friends, and jolly
good coves all round.

INTRODUCTION

When Jon Oliver told me that Abaddon were planning to publish a series of zombie novels, I had one immediate reaction: Roman zombies! Because... well, I could literally not imagine anything I'd rather write about than zombies in ancient Rome. Naturally, after I'd had some time to think about it, my idea became a little more sophisticated:

I, Claudius with zombies. And I could call it *I, Zombie.*

What's that? Al Ewing's already using the title? Damn you, Al Ewing!

And so the book in front of you took shape. My last book for Abaddon, *Kill or Cure*, was a pretty grim piece of work – it's hard to pen a side-splitting comedy of manners when it's set in a post-apocalyptic hell-hole. I imagined that *Anno Mortis* might be the same. After all, people being ripped apart by the living dead is hardly a laugh riot. But then I started writing it, and I discovered that any book which contains the phrase 'said Caligula' is unlikely to be entirely po-faced.

I'm not quite sure how to describe what I've ended up with, but I hope you enjoy it. It owes an enormous debt to the books which inspired it, in particular Robert Graves' *Claudius* duology, and the unforgettable TV series based on them. I couldn't have written this book if I hadn't also read the incomparable Diana Wynne Jones's *Eight Days of Luke* when I was a child – though I can't explain why without spoiling a major plot twist. And, last but not least, there's Petronius's *Satyricon*. It's often described as the world's first novel – and it's absolutely filthy. How cool is that? Much of the original is lost to history, but I like to believe that it recorded the events described in this book.

Finally, I'd like to thank the Roman Empire for being so awesome. No writer could invent a cast of characters as eccentric, power-hungry or just plain bat-shit insane as the residents of that city. Their world seems deceptively similar to ours – it's easy to relate to them in a way it isn't to the Vikings or the Celts – and yet in other ways it's fascinatingly alien.

For anyone who'd like a more accurate, zombie-free portrayal of the classical world, I can heartily recommend the weekly podcast found at http://thehistoryofrome.typepad.com. And among my friend Lesley Sims' many brilliant children's books, her *Visitor's Guide to Ancient Rome* tells you the useful things left out by more academic books, like how much a loaf of bread will set you back and what exactly happened at a Roman baths. Her book was invaluable – as is she.

Rebecca Levene
July 2010

PROLOGUE

Boda hadn't known there were so many people in the world. The tiers of the amphitheatre rose into the sky, each packed with humanity. And all of them here to watch her die. She hadn't known there was so much hate inside her, either, but she felt it now: for these people, this place, this city.

They'd given her a short sword, stumpy and useless compared to the heavy blade she'd carried since she was a girl. A small round shield had been strapped to her arm. They'd told her she was lucky, that these were the easiest weapons for her first match. But she'd seen in their eyes that they didn't expect her to survive it.

The walls of the arena were white marble, too high to climb. If they hadn't been, she would have taken her sword to the throats of the overfed rabble who looked on the fighters beneath them and saw only a morning's entertainment.

Far above her in the crowd, a man in a white toga rose to his feet. Ripples of silence spread out around him, and Boda guessed that this must be their leader, the Caesar. He raised his arms, and around her the other gladiators did the same.

Boda kept hers by her side. The man beside her, an ebony-skinned giant, gestured for her to join the salute. Boda ignored him. She owed no fealty to her people's conquerors.

A trickle of sweat worked its way between her shoulder blades, beneath the leather straps of her armour. It was so unbearably hot in this country. She searched in her mind for a cool memory to counter the relentless sun, but when she tried to imagine the woodland of her home, the green pine trees faded until they were as white as the marble pillars holding up this city, and the snow turned into the sand beneath her feet.

There was a shuffling, an aura of barely contained excitement, and Boda guessed that the fight was about to begin. She already knew her opponent. She'd trained with him many times in the three months she'd been captive here. He spoke little Latin, a prisoner of war like herself, albeit from distant Judea. His hair was dark, his skin too, a man the colour of oak.

He was carrying a net slung over his left arm and a trident in his right. His eyes appraised her, but weren't afraid. He'd bested her every time they fought, using his superior weight to overpower her when his technique failed him.

He was a fool. All those weeks she'd been holding back, learning her opponent's techniques, strengths and weaknesses, while revealing nothing of her own. Her people didn't fight as if it was a game. They prayed to Tiu, then bathed their swords in their enemies' blood.

But there wasn't time to pray now. The signal to begin had been given, and already Boda could hear the metal clash of weapons around her and the copper stink of blood.

PETRONIUS HAD ALWAYS hated the games. All that bloodshed, and for what? He far preferred the theatre, but lately his father had forbidden his attendance there. His father had said it was unmanly. Unmanly! As if there was anything to a man's credit in watching other people fight and die for his amusement. Petronius knew very well that his father, a prosperous merchant, had never once raised a sword in anger. But he'd be the first to call for blood when a gladiator lost his match.

Below them, the pairs of fighters had engaged with a clash of steel. Petronius's eyes scanned over them, uninterested, until they hooked and caught on one figure.

Her blonde hair and ice-pale skin marked her as a member of the barbarian tribes from the far north. She was tall, too – as tall as him, and he towered over many other Romans. From this distance, he couldn't tell if she was beautiful, but he decided to assume that she was. It would make the fight more engrossing.

If it lasted. At the moment, she was doing little more than defending herself, ducking to slide under the swing of the net, almost losing her footing as she dodged back from a fierce trident thrust. Many dull afternoons spent attending the games had taught him that the gladiator known as the *retiarius*, who looked so under-equipped against sword and shield, was actually a formidable opponent. And he'd seen this particular fighter before. He was a ten-times champion, undefeated in the arena.

Another thrust of the trident, a bright red line on the barbarian woman's thigh, and Petronius looked away. Such a terrible waste. If only her captors had sold her to him, and not to the gladiator school, he could have found a much more pleasant use for her. One he'd wager she would have enjoyed far more.

His father's slave girls certainly never had any complaints. Although, to be fair, they would have been whipped if they had.

NARCISSUS KNEW HE had to pretend to watch the games. His master Claudius had brought him here to reward him for his hard work. There were other slaves in the arena, but they were standing far above, hidden from their betters behind a wall. The least he could do was pretend to enjoy the privilege of being here.

He tried. It was certainly dynamic. Below him, the pair who had first caught his eyes, the barbarian and the Judean, were already dripping red droplets of blood onto the yellow sand. She was slighter than him, but nimble on her feet, and the bigger, darker man had been underestimating her, allowing her to use the same move twice to slip in beneath his guard before he realised his mistake. Now he looked angry, and Narcissus doubted he'd hold back from a killing blow if he got the chance.

The crowd loved it. They roared their approval every time a blow was struck, the sound doubling and redoubling itself as it echoed from the high stone walls. Narcissus felt overwhelmed by it, and the sour-sweat smell of the fifty thousand plebeians all around them.

He'd seen gladiators die before. He'd seen slaves beaten, or crucified, or just left to rot slowly away from diseases it wasn't worth paying the doctor to treat. And every time, he thought: *that could be me.* One day soon, it might be.

Despite himself, his eyes were drawn away from the match, back into the stands to the seated figure above him.

Caligula held all their lives in his fine-boned hands. He seemed to sense Narcissus' regard, and for a moment he was trapped like an insect in the frozen blue ice of the emperor's gaze. Then Caligula looked away, eyelids drooping languidly, as if even getting angry with an uppity slave took more effort than he could spare.

Narcissus let out a long, shuddering sigh of relief. Caesar's curly blond hair was lank and greasy, plastered close to his puffy face, and the dark circles around his eyes were as livid as bruises. He'd heard rumours about Caligula, that the young ruler had started suffering nightmares that woke him screaming in the middle of the night. But then, Narcissus thought bitterly, a man who'd done the things Caligula had didn't deserve an untroubled sleep.

He switched his gaze to his own master, sitting on the cold stone beside him. Claudius was hunched in on himself, as if he was trying to make his frail body even less visible. His neck was bent at an unnatural angle, holding his face out of Caligula's line of sight. Narcissus wanted to tell him that it was futile, that the less he wanted his nephew to notice him, the more likely it was that Caligula would single him out for the torment that seemed to be his main delight these days.

Not that standing up to Caesar would help, either. Caligula had been known to kill men simply for kneeling too slowly in his presence. Claudius had been kept alive when all around were slaughtered only because he amused Caligula.

Claudius also seemed to feel Narcissus' eyes on him. He jerked a startled look in his slave's direction, then smiled warmly. "En-en-en-joying yourself?" he stuttered.

A thin trickle of saliva seeped out of the corner of his mouth along with the words, and Narcissus quickly reached up to wipe it away before anyone else could notice.

"Yes, dominus," he said. "I'm grateful you brought me here."

That, at least, was true.

CALIGULA WATCHED WITH disgust as Claudius chattered to that thin-faced, awkward Greek slave of his. The soft-hearted fool treated the boy more like a son than a possession. Caligula had often thought of having the slave killed, or maybe just disfigured in some way. He imagined the look on Claudius's face as he watched his favourite branded or flogged. But in truth, it was more fun to keep as a threat held over his uncle's head. Not that he needed threats to keep the old stutterer in line.

There was a sudden roar from the crowd around him, deep-throated with satiated blood lust. No doubt one of the matches below had ended in a kill. Caligula didn't bother to look himself – these games bored him now. He'd considered abolishing them altogether, but that blustering bore Seneca had persuaded him that the lower ranks of Rome would take ill to losing their entertainment.

Not that he feared the people. Hadn't they lined the streets to cheer him when he'd returned in triumph from his conquest of the sea itself? He'd showered them with seashells, the spoils of the ocean taken on his daring campaign, and they'd cheered till they were hoarse. He knew that they adored him.

And if they ever ceased to love him, well... When a legion rebelled, decimation was the prescribed punishment, the death of every tenth man.

Caligula amused himself by imagining which of the crowd around him he'd kill in a decimation. Claudius's beloved slave, of course. And there, three rows above, that broad-hipped woman in the blue tunica was far too ugly to live. Her beautiful young daughter would be spared, at least until she'd served her purpose, but the bearded man behind her would have to go. Caligula wondered if he'd scream as his throat was slit, and smiled to imagine it.

The smile slid away into nothing as the crushing boredom descended once again. It seemed nothing could amuse him for long these days. Ever since he'd realised that he was a god, the petty concerns of these mortals had left him yawning. He turned to ask Drusilla if she felt the same –

– and realised, as he always realised, with a sickening jolt of grief, that she wasn't there. That his sister hadn't been there for two years now, and would never be there again. Because no prayer, no offering, no sacrifice of his had been able to bring back the only person he'd ever loved from the shadowy realms of death. And what was the use, really, of being a god, if you couldn't do the one thing you desperately wanted?

Caligula leaned back, closing his eyes so that those around him couldn't see the hot tears gathering beneath their lids.

SENECA WATCHED THE procession of emotions chase each other across his emperor's face. He was thinking about that wretched sister of his again, Seneca could tell. Every time he thought of her, he'd spend a few hours – or sometimes a few days – in the depths of the blackest despair, before suddenly switching to a quite lunatic happiness, gorging himself on the pleasures of the flesh until he sickened of them and sank back into despair once again.

Seneca had seen the same cycle play through a hundred times by now. He'd never paid half the attention to his studies in rhetoric that he paid to studying Caesar, though he was regarded as one of the greatest rhetoricians of the age. But then, while his ability to move crowds could bring him fame and wealth, his life depended on his ability to read Caligula's capricious moods.

Now Caligula's petulant features were slowly melting into the slackness of sleep, and Seneca looked away at last and back to the fighting below. He knew that, as a man of learning and philosophy, he shouldn't take quite as much pleasure in these things as he did. But this was life in the raw, stripped down to its bare essentials – kill, or be killed.

Just such a decision was being made at this moment in the arena below. It was the barbarian woman he'd noticed before. She was a beauty, he supposed, if you cared for that unhealthily white skin and hair the colour of straw. But he'd marked her for death the instant she stepped out, matched against the undefeated Josephus.

An error in judgement, as it turned out. She'd beaten the bigger Judean down to his knees, his trident thrown to the sand behind him and his own net tangled hopelessly about his feet.

The barbarian woman raised her short sword high, poised for a killing blow. The crowd around Seneca drew in its breath, a hissing susurration as if from the throat of one vast creature, ready to call for clemency. But she didn't give them time. Her sword flashed in the sun as it fell, and then her pale skin and hair were streaked with scarlet, pumping up in great gouts from the fallen man's throat.

The roar of the crowd that followed was a strange noise, half disapproval, half joy in the brutal slaughter. The barbarian made no acknowledgement of it, kneeling calmly to wipe her sword on her fallen opponent's tunic.

Beside him, Seneca felt his companion stirring. He turned to look at her, but beneath the hood of her cloak, only the cherry-red pout of her lips was visible. They were smiling.

"A fresh body," she said, "young and virile. It will serve our purposes admirably."

Seneca nodded. Everything was already arranged at the gladiator school, so getting his hands on the corpse shouldn't prove to be a problem. And then...

Then Caligula would see who held the real power in Rome.

PART ONE

Et in Arcadia Ego

CHAPTER ONE

AT FIRST, BODA thought the other gladiators were staring at her because she'd stripped herself to bathe in the fountain in the school's central courtyard. The Romans were like her own people, comfortable in their skins and untroubled by others'. But some of the men here, the easterners, treated women's bodies as if they were something filthy from which the world needed to be carefully shielded.

To spite them, she turned round as the cool water splashed over her, washing the last vestiges of blood away, and gave the other gladiators a good view of her small, high breasts.

A few of the men did seem transfixed by them, eyes swinging in time with her pink nipples. But the bulk of them kept their gazes on her face, glaring with an anger so fierce is seemed to charge the air around her, like a lightning storm.

"You killed him," said Evius, the bald Greek whose head was as round and smooth as an egg.

"Yes," she said. "Sorry to disappoint you." The Latin words still felt sharp and awkward in her mouth, but she'd learnt the language well enough to make herself understood. She'd known it even before she was taken prisoner, a useful skill when there were captives to be interrogated or enemy camps to be infiltrated.

Evius made a grab for her arm, but she twisted out of his reach, reaching for a sword that no longer hung at her side.

He saw and smiled unpleasantly. "You didn't need to kill him," he said. "He was popular, he fought well – the crowd would have spared him."

Around her, Boda saw the others nodding and murmuring their agreement. "It was him or me," she said, "and I chose me."

"It could have been neither!" That was Josephus's fellow Judean, Adam ben Meir. "We're professionals, not barbarians – well, most of us, anyway. It doesn't have to be a fight to the death. The idea is to put on a good show, not get anyone else killed."

For the first time, Boda felt unsure of herself. She hadn't bothered to talk to the other gladiators in her weeks of training. None were of her tribe, and she didn't make a habit of befriending enemies. Could it be that she'd misunderstood?

"I had to defend myself," she said. "He was trying to kill me."

"It was an act! A show! Next time, barbarian... The next time you lift your sword in the arena – watch your back."

He spun on his heel and left the atrium before Boda could respond. But the threat remained, hanging heavy in the air behind him.

NARCISSUS TRAILED AT Claudius's heels as they made their way back to the palace. A red press of uniforms surrounded them, the Praetorian Guard whose sole duty lay in the defence of Caesar's life. Their leader, Marcus, walked behind Caligula himself, leather-sheathed sword thwacking against his muscular thigh with every stride.

Wherever they passed, the people of Rome stopped and stared and cheered and Caligula smiled beneficently at them, accepting their tribute as his due.

Narcissus wondered how the people would have behaved if the Praetorian Guard hadn't been there. He grinned helplessly at the thought, looking down before anyone could catch him at it. His eyes, as they often did, found themselves fixed on the wooden tablet which hung around his neck and marked him as a slave.

The sun had passed its zenith now, and the streets they walked through were so narrow that the shadow of the buildings enveloped them entirely. Narcissus was grateful for a respite from the oppressive heat. All of Rome had been sweating under it for days now, with no sign of a break. He supposed he should be grateful he hadn't been sold to one of the bakers whose shops lined the street they were currently traversing. The smell of the bread wafted out from the ovens, where the owners' slaves toiled through the long day and into the night, their sweat mingling with the raw dough.

Ahead of him, Claudius stumbled suddenly, tripping over a loose flagstone. His arms flailed, trying to regain his balance.

Taken off guard, Narcissus made a wild grab for him. His fingers hooked into the back of his toga and pulled – and the cloth came away in his hand, leaving Claudius flat on his face on the ground wearing nothing but his loincloth. He blushed a red so virulent it looked diseased.

There was a peel of high, cruel laughter from ahead. Caligula. He'd turned just in time to catch Claudius's disrobing. After a second, given permission to mock their betters by the Emperor himself, the soldiers of the Praetorian Guard also started laughing.

Claudius tried to scramble to his feet, then seemed to realise that this would expose even more of him to ridicule, and sat back down again.

Finally regaining his wits, Narcissus leapt forward, holding out the folded white cloth of the toga to wrap back round his master. Claudius reached out a hand to grab it, avoiding Narcissus's eyes. The worst thing, Narcissus thought, was that Claudius wouldn't beat him for this. His master wasn't angry, he was upset that Narcissus had seen him so publicly humiliated.

"Oh, there's no need for that," Caligula drawled. "I'm sure my uncle will appreciate the breeze without one." And he held out his hand too, demanding the toga.

And this, Narcissus thought, was the moment. This was his chance to prove himself a man, no matter that he was one who could be bought and sold. This was when he could repay Claudius for all his kindness over the years.

He imagined, for a moment, the gratitude in Claudius's eyes. The pride, as Narcissus ignored the demands of his emperor and handed the toga to his master instead.

And then, even more vividly, he pictured Caligula waving at the Praetorian Guard in that uncaring way of his. He saw them falling on him with the pommels of their swords until they'd beaten him into unconsciousness. Dragging his limp body to the Esquiline Gate. He felt the terrible agony as the nails were driven through his wrists, and the cross raised.

He took two steps forward, and handed the toga to Caligula.

The Emperor smiled. He shot one sly, triumphant look at Claudius, still sprawled on the paving slabs where he'd fallen, then slung an arm around Narcissus's neck.

"What's your name, slave?" he asked.

The words stuck behind the lump of shame in his throat. He forced them out with a cough. "Narcissus, dominus."

"Narcissus. Well, not really as beautiful as the myths say, but..." He ran his hand down the slope of Narcissus's shoulder, down his back to cup his buttock beneath his thin tunic. "You'll do."

Narcissus lowered his eyes submissively, afraid of what Caligula might read in them. "I am at my Emperor's command."

"Of course you are!" Caligula said, suddenly pulling away. He turned back to Claudius, who had finally dragged himself to his feet. "Uncle, I want your slave. Give him to me."

Narcissus knew that Claudius was very good at keeping his real feelings from his face. It was how he'd survived so long in the court of the mad Emperor, virtually the only member of his family who had. But he couldn't disguise his expression of dismay now. "He's been with me si-si-sixteen years!" he said. "I bought him when he was just a b-b-boy!"

Caligula shrugged. "Then he must be more than ready for a change of scene. Really, uncle, it's terribly selfish of you to want to keep an energetic young man like this all to yourself."

"B-b-but –"

"I'll go," Narcissus blurted out. He hung his head, because what did it say about him, that his poor, crippled master had the courage to stand up to Caligula for his sake, and Narcissus had none? "I'll gladly go with you, dominus."

Caligula beamed and Narcissus looked only at him and never at Claudius, so he wouldn't have to see the betrayal in his master's eyes.

BODA TOOK HER flatbread to a quiet corner to brood. Now that battle was no longer heating her blood, she could think more clearly. She closed her eyes and watched a memory unfold behind her eyelids, the moment when the Roman soldiers had found her, miles from her tribe and without hope of help.

There had been four of them, two so young they'd barely started shaving and all of them shivering in the northern cold. But their swords were sharp and clean and there had been only a moment of hesitation before they were all pointed at her.

One she could have taken. Maybe two. But four? For a second she'd considered charging forward anyway, dying a glorious death. It would have been the honourable thing to do, and her tribe would have sung songs and drunk mead to her memory.

Honour and glory. In that instant, Boda learnt a shameful thing about herself. She cared more about life than either of them.

Her sword had left a deep imprint in the snow as she dropped it. She remembered seeing the yellow petals of a newly sprouted daffodil, crushed beneath the tip.

And she realised now that, in that moment, she'd stopped thinking, because her thoughts were too painful. She'd let instinct alone and long years of training carry her through the terrible journey back to Rome, the pain of branding, the humiliation of sale at a slave auction and the long, bruising training at the gladiator school.

Instinct had told her that the other gladiators were enemies, only to be fought, and she hadn't questioned it. And now a man was dead because she had never thought that he too was a slave. She'd never seen that these people were her brothers, not her adversaries.

The people of Rome were not all of one tribe, and it was wrong to treat them so. Who was she, without honour or kin, to look down on others who had made choices no worse than hers?

And there was something else, now that she was thinking again, now that she'd stopped drifting through the world like a spirit, as if she really had died in the dark and ancient woodland of her home.

Why had no one told her that the games were a performance, no more real than the spear-shaking dance that initiated the youths of her people into adulthood? Why had Quintus, the trainer of the gladiator school, not told her? His employers had paid much gold for her and all the others; he should be the most eager of all to save the lives of their possessions.

She saw him now, a fat, silver-haired old man who always stank of violets. He glanced quickly at her, then away, and his pace increased, little mincing steps turning into a half trot as he moved away from her.

She sprang to her feet, intercepting him before he could enter the private quarters where the gladiators weren't allowed.

"Quintus – a question."

He turned with an oily smile. "For you, my barbarian beauty, anything."

"The games today. The others – they told me I wasn't supposed to kill Josephus. Is that true?"

"You're a warrior, my petal, my thorny white rose. Fierceness is what the crowd expects of you." He turned away, obviously hoping she'd be satisfied with that.

She took two long paces to put herself back in front of him. "Fierceness, yes. But is it supposed to be real, or a show?"

He waved an expansive arm in the air. "How are such things to be distinguished? All life is a performance, or so they say."

"Real, or not?" she persisted grimly.

He sighed and his eyes darted to left and right, as if checking to see whether anyone was close enough to overhear. They weren't. "There is perhaps an element, the merest hint of showmanship, my dove..."

"Then why in Odin's name didn't you tell me?"

His eyes shifted again. Not looking for anything this time, just avoiding hers. And she knew that whatever he said next would be a lie.

He was saved from voicing it by a commotion, over by the door to the school. "How painful it is to leave you mid-conversation," he said. "But alas, that terrible task-master duty calls."

He slid from her side quicker than a man his size should have been able to move, and headed towards the source of the sound.

Boda considered letting him go. She'd discovered that he was hiding something. Anything beyond that he was unlikely to reveal. But there was something about the noise from the doorway – not any words she could make out, just a tone that was hauntingly familiar – and she found herself following Quintus.

"What's this?" he said. "A fox in the hencoop? Someone come to disturb the peace and tranquillity I've worked so hard to foster?"

"Just a beggar," said Aulus, the youngest and meekest of Quintus's household slaves.

"Then give him some bread and send him on his way."

"I've tried, dominus! He says he won't go without bread and wine."

"Does he now?" Quintus turned back to the door, an unpleasant expression on his face.

Boda moved beside him, getting a clear view of the beggar for the first time.

"Absolutely," the beggar said. "And make the wine something decent – none of that Spanish crap!"

He was tall, red-haired and pale-skinned, with a fine dusting of freckles over the sharp spike of his nose. Boda felt a flare of something warm and hopeful in her belly. She had never met him before, but she knew his face all the same. This was a man of the Cimbri, of her people. She could hear it in his voice, the accent as he spoke Latin a mirror of her own.

She knew he recognised her too. His gaze appraised her and seemed pleased with what it found. "Greetings, clanswoman," he said in her own language.

She lowered her head, to acknowledge him and to hide her face. She didn't want Quintus to read whatever might be written there. She knew that it was too open, a vulnerability she didn't want to show.

Quintus must have guessed some of it. "One of your own?" he said. "How fortuitous, my virgin huntress. Then you may find him the stalest bread and the dregs of last night's wine, and send him on his way." He smiled thinly and left, clearly glad to be rid of them both.

"I am Vali," the beggar said. His eyes, she saw, were a startling red-brown, unusual for her people. They stared into her own blue ones with amused frankness.

"I am Boda, daughter of Berthold," she said. "A captive here."

"Will you show me to the kitchen, then, and the food I've been promised?"

She nodded. "I'm sure I can find something a little better than stale bread for a hungry man." There was a hungry look about him – in the thin, sharp angles of his face.

"And in return," he said. "I have something to show you."

She paused to shoot him a puzzled look. He was wearing nothing but a tunic, too light to hide anything beneath it.

"Something here," he told her. "A secret darkness in this place."

He walked ahead before she could ask him what he meant. Straight towards the kitchen, as if he already knew where it was.

PETRONIUS SPRAWLED ON the bed, wondering if life could get any better. A slave girl under one arm, a slave boy under the other, and food and wine enough to sate the entire Ninth Legion. Best of all, he could feel himself beginning to recover from their previous exertions. More pleasure, he felt, was definitely imminent.

Which was why he was particularly displeased when his father strode through the doorway, throwing the two slaves such savagely disapproving looks that they instantly slunk from the room.

"What?" Petronius said. "We were only just getting started!"

His father glared. "You've been in here two hours."

"Exactly."

"You're a disgrace."

"That's not what they were saying half an hour ago."

It was a familiar argument, and one they'd had so often before that Petronius felt his father hardly needed him there to supply his half of the exchange. Except this time, the other man veered wildly off script.

"It's over," his father said. "Enough. You're a man, or" – a pause for him to slowly eye Petronius up and down – "so the calendar tells us. Fifteen years old, and no achievement to your name bar the impregnation of five slaves and the debauching of Jupiter knows how many others."

"That's what they're for," Petronius protested. But he rose to his feet, clutching the bed sheet around him. He felt, though he wasn't quite sure why, that he was about to get some news which needed to be received standing up. His curling black hair was a tangled mess, and he raked a hand through to tidy it, then gave his father the most meltingly innocent look his big brown eyes would allow.

"You're no use to me, you're a disgrace to the family name," his father continued, clearly unmoved. "And it's my fault. I've indulged you. I've allowed you to laze around the house, doing nothing more productive than scribbling a few words when the fancy takes you and claiming you're planning to be a playwright. A playwright! No, it won't do. It's time you started a profession suitable for a man of your station."

A beam of light crept through one of the house's high windows as his father spoke, casting his shadow onto the wall behind him like a harbinger of death.

Petronius shivered involuntarily. "Writing is an honourable profession. Phaedrus is a highly respected man."

His father sniffed. "By the plebeians, maybe."

Petronius forbore to point out that their own family had been plebeian themselves a mere two generations ago. He didn't think now was a good time to be antagonising his father. "I'm not suitable for anything else," he tried instead. "You've said so yourself – who would put up with a no-good wastrel such as myself?"

"A very good question," his father said ominously. "Happily, today I found the answer. Seneca is in need of an apprentice of good family, and despite having heard every sordid tale of your behaviour buzzing through Rome, he declares himself happy to take you on. No doubt it's because he's a Stoic – they're said to crave hardship and unpleasantness."

"Seneca?" Petronius said. "What can that dusty old bore possibly teach me?"

His father smiled for the first time since entering the room. "Rhetoric. I've thought long and hard, and there's only one career in which you can possibly excel – politics. With your propensity for lying and lechery, the Senate should feel like a home from home."

Petronius let himself fall backwards onto the bed and closed his eyes. He was hoping that when he opened them again this would all prove to have been a dream.

CALIGULA TALKED TO Narcissus all the way back to the palace. It was the longest twenty minutes of his life.

The rest of the Emperor's hangers-on held back, and Narcissus sensed that they were glad of the chance to leave the conversation to someone else. Caligula's mood seemed good at the moment – almost too good, as he laughed raucously at his own jokes and commanded his guards to throw coins to the prettiest of the women they passed. But Narcissus knew that Caligula's moods were as changeable, and as deadly, as a maritime wind. One wrong word and he'd find himself wrecked on the rocks of Caesar's displeasure.

He tried to confine himself to yes or no answers, but he soon realised that even this was angering Caligula. The tenth time he smiled and agreed, the Emperor pouted and pulled away from him. "You're no fun," he said. "I thought you wanted to be my friend."

There was no possible reply to that. Narcissus bowed his head and hoped that would be enough.

It wasn't. "If I wanted silence," Caligula said, "I'd have cut out your tongue."

"I'm sorry, dominus," Narcissus whispered. But he could see that this only angered Caligula more. What did he want? Impertinence, perhaps, a witty retort – but it was far too great a risk.

"He's d-d-dazzled by you, nephew," a voice spoke up behind them.

Claudius, protecting him still. Narcissus was too ashamed to turn round and face him.

Their procession finally swept through the entrance to the palace, purple-painted marble pillars looming on either side. Caligula frowned at Narcissus in the sudden shade. "Are you? Dazzled by me, that is?"

"Yes, dominus." Narcissus said. And then, through a mouth numb with fear, "I've admired you so long from afar. To be suddenly so close to a living god is too much for a humble slave like myself."

"Well," Caligula said. "Understandable, I suppose. But disappointing. As you're such a hopeless conversationalist, I suppose I shall have to find another use for you."

"I live to serve," Narcissus said, and this time it seemed to be the right thing.

Caligula nodded. "Naturally. And I think I have just the job for you." There was a cruel twist to his lips as he spoke. "The importation records for the Empire are in a most desperate state. I had a slave looking over them, but her handwriting was just dreadful. So I cut it off. Her hand, that is. And then I couldn't have her bleeding all over the parchment, so since then there's been no one to sort it out."

"But dominus," Narcissus croaked. "I've no training in accounting. My master –" He caught Caligula's frown just in time. "My former master had me tutored in music, to play the lyre and the flute at his dinners."

"A musician – how wonderful! I play myself, you know. It's a career I could have pursued professionally, if I didn't have a higher obligation."

"The whole Empire speaks of your skill," Narcissus said.

Caligula eyed him coldly. His expression said that he knew he was being patronised, and Narcissus reminded himself that the Emperor wasn't stupid, just mad.

"That's as may be," Caligula said. "But as you can see, I need an accountant, not a flautist. You're a clever man – or so my uncle's always boasting. I'm sure you'll pick it up in no time. And if you don't..."

Caligula's eyes were already drifting away, searching the palace for some other entertainment. "But we don't need to worry about that, do we? I'm quite sure you won't disappoint me."

PETRONIUS HAD THOUGHT he might be given some time to prepare himself. But once his father had made up his mind, he'd always been quick to put his plans into action. It was what made him so successful as a businessman. And it was the reason that, a mere half hour after he'd learned his fate, Petronius found himself at the door of the most tedious man in Rome.

Seneca looked at him sourly after his father had effected the introduction and then hurriedly left, presumably before Seneca could change his mind.

Petronius didn't know what the other man found so displeasing in his appearance. He'd often been told that he was a well-developed young man – and not just by the slaves – while Seneca himself was quite an unappealing sight. With his stringy, greying hair and gnarled limbs, he had the look of a man who'd suffered some debilitating illness as a child, and been slowly decaying into middle age ever since.

"So you're the young reprobate Anthony wants to palm off on me, are you?" he said, in a thin, reedy voice.

"I am Petronius son of Antonius of the Octavii, yes."

Seneca looked even less impressed. "Jumped-up plebeians, the lot of you."

Since this was exactly what Petronius himself had been thinking a short while ago, he elected not to respond.

"Well," Seneca said, "I suppose you'd better come in." He stood aside, ushering Petronius into the room beyond.

Dusk was beginning to fall over the city, but that didn't fully account for the gloom Petronius found within. Most Romans of Seneca's station filled their houses with light, a central atrium for greenery and direct sunlight, and windows elsewhere with bright painted plaster and mosaics for colour and life.

Not here. There were no windows in evidence, and the walls and floor were painted the same stark, gloomy red. The colour of dried blood, Petronius thought, and shivered. The whole place felt old, as if it was a relic from a more ancient city on whose bones Rome had been built.

Seneca led him through at a slow pace, slow enough for him to inspect the clutter of furniture and objects that filled every room. "You've spent time in Egypt?" Petronius said.

Seneca turned to stare at him, brown eyes bright and unfriendly. "Yes. How did you know?"

Petronius laughed. When that just made the other man frown, he gestured around him. A figurine of a cat sat on top of a wooden chest, half-decayed but still inscribed along its length with the little squares and pictures of the Egyptian hieroglyphs. A pile of papyrus teetered in one corner, while the other was taken up with the life-size statue of a cow-headed woman, a half-moon balanced on her crown.

"Yes, I see," Seneca said. "I'm surprised you recognise it."

"I have had some education."

"Little enough, your father tells me. But no matter. With me" – he gestured Petronius through to another room, its door half-hidden behind a thick blue cloth – "you may begin to study those things which really matter."

Here, at last, was a window. High in the far wall, it cast a wan light down on the stacks and stacks of scrolls which sat on every available surface. In the centre of it all was a rickety wooden chair tucked beneath a small desk. The desk too was piled high. Seneca swept an impatient arm across it, pushing the scrolls onto the floor and a cloud of dust into the air.

"I did my own studies here, you know. This room made me the man I am."

"I can certainly believe that."

Seneca ignored – or perhaps didn't notice – his sarcasm. "Your first task will be to copy some of my more famous speeches. Many of my friends have been begging me for their own editions, and you'll learn a great deal in the process."

Petronius eased himself into the chair, sending up another cloud of dust from beneath his buttocks. "About what, precisely?"

"How to address your betters, for a start!" Seneca snapped. He rifled through one of the many piles of scrolls, pulling three out to hand to Petronius. They stank of mildew and old leather. "You may start with these. And I hope your hand is fair – if they're not readable, you'll simply have to start again."

The door slammed behind him as he left, the impact toppling one heap of paper to slide sibilantly to the floor. Petronius sighed and knelt to put them back in some kind of order. But his hand froze, hovering in mid air, when he saw that these too were covered in hieroglyphics.

Seneca had scoffed at him, at the idea that he might have attended to any of his education. And it was true that when the Greek slave his father had bought to tutor him had droned on about the history of the Roman republic, or the conquest of the barbarian tribes on its borders, he had closed his ears. But words, language, stories – these were things he cared passionately about. And when he cared, he applied himself. By the time he was thirteen, he could understand nearly every tongue spoken in the Empire.

He had never told his father, of course. If he'd known, the old man would have sent him off to manage a field office somewhere dreadful like Gaul and that would have been unbearable. A writer of Rome must live at its beating heart. So he'd kept the knowledge to himself, studying by the light of a candle after the rest of the household had retired to their beds.

He could speak all the languages of Rome. And he could read hieroglyphs, too.

He placed the fallen scroll on his desk and ran a finger along the first line, mentally translating it. 'And Osiris says, my hiding place is opened, it is opened. And the spirit falls into darkness, but I shall not die a second time in the land of eternal fire.'

He leaned back, rocking his chair on its legs. This was intriguing. Certainly far more interesting than Seneca's speeches. If he wasn't mistaken, those were lines from the Egyptian *Book of the Dead*. He'd tracked down a fragment once, in the shop of a shady Syrian who dealt in rare artefacts of questionable provenance.

Even those fragments had cost him a small fortune, gold coins he's pilfered from his father when he was too drunk to notice. The Syrian had claimed he was lucky to find anything at all. *The Book of the Dead* had been banned in Egypt two centuries ago, all the known copies burned.

So what exactly was Seneca doing in possession of one?

VALI TOOK THE bread and olives that Boda gave him without a word. But his red-brown eyes watched her the whole time he ate, thoughtful and assessing. She felt her pulse quicken, though she wasn't quite sure why.

"How did you come here, clansman?" she asked, when the silence had stretched on too long.

"I'm a wanderer." He shrugged, as if that was explanation enough.

"You've wandered very far from home."

"The world is wide and my time short. I've travelled as far as I can."

"And who are your parents?" she asked. "Your cousins? Where is your people's hearth-home?"

His head tilted to one side as he quirked a crooked smile. "You don't trust me, clanswoman. You're right to be suspicious. This place is full of lies – but not mine."

He was speaking in riddles, like a bard. Could that be what he was? It might explain his presence here. The most famous storytellers among the Cimbri had been known to travel thousands of miles in search of a rare poem or a lost tale.

"You spoke of a secret hidden here," she said to him. "What did you mean?"

He finished the last of the bread before he answered, chewing each mouthful deliberately before washing it down with a mouthful of wine. His lips were stained dark red with it, and when his tongue flicked out to lick them clean it looked very pink in contrast. "There are secrets," he said. "But are you sure you want to know them? Ignorance is safer."

She thought about Josephus, dead by her sword because no one had told her the truth. "I don't care about safety. I want to know."

"Even if it might lead to your death?"

"Even then."

"Good." He smiled, as if she'd passed some sort of test, and his long legs uncurled from beneath him as he rose to his feet. A white litter of crumbs fell to the floor around him and she saw a small brown rat dart from beneath the table to seize them.

"It's through here," he said, moving quickly towards the back of the school, where the weapons and armour were stored between fights.

There were half a dozen other gladiators in the room and they all turned to stare as Boda walked past. Their gaze felt like a physical blow, filled with hostility. She wanted to tell them that she hadn't known Josephus was meant to live, that if they wanted to blame someone they should blame Quintus. But it was her sword that had been the instrument, and even by the laws of her own people the blood guilt was hers.

At the far door, Vali paused, his fingers brushing over the iron keyhole. "The key?" he said, and Boda saw that it was locked. That was new. Only last week she'd been in the place herself, trying out different helmets for the match in the Arena.

She shook her head. "Quintus must have it."

The other gladiators were still watching. If she tried to kick down the door, they'd stop her. She could already hear them murmuring, no doubt wondering why she was giving this beggar a tour of the place. It was probably only a matter of minutes before Quintus himself was summoned. Vali hadn't said so, but she was quite sure that the secret he spoke of concerned the old man.

"We don't have much time," she told him.

He looked skyward for a second, either praying or thinking. Then he shrugged, and turned the door handle.

The door swung open, creaking a little on its rusted hinges. He slipped through, holding it open only a crack for her to follow. When he pushed it shut again, she heard a click that sounded like a lock turning.

She grabbed his arm. "How –"

He put his finger over her lips. His skin was dry, and hotter than she expected, as if he had a fever.

"There's not much time," he whispered. "You can ask your questions when I've shown you what you're here to see."

She could hear nothing except the gentle sound of her own breathing and the harsher rasp of Vali's. The sun had set outside, and the room's two windows were dark and blank. But there was a flicker of golden light, illuminating the neat racks of swords and the shelf after shelf of breastplates and helmets and greaves. The light seemed to be coming from behind them, in the far corner of the storeroom. Candles, she realised, smelling the honey-scented wax in the air. But why leave them burning in an empty room?

Vali nodded at her, as if he knew what she was thinking.

She crept forward, bare feet cold on the marble floor. Vali's footsteps slapped softly beside her. If there had been anyone else in the room, they would have heard him. But there wasn't. There was no one else living inside.

Josephus had been laid on a slab of stone at the far end, wedged into a corner beside a row of tridents. The candles were arranged around him, two of them already burned out and one guttering near extinction.

His body had been mutilated. Her sword had pierced his heart, but it had left a neat hole when she withdrew it. Now his chest had been cut open entirely, the ribs peeled back to emerge from the red flesh beneath like a row of jagged white teeth. She could smell rotting meat and shit combined, but there were no flies buzzing around this feast, though she could see them thick on the window above. It was as if something about the corpse repelled them.

Boda felt bile rise into her throat, acrid and burning, but she forced herself to move closer. She peered into the wide cavity of the chest, and saw that the wound in his heart had been repaired, the jagged edges sewn together with small black stitches. The heart should have nestled between the two lobes of his lungs, but those were gone, nothing but a bloody vacancy in their place. The folds of the intestine were also missing and the great purple disc of his liver.

His face was mostly intact, but his nose was bloodied and broken. A thin white gruel dripped from one of his nostrils and Boda realised with a nauseous shock that it was what remained of his brains.

Set on each corner of the slab on which he lay were four earthenware jars. Up close, she could see that their lids were fashioned in the form of heads: man, monkey, fox and something that might have been a hawk. The smell of shit came most strongly from this last, and after a moment's hesitation, she lifted its lid.

Josephus's intestines lay coiled inside, like a slick brown serpent.

She dropped the lid, hardly noticing as it smashed on the floor beside her foot. Vali shifted beside her and she wrenched her eyes away from the corpse to look into his grave face.

The sound of the key turning in the lock was startlingly loud in the silence.

Boda spun to face the door. The rack of tridents was beside her, and she snatched one to defend herself, though the foreign weapon had always felt clumsy in her hand.

There was a slight hesitation before the door opened, as if the person on the other side was equally nervous about what he might find inside. Boda placed herself in front of Josephus's body, though she wasn't sure what she could defend him from, except further desecration.

Finally, the door flew open. The light was far brighter behind it, blinding her for a moment so that all she could see was the dark silhouette of a man. A spear of cold fear shot down her spine and she tightened her grasp on the trident, fingers suddenly slippery with sweat. Then the figure stepped forward. Two steps and the softer light of the candles washed over his face.

It was Quintus. For just a second his expression was closed and hard. Then his eyes met hers and his face sagged into its usual weak, ingratiating lines.

"Boda, my lioness, what are you doing here?"

"We were looking for a fresh sword," she said, knowing that a quick lie was always more convincing than a slow one. "My old one is nicked from the fight."

"We?" Quintus said.

Boda turned to Vali – only to realise that he was no longer standing beside her. She jerked a look behind her, thinking he might have tried to hide, but the room was empty save for her and Quintus.

Then a waft of air blew into her face, from a window that she was sure had previously been shut, and she saw the edge of a booted foot slide across the sill and out of sight. But the window was high above the floor. How could he possibly have reached it?

"Boda, sweetness," Quintus said. "Are you quite all right?"

"Yes," she said, turning back to him. And then: "No! Quintus, what have you done to Josephus?"

"I? It was you who dispatched him to a better place, my treasure."

She stepped to one side, so there'd be no question that he saw the body.

His eyes widened in shock. But there was something theatrical about it – too rehearsed to be quite real. "For the love of Mars, what has happened here?"

"Yes," Boda said icily, "what has happened here?"

He studied her for a moment, no doubt gauging the probability that she'd believe a denial. He must have realised that she wouldn't. His eyes returned to their normal size and his mouth to its customary greasy smirk. "I'm sorry that you had to see this, truly," he said. "Josephus begged me to do this for him, in the event of his death. It's the death ritual of his people, you see. Without it, he told me he'd be condemned to wander the near shore of the afterlife forever."

Boda looked back at the body, lying with candles all around it, nearly all extinguished now, and the four jars at the four corners of the slab. There was a ritual look to it, that was true, but a deeply unholy one. "His people?" she said.

"The Egyptians."

"But Josephus was of Judea," she said. "A Jew."

Quintus shrugged with a look of careful unconcern. "Once, maybe. But he converted to the worship of Osiris. You know those Jews, a flighty lot, changing gods as easily as the rest of us change tunics."

He looked at her, face bland and composed and eyes so unreadable it was as if he had shutters behind them. She could see there was nothing further to be gained from doubting his word, and much to be lost. By Roman law, she was property, with no more rights than a table. If she became too troublesome, he need only dispose of her.

She bowed her head. "I apologise for questioning you, Quintus. It... disturbed me to see a body treated this way, that's all."

"Understandable, my northern star." He smiled and slipped an arm around her shoulders to guide her from the room. She stiffened, but managed to stop herself from shrugging it off.

Outside the room, he noticed her watching him as he carefully locked the door and pocketed the key. "To spare anyone else the shock you've had," he said.

She nodded, as if she understood, and he turned and walked away. She watched him go, wondering how much he guessed of what she believed. And what exactly he might do about it.

CHAPTER TWO

THE NEXT DAY began as the previous one had ended – with Petronius banished to the musty room at the back of the house with nothing but a stack of scrolls for company. Seneca left him with a slice of flatbread, a pot of honey and the suggestion that he might like to try working a little harder than yesterday.

By the time the old man returned, Petronius had uncovered five other pages from the *Book of the Dead*, as well as three papyruses so ancient even he could barely decipher them. He heard the old man approach a few seconds before the door opened, and hurriedly re-seated himself at his desk, pulling a scroll open in front of him at random.

He remained bent over it, pen poised, as the door opened.

"Young man," Seneca said.

Petronius raised his head, blinking. "Oh, I'm sorry. I was so engrossed I didn't hear you enter. I've never read prose of such fluency before."

Seneca smiled. "Really? Well, I have been told my talent is quite unique."

It said something about Seneca, Petronius thought, that he was ready to believe so egregious a lie. Some people's opinion of themselves was so high that no flattery seemed too outrageous.

"I stand in awe," Petronius said, carefully shifting his elbow to cover the blank scroll on which he was supposed to have been writing.

Seneca nodded, taking this as his due. "I came to tell you that I have a meeting to attend. The rest of the morning is yours, though your father has instructed me that you're not to leave this house except in my company."

Of course he has – the old bastard. Still, Seneca must have some household slaves working for him. Petronius would simply have to make his own entertainment. He managed a smile. "Don't worry, sir. Despite what my father may have told you, I value nothing more than quiet study and contemplation."

That, he quickly realised, was a lie too far. The old man frowned at him disbelievingly, then shrugged. "Your may spend the day in your sleeping quarters, or in the public areas. My own rooms, of course, are out of bounds." And with a curt bow, he was gone.

He left the door open behind him, and Petronius remained in his seat, listening to his retreating footsteps until he was quite sure the other man had gone.

His bones clicked as he stood, stiff after so long crouched on the floor. He looked down longingly at the scrolls he'd discovered, but he couldn't risk taking them. If Seneca discovered they were gone, Petronius might find himself out of an apprenticeship – with no guarantee that his own family would take him back.

No matter. He imagined he'd be spending quite some time in that room. Plenty of opportunities to uncover any other treasures that might be hidden there. He could make copies for himself when he had more time – or, if he was careful enough, leave the copies and take the originals for himself. Now he had an opportunity to explore the rest of the house without the old bore around, he should make the most of it. His quarters were to the left, the common areas lying between there and the door. That must mean that Seneca's own quarters were on the right. He'd start there.

His head was down, deep in thought, and he didn't see the slave until he'd walked right into him.

The man was so massive, he had to slope his shoulders to fit beneath the stuccoed ceiling. His arms were as thick as Petronius's thighs, knotted with muscles beneath the bronze skin.

"Where are you going?" the slave said. His voice was so deep it felt more like vibration than sound.

"Looking around," Petronius told him. "Seneca said I could have the run of the place."

The man nodded his head, like a rock teetering on the edge of a cliff before an avalanche. He was standing foursquare in front of the doorway leading to Seneca's quarters, blocking it entirely. It would have taken a small siege engine to move him. "The dining room is behind you," he said. "Food can be prepared, if you wish it."

"Of course," Petronius said.

He remained where he was, and so did the slave. They stared at each in silence for a few moments.

"Well," Petronius said eventually. "Perhaps a prayer before I eat. I'm a deeply religious man, as I imagine Seneca has told you."

The slave didn't respond. He shifted a little, moving his weight from one plate-like foot to the other.

"So where," Petronius persevered, "might I find the lararium?"

For the first time, something resembling an expression crossed the other man's face. He frowned. "There is no shrine to your gods here."

"My gods?" Petronius said. The lararium held household gods, not the great deities of Rome. "Well, no, of course, but as the newest member of this household, I'd like to pay my respects."

"No shrine here," the slave repeated, face mask-like once again.

"Then," Petronius said, "perhaps I'll head out to find a suitable temple. My day doesn't feel complete without a prayer."

He expected the slave to try and stop that too, but he just looked away, as if the conversation no longer concerned him. His massive arms remained folded in front of his smooth chest, and it occurred to Petronius that he looked like a statue of a god himself. One of those frightening Eastern ones who was terribly keen on sin and purity.

He gave the slave one last smile and backed away, unwilling to take his eyes off him. When he felt the door against his shoulder he slid round it and away, letting out a breath he hadn't known he'd been holding.

This stay with Seneca was proving to be considerably more interesting than he'd imagined. And considerably more nerve-wracking.

CALIGULA HAD BEEN right: the Empire's records were a mess. Narcissus thought about Hercules, challenged to clean out the Augean stables in just one day, and decided that he'd had the easier task. The Emperor had left Narcissus in a room with a thousand sheets of parchment and one abacus. He flicked the beads from side to side, the click-click-click a distraction from the roaring of panic in his mind. He didn't know how to do this. He didn't even know how to start.

"It's pointless, you know," said a voice from the shadows.

Narcissus yelped and spun round so fast that he fell off his chair. Paper wafted in the air all around him as a figure appeared through the storm of white, brushing the sheets impatiently aside. It was a woman, a young one, face as pale and blank as the paper which surrounded her.

"Who – ?" Narcissus said.

She held an arm out to him, and after a moment's hesitation he grasped it to lever himself off the floor. Only when he was on his feet again did he realise that he'd been holding a wrist – that there was no hand at the end of it.

"I'm your predecessor," she said.

She was quite pretty, he realised, her curly hair a shade darker than honey and her cheekbones high and sharp. But her skin had the unhealthy pallor of someone who didn't see the outside world enough, and there was a feverish brightness to her eyes.

"Your hand," Narcissus said.

She snatched the stump behind her back. "He took it."

"Caligula?"

She nodded, twisting her face away so that he couldn't read her expression. It brought the mutilated arm back into his line of sight, but he was careful not to look at it again.

"The Emperor told me about you," he said. "What he'd done."

She moved with startling quickness, slipping past him to perch cross-legged on the table in front of him. "I showed him. I showed him what was wrong, but he wouldn't listen. They told him I was lying, and he listened to them instead."

"He said..." Narcissus cleared his throat and looked away, embarrassed. "He said he didn't like the way you wrote."

She laughed at that, a high, jarring giggle that didn't sound entirely sane. "He didn't like *what* I wrote."

Narcissus nodded. He could well believe it. Caligula had a talent for seeing those things he chose, and overlooking the ones he didn't. How else could he believe that the people still loved him?

"And you?" she said. "Down here in the darkness with all the numbers. The rows and rows of numbers all lined up, like soldiers on parade. What is it you did that displeased him so?" The mounds of paper in the room muffled the sound of her voice, smudging it like ink on a page.

Narcissus picked up his chair from the floor, setting it in front of her before gingerly sitting down. She immediately shuffled backwards, her eyes wide and fixed fearfully on his.

He held out a hand to her, palm up, as he would have done if she'd been a skittish horse in need of gentling. "I'm not going to hurt you."

"Aren't you?" She frowned. "But you're here to replace me. If he has you, he doesn't need me. If he doesn't need me..."

Narcissus imagined her, all these weeks in this room, in the dark. Waiting for Caligula to finish the job he started with her hand. To break her apart, piece by piece, until she wanted to die.

"I won't let that happen," he said. "I promise you."

"Oh, you promise." And now she looked entirely sane and far too knowing. "You've been promoted, have you, *slave?*"

"No. But I can help you, if you help me. I need you. I was never taught to calculate. I can't do the thing Caligula's ordered me to do – which is why he asked me to do it, of course."

She reached out suddenly, moving as quick as a striking snake to grasp his hand. He tensed then relaxed, letting her pull it towards her. She cradled it in hers, turning it from side to side, as if it was some rare and delicate artefact. Her fingertips trailed along the lengths of his fingers and over the ball of his thumb, a sensation that was half ticklish, half something else.

"Soft hands," she said. "But calluses, here, here and here." She touched the very tips of his fingers. "You're a musician."

"Yes," he said. "I understand songs – not numbers."

"Numbers are easy," she said. "Eight hundred and twenty-three thousand, five hundred and forty-three."

Narcissus paused, waiting for more, but that seemed to be it. She tilted her head to the side, waiting expectantly.

"That's... a very large amount," he said.

She let out a *tssk* of frustration, jumping from the table with the same snake-quick speed she'd shown before. She leaned towards him, bringing her mouth so close to his ear he felt the whisper of her breath in his hair. "The days of the week multiplied by themselves, of course. Numbers are easy – it's people who are difficult."

He pulled away so he could look her in the eye. "Then will you help me? So the same thing doesn't happen to me as happened to you?"

She shook her head, backing away until she was in the far corner of the room, half hidden behind a stack of ledgers. "Maybe that's what I want," she said. "Maybe I'd enjoy watching someone else suffer the way I did."

He could feel himself shaking as he studied her. She was what he might become, if Caligula had his way. "No," he said. "I don't think you would."

After a moment she sighed and nodded. He noticed that she was wearing a beautiful chiton, blue trimmed with gold lace, but it was torn and stained. He wondered who she'd stolen it from. Or had Caligula given it to her, back when she'd still been in his favour?

"What's your name?" he asked.

She smiled, a bright and carefree expression that made her look suddenly very beautiful. "I'm Julia. And you're Narcissus. Do you find your reflection as pleasing as he did?"

He felt himself blushing. "My mother named me for my father. She was sold away from him before I was born."

"Greek, yes. I will help you. Or, anyway, I'll tell you. Whether that will help, only the gods can know. Come – over here."

She led him to a shelf halfway along one wall, the wood buckling under the weight of the years of ledgers lined along it. She picked the furthest of these, its paper still pale and new, and pulled it to the floor, crouching in front of it on her heels. Narcissus knelt beside her, reading over her narrow shoulder.

"My work," she said, gesturing at the whole row of books. "Twenty-five years of records. Tiberius kept none while he reigned, there was nothing but disorder when I started. And here – look what I found."

She'd flipped to the back few pages of the ledger. Narcissus studied them, the lists of goods and money and what might have been ships' names beside row after row of figures, some large, some small – all incomprehensible. The only conclusion he could draw was that Caligula had a point about her handwriting.

"I'm sorry," he said. "I don't know what I'm supposed to be looking for."

"Here – just here!" She jabbed her finger down on one line: *The Khert-Neter.* "Every week this ship travels from Egypt to Ostia, empty, and every week it returns home with a hold full of oil."

Narcissus kept looking at the figures as if, given enough time, they might explain themselves. But nothing made sense and he began to wonder if this imagined finding was nothing more than a delusion. "So? Hundreds of ships trade with Rome every week. It's the lifeblood of the Empire."

"Idiot!" she said. "As foolish as him! Listen. They travel the sea every week, three days' journey across wave and through storm and all to bring a hold full of air?"

And, finally, Narcissus thought he understood. "Yes, yes. I see. Why not carry something on the way there as well as the way back? They're halving their profits – it doesn't make sense."

"Exactly," she said. "He understands." She rocked back on her heels, looking up at the ceiling with her eyes half lidded. "And when a thing makes no sense, what do we conclude?"

Narcissus could feel the excitement building in him now. "That it's not what's really going on. That ship wasn't empty – it was carrying something on every trip. But whatever it was, they didn't want it entered in the Empire's records. Smugglers, I suppose."

"Maybe. Possible, yes."

"And you told Caligula about this?"

Her eyes closed completely for a moment and she shuddered. "Yes. But the ship belongs to Seneca – an honoured man. A free man, a citizen. He told the Emperor I lied."

"And the Emperor believed him and not you," Narcissus said bitterly. And, of course, if he made the same accusation now, the outcome would be the same. Worse, probably. He knew that Caligula didn't care about him – he enjoyed tormenting his uncle. The more he made Narcissus suffer, the more it would torment Claudius, so he'd make that suffering as terrible as he could contrive.

She must have read something in his face, because she nodded sadly. "Proof. We need evidence – something more concrete than this."

He looked back down at the ledger. "Am I reading this right? Does the ship follow the same schedule every week?"

She nodded. "Into Ostia on Mercury's Day. Loaded and leaving again that same night."

He jumped to his feet, wishing this room had windows so he could judge the position of the sun. "It's Mercury's Day today, isn't it? The ship might be in port now."

"It arrives at midday, leaves at midnight," she said. "There's still time."

And something in the tilt of her smile, or the way her eyes wouldn't quite meet his, told him that this had been her intention all along: for him to finish the job she'd started. He was being used, but then he'd intended to use her, so he supposed it was only fair. And saving her might be the only way to save himself.

"Fine," he said. "I'll go to the docks. And hope that Caligula doesn't come looking for me in the meantime."

TRAINING WAS BRUTAL for Boda that morning, the other gladiators taking every opportunity to bruise and wound her. By the time lunch approached she was exhausted and aching and only a few lucky blocks away from losing an eye. But the dusty training ground felt solid beneath her feet, and in the light of day the horror of last night seemed more tolerable, the memory already losing its vividness, like a painting that had been left out too long in the sun.

And yet she couldn't quite forget. Every time she looked up after a fight, wiping away the sweat that dripped into her eyes, there was Quintus. He lurked in the shadows, a measuring look on his face as he watched, and she knew that whatever business had begun between them last night wasn't finished.

When midday approached, a messenger came for him. A slave, young and round-cheeked, he drew the older man aside and whispered in his ear. She was resting when it happened, pouring a handful of water over her head to try and cool off in the endless heat.

Quintus's eyes flicked to her, as they often had during the morning, but this time they didn't flick away again. "Boda, my somnolent Siren, are you worn out already? Truly, your stamina must improve if you're to last another bout in the Arena. Vibius there – give our barbarian queen a work-out."

Vibius eyed her balefully as he picked out the sharpest of the wooden practice swords and gestured her towards him.

Quintus smiled and executed a small, mocking bow – then turned to follow the messenger slave towards the entrance.

Trapping her here so she couldn't follow him, she thought. Which was foolish. It might not have occurred to her that he was worth following, if he hadn't gone out of his way to ensure she couldn't.

She threw her short sword to the ground. "Sorry, Vibius, I have something more important to attend to."

The jeers and catcalls of the other gladiators followed her as she left the training ground, but she didn't let it bother her. If she could prove that Quintus had lied to her, that – for some reason – he'd deliberately arranged to have Josephus killed, then maybe she could restore her honour in their eyes. Maybe she could restore it in her own.

Outside, the streets were crowded with slaves and citizens too poor to make others work for them in the noon heat. Quintus was already far ahead and she let him stay there, sticking to the shadows as she trailed him past the austere Temple of Serapis and towards the heart of Rome.

He stopped several times, forcing her to hang back too, but she didn't think the people he spoke to were the reason for this trip. His expression was too unguarded, and theirs too open. They were probably just spectators from the games, she thought bitterly, congratulating him for putting on such a fine and bloody show.

She'd seldom been outside the gladiator school since she was brought to the city and she was struck once again, as she had been on her arrival, by the sheer size of the place. Even the simple tenement houses were bigger than the chief's mead hall in her own village, and towering above them were great edifices of marble, their purpose unknown to her but their message clear: here sat the wealth and power of the world.

What was wrong with these people, to want to live so close together, without trees or grass to remind them of their roots in the ground? This was a city of strangers, where every day unknown faces passed on the street. No wonder they were so cold, so in love with blood for its own sake. In a place such as this, one could forget how to be human.

She was so lost in her own thoughts she almost failed to notice when Quintus finally reached his destination. And when she saw where it was, her spirits sank. The bath house. She'd wasted an hour and more following him to no purpose.

Except, no. Instead of going straight inside, Quintus paused, turning to survey the street around him. Boda hurriedly ducked her head, hiding her face from sight and hoping that her yellow hair wouldn't draw his eye.

It didn't seem to. When she looked up again, Quintus had moved. She could just make out the back of his head, thinning hair dripping with sweat as he entered the bathhouse between two tall white columns.

A man who didn't want to be observed had something to hide. She waited a few more moments to be sure he didn't leave, then crossed the street to follow him inside.

PETRONIUS LAY BACK, eyes closed, as the attendant scraped the oil from his shoulders. She was red haired, with a pert nose and the largest breasts he'd ever seen, and he was having to concentrate quite hard on not getting an erection.

When he'd left Seneca's house, he'd fully intended to carry on his investigations, perhaps ask around his father's friends to see what rumours might be circulating about the man. Rome was a city of sins, but they seldom remained private ones for long.

He'd headed towards the Forum, where his father's cronies were usually to be found, tallying the latest goods they imported from all over the Empire. But then his route had taken him past the bath house, and just the sight of the steam wafting through the window of the sudatorium reminded him that he hadn't washed himself in nearly two days.

Before he realised, he'd made the decision; he found himself inside, stripping off his toga in the apodyterium and handing over the two denarii that bought him a personal attendant for the duration of his visit. And, really, if Seneca was going to keep him cooped up inside for days at a time, he had to take advantage of opportunities like this while he could, didn't he?

Still, his conscience had continued pricking him until he'd plunged into the scaldingly hot water of the caldarium. After that, his worries seemed to float away on the steam.

Only to return with a sharp stab of guilt when he heard a familiar, grating voice not three paces from where he was lying. His eyes flicked open, then quickly shut again as soon as they lighted on the man's face.

Seneca. Petronius didn't think the other man had seen him, but he wasn't risking another look to see. He mock-casually raised an arm, throwing it across his face to shield it from view and hoping the movement itself didn't attract the old man's attention.

There were three bath houses within far easier reach of his home – why in Saturn's name did the miserable fool have to come and visit this one?

After a second of lying statue-still, heart like a galloping horse in his chest, it occurred to Petronius that this was a very good question. Just what was Seneca doing so far from home?

He opened one eye a crack, peering out from beneath the shelter of his elbow. Seneca was still dressed, the cloth of his toga sweat-soaked and clinging to his spindly limbs. He wasn't lying down and it was clear he wasn't here to bathe. A few of the other occupants shot him puzzled looks – no one ever came into the heat of the caldarium dressed.

Seneca ignored them, stooping to whisper in the ear of a man lying on the bench beside Petronius. The man, plump and red like a ripe plum, listened in silence for a few seconds. Then he rose to his feet and the pair of them hurried from the room. Petronius only hesitated a second before following them, snagging an unattended tunic to pull on as he passed.

After the hot bath, most people headed for the lukewarm tepidarium before going outside to brave the frigidarium. Seneca and his companion were certainly walking in that direction, past the massage room and into the central atrium with its burst of sunlight and mosaic-covered walls. But at the end of the atrium they turned left instead of right, towards a small side room that Petronius had only ever seen used by slaves before.

At the doorway they paused – and then turned back, eyes sweeping the room behind them. Petronius spun around so quickly he made himself dizzy. He rested an arm against a pillar for support, slowly easing himself around until his back was pressed to the far side and there was no way that Seneca could see him.

When his breathing had returned to normal, he leaned his head back against the cool marble and cursed. That had been far too close.

It was only when he looked around that he realised he wasn't the only one hiding there.

The woman was being more subtle about it than he was, leaning forward on her elbows as if she was taking a rest, but the darting glances she kept shooting past the pillar gave her away. She caught him looking at her and met his eyes for a moment, her own a bright, light blue beneath her barbarian-pale hair. Her face was pleasingly rounded but somehow not soft. There was something familiar about it, though he couldn't place her. Then she turned away, clearly dismissing him as irrelevant.

"Well," Petronius said. "I know what I'm doing skulking behind this pillar. How about you?"

Her mouth pulled into a tight, tense line as she turned to look at him, but otherwise her expression remained impressively blank. "Apologies dominus," she said in heavily accented Latin. "I'm afraid I don't know what you're talking about."

"I'm definitely up to no good," he told her. "So I can only assume you are too. The question is whether our nefarious activities happen to coincide."

She stared at him silently for a long moment, and he was just about to say it again using shorter words when she smiled slightly and shook her head. "You speak as if I trust you – a strange assumption."

"I can always find your master and tell him what you've been up to," Petronius said, and instantly regretted it when he saw the flare of anger in his eyes. The muscles in her right arm tensed from shoulder to hand, as if grasping for a sword that didn't hang at her side – and he realised suddenly where he'd seen her before.

"You're a gladiator!" he said. And then, that memory jogging loose another one, "And that man with Seneca is... I can't remember his name, but he trains half the fighters in the Arena."

She looked at him for a long, cold moment. Then her hand unclenched and she nodded sharply. "Quintus, yes."

"You're following him – from the school, I suppose."

Another nod, then her head tilted to the side as she studied him. She really was very pretty, in an exotic sort of way. "And you were following him too?"

"No. I know the man he's with – Seneca."

As if by mutual agreement, they drew apart again to dart their heads round opposite sides of the pillar – just in time to see Quintus and Seneca disappearing through the doorway, accompanied by a middle-aged man and woman whom Petronius was sure he'd never seen before.

"We must follow them," she said.

Petronius frowned. "Are you sure that's safe?"

He only caught the edge of her smile as she turned away. "Probably not." And then she was walking calmly across the atrium towards the door, not waiting to see if he'd follow.

After a second's hesitation, he did. There was no point coming all this way, only to balk at the last hurdle. And besides, if he didn't follow her, he might never see her again – and that would be a terrible shame.

THE PORT OF Rome lay on the right bank of the Tiber, in the long shadow of the Theatre of Marcellus. Narcissus's breath was burning in his lungs by the time he reached it, and his clothes were plastered to his body with sweat. The crowded streets of the city didn't allow a man to run, but he'd pushed through them as fast as he could, desperate to complete his mission and return to the palace before Caligula noticed he was missing.

Narcissus felt a tight, hard knot of fear in his stomach, knowing there was every chance the Emperor had already noticed. He couldn't let himself think about it, though. He had no choice. Better to risk possible punishment now than face certain torture later if he didn't find what he was looking for.

The great seagoing ships didn't travel this far up the river, its bed too shallow to allow them passage. But barges brought their wares to the gates of the city, labouring day and night to supply the needs of the million people who called it their home. He could see three of them now, floating amid the debris of crates and rotten vegetables strewn across the ruffled green surface of the water.

If the *Khert-Neter* was bringing a cargo from Egypt as well as sending one to it, the goods would pass through here. Illegal or not, there was no other route. By land the journey from Ostia to Rome was fifteen miles, a weary ride for any pack mule and far more conspicuous than simply bribing a port official to look the other way while the barge was unloaded.

The waterfront was a filthy place. The slaves who worked it were treated little better than the field slaves who broke their backs tilling the rural estates of many Roman notables. Narcissus could see a group of them now, bowed under the weight of a huge crate as they hauled it from barge to shore. One slip and they'd all be crushed beneath it, but the citizen who commanded them didn't seem to care, flicking his whip against their calves as he shouted at them to move faster.

If the port master was being bribed, there would be no point asking him about the missing cargo. And the freemen here all worked for him, so Narcissus doubted he'd get anything from them, either. That left the slaves. He watched them working, waiting for a pause, a break for them to recuperate when he could question them without interruption.

It was only after half an hour that he realised there wasn't going to be one. The anger he felt surprised him. He'd known all his life the way things were, that some were born free and others into servitude and the gods said this was just, though no one had ever been able to explain why. But cosseted by Claudius in the Imperial Palace, it had been easy to ignore what that really meant. Here, there was no denying it.

Five more minutes and he snapped.

He strode to the nearest overseer, wrenched the whip from his hand and threw it to the ground. "Enough."

The overseer's cold gaze took in his simple tunic, the wooden tag on his neck that marked him as a slave. He raised his arm to strike Narcissus in the face.

Another arm caught it. A stringy, wire-haired man pulled the overseer back, holding on tight until he could see the fight had gone out of him. "This is Claudius's man," he said. "Have a care."

The overseer's eyes widened and he turned to Narcissus, suddenly abject rather than arrogant. "I didn't know. If you'd said you were here..." He held up his hands, backing away. "Apologies."

It was the first time in Narcissus's life he'd ever inspired fear. He wasn't sure he liked it, but it had saved him a beating, or worse. "Thank you," he said to the newcomer.

The man inclined his head. "Sextus. You won't remember me, but I'm an old friend of your master's. It's my ship they're offloading right now – and putting my cargo at risk by working the men doing it into the ground. I've had two crates of fine Syrian glassware shattered by these oafs, and not a hint of compensation."

"Shattered glass," Narcissus said. "Of course."

Sextus looked at him through narrowed eyes. "And men maimed or killed to no purpose. A waste all round."

Narcissus felt himself relax a little. "Indeed, dominus."

"Even watching this is thirsty work. A drink with me in the shade, perhaps?" He slung an arm over Narcissus's shoulder without waiting for an answer, leading him to a low table in the shadow of the docks.

The wine was welcome after the long walk, and Narcissus gulped it gratefully. When he looked up again, Sextus's eyes were sharp on him. "So, what interest of Claudius's brings you to these parts?"

Narcissus looked away. "I'm not here for Claudius, dominus. I'm on the Emperor's business."

"Ah." Sextus leaned forward, steepling his fingers on the table in front of him. "The *Khert-Neter*, perhaps?"

Narcissus knew the answer was written on his face. The other man smiled and clapped a companionable hand on his shoulder. "It's no secret round here, boy. We all drop some gold into the harbour master's hand now and again, to see our cargoes unloaded first or fastest. But every week, when that ship comes in..."

"We think..." Narcissus hesitated, but Sextus had given him no reason not to trust him. "It's been suggested they might be smuggling something in to Rome."

"Bringing a cargo they don't want examined, that's for sure." Sextus nodded to his right, to the far side of the docks where a lone warehouse sat separate from the rest. "They put it in there, and that's the last we see of it. Don't ask me what it is; I doubt there's a man on this dock who knows. And whoever runs that ship has enough gold to ensure it stays that way."

Narcissus studied the warehouse. It looked newly built, the wooden slats still pale where the axe had shaped them, untarnished nails holding them together. "In there?"

"Yes." Sextus tipped another splash of wine into Narcissus's goblet. "The owners of the *Khert-Neter* are powerful men, influential. And that warehouse is tucked away out of sight, hard to find unless you're looking for it. If I hadn't been here, you might never have discovered it. If you returned to the Emperor and reported that you had found nothing, no one would ever question you."

Narcissus wondered for a moment if he was being threatened, but he saw only kindness in the other man's face. "Thank you, dominus. I understand. Unfortunately, I have to know."

"Your choice," the other man said, but he didn't look as if he thought it was a wise one.

THE DOOR WAS locked. Well, of course it was. Boda shot a look at the young man she'd met behind the pillar – who'd introduced himself as Petronius of the Octavii – but he was frowning in obvious bafflement. She didn't think he could have seen more than sixteen summers, his body gawky and angular as if he hadn't quite grown into it yet, but the potential for beauty was there in the soft, half-formed lines of his face.

"Well, I suppose that puts a stop to our plans," he said. He scratched a hand back through his mop of dark, curling hair.

She shook her head disbelievingly at him. "If the door needs a key, we'll find it."

"How?"

"You!" She grabbed a passing slave, pulling him round to face them. "My master wants entry here."

The slave's eyes flicked between her and Petronius nervously, finally settling on him. "But there's nothing there, dominus," he stammered. "It's a store cupboard for towels."

"And a fresh towel is precisely what I need." Petronius's smile was charming, and he obviously knew it.

"I can fetch you one –"

"Open it," Boda said coldly. "Or my master will be displeased."

The slave studied Petronius, as if trying to work out what form his displeasure might take. Then he looked at Boda and swallowed hard, perhaps realising that her own was likely to be more immediate and painful.

"At once." He bowed and scurried off.

"Well," Petronius said when they were alone. "Now we've alerted everyone to what we're doing, it only remains for us to be denied entry and our mission will be complete."

"Tell them you belong inside, and they'll believe you," she said.

"Why?"

She sighed. "Because you're a free man, and they are slaves, and they've been raised their whole lives to obey."

He looked dubious, but she was right. A minute later another man approached, older and less nervous, and pressed a small iron key into Petronius's hand. "Apologies, dominus," he said. "I thought all were inside today."

He backed away, bowing, as Petronius bent to put the key in the lock. But when he drew level with Boda, he paused. "Don't go in," he whispered, too low for Petronius to hear.

She spun to face him, but he wasn't looking at her. He shook his head, a warning. "Listen to me, woman. Our kind go through that door, and they never come out again." And then he was gone, quick strides carrying him to the far side of the atrium.

"What was that about?" Petronius asked, peering back over his shoulder.

"Nothing." She shook her head. "Nothing important."

Petronius shrugged and turned back to the door. It swung open silently, revealing a dim cavity beyond. He gestured her before him, but she shook her head and after a moment he strode through. She took one last look behind her, searching for the other slave in the crowd, but he was long gone. Then she sighed and walked in after Petronius.

Only to find herself pressed up against his back, a mere two paces from the door. It slammed shut behind them, plunging them into darkness.

"Why have you stopped?" she said.

Petronius sighed. "Because we are, in fact, in a cupboard. With a lot of towels."

She reached forward, ignored his yelp as her hand collided with his hip, and eased herself round his slender body. He was right – in front of him there was a shelf and her questing fingers found soft folds of material stacked on top of it.

But Quintus had come through here, and those other people. This couldn't be what it appeared. She braced her feet against the floor, then pushed forward against the shelf with all her strength.

For a moment, her feet slid backwards on the marble floor and the shelf remained stubbornly as it was. Then her heel caught in the gap between two slabs and she stopped moving backwards as her arms started to move forward. The shelves groaned as they slid back, splinters of wood shaved from the sides by the walls.

When she'd finished, the cupboard was five paces deeper and the trapdoor in the floor beneath was fully exposed. Boda pulled on the metal ring set in its centre, and it swung open with little effort. A waft of dank and unwholesome air swirled through the gap. Beneath, the darkness was almost absolute, only the faint orange hint of torches somewhere in the distance.

Petronius swallowed hard. "After you," he said.

THERE WERE GUARDS on the warehouse, but only two of them, fine-boned Egyptians in short white kilts. Every five minutes their patrol route took them to opposite ends of the building, the entrance unwatched between them. Narcissus waited until the second time it happened, then darted though the doorway, sending up a silent prayer of thanks that it was unlocked.

Inside, the overriding smell was of wood sap and saltwater, strong but not unpleasant. There weren't as many crates as he'd expected, only ten or so scattered over the floor, with smudged footprints in the sawdust between them. He circled them cautiously, looking for anything hidden between them, but there was nothing there. All the way from Egypt, and they'd only brought ten crates. It didn't look like a major smuggling operation at all.

At first, he barely noticed the sound. But gradually it began to intrude on his consciousness, a dry, high-pitched chittering. He tilted his head, trying to identify the source, but it seemed to be coming from all around him. It was, he realised with an unpleasant shock, coming from inside the crates.

There was something alive in there.

A thin, cold sweat broke out on his chest and arms. His body rebelled at the thought of getting any closer to the source of that sound and he found himself backing away until he was leaning against the wooden wall of the warehouse.

But this was ridiculous. Finding out what was in those crates was exactly why he'd risked so much to come here. And Julia had been right. There was something coming into Rome from Egypt that wasn't being recorded. Something living.

It took a fierce effort of will to force himself forwards. His feet dragged through the sawdust, leaving long thin scuff marks behind him. He realised that he'd balled his hands into fists, and concentrated on unclenching them, one finger at a time.

By the time he'd finished, he was standing beside the first crate. The sound was louder close to, a clicking and a scratching that grew more frantic as he approached, as if whatever lived inside could sense him. He licked suddenly dry lips, wishing he'd drunk more of Sextus's wine before he came here.

The crate would be very easy to open. It was held shut with nothing but twine and a couple of small rocks on top to weigh down the lid. He removed one of these, paused, removed the other – and now he could see the crate shaking. Vibrating, as if whatever was inside was flinging itself against the walls in a desperate attempt to escape.

He waited a lot longer before starting to untangle the twine. It was only the sound of voices outside that startled him into action, and his fingers fumbled as he worked, shaking too hard to get a firm grip. He bit down on his lip, trying to get himself under control, and finally the knot began to work lose.

He was pulling the last twist of twine free when the lid of the crate rose under its own power. He gasped and stumbled back, an instant later moving forward again, throwing himself against the lid to keep it closed.

Too late. The crate gave one final shudder and the lid fell to the floor with a crash.

For a second, Narcissus thought there was nothing inside but earth, little round balls of it, packed so tight the crate bulged at the sides. Then the first ball moved, stretching translucent brown wings behind it. The chittering grew in volume, louder and louder, and now Narcissus understood that it was the sound of legs rubbing against each other, against ridged carapaces, scratching against the walls of the crate.

The first beetle launched into the air towards him, and a moment later a thousand more followed behind.

CHAPTER THREE

THE BEETLES WERE everywhere, small dry legs pattering over his stomach and back and neck, crawling through his hair and under his clothes. They stank of the worst kind of filth. Narcissus froze into horrified immobility. And then, before he'd consciously decided to do it, he ran.

He could see nothing, one hand over his eyes to protect them from the razor-sharp jaws of the beetles, and he hit the far wall with an impact that jarred from his elbows to his backbone. His fingers scrabbled, desperately searching for a door that wasn't there. Splinters of wood lodged painfully beneath his nails and he realised with a sick shock that he was making exactly the same sound the beetles had made inside the crate. Mindless creatures fighting to escape.

Sweat was running down his back. He felt some of the beetles slipping, legs floundering for purchase in the moisture. It was the most horrible sensation he'd ever experienced. After that he couldn't think at all. He just ran, into another wall, then another, stumbling to his knees halfway across the floor only to push himself upright as a torrent of insects headed towards him.

It was sheer chance that led him to the door, and for a second he didn't realise what it was. He'd almost pushed off again, driven by the overwhelming urge to run, run, run when he realised that it was metal beneath his fingers, not wood. Hinges.

He felt the bodies of beetles squashed to a pulpy liquid beneath his hand as he fumbled, trying to find the handle, trying to get out. But all he found was more wood and eventually he was forced to take his hand away from his eyes.

When he opened them, it was like a vision of Hades. The beetles were everywhere, blunt and brown and clinging. His own body crawled with them, five or ten thick so that he could barely see the skin beneath. He let out a muffled whimper of horror, unable to open his mouth for fear of letting the creatures in. But there, finally, he could see it, and he yanked the handle down with the last of his strength and tumbled out into daylight.

All around him the beetles took flight, a black seething cloud heading high into the sky. A moment later they were gone, over the warehouse and away.

He drew in a deep, shuddering breath of relief and fell to his knees, lifting his face to the sun and shutting his eyes.

When he opened them, he saw the two guards. They were staring at him with expressions of shock slowly transmuting into rage.

He didn't think there was any strength left in him. But he used what little he had to drive himself to his feet and stumble away, back towards the docks. He could feel runnels of liquid coursing down his cheeks and arms and he knew that not all of it was sweat. The creatures had bitten and scratched him, a thousand wounds that suddenly started to tell him how much they hurt.

He had no breath left to cry for help, even if he'd been certain it would come. He could hear the guards at his heels. He didn't dare waste the time to snatch a look behind him, but he knew they'd been armed. He imagined their swords, poised above their heads for a killing blow, and his heart somehow found the strength to pump a little harder and his legs to run a little faster.

A second later and he was in the maze of port buildings. He dodged right and left, jumping over abandoned barrels and sometimes weaving in and out of the buildings themselves, his breath like fire in his lungs. He didn't know where he was going – nearer the city, further away – only that he had to escape.

Another warehouse loomed straight ahead of him, and he wrenched open the door and flung himself inside. He was so intent on his pursuers behind that he didn't notice the man in front until he'd run straight into him. They fell to the floor together in a tangle of limbs and Narcissus struck out without thinking, the primitive part of him that cared only about living overriding all civilisation.

The other man caught his fist in his palm, wincing at the impact. "Easy," he said. "I can help."

Narcissus tried to wrench his hand free, and after a moment the other man let him. "Who are you?" he gasped.

The other man laughed. "Does it matter?" He was red-haired, a barbarian, with a sharp nose and a mobile, mocking mouth.

Narcissus scrambled to his feet and the other man followed, moving with a grace that Narcissus couldn't emulate. "It matters to me," he said.

The man bowed. "Then I am Vali, a stranger here. And you are about to be caught, unless you do precisely as I say."

Narcissus opened his mouth to argue – then closed it again as he heard the sound of the warehouse door opening and guttural shouting in Egyptian. More than two voices now; the guards must have found reinforcements.

He turned to Vali, though he didn't know how he could help. The man wasn't even armed.

Vali smiled. "Some fights can't be won – only avoided." And then he stepped aside, and Narcissus saw that there was a crate behind him, half-filled with jars of olive oil. "I threw the rest out earlier. Plenty of room for both of us in here."

There wasn't time to argue. Narcissus scrambled in, bleeding arms and legs jarring painfully against the awkwardly shaped glass, worse when the other man climbed in after, pulling the lid shut behind him.

A second later he heard the Egyptians, moving through the building as they shouted incomprehensibly to each other in their own language. He held his breath, too afraid of being heard to ask Vali the hundred questions clamouring for answers, but they circled in his mind as he crouched and shivered. And the loudest of them was: if Vali had already prepared their hiding place in advance, how had he known that they'd be needing it?

THE STEPS BENEATH the baths led a very long way down. Boda descended without any sign of fear, but Petronius could feel a sour lump in his stomach, threatening to head north. He paused a moment to swallow it back, then scrambled to catch up. The only thing worse than being down here would be being down here alone.

Boda waited for him at the bottom, squatting on her haunches with a look of supreme unconcern. They were in a natural cavern, chill and wet. It was too dark to make out much detail, but he saw the shadows of paintings on the wall, relics of a civilisation older than Rome's.

"What is this place?" he whispered.

Boda shrugged. "I don't know. But whoever built the bath house must have known about it."

That was a sobering thought. The bath house had been here as long as Petronius could remember. He vaguely remembered his father telling him that it had been constructed as part of the public works Emperor Augustus had commissioned in the city. Thirty years ago? Fifty? Whatever Seneca was involved in, it didn't seem likely that it was just smuggling banned books from Egypt.

Boda pointed to the far side of the cavern, where a tunnel could just be seen, snaking up. "The light's coming from that direction."

Petronius was prepared to take her word for it. She seemed to know what she was doing. In fact, she didn't really seem to need him there at all. For a brief moment he entertained the thought of turning round, climbing back up the wooden ladder and leaving her to it.

He'd never been this afraid before. He'd thought he had – he thought he was frightened last year when his father very nearly caught him in bed with his business partner's wife. This, though, was the real thing. His father would just have given him a beating. He had no idea what would happen if he was caught snooping around here, but he didn't think it would be good. His body could rot down here a very long time before anyone found it.

Some of what he was thinking must have showed in his face. Boda was staring at him narrow-eyed and impatient. "Are you coming?" she snapped. "Or are you going?"

And then again, he thought, Seneca could have come down here for some innocent – or at least safe – reason. Sexual recreation, perhaps. At the end of that tunnel he might be confronted with nothing more than the sight of the old man balls-deep in a woman, which would certainly be unpleasant, but definitely not fatal.

"I'm coming," he said.

She took his arm, guiding him over the uneven floor of the cavern. His sandals slapped on the wet rock, echoes of the sound bouncing from the walls. She frowned and motioned to her own feet, showing him how she slid them forward without lifting them. He copied her, and as the fear receded he realised that he was starting to enjoy himself. He was having an adventure, something he could tell Flavius the next time he boasted about his convoy being chased by Gauls all the way to the Rubicon.

She released his arm when they came to the tunnel, too narrow for them to walk side by side. There was a sound from up ahead, a muffled babble of voices that implied more people than the four they'd seen enter, a lot more. Still, their chatter should cover any sound that he and Boda made.

"So," he whispered, "what brings a lovely girl like you to a place like this?"

She turned to frown at him, then said: "Quintus is hiding something, I know it."

"Well, obviously." Her body blocked the dim light that shone back through the tunnel, and he trailed a hand against the wall to guide himself through the darkness. "What exactly do you think he's hiding?"

"A reason why he'd arrange for one of his own gladiators to be killed. And why he'd mutilate the body afterwards."

"Oh." He stopped, suddenly very sure that turning back was a good idea. Dead bodies, mutilated ones – these weren't the sort of adventure he had in mind.

He turned to go, and found her hand clawing at his arm to stop him. He opened his mouth to protest and her other hand clapped over it. Her eyes bored into his, demanding something. Silence, he supposed. When he blinked acknowledgement she released him, dropped to her knees and gesture to him to do the same.

Without her body to block it, he saw what lay ahead. The tunnel opened into another chamber, broader than the first, its walls carved flat and smooth. He couldn't see Seneca, but that wasn't very surprising. There were at least fifty people here and Petronius recognised a large number of them, the great and the good of Rome. They were chatting, laughing and drinking wine from crystal goblets, as if this was just another social gathering, an informal dinner party for close friends.

But it wasn't. He counted twelve coffins, leaning against the walls at regularly spaced intervals. The guests ignored them, but Petronius was unable to look away, however much he might have wanted to.

The coffins were open. Inside each, he could see bandage-wrapped corpses, and even from his hiding place in the tunnel he could smell the stench of death that wafted from them. All that, though, all that might have been bearable, if the corpses hadn't been moving.

PUBLIA TRIED NOT to look inside the coffins. She could see the movement out of the corner of her eye, the white flicker as bandaged arms and legs twitched, but she did her best to ignore it, as everyone else seemed to be doing. It wouldn't do to look like naïve yokels gaping in shock at these big city ways.

Which was precisely what her husband was doing. "Antoninus!" she hissed, stamping on his foot to stop him gawping quite so openly.

He turned to her, face blank with shock. "They're alive. They're dead – but they're alive."

"Of course." She laughed gaily, in case anyone more important was listening. "I'm sure this sort of thing goes on in Rome all the time."

"Does it?" He looked a little sick, though it had been his idea to join the Cult of Isis in the first place, and his business partner who'd proposed them for membership. Antoninus had seen it as a way of expanding his network of contacts, perhaps securing a few more lucrative contracts for his slave-importation business.

Publia had understood that it could be much more than that. The Cult could be their route to social acceptance, to a class above the one they'd been born to. She couldn't say that she liked everything they stood for. She'd been brought up traditionally, to honour Jupiter and Juno, the divine parents of them all, and steer clear of foreign gods, who were seldom to be trusted. But all around her she could see evidence of the power of the Egyptian deities – and more importantly, of the power of those who worshipped them. If she and Antoninus played it right, her four-year-old son might not grow up to be a merchant like his father. He could be a senator, or even a consul. They just had to ingratiate themselves with the right people.

There was one of them now: Seneca, who was said to have the ear of the Emperor himself. He didn't look like much, skinny and stooped, but Publia put on her best smile as she approached him. "An honour, sir – I can't tell you how thrilled my husband and I are to be here."

Seneca looked at her and Antoninus a long moment, clearly trying to remember who they were. Then something seemed to click in his memory and he smiled back. "The slave traders, of course. You're most welcome."

"I've long venerated Isis," Publia said, gesturing to the cow-headed statue behind the altar. "It's such a relief to find others of a like mind."

"Indeed. And for us it was like a blessing from the goddess herself to find a supplicant with such a plentiful supply of slaves."

"I'm sure it was," Antoninus said dryly, and Publia stood on his toe again. She knew he'd bitterly resented the five slaves they'd been told they needed to offer to the goddess to secure their membership. And a final one tomorrow night, before their initiation would be complete. Expensive in terms of gold but cheap when you thought what it might buy them.

"We were glad to dedicate them to the service of Isis," Publia said. "I hope they've proven useful – we did send you our very best."

"Oh yes." A slight smile twitched at the corner of Seneca's mouth. "They were exactly what we required." His eyes wandered the room, sweeping over the twitching bodies in their coffins, and his smile widened.

Publia followed his gaze. There were slaves mingling with the crowd, pouring the wine and handing round small snacks, oysters and stuffed dates, but she didn't think any of them were the ones Antoninus had supplied. She distinctly remembered that one of them had been a Nubian – she'd been fascinated by the deep blue black of his skin – and no one here looked like they hailed from south of the Mediterranean.

"And now your initiation is almost complete," Seneca said.

Publia paused, her eye caught by a flicker of movement to her left, in the entrance tunnel. Was it her imagination, or were there two figures crouching there?

Seneca raised an enquiring eyebrow.

"I think," she said, "that we have some uninvited guests."

*   *   *

IT TOOK BODA a second too long to realise they'd been spotted. She'd been watching Quintus as he circulated through the crowd, trying to figure out his place among them. Respected, she decided, but not honoured. He bowed too low and smiled too ingratiatingly to be among equals.

And then she saw the smile drop from his face, and his eyes darted towards her – just for a moment – before darting away again. He knew she was there and he'd been told not to show it.

"Move," she said to Petronius. "Get up – we've been seen."

He froze as a flash of terror crossed his face, already pale from what they'd witnessed. She knew she was faster and stronger than him. She could outrun him and leave him to slow their pursuers. He was a citizen of Rome, one of those who'd enslaved her, and she owed him nothing.

But she still found herself dragging his arm to get him moving, then pushing him in front of her. Maybe it was because he was still so young. Or maybe it was because no one should be left to those things they'd seen, the twitching corpses in their wooden boxes.

They were behind her now. She could smell the death-stench of them and hear the rustle of their bandages as they ran. Petronius stumbled on the uneven floor, falling to his knees, and she had to waste precious seconds hauling him to his feet. She felt the brush of skeletal fingers against her back, and despite herself she cried out in fear, a base animal reaction to a thing that should not be.

The creature behind her answered, its voice a dry rattle. She heard its teeth snapping together, the clash of bone on bone, and she knew that if Petronius fell she wouldn't stop for him again.

But the boy kept his feet and fear drove them both through the tunnel and into the cavern beyond. Petronius was chanting a Latin prayer between desperate pants of breath. She realised she was doing the same, begging Tiu to spare her this death – to grant her any death but this.

When they reached the ladder and began a desperate climb, she looked down at their pursuers for the first time. The bandages had begun to loosen in the flight through the tunnel. She could see skin beneath at shoulder and waist and hip, grey-green and rotting. A hand reached up to grab her ankle, putrid flesh falling away as it grasped to reveal the white bone beneath.

She kicked out. The toe of her sandal caught the thing beneath its chin and the head snapped back, spewing corpse fluid through its jagged teeth. Another kick and it fell back the twenty feet to the floor below, leaving its hand still clamped to her leg.

The hand twitched and started to inch its way up her calf, and this time Boda couldn't control the scream that bubbled out of her throat. She scraped her other foot along her leg, peeling skin and not caring because a second kick dislodged the hand to fall and shatter on the rock below. Droplets of blood from the raw scrape on her leg splattered on top of it, falling faster as she pulled herself up the ladder, sending the blood racing through her veins.

And then, finally, she was at the top, pressed against Petronius as he shoved at the trapdoor. One of the walking dead was only eight rungs below and closing fast. The rest clustered at the foot of the ladder. When the corpse that was pursuing them pulled them down, the others would be waiting. She couldn't see their eyes beneath the bandages, just the blank white of their faces as they looked up. And still Petronius was pushing against the closed door.

"Hurry!" she shouted.

"I'm trying!" he gasped. But then he gave one final shove and the trapdoor swung open with a hollow thud.

She lifted her arms from the ladder to push him through, ignoring his grunt of protest. Her own feet wobbled and slipped on the slick wood of the rungs and for a terrible moment she thought she was going to fall, into the waiting arms of the dead below. Then Petronius's hand reached through, grasping her wrist and jerking up hard enough to tear the ligaments in her shoulder.

She stifled the cry of pain and used the last of her strength to leap up, fingers scrabbling for purchase on the marble floor around the trapdoor. They slipped, slipped again, and then held in a crack between slabs. And finally she was able to lever herself up and through and she didn't even pause for breath, just slammed the trapdoor shut behind her.

A second later the door bounced on its hinges as the thing below pushed up with inhuman strength. Petronius flung himself on it, an act of bravery that seemed to take him by surprise. His eyes widened in horror as he realised what he'd done.

And it wasn't enough. A decaying hand crept round the edge of the wood to fumble at his arm. He shuddered and drew back.

Boda stepped over him, ignoring his yelp of pain as his fingers were caught beneath the heel of her sandal. The shelves were even heavier than she remembered and she was at the last of her strength. One tug, two, and they remained stubbornly in place. Then another body was pressed up behind her, two big male hands over her own, and finally the shelves were moving, grating over the stone floor with a nerve-jangling screech.

Boda had one last, brief glimpse of the undead creature. The bandage had ripped from half its face and she could see the flesh beneath, hanging in decaying strips from the hinge of its jaw. Its eyes, the milky-white of blindness, glared malevolently at her. Then the weight of the shelves slammed the trapdoor shut.

* * *

CLAUDIUS TRIED NOT to worry. He knew that his nephew could read every emotion on his face. The more concerned he seemed for Narcissus, the more Caligula would torment him.

But he'd been down to the records room twice now, and there was no sign of the young man. The other slave there, the head-touched one whom Caligula had maimed, claimed that Narcissus had been sent on an errand and would be back any minute. Claudius had been prepared to believe that the first time. Now... He pictured Narcissus's thin, not-quite handsome face, his cautious smile, and his stomach clenched.

"You look troubled, uncle," Caligula said.

Claudius's head jerked to the doorway, sending a fine spray of spittle from his open mouth. He'd thought the Emperor would be kept busy entertaining himself with his latest lover, the sixteen-year-old wife of Senator Flavius. He thought he'd have longer.

"No t-t-trouble," Claudius said. "Merely moved by the t-t-travails of Troy." He set aside the scroll of the *Iliad* he'd been trying to read to distract himself from his fears.

The light had fled the atrium this late in the day, and his nephew's face was in shadows. A lone sparrow twittered in the silence, the water of the fountain behind it wetting its drab wings.

"Well," Caligula said. "I must say, your man Narcissus is proving a disappointment. You always spoke so highly of him, but I set him a task and he's shirking already. You don't happen to know where's he's hidden himself, do you?"

The Emperor's expression was bland, but Claudius had long practise at reading the malice lurking in the depths of his light eyes.

He nodded. "I sent him to the market, nephew. W-w-was that wrong?" He kept his face open and guileless as Caligula studied it and, after a second, the other man let out an annoyed huff of breath and turned away.

"He's my slave now, uncle – *mine!* In future, you must ask my permission to use him."

"Of course." Claudius bowed his head in submission, and when he looked up again, his nephew had gone. But the lie would only satisfy him for an hour or so. If Narcissus didn't return before the sun set, there would be nothing Claudius could do to protect him.

PETRONIUS AND BODA didn't stop running until they reached the Forum. Lost in the crowd there, and in the fading light of day, they finally felt something like safety.

Petronius leaned against a marble wall, beside a red-and-blue-painted statue of Minerva, and gasped for breath. Someone had set the stuffed body of a snowy owl by the goddess. A faint smell of badly preserved flesh drifted from the offering, and he had to swallow hard to keep the contents of his stomach down.

He could hear Boda's ragged breathing beside him, keeping pace with his own. When he turned to look at her, he realised that she was laughing. A part of him wanted to join in, a desperate release of tension, but he was very much afraid that what started as laughter might dissolve into tears.

"So," she said. "We can at least be certain that something is going on."

"That was..." Petronius didn't know how to complete the sentence. Terrifying? Impossible?

"Raising the dead is forbidden among my people. Is it different here?"

Petronius did laugh at that, a jagged bark quickly cut off. "Of course it's forbidden here. It doesn't happen here! That must have been... I've heard about these cults, the shows they put on to impress initiates. It's all smoke and mirrors – a con trick!"

"A con trick?" She stared at him incredulously.

He nodded, convincing himself as he failed to convince her. "Yes – of course. Keep the light low, dress up a few followers in bandages and there you have it. Something to scare the plebs."

"And us," she said dryly. "This was no trick. The things that attacked us were the bodies of the slain. I saw the flesh falling from their bones!"

"No," he said. "No. The peasants still believe that sort of superstitious nonsense. But we're educated people, or at least I am. I've found out Seneca's secret, and it's nothing that matters. The mystery cults have never been banned. If he wants to take part in their theatrics, it's his business. I had no right to follow him, and I won't do it again."

Now she simply looked disgusted. Petronius started to turn away from the contempt in her blue eyes.

She didn't let him, grabbing his chin and forcing him to face her. It was a whipping offence for a slave to treat a citizen that way, but he didn't say anything. A twist of her wrist would snap his neck like kindling. He'd seen it happen in the Arena often enough.

She must have read something in his face, because she abruptly released him. "That's not good enough. The man outside the door, the one who gave us the key, he told me that slaves disappear in those caves. They go in but they don't come out. Don't you wonder what happens to them?"

Petronius shrugged, drawing a deep breath to steady his voice. "They're just slaves."

He had a minute of long cold silence to regret saying it. Then she nodded. "Of course. Roman, I understand." She looked at him a moment longer, then spun on her heel and stalked into the crowd.

Petronius watched her go, her blonde hair a beacon that drew his eyes as she moved away. He thought about chasing after her, but he knew that he wouldn't. She was beautiful but dangerous, and the world was full of men and women who were only the former. And in the end she was just a barbarian and a slave. Her problems weren't his, and he'd be a fool to make them so.

NARCISSUS DIDN'T KNOW how long they lay inside the crate. Long enough for the arm trapped beneath him to go entirely numb, and for the pervasive smell of olive oil to transmute from pleasant to unbearable. At one point, he felt the crate being shifted, rattling the jars together and pushing his face so hard against the wood it left the imprint of the grain on his cheek.

His heart clenched tight in his chest, but the lid never lifted and as the rattling went on and on, he realised that the crate was being moved, not searched. Five more minutes and it was set down again, somewhere so dark that not even a sliver of light penetrated between the wooden slats.

He was painfully aware of the second body pressed up against his, an elbow in his ribs and a knee digging into the soft flesh of his thigh. He could hear the other man's breathing, slow and steady, but he didn't say a word and Narcissus didn't either. He pictured the Egyptian guards in their white kilts, standing by the crates and waiting for them to give themselves away.

Time lost all meaning in the darkness. A day could have passed or only an hour, but the waiting finally became too much, and the risk of getting caught here less than the risk of being found missing from the Palace. He didn't give himself time to worry about it, just braced his feet against the slick glass of the bottles and pushed up.

The lid instantly lifted, far faster than he'd anticipated. He made a desperate grab for the wood before it could fall. His fingers clutched and missed but the lid stopped anyway and he saw that another hand, paler and finer than his own, was slowly easing it to the ground.

Vali smiled at him, a wide grin under his sharp nose.

"Where are we?" Narcissus whispered. The room they were in looked like part of a warehouse, with wooden walls and a sawdust-covered floor stacked with similar crates, but it wasn't the same one they'd entered. Had the crate been shifted to another part of the docks?

"Listen," Vali said.

Narcissus tilted his head, straining for the sound of pursuit. Nothing at first, and then footsteps, coming from above. "Do they know we're here?" he mouthed.

Vali shook his head. "Listen," he said again.

The feet were still pacing, more than one pair of them, but Narcissus tried to hear beyond them. Nothing. It was quiet here, no voices, only the soft sound of the wind, rising and falling outside the walls. Except, no, there was something too regular about that noise, a push and pull that the wind never had. And something else, too, a gentle slapping that sounded like water.

And as soon as he became aware of that, he became aware of the motion too. The floor, the whole building, was swaying from side to side. He'd only failed to notice it because it had been going on so long – since the crates had been moved.

It took him five minutes of frantic searching to find a knothole in the wall big enough to see through. He pressed his eye to it, blinking against the stinging salt spray.

The horizon was miles distant, a dividing line between blues, one dark and troubled, the other light and clear. The ship was already a long way out to sea, not a speck of land in sight.

CHAPTER FOUR

When Quintus told Boda she was to fight in the Arena that day, she knew he'd seen her in the Cult's hideaway. She could read it in his face, the calculating look in his watery eyes. And she knew it because she wasn't supposed to be fighting. No gladiator was expected to do battle on two consecutive days. There could be only one reason he was sending her out there. This time he meant for her to die.

Her shoulder still pained her from when Petronius had yanked her to safety. The tendon was inflamed and she barely had the strength to lift a sword. Not that that would matter. She wasn't to use a sword this time – Quintus had decreed that she was to fight as a Retiarius, with trident and net.

She'd never practised with those weapons. Quintus knew it, and so did the other gladiators. She saw them watching her as she stretched her muscles in the training ground. There was no warmth in their eyes and she knew that they'd give her no quarter. Quintus had whispered to them too, no doubt giving them permission to go for the killing stroke. He needn't have bothered. They hadn't forgiven her for Josephus's death, and this was their chance for revenge.

When she stepped into the Arena the sun was at its peak and the same crowd thronged the stands. Boda hated them even more, because they'd come to watch her die, and she was afraid that today they'd get their wish. The ache in her shoulder throbbed in time with her strides, and the trident felt clumsy and too heavy in her hands.

The gladiators weren't the first spectacle that day. A group of prisoners from Gaul had been set against a pride of lions, and the carnage of that unequal battle lay all around: a severed hand already black with flies, gobs of blood and torn hair. Boda remembered Josephus's body, torn open on a slab, and wondered if hers would end the same way.

The crowd roared when their fight began. She'd been paired against Adam ben Meir, a close friend of Josephus's and the most skilled of them with a sword. He swung it now, too swift to parry with the longer trident, and it cut across her ribs. She saw the blood a moment before she felt the pain. Another slash of his sword and a line of fire opened high on her chest.

If she let him rule the fight, she was finished. Though it pulled agonisingly at her torn shoulder, she flung the net low at his feet, as she'd seen the other gladiators do.

He was already moving, leaping over the net and inside the reach of her trident. She used it as a stave instead, knocking aside his sword arm when he drove it towards her leg. In the second it bought her she rolled out and away. But her feet tangled in her own net, and when she regained them she'd lost her hold on it. Now she had nothing but the trident to defend herself with.

There was a shriek from the crowd, half fear, half pleasure. They knew that she was finished. She knew it too, but she refused to give in. This time she would face her death with honour.

Another slash of Adam's sword, and this time her forearm took the blow. The flesh parted in a neat line, exposing the thin yellow layer of fat beneath before blood bloomed red and covered it all.

It was her weapon hand. Her trident drooped and nearly dropped and she shifted it to the other hand. But this arm was weaker still and she could do little more than jab and retreat, never hoping to strike a killing blow.

Adam knew that he had her. The crowd groaned as he toyed with her, driving her first right, then left, knowing he could finish it at any time. A few more contemptuous strokes of his sword, and cuts opened on her thighs and stomach. His eyes glared into hers, with battle-rage and something else, something more personal. He wanted her to suffer before she died.

She knew that in a minute more she'd be too weak to fight, her wounds leaking her life away drop by drop. There was only one chance. She darted forward with the trident, a reckless but unexpected move that forced Adam back. She retreated herself, ten places clear of him and maybe far enough for what she intended. Her shoulder screamed in agony as she drew her arm back, but the heat of battle overcame the pain.

Adam knew what she was doing. He charged forward, snarling. No more games – he meant to kill her now. And then her arm moved forward and she threw the trident as hard as her abused body would allow.

For just a second, she thought she'd succeeded. Adam's eyes widened in shock, and the trident caught his sword on the down-slash and knocked it aside. Then it was through his guard and the metal tines were heading for his chest. And in an acrobatic move she wouldn't have expected from a man so large he twisted to the side, and the trident passed beneath his arm and behind him.

He smiled as he raised his sword and walked slowly towards her. Boda raised her head. It was over now, and in a way that was a relief. If death was inevitable, then fear became pointless.

"This is for Josephus," he hissed when he stood in front of her.

She nodded, accepting that, then bared her throat to him.

NARCISSUS SAT ON a crate, head cradled between his hands. This was worse than he could have imagined. Caligula must know he was gone by now, and if he didn't he soon would. Even if the ship turned straight round, he'd never get back to the palace in time. And if he simply left the ship at the end of its journey, kept on travelling, he'd be condemning himself to spend the rest of his life on the run. Crucifixion was the punishment for runaway slaves.

"I'm sorry," Vali said, sitting on the crate beside him.

Narcissus tilted his head, looking at the other man through one eye. He remembered that it had been his idea to hide in the crate. "It doesn't matter. If they'd caught me they would have killed me anyway."

"Probably." Vali stretched, then rose to his feet. "Since we're here, I suppose we may as well explore."

Narcissus remained seated. Now the first panic was over, the questions returned. "Who are you, anyway? Why did you help me? If that's what you were doing."

Vali tilted his head, considering, and Narcissus was quite sure he was deciding how much of the truth to tell him. Then he shrugged. "I heard of your investigation, and it matched my own."

"You're looking into smuggling?"

Vali shook his head. "No. Well, yes, but only as a by-product. I'm interested in the Cult of Isis."

"The Cult?" Narcissus had heard of them, of course. Claudius had attended a meeting once, but he hadn't gone again. Decadent and meaningless, he'd said. "They're Egyptian, I know – but shipping in crate-loads of beetles? Why?"

"They were scarab beetles," Vali said. "Carriers of death."

Narcissus stared at him, but that appeared to be as much of an answer as he was going to get. "And how did you know I was looking into this?

I didn't tell anyone." But as soon as he said it he pictured her sitting in the dark, with her pretty face and broken mind. "Did Julia tell you?"

Vali smiled and shrugged. "She is one of mine."

That was a non-answer, too, but the bland, unreadable expression on the other man's face told Narcissus he'd have to be satisfied with it. He sighed and rose to his feet, pacing the length of the storage room. "None of that matters now, anyway. Neither of us can do what we want until we get off this boat and back to Rome." He tried the handle of the door at the far end of the room and smiled to find it turning, unlocked.

Vali moved up beside him, placing a hand on top of his to still it. "Why would we want to leave here? This boat is taking us exactly where we want to go. We're on the *Khert-Neter* itself, didn't you realise?"

BODA SHUT HER eyes, waiting for the killing blow. She knew it would hurt, but not for long.

After a minute, as the noise of the crowd grew, she opened her eyes. Adam wasn't looking at her. He was frowning up into the stands, his sword slack at his side. She couldn't work out what had caught his attention at first. And then she saw him, high above and to the left, a lone figure on his feet and shouting, his fist raised in the air.

She couldn't make out what he was saying, but after a while the crowd took up his words and then she could hear them chanting: "Let her live, let her live, let her live!"

Something unfolded in her chest, sharp and painful. She thought it might be hope.

Adam looked back at her, his sword raised once again. She knew he was wondering if he could chance a killing blow before the demand to spare her became too loud to ignore. But the words were so clear now he couldn't deny them, and in the Emperor's box, she saw an upraised arm.

Adam flung his sword into the sand and walked away.

The spectators roared their approval. Boda found that she didn't know what to do. She tried to locate the original figure, the one who'd begun the cry to save her, but the whole crowd was on its feet now and he was lost in the multitude of white togas and brown faces.

So she just bowed, and hurried to the great gateway that led out of the Arena. The other fights were finished – none of them fatally – and the gladiators crowded around her. They stank of sweat and blood and she knew that she did too. But she was alive, when she hadn't thought she would be, and that warmed her stomach like beer.

There was a ceremony after, gold and a laurel wreath to the victor. Boda smiled and drifted through it, ignoring the hate-filled looks the other fighters gave her. But the expression on Quintus's face when they returned to the school was more troubling.

She knew he'd been in the crowd. He already knew his plan had failed, but in the hour since his rage had built. The instant she stepped through the door he struck her across the face.

She gasped and reeled back, more shocked than hurt. The old man had little strength in him.

"Useless bitch!" he said. "You call that a fight?"

She lifted her chin. "As much of one as you allowed me."

"You disgraced me! You made my school a laughing stock!" There were little flecks of spittle at the corner of his mouth. He wiped them away with a quick hand and struggled to compose himself. The fury in his eyes faded to be replaced by a more calculating light. A more dangerous one.

"You must be punished, of course," he said. "Two hundred lashes should suffice."

Two hundred lashes was near enough a death sentence – and a far worse way to die than sword-stuck in the Arena. Even some of the other gladiators murmured their protest.

Quintus ignored them. She guessed he'd have preferred to dispose of her more subtly. A death in the Arena would have aroused no comment while this might spark some questions. But she wouldn't be around to answer them, and that was what mattered to him. He gestured at two of his household slaves and they moved forward to seize her hands. She tensed her arms but didn't try to shake them off.

"Wait," Quintus said, as they began to drag her to the whipping post in the centre of the training ground. He leaned in, his mouth so close to her ear that she could feel the moist brush of his lips. "I'm sorry, my petal. Truly. But you've seen too much."

When he pulled back, she saw that his eyes were misty with tears, and she realised that he meant it. It was almost funny.

"Stop!" a new voice said. She thought it must be one of the other gladiators, their conscience pricked, and didn't bother to look up. There was nothing they could do. But the man spoke again and the men dragging her away stumbled to an uncertain halt.

It was Petronius. His deceptively guileless brown eyes darted towards her, and he sent her a brief, tight smile. Then he looked back at Quintus. "I can't have you whipping her."

Quintus looked baffled and Boda guessed that Petronius hadn't been spotted at the Cult meeting. Quintus didn't understand why the young man would want to intervene.

"It can be distressing, young sir," Quintus said. "But disobedient slaves must be punished."

Petronius nodded. "By their masters."

"Indeed." Quintus licked his lips, nervous, because although Petronius was agreeing, he wasn't going away. Instead, he walked to Boda and put a hand on her arm, drawing her gently away from the men holding her.

"Even when the crowd has chosen to spare them for their valiant display?" Petronius said. And something in his voice, some intonation, sparked Boda's memory. It had been Petronius who called for mercy in the Arena. He was the one who'd saved her life.

"Even then," Quintus said.

"Well, clearly you're a hard master. I, however, am more lenient. And as this slave is now my property, I choose to spare her this punishment."

Quintus's eyes bulged from his face. "Your property?"

Petronius smiled brilliantly, at Quintus and then at her. "That's right. I bought her from the school half an hour ago."

NARCISSUS DIDN'T WANT to explore the ship. Now he knew where they were, he didn't want to leave the safety of their crate for the remainder of the voyage. But Vali clearly intended to poke around, and Narcissus felt safer with him than he did on his own. So when Vali pressed his ear against the door, listening in silence, then pulled it sharply open, Narcissus found himself following behind.

The other man seemed to have some idea of where they were going. The below-decks area was cramped and crowded, a maze of storerooms filled with crates, all seeping a rich olive oil smell into the air. Vali wove a course that, five minutes later, took them to what appeared to be the ship's armoury. One wall held a rack of swords, polished and sharp, the other rows of round leather shields.

Vali took one sword for himself, pushing the scabbard through the belt of his tunic. He looked back at Narcissus, holding out another.

Narcissus shook his head. "I've never handled one. I don't know how."

Vali continued to hold out the sword. "Perhaps now would be a good time to learn."

But Narcissus stepped back, hands by his side. "I'd be more of a danger to myself than any enemies," he insisted.

The other man smiled at that and returned the sword to its rack. "As you wish."

Narcissus could hear footsteps again, above them on the deck. No more than four sets, and he was beginning to wonder if that was all there were. "What now?" he whispered. "Do we try to overpower them?"

Vali raised an eyebrow. "Can you sail a ship?"

Narcissus shook his head.

"Then it would probably be inadvisable."

He was right, but Narcissus couldn't stand the thought of being cooped up below decks for the entire journey, constantly wondering if they were about to be discovered. Fears, he was beginning to discover, were less frightful if you turned and confronted them head on.

"The sun's set," he said. "It should be dark enough to sneak on deck unseen. We could try to overhear what the sailors are saying."

Vali looked amused. "And do you speak Egyptian?"

"No!" Narcissus snapped. "But if you have a better plan, feel free to share it."

Vali's smile widened. "I do speak Egyptian, and I think your plan is absolutely fine."

It took them a while to locate the steps leading up; the narrow treads glistening white with caked salt. The crystals crunched gently beneath their feet and Narcissus winced at every step, but Vali didn't hesitate.

The moon was only a silver sliver in the far corner of the sky. A million stars shone bright around it, but none shed enough light to reveal Narcissus and Vali to the others on deck as they crept through the hatch.

Narcissus could hear the sailors, muttering softly near the sharp prow of the ship. He wanted to ask Vali what they were saying, but didn't dare risk it. Sound carried too clearly on the open water.

Vali laid a soft hand on his arm, then gestured forward.

The wind sighed through the rigging, a haunting, mournful sound. A haze of sea-spray hovered all around, and the deck beneath was spongy and slick. Narcissus trod carefully, securing one foot before he moved the next. The sailors were visible now, dark silhouettes against the distant moon, though their faces were hidden beneath deep cowls. He kept his eyes fixed on them, alert for any sign that they'd been spotted.

And because he was looking at the sailors, he didn't notice the tangle of ropes strung across the ship. They whipped his legs out from under him so fast he didn't have time to put out his hands to break his fall. His head met the deck with a meaty thud and he couldn't stop himself from calling out.

The sailors were on them before he'd regained his feet, moving faster than he could have guessed. A wicked-toothed knife jabbed towards his ribs and he rolled desperately. The blade sliced through his tunic and into the skin beneath, but the point hit wood and stuck there and he managed to scramble clear.

There were four of them, as he'd thought. Black-cloaked in the darkness, only the silver of their blades shone bright, and deep within their cowls the sparkle of eyes.

He dragged himself backwards and away from them. Splinters of wood drove beneath his skin, and he tried to regain his feet but his legs were wobbly with fear, and as the hooded figures approached he fell to his knees again. There was nowhere to escape to, anyway – nothing but sea all around.

He understood for the first time why people spoke about dying with dignity. He longed for the sword he'd refused earlier. He didn't want it to end like this, with him cowering in front of his killers.

And then Vali attacked. His sword carved graceful arcs through the air, a moonlit blur of movement. His aim was true and the metal bit deep into the chest of the nearest sailor.

It didn't even slow him. The man turned, jabbing his own blade forward in a less elegant but equally deadly thrust.

Vali leapt back, but now there were hidden ropes behind him. He stumbled, his sword arm flailing wildly as he fell. His blade missed flesh and instead caught and hooked in the hood of the nearest sailor. The material parted and fluttered to the ground.

At first, Narcissus thought it was a trick of the moonlight, the long blackness at the front of the man's face, the hint of curved teeth within. But then the man shifted slightly, the remainder of the hood fell away, and there was no more hiding what lay beneath.

The sailor had the head of a jackal on the shoulders of a man.

CHAPTER FIVE

NARCISSUS CRINGED BACK, crying out in fear. The jackal head swung towards him, jaws parting in a wide grin. A long pink tongue snaked out to lick the purple lips.

"You have seen us, mortal," the creature said. Its voice was slurred, as if the mouth wasn't made for human speech.

"I'm sorry," Narcissus babbled. "I'm sorry. I meant no blasphemy."

"These creatures aren't gods," Vali whispered.

Narcissus felt his bowels loosen. If these creatures weren't gods, then they must be something darker, the enemies of divinity – because they surely weren't human.

The creature let out a laugh that was almost a howl. "You are right to fear us, child of man. None who see us live to speak of it."

It knelt in front of him, reaching out to clasp his chin. Its hands were human, black and thin, but their touch burned like fire. Narcissus flinched and the creature's grip tightened.

"No escape," it said. "You will lie in these deep waters for all eternity and time will turn your bones to rock."

"Or," Vali said, "you might like to think about this for a minute." He sounded strained but unafraid.

The sailor released its grip on Narcissus and swung to face the other man. "In such a hurry to die? We care not which throat we slit first." It loomed over Vali, spittle dripping from its open mouth onto his cheek.

Vali brushed it away and Narcissus could see that it had left the skin red and blistered beneath. "But does it matter to you," he said, "why we're here? Or how we found you? If you kill us now you'll never know."

The sailor reared back while his comrades clustered closer, whispering in a guttural language that Narcissus didn't think was Egyptian or any other human tongue.

The one who seemed to be their leader turned back to Vali. "And will you answer those questions?" it said.

Vali smiled. "Will you kill us as soon as I have?"

The creature didn't answer, but its fangs shone white in the moonlight as it smiled.

"In that case, no."

Narcissus wanted to scream that he would answer, that he'd tell them anything they wanted to know. But Vali was right. Silence was their only hope and he bit his tongue to still it, hard enough to draw blood.

"So be it then," the sailor said. "It is as well. Only answers found in pain are to be trusted. You will tell us what we want to know, when even death seems sweeter than what we offer you."

"You intend to torture me, then?" Vali said. Narcissus couldn't see his face, but his voice sounded calm, almost as if this was what he had expected.

"Not you," the sailor said. "Your mouth is full of lies."

As one, the jackal heads of the sailors swung to face Narcissus.

IT WAS DARK as Boda and Petronius walked from the school to his home. Boda had never been out at this time of day before, and she was shocked to find the streets crowded with wagons, their wooden wheels the cause of the deep ruts in the road's surface which had baffled her before. The noise was unimaginable, ten times the volume of the yearly fair at which her people traded their cattle with other tribes.

"What is this?" she shouted to Petronius above the din.

He looked puzzled and she gestured around her as they squeezed against a wall to let a heavily laden wagon through. The horse paused to shit as it passed, the pungent smell quickly buried in the cacophony of other odours.

"What occasion is it tonight?" she asked. "Why do they all gather?"

His expression cleared. "Oh, it's like this every night. An edict forbids wheeled vehicles by day."

"Every night?" Boda could hardly believe it. She knew that trade was the lifeblood of the Empire, but to see it like this! How could so many people want so many things?

Petronius nodded and Boda looked away from him to study their route, trying to memorise it. She was used to fighting on her own ground, where she knew the place of every tree and twig. Here she'd be fighting blind, and if – when – Quintus came after her, she needed to be prepared.

After a long space of silence, Petronius turned to her. "So, are you really not going to thank me?"

Boda's muscles tensed. "I don't know how much gold you spent, but don't expect repayment in another coin."

Petronius laughed. "I'll take that as a no. I did save your life, you know."

"Yes," she said. "Why?"

He shrugged and looked away. "Maybe I think the world would be poorer without you in it. Or maybe I'm just desperate for company."

She laughed at that, though she still wanted to know the real answer. Guilt? Perhaps, though he hadn't struck her as a person who heard the voice of his conscience very loudly.

"I did spend a lot of gold," he said. "But it wasn't, in fact, mine."

"Your father's?"

"Seneca's."

She frowned. "Wasn't he the man you were following when I met you? He was one of the cultists."

He nodded.

"Was it wise to steal from him?"

"Probably not. It's probably not very wise to take you back to his house, either, but I don't have much choice. There's nowhere else I can go. I'll try to sneak you in when he's not looking, hide you in my quarters."

"I've heard more impressive plans," she told him. But there wasn't much heat in it. He had, as he said, saved her life.

When they reached it, the house was grand but dark, the white marble blank and unwelcoming. It took her a second to realise why. There were no windows facing out, only a metal-studded wooden door.

Petronius read her expression. "I know, and it's no better on the inside. Wait here for a minute."

He disappeared through the doorway, only to reappear again a few seconds later.

"Empty," he said. "Even that ten-foot-tall slave of his is missing. Hurry now, while we can."

He'd been right about the interior. A few candles flickered in sconces high on the wall, but they did little to dispel the general gloom. There was a musty smell to the place, and she wondered if it was ever cleaned. It would be a hard job to shift the dust from the piles of books and statues and trinkets which covered every surface and crowded every corner. It looked more like a warehouse than a home.

"This way," Petronius whispered.

He led her to the left, through a low doorway and into another wing of the building. Where the other parts of the house had been full to overflowing, these rooms were so stark they barely looked lived in. The first held a low table with just one cushion on the floor beside it, and she glimpsed a narrow wooden bed through an archway ahead.

Petronius caught her expression and shrugged apologetically. "I think the old man's trying to teach me a lesson about the worthlessness of material things."

"A lesson he clearly hasn't learned himself," she said.

He choked off a laugh as they both heard the hollow sound of the main door closing. A second later there were voices, one quavering and male and the other low and sweet and female.

"He's back," Petronius whispered.

THE SAILORS WERE quick, but Vali was quicker. He flung himself on Narcissus, toppling him to his back and out of their reach.

For a moment the two men were face to face. A trick of the moonlight shaded Vali's red-brown eyes to scarlet, the exact colour of fresh blood. For a split second, Narcissus was more afraid of him than of the jackal-headed sailors. Then he felt Vali pressing something small and cold against his palm. He looked down to see that it was a simple silver coin.

He would have dropped it, but Vali squeezed his hand, closing his fist tight. "You'll need it," he said. And then the sailors had hold of him, and they pulled him away and Narcissus had no one left to defend him.

He slipped the coin inside his mouth in the brief moment before the sailors came for him. He couldn't imagine what good it would do. No bribe so small would turn them away from their course. But he needed a talisman to ward off what was to come.

When the sailors descended, he fought. He knew it was futile, but the panic consuming him was beyond rationality. He bit and thrashed and clawed with his nails and it was all for nothing. Each of the sailors took a limb, pulling with inhuman strength, and when he was spread-eagled between them, they carried him to the prow of the ship. Face up to the sky, Narcissus could see nothing but the ghostly white of the sails as they slid in front of the waning moon.

They tied him to something flat and wooden, the ropes tight enough to cut off the circulation in his hands. He clung on to that small pain, hoping it would drown out the greater to come. He could feel hysterical laughter bubbling inside him, at the thought that he'd once feared Caligula's wrath. That escaping it had brought him to this.

The laughter died as the stars above him were blotted out by the dark dog-shape of the sailor's head. "You may speak now, and spare yourself this," it said. "Who sent you to us, boy?"

The words were in his throat, pushing to come up. It would be so easy to speak. But he remembered what Vali had said and he didn't think he was ready to die. Not yet, not before his twenty-second birthday.

"I won't tell you," he whispered.

They didn't ask again. He'd been expecting blows and that was what they gave him. The first drove into his stomach, leaving him so empty of air that he couldn't scream when the others followed, against his chest and groin and on his face. His left eye swelled shut and he could feel the blood trickling from a cut on his forehead where his skin had split like a ripe peach.

The agony was so intense that he was certain it must end soon. It didn't seem possible that anything could hurt this much for this long. But it didn't end, and when he had enough breath to scream he did. He screamed his throat raw and still they carried on.

When they finally stopped, he was too dazed to realise it. His mouth was still open in a voiceless cry. The pain didn't abate, every part of his body joining in the chorus. But gradually sense returned and he knew that there were no new injuries being inflicted.

"We ask again," the sailor said, voice so calm it was as if the preceding torment had never happened. "Who was it who sent you here?"

Narcissus had no voice left to answer and the sailor took his silence as a refusal. He saw the dark space inside the creature's maw as it snarled.

"They sent you to this," it said. "You owe them no loyalty."

Narcissus agreed. He wanted to tell them, but only a dry croak emerged. He shook his head to clear it, and the creature thought he was refusing it again.

"Very well," it whispered. "Then the torment will be increased."

Narcissus saw a flash of silver as it brought its knife to his hand, and though he hadn't known he could feel any more terror he felt it now, at the thought that he was about to lose a part of himself. He remembered Julia, hiding the stump of her hand behind her back. Was that his future? Would his mind crack, as hers had?

The blade slid over his forearm, leaving a slick trail of blood behind. It pressed into the bone of his wrist for a moment, a sharp agony, then slid down the length of his hand to his fingertip. A pause – and then it drove inches deep beneath his fingernail.

His body convulsed and his back arced from the board, straining against the binding ropes. For one second the stars blazed so bright they blinded him, pinpoints of white fire in the darkness. And then everything was black.

PETRONIUS AND BODA stood face to face, ears pressed against the door as they listened to the conversation beyond. He'd begged her to hide in the relative safety of his bedroom, but she'd ignored him, and he couldn't risk further conversation to make his point.

She was utterly infuriating. What did these barbarians teach their women? He'd never met another like her, and certainly not one who was a slave. She'd asked him earlier why he saved her life, and the truth was he didn't know. Oh, he'd felt guilty about leaving her to her fate, but not guilty enough to steal a purse full of Seneca's gold to rescue her. And she was pretty, but Rome was full of beautiful women who could be had a lot more cheaply.

Now, though, he was glad he'd brought her here. Seneca and his female guest were talking in low, guarded tones, but they'd chosen to seat themselves right next to the door to Petronius's quarters, so that almost every word was clear. And the more he heard, the less he liked.

"It's all prepared, then?" Seneca said. He sounded almost meek, a tone of voice Petronius had never heard from him. Whoever this woman was, she seemed to make the old man nervous.

"Everything's in place."

Seneca grunted. "We've cut it fine this time. One night to spare 'til the dark of the moon."

"True. But this is the thirteenth, the most important. Everything must be perfect – the goddess demands it."

Petronius heard a grating sound, as a chair scraped back against the floor. When Seneca spoke again, his voice was more distant. "And you're satisfied with the body?"

"Indeed," the woman said. "The body is ideal – young and strong. And the man died a violent death. The power of it will fortify the spells."

"Excellent," Seneca said. "Quintus may be ill-educated and vulgar, but he's proven his value to us."

Boda gasped, a voiceless puff of air Petronius felt against his face.

Outside there was a sudden silence. It stretched on so long that Petronius begun to wonder if Seneca and his companion had left, though he was sure he would have heard that.

A moment later, the door was wrenched open and he and Boda fell forward into the main room. She kept her feet, but Petronius stumbled to his knees. From there he looked up at Seneca's furious face.

"So," the woman said. She was Egyptian, he could see that now, though there was no trace of it in her voice. Her face was perfectly round and very smooth but still not quite young. She could have been any age from fifteen to fifty. She smiled when she saw him looking, a delicate pout of her rosebud lips. "You heard us speaking, I suppose?"

He nodded. There was no use denying it.

"And do you know who I am? Who we are?" She was looking at Boda now.

The gladiator glared back, blue eyes as dark as midnight in the ill-lit room. "Worshippers of the gods of Egypt," she said. "And you are their priestess."

The woman looked momentarily startled. Then she smiled – a dazzling expression that transformed her face from serenity to almost unearthly beauty. "Indeed. I am Sopdet, high priestess of the Cult of Isis, and when you spied on our meeting last night you trespassed on secrets which only the initiated may know."

"We didn't hear anything!" Petronius said. Sopdet gave a small satisfied nod, and he realised he'd been played. Until he'd spoken, she hadn't been entirely certain that he'd been at the cult meeting.

"I tried to keep you out of this, boy," Seneca said. "What concern was this of yours?"

It was a good question, so Petronius just shrugged and looked away.

Sopdet put a restraining hand on Seneca's arm. "This boy – he's of good family, is he not?"

Seneca sniffed, but nodded grudgingly. "Good enough."

"Precisely," she said. "Good enough for him to be eligible to join the Cult. And if he were an initiate himself, the secrets of the Cult would be open to him. No need to punish him for his intrusion then." Her face was friendly as she looked at Petronius, her expression almost conspiratorial.

He felt a flood of sweet relief coursing through him. He had no particular desire to prance around in subterranean caverns with bandage-wrapped lunatics, but it was definitely preferable to the alternative.

Seneca frowned. "And what of his joining fee?"

Sopdet's eyes swung to Boda and her expression shifted, only a subtle movement of muscle beneath skin, but suddenly her face didn't look friendly at all. "This slave will do very nicely," she said. "The dark of the moon is in three nights' time. Let her be sacrificed then."

WHEN NARCISSUS WOKE he was by a river. It was dark all around and that made sense, because it was still night, but then he realised it was the darkness of an underground world. The river ran through a cavern, more vast than any he'd ever seen.

The air was full of a gentle hissing sound. After a moment he understood that it was voices, thousands of them. He strained to make out the words but they remained, tantalisingly, always at the edge of his consciousness. And whoever whispered was hidden from him, though his eyes strained into the outer reaches of the enormous, dim cave.

There was only one person visible. An old man stood by the banks of the river. He was ankle deep in the brown-green mud, an unclean smell oozing into the air around him. The slapping of small waves against wood grew louder as Narcissus approached, and he saw that there was a boat in the river. It looked half-decayed, and a foot of water sloshed inside, but it was the only way to cross.

The old man wore a cowl, like the sailors. Narcissus thought he might be human, though. He caught glimpses of a thin white nose and the gaunt curve of a cheek in the darkness. Sometimes it looked like a skull beneath the hood.

Narcissus needed to cross the river. He wasn't sure why, but he knew it was important. If he stayed on this side, he was in danger. Something awful was following him, a person or maybe just a sensation. An agony he had to escape.

The old man looked up as he approached, though his face remained hidden.

"How much to take me over?" Narcissus asked.

He'd expected a dry croak, but when the old man's voice came it was high and light. It sounded like birdsong. "One piece of silver, son."

Narcissus felt for the pouch that usually hung at his neck, but there was nothing there. His money was gone. Only... what was that sharp metallic taste in his mouth? He probed his tongue between gum and upper lip and felt the edge of something solid. When he spat it out he saw that it was a small silver coin.

"Will this do?" he asked.

The old man took it from him, bone-thin fingers ghosting over his as he picked it up. "This will get you there – and back."

Narcissus looked behind him. Something seemed to be resolving itself out of the darkness. It almost looked like the deck of a ship. There was a body on it, tied down and bleeding. Whoever it was must be suffering terribly. "That's all right," he said. "I'm not sure I want to come back."

"You will," the old man said. A yellow slice of teeth smiled beneath his hood. "Everyone wants to return while they still can."

Narcissus nodded, and stepped into the rickety boat...

...And on the deck of the *Khert-Neter*, the jackal-headed sailors prodded and struck his unconscious body, but nothing they tried could wake him.

PART TWO

Morituri Te Salutamus

CHAPTER SIX

Petronius woke, sweating and frantic, from a dream he'd already forgotten. There was no light in his room, so he didn't know what time of day it was, but he suspected it was late. A painful stab of guilt told him he should have been up with the sun, searching the streets of the city for Boda. But he'd been doing that for the last two days, and to no avail. Wherever Seneca and Sopdet had hidden her, he was pretty sure it wasn't within the walls of Rome.

He didn't know why he felt responsible for her. She had, after all, got herself into this mess all on her own, and if it hadn't been for him, she'd be crow-meat already. But the thought of her dying was unbearable to him. And now time had almost run out. Tonight would be the dark of the moon.

He'd managed to track down a few cultists, but they'd said nothing, only reported back to Seneca everything Petronius had asked them. After that he'd tried to talk to his father. The old man hadn't listened past the point where Petronius described following Seneca to the secret meeting. Then he'd offered a beating if his son ever did anything so disrespectful again. And it turned out he'd been a fool to buy Boda with Seneca's money. That made her Seneca's possession, to do with as he wished. No one would help him, and no one but him could help Boda. However futile it seemed, he had to keep trying.

He rose from the bed, joints creaking, and splashed some cold water onto his face, but didn't bother to shave. His dark, curling hair hung limp with grease. He hadn't been to the baths since Boda was taken. What was the point?

There was no one in the main room when he entered. The door to Seneca's quarters stood at the far end, enticingly unguarded for the first time in three days. Could this finally be his chance?

He sidled up to the entrance, glancing behind him for any sign of the old man's huge, silent slave. No one. Not quite believing his luck, he put his hand on the doorknob and turned.

The door was yanked out of his hand as Seneca pulled it inward. He paused when he saw Petronius, eyebrows raised. "Something I can do for you?"

Petronius felt a sudden flare of rage. The old man was treating this like a joke. As if he found the death of a woman nothing to get too worked up about. "You know what you can do," he said. "Release Boda."

Seneca shook his head. "Really, boy. I don't understand why this concerns you so much. She is, after all, only a slave – and a barbarian at that."

Petronius opened his mouth to give a heated response. A second later, he closed it again. A slave, yes. How could he have forgotten?

"You're right, of course," he said, bowing. "I shan't trouble you again."

The old man smiled cynically. Petronius could tell he didn't believe a word of it. "Won't you? Well, just be sure to be here before sundown tonight. I wouldn't want you to miss the ceremony." And he slammed the door in Petronius's face before he could say anything further.

Petronius didn't mind. The sooner he got out of there, the sooner he could start searching for someone who really could help. Someone who not only knew Boda's location, but might have some motivation for revealing it. He couldn't suppress a wry smile. No doubt it would amuse Boda to hear that it had taken him three days to realise the best person to ask about the fate of a slave was another slave.

NARCISSUS WOKE TO a wavering blue-green light. He was aware of pain, but it was faded and dull, and when he rolled to his feet he felt only a residual discomfort.

"Awake at last," Vali said. The other man was sitting cross-legged on a small crate. When Narcissus looked around him, he realised he was back in the ship's hold.

"What happened?" he said. His voice was a dry croak, rusty with disuse.

"You passed out when they started torturing you, and they didn't seem able to revive you. So they left you in here to deliver to their mistress when we reach our destination."

Torture. Yes, Narcissus remembered that. He examined the blue-brown bloom of bruises on his arms, and when he lifted his tunic he saw that his stomach was covered in them, barely an inch of pink skin showing through. His eyes were caught by the index finger of his right hand, the red blood clot where his nail had once been.

He let his tunic drop and looked back at Vali. "So why didn't they torture you?"

Vali hesitated, then lifted his own tunic, exposing a white, lightly muscled chest. Tattooed in its centre was a five-pointed star. "A hex of protection," he said. "They couldn't harm me."

Narcissus thought about the silver coin which seemed to have bought him these three days' respite from torment. He'd heard that the northern tribes had powerful sorcerers among them. "And have we reached our destination?" he asked.

Vali nodded to the far wall, and Narcissus saw that he'd somehow managed to carve a large chunk out of the ship's hull. The sea surged in choppy little wavelets only a few feet beneath. And closer than the horizon, a broad low land began. Narcissus held to the side of the gap, leaning out to enjoy the warm sun and refreshing sea-spray.

"It's Egypt," Vali said, which wasn't much of a surprise. "Alexandria."

"And what will happen to us when we arrive?"

Vali shrugged, leaning into the space beside him, arm to arm. His flesh where it touched Narcissus was surprisingly hot, as if he'd already basked in the sun for hours. In daylight, his face looked even paler, a fine dusting of freckles visible over his high cheekbones and sharp nose.

"Will I be able to... go wherever it was I went if I need to?" Narcissus asked him. "Can I hide there if they torture me again?"

Vali continued to look out, frowning slightly against the glare. "You're assuming their leader will try the same technique. I would guess that, violent persuasion having failed, they will try something else."

"What sort of thing."

Vali's mouth turned down. "You've seen what those sailors are. They're not of this world. And their mistress... Who's to say what she might be capable of?"

Narcissus felt an icy chill, even in the baking midday air. "Then what do you suggest?" He didn't know when the other man had become their leader. Probably right from the moment they'd met. A lifetime as the pampered house slave of a Roman patrician hadn't prepared Narcissus for command in a crisis.

"I think," Vali said, "that it would be best if we didn't arrive in Alexandria in the company of our captors."

Narcissus looked out at the mile of sea between the ship and the shore. He thought he understood what Vali was suggesting, but the idea was impossible. "I can't swim."

Vali's red-brown eyes remained hooded as he slung a friendly arm around Narcissus's shoulders. "I expected as much. Fortunately, I can. Tell me – do you trust me?"

"No." Narcissus said. "Not entirely."

Vali smiled. "That's very wise."

It took a second for Narcissus to realise that the arm on his shoulder was no longer loose. It was pushing him, and somehow Vali's leg was tangled with his own, tripping him as he tried to regain his balance.

He fell forward, into space and sunlight. A second later, the sea rushed up to grab him. There was a moment when his head was still above the surface and it seemed that he might float. Then a wave curled over him and he was lost beneath the water.

IT TOOK PETRONIUS an agonising three hours to track the man down. Boda had said a slave working in the bathhouse warned her against exploring the hidden chamber, but there must be a hundred slaves employed to clean and pamper the citizens who washed there, and he could hardly go around asking each of them what they knew about the Cult of Isis. He bathed instead, spending just long enough in each pool to study the slaves who serviced it.

In the end, he recognised the man. His beard was short and square in the Syrian style, but it was his eyes that gave him away, sliding shiftily away when Petronius glanced at him.

Petronius followed him outside the next time he took some towels out to dry, then pinned him against the wall by his shoulders. The man didn't fight back. A citizen could treat a slave as he wished.

"You know about the Cult," Petronius said.

The man opened his mouth in what was obviously going to be a denial. Petronius cut him off. "I know you do – you said something to my friend about them."

"Your friend?" The man relaxed a little.

Petronius hesitated, then released him. "Yes. You told her it was dangerous for slaves to get involved, and you were right."

The man nodded. "Been taken, has she, your woman?"

"And not to their meeting place here – I've already checked."

There was a painfully long silence as the man considered. Petronius didn't try to force him. The slave had cared enough to risk exposure when he warned Boda before. Petronius had to hope that the man would risk it again.

Finally the Syrian licked his lips, looked right and left, then said in a low whisper: "Here is where they meet. They hold their ceremonies elsewhere."

Petronius felt a rush of hope. "And is that where they're keeping her?"

He shook his head. "I don't know. But every month they gather there, in the catacombs outside the city. Every month on this day."

ONCE WHEN HE was three and his mother still took care of him, Narcissus had fallen in a river. He remembered the terror he'd felt then and he felt it again now. It was a panic so unreasoning that he could do nothing to save himself, just flail helplessly. He screamed and his open mouth let the salt water flood in. He gasped in fear and it was in his lungs, and a blackness began to press against the edges of his mind.

There was sound, something beyond the murmuring of the waves, but though he knew it was speech, he couldn't resolve it into words. Something was holding him and he kicked out against that too, but it kept its grip and then his head was above water and he was choking up a froth of seawater and vomit. It trickled noisomely down his chin and the sharp smell of the bile stung his nose and cleared his head.

"For the love of the gods, stop wriggling about!" Vali shouted.

His voice was right by Narcissus's ear, and after a moment longer of futile struggle, Narcissus realised that it was Vali who was holding him up. It was Vali's arm around his neck. Vali's grip loosened as Narcissus's legs kicked out in a spasm of panic that seemed outside the control of his conscious mind.

"Calm down!" Vali said. "Just relax."

With a supreme effort, he forced himself to stop struggling, tensing every muscle until it submitted.

Now that he wasn't moving, he felt the whisper of air over his ear as Vali sighed. "Go limp – as if you're unconscious. I can't swim with you otherwise."

That was even harder, but as the minutes passed and the water didn't rise to cover his head, he slowly let the tension drift out of him. His legs floated behind him, and his head lay back, pillowed on the water and Vali's chest.

It was a long way. Narcissus was astonished that the other man had the strength. He had nothing to look at but the perfect blue sky above, blurred now and then as one of the larger waves washed over them. The water stung his eyes and in the barely-healed cuts on his face and chest, but this was almost comfortable. There was something easy for him in giving total control of himself to another. It was what he'd been trained to do all his life.

After an uncounted space of time, he felt the drag of sand beneath his feet.

"We're there," Vali said breathlessly, and released him.

He floundered a moment, panic returning full force, but when he found his feet the water only came to his chest. They were some distance from the docks, on the outer edge of a city that rivalled Rome for size, but was full of angles and colours that marked it as the product of another land and culture. On an island near its entrance stood a huge tower, a light as bright as the sun blinking at its peak. It must be the famous Pharos of Alexandria, a warning to shipping that approached the east's greatest port.

When Narcissus reached the shore above the waterline he fell to his knees. Though he'd been doing none of the work on their swim he was wrung-out with exhaustion. He could only imagine how Vali must be feeling.

The other man remained standing, though he leaned over with hands on knees, gasping to regain his breath. As soon as he had, he reached down to draw Narcissus to his feet. "We can't stay here," he said. "I think the sailors saw us leave the ship. They'll be looking for us."

And as if Vali's words had summoned them, Narcissus heard the shouts of their pursuers, and the scrape of swords drawn from scabbards. They were very close.

Vali released his arm and ran, away from the sea and the shore. Narcissus staggered after, trusting the other man to find his way, though he was no more Egyptian than Narcissus was.

Their pursuers spotted them almost straight away. They let out an ululating cry – high and unearthly – and followed on their heels.

PETRONIUS HAD ONLY been to the catacombs once before, to witness the internment of his father's father. Then he'd been in the company of a crowd of mourners, brightly dressed and loud, if not exactly cheerful. Now he was all alone, and he hesitated at the entrance to the tombs and wondered if he really had the courage to go in.

He'd brought a torch, a spare in the bag slung over his arm. He lit it now, its flame a translucent wavering in the air. The sun wasn't yet close enough to the horizon for its rays to turn the red-orange of a dying day.

Petronius drew a breath, then walked forward into the dark mouth of the cave. He kept his eyes on the flame, which seemed to brighten and brighten as the light around it faded. Finally he was in darkness with only the yellow flicker of the torch to show him where he trod.

For the first hundred paces he saw nothing around him but earth and rock walls, gradually narrowing as he descended. Side tunnels snaked off at irregular intervals, but he ignored them. The whole vast place was a maze with no map. If he stuck to the straightest route, he stood the least chance of getting lost.

He wished that, like Perseus in the Labyrinth, he'd thought to bring a thread to mark his path. Too late now – the catacombs lay outside the walls of Rome. If he went back he'd never find Boda before the moon rose.

Deeper down, beyond the reach of any daylight, he saw the first urns, tucked into alcoves low in the walls. The fashion had been – still was, in the more traditional families – to burn the dead before they were buried. He thought of all the generations of Rome, reduced to the same black ash.

The bodies were worse. He came to them deeper inside. The freshest were first, stinking of rotting flesh. The light of his torch shone briefly into one of the shallowest crevices and he saw the corpse of a little girl inside, so recent that he could still make out the structure of her face, though the flesh was beginning to green and hang away from it. She'd been a pretty little thing.

After that he kept his eyes on the path. He was looking for other footprints, the hint that a large group of people had passed here recently. It was futile. Too many funerary parties had come this way, obscuring the marks left by anyone engaged in less respectable activities.

The tunnel was barely head-height this deep in, and soon there was no obvious main path to take. He stood for a moment, looking at the three-way fork that faced him, then decided to take the right-hand turning. If he did the same at every junction, he should be able to reverse his steps without getting lost.

The bodies were fewer here, and older. He'd heard that the catacombs had been in use since the founding of the Republic. These bones were brown with age and it was hard to imagine that they'd ever walked and talked and fucked. It was damp here, too. Rank moisture dripped onto his bare neck and when he brushed it off it left a green streak on his hand.

Then he came to a turning that led to a tunnel which narrowed and narrowed. At first he stooped and then he crawled forward on his hands and knees until finally he realised that he could go no further. For a moment of clenching fear he thought he was stuck tight. But he wriggled and drove himself backwards with his hands, and eventually he made his way back to the original turning.

He took the middle turning this time, but soon he found another blocked path and then another. By the fourth time he'd reversed himself and headed down a different path he realised that he had no idea which way would lead him back out.

THERE WERE NO dead ends in Alexandria, no gently curving roads and nowhere to hide. The entire city seemed to be laid out on a perfect grid, parallel streets meeting at right-angled crossroads. And there was nowhere to escape to, no refuge outside the city limits. At either side lay water, the sea on one and a great inland lake on the other.

Narcissus and Vali were fleeing down the broadest avenue, a hundred paces wide and lined with marble palaces that would have put most Roman villas to shame. Only the crowds shielded them from their pursuers. Filling every street, they moved at the sluggish pace of those who'd rather not be out in the midday sun. No amount of shouting induced them to move aside.

Narcissus dodged between black-robed old matrons and naked street children and heard cursing behind them as their pursuers tried a more direct route through. The salt water soaking his clothes and hair never dried, just slowly gave way to a sheen of sweat in the unbearable heat.

At the next crossroads he snatched a quick look back and saw that the men chasing after them weren't the jackal-headed sailors from the boat. No doubt they'd have been too conspicuous, even here. Alexandria held the same mix of peoples as Rome herself, only the shades of their skin a little darker. But all of them were human.

The shouting behind continued and now the strangers on the street began to notice. The city was full of Greeks like Narcissus, but Vali's pale skin and flaming red hair stood out like a beacon. The men behind them wore the clothing of local guards and spoke the Egyptian tongue. It was clear whose side the crowd would take and hands began to reach out for Narcissus, snatching at his tunic as feet sought to trip and stop him.

He fell to his knees and cried out in pain as the impact jarred every bruise on his body. Ten paces ahead, Vali heard the sound and turned. He ran back, dragged Narcissus to his feet and pulled him on. Another hand reached out to grab them, dirty nails on the end of blunt brown fingers. Narcissus kneed its owner between his legs and the arm dropped away.

Their pursuers were only a few paces behind them now. But the mood of the crowd was starting to turn ugly. People pushed aside fell into others, and those others turned and shouted and shoved back. It was close to a riot, but thankfully it was happening behind them – slowing their pursuers and not them.

A few more paces and they found themselves in a market. Stalls stood everywhere, piled high with produce from all of Africa. Narcissus dodged the first and brushed against the second. A hail of apples tumbled into the street, bouncing between his feet.

The next stall they came to, Vali deliberately kicked. One supporting leg came away, and a cascade of oranges joined the green apples. Seconds later they were trodden underfoot, releasing a strong smell of citrus and cider into the air. The stall keeper shouted and swore but was more worried about rescuing his wares than chasing after the culprits.

Vali kicked over the next stall and the next, while Narcissus did the same to his left, sending dates and peaches to join the other fruit on the pavement. A display of small red and black pots smashed to pieces in their midst.

Now a full riot was in progress. Narcissus could see Egyptian soldiers rushing to quell it, but he and Vali were clear now, and there was no one close to point to them as the cause of it all.

The crowds thickened as the broad avenue opened out into an even wider space where it met a road of the same massive breadth. A huge structure stood in its centre, caked with gold. The sun glittered from every angle of its intricate carvings, reflecting distantly on the great buildings that ringed the square.

Vali stopped abruptly in front of Narcissus, and when he tried to run on the other man laid a hand on his shoulder to pull him back. "They've lost us," he said. "Try not to draw any attention."

Vali himself ambled easily on, looking around as if casually shopping for food. Narcissus tried to do the same, though he imagined his performance was rather less convincing. His heart was pounding so hard he could hear the pulse in his ears, and the lingering terror of his torture aboard the ship tensed his muscles whenever he thought of it.

Vali kept an arm slung over his shoulder companionably as he guided them both to the centre of the vast crossroads and the gold-inlaid building that stood there.

"The Sema, the tomb of Alexander," Vali said. "We'll be safe if we hide in there."

"Really?" It seemed to Narcissus like the most obvious landmark and therefore the first place they might look.

"It's sacred to them," Vali explained. "No Egyptian will enter a resting place of the dead. Only your Roman rulers come, to gawp at the remains of the greatest general who ever lived."

A moment later, as they entered the cool of the building, Narcissus could see why. The interior was empty and echoing, vaulted spaces leading to a high, thin spire. The tomb stood in its centre and he found himself drawn helplessly towards it. The whole thing was made of crystal, its facets sparking back a thousand glints of light until Narcissus had to shade his eyes as he looked at it.

"A hero of your people, I believe," Vali said.

Alexander was there, entombed in the shining centre of the crystal. His body had been preserved in the Egyptian way and someone must have painted colour on his lips and cheeks. His eyes were shut, but it seemed possible that they might open at any moment.

Beside the fallen hero, Narcissus caught his own dim reflection in the crystal. His face was too thin and too serious, but then it always had been.

"Good," Vali said. "We'll leave it for a few minutes, then head back out and try to track down our sailors and their friends. It shouldn't be too difficult with the ruckus we've caused out there."

Narcissus stared at him. "Track them down? But we've only just escaped!"

"Exactly," Vali said. "So now the pursued can become the pursuers." He tilted his head to the side, studying Narcissus quizzically. "This was the whole point of coming to Alexandria, you know. We have to find out what they're up to."

THE CAGE WAS too small to either stand or sit. After three days inside it, every joint in Boda's body was a screaming agony, and she feared she'd never be able to walk again.

The worst thing, though, was the darkness. It was so absolute that she couldn't see her finger when she held it an inch from her nose.

She thought that her last visitor had been a day ago, though it was hard to tell time here, with nothing to mark it. A group of cultists had come to bring her food and water during a brief interval of torchlight. After they'd gone she'd had nothing but sound for company.

The tombs were alive with it. There was dripping near and far, water seeping through the ceiling to the rock below. And she could hear a perpetual soft sighing that she eventually decided was an echo of the wind in the tunnels far above. The skittering sound of nails against rock must be the rats, hurrying to their latest feast of dead flesh.

And there were other sounds, harder to place and therefore more frightening. What was that sudden dry snap, over to her left? Was it a human voice she could hear humming that tune somewhere in the distance, or was it something else?

Boda was unused to such unreasoning fear. She'd been training as a warrior since she was big enough to hold a sword, and killed her first man before she saw her first moon as a woman. She'd screamed and cowered when the men danced round the fire at midsummer and midwinter, wearing the masks of the tribal gods, but she'd known it was only in sport. She knew the stories of Asgard, the home of the gods, and Hel, where the evil went when they died. She knew that the world was filled with demons; she'd just never expected to meet any.

She never thought she'd see the dead walking. She didn't know if they walked here, but she imagined them, lurking in the darkness her eyes couldn't penetrate. And now she heard footsteps, echoing through the caverns. She told herself they were just a product of her mind, giving flesh to the spectres of her imagination.

But the footsteps grew louder and nearer and soon they brought with them a glimmer of light. Her captors, then. Were they coming to feed her again? Or was this finally it, the moment when they would spill her blood in a sacrifice to gods who were not her own?

As the light grew nearer she could see the slab over which she hung suspended. A body lay on top, wrapped in fresh bandages. Four animal-headed jars surrounded it. She couldn't say how, but she knew that Josephus's mutilated corpse lay beneath the white cloth. Around him, the ancient rock was splattered with the black of old blood.

The torchlight grew nearer and brighter, and the bloodstains brightened to a rusty scarlet. She couldn't take her eyes from them, even as she heard the newcomer walking towards her.

"Boda!" he said.

It was Petronius. She was shocked into silence. It had not occurred to her, even in a second of desperate hope, that the Roman would come for her.

Now he was here, of course, he was looking characteristically clueless. "How do I get you out of there?" he asked helplessly.

The cage locked from the outside. She'd tried to force it in the days she'd been here, but it was solid iron and impossible to shift. No doubt her captors had taken the key with them. "Try breaking the lock with a stone," she said.

He fumbled on the floor for a loose rock, then juggled his torch uncertainly when he found one.

"There's a sconce on the wall behind me," she told him, trying to keep the impatience out of her voice.

"Oh, yes, right." He fumbled for a second before finding it, and the quivering yellow light settled into a steady, comforting glow. She realised that he was shaking and terrified.

"Thank you," she said, meaning it.

He grinned at that, suddenly looking very young. "I knew if I put myself in enough danger for you, you'd say it eventually."

He had to balance himself on the slab beneath her to reach the lock. He braced his feet to either side of Josephus's corpse, averting his eyes from the body. It took him three strikes with the rock before the lock broke.

Then the side of the cage fell open, hitting Petronius on the head and knocking him to the cavern floor. Boda tumbled after, landing beside Josephus on the stone slab. She groaned in pain as cramped joints slowly unknotted. Petronius groaned too, rubbing his hip and thigh as he stumbled to his feet. Metallic echoes of the lock breaking washed back into the chamber.

They masked the sound of approaching feet. Boda didn't realise they were no longer alone until the light in the cavern brightened unexpectedly and she heard a coughing laugh.

"So," Seneca said. "It seems you couldn't wait to get started."

Behind him, the other cultists began streaming in. They were dressed in their festival best, chatting and smiling, but a dark current moved beneath the civilised surface.

"I won't let you get away with this!" Petronius said. His throat bobbed as he swallowed nervously.

Seneca smiled. "My dear boy, there's absolutely nothing you can do to stop it."

CHAPTER SEVEN

THE SAILORS HAD gone to ground in the Royal Library. It took Narcissus and Vali an hour to trace them there, by which time the sun had set and the insect-rich African night had descended. The chirping of crickets was louder than the daytime crowds had been.

Every monument in Alexandria seemed to be built on a grand scale, but the library dwarfed them all. Narcissus had heard of it – everyone had – but he'd always pictured it as just one building. It wasn't. There were scores of interconnecting structures arranged around courtyards both open and closed. The place was almost a city in its own right.

The fifty-foot high wooden doors stood open even at night, the warm glow of torchlight spilling out from within. He expected trouble when they entered, but the bored-looking guards didn't even glance their way, just stayed crouched on the marble floor over their dice. Red-kilted librarians were everywhere inside. Deep-set black eyes peered suspiciously out of the palest Egyptian faces Narcissus had yet seen, but nobody moved to stop them.

"This place is huge," Narcissus said.

Vali nodded. He asked a librarian if there was a map they could follow, but the man sneered that any true scholar would know his way around. He strode off before they could ask him anything further. And the endless rooms of the library stretched away to either side, doorways framed within other doorways like reflections within paired mirrors.

Narcissus looked around him in despair. "We'll never find them here."

Vali nodded gravely. "You're right. We may as well give up now."

Narcissus glanced at him from the corner of his eye. "You're mocking me, aren't you?"

"Yes." Vali strode forward, deeper inside. To his left, a doorway led to a circular lecture hall, ranks of stone seats surrounding a central podium. There was a lecture in progress now, a stooped professor holding court over three hundred or more students. Narcissus only caught a few words as they passed, but he thought the man was talking about the work of Archimedes. It was here, of course, that the mathematician had laid down the principles for calculating the surface of a sphere, and invented the device used throughout the empire to pump water.

"So you know where we're going?" he asked as they walked on.

Vali shook his head, and Narcissus repressed the urge to hit him.

"This is just aimless wandering, then? A pleasant walk on a quiet evening?" He'd never spoken to a freeman in such a tone before, but the barbarian was infuriating.

Vali stopped at last, turning to face Narcissus. "We don't know where they are," he said, "but we know something. We know that they like to carry out their business in secret."

Narcissus looked around him, at the shelves stacked high with scrolls and the never-ending progression of rooms. All the knowledge of the world was here. "Yes, but there could be a million places to hide and we'd never find them."

"True, but remember this is a library. There are books here that are meant to be read – and some that aren't."

Narcissus began to see what Vali might mean. "You think they're hiding among the banned works?"

Vali shrugged. "These are people who covet the forbidden. And only a select few are allowed to read the texts that are held to have the power to corrupt."

"A select few that doesn't include us," Narcissus pointed out.

The other man smiled crookedly, and the smile somehow transformed his face. Maybe it was just a trick of the light, but his skin seemed to darken, and his hair too, and Narcissus couldn't believe he hadn't noticed before how long his tunic was. Long and black. Only his eyes remained the same, the colour of banked flames.

He winked at Narcissus, then turned into the path of an elderly man walking head-down towards the library's exit. "Teacher," he said. "May I beg the favour of a word?"

The old man stopped and stared. He was dressed in the same long black tunic that Vali now wore, and over it a fringed shawl that draped his head and shoulders. "Of course, my brother. What is it you would ask?"

His accent was lilting and round and Narcissus realised that he was a Jew. There were said to be many here in Alexandria, a community second in size only to the Greeks.

"It's knowledge, I seek," Vali said. "I've heard that treasures are held here, lost books of the Torah. I seek the Martyrdom of Isaiah, and the Fourth Book of the Maccabees, which speaks of reason's triumph over the body. But the librarians will tell me nothing."

The old man's face lit up at this, the gleam of enthusiasm in his eyes. "You've heard the truth. They are indeed here, if you know where to look. But –" and a flicker of suspicion played over his face. "Their words are not for everyone. The unwary may be led off Hashem's true path. Is your virtue strong enough to withstand that which is inside them?"

Vali bowed his head. Narcissus strongly suspected it was to hide a smile. "If Hashem is willing, I will keep to the Law and gain only knowledge, not sin."

It seemed to be the right thing to say. The man nodded approvingly, and slipped a small silver key into Vali's hand. He told him to come to the Room of Anatomy when he wished to return it.

When the man had gone, Vali turned back to Narcissus. His face looked the same as ever, pale and freckled, and how could Narcissus have thought that his tunic was long and black? It was quite clearly knee-length and a light brown.

"So," Vali said, flipping the silver key from hand to hand. "Now we know where to look."

PETRONIUS DIDN'T THINK Seneca could have devised a better way to torment him. He could see Boda the entire time. They hadn't put her back in the cage, just closed a metal collar around her neck and chained her to the wall. She glowered at the people around her, but they stayed out of her reach, and Petronius could see that her neck was already chafed raw from her futile efforts to escape.

He thought he could have borne it if they'd just got on with it. But the fifty or more people crowded into the small cavern didn't seem to want to do anything more than sip at goblets of wine and exchange small talk. A particularly irritating woman to his left was coaching her husband on what to say if Senator Trebonius should deign to speak to them. Her voice was shrill and affected and it grated on his nerves like a serrated knife.

Seneca was looking at him with a smug smile he very much wanted to wipe off his face.

"Why don't you just get on with it!" Petronius hissed. "Do you think killing her is some kind of entertainment?"

"No. Unlike that vulgar spectacle in the Arena, this is not for pleasure. It's an act of worship."

"For some jumped-up African god!"

"Not a god," Seneca said coldly. "A goddess. And you should be wary of offending her. You've already seen the evidence of her power."

He nodded to the side of the room, where the bandage-wrapped corpses once again twitched in their coffins. Petronius had stopped pretending to himself that it was all some kind of trick. He felt a trickle of cold sweat down his back, because Seneca was right. Any goddess who could do that was indeed to be feared.

Seneca bowed sardonically and moved away as a white-haired slave sidled nearer, offering Petronius a plate of delicacies. He raised his hand to slap him aside, then let it fall again. Boda would hate to see him do that. And none of this was the slave's fault.

"You're a new face here, aren't you?" someone said behind him. It was the woman he'd heard before, with the annoying voice and meek husband.

He nodded and looked away, hoping that would end it.

It didn't, of course. "I'm Publia," she said, extending a hand, "and this is my husband Antoninus."

"I'm Petronius of the Octavii," he said stiffly.

"And this is your first time, is it?" Her tone had shifted to become a little patronising, a result of his family name, no doubt. Not prestigious enough for sycophancy, but too rich to offend.

He sighed. "This is my first meeting as a member of the Cult."

"How exciting for you," she gushed. "I remember our first time. Don't you, Antoninus?"

Her husband nodded glumly. He had grey-sprinkled hair and the sort of long, morose face that always looked faintly equine.

"I was terrified, of course." She giggled, and he wanted to tell her that she didn't know what terror was. That perhaps she might like to ask the woman who was about to be sacrificed for her amusement. He looked at Boda, blonde hair awry and cheek bloody and bruised where they'd subdued her, and felt a boiling anger like none he'd ever experienced.

"And they were all like this, were they?" he asked, biting back on his fury. He nodded at the coffins – and then at Boda. "They all ended the same way?"

She must have detected something in his tone, because her expression grew more serious. "Yes. The goddess demands a heavy price of her worshippers."

"Of her worshippers?" Petronius said incredulously. His hands balled into fists and he thought that it would be worth it, worth any consequence, to wipe that sanctimonious look off her face.

"Don't listen to her," Antoninus said suddenly. "We've been to several meetings, but never a ceremony before. This is our first time, too."

"So you don't actually know what's going to happen tonight?"

Antoninus shook his head as Publia said sententiously, "The mysteries of Isis reveal themselves to mortals only gradually."

Petronius felt marginally less like hitting her this time. His eyes met Boda's across the room and he felt the first faint stirring of hope. If these people didn't know what the ceremony involved, then perhaps they might object to it. Perhaps they'd help him to stop it.

"Listen," he said. "I do know what—"

"Brothers and sisters in Isis," Seneca's voice cut across him. All around, the cultists turned to look at the old man as he approached the stone altar where the bandage-wrapped corpse lay. Petronius realised for the first time that it was the only one that wasn't moving.

"I'd like to welcome our newest initiate," Seneca said, smiling sardonically at Petronius. Then he looked back at the crowd, watching him with rapt attention. "And I'd like you all to take your places. Tonight's ceremony is about to begin."

WHEN NARCISSUS AND Vali found the room the elderly Jew had directed them to, it seemed like a dead end. The only door was the one through which they'd entered, and all four walls were lined with shelves, each stacked high with scrolls.

"The stories of the gods of Egypt," Vali said, reading a sign written in both Greek and hieroglyphs.

Narcissus glanced along the shelves. There were labels beneath the scrolls, and he saw that they were arranged according to era. The very oldest drew him, so brown and frail it seemed the slightest breath of air would crumble them.

"These are an ancient people," he said.

Vali nodded. "A civilisation older than your own, and gods more powerful and strange." He picked up a scroll and unrolled it. The papyrus crackled but it didn't crack.

Narcissus studied it in fascination. The old writing was interspersed with illustrations, animal-headed beings who strode through a world of sand. He saw a picture of the sun, carried on a barge down a great river.

"Can you read it?" he asked.

Vali made a non-committal sound and replaced the scroll on the shelf.

Narcissus turned away, scanning the room. "This can't be the place he meant, can it?" There was nothing to stop common entrance here, no lock that fitted the silver key.

"The entrance must be hidden." Vali said.

Narcissus searched the floor first. An ornate mosaic covered the whole thing, satyrs at each corner and a depiction of Dionysus springing full-grown from Zeus's thigh in its centre. The lines of a trapdoor could easily have been lost in the pattern, but Narcissus stamped on every square yard of it, and nothing rang hollow.

It was only when he reached up to straighten a crooked scroll – the instinct for tidiness of a house slave – that he realised what the trick was. The scroll didn't move, stuck fast to the shelf beneath. He ran his hand along the edge of the wood until he came to the gap that he knew he'd find, and when he looked above it, the keyhole was there.

"This is it!" he said excitedly. "The old man was right."

Vali fitted the key in the lock, and the whole wall swung out, shelves and fake scrolls attached.

There was light within. Torches lined a short flight of steps leading down to another, larger room. When Narcissus and Vali followed them down, they found themselves in a hall so large the far end was lost in darkness.

There were more books, thousands of them, some more ancient than those above. Down here they were separated by nation rather than age. Within that category Narcissus saw that they'd been subdivided further, each different heresy with a section of its own.

"Imprisoned knowledge," Vali said. "Locked up for its sins." His words echoed loudly from the vaulted ceiling, and Narcissus looked around nervously, though there was no one to hear.

Vali scanned the shelves, drawing out volumes here and there and reading them with raised eyebrows.

"Anything interesting?" Narcissus asked.

Vali smiled. "Well, the old man was right. They do have a copy of the *Fourth Book of the Maccabees.*"

"And does it, in fact, explain how reason triumphed over the body?"

Vali laughed and put the book back. "Possibly." He moved deeper inside the room, where the shelves lay parallel to the walls, row after row of them that left little space to slide between.

"This one's more along the lines we want," Vali said, drawing out a thick scroll, bound with a black silk ribbon. It was ancient, but unlike the others it didn't seem to be made of papyrus. The scroll was parchment, old and grey, and it gave off a putrid smell as it was unrolled.

The first image Narcissus saw was a jackal-headed man, holding a flail in the crook of his arm. "One of the sailors!" he said.

Vali nodded. "Or their master."

"What is that book?"

"*The Book of the Dead*, banned but not forgotten these many years."

He unrolled the scroll further, and Narcissus flinched when he saw the picture of a beetle. There was a red-gold sphere clasped between its mandibles, and he realised after a moment that it was a symbol of the dying sun.

"A scarab," Vali said. "Born spontaneously from the dung in which it lives. The Egyptians believe it's a messenger of reincarnation."

He rolled the scroll on, and Narcissus was glad when the creature was lost to sight. The next image was of a lizard, its long strong body emerging from a river. A mouth full of razor-sharp teeth grinned out of the page.

Vali frowned. "Crocodile. The Nile is infested with them. They're said to guard the gateway to the underworld."

"Really?" Narcissus tried to keep the excitement out of his voice. "Crocodiles like those ones, you mean?"

They were at the far end of the room, another fifty paces on. The marble they'd been carved from was the same mottled green as a living creature's skin, and as Narcissus approached he got a true sense of the scale of them. Their heads, filled with the same brutal teeth as their picture, were at the same height as his. Their eyes glittered black in the light of the torches.

They stood face to face against the wall, a gap wide enough to admit two men between them. But there was nothing there, just blank white marble. No entrance, and this time no hidden keyhole either.

Vali moved to join him, rolling *The Book of the Dead* back into a cylinder and tucking it beneath his tunic. "You think this is a doorway?" he said.

It seemed absurd to be so certain, but Narcissus was. "Everything we know so far links back to *The Book of the Dead*. Wouldn't it make sense if this did too? And" – he looked around the vast room – "where else do you think the sailors could have gone?"

Vali shrugged. "I was only guessing that we'd find them here."

"It was a good guess," Narcissus insisted. The floor was plain marble, a scuffed white, but he checked every inch of it for a trapdoor anyway. There was nothing. And the wall between the crocodile statues was a total blank. He clenched his fist in frustration.

"Maybe it only opens from the inside," Vali suggested. "A way to stop unwanted intruders."

"Yes," Narcissus said. "But then how does anyone on the outside let them know they want to get in?"

Vali shook his head, but Narcissus knew the answer to his own question. He raised his fist and knocked on the wall between the two statues.

The sound rang loud and musical, as if a gong had been stuck. Narcissus flinched and backed away from the wall. But the sound went on and on, ringing through the whole room. Then, as abruptly as it had started, the ringing stopped.

At first, the line that appeared in the plaster between the statues was barely visible. Then, gradually, it widened and darkened until it was clearly the outline of a door. A polished gold handle protruded from the wall where no handle had been before.

Narcissus froze, afraid now to finish what he'd begun. Vali looked at him a long moment, then shrugged, reached forward and turned the handle.

The door swung silently open. Ice-cold air wafted out, raising goosebumps on Narcissus's bare arms. There was a noise inside, too quiet to place. Was it the murmuring of water, or voices? And were those skittering footsteps human or something else?

"You were right," Vali said.

Narcissus nodded, but he wished he hadn't been. Everything in him rebelled at the thought of stepping through that doorway. He thought suddenly of the ancient ferryman on the river of his dream. This library room was nothing like that bleak cavern, but he sensed a kinship between them he couldn't explain.

Anything could be waiting beyond those doors. And the jackal-headed sailors who'd tortured him didn't seem like the most frightening possibility.

"Do you want me to go first?" Vali asked.

It was the hint of pity in his voice which spurred Narcissus to find his courage. "No," he said. "Side by side."

Vali nodded and they stepped forward together, between the watchful black eyes of the crocodiles.

The moment their feet crossed the threshold, all four eyes blinked.

PETRONIUS FOUND HIMSELF squeezed between Seneca's large, silent slave and another man with darker skin and an even more forbidding face. Each held one of his hands tight behind his back, where the other cultists couldn't see. He was sure if he tried to protest he'd be silenced, maybe even removed. Better to keep quiet and stay and hope desperately that he'd have one final opportunity to rescue Boda.

She'd been moved again. They'd tied her arms and legs to a light metal frame, then hung it from the ceiling above the bandage-wrapped body. He'd seen a similar arrangement at the Temple of Mithras once. Only then it had been a bull, hung above the worshippers so that when its throat was slit they could bathe in its blood. The thought brought a sour lump of bile into his throat.

At least the ceremony preceding the sacrifice seemed to be a long one. Long and dull as most religious observances were. The priestess Sopdet officiated as the corpses surrounded her, swaying in time to her atonal chanting.

Some of the cultists had joined the chant, eyes shut in either ecstasy or boredom. The sound reverberated from the walls and echoed back, low and distorted.

Seneca knelt in front of Sopdet, head lowered and hands raised, a curved bone dagger resting on top of them. He was shaking, but Petronius thought it was with excitement, not fear.

Boda was shaking too, rattling the frame from which she hung. Her eyes were wide and her pupils huge. They'd made her drink something before the ceremony began, holding her nose until she swallowed. Petronius thought it might have been an hallucinogenic. Maybe that was better. If his life had been about to end this way, he'd have preferred to be out of his head while it happened.

Without warning, the chanting stopped. The circle of corpses shuffled back until they surrounded not just Sopdet but the stone altar and Boda's body above it. The priestess moved to each of them in turn, daubing a spot of red on their brows and chests. Petronius thought it might be her own blood.

When the circle was complete she returned to Seneca and took the bone knife from his hands. Her eyes caught Petronius's for one second. Then she raised the knife and walked towards Boda.

For things so large, the marble crocodiles moved with lightning speed. Narcissus heard stone rasping against stone as their jaws snapped just behind his ear, and he tucked his head down and fled.

Vali ran at his side, though he sensed that the other man could have outpaced him if he'd chosen. A vague gratitude floated somewhere in his mind, subsumed by the overriding panic. His muscles burned with the poison of over-exertion. Today felt like one endless flight, and he was losing the energy for it. After a while, he'd discovered, even abject fear becomes boring. He longed for an end to it – even if it cost him his life.

He didn't have time to examine the place they were fleeing through. But he caught flashes of it from the corner of his eye, mismatched and baffling.

The first time he looked, he thought he saw sand, a vast undulating sea of it glittering white in the moonlight. But he blinked and looked again and no, they were inside as he'd thought. Though that marble pillar, twined with vine leaves, seemed to stretch too high to fit anywhere inside the library.

A left turn down a corridor that somehow was also a woodland path, and the crocodiles were still behind them. Their breath was pure and odourless as no living beasts' would have been. Sometimes Narcissus felt them far above him, as if they'd grown since he'd last seen them. Other times they were low to the ground, snapping at his heels.

Only the sound of their claws remained constant, nails scratching across marble.

There were other noises here, too. That murmuring might have been the river they ran beside now, though when the water disappeared the sound remained. It was growing louder, and Narcissus began to think he could make out words. He strained to hear them, but they remained elusive, like a half-remembered song.

He could feel himself slowing. It wouldn't be long before he could run no further. He decided that he'd turn and face the creatures. He might buy Vali some time, and it would be the closest to a dignified death he could contrive.

He braced himself, ready to surrender. They seemed to be indoors again, running down a mosaic-lined corridor that might actually be hidden beneath the Library of Alexandria. But in the moment before he stopped and turned, he saw something else – something that didn't belong.

It lay fifty paces ahead of him, a perfect circle of rock, its rim carved with hieroglyphs, and a milling crowd of people visible through its centre. But when Narcissus looked to either side of the ring there was nothing but bare rock. It was a doorway in space.

Hope filled Narcissus with energy. He pushed leaden legs for one last burst and saw that Vali was doing the same beside him. The crocodiles fell a little behind, the harsh susurration of their breath like the sound of wind across rock.

When they were ten paces away, Narcissus could see what lay through the round portal. It was another chamber, a cave by the look of it, deep underground. Figures wrapped in bandages circled a woman holding a knife. And there was another woman, hung upside down above a stone altar.

Narcissus realised with a sick shock that he was watching a human sacrifice. He flung himself at the portal, not sure if he was trying to save the woman or himself.

The air between this place and that was as hard as stone. He bounced from it, face already swelling where he'd struck. Vali grabbed him as he tumbled, arresting his fall before it took him into the mouths of the waiting crocodiles. The other man's face was grim.

There was nothing to stop the animated statues now. They slowed, as if taking the time to relish their victory, and the nearest yawned wide, displaying every glistening tooth in its long mouth. There was a thick black tongue inside, and then the darkness of its throat.

It was big enough to swallow them whole. Narcissus supposed he should be grateful. It would be better than being torn apart piece by piece.

But there was something else behind the crocodiles, something that made even them pause. It seemed to float in the air, a suggestion of a face that might almost have been a trick of the light. As it came nearer it grew more substantial, resolving into the form of a young woman with pale hair and something trailing from her back that might have been wings. She screamed soundlessly as she approached.

"Grab hold of it!" Vali said.

Narcissus didn't know why he obeyed. The spirit horrified him. But he found his arm clutching at one of hers. Her skin was clammy and cold but he held fast and then he was being dragged after her, towards the portal.

BODA SENSED THAT the ceremony was over. Her head felt so light she wondered if it might float away. She could see Petronius, helpless between two full-grown slaves. She knew he would have helped her if he could.

Then Sopdet stepped closer, bone knife raised. The blade shone white, but Boda could see flecks of red on its edge from the last time it had been used. It was sharp, at least. Her blood would drain quickly and then she'd know nothing.

The priestess's eyes locked with hers. There was no more fellow feeling in them than Boda felt for her father's cattle. She was just a beast to this woman. Boda turned her gaze on the cultists instead. Let them see the light die in her eyes and know whose life they'd taken.

There was a collective indrawn breath from the crowd, a poised moment as the knife hung at the apex of its arc – and then the breath turned to screaming as something entirely unexpected happened.

The air behind the priestess shifted and changed. Where Boda had seen Seneca behind her, still on his knees, now she saw two other men, standing somewhere else. She realised with a jolt that one of them was Vali. The other was young and thin-faced and looked as terrified as she felt.

There was something between them, too insubstantial to make out, though the two men seemed to have hold of it.

The men knocked Sopdet to the floor as they fell through air and on to the sacrificial slab, squashing Josephus's body beneath them. And behind them came something else, lizard-like creatures larger than any Boda had ever seen.

The cultists were already fleeing, but Boda was unable to escape, and she hung right in their path.

CHAPTER EIGHT

AT THE LAST minute, the great beast turned its head, and snapped its jaws at Sopdet. The priestess scrambled back. She didn't look so elegant now, with her mouth stretched tight with fear and her dress torn where the crocodile's teeth had caught it.

Petronius heard somebody whimper and was rather surprised to discover it wasn't him. He saw the faces of the slaves holding him, frozen in fear, then they released his arms and fled. Seneca fell to the floor beside him, huddled into a ball. The keychain hanging from a belt at his waist jangled as he shook. Petronius snatched it, kicking Seneca when the old man tried to stop him. It felt good.

The two men still lying on the altar grunted when he trod on them. He ignored them, fumbling through the keys as he tried to find the one which would unlock Boda's chains. The crocodiles glared balefully at him. Their scales scraped across the floor as they slunk nearer. Most of the cultists had fled, but the living corpses remained. They too were closing in, blank white faces watching what he did.

To his surprise, one of the men on the altar – the red-haired barbarian – rose to help him. "I think it's this one," he said, picking out the slenderest key. He was right. The lock clicked open and Boda tumbled from her chains, bowling Petronius and the other two men to the floor beneath her. The giant crocodiles' jaws snapped shut on empty air.

Behind them Petronius saw Sopdet. She still held the bone knife in her right hand and there was murder in her eyes. The circle of corpses closed around them.

Boda flung herself at the nearest with a roar of rage, but she staggered as she moved, weakened and disoriented by her hours chained. The corpse fell back a step, then steadied. Its arms closed around her and she let out a choked gasped as the breath was squeezed out of her.

But she'd had the right idea. Petronius closed his eyes so he wouldn't have to see what he was doing and flung himself forward. His strength was greater than hers and both Boda and the corpse fell to the floor beneath him. A hideous green fluid oozed between the bandages but its arms fell away and Boda was free.

They ran. The others followed, though Petronius was no sort of leader. He had no idea of the route out of the crypt, and even if he had, he wouldn't have been able to follow it. At every turning, bandage-wrapped corpses or fear-crazed cultists loomed to block their way. And within a minute they were running in darkness. Petronius hadn't thought to grab a torch as he fled and nor, it seemed, had any of the others.

He could hear them behind him, breath panting as hard as his own. But one false step and they'd be lost to him. He reached back and grabbed a hand. Thin and damp, it probably belonged to the younger of the two men who had somehow saved Boda's life. Petronius pulled and after a moment's resistance the man's hand tightened on his and he followed after.

Running was impossible in the darkness. When Petronius tried it he rebounded hard from a wall he hadn't seen, then tripped over a shelf in the rock beneath his feet. After that he slowed, sliding his feet forward and holding out his left hand to feel the way. The catacombs were huge and he knew that he could wander them this way for hours or days, until he died of hunger and thirst in the never-ending night. He tried not to think about that, or about the fact that his groping hand sometimes touched bone rather than stone.

At least, moving slowly and near silently, they stood some chance of hearing their pursuers before they stumbled over them. For a while the voices were all around them, crying out in fear and sometimes screaming. There was a softer, darker sound too, of stone scraping against stone. Petronius thought it might be the crocodiles that had fallen through the gateway to nowhere along with the two men. He knew that the creatures weren't flesh and blood. He was choosing not to think about that, either.

After an unmeasured time, words floated forward out of the darkness. "Head upwards. That's bound to take us out of here." There was the trace of a harsh, foreign accent in the voice. It must belong to the barbarian.

"What a brilliant idea," Petronius hissed irritably. "Obviously, that hadn't occurred to me."

"No, he's right," another voice said, the second stranger. "There's a slope to the floor, I can feel it."

"You lead the way then, if you think you can do better."

Petronius hadn't meant it seriously, but after a moment he felt the other man fumbling along his arm, pressing close as he inched along his body to overtake him. For a moment the man's breath was in Petronius's face, hot and moist, then his other hand was clasped and pulled as the man started moving forward again. For a moment Petronius's trailing hand was empty, then another reached forward to take it. It was harder and more callused but small and fine-boned.

"Boda?" Petronius said.

He heard her breath huff out in what might have been a laugh. "I should have listened to you back at the baths," she said.

"And miss out on all the fun?" the barbarian said behind her. Unlike them, he wasn't whispering, and his voice echoed too loud through the tunnel. Petronius cringed and kept his peace, hoping that none of their many pursuers had heard.

The minutes stretched on, but gradually Petronius realised that the man leading them had been right. They were going up. Around them, the tunnel was broadening, changing the quality of sound so that their footsteps seemed to ring a little louder while their breath faded into nothing. Petronius remembered the wider tunnels near the entrance and felt a relief so intense it left him faint.

Soon a glimmer of light seeped in. It must be night still, and moonless, but after the absolute darkness of the catacombs the faintest illumination shone bright. Twenty more paces and they were out, the sky spread broad and star-speckled above them.

Though Petronius would have lingered to enjoy the freedom, the barbarian hurried them on. "We don't know how close behind they are," he said. But after a few more minutes he stopped and looked around. "Where are we, anyway?"

The question was directed at Boda but she shook her head. Petronius guessed that she'd been unconscious or blindfolded when they brought her to the catacombs. "The walls of Rome lie that way," he told the barbarian. "No more than fifteen minutes' walk."

The man nodded and they carried on in silence. The thought of people and noise and light drew Petronius. And there was safety in a crowd, too. The cultists hid what they did. He doubted they'd dare attack in a public place.

Soldiers guarded the gates of the city. They eyed Boda and the barbarian man askance, but Petronius lifted his chin and told them he'd been visiting his family's tomb, and after a moment's hesitation they let him through. He heard them mutter something about the catacombs being crowded tonight and wondered how many cultists had made it back to Rome before them.

The younger man looked about him in wonder as they walked down the Appian Way towards the heart of the city. He wasn't much older than Petronius, but his long, bony face looked like it had seen a great deal more unpleasantness. He had the sort of ugliness that could be almost attractive, in the right circumstances.

"Your first time in Rome?" Petronius asked him.

The man laughed, a disbelieving gulp. "I live here. I was here three days ago. I just didn't expect to be returning so soon."

Narcissus took them to a tavern he'd sometimes been allowed to visit with Claudius's other household slaves. It was dark and dingy, the torches inside filling it with a choking smoke – a place for plebs, not patricians. The owner recognised him and cleared a table by the door.

After they sat down, they stared at each other for a minute in silence. Narcissus found his eyes drawn to the barbarian woman. She looked ill-used, face blood-stained and limbs bruised. She sat as if it pained her but held her back straight and proud. Beside her, her friend slouched. His face was still soft with youth, but his large brown eyes and full mouth had the arrogant cast of a high-born Roman. Narcissus wondered if the woman was his lover.

The youth saw him looking and raised an eyebrow. "I'm Petronius of the Octavii," he said. "And this is Boda, my –". He caught her eye and swallowed whatever he'd been about to say. "Boda, a woman of the northern tribes."

"That's Vali, also of my people," Boda said. "He was the one who first told me about the Cult."

Narcissus glanced between them, shocked. It hadn't occurred to him that they knew each other. Was it a coincidence, or had Vali planned to rescue her all along? He looked at the other man, but his face was unreadable as he nodded a greeting to the barbarian woman. Narcissus was sharply reminded of how little he actually knew about him. *Do you trust me?* Vali had asked, and Narcissus was fairly sure that he didn't.

"And your name and clan?" Boda asked. "You're not Roman, are you?"

"I'm Greek," Narcissus said. "I'm Narcissus, a slave of the Emperor Caligula and Vali's travelling companion. Though you seem to know more about him than I do."

Petronius studied Narcissus and Vali closely. "You saved Boda's life, so I suppose I should thank you. But on the other hand, I don't think you actually meant to. What were you doing in the catacombs?"

"And how did you get there?" Boda asked.

Narcissus shrugged, helpless to answer. His head was still spinning from everything that had happened, and he saw flashes behind his eyelids of the strange place they'd travelled through to return to Rome.

"We've been to Alexandria," Vali told her. "In the hold of the Cult's ship."

Petronius frowned. "They own a ship? Smuggling, I suppose, but what could they want?"

"Beetles," Narcissus said. And then, remembering what Vali had told him, "Scarab beetles, which the Egyptians believe carry messages from the dead."

"Everything comes back to that, doesn't it?" Boda said. "Everything we know about the Cult. We know they animate the bodies of the dead. And we know they sacrifice the living – maybe to help them raise the dead. I think if you hadn't saved me, my blood would have revived Josephus's corpse."

Petronius shuddered, then nodded. "We know that they venerate Isis, of course, and maybe the other gods of Egypt."

"We know they have powerful friends," Narcissus added. "The previous slave who investigated their ship was – she was stopped and punished."

"Yes," Petronius said. "Seneca's a member, and many others of high family."

"But what do they want?" Narcissus said. "Why sacrifice the living? Why bring back the dead?"

Boda shrugged. "Perhaps their goddess demands it. I've heard that foreign gods can be cruel."

Petronius smiled a little. "Whereas your own, of course, are masters of rationality and kindness."

She glared at him a moment, then looked away. "War isn't kind, but Tiu and Odin reward those who fight it with courage and honour."

"Isis isn't cruel either," Narcissus said. "Some of Claudius's other slaves used to make offerings at her temple. They told me she's the sister-wife of Osiris, ruler of the Egyptian gods, and she's said to take a special care of the poor and downtrodden. If she's demanding these sacrifices it isn't because she enjoys blood for its own sake. There must be some other reason."

"But her husband is lord of the underworld, who sits in judgement on the dead. Perhaps he's the one who wants this," Vali said.

"And just how," said Petronius, "does a barbarian like you know so much about the gods of Egypt?"

It was a good question. Suddenly Vali had three sets of eyes trained on him, none of them entirely friendly.

He shifted uncomfortably. "I could just as easily ask each of you what your interest is in this."

"You know what my interest is," Boda said. "You were the one who showed me where to find Josephus's body."

"And I was auditing the Empire's records," Narcissus said. "I travelled to the docks to track the missing cargo, and you rescued me there."

Their gaze switched to Petronius, who shrugged. "I was bored. And Seneca was clearly up to something much more interesting than sitting on my arse copying out his quite extraordinarily dull speeches." He looked back at Vali. "So that's us explained. How about you?"

The other man lowered his eyes and smiled crookedly. "I could tell you the truth, but you wouldn't believe me."

"I think we would," Petronius said. "How much more improbable could it be than walking corpses and gateways to nowhere?"

Vali gazed at him a long moment. The lone torch by their table cast the shadow of his nose sharply across his cheek. "Sopdet is my sister," he said finally.

Petronius snorted. "You're right – I don't believe you. You're about as Egyptian as I am."

He was right. With his pale skin and fiery hair, Vali was clearly a man of the far, cold north. And yet... Narcissus remembered the way the other man's face had seemed to shift and change in the library of Alexandria, and suddenly it didn't seem quite so unlikely.

But Vali just shrugged and raised his palms, as if he'd been caught out in a lie. "Very well. Then this is the truth. I'm the Cult's enemy. And I'll do anything that's needed to stop them."

Boda's tilted her head as she looked at him. "Stop them doing what?"

"Opening the gates of death."

"They've done that already," Petronius said. "We've all seen it."

"They have," Vali said. "But only very briefly, just long enough to revive one body."

"You think they want to do it for longer? To let more dead spirits through?" Boda asked.

Vali shook his head, expression grim. "No. I believe they want to open them permanently – to erase the barrier between life and death for ever."

Petronius clicked his fingers suddenly, face lighting up. "When we overheard Sopdet and Seneca talking, she said something about tonight's ceremony being important – special somehow." He turned to Boda. "Do you remember?"

She frowned. "I think so. She said that the sacrifice..." She laughed humourlessly. "That *my* sacrifice would be the thirteenth."

"That's right," Petronius said. "It sounded as if, whatever they're trying to do, tonight would have completed it."

Boda nodded. "And it had to be done at the dark of the moon, they said that too."

"That means they can try again in a month, doesn't it?" Narcissus said. "And even if we aren't sure what they want, we can be pretty certain we want to stop it."

"How?" Petronius said. "The great and the good of Rome are members of the Cult. Why should anyone listen to us?"

"Why indeed?" said another voice, one Narcissus instantly recognised. If he hadn't been so caught up in the conversation, he might have noticed that all the others around them had stalled.

"Narcissus," Caligula said. "What a surprise to see you here."

The Emperor was surrounded by his Praetorian Guard. Their scarlet cloaks looked black in the dim light. Narcissus knew them all by name but none of them would meet his eyes as he fell to his knees in front of his master.

Caligula slid into his empty chair. "I must say, this was the last place I expected to find you. Runaway slaves usually have the good sense to, as the name implies, run away."

Narcissus tried to swallow past the dry lump in his throat. "I wasn't trying to escape, dominus."

Caligula's face tightened with displeasure but Narcissus ploughed on. It wasn't as if he could make this any worse. "I found a discrepancy in the audit, and I went to the docks to investigate."

"Yes," Caligula said, "so Julia told me when I had her tortured."

Narcissus squeezed his eyes shut to banish the images this conjured. When he opened them again, Caligula was staring at him.

"And what happened at the docks?" the Emperor asked. "It must have been truly fascinating, to keep you so long from your duty."

"I was trapped on board a ship. It put to sea before I could escape. But I found what I was looking for, dominus – evidence that the Cult of Isis have been smuggling scarab beetles into Rome to use in their ceremonies to raise the dead."

Caligula rocked back in his chair, eyebrow raised. "I'm amazed. My uncle never told me you were such an accomplished storyteller."

There was a muffled sound as Boda tried to speak and Petronius clapped a hand over her mouth. She mumbled indignantly behind it as Caligula turned to look at her.

"You have something to say?" he asked.

Petronius shook his head. "Nothing, Caesar. My slave merely intended to denounce this villain. Had we known we were drinking with a runaway slave we would, of course, have reported him to the authorities. I feel sullied."

Caligula studied him for a long time. Then he smiled. "I'm pleased to hear it. Cowardice has always been something I cultivate in my subjects. It causes so many fewer problems than bravery. You, your slave and your barbarian friend may go."

It was a dismissal, and Narcissus's three companions didn't lose any time in obeying it. He watched them disappear through the door of the bar and knew that his last hope went with them.

"And you," Caligula said, "will come with me. It's been far too long since I've seen a crucifixion and I'm looking forward to yours immensely."

CHAPTER NINE

BODA WALKED IN silent fury through the bustling night-time streets. She kept her mouth clamped tight shut. She knew if she opened it something would emerge which was likely to get her killed. Petronius still owned her, she needed to remember that. The fact that he'd fought briefly by her side didn't make him her friend.

"I know what you're thinking," he said. "If you'd spoken he would have killed us all."

She couldn't control herself. "And preserving your life is, of course, your first concern."

"Yes," he bit out. "My life – and yours too."

"And Narcissus's life," Vali said, and she jerked a startled look at him. She'd forgotten he was there. He drew to a halt, pulling them beneath the awning of a baker's, shut for the night. "Caligula won't give him an easy or a quick death – there's no fun in it for him."

Petronius flinched, but Vali put a comforting hand on his shoulder. "Which means you've bought us time to try and save him."

"Oh," Petronius said. "Of course – naturally, that was my intention."

Boda shot him a disparaging look and he blushed and dropped his eyes. "How can we save him?" she said. "That man was the Caesar, wasn't he? God-king of the Romans. There's no power in this city greater than his."

Petronius shook his head, smiling beneath his curling black hair. "You've got it back to front. Caligula's weak, not strong. All my father's friends said so, when they thought there was no one near to overhear. He's terrified he'll be killed and replaced like Julius Caesar was. Any other power – any rival power – is a huge danger to him."

Vali was smiling too, the expression less joyful and more sly on his angular face. "You think he'd see the Cult as a threat."

"The Cult is a threat, isn't it? If the dead rise, what becomes of Rome or its rulers?"

Boda understood. There had been a king of a neighbouring tribe who ordered killed every boy child whose height or strength exceeded his. In the end, his wife had put a knife in his back before he could murder his own son. "But we need proof," she said. "The Emperor won't take our word."

"Even with proof, he might not listen to us," Petronius said, suddenly despondent. "He's a lunatic."

"But there is someone he listens to," Vali said. "His uncle, Claudius, who was Narcissus's master before him. If we brought our story to him, he might convince his nephew we're telling the truth."

Petronius shrugged. "It's worth a try, isn't it? It's not as if Narcissus has anything else to lose."

THEY LED NARCISSUS outside the walls of Rome again, through the Esquiline Gate. The soldiers on guard saluted as they passed, fists thumping against the leather of their cuirasses. The sound rang loud in his head.

Outside the gates, the rows of crosses began. Only slaves and foreigners were crucified. The punishment was considered too humiliating, too agonising for a citizen to endure. He could hear the sobs of some of those hanging above his head. They were begging for a mercy they knew they wouldn't be granted. Narcissus was sure he'd be begging too, before the end. The line of crosses stretched into the distance. Even Tiberius hadn't killed so many and he'd been notorious for his love of slaughter.

Caligula kept snatching glances at him. The Emperor was relishing his fear. His mouth was twisted in a smile of cruel pleasure.

Narcissus's steps began to drag. He tried to keep walking, to keep his dignity, but his body rebelled against him. It didn't want to die, and especially not this way. In the end, the Praetorian guards to either side dragged him by his arms. He wished they'd look him in the eye. He wished that Vali were there, even if there was nothing he could do to help, or Petronius, or Boda. It would have been good to see a friendly face.

When they reached their destination, a cross lay on the ground waiting for him. The wood was newly cut and he could smell the sweet sap as they laid him against it.

Caligula stood beside his head. When they brought the nails he held out his hand. "Give them to me," he said. "I want to do it."

The soldier hesitated, glancing uneasily between Caesar and his commander.

Marcus, the captain of the Praetorian Guard, stepped forward and bowed. "It wouldn't be wise, my lord. The placing of the nails needs to be exact. If they don't fit between the bones of the wrist they're likely to come loose."

Caligula pouted, but he dropped his hand. "Go ahead then. I'll just watch." He knelt on the ground beside Narcissus's head, his purple toga trailing in the dust.

Narcissus shut his eyes as Marcus crouched beside him. A moment later rough fingers pinched his eyelid and pulled it open. He gasped and tried to blink but it was held fast.

"Oh no you don't," Caligula said. "I want you to watch. I command it."

For a wild moment, Narcissus thought of asking what Caligula could threaten to oblige his obedience. What more could the Emperor do to him? But he didn't ask the question because he feared the answer.

Marcus gripped his tongue between his teeth as he positioned the nail against Narcissus's wrist. His eyes flicked up a moment and Narcissus flinched at the sympathy in them. Then he screamed as the nail was hammered home.

He thought he'd known what pain was on the Cult's ship, but it didn't compare to this. Each strike of the hammer rang up the nerves of his arm to resonate in his mind. And the pain went on and on, even when the nail had been driven home. The slightest shift, the slightest movement, grated the metal against the nerve and launched a fresh spear of agony.

His left arm was stretched out and then the other nail was hammered in. Now he could think of nothing but the pain. His mind seemed to expand to encompass it. He could see Caligula saying something. The Emperor's lips moved and there was a hum of sound, but it meant nothing.

Then they began to lift the cross. As Narcissus rose, his weight pulled down on his arms and the pain increased still further. He hoped he'd pass out, like he had on the ship. But he'd lost Vali's coin when he swam to Alexandria and there was no escape into darkness here.

His cross had been placed on a hill. When they'd pulled him upright, the soldiers grunting at the strain, he had a view over the whole of Rome. The city's streets were arteries of light, and the clamour of traffic reached even this far outside the walls. A million people lay in front of him, but he would die alone.

ONLY VALI'S FAST-TALKING and Petronius's charm saw them through the gates of the Imperial Palace. After ten minutes of confused wandering, they found Claudius deep inside, sitting in a room lit by the faint pre-dawn light of the unseen sun. The old man looked up as they entered, eyes watery and wary.

Petronius had heard his father talk disparagingly about Caesar's uncle. They said he was a simpleton. "My lord," he said, bowing, "may we beg an audience with you?"

"With me? D-d-do I know you, young man?" The words sounded like they were sticking on something in his throat, and a thin line of drool trickled down Claudius's chin as he spoke.

Vali stepped forward. "We've come to ask for your help. We're friends of your slave, Narcissus."

"Narcissus? Are you here from m-m-my nephew?"

"Your nephew is the Caesar, isn't he?" Boda said.

"He is. And you're a gladiator, if I'm n-n-not mistaken."

Boda moved forward to kneel at his feet. "You're not. We're told you treated Narcissus kindly. That you cared for him. Is that true?"

Claudius's eyes narrowed as he studied her, and suddenly he didn't look like such a fool. "I love him like a s-s-son. And you've come with bad news. I can see it in your faces."

"Narcissus is being crucified," Vali said.

Claudius flinched and so did Petronius. These barbarians had no tact. But Claudius only rested his head in his hands for moment. "Thank you for t-t-telling me," he said when he looked up.

"But listen." Vali grasped Claudius's arm. "He's not dead yet. He could last a day or more – there's time to save him."

"From my nephew's cruelty?" Claudius shook his head. "There's no stopping it. I'm sorry – m-m-more sorry than you can know."

"There is a way," Boda said. "Or are you simply afraid of what Caligula might do to you too?"

For the first time, something like anger twisted the old man's face. His cheek twitched, pulling his mouth to the side and widening the stream of saliva seeping from it. "Of c-c-course I'm afraid of him. I've s-s-seen what he's capable of. I know it b-b-better than any man alive."

Vali didn't release his arm. "But will you risk his wrath for Narcissus's sake?"

This was the question and Petronius tensed as Claudius considered it. He didn't care about Narcissus, of course. He barely knew him. But he found that he cared about Boda's good opinion. He cared about it far too much, and he suspected that if the Greek slave died he'd lose it for ever.

Finally, Claudius bowed his head. "I've lived too long already, and s-s-seen too much. Yes, I'll do what I can for my b-b-boy. But how do you think I can help him?"

This was where Petronius came in. He'd been considering it carefully on the walk over. "It's all about the Cult of Isis," he told Claudius.

Claudius nodded. "There have been rumours about them for a long time. And they've grown very strong this last year."

"Yes, that's because they're..." Petronius remembered how Caligula had reacted to hearing the same story. "Well, they're up to no good, and that's what Narcissus was investigating. All of us were. The trouble is, when Caligula found us we had no proof. But I think I know where we can get it."

"You do?" Boda frowned sceptically at him.

He gave her a triumphant smile. "Seneca's something big in the Cult – its high priest, it seemed, judging by that ceremony. He's bound to have more information about them. And the last we saw him, he was trapped in the catacombs being chased around by" – he caught Claudius's puzzled expression – "something he couldn't escape from in a hurry. And that enormous slave of his was at the ceremony too. While they're down there, his house stands empty."

"While they're down there," Boda said. "We found a way out – why shouldn't they?"

"No reason at all," Petronius said. "But that's the only idea I've got. Do you have a better one?"

It was clear from her face that she didn't.

CALIGULA HAD STOPPED enjoying himself about half an hour ago. He always forgot how long it took people to die of crucifixion. That was part of the fun, of course, but a warm bed and the terrified son of one of his enemies in the Senate were waiting for him, and as dawn approached the air was chilling unpleasantly.

He thought about his sister Drusilla, who loved this time of day. She used to say that beginnings were better than endings. Caligula had always taken exception to that. He'd liked the end of things, which made them complete and whole. But then she'd died and he'd thought that maybe he'd been wrong all along. There were some things that should never end.

He looked up at Narcissus on the cross. He was writhing, lifting himself up on his toes to take the strain off his arms, then falling back down when his strength failed him until the pulled-down position of his chest stopped his breath and he had to try to stand upright once again. Caligula sighed. There was clearly plenty of life in the boy yet.

He turned to Marcus. "I'm bored. This is failing to entertain me."

"Should I bring him down then? Has the punishment sufficed?"

"Don't be absurd!" Caligula snapped. "He disobeyed me. He needs to die. I just want him to get on with it. Isn't there something we can do to speed the process along?"

Marcus bowed his head. Caligula suspected that he liked the slave and didn't approve of what Caligula was doing to him. That was a shame.

Caligula had always thought highly of the guard captain, and he didn't particularly relish the thought of killing him. Still, disloyalty couldn't be tolerated. Bad enough when he was just a man, but now that he was a god, it amounted to blasphemy, didn't it?

When Marcus looked up, though, his expression was blank. "A spear in the side would hasten things, Caesar. Or if you broke his legs he'd be unlikely to last out the hour."

Caligula squinted up at Narcissus. The young man was looking down at him, eyes wide in his pale, innocent face. It looked like he'd heard. Would he beg for his life – or for death?

"Well?" Caligula asked him. "Which would you prefer? I imagine a spear in the side would be quicker. Though stomach wounds can be awfully painful, I'm told."

Narcissus opened his mouth, but only a rasping croak emerged. His lips were chapped and bleeding. He moistened them with a swollen tongue, then spoke again. "Whatever you wish, dominus. I live to please you." He let out a dry rattle that might have been a laugh.

Caligula almost spared him for that. Except was the slave actually mocking him? It seemed hard to credit, but Caligula thought he probably was. A slow death, then. "Break his legs," he told Marcus. "One at a time."

Marcus nodded, then signalled a legionary to bring over his shield. He'd use the edge of it to shatter the bone. Narcissus turned his face away as Marcus drew the shield back.

"Stop," a voice shouted. "S-s-stop this, nephew."

Marcus dropped the shield, looking almost as glad of the reprieve as Narcissus.

Caligula scowled at Claudius and the small group of people behind him. The same three who'd been with Narcissus in that bar.

Claudius was shaking and twitching. He always twitched when he was nervous. But he raised his head defiantly when Caligula approached. "You h-h-have to listen," he said. "This isn't a game any m-m-more."

Caligula looked him up and down, his frail, twisted body and thinning hair. Was his uncle really defying him? And over a slave? "You think this is a game? He ran away! He shamed you!"

"That's not what happened," Claudius said. "Nephew, if you've ever t-t-trusted me, t-t-trust me now. We're facing a terrible threat. Only you have the p-p-power to stop it." His face was drawn and serious and Caligula suddenly realised, with a strange jolt, that it wasn't him his uncle was afraid of.

He swallowed. "A threat? From where?"

Claudius gestured at one of the three behind him, the red-haired barbarian, and he stepped forward to hold out a stack of documents. "The Cult of Isis," he said. "Caesar, we bring evidence that they mean to do an unspeakable thing."

"To me?" Caligula said, voice high with fear.

The barbarian shook his head. "To your Empire."

"Oh, that." Caligula frowned.

"And through it, to y-y-you, nephew," Claudius said quickly. "If you don't p-p-prevent it, it's the end of all of us."

Caligula looked in his eyes. Usually so watery and weak, they were hard and determined. He couldn't see the shadow of dishonesty in them. He fell to his knees, cradling his head in his hands as he rocked back and forward. "Oh, Jupiter. Mighty Jupiter, save me. Save me, I beg you."

Claudius knelt beside him, resting a warm hand on his shoulder. "Don't fear, n-n-nephew. There's time to s-s-stop this. A full month."

Caligula's paralysis lifted as quickly as it had descended. He was Caesar. He was a god! He could deal with this, as he'd dealt with all threats to his rule and person – ruthlessly. He leapt to his feet. "Then we'd better get started. Oh, and take your slave off that cross. He might be useful."

THE SUN WAS rising when Seneca finally emerged from the catacombs, Sopdet beside him. The shattered remains of the marble crocodiles lay in the darkness behind them. She'd found the spells to destroy them eventually, but not before several cultists had been killed and the whole ceremony ruined. Seneca had never felt so weary – or so furious.

Sopdet caught his expression and rested a finger on his arm to draw him to a stop. Her own round face was smooth and calm but he sensed that she was angry too. Everything had been leading up to the sacrifice tonight. *Everything!*

"That boy..." he said. "When I next see him, I'll kill him. I don't care how rich his father is."

"It wasn't the boy who ruined it," she pointed out. "It was those two men, who came through the gateway from the other world."

"Who were they?" Seneca asked. "The younger one I've seen before, I think. A slave at the palace. But the red-haired barbarian..."

She frowned. He'd known her for twenty years, since he'd lived in Egypt as a youth. The Cult had been nothing then, a mere social club for bored Romans in a foreign land. He'd seen her lead it from obscurity to unrivalled power at the heart of the Empire. And in all that time, he'd never seen her age a day, and he'd never known her look as uncertain as she did now.

"Did you recognise him?" he asked.

"I thought perhaps I did, but it was too dark to be sure..." She shook her head. "It doesn't matter. They stopped us once; we won't let it happen again. That fool Publia will need to persuade her husband to part with a new slave. The gladiator's body was damaged but there's time to mummify another. We can ask Quintus to provide us one by midday. A terrible accident in training, or some such."

Seneca felt a rising excitement banishing his tiredness. "So we can do it again? The ceremony can be completed?"

She smiled. "Yes. The dark of the moon lasts three nights. We've missed the first, but tonight another sacrifice will honour the goddess. And nothing will prevent us from opening the gate."

CHAPTER TEN

Narcissus was burning up with fever. The wounds in his wrists had festered where the nails had driven dirt deep into his flesh. He knew that he was being supported as he walked, Boda under his left arm and Vali under his right, but he felt as if he were floating. Sometimes he thought he was walking beside the bank of that dark river once again. Sometimes he wondered if it was all a fever dream, and in reality he was still dying on the cross.

The city was painted in shades of grey. A dark hole loomed in front of him and he flinched back from it. The pressure on his arms increased, forcing him through, and when he blinked against the new light he realised that it was just the gateway to the Imperial Palace. He was home.

He was laid on a bed, and something cool was placed against his forehead. Liquid dripped into his eyes and down his cheek and he tried to catch it on his tongue. His throat felt like it was coated with sand. Someone seemed to sense what he wanted, because he felt an earthenware cup pressed against his lips and gulped the water down greedily.

He realised that it was Claudius ministering to him. His face swam in and out of focus, sometimes looking so old he seemed seconds away from death, other times like the anxious young man he must once have been.

"Dominus," Narcissus said. "You saved me."

Claudius smiled, but even in his delirium, Narcissus could see that there was something a little false about it. He was still dying, then. Oh well. "You tried," he said. "You faced Caesar for me."

Claudius swept a strand of sweaty hair away from Narcissus's forehead. Even the light touch of his fingers was painful against burning skin, but Narcissus didn't flinch away. He was grateful for any contact.

"It was a very brave thing you did," Claudius said. "Stowing away on that boat."

When Narcissus smiled, his lips cracked and bled. "It wasn't deliberate. I was just hiding."

Claudius's hand kept stroking his hair. "You've saved Rome, all the same. You've paid for your freedom a thousand times over. I always meant to free you, you know. I only kept you as a slave because I thought you'd be safer that way. Protected from Caligula's malice by your insignificance." His voice drifted into silence and Narcissus's mind floated away with it, somewhere dark and filled with a terror that lingered when he startled awake and opened his eyes. He must have made some noise, because Claudius was leaning over him again. Or maybe he'd never left.

"Don't be afraid," Claudius said. "They tell me this is the crisis. When it's over, the wounds will heal and you'll be well."

Narcissus wondered why his master was speaking so clearly, without the trace of a stutter. But the thought faltered, burning up in the blazing heat of his fever, and he didn't ask the question.

"I'm sorry," Narcissus said. He meant to tell Claudius that he regretted allowing Caligula to laugh at him after the games in the Arena. That if he'd stood his ground then, and defended his master, none of this would have happened. But his memories were all jumbled, the short years of his life merging together. "I lied," he said in a childish voice. "I told you that Nerva stole the honey, but he didn't. It was me."

"I know," Claudius said in a strangely tight voice. "That's why I didn't whip him for it. You were always a terrible liar, even when you were only seven."

Tears were trickling down Claudius's face, and Narcissus didn't know why. Why was he sad? It was a beautiful sunny day and tomorrow they'd be travelling to the villa in the country with the swing he loved to play on. Dominus had promised him. "What's the matter?" Narcissus asked. "Why are you crying?"

Claudius took his hand and kissed the palm. "Because I love you. I love you and I don't want to let you go."

Narcissus nodded and closed his eyes, trusting his master absolutely. A darkness was waiting for him, deep and restful, and he let himself sink into it.

* * *

PETRONIUS HAD BEEN drinking since dawn, huddled alone in a corner of the same dingy tavern where Caligula had found them. He caught his reflection in a silver platter and saw that his lips were stained dark red with wine. There was a lot more of it inside him. His head was spinning in a way which he knew would remain pleasant for another hour or so, then swiftly become unbearably nauseating, before finally triggering a relentless, pounding headache. As his father had often complained, he had extensive experience with inebriation.

His father. He, of course, was the reason that Petronius had been drinking so long and so hard. Because Petronius had realised, some time during the euphoria of convincing Caligula that they were actually telling the truth, that he'd completely destroyed any possibility of going back to Seneca's. That left him really only one option: being welcomed back into the bosom of his family.

He didn't anticipate an effusive welcome. For one mad moment he'd contemplated asking Caligula to vouch for him. To explain that, just this once, he really had been acting entirely selflessly. However, one look in the Emperor's over-bright, half-crazed eyes had convinced him that would be a bad idea. He'd wanted Boda with him, too, to provide moral support – or, if necessary, muscle. But did he really want her to know how little his family thought of him? No. So he'd left her being questioned by Caligula with her barbarian clansman and headed off alone. He'd only stopped for a quick drink to fortify his nerves.

That had been half a day ago, when the sun was just rising. It was setting now. If he didn't go soon, the doors of his home would be bolted against everyone. He sighed and heaved himself to his feet. The room staggered, or maybe he did, and he grabbed the edge of the table for support.

It took him two tries to find the door, by which time he had a bloody nose from walking into the wall and a bruised arse from bouncing back onto it. That was good, he decided. If he looked like he'd been roughed up, his father might treat his stories of rogue cults and raised dead more seriously.

"What do you think you're doing here?" his father said coldly, and Petronius blinked. Hadn't he just left the tavern a second ago? He swayed and put a hand out to steady himself, grabbing his father's toga rather than the doorframe by mistake. His father looked down at Petronius's hand as if it was a cockroach which had just landed on him.

"I've come to..." Petronius trailed off, temporarily forgetting what it was he had come to do. "I've come to be welcomed back into the loving arms of my family!" he shouted, pleased to have remembered.

His father brushed his hand away and stepped back. "You're no member of this family, boy. Seneca told me how you disgraced yourself."

"He did?"

"Caught in bed with Seneca's own niece – for shame! How can your mother and I show our faces in public after that?"

Petronius frowned, confused. It certainly sounded like the kind of thing he would have done. But he was fairly sure he hadn't. "I don't think that's true," he said.

His father made a disparaging noise.

"I mean, I know that's not true! That's really, really, not even the tiniest, slightest bit true." Inspiration suddenly struck. "Think about it. Why on earth would I do something so stupid?"

"Because you always do?" his father suggested.

"Yes, but... But I didn't! I did nothing wrong there. It's Seneca who's the villain!"

"Really."

He realised that his father had started to swing the door shut and stuck out his foot to stop it. He yelped as it slammed into his toes. "No, honestly, you have to believe me. Seneca's running this Cult, you see. The Cult of Ishtar. No – the Cult of Isis! He's sacrificing virgins. I saw him do it. Well, try to do it. And he's raising the dead."

Now his father looked disgusted. "That's the best you can do, is it? I'd hoped your time with Seneca might at least have improved your powers of invention."

"I'm not lying!" Petronius said desperately. But his voice echoed too loudly in his own head, resonating against his skull and down into his stomach where it threatened to send his dinner back up. He swallowed with difficulty, feeling a cold sweat start on his face.

"You've shamed me and you've disgraced your family," his father said. "But no more. From now on, you're no longer Petronius of the Octavii. You're Petronius the wastrel, the orphan – the man without family or name!" He kicked Petronius's foot aside, and slammed the door in his face.

Petronius stared at the closed door for a few minutes. Then he knelt down and was violently sick on the doorstep.

ONCE IT BECAME obvious that Narcissus was too ill to speak, Caligula summoned Boda and Vali for questioning. Boda had heard much about the Emperor's madness and lust for blood. They said he'd bedded his own sister, and made his horse a consul of Rome. She'd been prepared for his erratic mood and knife-edge temper – but not for the sharpness of his mind.

He kept them with him for hours, going over their accounts again and again to wring every drop of information from them – and, she suspected, to test them for any inconsistencies. There were none in hers, she knew that. She had nothing to hide and told him the unvarnished truth.

When it came to Vali, she wasn't so sure. His narrative remained unchanged with each retelling, but there was something too perfect about it. It had the neat structure of a story, not the messiness of real life. He claimed he was a bard of the Cimbri, that he'd heard tales of the Egyptian gods and come to Rome to learn more. He said he'd been searching for new stories to tell and instead found a conspiracy to uncover.

Caligula believed it. Why wouldn't he? He knew nothing of her people or their ways. But she did, and no bard she knew would have acted as Vali did. And he'd also told them that Sopdet was his sister. Both couldn't be true, but each explanation was equally plausible. Or implausible.

She saw Vali's sly, relieved smile as they left the Emperor and knew that she was right to suspect him. His smile widened when he caught her expression and she also knew that he would never tell her the truth.

"A fine performance," she said dryly.

He bowed mockingly, red-brown eyes glinting in the sunlight. "I live to entertain. And now the Emperor will act against the Cult."

Boda frowned. "If he's to be trusted – or relied on."

"You think we should continue our own investigations, then?"

"I think we'd be fools not to."

They searched for Narcissus, but a guard on his door told them he was too sick to receive visitors. Boda had seen the waxy pallor of his face when they brought him down from the cross and could well believe it. She wasn't sure he'd last the day. Vali looked like he thought so too. His mouth turned down but he didn't say anything, just led them in search of Petronius instead.

He was absent too – still not back from visiting his family.

"We won't see him again till the whole thing's over," Boda said dismissively. "Now he's passed the responsibility on to someone else he can get on with what he does best – drinking and whoring."

Vali shook his head as they settled onto cushions in a small back room of the palace. "I wouldn't be so sure about that." Boda could see his eyes studying her from beneath lowered lids. His hair looked darker in the shaded room and the angles of his face sharper. There was something curious about it – she couldn't decide if he was very handsome or profoundly ugly.

"The boy is in love with you, after all," he said.

She snorted. "In lust with me, you mean."

"No, I don't think so. He risked his life for you, or so you said."

Yes, he had, and it made her uncomfortable. She didn't want to be indebted to any Roman, much less the one who owned her. And she definitely didn't want to like Petronius. But she found that she did, his irresponsible laughter and quick wit. He was nothing like any of the men of her own people. Except, she realised, for Vali. There was mischief in both their eyes.

There was mischief in his eyes as he looked at her now. "A love requited, perhaps?"

"Don't be ridiculous, he's a decade younger than me!"

The shadows disguised Vali's expression, but she thought perhaps he looked pleased.

"Besides," she said. "Love is a bad reason for heroism."

"Is it?" Vali titled his head, puzzled. "And what would be a good one?"

She shrugged. "Loyalty. Honour."

Vali laughed. "Loyalty is reciprocal – it demands something in return. And honour is for the self alone. Love is the best motivation of all, the only one that's purely for another."

There seemed to be some message in his words, but Boda couldn't decipher it. Vali's riddling talk infuriated her. He was the first man of her own people she'd met since being taken captive, and he ought to have been the first with whom she felt the bond of shared knowledge and beliefs. Instead, he baffled her. She understood Petronius better.

"It's no matter," he said, almost in answer to her unspoken thoughts. "The boy will return, and in the meantime, I have something we should look at."

He pulled a scroll from beneath his tunic. An old, unpleasant smell fluttered out with it. "The Egyptian *Book of the Dead*," he told her. "We found it in the Library of Alexandria."

"And you believe it has some clue to the Cult's purpose?"

"I believe it's their holy book – the thing which guides them."

She shuffled nearer to peer at the parchment over his shoulder and its musty odour was swamped by the sharp, almost spicy scent of Vali's body. He smelt like burnt cinnamon.

She shook her head and glanced back down at the scroll as he unrolled it. Images flashed quickly by – a beetle, animal-headed men, the moon between the horns of a cow – but he didn't pause over them and she guessed he must have studied that section already and found nothing useful. He seemed able to decipher the strange script of the Egyptians, though her own people had no written language and she herself could barely make out the letters of the Roman alphabet. Yet another of his mysteries.

Finally, he paused. She could see what had caught his eye, a drawing of twelve bandaged-wrapped figures circling a thirteenth corpse laid out on an altar. A screaming woman hung above them all. It was her own intended sacrifice in every detail, and she couldn't repress a shudder at the memory.

"Last night's ceremony," Vali said. "'And the blood that is spilled shall waken the thirteenth, for the thirteen months of the greater year. And as the year is completed so shall the gate be opened, when the moon rises where it is not seen.'"

"But does it say what the gate is?" Boda asked.

Vali unrolled the scroll further, scanning it, until he read: "'The souls of the dead shall fly out, and the mortified flesh will rise, and the river that is life will flow backwards, taking from the sea and giving to the land a harvest of destruction, and the life before shall be as the life after.'"

"Well, that's as clear as mud," she said.

He laughed. "I think it's as I said, a permanent portal between the underworld and this world."

"Even if it isn't," she conceded, "it certainly doesn't sound good. But if it has to be done when the moon's hidden, they have to wait another month. The difficult thing will be tracking down all the cultists. If we leave any out there, they can still perform the rite. It doesn't stipulate the number of worshippers who have to be present, does it?"

He shook his head. "Just the number of corpses." He continued to shuffle forward through the scroll as he spoke, sometimes hesitating over a word or image before moving quickly on.

When he stopped, frozen into immobility, Boda immediately understood why. She didn't need to read the Egyptian script to understand the drawing in front of them. A circle of circles, it was clearly a chart of the phases of the moon.

Three of them were entirely black.

"Allfather!" Boda hissed. "This says – does this really say that the dark of the moon lasts for three nights?"

She could see Vali's eyes flick from side to side as he scanned the text beneath. When he'd finished he didn't need to say anything; she could read the answer in his face.

"When does the moon rise tonight?" she asked, voice harsh with panic. It was already dark outside, the first stars struggling to shine through the lights of the city.

"I'm not sure," he said. "Last night it was a few hours after sunset."

"And will it be the same tonight?"

He spread his hands hopelessly. "It might be. We have to hope it is."

"If Caligula sends a regiment of his soldiers, there's time for them to stop it."

"We'll have to hope so," he repeated.

But Caligula was nowhere to be found. Eventually they tracked down a slave who knew his location: a large house on the far side of Rome. The slave didn't think Caesar would want to be disturbed. Boda didn't care what Caesar wanted, but the house was too far away. The moon might rise unseen while they searched for it.

This time they didn't listen to the guard outside Narcissus's room, pushing past him to get inside.

Claudius glanced up sharply as they entered. Boda could see the faint glimmer of tear tracks on his cheeks.

"Is he...?" she said. The figure on the bed looked very still, arms and torso bare where he must have tossed the sheets aside in a fever sweat.

Claudius lowered his eyes again. "Gone," he said.

Boda bowed her head for a second. "I'm sorry. But we've made a terrible mistake."

"Have you?" Claudius's voice was flat and dull, as if he wasn't really listening to his own words.

She turned to Vali, hoping he could rouse the old man, but he was staring at Narcissus, an unreadable expression on his face. She dropped to her knees beside Claudius and grasped his arm. "The moon is dark again tonight," she told him. "The Cult can hold their ceremony. They might be holding it right now!"

Claudius laughed, a horrible, joyless sound. "So the w-w-world will d-d-die on the night my Narcissus has."

She tightened her fingers on his arm. "But there might still be time! If you order the Praetorian Guard to the catacombs, we could stop them."

"If I did..." He pried her fingers away without looking at her. "And why sh-sh-should I? Why sh-sh-should I save my n-n-nephew's city when my boy is no longer in it?"

His eyes finally met hers, bleak and hard.

"Please," she said. "Everyone will die – *everyone* – if we don't stop this."

"Let them," he said. "Let tonight be the end of it all."

Petronius returned to consciousness with a cry of pain as someone trod on his hand. They'd moved on by the time he was able to pry his gummy eyes open and he remained lying on his back for a moment, trying to piece together the shattered fragments of his mind.

He'd had another argument with his father, he remembered that. No – he'd had a terminal argument with his father. Which meant – yes. He rolled over on his side and looked around him. He was lying in the gutter, somewhere in one of Rome's less salubrious neighbourhoods. He thought he must have continued drinking after his father disinherited him, but the memory was as blurred as rain on glass.

He wanted to carry on lying there. It wasn't comfortable, but it was flat, and it wasn't as if he had anywhere else to lay his head. He had no home, and no apprenticeship. His head felt like an elephant had urinated in it, but his thinking was a little clearer. He knew he had no choice left but to throw himself on Caligula's mercy.

He didn't anticipate that going any better than the encounter with his father. In fact, he suspected it might go considerably worse. At least his father wouldn't actually kill him.

Two more people walked past him, stepping over rather than on his body this time. They were too well dressed to be out at this time of night in this neighbourhood, he thought, as their trailing togas swept over his face.

With a groan of effort and pain, he rolled onto his stomach, then heaved himself up to his knees. He knew those men. They were cultists. And so were those three women scurrying past on the other side of the road. Now he thought about it, he suspected the man who'd trodden on his hand had been a cultist too.

His heart started pounding and he felt a wave of nausea that had nothing to do with the wine he'd been drinking. He didn't think they'd seen his face. He was just a drunk in the street and they hadn't paid him any attention. He had to make sure it stayed that way.

Head lowered, he staggered across the road, into the shadow of a statue of Tiberius Caesar. A few eyes flicked over him but none of them paused. He still looked like a hopeless drunk. He *was* a hopeless drunk, he thought angrily. If he'd had his wits about him he might have noticed this far sooner.

The cultists were being clever about it, he could see that now. They came in twos and threes, leaving a gap between each group. No one who didn't know who they were could possibly suspect anything.

But Petronius did know. He just didn't know what he could do about it.

BODA WASN'T SURE why she was doing this. She and Vali couldn't defeat the cultists alone, and they hadn't been able to persuade a single soldier to accompany them from the palace. She would have welcomed even Petronius's presence. He, at least, might have some idea of where the Cult's chamber lay inside the catacombs. In his absence, she and Vali were trusting to blind luck.

Vali was leading, the torch in his hand casting long shadows behind them on the grey, uneven rock. His footsteps were nearly silent, hers a little louder. She was glad of even that low noise. It made this place seem real, not the half-dream it had been when she'd last been here, still shaking off the effects of the drug they'd made her drink.

The dead lay all around. Some of the bones had crumbled to dust, but many skeletons were intact, curled inside their niches in the wall. The Cimbri burnt their dead. She thought that better – a quicker route to the other side than this slow rotting away.

They hadn't seen anyone else approaching the catacombs when they came. Even deep inside as they were she could hear no breathing except their own.

"This is a good sign," she whispered to Vali.

"Is it?" His head was bowed as he walked in front of her, the tunnel too low to accommodate his full height.

She nodded, even though he couldn't see it. "I don't think any cultists are here yet. We might be able to sabotage the ceremony before they arrive. If we burn the body they won't be able to reanimate it, will they?"

His narrow shoulders shrugged. "Maybe not. Or maybe it's over, and we're already too late."

They stumbled on. From time to time the torchlight revealed their own footprints in the dust ahead of them, and they knew that they'd doubled back on themselves. And all the time Boda felt a prickle of fear between her shoulders, as if some primordial instinct sensed the hidden moon nearing the horizon – or already over it.

Then, finally, they stumbled on a chamber that Boda recognised. She'd stared at that rock formation – the one that looked like a rider on a bucking horse – for long minutes while they chained her arms and legs to the grating.

She grabbed Vali's arm, pulling him to a stop. "This is the place they prepared me for the ceremony. The chamber's very near here."

He looked around, frowning, and she knew what was worrying him. It worried her too. There was no sign of any cultists, no glimmer of light from the surrounding tunnels. And the grating itself and the chains with which they'd bound her were gone.

Five minutes later, when they found the central chamber, that was empty too. There were bloodstains on the slab of rock that served as an altar, but no body. Boda could see marks through the dust on the cavern floor where Josephus's corpse had been dragged away.

Vali and Boda looked at each other with the same horrified understanding. The cultists were gone from here, and they weren't coming back. Tonight's ceremony would take place somewhere else.

CHAPTER ELEVEN

PETRONIUS HOVERED ON his toes, wracked with indecision. Two more cultists were passing him now, the first he'd seen for several minutes, and possibly the last. If he let them go, he might lose them altogether. But if he followed them, they'd be bound to spot him. They still needed a sacrifice, and they'd lost Boda. He didn't want to volunteer himself as a replacement.

The second of the pair paused to adjust the shoulder of her white peplos, then disappeared round the corner. Petronius hesitated only a second more, then hurried in her wake. He'd been introduced to the Cult as just another member. There was no reason for them to suspect him – only Seneca and Sopdet knew his part in Boda's escape. As long as he didn't run into them, he should be safe.

Still, he hung back, keeping to the shadows as he slunk after them. He didn't have far to follow. In fact, he guessed their destination several streets before they reached it. The Temple of Isis. Its ornate marble façade loomed ahead, crowned with a silver dome.

He hovered at the edge of the wide square which held the Temple. A tradesman's horse, forced to a halt by the crowds of wagons which crowded the roads at this time of night, pushed its nose into his palm. He stroked its long, silky face absentmindedly.

He didn't know what the cultists were doing, but he could guess. They intended to complete tonight what they'd started the night before. Why else risk a meeting when they must know that the authorities had been warned against them?

Last night the ceremony had seemed to drag on for ever, but he thought that it had actually lasted less than an hour. It might be shorter tonight. There might be no ceremony at all, just a quick knife across the throat of some poor unfortunate and it would all be over. Petronius had almost no time to find help.

The palace was on the other side of Rome. It would take him half an hour to reach it – out of the question. He'd have to persuade someone nearer at hand to intervene. There were a few soldiers outside a building on the far side of the square. He could see their blood-red cloaks and the glimmer of their armour and weapons in the torchlight. They'd be members of the Praetorian Guard, of course. No other legion was allowed to bear arms within the walls of Rome.

He was already crossing the square towards them, shouldering the crowd of pedestrians aside, when he realised what that meant. The Praetorian Guard protected Caesar. If they were outside that building, Caligula was almost certainly inside.

The soldiers didn't want to let him through the door. When he tried to push past, he felt the point of a sword piercing his tunic to prick a drop of blood from his stomach.

"Please," he said. "Caesar knows me and he'll want to hear what I have to say. Just send to ask him."

The guards – one short and dark, the other tall and fair – exchanged a look.

"Caesar's busy right now," the shorter one said. "Not to be disturbed."

Petronius felt a rising tide of exasperation and fury swamping his good sense. He pushed the guard's sword aside with a violent jerk. "Listen to me, you idiots –"

"Now, now," the taller guard said. "There's no need to be insulting." He grasped the front of Petronius's tunic and pulled him high on his toes until they were face to face. The soldier's breath smelled of fish, and there was a half-moon of pimples round each corner of his mouth.

"Oh, leave him be," the second guard said. "Send him in and let Caesar deal with him – however he chooses."

The tall guard smirked as he dropped Petronius, who teetered for a moment on his heels before regaining his balance. He ostentatiously smoothed down his tunic. "I can pass then?"

The short guard scratched a hand through the rough stubble on his chin. "Go ahead – it's your life, citizen."

The other man held the door open with a mocking bow. Petronius hurried through, his heart pounding. Caligula had listened to them earlier, but there was no guarantee he'd do it now. The unpredictability of his moods was notorious. And Petronius had no evidence of wrongdoing tonight, only instinct. He just had to hope that would be enough.

"THEY'RE MEETING SOMEWHERE else," Boda said. And as soon as she said it, it was completely obvious. The cultists would have been fools to return to a known location to hold their ceremony. She and Vali were fools for assuming it.

Vali's face looked very pale in the torchlight and she could see the strain in the lines around his mouth. "Where then?"

She shrugged. "Back in Rome? The chamber under the baths, maybe? Not here, anyway."

"We can still find them," he said. And though neither of them really believed it, they started moving again, retracing their steps back. They had to try. What else was there to do?

But they had no more idea how to leave the cavern than they'd known how to find it. Following their own tracks was impossible. Nearly a hundred cultists had fled from here yesterday, setting off in every direction and leaving footprint on top of footprint throughout the surrounding tunnels.

"Up," she said, because that had worked before. Vali nodded and reached out to clasp her hand. His was warm and she could feel his pulse beating a comforting rhythm through his palm. Then he pulled and they started to run, heading down the broadest of the tunnels that led from the sacrificial chamber.

The air down here was stale. Within a few paces she felt as if she'd already sucked all the nourishment out of it. Her lungs burned as they strove for more and her legs wobbled but she forced herself to keep moving. Vali's torch cast an uncertain light ahead of them, flickering and nearly dying as they moved.

Its flame was little more than a spark when the pit opened in the rock floor in front of them. Neither of them saw it in time. A stride ahead of her, Vali fell in first, and his grip on her hand dragged her in after.

The bottom was a very long way down and when she hit it, she hit it hard. There was a brief bright flash of red behind her eyes, then darkness.

CALIGULA WAS NAKED, and so were the three women with him. The youngest sat astride him, brown hair flowing down her shoulders as her head was thrown back in – Petronius suspected – feigned ecstasy.

The second squatted athwart his face and looked like she might genuinely be enjoying herself. It was probably the most fun she'd had in years – her hair was bone-white and her cheeks seamed with wrinkles. They crinkled further as her lips spread wide in a rictus of pleasure.

The third woman, a portly matron, lay sprawled alongside Caligula's lean body. She wasn't participating, just gasping for breath as if she'd recently been exerting herself.

There was something curious about the women's faces, and after a moment Petronius realised what it was. They all had the same upturned nose and rounded cheeks, the exact same shade of hazel eyes. They looked like the same woman pictured at different stages of her life. They were clearly a family, mother, daughter, and grandmother.

The mother opened her eyes and saw him staring. She screamed and sat up, clutching her hands to her breasts. The daughter jerked round at the sound, pivoting on Caligula's cock, and the grandmother fell backwards against the headboard, uncovering his face.

He looked murderously angry. "Get out!" he said. "Get out, and I'll kill you when I've finished!"

Petronius took a step back. He wanted to take more. He wanted to get out of there as fast as he could, and most of all he didn't want the image of the four of them seared on his mind for whatever remained of his life.

His hand trembled as he covered his eyes, but he didn't retreat. "I'm sorry, Caesar. I didn't mean to interrupt, but this couldn't wait."

Petronius heard the bed creaking and risked a peak between his fingers. Caligula had sat up, drawing the sheet around him. "Wait," he said. "You're one of them – a friend of those barbarians who told me about the Cult." He frowned. "Is something wrong?"

"Yes!" Petronius's voice was breathy with relief. "Yes, something's *very* wrong. They're gathering, Caesar. Tonight – in the Temple of Isis."

Caligula's petulant mouth turned down. "But you told me they wouldn't meet for another month. You lied to me!"

Petronius bowed his head. "I'm sorry. We didn't mean to – we didn't know. But tonight I was walking through the streets and I saw them, and I thought..." He swallowed as he looked into Caligula's pale, unreadable eyes. "I thought there was only one man in Rome with the power and wisdom to deal with this."

Rage twisted Caligula's mouth and Petronius stumbled against the wall as he backed away from it. He could feel his heart beating in his throat. Then, like a storm cloud in a high wind, the expression passed swiftly across the Emperor's face to be replaced with one of mild irritation. He flung the covers away from him and, buck-naked, strode across the room and through the door.

He paused on the other side and glanced back over his shoulder at Petronius. "Well, come on then. We haven't got time to waste!"

*　　*　　*

BODA KNEW THAT she'd only been unconscious for a few seconds. She could still feel the reverberation of the impact through her bones. She struggled to sit up, squashing something soft beneath her. It let out a groan and she realised that it was Vali. He must have cushioned her fall.

"Are you all right?" she asked.

"I'd be better if you took your knee out of my crotch," he told her.

Clearly not hurt too badly, then. She rolled away, onto her back. There was still light and she realised that the torch had fallen to the ground beside them, weakly aflame. It illuminated the sheer rock walls of the pit, stretching three times the height of a man above them. The small square of darkness at the top looked very distant.

Vali grunted as he sat up beside her and propped the torch against the wall. She saw that there was a smear of dirt on his left cheek, and his hair was sticking up at wild angles, glinting red in the torchlight. He caught her expression and asked: "What?"

She shrugged, smiling. "You're not always perfectly in control, then."

He laughed. "Very seldom, in fact."

She climbed to her feet, wincing as muscle and bone protested. She didn't think anything was broken, but she'd barely recovered from her long imprisonment in the cage, and now she felt as slow and inflexible as a woman of seventy. She sighed and let her fingers trail over the wall, searching for finger-holds.

Nothing. "Do we have rope?" she asked Vali, but she knew the answer before he shook his head.

He was sitting cross-legged, staring down at the ground rather than at her. She saw him prod it tentatively with a finger.

"I don't think we're going to be able to dig our way out," she told him.

"They're bones," he said. "Look."

He was right. When she knelt beside him she saw that the five white lumps she'd mistaken for pebbles were the fingers of a skeletal hand. And there beside them, half buried in the dirt, was the dome of a skull. There were still scraps of skin attached to it and strands of brittle black hair.

He picked up the torch and swept it over the floor and she could see suddenly why it was so uneven. The bodies must have been piled on top of each other, who knew how deep? There was only a thin layer of grit and dust on top of them, barely hiding the withered arms and sunken chests. There was nowhere to stand that wasn't on the dead.

She could hear her own breath, harsh and rasping. She'd never been afraid of death. She'd seen enough of it, over the years. But when she looked down at the piled bodies beneath her she remembered the corpses the cult had raised and her stomach heaved. The torchlight flickering over the bones seemed to make them dance. She was afraid to take her eyes off them in case they actually did.

She looked up again at the walls of the pit. Even if she climbed on Vali's shoulders, she'd barely reach halfway to freedom. And she'd never been much of a climber. She preferred to feel the earth beneath her feet. Unable to help herself, her gaze dropped back down to the carpet of bones. In a few months, their own might be among them.

In the end, Caligula was only able to muster twenty of the Praetorian Guard. The rest were at the palace or off duty, and there was no time to gather them.

When they marched across the square to the gates of the temple, people stopped to stare. They were mute, but their faces spoke volumes. Petronius wondered if Caligula knew how much his subjects hated him. Or did he only care about their fear?

The cultists guarding the entrance to the temple were afraid. Petronius could see that they wanted to bar Caligula's way. They'd no doubt been told to stop all comers, but whoever had given them their orders couldn't have anticipated that Caesar himself would demand entrance.

"Let me through," he said imperiously, and they glanced at each other and stepped aside.

The gates were guarded by silver statues of the goddess, horned head looking down at them. Petronius looked up at her face as they passed. Narcissus had said she was considered kind, but he didn't think whoever sculpted these statues had thought so. Her face was beautiful but remote, as if no human troubles could touch her.

The interior of the temple was dark, despite the torches lining the walls. Petronius saw that there was a vast round hole in the ceiling, a few stars glittering distantly through it. He guessed it was meant to let in the moonlight, when the moon could be seen.

More cultists rushed towards them as they marched on. Their sandals slapped against the marble floor and they brought the smell of incense with them, and a faint copper whiff of blood. Petronius felt his gut clench. Were they too late? Had the sacrifice already happened?

"Caesar," the first cultist said. "You come at an inauspicious time."

Petronius recognised the vacuous woman he'd spoken to at the last Cult meeting. She was pale and sweating and he could hear her yellow robe rustling as she trembled. She must know the risk she took speaking to Caligula this way.

He ignored her, striding onward and forcing her to trot along beside him. "There's a ceremony in progress," she gabbled as she ran. "Initiates only."

He did stop at that, his glare freezing her tongue. "Are you denying your Emperor entry? Do you really think that's wise?"

He pushed past her as she stammered an answer, and then they were at the heart of the temple. Another statue of the goddess towered in front of them, far larger than those at the door. Its face was nearly lost in shadow high above, but Petronius didn't think it looked any kinder than the others.

When they'd first entered, the low hum of Sopdet's chanting had drifted through the temple. That had stopped, but as they drew nearer to the gathered cultists, another sound grew louder. Petronius thought it was the cultists chattering until he saw that they were silent, turning from their circle to watch Caligula's approach. The ring of corpses surrounding them stood so still they might actually have been dead. Only their bandages fluttered in the slight breeze.

The sound was coming from a stack of crates behind them. As his eyes adjusted to the light, Petronius could make out something moving inside them, brown and restless like a muddy puddle in the rain. Two more paces and he flinched as he realised that the crates were entirely full of beetles.

Caligula noticed them too. He shuddered and turned to Sopdet. Petronius saw with relief that the knife in her hand was still clean and white. Above her head, a black slave writhed on the grill to which he was chained. The body beneath him on the altar was motionless.

Sopdet lowered the knife as Caligula approached.

"So it's true then," Caligula said. Around him, the Praetorian Guard drew their swords, scarlet cloaks swirling back to free their arms.

Sopdet bowed her head in submission, but when she raised it again, her eyes were unapologetic. Petronius saw that the cultists, pale and frightened, were watching her rather than Caligula – as if the high priestess represented the greater source of danger.

"Caesar, this isn't what you think," she said.

Caligula glanced around him. The Temple was bare, no ornamentation or treasure except the vast statue of the goddess and the bare stone of the altar on which a freshly wrapped corpse lay. Beyond the light of their torches, the room faded into darkness. Anything could have been hiding in it, and the soldiers shifted uneasily, moving until both Petronius and their Emperor were ringed by a circle of steel.

At the outer edges of the light, the twelve corpses suddenly moved, taking shuffling steps forward as if they intended to fight the soldiers for their mistress. Petronius saw the men's eyes narrow – then widen as they realised what the bandage-wrapped figures were. The stench of death hung heavy around them.

Caligula noticed them too. His fingers fluttered nervously, then tightened into a fist. When he looked back at Sopdet he seemed both more frightened and more determined.

"But you are raising the dead, I can see it."

She held out her hands, palm up, letting the bone knife clatter to the marble floor. "We have opened a gateway to the other world, yes."

Petronius pushed forward till he was standing level with Caligula. "And you plan to keep it open, don't you? To break down the barrier between life and death?"

The thousands of beetles hissed, as if in agreement, and Sopdet nodded. Behind her, several members of the Cult gasped. They hadn't known and – judging by Seneca's worried frown – they hadn't been intended to know.

"I don't think I can allow that," Caligula said. "I know offering you a trial would be the decent thing to do, but let's be honest" – his eyes swept the crowd of cultists cowering away from him – "there are for too many important people here for a trial to be politic. So I'll just put you all to the sword now, and make up an excuse afterwards."

He gestured at the Praetorian Guard, a negligent flick of his wrist. There was a moment's hesitation – there were Senators among the crowd, and two of the richest men in Rome – but only a moment. The soldiers could see the corpses rotting beneath their bandages. They understood why these people had to be disposed of.

Some of the cultists screamed. Petronius saw a man with a big, sweaty face and hairy arms cower behind a petite woman, probably his wife. Another dropped to his knees and then his side, curling his arms round his head as if that might somehow protect him. He smelt the sharp stench of urine as one or more of them lost control of their bladders. And these were the people who had planned to end the world? Petronius almost felt sorry for them. But he saw the slave struggling, suspended above the altar, and he remembered Boda's face when she'd thought she was about to die, and his pity curdled into contempt.

Only Sopdet seemed unafraid. Her face was as beautiful and serene as the statue's she stood under. "Kill us," she said, "and you'll never see her again this side of Hades."

Petronius had no idea what she meant, but he could see that Caligula did. His face twisted, though it was impossible to tell if it was with anger or pain. "Stop," he whispered.

The Praetorian Guard hesitated, looking around. They didn't know if the order had been for them, or for the priestess.

Petronius didn't think Caligula knew either. In the taut silence he left, Sopdet took a step forward. She was barefoot, her feet startlingly brown against the white marble beneath them.

"Think, Caesar," she said. "If the gates are open, all may return. We have only to call them through. There will be no more mourning, or grief. Mother and daughter, husband and wife, brother and sister – need never be parted."

Caligula licked his lips, a nervous flick of his tongue. Petronius realised with a jolt of terror that the Emperor was actually moved by these arguments.

Petronius clasped Caligula's arm, hard enough for his nails to bite into flesh, not caring that he could be killed for it. They'd all be dead anyway, if Caesar gave in. "Don't listen to her," he said. "The gate between life and death is barred for a reason."

Caligula turned to look at him, a wild, almost pleading look in his eyes. "Is it? And why do people die, tell me that?" His voice thickened. "Why did she die when I loved her so much? What's the point of being Caesar if I can't open the gates of death when I want?"

Petronius shook him a little. Some of the soldiers shuffled their feet, a few pointed their swords at him. But nobody moved. Everything balanced on this one man's decision – this one, selfish, cruel, half-crazy man.

"The gods forbid it," Petronius said. "They'll punish you."

Caligula wrenched his arm free. Petronius could see the red half-moons where his nails had bitten in, and Caligula rubbed them absently as he spoke. "I am a god, you fool."

"Indeed you are," Sopdet said, and Petronius could hear in the feline satisfaction of her voice that she knew she'd won. "And Isis is a goddess, the mother of the sun, and this is what she commands."

"Then let it be done," Caligula said. "Let the gates of death be opened."

Sopdet moved as quickly as a striking snake, stooping to pick up the bone knife from the floor, then jumping to balance on the edge of the altar. The knife swept out, a white blur through the air, and its keen edge ripped through the slave's throat.

At the same moment, something opened in the darkness behind the altar – a deeper darkness like the gateway to nowhere Petronius had seen in the catacombs, the one Vali and Narcissus had tumbled through at the most opportune moment.

There was no similar reprieve now. Something flew through the dark gate, but it wasn't human. It was barely there, like the sketch of a man in the air, strokes of pale light picking out his nose and wild hair and silently screaming mouth.

The slave above the altar screamed too, a horrible bubbling sound. His limbs jerked and spasmed against their chains and his eyes rolled back in his head as the cut in his throat gaped like another mouth, wide and red.

Some of the blood sprayed on Sopdet's face, dotting it with red freckles. Petronius saw her raise her other hand to wipe herself fastidiously clean while the rest of the blood jetted down. When it struck the body lying below, it stained the bandages scarlet.

Petronius didn't realise he was running until he was right there, heaving at the corpse's arm, trying something – anything – to stop this before it was too late.

But it already was. The red of the blood soaked into and then somehow *through* the bandages, leaving them pure white again, and the apparition from the gate followed, sinking into the bandaged corpse. For a moment a face was overlaid on the blank bandages, snarling and savage. Then that too disappeared.

The corpse began to twitch, limbs jerking in a horrible echo of the slave's death throes.

Sopdet smiled mockingly at Petronius as he backed away. Even Caligula looked horrified, finally realising what he'd allowed. Sopdet seemed to sense his doubt. "Wait," she told him. "Just wait."

The corpse juddered one last time, arching its back until only its head and heels touched the altar before falling back down. Then its arms flexed and stiffened, reaching out to lever it upright. Its legs swung round, landing on the floor with a muffled thump.

Sopdet flung her head back, letting out a scream of triumph that was high and strange, hardly human. Even the cultists flinched away from it, but the corpse moved on, joining the ring of twelve that now circled them all.

Behind them, Petronius saw that the gateway to another world – to the underworld – was closing. The darkness within darkness narrowed, until only a man's arm could have fitted through.

"In the name of Osiris, brother-husband of Isis!" Sopdet called.

There was an echo, a buzzing sound that came both from the walking corpses and the insect-filled crates.

The gateway in the air stopped narrowing. And now there was a light behind it, sickly and green. It glowed on the cultists' pale faces and on the blood-streaked knife Sopdet still held in her hand.

"In the name of Horus, god-child of Isis!" she shouted, louder still.

The corpses stretched out their arms and the air crackled between them. At first it was no more than a sensation, something that prickled the hairs on the back of Petronius's neck like the build-up to a storm. Then it broke. Streaks of blue-green lightning shot out from the corpses' arms, linking them together and encircling the living in an impenetrable, brilliant barrier of light.

Petronius fell to his knees, Caligula beside him. The Emperor looked terrified. If the crackle of supernatural energy hadn't been so loud, Petronius thought he would have heard him sobbing. And so he should – he could have stopped this, if he'd chosen to.

Behind Sopdet, the gate widened, the green light behind it brightening until it rivalled the lightning pouring from the corpses' hands.

"In the name of Isis," she roared, "widow of Osiris, mother of Horus, guardian of life and death!"

There was a crack as loud and sudden as thunder, and the gateway seemed to freeze in place. At its rim, the green light swirled and congealed, hardening into a gritty grey marble. It was a true gateway now, and the landscape beyond could finally be seen, a vast dark cavern, sprinkled with sharp rocks. In the distance, a broad and sluggish river flowed.

There was something there, gathering. Petronius couldn't quite make them out, the forms tickling at his mind, like the half-remembered words of a song. Although they became no clearer as they drew nearer, flying at a terrible speed towards the gate, he realised what they were – spirits, like the one that had animated the corpse.

He would have run if he could, if there'd been any possible escape. But the ring of corpses still circled them, although the lightning that linked them was fading, sparking away to nothing.

The insubstantial spirits of the dead flew through the gateway into the living world. Petronius thought they'd come for him – that they'd possess his body as they'd animated the corpse on the altar. But they stopped behind Sopdet, hovering for a moment in which their faces became clearer, blank and hopeless, and then they plunged down and fell into the beetle-filled crates.

Behind them, the landscape of death was lost once again behind a sick, green light.

Sopdet lowered her arms, groaning, as if it was her own energy which had been used to power the ceremony, and was now drained. And, suddenly and unexpectedly, the circle of corpses slumped to the floor.

Petronius watched, expecting a trick. Expecting them to rise again, stronger and more lethal than before. But instead they seemed to deflate, the bandages slowly sinking in on themselves until there was nothing more inside them, only a fine grey dust.

There was a collective sigh from the cultists and the soldiers of the Praetorian Guard, part relief, part fearful anticipation of what might come next.

"Is that it?" Caligula asked, voice quavering. "Is it over?"

The captain of the guards shook his head. He was one of the few soldiers still standing, sword in hand. Most had dropped to their knees beside their Emperor. A few were sobbing. One was clinging to a young female cultist, his eyes darting from place to place, alert for the next threat, the next terrible, inexplicable occurrence.

And for a moment, nothing at all happened. The loudest noise was the chittering of the beetles in the crates where the spirits of the dead had vanished, almost lost beneath the clash of metal against leather as the soldiers struggled to their feet. But gradually, the sound began to change.

The hissing of wing casings rubbing against each other transmuted into the whisper of voices, thousands upon thousands of them. Petronius couldn't make out the words, but the tone was clear – cold and angry. Leaning on the altar, gasping for breath, Sopdet looked up and smiled.

Petronius took a step back, then another, almost tripping over Caligula, crouched on the floor behind him. He kept his eyes on the crates, guessing what was coming, dreading it and powerless to stop it.

Finally, like a cloud of darkness, the beetles rose into the air. A stench of shit and death rose with them and there was a blaze of green light from the gate behind. It lined their wings and sparked from their twitching antennae. And in the light Petronius could see faces, one face hovering over each beetle, and then narrowing, disappearing, somehow being sucked inside it.

The beetles, he finally understood, were carriers – transporting the spirits of the dead through the living world. The buzzing cloud, thousands strong, hovered above their heads one final moment as the light within it died. And then the beetles stretched their wings and flew from the temple out into the streets of Rome.

PART THREE

Deficit Omne Quod Nasciture

CHAPTER TWELVE

WHEN BODA FIRST heard the sound, she thought it was voices. They sounded angry and hateful, but after two hours in the pit she didn't care.

"Help!" she shouted. "Please – we're in here!"

"I don't think they can hear you," Vali said. He had spent the last hour sitting cross-legged on the ground, seemingly untroubled by their situation. Now she saw his face drain of colour, and a sheen of sweat stood out on his pale forehead.

"Down here!" she yelled, making a trumpet with her hands to amplify the noise.

Vali stood up, his long legs creaking as they unfolded. He grasped her shoulder hard, and shook. It startled her enough to silence her momentarily. He'd never laid hands on her before.

"Don't attract their attention," he hissed.

"Why not? We can't get out of here on our own. Even if it's cultists, we'll have a chance to fight them once they've rescued us. Down here we've got no chance at all."

"It's not cultists," he said. His voice sounded weary, almost defeated. "It's nothing human – nothing living."

And as soon as he said it, she knew that he was right. Why had she thought that those were voices? Now she could hear that it was the chittering of insects, thousands of them. The beating of their wings echoed down the tunnels until it was impossible to tell what direction they were coming from.

Then they were there, a dark cloud hovering over the mouth of the pit. Boda didn't know why they frightened her so much. They were just insects – what could they do? But she remembered the beetles in *The Book of the Dead*, and guessed these were part of the Cult's plans.

"We're too late, aren't we?" she said. "It's already happened."

Vali just nodded as the cloud of beetles flew on, a smaller group detaching and swooping down towards them.

Boda crouched, covering her eyes. The wings brushed her cheeks as they passed, but they didn't settle on her. She waited a second for something more, something worse. When it didn't come she slowly uncovered her eyes.

Vali was still standing, looking down at the ground. Boda followed his gaze and saw the beetles burrowing – into the pile of corpses.

A moment later, the corpses stirred. The earth covering them shook and slid aside, and the brown finger-bones of a dead hand curled around her ankle and pulled.

A FEW OF the beetles remained, hovering around the altar as the cultists slowly rose to their feet. Most were white and shaking, but a few were beginning to smile. Caligula dismissed them from his mind. They were merely Sopdet's tools, as she had become his. They could be rewarded or punished later as he saw fit.

Sopdet looked at him, half smiling. "It's done," she said. "Thank you, Caesar."

The Praetorian Guard were beginning to collect themselves, forming up in ragged ranks on either side of him. They hadn't exactly covered themselves in glory during the last hour or so, and their faces suggested they knew it. He'd have to punish some to educate the others, and from the grim set of their mouths several of them knew that too.

"It's not done," he told Sopdet. "You have what you want. Whereas I..."

She nodded. "Your sister, yes. I can sense her, waiting on the other side of the gateway. She's been waiting for you there from the moment she died. I can summon her through, but we need a body to house her. Although the spirits can animate anything that was once flesh, I imagine you might want a fresh corpse for her."

Now that it was almost here – now that it was finally possible – he found himself shaking with excitement. Or was it fear? He couldn't tell. For a moment he thought about telling Sopdet that he'd changed his mind, that he wanted to wait a little longer. But what if the opportunity never came again?

The cultists were an unpromising looking bunch. There were more men than women and the few women were more notable for their wealth and power than their youth and beauty. "You," he said, pointing to the prettiest and youngest of them. "Come here."

She hesitated.

"Your Emperor commands you," he said, and the soldiers to either side of him drew their swords.

A man approached with her, probably her husband. She bowed, so low that her thick brown hair brushed the floor. "I am Publia of the Julii, and this is my husband, Antoninus. Your loyal servants." When she rose from the bow her eyes met his, desperate and pleading.

Her husband gripped her arm. His long, melancholy face was pinched tight with fear. "Please, Caesar," he said. "We have slaves – young ones, pretty ones. I can bring them here in less than an hour."

Claudius turned to Sopdet. "Tell me, once a spirit is embodied, can it move? Or is that it – stuck forever in the new body?"

She smiled. "Once inside a scarab, the spirit is a free agent in the living world. It can move at will."

"Good," Caligula said, and then to Antoninus. "Yes, bring your slaves. I'll choose the appropriate vessel for myself."

The man sagged with relief as Caligula turned to his soldiers. "In the meantime, kill that woman for me. But do try not to damage her too much – a knife through the back would probably be neatest."

Antoninus let out a choked cry of protest. He flung himself towards Publia, but it was already too late. She opened her mouth on what might have been a scream. Only a soft cough came, and then a flood of red-purple blood.

Caligula looked down at her corpse, as the last of the life twitched out of it. To one side, his soldiers were holding back a sobbing Antoninus, but that didn't interest him. Publia's blood was gently steaming as it pooled around her. He watched and watched, waiting for his sister to appear. Nothing.

"You lied to me!" he screamed at Sopdet. "You said that she'd come back!"

The cultists surrounding her backed away, but Sopdet herself seemed unmoved. "Patience, Caesar," she said. "She's found her carrier – look."

And there she was at last – *at last*. He could see the outline of her in the air, sketched in pale blue fire. She was screaming and his heart clenched. Did it hurt, coming back? But it didn't matter. She'd be here soon, whole again, and then he could ask her himself.

Drusilla's spirit hovered for a moment, high above them. Then one of the cult's beetles flew to meet it and her form twisted and narrowed and slipped inside, between its wide mandibles.

The beetle's wings whirred as it flew down towards Publia's body. Her mouth was still open, only a trickle of blood seeping from one corner. The beetle's legs pattered through the pool of fluid, leaving little red pinpricks on her cheek. Then it was inside her mouth. For a moment its back legs were visible, waving at them. There was a sudden stronger smell of blood and something meatier, the sound of chewing, and the legs disappeared.

The smell of bile joined the stench as Antoninus fell to his knees and vomited, dry-retching when there was nothing left inside him to bring up.

The chewing inside Publia's head went on for a few more seconds, and Caligula tapped his foot impatiently. Then, finally, she sat up.

One of the cultists screamed, and a soldier dropped his sword. Even Caligula found himself jumping back. For a moment Publia's eyes were blank and staring, as if no more than a beetle's intelligence lived behind them. Her head swivelled, stiff on her neck, until her unseeing gaze settled on him.

"Drusilla?" he said. His voice was a dry croak.

Publia's dead body smiled. "Hello again, brother."

VALI SAVED HER, stamping on the skeletal hand and grinding its bones to dust. But there were more, hundreds more, a pit filled with them, and one by one they were all waking.

"We've got to get out of here!" he said.

Boda laughed, high and hysterical.

He shook her, rattling her teeth. They made the sound of bone on bone, just like the bodies beneath them. She shivered convulsively and he shook again, shook her until she put her hands on his arms and pushed him away.

"We can climb," he said. "The rock's soft – look." He dug his fingers in, above his head, and the stone flaked away until there was enough room to fit the tips of his fingers inside, but no more. "Your feet too!" he said, and she saw him kick a hole in the pit wall a foot above the floor, then hook his foot in it, using the finger-hold to heave himself up.

But the corpses were pulling themselves up too. She saw one, skull bobbing on its narrow neck as its legs struggled free of the earth. She lashed out in terror, kicking the dome of the skull, and it broke off and flew to imbed itself in the wall behind.

For the first time, something like reason triumphed over blind panic. They weren't invulnerable. They were just bone, and she'd hacked enough of that, even if it had been wrapped in flesh at the time.

She drew her sword from its scabbard and swept it around her. Vali was four feet up now, above the blade's path, and she was able to spin in place, clearing the pit of everything that had emerged.

There were more, though, and still more beneath them. Another skeletal hand grabbed her foot, then another, and though she stamped them into fragments she knew they'd overcome her eventually. There were far too many of them.

"Boda!" Vali shouted. "Climb!"

She hesitated a moment, sword in hand. To climb she'd have to sheath it, and the thought of facing the legions of dead without a weapon was horrifying. But in the end, she had no choice. She slashed with the blade one last time, low and wide, giving herself a second's grace. Then she dug her fingers into the stone above her and pulled.

Her legs flailed gracelessly against the wall. She hadn't thought to make a hole for them first and without any leverage there was no force behind her kicks. As she struggled something brushed against her leg. She looked down and saw an arm, brown and rotten, reaching towards her. It was blind, the head still buried beneath the ground. But she could see the skull's dome rising from the earth and soon it would see her.

One more wild kick and her foot stuck in something. She realised that it was a hole Vali had dug on his way up. In the panic of battle she hadn't thought to literally follow in his footsteps, but she thought of it now. She could see him hanging, fifteen feet above her and slightly to her left. The pale oval of his face looked down on her as she reached her left arm out, running her palm over the wall until she found the dent he'd left.

His fingers were broader than hers and the hole threatened to be too big, spilling her back to the pit's floor still far too close below. She grimaced and dug her nails in, then stretched her leg out and found a foothold before her handhold gave.

Bone fingers closed on her calf. Every instinct screamed at her to kick out at them. She bit her lip and forced herself to stay still, only her right hand grappling above her for another hold.

But she couldn't stop herself from looking down. The floor of the pit was full of the dead. And escape lay twenty feet above her. She fumbled for another handhold, closing her eyes so she wouldn't have to see what waited for her below.

Caligula held out his hand, drawing Publia's corpse to its feet. Its face smiled but the expression looked wrong, as if whatever lived inside it now didn't quite know how to move its features naturally. The Emperor didn't seem to care. He leaned forward and pressed his lips against the corpse's, ignoring the blood smearing across his mouth and cheek.

To one side, held fast between too beefy soldiers, Antoninus yelled a wordless, helpless protest.

Petronius didn't think he'd have a better opportunity to escape. He toed his sandals off, leaving bare feet to pad soundlessly across the temple floor. Untended, most of the torches had burnt to cinders in their sconces, and he found himself walking through darkness. He curled his arms around himself, shivering, and quickened his pace. The great arched doors were ahead of him, within reach now. But they didn't represent any sort of sanctuary. He'd seen the beetles fly through them. Who knew what they'd woken outside?

He was almost at the door when he heard Caligula's voice shouting something that was probably "Stop!"

Petronius hunched his shoulders, pretending not to hear. Ten paces to the door, and now he could hear the beat of approaching footsteps running towards him. Two, maybe three people. There was a jingling too and the slap of leather against skin. Soldiers. A shiver of fear ran down his back, but he forced himself not to look. If he didn't look, he could pretend he hadn't heard. And now the door was only five paces away.

He was almost through it when the soldiers caught him. They took his arms, holding them behind his back as if they expected resistance, but he didn't struggle. What would be the point?

"Leaving us so soon?" one of the soldiers asked. It was the same man Petronius had seen earlier clinging to one of the cultists, sobbing.

"When the party's over..." Petronius said, trying for insouciance. His voice only shook a little.

There were more footsteps drawing near. The soldiers turned him around between them, an ungainly manoeuvre, and he saw that Caligula was approaching, Sopdet and the cultists trailing behind.

Publia's body walked by his side. The thing that lived inside it already seemed to have better control. The stride was easy, only the arms a little too stiff at the body's sides. "Is this the one?" she asked Caligula. Her voice was mushy, as if her tongue kept getting in the way.

"Indeed he is," Caligula told her and then, to his soldiers: "Bring him."

THE MARCH THROUGH the streets of Rome back to the palace felt like a dream. It was past midnight now, and the streets were less busy. The crazy clatter of horses' hooves and wagon-wheels on flagstones had faded, leaving individual sounds easier to distinguish.

At the far side of the square, a couple were arguing. Her voice was high pitched, teetering on the brink of a sob. His was deep and abrupt, curt words interposed here and there into her long diatribe. Petronius couldn't hear what they were saying, but he could imagine it. *You're still seeing her when you promised me not to! That's a lie. You treat me like a vassal, like a slave! I love you. You never have.*

Nearer to them two traders were locked in their own argument, quieter but every bit as fierce. *I wouldn't pay ten denarii for this crap. Five is the most I'll give. You're a thief and the son of thieves. Seven then, but my children will starve.*

This was Rome, a city Petronius had known his whole life, but it seemed like an alien place tonight. When he looked at the squabbling couple, the haggling merchants, he imagined them dead. He could see the bones beneath their skin. How long before they looked like Publia, walking along at Claudius's side with some other woman peering out from behind her eyes?

Another ten minutes and they were passing the Senate House, white and austere. It stood empty now, and Petronius imagined it fallen, the tall columns cracked in two and the roof caved in, rain dripping through and plants growing out.

The next street was lined with domi, the houses of the rich. The doors were bolted, slaves posted outside as guards. A flickering yellow candlelight shone from within and there was the sound of laughter and music. Petronius had spent many similar evenings and knew this one would stretch on for hours yet, the guests drinking and eating and later fucking – if a guest or a slave had caught their eye – and they had no idea, none at all, of the devastation that was to come.

As they walked on, the cultists began to slip away, one by one. The first glanced behind him, expecting Caligula to order him back, but the order didn't come. The Emperor had eyes for no one but his resurrected sister. A flood of them left after that, scurrying away to their holes, like rats. Only Sopdet remained, smiling that tranquil, unreadable smile, as if she was enjoying some private joke.

The soldiers had dropped Petronius's arms long ago. But when he too tried to slip away they grabbed him, and the taller sour-faced man tutted.

And there, finally, was the palace. The building had stood since Augustus's time, renovated and enlarged by Tiberius, gilded by Caligula. Statues of each Emperor lined the path that led to it. The sculptor hadn't flattered. The Emperors were clearly people. There was Julius's furrowed brow and thin lips, and Augustus's weak chin. And there was Tiberius, as frightening in marble as he'd been in the flesh. His eyes were round white nothings, but Petronius thought he could see the rage in them. He wondered what the old Caesar would have thought of what his nephew had done. Would he have understood? Maybe he would. Maybe they all would. There was something wonderful, Petronius imagined, in knowing that you were the last Emperor of Rome. That yours was the last golden age.

The palace was a domus writ large. In place of one atrium there were a score, filled with bright-flowering plants from every corner of the Empire. Petronius almost smiled as they passed the lararium, where the household gods lived. Caligula had ordered his own image set up there, above all the others. His empty eyes seemed to follow Petronius as they moved on.

The Praetorian Guard had started to melt away, too, taking their usual places around the palace. Or maybe sneaking home to their wives and children. Perhaps warning them what would come, when the beetles found the graves that lined every road outside Rome. When the dead came back for the living.

Finally, they reached the great triclinium, where Caligula's infamous banquets were held. Now only Sopdet, the Emperor and his sister, and Petronius's two guards remained. And the slaves lining the walls, waiting on the Emperor's pleasure. It shamed Petronius how nearly invisible to him they'd become. But Boda had taught him to see that they were people too. He was trying very hard not to think about what was happening to her, wherever she was.

The Emperor looked at Petronius, as the soldiers forced him to his knees. Caligula's hand was twined with Publia's. Drusilla's now, Petronius supposed. Publia's face had worn an expression that hovered between haughty and ingratiating, ready to switch at a moment's notice depending on the company. Drusilla was entirely different. There was a self-indulgence about her mouth that a woman in Publia's position couldn't have afforded. Publia's plump lips pouted a shape they'd never made before.

"So he was the one who brought you there, brother," she said.

Caligula nodded. "But not to bring you back. He wanted to stop the ceremony. Isn't that right?"

Petronius thought about lying. The Emperor was crazy, he might believe him if he claimed that this had been his plan all along. "That's right, Caesar," he said. "I didn't want this to happen."

"You see!" Caligula said.

But Drusilla was still studying Petronius. She ran her fingertip up the bridge of his nose and then along the curve of his cheek beneath his eye. He forced himself not to flinch away from the ice-cold touch.

"He isn't frightened," Drusilla said.

Caligula's mouth drooped. "Isn't he? That's disappointing."

"It makes him more of a threat, Caesar," Sopdet said.

Petronius laughed, he couldn't help himself. The only things he'd ever threatened were his family's good name and his female acquaintances' virtue.

Caligula scowled at the priestess. It occurred to Petronius that the Egyptian didn't know him terribly well, although she'd managed to manipulate him earlier. She didn't understand his perversity, how little he liked being told what to do.

"The boy's intentions were good," Caligula told her. "He had the interests of Rome and his Emperor at heart. Didn't you?"

"Yes, Caesar," he said. "Only that."

"We should let him live," Drusilla said. She moved her hand to cup Petronius's chin, turning his face up to her. "He's a handsome thing. I could enjoy him."

An expression of mingled shock and pain crossed Caligula's face.

Drusilla laughed, and released Petronius to embrace her brother. She rubbed her face against his, like a cat begging for food. There was no real warmth in it, only self-interest, but Caligula's expression softened.

"How about it?" he asked Petronius. "Do you deserve to live?"

Sopdet glared and Drusilla smiled, cruelly amused. Would he talk his way out of this, or fail and die? It was clear she'd be entertained either way.

"No one deserves to live," Petronius said. "Life is a gift – from our gods and from our Emperor."

Caligula laughed delightedly. "A poet in the making! Indeed, life is a gift, and one I intend to grant you. After all, if it weren't for you,

Drusilla wouldn't be here – even if it wasn't quite what you intended."

Drusilla jumped up and down like an excited child, clapping her hands in glee. Only Sopdet glowered her displeasure, but she had the sense to keep it to herself.

"Caesar, your generosity undoes me," Petronius said. He didn't have to fake the tears in his eyes. He wasn't sure how much more he could take. "And now I beg leave to return to my family."

"Return?" Caligula said. "Don't be absurd – the day's just beginning." He snapped his fingers, bringing a slave scurrying to his side. "Send an invitation to all the top families in Rome. Tell them refusal is not an option. We're celebrating the return of my beloved sister, and there will be more food, more drink and more copulation than this palace has ever seen."

He turned back to Petronius, drawing him to his feet and slinging an arm around his shoulders. "And you," he said, "shall be the guest of honour. What fun we're going to have!"

THE DEAD REMAINED in the pit when Boda and Vali finally struggled out of it. They were too weak or stupid to scale the walls, but it didn't matter. The catacombs were full of corpses. In every nook they passed a body was uncurling, strips of rotting flesh falling as bones jerked into new life.

Boda drew her sword and swung wildly. She soon discovered that a blow to the arm or leg wasn't enough. The severed limb dropped and the dead carried on. Only a blow to the head, smashing the skull, finished them off. Her arm ached with the effort of heaving it. Vali ran beside her, wielding his small belt knife, but it wasn't much use. The blade passed through putrid flesh and between bones and did no harm at all. And the dead loomed in front of them, at every turn in every tunnel, skulls swaying on their bony necks.

They found the exit from the catacombs by sheer luck. The entrance loomed, a midnight blue within the black and then they were through and the dead were shambling after, too slow to catch them.

When they'd left them out of sight behind, Boda and Vali finally stopped. He reached out to touch her arm and when she saw the red on his finger she realised she was bleeding. The pain immediately hit, as if it had been waiting for her to notice it.

"It's nothing," she told him. "Just a scratch."

His face was more sombre than she'd ever seen it. "We failed."

"Yes. So what do we do?"

"We failed," he repeated.

Now she wanted to shake him. "We failed to stop the seed being planted. That doesn't mean we can't uproot the plant that grows."

"You really think so?"

"I have to. Or would you rather stand back and let this happen?"

"It's Rome," he said, eyebrows dipping as he frowned. "Why should you care if it's destroyed?"

"Is it just Rome?" she said. "Do you think it will end here?"

He sighed. "No. The dead will spread like a plague over the whole world."

"Then we have to stop them."

He didn't argue, but he didn't look convinced either. She could see the doubt in his face more clearly now. The sun must be nearing the horizon. The light grew and their view widened from just a few paces in either direction to ten and then twenty, and then all the way to the walls of Rome on one side and the farmland ringing it on the other.

"Odin protect us," Boda whispered.

Ahead of them, the Appian Way was lined with graves. She hadn't seen them on her journey to the catacombs but they were obvious now, a line of white pillars marching into the distance. Beside each one, the earth was churning. Some corpses had already pulled themselves free. They were fresher than the bodies in the catacombs, more whole. In the dawning light they could see Boda and Vali too. Their heads swung, nostrils flaring as they sniffed the wind.

To their left ran the Esquiline Way, lined with crosses. Some of those nailed to them were still living. During the long nights they'd been slumped and motionless, waiting for the end. Now they were twisting against the metal that held them, though it must have been agonising.

On the crosses beside them, men and women who'd already surrendered to death opened their eyes. They struggled too, harder and more determinedly. From their blank faces, Boda guessed that they felt no pain. The heads of the nails in their wrists and feet were broad. They ripped flesh and chipped bone but then the corpses were free and they fell to the ground beneath them. Blood flowed but didn't spurt with no heart to pump it.

The bodies lay crumpled as the living crucified around them screamed, and Boda hoped for a futile moment that they were too broken to move. Then bleeding hands pressed beneath the corpses to push them to their feet. A hundred heads swung towards Boda and Vali.

And nearer still there was a heap of earth taller and broader than the Senate House itself. That was stirring too. Unlike the silent human corpses, whatever lay under here was growling and hissing and braying.

Then the first animal emerged. It was a lion, killed in the Arena as everything in that charnel pit had been. A tiger followed and then a grey barrel of a monster with a single horn whose name Boda didn't know.

In her short time as a gladiator, Boda had seen thousands of animals killed. They'd all been buried here, and now they were all rising. The lions snarled round mouthfuls of sharp white teeth while the grey creature put down its head to charge.

Vali grabbed her arm, pulling her back, though nowhere was safe. The dead were everywhere. "Tell me, Boda," he said. "How can we stop this?"

CHAPTER THIRTEEN

THE GUESTS STARTED to arrive as the sun rose, bleary-eyed and desperately trying to seem happy. It was a lunatic time to hold a feast, but their Emperor had never been known for his sanity. Petronius watched them bowing and laughing and pretending they were honoured to be there.

Caligula looked happier than Petronius had ever seen him. While he talked to his guests his fingers were constantly brushing Drusilla – her arm, her waist, her face – as if he was afraid she'd disappear. The guests heard Caesar calling another woman by his dead sister's name and smiled politely, no doubt taking it for another manifestation of his madness.

The Emperor insisted on seating Petronius at his right hand, with Drusilla on his left. From there he had a fine view down the table as it was heaped high with food. When he tasted it, Petronius discovered that the suckling pig centrepiece was actually cunningly disguised fish meat. And the enormous pie no one quite dared to cut into was said to contain live sparrows. The slaves in the kitchens had outdone themselves. Amazing how motivating abject terror could be.

The Cult had been summoned to attend, too. Unlike the rest of the guests, none of them could meet Drusilla's eye. And they had even less appetite than everyone else, desultorily picking at morsels of chicken disguised as lamb or wood pigeon stuffed with humming bird whenever

Caligula looked their way.

Sopdet was seated beside Drusilla. She didn't even pretend to eat, just watched the gathering with haughty eyes. Petronius smiled smugly when she looked at him. His continual existence was a pretty small victory in the scheme of things, but he was very pleased with it.

Seneca had been seated beside Petronius. He turned and smiled at the old man. "Enjoying yourself?"

Seneca returned a smile that looked more like a grimace. "Immensely."

"Tell me," said Petronius, "because I've been wondering. Just what did you think would happen when the Cult got its way?"

Seneca paused, a wizened chicken foot halfway to his mouth. He chewed it whole before answering. "You're too young to understand."

"Funny, I don't feel as young as I was yesterday. And I want to know."

"Very well then. I wanted exactly what's happened, a breaking down of the barriers between life and death."

"But why?" Petronius leaned forward, genuinely interested. The other cultists seemed to have been in it for the prestige, the social lubrication. Many of them had seemed entirely ignorant of the actual purpose of the ceremonies. But Seneca – Seneca had known.

The old man shook his head. "When I say you're too young, it's not an insult to your intelligence or understanding." Petronius raised a disbelieving eyebrow and Seneca almost smiled. "Don't misunderstand me, I think very little of your intelligence. But what I meant was that you can't have felt the approach of your own death, felt it colouring every moment of your life. And I doubt you've lost anyone who mattered to you, not yet."

Petronius thought of his twin sisters, who'd died shortly after their birth. Or his elder brother killed in bread riots during the last emperor's reign. None of them had really meant anything to him. But he looked across at Caligula, gazing into his dead sister's eyes. "You're wrong, I do understand that. But death is long and life is short. Why not wait until you're reunited?"

"When you're grieving, every second seems like a year. A year stretches into eternity."

"Then slit your wrists and join them that way. Why should the world be changed to fit your needs?"

Seneca was scowling at him now. "I've seen the other side, boy. I know what waits for us there. When I was young I was very sick, did you know that?"

Petronius looked at the other man, the way his stick-thin limbs seemed to struggle to support even his own frail body. "I can believe it."

Seneca smiled bitterly. "My parents thought I'd die – and I did. For two whole minutes illness took me out of this world and into the next, until the doctors brought me back. And I saw..." The focus of his eyes shifted outward as his thoughts turned inward. "You've heard the legends, but like every educated man today you probably don't believe them. You laugh them off as superstition and metaphor. Idiots, all of you. The afterlife is exactly as the legends say, a bleak darkness where the sun never shines and the rivers that run are icy cold and empty of life. And the people... they've forgotten what it is to feel, or think. They're shades indeed, mere shadows of who they once were, waiting for judgement from a god who has no patience with human foibles or needs. At the age of seven, I swore I'd never return there – and Sopdet offered me a way to ensure that I never did."

Petronius was left momentarily silent by the old man's passion. His narrow, sagging cheeks were flushed and there was a light in his eyes Petronius had never seen before. And he almost agreed with him. Almost. "But this is no kind of escape," he said. "Without the barrier between them, won't this world become like that one?"

Seneca shook his head, but for the first time he looked a little doubtful. "Sopdet promised me that it's this world which will change the other."

"Did she?" Petronius looked across the half-eaten heaps of food to find that Sopdet was watching them closely. "And did you ever ask her why she wanted this? Or did you just assume her motives were the same as yours?"

Seneca's mouth thinned, and it was obvious he didn't have an answer.

BODA WAS USED to fighting other men, and the vacant look in the corpses' eyes made them easier to hack and dismember. Her arm was smeared with blood up to the elbow from the recently dead and she was splattered with fouler fluids from those who'd been lying in the ground longer.

But her people had taught her to respect animals, and the tiger was the most astonishing creature she'd ever seen. Powerful muscles moved liquidly beneath its fur and it could only have been dead a day. Despite her knowledge that it meant her harm, she couldn't bring herself to strike it. And then it leapt, lethal and beautiful.

Without thinking, she raised her sword, the point positioned precisely to skewer its heart. The sword sunk in to the hilt but the tiger didn't even slow. Its body landed on hers, knocking her to her back beneath it. Close to, she could smell the earth caked in its fur and the first hint of putrefaction.

The creature's jaws snapped shut, inches from her face. She braced her arm beneath its neck and pushed desperately, but it was no good. The tiger was stronger than her, and it had the leverage. When its jaws closed a second time its teeth grazed her nose, scraping the skin and flesh from its tip. Then its front leg slashed out, claws digging deep grooves in her arm. She gasped and her hand loosened, an involuntary reflex she couldn't control.

Instantly, the tiger lunged. She twisted her body and jerked her head to the side and this time its teeth caught her ear. They closed and pulled and she felt the lobe tear away. The agony was instant and almost overwhelming. But the moment the tiger took to swallow its morsel gave her a chance.

Her sword arm was hopelessly pinned beneath its left leg. She dropped the blade and rolled to one side, away from its terrible jaws. It tried to stop her, legs scrabbling to keep their hold on the ground, but the force it could exert sideways was weaker than the pressure of its massive weight bearing down. The leg gave and she was free.

Her own sword sliced her back as she rolled over it and her first grab took the blade and not the hilt, opening a deep cut in her palm. The hilt was slippery with her own blood when she finally grasped it, but she held on tight and swung. This time she was aiming for the neck, and her blade bit deep and stuck fast in the tiger's spine.

The tiger writhed on the end of her blade like a fish on a hook. She braced her feet on the ground and held tight. The metal rang as its teeth snapped against it but the blade held. A stalemate.

A quick glance to the left showed her that Vali had his own troubles. He faced the wickedly hooked tusks of a great black boar as a skeletal monkey gibbered on his shoulders and tore at his hair. There'd be no help for her there.

The tiger was still twisting and turning and she realised that it would never tire or stop. But she would. Her hand could barely keep its grip on the hilt of her sword and the blade was already beginning to loosen, working free of the bone.

She only had one chance. The next time the tiger's head swung round she pulled against the motion rather than moving with it, allowing the creature's own strength to wrench the metal out of its neck. The flesh and bone gave grudgingly and for a moment she thought the sword would stick fast. She was unbalanced and vulnerable – easy prey without a weapon to wield. She gritted her teeth and gave one final, desperate tug, straining her injured shoulder almost beyond endurance. And suddenly her sword was swinging free.

She scrambled desperately backwards, almost falling to her knees in her haste. The neck was still her only sensible target, beheading the tiger the only way to stop it. But she was weaker now than when she'd first tried that move, and her blade blunter.

The creature spun to face her, lips curled back as it snarled. In a second it would pounce. With a fierce yell, she circled her sword above her head – once, twice – before bringing it down with all her strength.

The blade sliced through flesh and bone and then flesh again to emerge the other side, nicked but whole.

The tiger's head flew a short distance through the air and landed neatly on its neck. Its eyes blinked and glared furiously at Boda as its jaw snapped on nothing. She stamped on its head, again and again until the bones of its skull cracked and splintered and the grey spongy mess of its brain oozed between her toes. When she finally took her foot away, the eyes were blank and the jaws still.

She took one deep, gasping breath, then turned to Vali. His short knife was buried deep in the boar's eye. Blood oozed around it and he was using it to hold the creature away from him. She wondered if he'd seen her own fight and decided to follow the same strategy. But with only a short belt knife he had no hope of administering the *coup de grace*.

Her shoulder ached fiercely and her arm burned with fatigue but she lifted her sword and brought it down behind the boar's ears. After three more strikes the creature's neck parted, and one quick thrust took the monkey's head from its shoulders, leaving the bones of its body to slither down Vali's back. There were deep scratch marks around his eyes where it had tried to gouge them out.

"You need a bigger sword," she said.

He gasped a surprised laugh. "Maybe we can ask them for one."

He gestured to their right and she realised for the first time that there were other living people nearby. Abandoned horses and wagons suggested they were merchants or farmers, bringing their wares to market. But some of them had swords and were fighting back against the dead. Boda could see small clusters of them scattered over the approach to the city's walls.

It was obvious the dead were winning. The living were hopelessly outnumbered.

"We have to get inside the city," Vali said. "The walls will keep the dead outside."

Boda nodded, looking at the struggling bands of living people. Some of them included children, huddled at the centres of groups. "Yes, we need to get to Rome. And we need to bring them with us."

PETRONIUS WAS EATING a concoction of strawberries and honeycomb when the messenger came from the city walls.

The man bent over to whisper in Caligula's ear, but he was panting for breath, and fear made his voice so loud that everyone at the table could hear it. "There's news, Caesar. Grave news..."

Caligula raised an eyebrow. "Grave enough to interrupt my dinner? To tear me away from celebrating my beloved sister's return?" His hand reached out for Drusilla but met empty air. She was leaning away from him and across Sopdet, whispering in the ear of the man beside her. The young, good-looking man with merry eyes and a full head of honey-coloured curls. Caligula's lips thinned and the messenger flinched back when he turned his angry eyes on him.

"Well?" Caligula said. "What is this news?"

The messenger looked like he wanted to turn tail and run, but he didn't, and Petronius shivered. News serious enough to risk the Emperor's wrath must be very grave indeed.

"It's... outside the walls of Rome, Caesar. There are..." He dropped his head. "The dead have risen from their graves. They're marching on the city."

Sopdet smiled gently. The cultists' eyes darted around the room, frightened or ashamed. There were a few gasps from the other guests, but mostly laugher and catcalls. Suggestions that the messenger was drunk, that he'd lost his mind.

Caligula laughed too. "The dead rising? How absurd."

The messenger's hands balled into fists. "I've seen them with my own eyes, Caesar. They're slaughtering everyone they can find. And the walls are barely defended. If they fall... You must send the Praetorian Guard to reinforce the soldiers there."

"I *must* send them? Whose command *must* the Emperor of Rome obey?"

"It's... it's... Caesar, it's..." The messenger stuttered into silence.

Caligula turned his back, flicking a finger at one of the soldiers who guarded the door. "Kill him."

The legionary stepped forward, sword drawn.

"Outside, you fool!" Caligula snapped. "We don't want to put people off their dinners. And while you're there, fetch that wretched uncle of mine. He's mourned long enough – the boy was only a slave, and a Greek at that."

The door closed behind them and it was only because he was listening for it that Petronius heard the messenger's muffled scream, quickly ended. The other dinner guests continued to gorge themselves. Caligula poured more wine for his sister. And Sopdet's eyes met his, spiteful and triumphant.

THE FIRST GROUP Boda and Vali found was completely unarmed. There had been at least twenty of them to begin with, but ten were dead now. The rest stood in a tight ring, arms held out to ward off the dead. In the middle of their circle crouched a boy and a girl, with fine light hair and open, trusting eyes. They couldn't have been older than five.

The dead weren't armed either. Unlike Boda's people, it seemed Romans didn't bury their warriors with their swords by their sides. It should have been an even match, but the walking corpses could shrug off any injury.

She saw one man kick out, the toe of his boot catching a shambling corpse between its legs. The blow was hard enough to lift it off its feet for an instant, but when it came down it leapt forward, its own arm lashing out to catch the man across the face. His head snapped back and he dropped to the ground, stunned. The circle of the living closed tight to fill the gap he'd left – and he lay helpless outside it.

Boda had to look away as the dead descended. But she smelt the blood they spilled, and the contents of his stomach as they ripped it open. She raised her sword and prepared to charge.

Vali's fingers clawed into her arm. "We can't help them. You'll just get yourself killed."

"We've got a chance," she said. "The dead are weak."

It was true these were less recent corpses, only dry skin covering old bones. When a woman kicked another in the chest, the ribs caved in, revealing hollow nothingness inside. Her sword would make quick work of them.

Vali didn't release her. "It's not just them. Look."

Behind the living, the undead animals were preparing to charge. She saw another tiger leading them, and a row of wolves behind.

"Then we save who we can," she said.

The merchants smiled as she approached, sword swinging. It cut through two corpses in one stroke and they crumpled to the ground, dead hands still grasping. Boda stamped on them as she pushed past a merchant and into the centre of the ring.

"What –" the man said.

She didn't have time to explain. Maybe these were his children. Maybe he'd understand.

Vali had followed her, though he was cursing her idiocy. Close by and getting closer, she could hear the roars and growls of the dead animals. She picked up the girl first and swung her little body high to settle it on Vali's shoulders. The boy she put on her own. His weight was almost intolerable on her injured shoulder but she made herself run, out of the ring of the living and away from the attacking beasts.

The shouts of the merchants followed them. She wanted to believe that some of them were thanks, but she couldn't worry about it. The girl was sobbing, wriggling on Vali's shoulders as she tried to look behind at her parents. Boda held fast to the little boy's legs, forcing him to face forward. She could hear the screams behind her and she didn't want him to see what was causing them.

If the animals had charged on, they would have been finished. But the creatures stopped to feast on the merchants and Boda and Vali managed to run clear, legs labouring under the weight on their shoulders.

The little girl fisted her hands in Vali's red hair and Boda saw him grimacing as he ran. A corpse lurched in front of him, teeth bared in a grin too wide for any living face. His small knife flash out and widened the smile still further, splitting the skull at the weak point of its jaw.

The corpse staggered to the side then made another grab for him – until Boda's blade took it through the stomach, sending its upper torso crashing to the ground and its legs running aimlessly in the other direction. She grabbed Vali's hand after that, keeping him within her sword's defensive range.

Ahead of them she could see another group of the living, larger and better armed than the previous ones. They even had shields, which they'd used to form themselves into a defensive turtle, the weakest members of the group crouched beneath as they shuffled agonisingly slowly towards the city walls. It was the same formation the legionaries had used when they defeated Boda's people in the western forest. Maybe there were soldiers in that group. They certainly looked like the best hope. But Boda and Vali would have to fight their way through fifty paces and hundreds of the dead to reach them.

CALIGULA COULDN'T STOP looking at Drusilla. It was amazing how quickly he'd come to accept that it really was his sister looking at him through another woman's eyes. But he knew Drusilla better than he knew anyone in the world. He was familiar with every expression that flicked across her face – the small polite smile that showed she was unbearably bored, the droop of her eyelids when she was planning some mischief, the arch of her eyebrows when she saw something she liked. He knew the way her hand would land, light but not innocent, on the arm of a man she was interested in. He'd always known what the spark of desire looked like in her face.

He knew her so well, how could he have forgotten how miserable she made him? She knew she was doing it, too. As she flirted with that son-of-a-whore Nerva, she kept shooting glances at Caligula out of the corner of her eye, gauging his reaction. Working out just how much she was hurting him. She'd always done this, *always*.

Another messenger came in, blathering something about the dead rising outside Rome. Caligula didn't bother taking his eyes off Drusilla, just clicked his fingers for a guard to dispose of him.

"Caesar," a voice drifted from further down the table. Caligula couldn't remember the man's name, but he was something big in the wine trade. "Perhaps, Caesar, we should listen to him."

There was a murmur – no, more than a murmur, a chorus – of agreement. Caligula finally wrenched his attention away from his sister to look at his other guests. They were staring back at him with expressions ranging from fearful to angry, with every shade of alarm in between.

"What is this?" he said. "Are you questioning my judgement?"

The soldier left the door open this time, and the scream of the dying messenger was very loud in the near-silent room. The only other sound was the chink of silver against ceramic as one grey-haired, barrel-chested guest continued eating, oblivious. Outside, the pile of bodies had grown quite high. Flies were beginning to buzz around them.

"Please, Caesar," the wine importer said. "Killing the messenger won't change the message. You need to do something."

Instead of gasps of shock at this treachery, there were nods of agreement from the other guests. Even some of the cultists were joining in – and they were the ones who'd caused the problem in the first place.

"I don't like that man," Drusilla said. "Get rid of him for me." She leaned back in Caligula's direction and trailed her fingernail from his shoulder to his wrist. Exactly the same trick he'd seen her using on Nerva earlier.

Caligula shrugged her hand off petulantly. Her face fell, a tear forming in the corner of her eye, and he instantly felt like a scoundrel. How did she do that to him?

"You heard her," he said to the nearest soldier. "Kill him." He looked around at the other guests, not cowed even by this, and thought that an object lesson in obedience wouldn't be out of order. "And you can leave his body where it is. Even dead he'll be better company than half the people here."

This time, the soldier didn't jump to obey him instantly. His hand hovered over the hilt of his sword as he looked across at his captain. But Marcus's face was as impassive as a statue, and he nodded without hesitation.

The man – what was his name, anyway? – rose to his feet as the soldier approached. "Don't do this, citizen. You know that I'm right. You should be at the walls fighting the enemies of Rome, not in here –" His last word tailed off into a choked gurgle as the sword took him through the gut.

The soldier pulled it free, resting a hand against the man's shoulder to ease the blade out as his knees gave from under him and he collapsed back onto the cushions. Caligula smiled to see his neighbours flinch away from his corpse. His blood pooled around him, viscous and red.

That should keep them quiet. And most of them did look cowed. Except that man there, Trajan. He had his face lowered, but Caligula caught a glint of his eyes glaring with hatred from beneath thick black brows. "Him too," he told the soldier. "And her – to the left there. Her nose has been distracting me since she got here. It's enormous."

The soldier's face was pale, but he didn't look for confirmation from Marcus before obeying this time. Trajan glared at him defiantly as the blade slid through his heart. The woman tried to flee, feet hopelessly tangling in the cushions. She held out her hands in mute pleading to the soldier, and Caligula saw him turn his face away as he killed her too.

He thought that would be an end of it, but now there was shouting all around the table. Some of the other guests were standing up, and one of them was waving a belt knife around. He didn't even have to tell the soldiers to finish that one off.

But as the chaos grew rather than abated, Caligula realised with a quiver of fear what he'd done wrong. He shouldn't have ordered that woman killed, even though she did have a quite absurdly large nose. Her killing had been too random – not the obvious result of questioning their Emperor – and now they all felt threatened. And they outnumbered the Praetorian Guard four to one.

Drusilla knew it too. Her strange new face was pale and when Nerva touched her arm she shook him off impatiently. "Do something!" she said to Caligula. "This is all your fault!"

The room was in uproar. Only Sopdet and Seneca were still sitting in place, and the youth Petronius. "You!" Caligula said to him. "How do I stop this?"

The boy looked round at the near riot, the soldiers in danger of being overwhelmed by the frantic guests. A huge, black, over-muscled man who had once been a gladiator appeared to be their ringleader. He'd managed to overpower one of the guards and take his sword, and was now laying about him with frightening efficiency. Caligula had a bad feeling he was the husband of the woman with the huge nose.

"Well!" Caligula snapped. "What can I do?"

"Not start this in the first place?" Petronius suggested. His eyes were wild, and Caligula realised he was close to hysterics.

Drusilla reached across to slap Petronius's face. "Don't be a fool! They saw my brother seat you at his right hand. Do you think you'll be spared if they win?"

The youth seemed to pull himself together a little. The hand rubbing his cheek shook as he nodded. "Let them go, then."

"They're traitors!" Caligula hissed. "They need to die."

"But we need to live!" Petronius shouted. "Didn't Julius himself say that you should never leave an enemy without an escape route? No one wants to fight a man with nothing to lose."

"He's right," Drusilla said, and smiled at Petronius with far too much warmth.

Caligula wanted to ignore his advice just for that, but then he saw the black ex-gladiator gut a soldier with his own sword. "Marcus!" he shouted. "Let them out!"

The guests heard. Some of them looked like they wanted to continue fighting. They knew they had the upper hand. But enough of them were soft and frightened and they stampeded for the door as soon as the guards moved aside from it.

For one terrifying instant, the Nubian gladiator stood in front of Caligula, sword raised for a killing blow. His mouth opened in a roar of rage – and instead of words, a torrent of blood poured out of it. Marcus had skewered him through his undefended back.

After that, the remaining guests turned tail and fled. They left behind a room littered with corpses. Some had fallen onto the table, heads buried in bowls of syllabub or resting on raspberry flans. The smell of fruit and cream and cinnamon almost overwhelmed the stench of blood. Four of the Praetorian Guard were dead, too, and several more injured.

Claudius, with his usual genius for ill-timing, chose that moment to finally join them. His eyes scanned the destruction with horror, lingering over the mutilated body of a fourteen-year-old girl. When they looked at Caligula, horror had been replaced with accusation. "What h-h-happened here, nephew?"

Caligula shrugged but couldn't meet his gaze. "There was a rebellion. They disobeyed me."

Some of the soldiers shuffled, and he heard a cough as if someone was about to speak, but nobody did.

Claudius leaned down to close the young woman's staring eyes. "A rebellion?"

"A very entertaining one," Sopdet said. She'd remained seated throughout the whole thing, untouched by any of the combatants. Now she rose gracefully to her feet. "I thank you for your hospitality, Caesar, but myself and Seneca have other things to attend to."

Caligula scowled. "You think you're going to leave? You're the one who caused all this!"

"I think you'll find," Seneca said, "that it was your own inability to control your temper which sparked it off. It really is quite extraordinary – the mightiest empire in the world ruled by a man with the self-control of a three-year-old."

Caligula was shocked into temporary silence. No one had ever spoken to him in that way. Even the people he had ordered put to the sword were too afraid for the families they left behind. "How dare you?" he finally said, voice trembling with rage. "You'll die for this."

Sopdet rested a hand on Seneca's shoulder as she stood beside him. "Really? Do you really think creating more corpses is a good idea?"

"Why not?" Caligula raged. "You're all ingrates – treacherous scum. Why shouldn't I kill you all?"

"Because," Sopdet said, "you're simply adding to the forces on my side."

Caligula stared uncomprehendingly at her as she snapped her fingers. But when the beetles flew through the doorway in answer to her summons, he knew exactly what it meant.

"Stop them!" he yelled.

The soldiers leapt to obey, swords flailing uselessly at the tiny, flying targets. Untroubled, the beetles buzzed past the metal and settled on the corpses.

Caligula dived at the nearest one, trying to brush the insect away from the dead gladiator's mouth. But he couldn't get a purchase on its slick carapace and then it was in the man's mouth and burrowing through to his brain. A moment later, the corpse's eyes opened, staring straight into Caligula's.

He screamed and jumped back, pressing himself against Drusilla. She whimpered and buried her face in his shoulder as all around the room the corpses of the recently dead woke.

The Praetorian Guard moved, ready to attack – and their own dead rose to face them. The soldiers' faces drained of colour and their swords drooped in their arms as they looked into their comrades' dead white faces.

"Your rule is over, Caesar," Sopdet said. "Soon there will be no one left alive within the Servian walls. And then the armies of the dead will march from Rome, until this whole world is a second kingdom of death."

THEY WERE ALMOST within arm's reach of safety when the horse attacked. At first Boda thought it was a stray, panicked by the fighting around it. Then, as it turned to face her, she saw the red gleam in its eye. Its hoof pawed the ground and its lips pulled back, baring yellow teeth. She saw that the flesh of its belly had fallen away, leaving the white arch of its ribs exposed as its entrails dangled in the dirt below.

The little boy on Boda's shoulders yelled and the horse reared, hooves lashing out towards Vali as flecks of spittle flew from its mouth.

Vali crouched, shielding his head. But the move was pure instinct, an animal reflex that didn't take account of the little girl sitting on his shoulders. The horse's kick caught her head straight on, stoving in her skull in one blow. She didn't even have time to scream, just slumped lifeless on Vali's shoulders.

Boda saw the moment Vali realised what had happened, as the little girl's blood trickled through his hair and into his eyes. He shuddered convulsively, even as his hands still clung tight to the dead girl's legs, holding her above him as the rest of her blood drained out of her.

The horse reared again, directly above Vali's crouched body. Boda couldn't reach the creature's neck, stretched taught with strain above her. Instead she swung her sword at the legs themselves, putting every atom of her remaining strength into the blow.

Her sword swept clean through the joint above the hoof and out, first the right leg and then the left. The horse screamed and began to fall, all its weight plummeting towards Vali's head.

Vali didn't move. His face was blank, no fear in it, no expression at all. Boda's heart raced. She'd seen this before – battle shock. It had paralysed him. The horse's legs were inches from his face now, and its balance was gone. Its whole body would fall on him.

She didn't think, just flung herself at Vali, knocking him to the side as she clung on desperately to her own small human burden.

The horse fell to one side of them, landing on the stumps of its forelegs. It screamed its frustration, but without its hooves it couldn't move and though its mouth foamed and snapped at them, they were out of its reach.

They lay, dazed, in a disorderly heap, Vali at the bottom, Boda on him and the little boy resting on her back, gabbling nonsense words that might have been his idea of a prayer. The dead girl's corpse was beneath them all. Boda could see the sloppy mush of flesh and bone that the fall had made of her little body.

When Vali realised what he was lying on, it seemed to snap him out of his stupor. He let out a cry of revulsion and rolled to one side, pulling Boda and the small boy with him. The girl's mangled body lay motionless where it had fallen. Vali couldn't seem to take his eyes off it. He wasn't weeping, but his silent grief and horror were harder to bear.

Then, as they watched, a beetle landed on the girl's lips. By the time Boda realised what it was, it had crawled inside her mouth and out of sight.

Vali whispered something, a wordless denial, but it was already too late. The light which had so recently gone out in the girl's eyes sparked back into life. Her knees were bent at the wrong angle, her chest squashed almost flat, her intestines oozing from its sides, but somehow she stumbled to her feet. And then, teeth bared, she came towards them.

Boda had to force herself to keep her eyes open as her sword separated the girl's head from her neck. Beside her, Vali fell to his knees and was copiously sick.

It was the little boy who pulled them out of their shock. Boda was horrified to realise that she'd forgotten him – forgotten to shield his eyes from what she'd done to his friend. But he wasn't looking at her. He pointed over Boda's shoulder. "Soldiers," he said.

He was right. In the minutes their fight had taken, the group of the living they'd been trying to join had changed their course to envelop them. There were no words exchanged. Boda didn't think she had any words left. But she, Vali and the little boy were absorbed into the centre of the shielded ring as, step by painful step, it edged its way nearer to the safety of Rome's walls.

Boda wanted to join the outer perimeter, the ones defending against the dead. But the leader of the group – Silvius, a former tribunus in the seventh legion – took one look at her bloody face and stumbling steps and told her she was too weak to fight, a danger to those around her. She didn't argue, just passed her sword to a man better able to use it. She knew he was right. Her sword arm was burning with pain and she barely had the energy to lift her head, let alone her sword.

Besides, she wanted to keep an eye on Vali. She'd known men choose death rather than live with the pain that lined his face. She'd tried to talk to him but he shrugged her off and so, on an impulse she didn't fully understand, she passed him the young boy to hold.

Vali rested his head against the child's. She wasn't sure which of them took comfort from it, but there was nothing more she could do. They marched on, one painful step at a time, until finally they stood before the gates of Rome.

The city wall was patrolled by archers and javelins prickled along its length. The gate itself was barred. Silvius pushed through to the front of the formation, and the others cleared a space around him so the centurion guarding the gate could see that he spoke for the group.

"Open the gates!" Silvius shouted.

The soldiers' faces on the battlements above remained grim and ungiving.

"Open the damned gates!" Silvius screamed. "For the love of Jupiter – there are women and children here!"

"I'm sorry," the centurion said. "It's too dangerous to let you pass." Then he signalled to his soldiers and, as Boda watched in horror, the gates of Rome were barred against them.

CHAPTER FOURTEEN

THE DEAD STOOD in a ring around them. But Petronius saw that some of them were swaying on their feet, while others stumbled to their knees when they tried to walk. He remembered how Drusilla had seemed to take a few minutes to gain full control of Publia's body, and he knew that right now was their only chance to escape.

"Be ready!" he shouted.

He couldn't see the remnants of the Praetorian Guard. If they were alive, they were outside the ring of undead. Caligula and Drusilla were still clinging and cowering together. Only Claudius looked up, face still clawed by grief. But the old man nodded and Petronius guessed that was as much encouragement as he was going to get.

In the wreckage of the dinner party, one item had survived unscathed – the huge, brown-crusted pie no one had dared cut into. Petronius launched himself across the table towards it, scooping up a knife along the way. The undead reacted but, just as he'd hoped, were too slow and uncoordinated to stop him. His knife bit through the crust, the pastry crumbled – and the terrified flock of living birds baked inside burst free.

For one moment, there was pandemonium. The living screamed. The dead flinched back. And even Sopdet crouched, covering her face, while Seneca turned tail and fled.

It was almost impossible to see through the flutter of wings and the flurry of loose feathers. The sparrows squawked and shat as they flung themselves against walls and windows. Petronius had been terrified of birds since he was a little boy and his aunt and uncle's geese had attacked him on their farm in the country. His flesh cringed at the light touch of wings or the sharp scratch of claws but he made himself ignore it, running straight for Claudius and grabbing his arm.

Caligula turned fearful, panicked eyes towards him. Petronius wasted a precious second in indecision. But then he took the Emperor's arm too. Caligula still ruled the city, and once they were outside the palace they might need his powers to command.

The Emperor in turn seized Drusilla's hand.

"Leave her – she's one of them!" Petronius yelled.

Caligula's expression was mulish as he held on tighter and Petronius couldn't waste the time arguing. The flock of birds was thinning as they stunned themselves to insensibility against the walls, and the dead were beginning to master their new bodies.

Petronius ran for the door, pulling the line of other survivors with him, and the dead tried to stop them. Some of them had swords and when one swung for Petronius's head he thought he was finished. But then another blade clashed with it, thrusting it aside, and he realised that the Praetorian Guard had gathered, the few that remained, ringing them as they headed to the door.

He saw a guard go down as three of the dead flung themselves on him. One of them had been a soldier himself, only the jagged, bloody hole in his leather tunic distinguishing him from his living comrade. Petronius thought the living soldier might have fought back if it hadn't been for that. Instead he screamed and shuddered as a blade pierced his own heart – only to rise a few seconds later, a new spirit lighting his eyes.

Another one took a knife to the face, cutting his cheek to the bone. But he managed to keep his feet, only hissing at the pain, and then they were at the door and the dead were penned inside the room.

There was a pause as both sides faced off against each other. For a moment, Sopdet's expression was a study in pure rage. Her eyes burned with it and her cheeks flamed redder than the cloaks of the undead guards around her.

"You bitch!" Caligula said. "You foreign whore! I should never have trusted you!"

Petronius bit his lip very hard to stop himself pointing out this was precisely what he'd tried to warn the Emperor.

Sopdet just smiled, as if Caligula's ranting had strengthened her.

"Laugh, will you?" Caligula hissed. "I've beaten you! You tried to kill me and you've failed!"

"It's true," she said, "that I can't prevent you leaving. But what difference does it make to me, if you're among the first in Rome to die, or the last? For, in time, die you will – every last one of you."

BODA SAW THE hope drain out of the eyes around her. She understood. Their fight through the horror around them had been sustained by the prospect of an escape from it. Now that had been taken from them, they were close to giving up. Already the dead were throwing themselves against the outer perimeter of the living, and she didn't think it would be long before that cracked like the shell of a nut, and the dead could rip through the soft flesh within.

She reached out to take the little boy from Vali. Vali was slow to release him, and the child wriggled and fussed, but eventually she had him cradled in her arms. She carried him forward to stand beside Silvius, facing the captain of the gate.

"You have to let us in," she said. "If you don't, you're condemning this child to die."

The captain's face reddened with shame. "I'm sorry. But until we know what they are... how can we know that you're not with them?"

"Because they're killing us!" Silvius snapped. "Can't you see?"

As if to underline his words there was a desperate scream behind them as another of the defenders fell, gored by the rolling remains of a black boar.

"But they're... they're dead," the captain said. "How can we stop them? If we open the gates they'll break through and the whole city will be doomed."

The small boy grizzled in Boda's arm and she rocked him, but he didn't take any comfort from it. She couldn't blame him. "Exactly," she said. "The city will be doomed with no warriors to defend it. There are nearly a hundred of them here. Can you afford to do without us?"

The captain's face was hard to read but she thought she saw him begin to soften. Then his eyes shifted and widened as they caught on something behind her. She spun round to see that a defender had hacked a corpse's arm at the shoulder, only for the dismembered hand to catch around his ankle. He tripped and fell, tumbling out of the defensive wall, and the walking corpse was instantly on him, ripping out his throat with its decaying teeth.

When she looked back at the captain, he was pale and shaking. "Nothing can stop those things. *Nothing.*"

But Boda remembered the little girl in the moment before she'd risen from the dead. She remembered the beetle, crawling into the girl's mouth. That was what had woken her. Without that, she would have stayed dead.

"It's in their heads!" she shouted, to the captain and the other defenders. She picked up a fallen sword and charged towards the armies of dead. "We can kill them."

Desperation gave her arm strength, and she took off the corpse's grey, rotting head in one swing. "Look!" she said. And a moment after it fell, the brown body of a scarab beetle crawled from the corpse's nose, its carapace smeared with the white meat of the brain.

"Look!" she said again and stamped down hard on the beetle. When she lifted her sandal there was only a brown mush left beneath it – and neither the beetle nor the body moved again.

"Help us!" she shouted to the guard captain. "Shoot them in the head!"

PETRONIUS BLINKED AT the brightness of the daylight when they emerged from the Palace. The streets of Rome were thronged with people, but the atmosphere had changed in the last few hours. There was fear in the faces around them, and sometimes hostility. The news from the walls must be spreading. And it looked like Caligula was being blamed.

The Praetorian Guard pushed through the crowds, clearing a path for their Emperor where once one would have opened spontaneously. Petronius was glad they'd managed to gather so many of the soldiers, more than two hundred picked up from around the palace or collected from various drinking dens as they passed. The mood of the people was ugly and there was an unhappy muttering as they passed. Caligula clearly sensed the anger. He kept his face down and mouth shut as he walked beside his sister.

Caligula had ordered Marcus to take them to the Temple of Saturn, though he hadn't bothered to explain why. Petronius guessed the Emperor thought that priests would be the least likely to turn against him. But the route led through some of Rome's poorest districts, and here the hostility was more overt. When they passed a stall selling elderly vegetables, some unseen hand liberated a few and threw them towards the Emperor's party.

An overripe tomato spattered against Petronius's tunic. He spat out the seeds and wiped juice from his eye, but it was impossible to see who'd thrown it. Caligula was hit with a mouldy peach, while a patter of grapes rained down on Drusilla's head.

Petronius expected the Emperor to react with rage, but instead he tucked his head tighter against his chest and quickened his pace. He seemed to have lost his pride – or maybe just his nerve – when Sopdet defied him and won. But Marcus drew his sword from its sheath and the other soldiers did the same and the crowd muttered, drawing back.

Part of their route took them close to the city walls. Here there were fewer people and those that were still around seemed intent on leaving.

Petronius saw some families outside their homes, hurriedly packing the contents of their houses into waiting wagons.

"Where are you going, citizen?" Petronius asked the father of one family.

The man turned wide, frightened eyes on him. "Away from the walls. They say they'll be over them soon. We're seeking refuge in the Temple of Jupiter."

Petronius didn't imagine the temple would be safer than anywhere else in the city but he just nodded and moved on. No need to create more panic than there already was.

Closer to the walls, they heard screams and the clash of weapons.

Marcus turned to Caligula. "Caesar, it seems the messengers spoke the truth."

"So?" Caligula snarled. "You killed them for treason – not perjury."

Marcus nodded, face carefully blank. "But now the people need us. The walls are only lightly defended – my men could make the difference between victory and defeat."

"Your job is to defend me!" Caligula screamed. "Not the good-for-nothing inhabitants of this rat-infested city! Me, do you understand – me!"

Petronius winced as the Emperor's voice echoed down the narrow street. Windows opened above them and someone flung a pitcher of liquid out of one. It missed Caligula and struck two of his guards, stinking of piss. The soldiers roared with anger, but Marcus called them back when they made to enter the house and Caligula smiled his satisfaction.

Only Claudius walked unheeding through it all, mouth and face closed. Petronius dropped back to walk beside him.

It took several minutes for the older man to notice him. When he did he attempted a smile, but it looked ghastly, a mere stretching of lips over teeth.

"I should thank you," Claudius said, "for t-t-trying to save N-N-Narcissus."

Petronius shook his head. "You don't need to thank me. What Caligula did to him was wrong."

For the first time, some life came into Claudius's eyes. He darted an anxious look behind him. "Don't speak so loudly. And d-d-don't be fooled by his cowardice. The most dangerous animal is a c-c-cornered one."

Petronius lowered his voice. "But he's not just a danger to those around him. Rome will fall if he doesn't act. Or if someone else doesn't act in his place..."

As suddenly as they'd filled with life, Claudius's eyes drained of it again. "Rome is not my concern," he said, and moved closer to his nephew to forestall any further conversation.

Petronius bit his lip in frustration. It wasn't just about preserving his own life, though it certainly was about that. But if Caligula continued this selfish, suicidal course, too many people would die.

He sneaked a look at the surrounding guards and found that Marcus was looking right back at him. Something about his expression told Petronius he'd overheard the exchange with Claudius. His heart thumped almost painfully hard against his ribs, but after a moment the guard captain looked away, the expression on his square face inscrutable.

At the tall, golden gates of the Temple of Saturn, the priests bowed and scraped and let them in. But they watched the Emperor from lowered eyes, and some of them whispered in corners, and Petronius would have bet good money that they knew about the trouble outside Rome, and the Emperor's refusal to do anything about it.

A statue of the god sat enthroned at one end of the main chamber. His face was bearded and kindly and his marble hands held marble stalks of corn. Beneath his feet and spread across half the floor of the temple, piles of fruit and vegetables teetered, some stretching almost to the ceiling.

"Excellent," Caligula said, rubbing his hands together. Now that he'd reached safety, he seemed to have regained both his confidence and his arrogance. "The god of the harvest has admirably lived up to his name. There should be food enough here to last us weeks or months, if we need it."

It was true – at this time of Saturn's great harvest festival, the Temple was better supplied with food than anywhere else in Rome. The smell of it all was overpowering, rich and sweet and just a little rotten.

"Bar the gates," Caligula ordered the nearest priest, a shabby young man in a dirty toga.

"But Caesar," the priest protested, "today is the lord Saturn's feast day. The poor must partake of the bounty provided by his grace."

"Listen to me, you jumped-up eunuch. That was an order, not the starting point for a debate. Now bar the gates!" Caligula's face reddened as he spoke, and this time the priest leapt to obey.

At the doorway, Claudius blocked him. "No," he said. "Y-y-your city needs you, nephew. Answer its call."

"Get out of his way, fool!" Caligula snapped, but Drusilla laughed and clapped her hands.

"Look, brother!" she said. "The dribbler's finally found some backbone. In fact" – she ran a teasing finger down Caligula's nose – "rather more backbone than you. I do believe you were actually shaking in front of that ghastly priestess."

"I was not shaking!" Caligula snapped. Petronius saw him struggle to master himself, and continue in a softer voice. "I was afraid for you, my love. As I am now. So stand aside, uncle – those doors will be barred whatever you say. Your only choice is whether you live to appreciate the safety they offer."

Petronius didn't quite know what possessed him. They would be safe inside the Temple. But he found himself stepping forward to take up position beside Claudius, blocking the doorway. "No. We can't cower in here while Rome burns. It isn't right."

"Oh," Drusilla purred, slinking up to him. "Handsome and brave. This one's a real find."

When she leaned in to Petronius, he had to restrain himself from leaning back. In the heat of the walk from the Palace, her flesh had begun to decay. He could smell its fetid odour, and he saw that the skin of her face was beginning to soften and sag, her lips drooping away from her gums.

"Get your hands off him!" Caligula yelled.

Drusilla turned to him, raising an ironic eyebrow. "Don't be silly, darling, I haven't touched him."

"And you're not going to," Caligula hissed. "I didn't bring you back for anybody else. I brought you back for me!"

"Really?" Drusilla's tone was icy now. "You expect complete fidelity, undying gratitude? I've only been gone two years, brother – can you have so quickly forgotten what kind of woman I am?"

"It seems I have," Caligula said. His voice was high and breathy and Petronius saw that he was shaking with rage. He wanted to step away from the pair of them, but he was terrified of drawing any more attention to himself. If Caligula's anger moved away from his sister, it would almost certainly be turned on Petronius.

"I'd forgotten everything about you," Caligula said. "I'd forgotten how self-centred you are. How selfish. I'd forgotten that you treat me like dirt, when all I've ever done is love you. And I'd forgotten that you have the morals of a two-denarii whore!"

Drusilla slapped him, the blow ringing through the suddenly silent temple. "How dare you! Love me? The only person you love is yourself! And that's just as well – because who else would love a scrawny, under-endowed, worthless little bastard like you? Even father despised you!"

Caligula let out a roar of mingled rage and pain that made Petronius flinch. He lurched to the side, towards one of the soldiers, and before the man could react, snatched his sword from his hand.

The Emperor wasn't much of a swordsman. His swing was wild but Drusilla was unprepared and unprotected. The blade sliced through her neck in one clean sweep. For a moment, only the line of red along her throat betrayed what had happened. Then her body toppled one way and her head tilted and fell the other. Her eyes stared accusingly at Caligula, still bright with rage. Then something behind them died, and a moment later a small brown beetle crawled from her mouth and scuttled across the temple floor. Caligula crushed it beneath the heel of his sandal.

There was a very long silence, finally broken when Caligula dropped his sword to the floor. He fell to his knees beside it, cradling his head in his hands. "Sweet Aphrodite, what have I done?"

It was Marcus who answered, stepping forward to scoop the fallen sword from the floor. "You've killed her, Caesar. Again. You risked everything – your whole Empire – to bring her back. And for what? For this?"

Caligula looked up, eyes streaked with tears. "You can't... you can't talk to your Emperor that way."

"That's true," Marcus said.

Unlike Caligula's, his sword-stroke was quick and efficient. It pierced Caligula through his heart and ripped downwards, opening his belly to spill his guts on the ground.

The Emperor looked down at the wreckage of his chest with disbelieving eyes. "What?" he said. "How?"

Marcus wiped his sword clean on Caligula's purple toga, then sheathed it. "Refusing the Emperor's command is treason. Luckily," he said, "we've just had a change in leadership." He turned to Claudius and saluted. "What are your orders, Caesar?"

WITH THE GATES barred against them and the living inside, the dead had retreated from the walls of Rome. The defenders took the opportunity to rest and eat inside the watchtowers; to regroup for a new offensive which everyone was sure would come.

Vali stared at the plate of bread and cheese in front of him, but his stomach rebelled at the thought of putting anything inside it.

"You should eat," Boda said.

She still had the little boy with her, clinging to her hand. Vali could hardly bear to look at him, but she wouldn't let him look away.

"He told me his name's Nero," she said. "He claims he's the Emperor's nephew, so we're keeping him here until Caligula can be found. I need you to look after him while I take my turn on watch."

Vali turned his face away. "You might want to leave him with someone safer."

She hauled him up by the front of his tunic, pushing him so hard against the wall that all the air was forced out of him. "Enough of this," she said. "Enough. You did what you could and the gods willed that you failed. Terrible things happen in battle – haven't you lived long enough to know that?"

How could he tell her he'd lived far longer than she knew, and understood the reality of the world far better than she could imagine? That he didn't know why he held himself responsible for one insignificant little girl's death, when he'd done far worse before and never felt a moment's guilt? That every time he shut his eyes he saw the girl's face, and he thought he probably always would, not because of what had happened but because of what she represented – the moment he became something both less and more than what he'd always been. He laughed, because he couldn't tell her any of that.

She looked puzzled, but she released her grasp on his tunic, letting him slide back down to his feet. She was still very close to him, her breath hot on his face. He felt a stirring of desire, but something else – more complicated and more troubling.

"You're right," he told her. "I've been here too long. This place is starting to change me."

She frowned, misunderstanding. "I thought you were newly arrived in Rome."

He nodded, because that was true, though not what he'd meant.

"I think I understand," she said. "I came to Rome as a captive, yet it seems I'm about to give my life to defend it. Maybe it's changed me too."

He looked away from the walls, towards the great city spread below him. He'd visited before, of course, many times, as he'd visited every city on earth. But that had been different – he'd been different, his full and wonderful self, not this cut-down version he'd been forced to adopt when he fled the punishment that awaited him.

The streets near the walls were empty, but he could see people deeper inside, milling in confusion and panic.

"The trouble is," Boda said. "Rome isn't just one thing, as I'd always imagined. Every nation of the world has a place here, and for all its cruelty there's something in it worth saving."

He turned back to study her face. Her blue eyes were wide and serious, but the lines around her mouth came from laughter, not anger. She was a contradiction, as all these people were. And she was right. It was easy to see them as simple, but embroiled in the centre of life rather than observing from its edges, the complications were inescapable.

She rested her hand against his arm, and his heart beat a little faster – a man's reaction to a woman. He struggled to see her through other eyes, the ones that had first chosen her. Had he made the right decision then? He didn't know. He'd lost all clarity.

A second later she abruptly released him. He saw her horrified expression before he saw what had caused it, and felt an icy flush of fear.

"Take Nero," she said. "They'll need me on the battlements."

Outside the walls, the dead had returned. There were far more of them than he'd seen before. The beetles must have flown far, finding every corpse they could animate within reach of the city. Their ragged legions were no match for the iron discipline of the soldiers defending Rome, but they outnumbered them a hundred to one. And there were soldiers among the dead – some in the scraps of uniform that had survived the grave, others in full armour, their faces intact.

Vali heard some names called in horror by those manning the walls and guessed that they recognised comrades among the dead. And then there were shouts of fear from everyone as the defenders saw what the dead had brought with them.

A grey wall of flesh marched behind the human corpses. Their trunks swung in time with their footsteps, so heavy they seemed to shake the earth. Smaller animals crowded around them, but the elephants didn't seem to care where they trod, crushing the bodies of wolves and tigers beneath them as they advanced.

As they came closer, Vali realised that they were drawing something behind them. Nearer still, almost within bowshot, and he saw that they were wooden towers topped with spikes – as tall as the walls of Rome and designed for scaling them.

All around him, men fell to their knees and prayed as the dead prepared to besiege the city.

CHAPTER FIFTEEN

WHEN THE DEAD attacked, discipline disintegrated. The word had been passed down the line and repeated by every centurion to his men. The dead could only be killed by a shot to the head. The men knew this, but in the fear and panic that accompanied the appearance of the elephants and their siege engines, they fired wildly. Hails of arrows flew into the rotting bodies below, most striking harmlessly at arms and legs and torsos. The dead didn't even bother to pluck them out.

Boda wasn't used to the Roman recurve bow she'd been given – she'd have preferred something longer and straighter – but an arrow was an arrow and at least she was aiming in the right place. Her first few shots went wide, but after that she hit her mark, time after time. It wasn't difficult. The walking corpses made little effort to defend themselves. Bodies must be like mules to them, she supposed, mounts that could be flogged to death and then replaced.

Vali was fighting by her side. He'd proved to be an able archer, too valuable to waste as a child-minder. Nero was being cared for by some of the refugees from outside the city while they fought.

She could already see that it was a hopeless battle. The siege engines remained out of bowshot for the minute, allowing the front ranks of the dead to advance unprotected. With nothing to shelter behind they were easy targets. They fell in droves, some still writhing, pinned to the ground by javelins through their chest, others truly motionless after arrows had pierced their heads.

But there were always more of them and they were fighting back. Some held bows, and though their aim was poor the defenders couldn't afford to lose a single man. Others flung head-sized rocks at the wall with inhuman strength and Boda saw several men brought down by them.

One rock flew towards her with terrifying speed. She flung herself to the ground and it missed her head by less than an inch. The man behind wasn't so lucky. She saw his skull caved in by the impact as he fell, limp, to the ground.

She couldn't spare him any attention. More dead were flocking to the walls and she grimly picked up her bow and prepared to thin their ranks. The focus of her attention narrowed to the corpses below, and there was none left over for the rock headed straight towards her. It caught her a glancing blow on the side of the head, momentarily stunning her. Her knees began to buckle and she saw that she was falling forward, towards the battlements and the lethal drop beneath. Her arms flailed but she couldn't seem to regain her balance and her vision was slowly fading to black.

Vali grabbed her arm and yanked her away from the precipice, and the pain in her injured shoulder shocked her back to full consciousness. She turned to thank him – and saw, a second before it struck, the sword that was heading for his back. He gasped in shock as she flung herself on top of him and the sword swung high over his head to clang against the ramparts.

She realised with a cold shock that the man attacking them was the same one who'd been felled by the earlier rock. In the moment of his death he'd left their side and joined their enemies. When she caught his eye he swung his sword again, but the spirit inside him was still clumsy in its new body, and it was an easy matter to evade the blow. One slash of her own weapon severed his head from its body. She tried not to look at the familiar face as she tossed it over the battlements.

And then the next wave came. They'd been hidden behind the main front, rows of undead carrying ladders between them. She could see a group approaching the section of wall she and Vali were guarding. Her bow sang as she picked off first one and then another. Beside her, Vali accounted for two more, but then they were at the wall.

The ladder thumped onto the parapet beside her and a hail of rocks accompanied it. She was forced to take shelter, cowering beneath the overhang as the lethal rain continued above. She could see the top of the ladder, only two paces from her head. It was shaking, and she knew that meant the dead were climbing it. How long before they reached the top?

She drew her sword, using the tip to prod at the top rung of the ladder. The metal pierced the wood but didn't shift it.

"It's too heavy," Vali said. "You'll break your sword."

She grimaced. "But they'll have to stop throwing rocks when their people reach the top."

She was half right. The rocks stopped but the arrows continued. She guessed the dead were unafraid of the damage the arrows could do to their brethren, or judged it trivial compared to the harm it would inflict on the defenders. Her heart raced, knowing it would take only one lucky shot to finish her off. But when she saw a skeletal hand grasp the top of the ladder, she knew she had no choice.

"Now," she mouthed to Vali, and didn't wait for his nod before launching herself to her feet, arms braced to lift the ladder. For a moment she strained alone, fighting hopelessly to push the wood away from the wall. It was crawling with dead, twenty of them at least and more waiting beneath to follow after those. Then Vali put his shoulder to the other side, and suddenly the weight was bearable and the ladder was tipping out and away, some of the dead still clinging, others plummeting to the ground below.

The day wore on, the sun climbing steadily higher to beat down mercilessly on the living and rot the flesh of the dead. Another ladder clanged against the wall and then another, and each time it grew harder to push it away and there were fewer men to do it. The ranks of the defenders were thinning alarmingly fast, and when the sun reached its zenith the attackers launched their final wave.

Boda heard the thump of the elephants' great round feet across the ground and the unearthly trumpeting when they raised their trunks skyward. The siege engines rattled behind them, and when they drew closer she could see that they were filled with the dead. When they reached the walls, it would be over.

She felt Vali standing beside her, shoulder-to-shoulder, and when she turned to look at him she saw that he'd been watching her.

"I'm sorry," she said. "If we'd run away... You said it was hopeless and you were right."

To her surprise, he grinned. Under his sharp nose and red hair, the expression was startlingly vulpine. "No, you were right. The dead aren't indestructible and they haven't broken through yet."

She looked at the siege engines, within arrow-shot now, but utterly impervious to them. "They will. There's nothing that can stop those things." She flung one of the last of their javelins at the approaching wall of flesh. It flew true and hit its target, striking the nearest elephant through its eye and sinking in almost to the grip.

The beast didn't even pause, just continued its lumbering, inexorable march onwards.

"Not the creatures," Vali said. "The engines themselves – and all the dead inside."

"But the walls are too thick too pierce."

His smile broadened. He flicked his fingers, and she couldn't see it but there must have been a flint hidden in his palm, because a flame sparked to life between them. "Fire," he said. "Wood burns – and so do the bodies of the dead. We'll give these Romans a proper northman's funeral."

He grunted in surprise when she flung her arms around him. A moment later, his arms met behind her back and squeezed briefly. His expression was strange when she released him but she didn't waste time puzzling it out.

"Silvius!" she yelled to the nearest battlement commander. "We need fire arrows, rags. Raid the nearby houses for their cooking oil if we need to – anything that burns."

She saw the white flash of his smile before he turned to his men. The soldiers he barked orders to scurried to obey, making a pile of everything usable within reach – a small stock of fire arrows as well as pots of oil made for throwing. But even as Vali fitted the first flaming arrow to his bow and sent it into the nearest siege engine, she knew it wasn't enough.

"We need more!" she called to Silvius. "They can douse single flames – we need to start too many fires for them to extinguish."

He shook his head, expression grave. "I can't spare the men. If I send them for supplies the walls will have fallen by the time they return."

He was right. Beside the siege engines, more ladders were approaching, and there were fewer and fewer defenders to push them away. Vali's plan had come just too late to save them. She shrugged and flung a pot of flaming oil at the monstrous engine. At least this way they'd go down fighting. They'd take some of the dead with them, and when the end approached she'd throw her own body on the fire so that it could never rise again.

The oil she'd thrown hit the siege engine at the apex of its tower. The flames caught and spread before any of those inside could scale the heights to douse them. She smelt the stench of burning flesh and, for the first time, heard the dead cry out in fear.

"The flames will consume the beetles as well as the flesh that holds them," Vali said beside her. "They dread a final return to the realm of darkness."

He was right. As the flames spread downwards, red and gold and bright even against the midday sun, a sudden brown cloud burst from the heart of them, hovering a moment in the sky above before diffusing to spread over the battlements.

"The rats leave a sinking ship," Vali said.

The tower was close enough to allow Boda to see what had happened to the dead inside. Without the beetles to animate them, the corpses were just corpses. Some of them crumpled and stayed where they were, slumped on the ladders and platforms inside the engine. Others toppled from the side to be crushed beneath the feet of the advancing army, careless of their own casualties.

The whole tower was aflame now, a beacon that belched an evil thick black smoke. The flames licked forward and the elephant too began to burn. The fat fried beneath its skin as the fine grey hairs singed and lit. The creature reared, a terrifying sight, its curved tusks gouging the air. And then it fell back to earth with an impact that shook the ground, and turned and ran. Its path took it sideways into another elephant and another engine that was not yet burning. Both toppled to the ground, and the ones behind were halted, hopelessly mired in the mess.

For one moment, Boda thought it might be enough. She sent another arrow into the engine to her left, and Vali joined her, but the dead quickly pounced to put out the flames and the engine trundled on. It was only forty paces from the walls now, and behind and beside it there were scores more, far too many for the defenders to burn. Soon the dead would come swarming over, and too few of the living remained to stop them.

And then, a sound she hadn't hoped to hear – the marching feet of reinforcements. The siege engine was thirty paces away and drawing closer and she didn't dare a look behind to see how many had come, whether it would be enough. She flung a pot of oil, then another – and when she flung a third a hail of arrows accompanied it, burning through the sky from behind her.

The dead screamed and the nearest engine caught, a thousand embers sparking a conflagration that they'd never put out. It spread too quickly even for the beetles to escape it. She saw a few of them try, but they were sparks of light, already burning, and then the whole structure sank in on itself, a blackened wreck.

Finally, Boda lowered her bow and looked behind her.

There were more men than she could have hoped for – it looked to be as many as a thousand. Some were in the uniform of the Praetorian Guard, others in civilian clothes. Claudius stood at their head, a slight, stooped figure with a new air of command.

Beside him stood Petronius, curling black hair plastered to his scalp with sweat. He grinned at her expression. "So," he said, "did you miss me?"

THE DEAD RETREATED when they saw the new force arrayed against them. They'd lost at least a third of their siege engines and the walls were now too heavily manned to overpower.

Petronius looked over the field of battle below and marvelled that so few had held the walls for so long. Then he looked at Boda. There was a bloody graze along one side of her head, the red bright against her pale hair. She stank of stale sweat and ash and she looked on the point of collapse. She was absolutely beautiful.

He'd told her what happened at the Temple of Isis, how he'd failed to stop the ceremony. He'd been expecting anger but she'd just nodded and when she saw his expression, told him, "you did everything you could." She was right, but he'd needed to hear someone else say it.

When it was certain the dead weren't merely regrouping for another attack, Claudius gathered a council of war. At Petronius's suggestion he included Boda and Vali as well as Marcus and two Senators – Flavius and Justinian – who'd joined them on the march to the walls.

The little boy Boda had rescued clung to Petronius's leg as if he never intended to let go. She'd said that he was Nero, Caligula's nephew, but no one among Claudius's party seemed to want to claim responsibility for him, including the new Emperor himself, and for want of anyone else to care for him he seemed to have attached himself to Petronius.

"We can arm the citizens," Claudius said. "Many have served in the legions. And those that haven't can still carry equipment, act as look-outs..."

Petronius realised that Claudius hadn't stuttered once since the Praetorian Guard had declared him Emperor. He seemed like a different man, confident and commanding for all his fragile body.

"But what about the dead inside the city?" Boda asked.

Nero whimpered, burying his head against Petronius's thigh. No doubt he'd seen his share of horror on the way to safety. Petronius picked him up and held him securely on his lap.

"There are very few dead inside the walls of Rome – only the ones Caligula killed and those guarding the gateway to the underworld." Petronius told Boda. "Our burials always take place outside the city gates."

She nodded. "Then we can hold the walls with the men we have."

"Don't be a fool," Vali said. "The walls will never hold."

Boda's head jerked to face him. "How can you say that? Less than an hour ago you told me I was right to fight."

"But this isn't an ordinary war," Vali said. "In battles soldiers fall and no one but their families mourns their loss. Here every man we lose is a defector to the other side."

"Yes," Claudius said. "I see. Their ranks swell as ours thin, making time their friend and our enemy."

Vali bowed his head in acknowledgement. "It's a battle we can't win."

Boda glared at him and Petronius had to suppress a smile at the other man's expression. He knew what it felt like to be on the receiving end of that glare. "You're counselling surrender, then?" she asked.

Vali held up his hands, placating. "No. I'm saying we should fight a battle we can win."

"We can't defeat the dead," Petronius said. "But the beetles that carry their spirits are easily crushed. Is that what you mean?"

Vali shook his head and Claudius said: "No. I believe his ambition is greater. You mean that we should try to shut the gateway itself, don't you? Close off the source of the infection rather than fight its symptoms."

"The dead will be guarding the gate," Boda said. "They won't be foolish enough to leave it undefended." But Petronius could see a spark of excitement in her eyes.

"That's the least of our problems," Vali said. "More importantly, the gates of death open outward – and close inward."

It took Petronius a second to understand what he meant. "You mean they can only be closed from the inside?"

The red-haired barbarian nodded, and the group erupted as everyone tried to talk at once. Petronius saw Vali lean back, a half smile on his lips as if the chaos he'd caused amused him.

Boda turned to him. "How do you know this?"

"*The Book of the Dead,*" Petronius guessed.

Vali nodded – a little too quickly, as if latching on to a convenient lie.

Boda frowned. "You went there, didn't you? You entered the gateway in Alexandria. If we went back there..."

But Vali shook his head. "That gateway wasn't the same as this, it's not meant to be crossed. You saw the guardians who followed us through – they'll be alert now, and ready to stop another incursion by the living. Besides, Alexandria is the centre of the Cult's power. They're still much weaker here in Rome, especially inside the city, where there are only a few of the dead."

"You think we should return to the Temple then?" Petronius said, and shivered. He still remembered, all too clearly, the terrible light that had shone from the gateway to the other world. The thought of passing through it horrified him.

But Boda nodded grimly. "It seems that we have no other choice."

IT WAS DECIDED that half the Praetorian Guard would remain to protect the walls and half accompany Boda and Vali to the Temple of Isis. Claudius had told Boda and Vali that they needn't go, that they'd already done enough for a city not their own. Boda knew the mission had little chance of succeeding, but she preferred to contemplate death in a near-impossible attack than a futile defence. And Vali had said that the underworld could hold little fear now that its worst denizens had entered the land of the living.

Petronius had also insisted on accompanying them. She could see him ineptly buckling on a sword he barely knew how to use. The little boy,

Nero, was trying to help him. He seemed to have taken a liking to the young man, a relief to Boda, who hadn't known what to do with the clinging, demanding infant.

Petronius seemed to sense her eyes on him. He looked up and smiled, but the expression looked strained. He didn't seem such a youth any more. The last few days had aged him in indefinable but definite ways.

Was Vali right that Petronius loved her? It seemed absurd, but when she'd seen Petronius's face as he realised she was still alive, she thought he might be right. And here he was, voluntarily putting himself in danger, when he'd always seemed to devote most of his energies to avoiding it.

She didn't love him – how could she? He was a Roman, and her master. He was ten years her junior and, until last week, had lived a life of unmitigated self-indulgence. The Boda who had first arrived in Rome would have thought him worthless. But she didn't, not now. The world was a more light-hearted place with him in it. And she couldn't bear the thought that he would die for her sake.

His smile widened when she approached him. Nero smiled too, holding out his arms to be hugged. She lifted the little boy, an awkward lump in her arms, but after a moment he wriggled to be free, and she released him to return to Petronius.

"He likes you," she told him.

Petronius shrugged. "Children and animals always do. It's adults who seem to find me objectionable."

"Claudius tells me his mother's in exile," she said. "He was travelling to Rome with his aunt and cousin, but..." She looked at Nero, happily playing at Petronius's feet.

"Yes," Petronius said. "He's seen too much for such a little one."

"He needs looking after."

Petronius nodded, stooping to stroke Nero's wispy blond hair.

"He needs you to look after him," Boda said.

Petronius's eyes snapped up to hers. "What are you saying?"

She rested her hand against his shoulder. "Stay here, Petronius. Keep him out of danger."

His shrugged her away angrily. "Don't treat me like a child. If you think I'll be a liability, just say so."

She sighed. "You're not a liability. If it wasn't for you, I'd be dead three times over. But I can't... Listen to me, we're accepting death, all of us who enter that gateway. And I know you're prepared to face it too. But I have no one here, nothing in Rome I care about – except you."

His face flushed with pleasure. "Oh. I... I care about you too."

"Then do this for me," she begged him. "I can enter that gateway and risk my life if there's something left behind that's worth saving."

He looked anguished. "But you're asking me to let you go to your death!"

He licked his lips, and she knew that she wouldn't like whatever he said next. "I still own you, if you recall. I could forbid you to go."

She felt a flare of rage, but tamped it down. She didn't want their last words to be bitter ones. "There is a chance we'll succeed, you know."

He just looked at her, and she dropped her eyes.

And then, before he could say anything else, the shout came from the walls. "They're back! The dead have returned!"

Marcus approached, the ranks of the Praetorian Guard waiting behind him. "We should go."

Though Boda knew he was right, she couldn't bring herself to abandon the walls without seeing what danger they were leaving behind. She nodded to Marcus but walked away from him, up the stone stairs that led to the battlements. She heard footsteps behind her and saw that Marcus had followed. It was clear from his face that he felt the same conflict she did. Claudius had ordered him to leave half his men behind to face an unbeatable enemy alone.

When they reached the top, the soldiers on watch saluted hand to heart and stepped aside. They'd been right to raise the alarm. Beyond the battlements, the dead had returned in force. They remained outside bow range, their ragged ranks stretching into the distance as far as the eye could see. There were more of them, Boda was sure of it. The beetles had had more time to fly, she supposed, and find fresh bodies to raise.

As she watched, the front ranks stirred and parted all along the line. The undead were bringing something new to bear on Rome. After a moment, as the great wooden mechanisms trundled into the open, she realised that they were catapults.

Marcus shrugged. "It's to be expected. The walls were built to withstand it."

She was sure he was right. The walls were thicker than she was tall and no rock, no matter how well aimed, would topple them. But she felt a stirring of unease all the same. The dead weren't fools. Whatever controlled them had proven to be a decent tactician. They must know that the catapults would fail – so why had they brought them?

Her disquiet grew as she watched the catapults being braced, hordes of the dead working together to pull the tightly coiled mechanisms back. And then there was a roar, the catapults leapt upright – and the loads cradled inside them flew through the air towards Rome.

Boda could see within seconds that they'd misjudged the trajectory. The rocks were heading high over the walls and would crash harmlessly into the street behind.

Except they weren't rocks. As they flew closer, Boda saw that, impossibly, they seemed to be moving. For one brief, horrible moment as she looked up she saw an eye look back at her. Then the thing was over and down and it landed on the street below with a horrible wet thump. Blood spattered all around it and around the scores of others that had landed close by.

The dead weren't throwing rocks – they'd thrown their own bodies over the walls. The corpses remained broken and motionless on the ground for only a second. And then, one by one, they began to rise.

CHAPTER SIXTEEN

THERE WAS CHAOS. The dead landed everywhere, more and more of them as the catapults did their work. Some of the defenders they killed as they landed, crumpling their bodies beneath them when they hit the ground. And then both corpses would rise to battle the remaining defenders.

A body fell to Boda's left, and she slashed out with her sword, severing its head before it could rise. The torso twitched and its dead eyes glared, and then the beetle crawled out of its mouth and it was still. She stamped down hard, but the creature was ready for her, on the wing before she could crush it. And soon, somewhere else, it would bring another corpse back to life.

Vali was at her back, hacking away with his own short blade. He was less skilled than her, but fearless. She saw him hack off the arm of a lurching corpse, then – as it kept advancing – its left leg. The body hopped another step forward, mouth open in a scream of rage, before losing its balance and toppling to the ground.

Petronius was already cut off from her, a horde of undead separating them. He'd drawn his sword but he couldn't wield it. Nero clung to his neck, his yells audible even over the din of battle, and Petronius couldn't use his weapon without hurting the boy. He shot her one last, desperate look, and then was lost to sight.

"To me!" Marcus shouted, and she saw that he was only ten paces away, gathering the ragged remnants of the Praetorian Guard around him.

The ground between them was thick with the dead. They'd strapped on swords and spears before they flung themselves over the wall. Boda saw a corpse which must have fallen on its own spear. Its hands pulled futilely at the long wooden handle protruding from its stomach, lacking the leverage to pull it out.

Boda stamped down on the spear, pinning the corpse in place as she lopped off its head. But behind it was one who'd landed better, his sword already in his hand. With a sick shock she realised that she recognised him. It was Silvius, the battlement commander who'd led them all to safety behind the walls of Rome.

Unlike many of the other undead, he knew how to fight. And, for the first time, she could see the intelligence shining behind his milky eyes. He didn't just want to kill – he wanted to kill *her*. His sword slashed low and lethal towards her legs.

She jumped clear of the blade only to stumble as she landed, tripping over the bloody remnants of another corpse. She brought her sword up just in time to counter the downward sweep of Silvius's blade. But he'd always been stronger than her and death had made him stronger still. His weight bore against her sword arm and pressed it down, bringing her own blade to within inches of her throat.

His face pressed nearer as if he wanted to be as close as possible to watch her die. His flesh had already started to rot, and a fetid smell washed off him. When he smiled she saw that his teeth were loose in their sockets, his gums brown and decayed. There was no spittle in his dry, dead mouth and his tongue looked as desiccated as an autumn leaf.

Her arm weakened and she let the tension seep out of it, allowing his face to come closer, closer... And when his cracked lips were within inches of hers she lashed her head forward, catching her forehead against his nose.

The blow forced the bone up and in, through what was left of his brain and the insect that had made a nest for itself inside it. Silvius's body gave one last, convulsive shudder and was still, his mouth gaping open to let his shrivelled tongue hang out.

A hand on hers helped drag Boda to her feet. It was Marcus, and she saw that while she'd been down the troop of Guards had moved to surround and protect her and Vali. There were pitifully few left now, and far too many among the dead attacking them.

"We should go," Marcus said. But she could see the conflict in his eyes. He didn't want to abandon the fight at the walls. He wouldn't forgive himself if the city fell because he wasn't there.

"Just get us a few streets away," she told him. "We can look after ourselves after that."

He shook his head. "I can't. Caesar's orders –"

"Were given before they started coming over the walls!" Boda snapped.

"You'll die!" Marcus yelled, but Boda was pulling away and the dead were already moving in to separate them.

"That's actually the idea," Vali said, and then the Praetorian Guard were lost in the sea of bodies, leaving them to face the dead alone.

PETRONIUS SAW BODA for one second, her eyes meeting his across the crowd of bodies. Then the tide of battle took her one way and him the other, and she was lost from sight. The little boy in his arms squirmed and cried and Petronius hugged him closer. Boda had asked him to look after Nero, and that's what he meant to do.

He'd given up on the idea of fighting altogether. After whirling his sword and nearly cutting off his own head – not to mention Nero's – he returned it to his scabbard and concentrated on running away.

He could hear the footsteps of the dead behind him. Why were they following? Did they know who he was? Sopdet knew his face, and she knew he'd opposed her. Was this her revenge?

When he chanced a look behind him, he saw that there were ten or more corpses racing after him. Some were long dead, staggering on flaking leg bones, sword pommels rattling in skeletal hands. But others were whole and strong and they were catching up. Nero's body was nearly a dead weight in Petronius's arms, dragging him down. The only chance he had to live was to drop the little boy.

He couldn't do it. How could he look Boda in the face if he did? He pulled Nero tighter against him instead, and turned left, swerving into a side street that he knew would take him to the Circus Maximus. He couldn't risk losing the time to look behind him again, but he could hear the undead following. It was clearly him they were after – or maybe the child in his arms. Perhaps they were trying to wipe out every drop of Imperial blood, leaving no one to rule Rome but Sopdet and her legions of the dead.

He could feel Nero's snot and tears running down his neck as he forced his legs to pump faster, harder. He forced himself to keep running when his body had already eaten up every morsel of energy inside it, and the breath was burning in his lungs.

The gates of the hippodrome loomed ahead of him, broad enough to admit four horses abreast. Petronius ducked beneath them, flinching for the moment of darkness while they hid the sun.

Then he was inside the great oval, at the bottom of the stands where the spectators sat. They were empty, as he'd expected. News from the walls must have reached here and the people had fled, but they'd left in a hurry. Petronius could see the detritus they'd abandoned: a cup of dates only half-eaten, one with teeth-marks visible in it; a dropped silk wrap, ripped at the hem; a child's doll, scuffed with dust where others had run over it. And below, something far more useful had also been left behind in the confusion – the chariots that would have raced today, if the dead hadn't intervened.

Petronius had nursed a dream of becoming a champion chariot racer for his whole childhood, until his father told him it was no job for a respectable boy. He'd watched every race religiously, bet on the Greens and joined in the riots when they lost. He knew everything there was to know about racing a chariot – without ever having actually done it. But how hard could it be?

The horses seemed to sense the unnaturalness of the dead. They snorted and pawed the ground as he approached and one let out that peculiar high neighing that was almost like a human scream. The dead let out a full-throated roar in response, and Petronius could hear that they were only paces behind, seconds away from catching him. Nero raised his golden-haired head and howled in fear.

But they were lucky. Petronius's gamble – his life-or-death gamble – had paid off. In their hurry to flee, the charioteers had left the horses in harness. The nearest team had begun to chew through the leather that imprisoned them, and the one beyond was hopelessly tangled in it, but the next chariot looked ready to go. As he drew closer, Petronius saw that it belonged to the Green team – and he took that as a good omen.

Nero yelled in shock as Petronius slung him onto the light steering platform, then hopped on beside him. The dead were close, but slowed by the horses, which reared and kicked as they passed. He saw one head crushed beneath a flailing hoof.

Then he had the reins in his hand, and they were off.

THE STREETS OF Rome here were eerily deserted. But as Boda ran through them with Vali at her side, she thought that they didn't feel empty. She could sense the people huddled silent and afraid in their boarded-up homes. She could feel their eyes on her, wondering if she was one of the dead. If she would be the death of them.

Her chest was tight with the effort of breathing and after five more minutes with no sign of pursuit, she slowed to a walk. Vali shot her a questioning look but dropped his pace to lope along beside her. The sunlight sparkled in his red hair and amber eyes.

"Can we really stop this?" she asked him.

He flicked her a surprised glance. "You were the one who told me we must."

She shrugged. "Even hopeless battles must be fought, if they're just. And you and I don't face the same death these Romans do. If we meet a warrior's end there'll be no endless darkness for us, but song and mead in the Halls of Valhalla."

He smiled, a sly, unreadable smile. "How dull. Imagine what the company will be like. All those over-muscled thugs bragging about their great deeds while drinking enough to poleaxe an ox. And at the head of the table, Odin himself – in all his dour, one-eyed, humourless glory."

She stared at him, shocked. "You insult the Allfather?"

"Believe me," he said. "If you knew him better, you would too."

Her smile died, unsure if he was joking. "So what is it you hope for, then, in the world that follows?"

"Ah, now there's a question. I intend to live for ever, of course."

"But we're about to step through the gates of death," she said incredulously. "Do you really think we'll be returning?"

He didn't answer, looking away before she could read his face. But she didn't like the flash of something she caught in his eye – was it pity, or regret?

And then the Temple of Isis loomed in front of them, white marble lips enclosing the hungry black darkness of its open mouth, the door that led to the gateway to death. She shivered as they approached it.

PETRONIUS HADN'T IMAGINED that the dead would follow. He'd – foolishly, he now realised – assumed they'd be incapable of mastering the chariots. But the rotting corpse behind him handled the reins with ease, and now he looked more closely, he thought he detected something familiar in the hollow curves of its face. Could that possibly be Porphyrius, the most successful charioteer ever to ride for the Greens? Petronius had a horrible feeling it was.

Nero stood clasped between his knees, wriggling to get free. The little boy had stopped crying. He was laughing and clapping his hands, as if this was all some entertainment put on for his benefit. "Faster!" he yelled in his high, clear voice. "Want to go faster!"

Petronius would have been happy to oblige, but the streets they raced through were too narrow. Their chariot was pulled by two horses abreast and there was barely room for them to pass between the high walls of the slums to either side. As he negotiated a sudden left turn the chariot tipped on its axis and the left-hand wheel scraped against the wall of a house, sending a shower of sparks into the air.

The chariot behind negotiated the turn far more gracefully, gaining ground. Nero gurgled with pleasure and slid from between Petronius's knees, forcing him to make a desperate grab that left the reins slack for a crucial second. The horses interpreted the sudden release of tension as an instruction to give it their all, and Petronius found himself thrown against the backrest as the chariot surged forward with a terrifying burst of speed.

At least the dead fell behind a little, unwilling to match their suicidal dash. Petronius could see that there were three chariots full of them, one two-horse affair like theirs and two more that were pulled by four. If they reached anywhere wide enough to let the horses have their head, the larger chariots would easily overtake them. But these narrow streets had dangers of their own.

Petronius pulled desperately on the rein with one hand as he clung to Nero's collar with his other. The horses were slow to obey. Maybe they'd been waiting all these years for a chance to truly let loose. Or maybe they could smell the stench of decay behind them. As they galloped into a small, statue-lined square, Petronius could see a desperate white froth around their mouths and knew they couldn't keep up this pace for long.

He yanked again, harder, and this time the horses obeyed – far too enthusiastically. They reared as they drew to a complete and sudden halt, neighing their fury. Behind them, the other chariots raced on, too surprised to stop in time. The dead were closing in, milky eyes glaring malevolently and mouths stretched wide in grins that anticipated victory.

But the horses they'd commandeered had other ideas. Well used, after years of training, to avoiding the collisions that could end a rider's life, they veered to either side of Petronius's stationary chariot, like fast-flowing water diverting round a rock.

For one second, the dead were abreast. Skeletal hands reached out, fumbled and failed to connect. But one body – faster than the rest – flung itself over the gap between carriages and landed sprawled across the chariot beside Petronius.

It was one of the older corpses, brown mummified flesh stretched tight over knobbly bones. The speed of its impact had broken some of them and Petronius saw its left hand hanging from its wrist by a thread of skin. Half its ribs had been crushed to powder but it only lay still a second before it rose and rounded on him.

It was Nero who saved him. The little boy squealed in fear – or maybe excitement – and the corpse's head swung limply on its neck to locate this new prey. In the second it bought him, Petronius hooked his hands beneath its armpits and lifted. His hands cringed away from touching the decayed flesh but the corpse was far lighter than he'd imagined, all the living juices long squeezed out of it. He lifted it up then flung it away to clatter against the pavement beside the chariot.

The corpse rolled and rose, even less whole than before. Its right hand was gone entirely now, and half its skull had caved in, lending its head a leering, almost comic appearance. But the same murderous intent was evident in its empty eyes and it braced its legs and shambled back towards them.

'Skellington!' Nero said, laughing and pointing as Petronius picked up the reins again and led the horses in a tight circle. He flicked them and they were off, in the opposite direction from the chariots of dead – but not for long. Already Petronius could see that they were slowing, turning their own circles in the next square along.

The race resumed. Petronius had the lead now but his chariot wasn't steering quite true. When he looked down at the left wheel he saw that it was warped. He'd probably bent it when he brought them too close to the wall. Now he had to constantly tug the reins to the right to keep moving straight.

He barely knew this part of the city. It was where the poorest citizens lived, and immigrants or former slaves without the full rights of citizenship. The houses that whisked by on either side were tall and thin and gloomy and he knew that they were packed with people, five or more to a room. The kind of people who survived on air and corn dole.

They were also the kind of people who strung their washing on lines across the street. Petronius saw it coming but there was nothing he could do to avoid it. If he stopped the dead would be on him and the road was too narrow to turn. The strung-out toga slapped him straight in the face, wet and smelling of the piss it had been washed in. The horses snorted and neighed and he knew that they were tangled too.

With the wet cloth pressed against his face, Petronius was running blind. One hand was tangled in the reins, but he raised the other to claw at the clinging fabric.

It didn't want to move. A little light seeped through the thick cotton but nothing else and when he breathed in it stuck tight against his mouth, the smell of urine acrid in his throat. The chariot was veering from side to side, almost tipping onto its axle, and he suspected that at least one of the horses had the same problem he had. And now, with so little control, he had to put two hands back on the reins just to slow the horses' wild flight and stop them overturning.

There was a sudden crunching sound beneath their wheels and then the desperate squawking of chickens. They must be in a market district, running through crates of the birds ready for sale. He felt one of them fly up into his face, its claws piercing the thick cloth over his cheeks to scratch the skin beneath and its beak pecking dangerously close to his eyes.

He released the reins again to flail at the bird. As if in retaliation, he felt something liquid squirt against his hand and then the strong smell of chicken shit permeated the cloth. But his reaching fingers found first a few loose feathers and then the bird's wing and when he gave it a fierce yank the creature finally flew away – its claws scraping the toga from his eyes as they passed.

He had one second to enjoy the fact that he could finally see. Then he registered what exactly it was he was seeing. Here, finally, just when it was most inconvenient, were some living people. They'd come to the market whose chicken coops he'd already destroyed and to either side they stared at his chariot through wide, shocked eyes.

The road was full of them too. It was early afternoon, well before sunset, a time of day when the pedestrians should have had the street to themselves. Petronius thought about pulling on the reins, but he couldn't afford to stop. He could hear the chariots of the dead behind him. The washing that had hit him must have missed them and they'd nearly closed the gap. If he stopped, they'd be on him – and then they'd slaughter these people too.

The terrified shoppers dived out of the way as his chariot weaved through them. The horses were as frightened as the people they almost trampled, rearing and turning their heads to nip at any who came too close. The market stalls crowded the street, too tight for the horses to fit through and they crushed them beneath their hooves. The air was thick with the smell of overripe melons and dates.

Another stall fell, this one selling spices. A brown, richly scented cloud of cinnamon enveloped them. Petronius coughed the dust of it out of his throat and wiped his streaming eyes. When they'd cleared, he saw that the people too had finally cleared the road – all but one.

The woman was very old and probably blind. From the pavement to either side of her, people were screaming at her to move, but though her head twitched from side to side in fright she didn't seem to realise where the danger was. The chariot was only twenty paces from her and closing fast. Petronius imagined it all too clearly, a vivid moment of blood as her frail old body was crushed beneath his wheels.

He'd leapt onto the horse's back before he even realised he'd done it. The creature bucked and screamed, unused to being ridden. Petronius set his teeth and clung on grimly. Behind him, alone in the chariot, Nero laughed. He'd handed the little child the reins, more to give him something to anchor himself than because he thought the three-year-old could steer. But the little boy had them in a firm hold and was pulling alternately right and left.

The horses didn't know that the person holding their reins had no idea what he was doing. They followed their orders as obediently as ever and the chariot swerved from side to side as they lurched first one way and then the other.

The old woman seemed finally to have realised the danger she was in. She was screaming, a high, thin desperate sound. But although Petronius could hear wails and sobs from the people to either side of her, no one was willing to risk their own life to save hers. She stood isolated in the centre of the road, rheumy eyes blinking up at him as the horse Petronius rode thundered towards her.

The weight of her nearly wrenched his arm out of its socket when he hooked it around her chest. He tried to lift, but his unsteady seat on the horse gave him no leverage and her sandalled feet scraped along the road as she screamed and screamed. His shoulder screamed at him to let go, but if he did she'd be lost beneath the wheels.

The horse carrying him felt the extra weight dragging it back and rebelled at this final indignity. It reared, Petronius's legs loosened round its stomach and he slid to the side, arm still dragged down by the woman he was doggedly holding. But in the moment when his mount's hooves left the road, he saw his chance.

The woman screamed even louder as he swung her, throwing her between the swift-moving legs of the horse to his right. Then he swung her back, the momentum and speed greater, towards himself, towards his own horse – and the temporary space beneath its rearing legs.

He got one final look at her shrivelled, open-mouthed face as his arms released her, and then she was flying out and away. The horse's descending hooves missed her by inches, but they did miss. And the landing must have hurt but the road was lined with people and the bodies the old woman barrelled into would have cushioned her fall.

Then she was lost to sight and Petronius was left on a furious, bucking horse, crucial paces away from the haven of the chariot. Inside it, Nero seemed to have become bored with holding the reins. As Petronius looked back, the little boy released them and began to clamber up the back, probably keen to see behind.

Petronius had a perfect view and was shocked to find that only one chariot of the dead still followed. They were close behind but not so close he needed to give them all his attention. There was a far more urgent problem - working his way back to the chariot in time to stop Nero falling off it.

The horse did everything in its power to stop him. Now that it had him on it, it seemed reluctant to let him off, and it reared and pranced every time he tried to shift himself, forcing him to cling tight with his legs around its withers.

He gave up trying to slowly wriggle his way back, and decided to opt for one desperate all-out attempt. He was running out of time, anyway. The road they followed ended ahead at a T-junction, and this place he did recognise. The left-hand fork dead-ended in a demolished tenement. If the horses, with no hand guiding them, decided to take it, they were finished.

Petronius's heart thundered in his chest, as if he was the one doing the running, not the horses. It pounded in time to their hooves as he braced his hands against the animal's neck and then – too quickly to give himself time to think about it – levered himself to his feet.

For one tottering, terrifying moment he stood there, balanced on his mount's back. Then it began to rear, he began to fall and he went with it, throwing himself towards the chariot and the little boy intent on clambering out of it.

His chest hit the chariot with enough force to drive all the air out of his lungs. Without his extra weight the horse leapt forward, the acceleration driving him even harder against the wood and he wondered if he'd ever be able to breath again.

The little boy reached the top of the chariot back at the moment Petronius reached for him. He startled to topple, yelling suddenly as he realised his danger, and Petronius grabbed his feet and pulled.

The abused muscles in his shoulder screamed their protest and so did Nero but a second later he was back in the very relative safety of the chariot –

– which was now starting to turn left into a lethal dead-end street. Petronius seized the reins and heaved, wrapping them around his own body as he'd seen the professional charioteers do.

The horses didn't want to obey. They pulled against him, determined now to have their own way. Petronius grimaced and flung himself to the right yanking the bit so hard into the horses' mouths that he saw flecks of blood among the spittle.

And finally the pain moved them. Their heads turned and their bodies followed after, down the road that led to freedom rather than death. The chariot turned too, but the circle of its path was broader and where the horses had missed the marble wall of the small temple of Aphrodite, the chariot caught it full on.

The impact flung Petronius against the shallow wooden side and Nero into his arms. It was the only thing that saved the boy's life. The chariot tipped and kept on tipping as the horses raced on. Astonishingly, it seemed to find stability at this crazy, acute angle, the right-hand wheel almost flat on the ground and the left-hand one high above it.

Petronius grabbed desperately for the side of the carriage with one hand and for Nero with his other. His fingers found a tenuous purchase on the thin wood, his arm a firmer grip around the little boy's waist. But he was still tangled in the reins and that saved him. Somehow he stayed in the chariot and when the horses took the next turn both wheels finally fell back to the ground.

Pain jarred all the way up Petronius's spine. Nero bounced from his knee and nearly out of the chariot before he made a desperate grab for him. The boy was still laughing, and Petronius was beginning to fear for his sanity.

And then, when he saw what was approaching, he feared for his own. Ahead lay a broad crossroads, the intersection of two of Rome's main thoroughfares. It was as deserted as the rest of the city had been; no old ladies to get in his way here. Instead Petronius could hear the clatter of approaching hooves.

The other two chariots of the dead had returned, as they must always have intended. They thundered towards him from opposite sides, meaning to trap him between them. They must have been waiting a while – they must have known a short cut – because they'd timed it just right. They'd meet in the middle at the perfect moment to crush his chariot between them. They'd be smashed to pieces in the impact too, but why should they care? There were always new bodies for them to move to.

"Race?" Nero said and Petronius choked out a laugh.

"Yes – I think we'll have to."

But he could already see that his horses were on the point of collapse. Their flanks were coated with sweat and their eyes were rolling as they galloped. The animals drawing the dead must have been equally exhausted, but as the two chariots raced towards him from either side, while the one behind continued to close the gap, he saw no evidence of them slowing. Perhaps fear of their dead passengers drove them on. And if the horses themselves died, they would simply be resurrected to continue the pursuit. If Petronius's horses died, they'd turn on their own passengers.

The dead were thirty paces and closing, and there was no way, just no way, that the chariot would make it through.

There was no way the *chariot* would make it through.

Nero yelped a protest when Petronius hoisted him onto his hip – then again when they both landed on the horse's back. The animal reared then bucked but Petronius was ready for it this time and he clung on grimly with one hand as he drew his sword with the other.

Fifteen paces. Petronius slashed down with the blade, and then again. The harness was only leather. It should have been no match for the steel of his sword. But there was no force in his blow, not twisted at that awkward angle, three-quarters of his concentration on keeping his seat.

Ten paces and the first strap parted. But the dead could see what he was doing. One of them threw a javelin, and he had to stop to pull himself and Nero out of its path. It missed them by a whisker to thump into the other horse's flank. The animal screamed and fell, dragging its harness-mate towards the ground with it.

Now Petronius had less than a second to free them or it was all over. He stopped trying to keep his balance, released his hold on Nero – trusting the boy to cling to him on his own – and brought the sword down against the remaining leather straps with all his strength.

It struck, caught and passed through. The momentum of his swing overbalanced him and the weight of the sword wanted to drag him to his death on the ground beneath his horse's hooves. He let the blade go, watching as it skittered and sparked along the pavement while his arms flung themselves desperately around the horse's middle.

Five paces, and it was up to the animal now. The reins had flown out of reach and Petronius could concentrate on nothing but keeping himself and Nero from falling to their deaths.

A second later, the undead were upon them. Petronius looked into the mad glaring eye of the nearest horse, and knew that it had already passed away and returned. The same fate that awaited him.

And then, spurred by something – fear of its own mortality, horror at its brother, slaughtered by its side – their own horse put on one final burst of speed. The spittle and blood from its mouth flew back into Petronius's face. He blinked his eyes to clear them and when he opened them again it was over.

The chariots of the dead had timed their approach exactly. They collided in perfect synchronicity, old human flesh and fresh horse and wood crashing together in an explosion of gore and splinters. The dead screamed their rage but Petronius's horse was through, it was past, and only the fine hair of its tail was caught in the carnage behind.

Petronius stayed, twisted round to watch it for a second more, then fumbled for the loose reins and guided their horse out of the square.

BODA HAD ONE foot through the door of the temple when she heard the rising thunder of hooves behind her. She spun and ducked, sword raised – then, a moment later, she sheathed it and smiled.

Vali raised his eyebrows, not looking altogether pleased.

Petronius's horse looked on the point of collapse, and she wondered what he'd been through to get here. The animal made a sound almost like a human groan as he dismounted and she could see that its eyes were bloodshot and its lips cut and bleeding where the bit had cut into them. One of the beetles which flew through the temple doors in a steady stream settled on the horse's flank, as if sensing a body that would soon be vacant for it to occupy.

It was only when Petronius strode towards her that she saw he held a small figure in his arms.

She smiled. "You saved him."

The child turned his wide eyes on her and grinned in return. "We raced against some skellingtons!" he said.

"Did you now?" Vali looked at Petronius and not the boy. "And you still managed to get here in time."

Petronius shrugged uncomfortably. "Actually, I was mainly concerned about running away. The fact that it happened to be in this direction was just a lucky accident."

"Indeed," the other man said dryly, and strode through the open doors of the temple to forestall further conversation.

Boda pulled Petronius into a quick embrace – Nero squashed between them – then turned away from the young man's blush to follow Vali inside.

As soon as she was through the door the noise hit her, the sound of a million beetles on the wing. It was a dry rasp that sounded just a little oily, as if the insects weren't entirely clean.

The interior of the temple was dark, lit only by the bright sun piercing the doorway and, at the far end of the long chamber, the sickly green light spilling out of the gateway to death itself. None of the Cult of Isis had stayed behind to guard the place. Maybe they couldn't bear to stare into that terrible portal for too long, with the buzzing of the dead souls all around. Boda could hardly stand to look at it herself.

She found her footsteps slowing as she walked through the darkness towards the gate. Petronius followed close behind her, but he kept casting nervous glances back at the doorway to safety and the outside world, brown eyes half-hidden behind the unruly tangle of his hair. She'd wanted to spare him this, but that was before the dead had flung themselves over the walls. Now there was no safety in Rome, and she found she was glad to face this with Petronius at her side.

Nero hid his face against Petronius's side, perhaps sensing the evil that lived inside the temple. Only Vali looked untroubled, his long strides drawing her on when her own would have faltered.

Then she was standing in front of the gate itself, with no further excuse for delay. The Cultists might return at any moment, and this was their only hope. She turned to Petronius, with the small, shivering boy by his side. "You can't bring him through here."

To her surprise, it was Vali who spoke. "Why not? He'll be safer inside death than facing it in the land of the living. If we succeed he'll be able to return, and if we fail, it's a pleasanter end than the one the undead will give him."

"Will we be able to return?" Petronius asked. He peered into the gateway, as if his eyes might penetrate it, but the green light hid everything behind it.

"As many as step though the gateway will be able to return through it," Vali told him. The light of death cast a ghastly pallor over his face, and dyed his red hair an unnameable colour.

Petronius looked at him out of suspicious eyes, and Nero out of round, trusting ones. "And how exactly do you know that?"

"Does it matter?" Boda asked. "My people's knowledge is different from yours. We know of the works of nature rather than those of man, but we know them deeply."

Vali smiled at her, then bowed and gestured forward. "Lead the way then, clanswoman. Your death awaits."

Boda swallowed, but she only allowed herself to hesitate a moment before stepping forward. Two paces and the green light was all she could see. She squared her shoulders and reached out her hand to feel her way blindly ahead of her –

– and when it met the gateway, it struck something solid. She frowned and pressed harder, putting her weight behind it, but nothing could move her fingers an inch past the rim of the gate.

"I'll go first, if you like," Petronius said, his voice shaking.

Boda realised that he thought she was afraid. She was, but that wasn't the problem. She turned to face the two men. "It's closed. It won't let me pass."

Petronius looked at Vali. "Is there some incantation, some ceremony we need to get through?"

Vali shook his head. "None that I know. The gates may only be closed from the inside, but it should be possible to enter them from either."

Boda took a step back towards them. "So we came all this way for nothing?"

Vali approached her, leaving Petronius and Nero behind. "Perhaps not. There are other ways to pass into death."

They were face to face now, and she saw that his was white with strain. He rested his hand against her shoulder and licked his lips.

"What other ways?" she asked him.

He pulled her closer still, and she thought for a second that he was going to kiss her, but he just rested his forehead against hers. "Do you trust me?"

She stopped her instant, automatic response, and thought about her answer. Did she trust him? She liked him, but that was far from the same thing. And she knew he hadn't always been honest with them. She still knew so little about him. In all the time they'd been together, she'd never been able to induce him to tell her his lineage or his chieftain. She shouldn't trust him – but she did.

"Yes," she said. "With my life."

He smiled at that, pulling back only a little. "That's generally considered unwise. But I promise you this, you'll have everything you need to get to the end. Everything you need you carry within you."

At first she felt the knife in her back only as a blow against her spine. A second later and what had seemed like an impact transmuted into a piercing pain worse than any she'd ever felt. The hilt settled snug against her skin, and she felt the prick of the blade emerging through her chest to dimple her tunic.

She looked down at it stupidly for a second. It was exactly where her heart lay, huddled in its cage of ribs. Then, as she looked back into Vali's eyes, he pulled out the blade and the blood gushed free. She had one moment to watch it spatter the white marble around her, and then she could see only blackness and the agony was nothing but a memory.

PART FOUR

Cineri Gloria Sera Est

CHAPTER SEVENTEEN

THE PHANTOM SENSATION of a knife sliding through Boda's flesh followed her into darkness. She thought she was screaming, but she couldn't feel her mouth. She couldn't hear the sound she made. Something that was her was still thinking, but it no longer had a head with which to do it, only a cloud of thought, of anger and betrayal.

The cloud was already dissipating. There was a wind, here in this lightless, loveless no-man's-land, and it wanted to blow her apart. She felt memories drifting away from her. Was that her childhood, seeping out? She was seven and she was climbing a tree, an oak deep in the old forest, she was happy and laughing – and then it was gone. Lost in the darkness.

There was something at the core of her, something the wind couldn't touch. But with all her memories gone, what would that thing be? Nothing that was Boda. Boda... was that her name? She was already forgetting.

No. No. Boda *was* her name. She had a childhood, a good one, and she wouldn't let it go. Her life had been full, though it had been short, and it had given her courage and strength. She used them now, pulling inward on the cloud of consciousness that was dissipating outward.

Something that wasn't her hand reached out for her childhood first. It struck other things, other memories – *a morning of brilliant sunshine on*

Crete; the pain of childbirth in the dark of a smoke-filled hut, and I've only seen thirteen summers, only thirteen, don't let this be my last – but they weren't Boda's memories and she batted them aside.

Then another flash, another moment. The weight of a sword between her two chubby palms and it's so heavy, so much heavier than she'd ever imagined. Will she one day carry it in her hand, wield it in defence of her tribe? It seems impossible and she sighs and hands it back to her father, who's smiling at her through his brown beard.

This, this is hers. She pulls it in and goes to collect more. Here's the moment when she first knew a man, fourteen years old and terrified that it would hurt as much as she'd been told. Three years later and there she is, bleeding the remains of her husband's child into the dirt. They tell her she's broken inside, that there'll be no more babies for her. Two weeks later and her husband cries as she leaves him for the life of a warrior. Another year and he's found someone else. Two, and she sees his fat, red-faced child, balanced on his wife's hip. Boda feels a moment of hurt, the pulling sense of roads not taken. Six months more and she's in her first battle and she knows this is what she was born to do.

More and more memories. Her sword sliding slick through blood. Boots in the soil of the forest, leaves churning beneath in a pleasant-smelling mulch. The hot-sweet taste of mead. Fire in her gut where a pike pierced it. The long agony of fever. Darkness – and then light. The feel of chains around her wrists as she's led to Rome.

The Arena. Josephus. His poor mutilated body. The catacombs, seething with corpses. The green light. The gateway to death.

The knife in her back.

All her memories, together once again. She gathered them inside her and slammed the door shut, locking them inside. And then she thought about her body, the one she'd had and lost.

She remembered how her hand felt, gripped around the pommel of a sword. The slight slipperiness of sweat on her palm, the coolness as the metal carried her heat away from her. She thought about water, the sweet relief of it in her mouth after a hard day's work, trickling down the valley of her thighs when she bathed. She pictured her own skin, pale when she first arrived in Rome, darkening over the months she spent there, but never the olive of the city's native sons. She pictured her skin, and she imagined it wrapping around her, enclosing all these sensations of body, these feelings of physical being.

She imagined ears growing from it, the improbable whorl of her lobes. Hair, fine and fair, the exact colour of her mother's. She felt it stirring in a breeze that wasn't there, itching with dust against her scalp. And lastly she thought of her eyes, their insensitive hardness behind her lids when she blinked. She pictured the little creatures of light that lived inside them when they were shut.

And then she imagined opening them.

She lay in a field of green grass, above her head a sky that was a different blue from any she'd ever seen. Reaching high, high into it, beyond where her new-old eyes could see, a great ash tree grew. Its leaves would have blocked the sun, had there been a sun here to block.

It was Yggdrasil, the world tree, which holds up every level of the world. And Boda lay in the lowest level of them all, the realm of the dead.

PETRONIUS STARED IN horror as Boda's body slumped to the ground, sliding through the arms Vali still held loosely around her.

He'd choked a protest when the knife went in, but now he found himself without words. His fingers fumbled at his own sword belt, but anything he could do would be no more than revenge. Boda was already gone. She was gone.

When his sword was trembling in his hand, the tip pressed against Vali's chest, he thought that revenge might feel pretty good. That sending the barbarian's blood to mingle with that of the woman he'd murdered would give him the closest thing to joy he was ever likely to feel again.

"Don't be a fool," Vali said.

Petronius knew that he was crying, and wasn't ashamed. She deserved his tears. "You low-born scum," he said. "She trusted you."

Vali bowed his head. Nero slipped from Petronius's side to stand beside Boda's corpse, and the other man rested a gentle hand against his head. Petronius saw with a sickening surge of rage that Vali left a bloody handprint in the child's fair hair.

Then Vali looked up again, and there was no apology in his eyes. There was – something. Something old and a little frightening and despite himself Petronius looked away.

"She gave me her trust," Vali said. "As I required. And now you must do the same."

"Why must I?" Petronius said.

The other man smiled, looking over his shoulder. "Because you have absolutely no choice."

Petronius's sword dropped as he spun. Somewhere in the back of his head, he'd heard the footsteps all along. He'd known they weren't alone. And now when he saw Sopdet, flanked on either side by the walking dead, he wasn't terribly surprised.

Her saw her shooting a troubled glance at the gateway between realms. But when she saw that the sick green light still shone through it, unbroken, she smiled. "A good plan," she said to Petronius. "What a shame that only I have the power to breach the land of death from this side."

Petronius was too shaken for bravura. He glared at her hatefully. "Then kill me. Kill me now, there's nothing left to live for."

She took a few more steps nearer, leaving her dead bodyguards behind. "I will, of course. But perhaps first I shall keep you a prisoner by my side, to share my full triumph. We'll walk the length of the earth, and where once the Pax Romana reigned, you'll see the Mortis Romana. Every person, every animal in the world will be a dead shell for the spirit living inside it. Only the trees and grass will remain as they were, green witnesses to the new world."

Her eyes were alight with a pleasure that was nowhere near sane. With her perfect rosebud mouth and fine high cheekbones and night-dark hair she should have been beautiful. But she wasn't. She was hideous.

And then, for the first time, her eyes gazed beyond Petronius, to the man she'd inadvertently stopped him from killing. Her already pale face drained of all colour and her mouth gaped open, a round black hole of shock.

"You!" she said.

Vali stepped forward until he was shoulder to shoulder with Petronius. He bowed ironically. "Fancy running into you here," he said. "What a pleasant surprise, sister."

BODA LAY FOR a while, staring up at the sunless blue sky between the long thin stalks of grass. It must be late in the year, in this realm without time. The seed pods had released their burdens, to drift in the gentle breeze across her face. She blew them idly away, watching the non-patterns the seeds made in the air, and thought that this was very pleasant. As she'd told Vali, she had nothing to fear from death.

Vali. He'd sent her here. And – she sat up, brushing the grass out of her way – he'd sent her here for a purpose. She must close the gates of death the only way a person could, from the inside. He hadn't had the courage to come himself, so he'd stabbed her in the back to send her here by the fastest route. His betrayal hurt more than she could have imagined, but it didn't alter the job that needed to be done.

She rose to her feet, and now she could see the grass, stretching into the distance. It seemed to go on forever, without horizon. No mountain or hill or landmark marred its endless sameness. Only its colour changed a little, as a breeze blew over and through it, and the stalks bent this way and that, exposing first their soft yellow underside and then their harsher, greener outer husks.

After a while the sameness of the grass began to oppress her. Would this be it, for all eternity, the only view she'd ever see? Would she have no company but her own? She turned from the grass, back towards the monumental tree behind. Its branches were far overhead, lost to distance. But its roots lay tangled all around, their arches as high as those brick roads the Romans used to carry water throughout their lands. The very thinnest of the roots was thicker than her body.

She stood at their outer edge, and inside she saw a darkness, stretching deep and far. There, for the first time, she thought she saw something – the glimmer of a red eye. She backed away, choosing to circle the tree instead.

It was a very long way. She wasn't sure how far she walked, looking at the peaceful plain of grass when the darkness under the tree began to trouble her, and at the shadows under the roots when the emptiness of the endless land became too much.

She'd almost given up hope of seeing anything different when she found it. She saw the well first. It was a simple stone structure, no bucket dangling from a rope above, but when she came closer she saw that a curved onyx drinking horn sat on its rim. The water came almost to its top, its blue as unlike normal water as the blue of the sky was unlike any sky she'd ever seen.

Still, she realised suddenly that she was thirsty. The horn felt solid in her hand, and cooler than she would have expected. She dipped it in the water and raised the lip to hers.

"Only poison, to those who drink without permission," a deep voice said behind her.

She span, sloshing water from the horn onto the grass. But there was no one there and she stood, irresolute, looking at the dregs of water and wondering if she dared quench her thirst with them.

"You must seek my blessing first, daughter of man," the voice said again – and this time she saw its source.

His head was huge, but still only a little higher than her waist, the reason her eyes had passed over it when she first searched for the speaker. His severed neck rested against the ground, bloodless. His smile was broad and might have looked friendly if it hadn't been nearly two-feet wide.

"Mimir," she said, because now she knew him, the immortal giant traded as a hostage to the Vanir, who sent back only his severed head.

She dropped to her knees, bringing her eyes level with his. Each was larger than her own head, but they were mismatched, the left brown and the right the most vibrant green she'd ever seen, so bright it made the grass around it seem drab.

"Do you wish to drink, child of Midgard?" Mimir asked.

Boda licked her lips. She did, but now she knew that it wouldn't be to quench her thirst. This well was the Well of Wisdom and its waters would tell her everything she wanted to know – and possibly many things she didn't. "Yes," she said eventually. "I want to drink. I need to."

The giant's severed head couldn't nod, but its huge eyes blinked in acknowledgement. "So said the Allfather himself, when the seasons turned. He needed my wisdom to save his son, but the sun was killed all the same. Is it the same business that brings you here? Do you wish to undo what even Odin himself could not?" His mismatched eyes studied her keenly.

"No," she said. "That's not what I want."

"Ah." The word was a deep rumble in a chest that wasn't there. "Then you wish for the opposite, do you? The keeping done of that which the Father of the Gods wished undone?"

She bowed her head but didn't reply. If Odin's son had perished, he might be the god Vali wished to remain dead. But she couldn't know for certain until she'd drunk the water.

Mimir seemed to understand what her non-answer meant. "And what price will you pay, for this knowledge you seek?"

"Price?" She looked down at herself, and realised for the first time that she was dressed in nothing but a simple tunic, like the lowest of Roman slaves. In all the vast empty landscape around her, there was nothing she could give for what she wanted.

The giant laughed. "There is always a price, girl, and yours will be high. The Allfather gave me his eye in return for the knowledge he sought. And you? What will you give me, that could equal the value of that?"

CHAPTER EIGHTEEN

PETRONIUS LOOKED BETWEEN Vali and Sopdet in appalled understanding. He was red-haired and she was dark, and she was dark-skinned and he was light, but for the first time, Petronius could see the resemblance between them. It was something in their eyes, something too ancient for their young faces. And the worst thing was, Vali had told them this truth right from the start, knowing that they'd never believe him. No wonder he'd murdered Boda. He must have been working with his sister all along.

But the look Sopdet gave Vali was far from loving. "You're too late," she said. "You can't stop me undoing what you've done."

He looked down his long, narrow nose at her. "If that was all you wished, sister, I wouldn't have gone to such lengths to prevent it."

Vali's words seemed to spark a conflagration inside her. Sopdet ignited with rage. Petronius took a step back, until he was pressed against the unyielding gateway to the other side. It was less frightening than this woman's anger, which seemed far larger and more pure than any woman should be capable of.

"You've already done all in your power," she said, "every single thing to keep us apart. You've walked the ends of the earth and beyond. You've done everything you can to keep him dead – but you can't do this!"

Vali seemed supremely calm. Petronius didn't understand how he could maintain that little half-smile in the face of Sopdet's fury. It could do nothing but provoke her. "It's certainly true, sister, that I can't step through this gateway unless you open it for me. But then you're going to do that very soon, so I see no problem."

"Am I?" Petronius could see Sopdet bite back her anger, struggling to mutate it into contempt. "There's a faster way to send you to the other side. Here in the realm of man, I can give you the same fate you gave my beloved."

Vali took a step back, until he was standing beside Petronius against the gates of death. Petronius flinched away from him, but Vali didn't seem to care.

"I think you'll open the gateway," he said. "Because you need to step through it yourself. And you need to step through it yourself, because my emissary has already crossed over." His eyes drifted down to Boda's body, on the steps beneath them.

For the first time, Petronius wondered why it had remained dead, when every other corpse in Rome had risen.

Sopdet looked at Boda and frowned. "That woman? Why should I fear her?"

Vali's eyes lingered on Boda, and Petronius thought he read regret in them. Or maybe it was just his own. "Because I've sent her to Mimir," he said. "And then I've instructed her to seek out our brother – and ensure he stays where he belongs."

Sopdet threw back her head and howled. The sound was so deep and so loud, the temple shook with it. Even the dead cringed away from their mistress, covering their decaying ears.

Petronius shrank back. His arms reached behind him, expecting the barrier of solid air that guarded the gate to death – and found nothing. Nero was pressed against his chest, the boy's wide blue eyes fixed on the howling woman. There were words in the howl, Petronius could hear that now, though he didn't know their meaning.

"Quick," Vali said. "Go through while you can – she'll close it behind her."

Petronius spun. He saw that one of his feet had already passed through the gateway. It disappeared into absolute darkness, invisible to him, only the sensation of his calf muscles clenching in fear to tell him it was still a part of his body. The green light had blinked out, but it left nothing behind, no clue to what lay beyond.

"Do you trust me?" Vali said.

Petronius laughed, almost hysterically. "What do you think?"

"Well," Vali said. "Do you trust me more than you trust her?"

Petronius couldn't help himself. He shot a look behind him. The noise cut out the instant he did. Sopdet's hair was suddenly white, and it took him a moment to realise why. It was full of the plaster flakes which had floated down from the painted ceiling with the strength of her howl. As if to compensate, her face was red, engorged with the blood of rage. And her eyes were luminous, blazing with the same sick green light that had once shone from the gateway to death itself.

As she lowered her head and raced for the gateway, Petronius grabbed Nero and leapt across the threshold into the darkness.

BODA SHOOK HER head. "There's nothing I can give," she told Mimir. "I've already lost everything I had."

"Your life, you mean?" the giant said. She could see his huge pink tongue moving inside his mouth, each taste bud the size of a coin.

"Yes. I brought nothing with me into death, not even silver for the ferryman the Romans believe in."

"Nothing at all?" There was a cunning note to his voice now. "What of your memories? Why did you fight so hard for them, if you hold them in no regard?"

Boda felt a heart that wasn't real pounding in her chest. "You want my memories?"

"Would you sacrifice them for this knowledge you seek?"

Would she? "No," she told him. "I need my memories to understand the knowledge. One would be useless without the other."

He chuckled. "A good answer. Then what will you give?"

She spread her hands. "What do you want?"

"I? It is the value of the sacrifice to the giver, not its worth to the recipient."

"Name any other price and I will pay it."

"So shall it be," the giant said, and his voice rang hollow with the sound of a vow given and sealed.

Boda hesitated, suddenly unsure of what she'd done.

"Drink then," Mimir said. "And you shall learn the price when you have the knowledge to understand it."

She raised the horn, watching the light sparkle on its carvings as she dipped the open mouth beneath the surface of the water.

"Fill it all," the giant said, "and drink it all. Your ignorance is far too wide, and only this can narrow it."

When the horn was full to the brim, she raised it to her lips.

"Drink," Mimir said. "Follow in the footsteps of Odin himself."

She shivered, knowing that once done, this could never be undone. That she'd made a bargain with a god, and that was never wise. Here in the realm of the dead, there was much she could suffer if it was decreed, and she'd suffer it eternally. But she'd sworn an oath as a warrior to protect her people. That oath didn't end at the gates of the otherworld.

The water felt cool as it gushed down her throat and it tasted of something she couldn't quite name. Was it rosemary? No, it was more bitter than that. Her mind chased the thought, chased the taste – and followed it out of the world of death and somewhere else entirely.

SHE LOOKED DOWN on a hall, a great hall filled with laughter and music and light, and at the table's head, a one-eyed man lifted a horn of mead to pass to the thunder-browed giant at his right-hand side. Odin and Thor and all the Aesir feasted in the halls of Asgard, and only one forehead frowned, only one mouth turned down instead of up.

Why was Vali sitting at the table of the gods? But the moment the thought was formed, Boda knew its answer. How had she confused this fierce, flaming being with the man she knew? This was Loki, god of fire and mischief and blood brother to Odin, but not brother of the heart. Not tonight.

Odin's gaze passed over Loki and didn't see the hurt in his eyes. They sought only one thing, only one man, the sun-gold face of Baldur, his beloved son.

He saw his son and didn't see the brother who scowled to see him smile. He didn't see the envy and the hate.

A wrench, a twist in time, and Boda was back at Mimir's well. For a moment she thought that it was over, that that was all she'd see. But then she realised that she was floating above the scene, a vantage point different from her body's. And she saw the Allfather standing by the water as he reached up to his face and plucked out his own eye, brilliant and green and knowing, to place inside the giant's empty socket.

Then Odin raised the horn, and as the water flowed in him and through him, so did she. She saw what he saw, the golden-haired Baldur dead, his red blood soaking the earth and his mother Frigga's face twisted in a grief that no goddess should ever know. Odin screamed with the same pain and rage and the scream carried Boda on.

Now she followed a horse, galloping the length of the earth. Frigga rode its back, tall and proud and full of love, and everywhere she rode she asked a vow of every living thing she met.

"Hazel tree," she said. "Will you swear never to harm my beloved son?" And the tree was filled with the same love she felt, and it took the oath. Next she asked a squirrel, a lion, an ant. Boda saw that there wasn't one thing in the world which didn't give its word.

But there was one beneath it, one little sprig of mistletoe. "I'll take the oath!" it said, but Frigga said it was too young.

And Loki – full of bitterness and envy – took the twig and nurtured it and grew it to a sapling. The god of fire looked on the spear he fashioned from the iron-hard mistletoe and smiled his crooked smile, beneath his long, sharp nose.

Another twitch in time, and now Boda saw the gods standing in the flower-filled fields of Asgard, with Baldur in their middle. The sun god stood and laughed as rocks and swords and hammers were thrown at him and not a single one could touch him. *We swore an oath,* the weapons cried and turned their points away.

Until, slinking and smiling at the side of the field, Loki placed a spear of mistletoe in the blind god Hodur's hands.

The spear flew, strong and true, into the sun god's heart. Laughter turned to screams and all the world gasped at the fall of this golden child. Even Hel, goddess of the underworld, cold and hard and without love, felt a moment of pity for Frigga, for a mother's pain. Hel swore that if every living thing wept for Frigga's fallen son, she'd free him from the realm of death to walk in Asgard's sunlit fields again.

Another twitch and Boda saw another horse, another journey the length and breadth of the earth. This time Frigga, tears streaming down her own face, looked for the same tears of mourning from every living thing on earth. The hazel tree wept, the lion, the ant, even the mistletoe which in its ignorant youth had killed her son.

But just one person refused – a giantess, with a face as stony as the rocks of the cave in which she lived. "I will not weep," she said. "I do not mourn him." And so Baldur was condemned to remain in the realms of death.

And when Frigga had passed on, cursing the giantess's name, the creature smiled a crooked smile beneath a sharp nose, and shape-changing Loki thought that his work was done.

Another twitch, stronger this time, and Boda found herself looking at a different scene in a different world – that she somehow knew was still the same as the one she'd witnessed before.

This time the sun-god's name was Osiris, and it was his sister-wife Isis and not his mother who mourned him so extravagantly. The god-murderer was named Set, not Loki, and sometimes he had the body of a man and the head of a beast, a composite of all the creatures that roamed the desert, the curved snout of a jackal and the long square ears of an ass. But sometimes he had a man's face, a crooked smile beneath red hair and a long, sharp nose. And here, as before, he was a stranger and outsider – a god of the foreign and the forsaken.

And then another twitch, and Boda saw that the Jews told the story a little differently, that Shaitan their red-haired desert god didn't kill the sun-god himself, but paid a living man thirty pieces of silver for his murder. And there were others – more and more images from all over the world until she thought her head would explode with them. A thousand and one stories but only one truth.

The god of mischief who was sometimes called Loki and sometimes Set and sometimes other things, murdered the sun-god out of jealousy and spite. And the goddess who had many names, of which Isis was only one, mourned the dead sun-god – sometimes as her husband and sometimes as her son, but always far too much.

She travelled the length of the earth, seeking a way to bring him back from the realms of the dead, where his mummified body sat in final judgement over the mortals who ended their short journey there. She failed, and her failure drove her mad and she hatched a final – fatal – plan.

Her husband was in the realm of death. She couldn't join him there because she was a goddess of the earth, of green and vibrant things, and her duty lay among them. The realm of death would spit her out if she stayed in it too long. And Osiris, being dead, could never cross to the living realm. But what if the two realms became one? What if the land of life became a realm of death too – not a single living man or creature still abiding there?

Then her husband could return. Then he could rule by her side.

But Isis would have to be careful – she'd have to be cunning. If the other gods knew what she was planning, they would stop her. If Set found out, he would foil her once again. And so she disguised herself as a human woman named Sopdet, and found followers among the mortals who had their own reasons to wish for the gates of death to be opened.

Sopdet, who was Isis – and also Frigga, and every other goddess who'd lost the god she loved – came to the realm of the living and opened the gateway to death. And only the trickster god Loki, who was also Set, and a red-haired man called Vali, could do anything to stop her. But he was the one who'd killed her husband-brother-son in the first place – and he was never to be trusted.

AND IN THE world of the living, the woman called Sopdet who was also the widowed Isis and the grieving mother Frigga, plunged through the gateway to death which she had created – the gate she was forbidden to cross.

Isis was the mistress of the moon, of bread and beer and all green things. And those who worshipped her as Frigga knew that she presided over the making of new life, through love and birth.

With the goddess gone from the land of the living, everything that she ruled went with her. The moon was on the far side of the world from Rome, invisible. No one in the city, huddled terrified in their homes, saw its silver light blink from the sky.

But even inside their brick and marble they heard the distant roar of the sea, surging wildly as the force that governed its tides was taken from it. Huge waves crashed against the shore, against the grass that grew there and was dying too, without its mistress to nurture it.

All over the Empire, at the height of summer, the leaves wilted on the trees and the flowers drooped and died, no pollen to spread on the wind and make new flowers. Without Isis in the world, there could never be new flowers again.

And in their houses in Rome, women looked at their husbands and husbands looked at their wives and where there had been love there was only indifference and where there had been indifference there was now hate, and no one remembered what it felt like to love another person, because the idea of love was gone from the world.

In Gaul, a man who'd been happily married for thirteen years passed the sixteen-year-old daughter of his best friend in the street. His cock twitched and suddenly he couldn't see why not. Why not take her right here, right in the street, if he wanted to? He covered her mouth to muffle her screams and the onlookers laughed and cheered as he had her.

In Syria, two brothers played a game of dice for coppers they could well afford. They'd played the game since they were children and they played it now to remember that happy time. But when one of them threw two ones and the other laughed, suddenly he couldn't bear it. How dare his brother laugh at him – his brother, who'd stolen his parents' attention from him when he was only four years old. The knife was only meant for cutting bread but it slid through his brother's chest like butter and he smiled to hear him scream in pain.

And in Egypt, a woman looked down in horror at this little creature suckling at her breast. What was this thing, this parasite, that was leeching the life out of her? She threw it away and stamped and stamped and stamped on it until there was nothing but a red and white mush on the floor and she could no longer remember what its little pink face had looked like.

And all around Rome, the dead raised their heads to the moonless sky and howled. Their leader was gone, and now there was no one to command them – and no one to rein them in. What had been a planned assault deteriorated into chaos, and what had been a focussed attack became a mindless slaughter.

All over the world, the green grass turned brown, the living forgot how to love each other, and the dead turned their mindless hatred on the living.

CHAPTER NINETEEN

BODA BLINKED HER eyes open, and found that she lay on her back, a strange blue sky above her and long, thin stalks of grass all around. Had she just arrived here? Was everything she had seen and heard a dream, the last imaginings of her dying mind?

A part of her hoped so, but when she struggled to her feet she saw the well and the giant's head beside it. "Daughter of Midgard, now do you understand?" he said.

She bowed her head, because she understood all too well. Her friend Vali, who had both saved and taken her life, was also the god Loki, who might have doomed them all when he contrived to kill his fellow god out of jealousy and spite.

"And can you guess the price I demand?" Mimir asked.

She shook her head. These were matters for gods, not mortals, and she couldn't see what her part in them would be.

"Look beneath the roots of Yggdrasil," he said.

She peered into the darkness, stretching miles beneath the vast tree, and for a moment a flash of lightning illuminated some of what was hidden there. She saw a slab of rock in a dark cave, and though the distance confounded all perspective, Boda knew that the rock was huge. The metal chains that lay on it were meant to hold a being more powerful than any that had ever been bound before. Above the rock the air seemed to twist and writhe and it took her a moment to realise that it was filled with snakes, hanging from the stalactites above, twining and twisting into each other and dripping their venom onto the slab below.

"Loki's prison," Mimir said, "meant to punish him for all eternity. But the god of fire and mischief fled and now someone else must suffer in his place."

Boda shuddered at the thought of lying there, in that impenetrable darkness, and knowing there would be no escape till the world itself had ended. She shuddered because she knew now what the price was to be. "You want me to take his place. He wanted it – that's why he sent me here."

Mimir's eyes flickered in acknowledgement. There was no pity on his vast face and that made it easier to bear. "A killing demands a blood price," he said. "Someone must pay it. And the death of a god is so vastly more consequential a thing than the death of a man, it demands a vastly greater punishment."

"I will pay it then," she said. "Though it was not I who did this wrong, I gave you my word and I'll keep it. But first you must let me complete my work."

"Must I, Midgard's child?"

Boda looked beneath the roots, but the darkness was complete again. She could remember it though, and always would, the rock and the snakes above it. She looked back at Mimir. "Yes. I took a vow to protect my people, to death and beyond."

"An oath more powerful than that you made to a god?"

"Yes," she said. "Greater even that that."

The giant sighed, a large sound louder than the wind. "Go then, and find your friends. Find the dead god and face his judgement, and when it is done, your mortal spirit will return here to suffer for all eternity."

She wanted to ask him how to find her friends – she wanted to ask him a lot of things – but his smile was already fading, and with it the rest of his face, and when it was gone entirely, she was somewhere else.

NARCISSUS THOUGHT HE'D been here a very long time, but he wasn't entirely sure. When he looked back into the past, it all seemed the same, the same wandering on the same grey and lonely river bank, and he wondered if he'd ever known anything else.

There were others here, by the shore of this underground river. Their faces would drift towards him, out of the endless mist, and he would back away. They looked so sad. He didn't think he could deal with their sadness as well as his own.

The rocky ground was uneven and he kept stumbling. His knees were raggedly cut and his hands abraded but there were no red beads of blood on his grey skin. Everything here was grey. He knew that soon he'd have forgotten what colours were. Maybe then he'd be content to stop wandering, and just sit still and wait for forever to pass.

But not yet. Not quite yet. He still remembered that his name was Narcissus. He still knew that his master had loved him. And he knew that he needed to cross the river. There was something better on the other side, if only he could reach it.

He found himself at the shore again, little wavelets lapping against the rocks at his feet. The ferryman was there too. He always was.

"I want to cross," Narcissus told him.

The man shook his head, hidden beneath his cowl. "You don't have the coin."

Narcissus felt for the purse that hung at his neck, but he already knew that the ferryman was right. It was empty.

"I'll pay you when I reach the other side," Narcissus told him.

The ferryman laughed and Narcissus saw a brief flash of yellow teeth in the shadows. "They all say that, son. And none of them can."

"I'm different!" Narcissus said, though he wasn't sure how.

"They all say that too."

"Then I'll swim." Narcissus looked down at the water. He had a memory, a bright blue one, of being dragged through the sea to the shores of Alexandria. He hadn't known how to swim then, but he thought he could manage now.

"Unwise, boy," the ferryman said. "This river will carry away more than your body."

"What choice do I have?" Narcissus asked him, and the ferryman had no answer to that. His flat boat drifted away, lost in the mist in moments, and only the long, slow-moving river remained.

Narcissus couldn't see the far shore, but it should be possible to reach it. And, after all, what more did he have to lose?

He drew in one breath and dived beneath the ice-cold surface before his mind could supply an answer to that question.

PETRONIUS FOUND HIMSELF on the bank of a great river. He could hear the waters rushing past, though they were hard to see in the gloom of the world that lay through the gate. Vali stood beside him – if that was even his name – and Nero lay limp in his arms. When Petronius put the little boy down, he clung tight to his thigh, his only anchor in this strange world.

Vali frowned at the river, its far shore lost in the darkness. "We need to cross," he said. "Before she follows us through."

"Who are you?" Petronius said. "And who's she?"

Vali smiled crookedly. "Gods and demons, beings from another realm. We're just people, Petronius, with many names and normal desires. And currently my desire is to survive. How about you?"

"Cold water!" Nero said, and Petronius saw that the child had knelt to dip his finger in the river.

Before Petronius could react, Vali swooped and lifted him back. Nero let out a little yelp of protest that faded into silence as he stared at the tip of his index finger, which he'd wetted to its middle joint. Petronius could see the middle joint. The water had withered the skin and flesh above it, ageing it a hundred years in a second.

The little boy began to cry, more from shock than pain, Petronius thought – and Vali hurriedly put him down. "This river runs with more than water," he said. "It carries the hours of the night, time passing in its ebb and flow."

"Then how can we cross it?" Petronius asked. He looked down at the water and felt a terrible temptation to dip his finger in it too – his whole hand. To feel time as a physical thing, flowing past.

Vali grimaced. "There was a day I could have swum it without fear of harm, but I've lived in the mortal realm too long. I fear time has caught my scent."

There was nothing else around them, a featureless plain stretching away from the river to a horizon that lay in darkness. Petronius suspected he could walk forever and never reach it. He could hear the gushing sound of what might be a huge waterfall, somewhere in the distance, but he couldn't see it.

"If these are the hours of night," he said, "can't we follow them into day?"

Vali laughed, a surprised and genuine sound. "How typically Roman – logic in the midst of unreason. No, the night here is endless, for all that it ticks on second by second like any other time."

Petronius found his gaze suddenly drawn behind them, back to the distant source of the dark river. "Then how about a boat? Could that carry us across?"

Vali's gaze tracked his until he saw the same thing. The barge was broad and high-sided, and it was the only thing in this gloomy land which carried its own source of illumination. The light from inside it spilled out on the water, and Petronius saw with a jolt of fear that the water itself was black. It absorbed the light that hit it and gave nothing back.

The barge sailed close to the shore, its double banks of oars sending the pitch-black water to splash against the land. The whole thing was painted in bright colours, daubed with the pictures and symbols the Egyptians used in their writing, a side-on eye and a falcon, a scarab and a bird. And there was a ladder leading up the side, Petronius could see that now. It should be possible to jump aboard it – possible, but frightening, if the aim was to avoid touching even one drop of the water beneath. The slightest stumble and they'd fall into the river and be burned to the bone by the waters of time.

Nearer still, Petronius caught his first glimpse of the oarsmen, hidden in the bowels of the barge. He flinched away from flashes of eyes slitted like those of beasts. One of the oarsmen smiled, a wide gaping in a mouth that was more of a muzzle. A pink tongue lolled over sharp white teeth.

Suddenly, climbing aboard didn't seem such an appealing prospect.

But behind them, there was another sound – a tearing in the air itself – and he guessed that Sopdet had followed them through.

"Our only chance," Vali said, and leapt aboard the barge.

His fingers caught on the rungs of the ladder, but the blue paint there must have been slicker than it looked. Petronius heard the barbarian gasp and his fingers slid until only his nails gave him any purchase. He was already leaning backwards – a second more and he'd fall into the rushing waters of the river below.

There was no reason Petronius should care. He had Nero to take care of, and himself, and Vali had lied to him from the start. But he found himself hooking an arm under Nero and flinging himself at the barge.

He aimed for the rung beneath Vali, the lowest that was still above the water. The river was smooth here but the slightest wave might splash and burn him. His feet scrabbled for their footing, finding the rungs already slick with water. The heel of his sandal saved his foot but when he risked a glance down he saw the leather rotting away.

Nero was as slippery as the wood beneath his feet, squirming in his arms. And his own hands could reach only the outer edges of the ladder, circling Vali's body between them in a loose embrace.

The initial force of the impact pushed all three of them against the side of the boat, saving Vali from falling and driving the breath out of all their lungs and rebounding from the slick wood of the boat. Petronius gritted his teeth and tightened his grip on the side of the ladder, hardly any power left in him after this long, strange day.

Vali was heavy, and the boat was swaying now – as if it knew it had uninvited riders, and was trying to buck them off. Vali fell back against Petronius with all his weight, and his elbow caught him beneath the ribs.

Petronius let out a harsh gasp of pain, but the pain made his hands convulse and clench and the extra strength of their grip saved him. Then the boat swayed back, they were pressed against it once again, and this time Vali didn't wait. His hands reached above him and he swarmed up the ladder towards the top of the boat and whatever awaited them there.

Petronius was only a little slower in following, hampered by the small boy clasped against his chest. The higher rungs seemed more robust, or maybe his diminishing fear made them seem that way, as he left the water below him.

As he neared the top, he began to hear a sound, a deep buzzing that was as much in his bones as in his ears. The light grew brighter too, but he was glad of that. Anything that pierced the darkness was welcome.

But when he finally entered the barge, the light was brighter than he could have imaged. He shut his eyes against it in a flinch of pain, but the light burned through his eyelids, seeming to pierce directly into his brain. He didn't dare open them again – wasn't sure that if he did, there'd be anything left behind his eyelids but burned-out black husks.

Only the image remained, almost as bright in memory as it had been of itself. He could feel the heat of it too, setting his skin smouldering – that great, burning ball of flame that he knew as the sun, carried here on a barge through the hours of night.

AND BODA, TOO, found herself facing a river. It traced a gentle curve through the endless field of grass, its waters a pleasant tinkle to counterpoint the wind whispering through the stalks. In the far distance, she could see something black stretching into the sky, and she guessed that it was Yggdrasil. She thought the source of the river might lie beneath the tree's roots, and she was afraid to touch its waters, however pleasant they sounded, and however blue they looked.

But there was a bridge, only a few minutes' walk along its course. The light here was diffuse, no one source to sparkle from the water or the bridge itself, but as Boda drew nearer she saw that the whole thing was constructed from rich, buttery gold.

When she reached the short flight of steps leading up to the bridge, she saw the figure standing astride it, one foot at one edge and one at the other, though the structure must be twenty paces wide.

The giantess didn't seem to sense her approach at first. The level of her gaze was high above Boda's head, and perhaps her ears were too distant to detect the sound of her tread. But when Boda placed her first foot on the bridge itself, the giantess shifted her gaze downwards, squinting as if she found it hard to focus on something so small. This close, Boda could feel the waves of cold rolling off her. Her armour had looked like silver from a distance, but now Boda could see that the whole suit was made of ice – intricately carved and near transparent, showing the blue skin beneath.

"Little mortal," the giantess said. "I am Modgudr, guardian of the bridge, and you may not pass."

Boda found herself pushed back a step by the enormous volume of her voice. The rasp as Modgudr drew her sword was louder yet, the sound of a mountain of ice breaking away to fall into the sea far below.

The blade steamed with cold and Boda fumbled at her side for her own, before remembering that in this realm she didn't wear one. She smiled at herself, because even if she had, how could she possibly have hoped to defeat this vast being?

"I must pass," Boda said. "Mimir commands it."

Modgudr huffed a breath that rolled over Boda like a freezing mist. "My bodiless brother is not my master. I chart my own course."

"Oh? Your learning must be great indeed, to exceed that of the master of the Well of Wisdom?"

"Do you mock me?"

Boda forced herself to look up and up, into Modgudr's distant eyes. "Perhaps. I've drunk from the well – have you?"

"I have no need of it! My understanding is deeper than the ocean, which Thor himself could not drain. My knowledge is broader than the plain of Vigrid, where the gods themselves shall die. How dare you question me, little ghost?"

"A contest, then," Boda said. "A test to see who's wiser."

"You challenge me?" Modgudr bellowed, the force of her words so strong, they blew Boda back to the edge of the bridge.

Boda clung on to the railing and set her teeth against the gale. "I do, riddle against riddle, and the one who can't answer must forfeit her life – or what life she has, in a place such as this."

"Hmmm..." the giantess said, a profound vibration. "But nothing must be asked that is not known by the questioner."

"Agreed," Boda said. "My word on it."

"Then mine is given too – and I shall ask my question first. Tell me this, daughter of worms, what is it that walks on four legs in the morning, two in the afternoon, and three in the evening?"

Modgudr smiled, clearly pleased with herself, but Boda smiled wider. Maybe if she hadn't spent those months in Rome, she might have been baffled, but she'd learnt their legends too. "Man crawls on four legs in the morning of his life," she said, "walks upright on two in the healthy afternoon, and stoops on two legs and a stick in the fading twilight of his years."

The giantess snorted, clouds of ice puffing from her nostrils to fall as snow on the bridge below. "Very well then – your question for me?"

Boda clenched her fists, then said: "Tell me, what did Vali whisper in my ear in the second before I died?"

There was a long silence. "This is your riddle?" Modgudr said eventually.

"Yes. Can you answer it?"

"Of course not! No one but you knows the answer."

Boda allowed herself the tiniest smile. "But I do know – which was the only condition you set."

The giantess's roar of rage seemed larger than the sky. Boda wondered if the white clouds would crack and the earth tear at the power of it. She fell to her knees, curling her arms around her head to block it out, but the noise was everywhere, in her and around her, and she thought if it went on a second longer it would melt her flesh and shake her bones apart.

When it finally ended the silence felt like a blow. Boda had a second to uncurl herself, and then Modgudr's sword began to swing. Boda flung herself to the side of the bridge, but the sword was broader than the walkway, broader than the river itself. There was no escaping it.

The point came towards her, blotting out the sky behind it, and she wondered if it would crush or pierce her. Closer still, and she could see the pits in the metal, the first huge specks of rust. It came level with her knees, her chest – and the outer reach of its swing whistled by a pace from her head, setting her blonde hair flying. Boda toppled backwards as the great blade continued to swing up, up and inward – towards the giantess's own heart.

The blade sank in without a sound, and Modgudr fell to her knees with only a low murmur of pain. Her aim was true and Boda saw the blood gush from the wound, as blue as the giantess's skin. Droplets as big as fists spattered against Boda's head. She was surprised to find that Modgudr's blood was as warm and sticky as human blood, though it smelt of wet ash.

The giantess's eyes were shielded behind lids as big as sails, but she blinked them open one last time. "Pass then, little ghost," she said. "Your wisdom is greater than mine."

HE DRAGGED HIMSELF from the water, wondering why he'd been swimming and where. The landscape around lay in darkness, the bare outlines of jagged rocks visible in the distance. Had he been here before? He couldn't remember.

He looked back at the river, and when he did he saw a boat, a flat-bottomed barge which was floating towards him. The man steering it had hidden his face beneath a deep black cowl, but he saw the ghost of a smile as he approached.

"So you crossed," the ferryman said. "Brave and stupid, boy."

"Crossed what?" he asked. He hadn't crossed anything, he was just standing there. Except, no. He'd just come out of the water, hadn't he? He must have swum the river. This new piece of knowledge about himself excited him, and he laughed.

The ferryman shook his head, lost in shadows. "The River Lethe is unkind to mortals. Do you know why you needed to be here?"

"No," he said. "Can you tell me? Can you tell me who I am? What I want? Where I came from and where I'm going?"

"So many questions – and I have only one answer to give. Which one would you like?"

He thought about it. He'd like to know his name – he seemed to remember that people needed names – but the ferryman was perfectly happy to speak to him without one. And he'd like to know where he came from, but he'd probably left there for a reason. On the other hand, if he found out where he was going, he might find what he wanted when he got there.

The ferryman nodded, as if he'd said all that out loud. "You're going to find the god who died, and persuade him to stay dead."

He frowned, because that didn't sound familiar at all. But why would the ferryman lie to him? "And where will I find him?" he asked. "It's part of the original question!" he added hurriedly, as the ferryman shook his head.

The boat was drifting away, already fading into mist, and for a moment he thought the ferryman wouldn't answer him. But the voice floated back, almost lost beneath the splash of the waves. "The dead god sits in the hall of judgement, as far from the river's bank as forgiveness and as near as guilt."

He wasn't quite sure what that meant, but it sounded like he needed to walk away from the river. After all, why else would he have swum it? He set off across the landscape of fallen rocks, the crushed remnants of a mountain that was long gone. The sharp edges tore his feet and his knees when he stumbled, but he didn't mind. He'd forgotten how to feel pain.

For miles and maybe years the landscape didn't change. But then, finally, he saw something, a greater darkness in the distance that resolved into a gateway as he drew near. Was that where he meant to go? If not, it must lead somewhere, and somewhere was better than the endless nowhere of this land.

He was almost at the cave-mouth when he saw the creature that lived inside. He fumbled for the word and found to his delight that he remembered it: 'dog'. But weren't dogs meant to be small, no taller than his waist? And did they normally have three heads?

The three heads swung to face him as he approached, and the creature rose to its feet, lifting them far above him. The heads seemed to be smiling at him, white teeth shining, but was it really a smile? He thought there might be another word for that expression, and for the deep growl that came from the creature's barrel chest.

Saliva dripped from the pink insides of its lips to the rocks below, burning where it landed, and he discovered that fear was an emotion he hadn't yet forgotten.

PETRONIUS HAD ALWAYS thought that blindness would be dark, but now he knew that it was as bright as the light that had burned his eyes. He wondered if he would see the sun for the rest of eternity, blazing behind his eyelids.

Nero still clung to his hip, though he didn't know if the boy had also been blinded. Only Vali seemed entirely unharmed. He'd taken Petronius's arm and led him ashore when the barge had neared the far bank.

Stepping off into nothingness had been terrifying – knowing that the waters of time might wait to drown him beneath. But he had to trust Vali. He had no choice.

"Where's Sopdet?" Petronius asked now. "Is she close behind?"

"She's swimming," Vali said, and Petronius thought he could hear a smile in the barbarian's voice. "It looks like she's finding it harder than she expected. Like me, she's spent too long among men. But she won't be far behind. We need to hurry."

Petronius did his best, stumbling over the rocky ground beneath him. All around him he heard voices, the sound of a thousand people, but he wondered if he would have been able to see them, even with his eyes. Their whispers seemed incorporeal, the murmured complaints of spirits who'd been worn away until they were nothing but air.

He didn't know how long the journey took. Away from the river that embodied it, time seemed to have no meaning here. But after a countless succession of moments, they drew to a halt.

There was another noise now, a deep and sibilant hissing that seemed animal, not human. Petronius felt Vali's hand claw into his bicep and shrank back, terrified by anything fearsome enough to frighten even the barbarian.

"Big snake," Nero said.

Vali choked a laugh. "A very big snake – and it has two heads."

"Well," Petronius said, "and this is only a suggestion, but perhaps we should run away from it."

"We can't," Vali told him. "We need to get past. This is the guardian of the halls of death."

"Then what do you suggest we do?" Petronius asked, and this time he couldn't stop his voice from shaking. He didn't want to face his end and not even see it. And what would it mean, anyway, for a person to die in the realms of death? Was there some deeper level, some worse hell he might be banished to?

"We hope that Boda really does trust me," Vali said, and then the hissing heads descended.

THE GIANTESS HAD barely finished dying when the wolf came. It looked tiny beside her vast corpse, but Boda backed away all the same, not trusting her senses in this world where nothing was quite as it seemed.

When the beast pounced, she knew that she'd been right to fear. Its back rose higher than her head and its head was the size of her whole body, each needle-sharp tooth as long as her arm. The saliva that dripped from them hissed and fizzled in the dirt.

But its size saved her. The soft hair of its belly brushed hers as she dodged underneath it, and the claw it sent raking towards her dug up a furrow of earth but barely missed her chest.

The beast realised she'd eluded it. Its back legs flicked up and round, trying to dance away from her, but she danced with it, keeping herself in the safe spot beneath its chest where none of its feet could reach.

A second later, the dancing ceased, and she had a sudden, upside-down view of its head as it tucked its muzzle beneath its own chest. She stumbled as she flung herself away from the wicked snap of its teeth and it saw her on the ground and knew this was its moment.

The wolf reared back on its hind legs, the great sweep of its tail raising a cloud of pollen behind it as it brushed over the heads of the grass. And then its front paws came down, claws unsheathed and slashing for a killing blow.

They caught her this time, low on the ribs, and she had a moment to wonder how a ghost could be injured, and then she found out. Her skin tore, not like flesh but something finer, the lightest silk. And when it did something leaked out of her, but it wasn't blood. She couldn't see it in the diffuse brightness of this world, but she sensed it. She was losing some essential essence, the thing that made her Boda, even when all her memories and all her life were gone.

She clamped a hand over the wound and flung herself forward to roll beneath the creature's legs. It roared its fury at her escape and slashed again, but she kept on rolling, flattening the grass beneath her and releasing a smell that was quite wrong, like sugar burning.

And then her back hit something else, something cold and hard – metal. She didn't make a conscious decision to reach for it, just incorporated it into her roll as she tumbled even further from the wolf, curling her hand around its smooth end and pulling up.

It was surprisingly heavy, wrenching at a shoulder that was somehow still tender, even in death. The wolf growled and lowered its head, hackles bristling on its back, and Boda only had one second to see what it was she'd taken. It was long and thin – sharp only at the point. It was a weapon, though like none she'd ever seen. But in this desperate fight she'd use whatever she could.

She hid it behind her as the wolf stalked forward. The creature's eyes were too wise to risk it understanding what she intended. Its tongue snaked out to wet its purple lips and she wondered what it might taste like, to eat a human soul.

Then, with no warning, the wolf leapt. Its paws descended towards her, each larger than her head, the pads like soft brown storm clouds. And, when the nearest was above her, she pulled the strange silver spear from behind and stabbed upward, into the animal's most sensitive flesh.

It yowled in agony and leapt away. The spear pulled in her hand but she clung on grimly and it came away with her and not the beast, leaving red blood to spurt from its injured paw, sticky and hot on her face and hair.

The wolf was crazed with pain and fury now, more lethal than ever. But it wasn't thinking clearly any more. It wanted to kill her, crush her – destroy this thing that had hurt it so badly. Its head snapped down towards her, snarling and spitting, and suddenly something even more vital was in her spear's reach.

And in the moment before she thrust it forward, Boda suddenly recognised the shape of her weapon – a hairpin, magnified a thousand-fold. It must have fallen from the giantess's head when she died. The realisation almost stayed Boda's arm but her will to survive was too strong.

The pin flew forward, past the wolf's snout, its snarling teeth – and straight into the great brown orb of its eye. Her arm went after, plunging into the glutinous fluid that spilled out, passing through it to pierce the orbit of the eye itself. And in the moment the spear punctured the wolf's brain, everything changed.

CHAPTER TWENTY

THE FIRST THING Boda saw was Petronius, Nero clinging to his left hip. The young man seemed oblivious to her presence, but the little boy stared at her over the corpse of something she was no longer sure was a wolf. The fur around its muzzle suddenly looked green, scale-like, and why had she thought it only had one head, when it so clearly had two?

No, not two, three – and of course those weren't scales, the fur was bristly brown. A dog's fur. The silver spear she'd used to kill it had pierced the central eye of its central head. And beyond the third head, staring at her in bafflement, was a face she'd never expected to see again.

"Narcissus!" she said, and he smiled uncertainly.

And then, as she watched, there was neither a wolf nor a serpent nor a three-headed dog lying between them all, but only a pile of freshly stripped bones, and soon even those faded from sight and the floor was just marble, black and white chequers receding down a corridor into an endless distance.

"Boda?" Petronius said, doubt and painful hope in his voice. His head swung from side to side, as if he was trying to seek her out by scent or sound alone. His eyes were as big and brown as ever, but they'd lost all expression. She realised with a shock of horror that he was blind.

"You found me –" she said, her words cutting off as he stumbled forward to fling his arms around her. She didn't know what else she would have said, anyway. How could she be pleased to see him, here?

"Are you're –" he said.

"Dead. Still dead." When she saw the sorrow on his face, she didn't say the rest. "And you? Did Vali kill you too?"

"No. Sopdet opened the gates of death. She's very close behind." His head twisted, as if he might be able to see her.

"I'm sorry, but who are you?" Narcissus asked. His blank face was as blind in its own way as Petronius's eyes, and Boda suddenly remembered the wind which had tried to rip her apart when she first crossed over into this realm. She feared that Narcissus had felt it too, and failed to resist.

"We're your friends," she told him, and he smiled and nodded, happy to accept her word.

"Is that Narcissus?" Petronius asked.

"Am I Narcissus?" he asked and Boda answered 'yes' to both of them. She turned to Petronius. "What happened to Vali?"

He shot a startled, blind look around him. "He was just here, a moment ago. Listen, Boda, he really is Sopdet's brother, and I don't think he's a man. I think he's –"

"A god," she said. "The god of mischief, whom the Egyptians call Set and my own people call Loki. I know. He's used us all, but he's still right. Sopdet must be stopped."

There was a sound behind them, footsteps echoing down the long corridor.

Petronius flinched, and Boda took his arm.

"She's coming," he said. "How do we stop her, if she's a goddess too?"

"We go on," Narcissus said. He spread his hands when they turned to face him. "The dead god must stay dead. It's the only thing I know."

The footsteps grew louder behind them, and Boda didn't argue, just pulled Petronius on, along the black-and-white tiled corridor, which led only into darkness.

When she saw the figures up ahead, she thought at first that they were more of the half-real shades who drifted through this place. But her footsteps stuttered to a halt when she saw their faces, glaring at her out from the most shameful corners of her own past.

"Josephus," she said. Death hadn't made him whole again. The cavities in his chest and stomach gaped raw and red, and there was a trickle of white brain matter from his nose.

"You killed me, barbarian," he said. "You condemned me to this place."

It was only the truth and she couldn't deny it. "I didn't know," she told him. "I'd change what I did if I could."

"But you can't. You can't!" said another voice and this time it was Petronius who flinched.

She was a young girl, not much older than him, ivory-skinned and flat-faced like the people of the far east. "I died of the child you got in me," she said, "and you weren't even there to watch me bleed my life away. Your father sold me to labour in the mines, and you never raised your voice in protest."

Boda could feel the shiver in Petronius' arm through the hand she rested against it. He took a step back, and she realised she had too.

Nero huddled against his legs, whimpering, and when Boda saw the little girl with the crushed head she understood. That spirit haunted her too.

Then another figure stepped forward, an older woman, grey-haired and sad-faced. "My son," she said to Narcissus, and Boda saw the resemblance between them, the too-thin, not quite pretty faces.

His remained blank. "Are you my mother?"

A single tear tracked down her cheek. "It broke my heart when they sold you away from me. I didn't last another year, and by then you'd already forgotten me. You loved the master who parted us more than your own flesh and blood!"

Boda winced at the pain in the woman's face, but Narcissus only frowned. "I'm sorry, I don't remember you. And I've forgotten how to feel guilt."

There were more spirits behind Narcissus, crowding back into the darkness. Boda saw faces she barely recognised but knew all the same; every Roman soldier she'd sent to his death stood beside the blue-eyed Celts she'd cut down when they tried to invade her land. Beside her, she felt Petronius begin to sob as more voices called out his name. And then she saw the smallest figure as it pushed itself to the front, the stumbling, awkward shape of a baby too young to be born. It mumbled a word that might have been "mummy."

Boda turned to flee, only to fall to her knees when a hand grabbed her. She didn't dare look back to see whose it was. It could be any of a hundred people. She hadn't realised she'd killed so many. So many lives unlived because of her.

But it was only Narcissus. "Close your eyes," he said. "And I'll lead you."

She didn't want to follow him. She couldn't bear the thought of passing those spirits, their dead flesh touching hers. But then she heard Petronius stumble to his feet beside her. He was already blind. If he could find the courage to face it, so could she.

Narcissus's hand was hot and dry in hers and she was reminded suddenly of their escape from the catacombs beneath Rome. Narcissus had rescued her, though it had been Petronius who led them.

There too she'd been afraid of what hid in the dark. Here she'd seen their faces, but did that really make it worse? Wasn't the unknown always more frightening than the known? Still, when the ghostly hands reached out and touched her, she couldn't stop herself flinching away, and only Narcissus's firm grip on her hand kept her from fleeing. She heard Petronius whispering words which might have been a prayer, but the spirits he faced were less malevolent than her own. He'd killed only tangentially – by neglect or ignorance. She'd set out to take life, and only now, as she felt them plucking at her clothes and whispering in her ear did she know the value of what she'd stolen, from so very many people.

She'd looked down on Petronius, because he'd never trained as a warrior and didn't know what it was to kill a living man. Now she understood that it made him the better person.

The journey seemed to take for ever. She wondered if perhaps it would, if they'd failed and this was their punishment. Could the prison that awaited her when this mission was done be any worse?

But it did end. The whispers faded into nothing and after a while she felt no more hands reaching for her. She sensed a greater emptiness around her, as if the corridor had opened into something far more vast.

"Can I look now?" she asked.

It took a moment before Narcissus replied, and when he did his voice sounded choked, as if there were tears in it. "Yes," he said. "They've gone. Everything's gone."

She opened her eyes to utter darkness. Narcissus's hand was still in hers. She could hear Petronius's breathing beyond, and Nero's quiet sobbing beside him, but aside from that nothing. She took a step forward and round, fumbling until she could catch Petronius's other hand in her own. His was softer and warmer than Narcissus's, and he gave her a grateful squeeze. His face alone was visible in the darkness, just the barest shadowed outline of his rounded cheek.

"What is it?" he said.

"All our ghosts left," Narcissus told him, "and they took the light with them."

There was something different in his voice, and after a moment Boda realised what it was. The blank innocence was gone. "You remember," she said.

She felt his nod travel down his shoulder to her hand. "When my mother left, the memories came."

"So what do we do now?" Petronius asked.

"We go on," she said grimly, releasing his hand, and they did, into the endless darkness. They went on and on and nothing changed, no hint of light ahead of them and no murmur of voices to either side. They might have been walking in place, and maybe they were.

"Are we there yet?" Petronius asked, after an uncounted time.

"We're nowhere," Boda said and saw his mouth twist down.

She saw it, when she could see nothing else. Why was he alone visible in this world? Her footsteps slowed as she pulled the others to a halt beside her and turned to face Petronius.

He was the source of the light. She could see its faint shine from beneath his eyelids. She reached out to touch them, soft skin with the hardness of his eyeballs beneath. He flinched away in surprise before leaning longingly into the contact. And suddenly she remembered what Vali had told her, in the moment before she died – that he'd make sure she had with her everything she needed.

"Petronius," she said. "How did you lose your sight?"

"I saw the sun, burning on the barge that carries it through the night."

"And do you see it still?"

His throat bobbed as he swallowed. "It's all I'll ever see again."

"Then let it out," she told him.

He shook his head, baffled.

"Open your eyes."

He hesitated, then flicked his eyelids open. "I'm still blind," he said after a moment. The disappointment in his voice was painful to hear, but she could see something, a golden light in the dark heart of his pupils.

"That's because you're holding the light inside you," she said. "You have to let it out. Let it go."

"How?"

"Just do it. Let the sun out. Give me the light, Petronius – please."

He looked almost wistful at that. But in his eyes the light burned brighter, and she thought she could see it now, the red-gold sphere of the sun trapped inside.

"Oh," he said. "Oh, I –"

And then the light roared out of him, blazing from his eyes and flattening his round face into blankness. Boda shielded her eyes but for an instant she was blinded too. And then she blinked them open and Petronius was in front of her, blinking back at her.

"I can see," he said. "I can see you."

And they could see everything else, too.

For a moment, Boda thought they'd somehow returned to the Temple of Isis. This marbled space shared its dimensions, its high vaulted spaces and its darkness. Behind the great, seated figure of the goddess, she could see the gateway to death, green light flickering at its rim.

But when she took a step nearer and saw the pale-faced spirits flooding through the gate, she understood. This hall was what lay on its far side. Then the figure on its throne stirred, and she realised with a shiver of fear that it was no statue. His form was lost in shadows, but she felt the power roll off him like a cold mist, the dead god who ruled this realm.

Boda fell to her knees, and beside her she felt Petronius and Narcissus doing the same. Only Nero remained standing, his head on a level with theirs and his eyes happy and unafraid as he looked up into the hidden face of death.

"So," Osiris said, "you have come to me, mortals, as my brother foretold."

There was a shifting in the darkness at his feet and Boda realised that there was another figure there, huddled and chained.

"Hello, Vali," she said.

He bowed his head, but she saw the shadow of a smile beneath his sharp nose and knew that his plotting wasn't over yet.

"We come to seek a boon, my lord," she said to the dead god.

"A boon?" His voice was as flat as a cracked bell, dying without echo in this vast dark space. "I know what it is you seek. And you too, my beloved."

Isis stepped forward to tower beside them, as tall as the god she'd come to redeem from death. Her face was as perfect and ageless as ever, but the desperate joy in her eyes made her seem almost human.

"I've come to reunite us, my love," she said. "To bring you back to the living world."

"The living world?" Osiris said, and for a moment the gateway behind him cleared and broadened until Boda could see the entirety of Rome spread out before her. The legion of the dead had swelled, and the streets were thick with corpses, but the living still survived, barricaded inside their houses or fighting in little, desperate clusters in the street.

Narcissus cried out, and after a moment Boda saw why. Claudius had gathered the free people of Rome into the Arena while the dead congregated outside. The Praetorian Guard held the gates, the gladiators she'd trained with beside them, but their defence couldn't last long. They were too few, and too tired. She saw Marcus, the captain of the guard, cut down by the risen body of one of his own men. Adam ben Meir, who once tried to kill her, stepped in to fill the breach.

And then, beyond the walls of Rome, throughout the whole world, she saw worse. There was no greenery anywhere, only the brown of dead grass and wilting leaves, and the same grey nothingness on every face she saw.

"The living world needs you, sister," Osiris said. "It is barren and loveless without you."

"I will return," Isis said, "when you return with me. I've missed you so much. Without you, my life is barren and loveless."

"So you killed the world to give me a place in it."

"It's not quite ready yet," she said. "But soon we can be together again – and for all eternity."

"And that is your wish. You have made your way to me, sister, which grants you the right to ask one gift, if it is within my power to give. But these others have journeyed here too, through obstacles more profound than you have faced, and they also earned that right."

Boda tried to meet Vali's red-brown eyes, but they were veiled beneath his lids, and Osiris's face was lost in shadows. Was he toying with them? Legend said the judge of the dead was fair, but then legend also said that Isis was loving and kind.

Boda didn't understand how she knew it, but she sensed the dead god's attention shifting to Petronius, his regard so heavy that she saw the young man buckle beneath it.

"And you, child of Rome," Osiris said. "You wish to close the gates of death, and condemn me to this realm for ever."

"Well," Petronius said, voice shaking. "Condemning you to this realm is really only a side effect of saving the world. It's nothing personal, if that makes any difference."

She felt a dank wind blow over them as the dead god shook his head. "And would you still wish it, if you knew what closing the gate entailed? For you live, and the woman you love has died, and if the world is restored she may not join you in it. But if you allow my sister to have her way, you and she may remain united for as long as you both desire."

The hope on Petronius's face was so naked that Boda had to look away from it. She understood suddenly that Osiris was both playing entirely fair and cheating horribly.

She tried to tell Petronius not to take the bait, but found her voice sticking in her throat. It seemed this was his decision alone to make, and she wouldn't be allowed to interfere.

The silence stretched on for a long time as he knelt with his head bowed. But when he looked up there were tears in his brown eyes. "The thing is," he said. "If I did that, she couldn't love me – so what would be the point?"

Osiris's laugh was as dry as autumn leaves. "A paradox indeed. And what of you, boy?"

Now Narcissus cringed under his unseen scrutiny. "The dead god must stay dead," he said. "Charon himself told me that, my lord."

"And is the ferryman's power greater than mine? If I go through to the living land, this realm requires a judge to take my place. Would you do it, slave? I could place you above every man and woman on earth. You would have the power to punish those who wronged you."

"Why me?" Narcissus asked, and Boda winced. He was tempted, she could tell.

"Because a ruler should know what it is to be ruled," Osiris said. "And who better to judge the sins of Rome than one who was their victim? Caligula is already in my kingdom, awaiting judgement. Would you like to deliver it? You could give him back a thousandfold the torment he gave you. It is in your power to make him suffer the pain of crucifixion every day for eternity."

Narcissus swallowed. "But not every Roman was cruel. My master..."

The dead god shifted in his throne with a sound like rock crumbling. "Yours would be the power to reward, too. You could bring as much pleasure to the pure as suffering to the guilty. What do you say, Narcissus?"

He stood up, looking as if he had to press against a great weight to do it. "But I'd have to choose, wouldn't I, who suffered and who didn't? I was born poor and powerless. I never had the ability to hurt anyone, so

I never did. But how can I be sure that if I'd been raised high, and not low, I'd have been any better than them?"

"Do you not know yourself, boy?" Osiris asked in his strange, flat voice.

Narcissus shrugged, but he didn't drop his gaze. "I don't think anyone can know that. And I won't stand in judgement on people for crimes I might have committed in their place."

There was a moment's frozen stillness, then Boda felt the dead god's attention shifting to her. It pressed against her mind, a power so strange and ancient that she could barely comprehend it. She knew that it was looking inside her, and that it saw everything.

"Woman of the north," Osiris said, "you have made a terrible bargain, but I can spare you its consequences."

Petronius's head swung to face her. "What bargain?"

She didn't reply, but the dead god said: "In exchange for the knowledge to complete her quest, she agreed to suffer for all eternity upon its completion. A vow to a god that may not be broken."

"It's true, Petronius," she said when she saw the denial in his face. "I had no choice."

"But what if your mission is never completed?" Osiris asked. "Then your vow need never be honoured. While the doors of death remain open, you remain free. What say you, daughter of Midgard?"

Now she understood the terrible temptation that had been placed in front of Petronius and Narcissus. The image of that prison hovered in the back of her mind, like a nagging pain that couldn't be ignored. She'd suffered enough in her life to be able to imagine what eternal torment might feel like. She could imagine it all too well.

And now, instead of that, she could be free – without breaking her word. The world would die, but why should she suffer to save it? She hadn't led a blame-free life, but she didn't deserve that. No one did, not even Vali.

She was shaking as she pushed herself to her feet, and she couldn't meet Petronius's eyes. She knew he'd want her to take the dead god's bargain, but the Boda he loved wasn't the woman who could accept what Osiris offered – another of the dead god's twisted paradoxes.

"No," she said. "I will keep my word. Let the gates of death be closed."

"Ah," he said, a bass note she felt in her bones. "Then it seems we have met an impasse, where I cannot grant one wish without frustrating another."

"Wait," Vali said suddenly. "Wait. Let me suffer the punishment, it's not Boda's to endure. The crime wasn't hers."

He crawled forward a little, chains rattling, until his face was in the light. He wasn't smiling now. His red-brown eyes looked wide and shocked, as if he couldn't quite believe his own words.

"Why?" she asked him, a desperate hope blooming inside her.

He shrugged. "Because I let a little girl die, and I can't forget her face. Because I spent too long as a mortal and forgot how to be a god, and if

I let you suffer for my sins, your face will haunt me for all eternity and even that prison might be easier to bear."

"Brother, your bargain is accepted," Osiris said. "The one who is responsible for this shall pay for it, in full."

In front of him, Isis smiled, a chilling expression.

"Sister," Osiris said, "you see that my killer is repentant. Will you forgive him?"

"Forgive him?" she hissed. "Never." While her love had looked human, her hate was larger and more terrible than that.

"Will you not remit one year of his sentence? Not even one day?"

"Not one hour," she said. "Not one second. Let him suffer the way he made me suffer."

"You?" Osiris said. "Yes, I see. It is your suffering you wish to end, not mine. So then beloved, is this your final word? Shall we be reunited at last?"

There was a sound like fingernails grating against glass as he rose to his feet. Vali skittered out of the way, awkward in his chains, and then Osiris stepped into the light.

Isis gasped as she recoiled. Boda shielded her face from the sight but it was seared on her memory. He was hideous, decayed and rotting. He was dead, and more monstrous in death than any mortal man could be.

"What happened to you?" Isis whispered.

"I died, beloved," he said, his shrivelled tongue visible through the holes in his gaunt cheeks.

"But... but you can be whole again! You can live!"

Osiris shook his head. "That can never be. But this world you mean to create, this world of death, there I can have a place and we may be reunited."

He took a step towards her, and she took one back. Boda might almost have pitied the horror in her face.

"No," Isis said. "I want you back as you were. Not this shadow, this mockery!"

Boda thought she read sadness on his rotting face. "The shadow is all that remains." He reached out a hand, swathed in bandages like the Egyptian dead. "Can you not love me as I am?"

She stared at his hand but didn't take it, and after a moment he let it drop.

"Then it has all been for nothing," he said. "And you must reverse what you have done."

Her mouth set in a mulish line. "Why should I? What care I for the world now?"

"The living world is your realm," Osiris said, "and you must return to it. Heal it, sister. It is your duty. Summon back the spirits of the dead to where they belong."

She stared at him a moment longer, but his decaying face was set in a severe frown, and after a moment she raised her hand. "Come then," she said, facing the gate. "It's over. It's all over."

Boda watched the gateway, waiting for the spirits to flood back through, but nothing happened. The green light buzzed at the edges and the dead only passed out.

After a moment, Isis stepped back. "I don't understand. They're not listening to me."

"Because you speak with hate, sister. They must be called with love."

She raised her arm again, then dropped it. "I can't. I don't love them. Now you're dead, I'll never love again."

"Ah," Osiris said, and Boda heard the same finality in his voice that had been in Mimir's when she made her vow to him. The dead god's milky eyes turned to her. "Then you must summon them, daughter of man. Or the world will remain a realm of death and your quest will have been for nothing."

It seemed impossible. How could she do what a goddess couldn't? But Osiris said they needed to be called with love and Boda thought that maybe she understood. When she'd found herself confronted by the spirits of those she'd killed, she'd tried to run from them. It hadn't been because she feared them. She'd run because she understood that all the people she'd killed were people who in another world might have been her friends. Someone had loved them, even if it hadn't been her.

And someone had loved all those spirits out there too. Isis had filled them with hate when she summoned them, with resentment against the living who had carried on when they had stopped. She understood that. Death was hard to accept. It wasn't meant to be easy. But it was necessary, because the living required it, and the dead were all people who had once loved the living.

She felt her mind, pressing outwards, expanding in ways she didn't understand. It travelled through the gate and into the outside world. Out there she could sense them, all the lost dead spirits, and she called their names. She knew them all, though there were a million of them. She knew them all individually, and though some of them had been terrible people, she found something in them that had loved or been loved, and she used it to call them back.

It was Petronius's voice which summoned her back to her body, crying out in fear as the spirits of the dead howled through the gateway, returning from the land of the living. A blue fire flickered around their peaceful faces as they flew past.

Beside him, Isis screamed. "No! What have you done? You've given her my power!"

Surrounded by the ghosts of the dead, Osiris shook his head. "I did not take it, you gave it up. You renounced it, and your right to it, when you sacrificed the world for yourself. But the world needs a goddess of love and life, and my brother has found a replacement."

"What?" Boda said. She shook her head, but the denial was pointless. She could feel the power inside her, too large for her small mortal frame. She felt it burning the mortality out of her, until she was something very different from what she'd always been. "But I'm a warrior," she said. "I know duty, and honour and war – not love."

"There is duty in love," Osiris said, "and honour too. Or there should be. Now –" He looked down at Vali, and the chains fell from him. Boda heard his joints pop as he straightened and when he had, he'd grown to the size of Osiris. She realised that she had too. But Isis had shrunk. She shivered beside Petronius. She looked human now because she was, everything godly stripped from her.

"Please, beloved," she said.

Boda did pity her then, but she could see in his face that the dead god felt nothing. There was only a cold, unyielding judgment in his eyes. "There must be a goddess of love," he said, "but it need not be you. And there must be someone to suffer in Vali's prison, but it need not be him. You said that the one responsible for this should be punished eternally, and so it shall be, not one day, not one second of the sentence remitted."

Isis screamed as the floor opened beneath her. The distance below seemed to stretch into infinity, but Boda knew what prison lay at the bottom, and she closed her eyes against it.

When she opened them again she found herself looking at Vali. "You knew," she said. "When you offered to take my punishment, you knew you wouldn't have to do it. You planned this all along."

His crooked smile was exactly the same whether he was a man or a god. "And if I did, you lived up to my expectations admirably. Or perhaps it wasn't like that at all. Perhaps it was my brother's scheming which lay behind all this. Maybe he planned everything, even his own death, because he knew that perfect order has no place in the living world, but the afterlife needs a judge who is fair and final."

She looked at Osiris, but his rotting face was unreadable, and Vali was never to be trusted.

"And the living world is the place for the chaos you bring, brother," Osiris said. "You must return to it now."

Vali bowed, seeming to shrink as he did. He sauntered to the gateway, but turned round to face them before he entered it, and his gaze found Petronius. "A word to the wise. If you value the new life you've been given, leave the child behind." Then he stepped through the gate.

"What?" Petronius said. He turned to Boda, craning his neck to look up at her, but the sight of her face seemed to pain him and he looked away.

"He speaks the truth," Osiris said. "This child is one of his, an agent of chaos. If he returns to the living world, he will grow to be the man who kills you. You may leave him in death if you choose, and I will not punish you for it. The world will be more orderly without him."

Nero seemed to understand something of what this meant. He looked up at Petronius with trusting eyes, and Petronius rested a gentle hand against his head. Then he looked at Osiris and shrugged. "I've still got time to change his mind, haven't I?"

Osiris didn't say anything, and Petronius seemed to take that as an affirmative. He smiled at Nero, then hoisted him onto his hip.

"And what of me?" Narcissus asked. "I'm dead. I belong here."

"It lies in my power to grant you reprieve, since you have earned it by voyaging to me," the dead god said. "Do you wish to live again? There is always more pain in life than the dead remember."

"I do remember," Narcissus said. "But yes, I want it. There's more I want to do, no matter what it costs me."

"Go then," Osiris said. "All of you. And Boda will close the gates of death behind you." He sank down into his throne, hiding his face in shadows once again, so that his last words floated out of darkness. "Farewell, sister. We shall not meet again until the final battle, when all the gods will fall."

Boda nodded, but didn't say anything. She knew that in that battle, Osiris and Vali would fight on different sides, and she wondered now whose she'd choose.

Then the gate stood before her and she realised that she was the size of a mortal woman again, though her skin contained a thousand times what it once had.

Petronius stood to one side of her, and she smiled when she looked at him. "So," she said, "we're not to be parted after all."

"Not by the gates of death," he whispered, then followed her into life.

They'd arrived back where they started, in the Temple of Isis. The moment the gate snapped shut, the marble beneath them shook and tore. For a moment Boda was just a woman, and then she felt her power stirring within her and flung it outward. The temple roof shattered and fell and she lifted her hands and brushed it aside, keeping the two men and the small boy by her side safe.

A cloud of white dust floated down around them, and when it had settled she saw that the sky was pale blue with the start of a new day. Around them, the streets of Rome were littered with corpses, but the corpses didn't move. And as Boda felt the world with senses she didn't used to possess, and the world felt her, the brown grass poking through a crack in the wall turned green, and everywhere people remembered what it was to love, and some of them screamed when they saw what they'd done in the hours her power had been gone from the land of the living.

She turned to Petronius, wanting to share these new feelings with someone, but his eyes looked straight through her and she realised what he already had. Though death didn't separate them, his mortality did. He occupied the land of the living, and she was part of a different realm.

"Well," he said to Narcissus. "That was memorable." His voice shook, but not too much.

Narcissus nodded. "We should find Claudius. He'll need help to clean up – rebuild."

Petronius looked around him, at the wreckage in the streets. "But first, we should find a bar." He walked away, stepping nimbly over corpses with Narcissus at his side and Nero slung high on his shoulders. The little boy giggled and pointed at the mutilated remains and Petronius shifted him till he was facing away from them, towards the rising sun.

Boda watched them till they turned the corner. There was much she needed to do, a burden she hadn't asked for and wasn't sure she could shoulder. She took one last second to enjoy the dawn on the streets of Rome, then closed her eyes and went elsewhere.

EPILOGUE

She was glad to find him surrounded by his friends. There was a feast laid out on the tables and though he didn't seem to have the strength to eat, he made sure that everyone else did. She lingered at the back of the crowd for a while, watching him.

"Well, Petronius," one of the men said, a fair-haired youth who might have been of her own birth people. "She was very tall."

"Just the right height," Petronius told him, "for what I had in mind," and the men and women around him laughed.

He'd changed, of course. He was a man now, the soft lines of his face sharpened, with threads of grey in his long black curls. His eyes were the same brown, though, and after a moment they picked her out in the crowd. Shock transmuted into a moment of unguarded delight. Then his gaze dropped and he quirked a private smile.

"My friends," he said. "I fear it's time for you to go."

There were expressions of regret, some genuine, some fake. Some of them looked embarrassed as they brushed past her, and glad of the reprieve. They didn't know what to say to a man on the day of his death.

When they were alone, she went to sit beside him. His arms hung limply over the sides of his chair, the blood draining slowly from his wrists to the bowls beneath them.

"Boda," he said. "Or is that no longer your name?"

"It's still one of them," she told him. Close to, the signs of age were clearer on him, the fine network of wrinkles just beginning around his eyes. And his smile was more cautious than it had been, though still not bitter. He'd chosen to spend his last day with company and in laughter, and she thought that he couldn't have changed that much.

"I wondered if you'd come," he said. "I hoped I'd see you again – at least this one last time."

"I would have stopped it if I could," she told him.

He laughed. "I tried to. I don't think you would have approved. I made myself Nero's closest friend, the one he could always rely on – who never questioned him. Even Seneca showed more backbone than I did, in the end. Did you know that Claudius called the old bastard back from exile to tutor Nero when he adopted him as his son?"

Boda nodded. "I heard Seneca had time to consider the error of his ways while he was away. That he wrote some thoughts on how to face your mortality. I always wondered why Claudius didn't just have him killed."

Petronius shrugged, then winced, as the motion jarred the wounds in his wrists. "I think he was so pleased to see Narcissus in the land of the living again, it put him in a forgiving mood. Narcissus rose very high, but I expect you know that too."

"Claudius freed him," Boda said, "and named him praetor. Gave him more power than almost any man in Rome. But Narcissus picked the wrong side in the battle for the succession, and Nero killed him – he killed them both."

"The boy's sanity snapped in the underworld. I should never have taken him there. But Seneca, he had some control over him. Nero wasn't a bad Caesar, while that old bore held sway."

"And then Nero killed him too," Boda said.

Petronius laughed weakly. "Last year. While I – the court favourite, Nero's Arbiter of Elegance – lived on. I thought I could cheat fate, but... Well, you know best of all how impossible that is. And now here I am, opening my veins on Caesar's orders. I've seen my last summer, and it was only my thirty-ninth."

His eyes glazed for a moment and she knew that his death was near. Then the bright light that had always shone from them switched back on and his hand twitched, gesturing towards the table. "I've written my last words too, a letter to Nero telling him just exactly what I think of him – and reminding him of all the fun we had together, most of which I suspect he'd rather forget."

Boda smiled. "I'm sure it's a masterpiece. I read your book too, you know."

"Did you? And what did you think of it?" He barely had the energy to lift his eyelids now, but she saw that he really cared about her answer.

"You turned our story into a comedy. A sex comedy."

"A boy can dream," he said. "Besides, who wants to read about the undead?"

"But you captured the voice of the people. The ordinary people, whom no one has written of before."

"You taught me to listen to them." He sighed, and she knew that it was almost over. "I've bedded a thousand men, Boda, and a thousand women. But in all these years, I've loved only you."

"I know," she said. "I felt it."

And now the man she spoke to stood beside her, the empty shell of his body still and silent on the chair in front.

"Is that me?" he asked. "I really am as handsome as I thought."

She laughed, but the sound died when she saw the expression on his face. "It was a short life," she told him, "but a full one. Like mine."

"And unlike most people, I've already been where I'm now going. But..." He looked away. "You can't join me there."

"That's true," she said. "The gates of death remain closed to me. So perhaps it would be best if you stayed here."

She smiled, as his head snapped round to face her. "I can do that?"

She shrugged. "Osiris owes me a favour. He's said that as long as your words live in this world, so may you."

"As long as my words live..." He looked into the distance, then switched his gaze to watch her from the corner of his eye. "That seems fair. And what shall we do, Boda, with all this time we have?"

"We should visit Vali. You're as much his as mine, after all."

"You speak to him?"

"Our paths cross. Love is a force for chaos too – I'm not sure Sopdet or Osiris ever really understood that."

He turned to face her completely, and now his expression was entirely serious. His spirit looked a little younger than his corporeal remains, but still a man, with a man's knowledge behind his eyes. "Why?"

She took his hand. "You've bound me to the mortal plane, and my mortal self – your memories of me, and your feelings. You help me to remember how it felt to be a living woman, and I don't want to forget. I don't want to become like Sopdet. You've earned a part of my godhead if you want it."

"I can be the demigod of pornography," he said.

"Of passion and pleasure."

"Why?" he said again.

She looked at his dead body one last time, then turned to leave. "Because the world's a more cheerful place with you in it."

REBECCA LEVENE has been a writer and editor for sixteen years. In that time she has storylined *Emmerdale*, written a children's book about *Captain Cook*, several science fiction and horror novels, a novelisation and making-of book for Rebellion's *Rogue Trooper* video game, and a *Beginner's Guide to Poker*. She has also edited a range of media tie-in books. She was associate producer on the *ITV1* drama *Wild at Heart*, story consultant on the Chinese soap opera *Joy Luck Street*, script writer on *Family Affairs* and *Is Harry on the Boat?* and is part of the writing team for Channel 5's *Swinging*. She has had two sit-coms optioned, one by the *BBC* and one by *Talkback*, and currently has a detective drama in development with *Granada Television*.